W9-CIJ-388

The Conan Chronicles

Tor books by Robert Jordan

THE WHEEL OF TIME
The Eye of the World
The Great Hunt
The Dragon Reborn
The Shadow Rising
The Fires of Heaven
Lord of Chaos

The Conan Chronicles

ROBERT JORDAN

The Conan Chronicles

CONAN THE INVINCIBLE

CONAN THE DEFENDER

CONAN THE UNCONQUERED

TOR® fantasy

A TOM DOHERTY ASSOCIATES BOOK
NEW YORK

This is a work of fiction. All the characters and events portrayed in this book are either fictitious or are used fictitiously.

THE CONAN CHRONICLES

Copyright © 1995 by Conan Properties, Inc.

This is an omnibus edition consisting of the novels *Conan the Invincible*, copyright © 1982 by Conan Properties, Inc., first Tor edition June 1982; *Conan the Defender*, copyright © 1982 by Conan Properties, Inc., first Tor edition December 1982; and *Conan the Unconquered*, copyright © 1983 by Conan Properties, Inc., first Tor edition April 1983.

All rights reserved, including the right to reproduce this book, or portions thereof, in any form.

This book is printed on acid-free paper.

A Tor Book
Published by Tom Doherty Associates, Inc.
175 Fifth Avenue
New York, N.Y. 10010

Tor® is a registered trademark of Tom Doherty Associates, Inc.

Design by Brian Mulligan

Library of Congress Cataloging-in-Publication Data

Jordan, Robert.
    The Conan chronicles / Robert Jordan.
        p.   cm.
    "A Tom Doherty Associates book."
    ISBN 0-312-85929-5
    1. Conan (Fictitious character)—Fiction.   2. Fantastic fiction, American.   I. Title.
PS3560.O7617A6   1995
813'.54—dc20   95-15461
                                                                CIP

First edition: July 1995

Printed in the United States of America

0 9 8 7 6 5 4 3 2 1

The
Conan
Chronicles

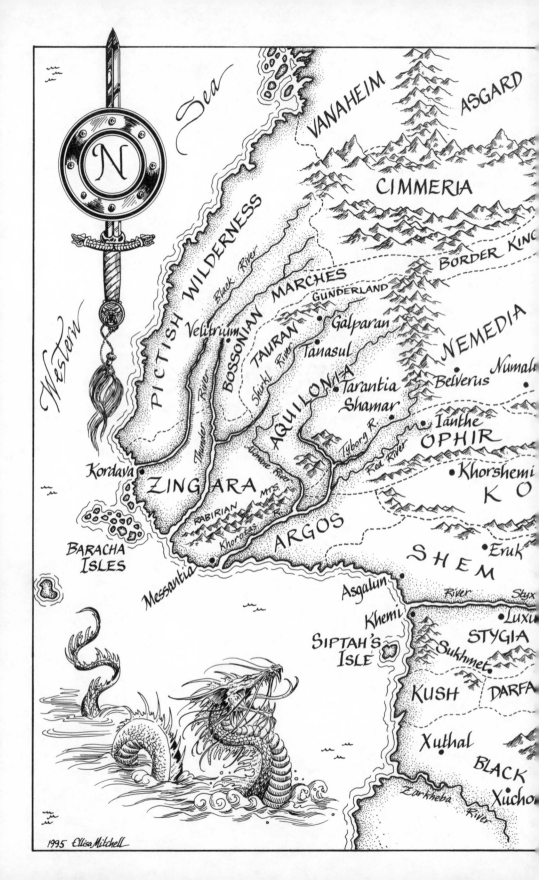

TUNDRAS

Haloga

HYPERBOREA

DESERTS

STEPPES

BRYTHUNIA

KEZANKIAN MTS.

HYRKANIA

CORINTHIA

ZAMORA

KARPASH MTS.

Shadizar

Avenjun

T H

KHAURAN

Sultanapur

TURAN

VILAYET SEA

KHITAI

KHORAJA

ISLE of
IRON
STATUES

Akit

DESERTS

Samara

Aghrapur

IBARS MTS.

Shangara

Xapur

Zaporaska River

Zamboula

Kuthchernes

Khawarism

Pteion

Ilbars River

lkmeenon

KESHAN

Kassali

VENDHYA

Keshla

PUNT

KINGDOMS

ZEMBABWEI

IRANISTAN

Conan
the
Invincible

I

The icy wind whipping through the brown, sheer-walled chasms of the Kezankian Mountains seemed colder still around the bleak stone fortress that grew from the granite flank of a nameless mountain in the heart of the range. Fierce hillmen who feared nothing rode miles out of their way to go around that dark bastion, and made the sign of the horns to ward off evil at its mention.

Amanar the Necromancer made his way down a dim corridor that violated the very heartstone of the mountain, followed by those no longer human. He was slender, this thaumaturge, and darkly handsome, his black beard cropped close; but a vaguely serpentlike streak of white meandered through his short hair, and the red flecks that danced in his eyes drew the gaze, and the will, of anyone foolish enough to look deeply. His henchmen looked like ordinary men, at first glance and from a distance, but their faces were vaguely pointed, their eyes glinted red beneath ridged helmets, and their skins bore reptilian scales. The fingers of the elongated hands that held their spears ended not in nails, but in claws. A curved tulwar swung at the hip of every one except for him who marched close behind Amanar. Sitha, Warden of the S'tarra, Amanar's Saurian henchman, bore a great double-edged ax. They came to tall doors set in the stone, both doors and stone carved with serpents in endless arabesques.

"Sitha," Amanar said, and passed through the doors without pausing.

The reptiloid warden followed close behind, closing the massive doors after his master, but Amanar barely noticed. He spared not a glance for the naked captives, a man and a woman, bound hand and foot, who lay gagged at one side of the column-circled room. The mosaicked floor bore the likeness of a golden serpent, surrounded by what might have been the rays of the sun. The mage's black robe was wound about with a pair of entwined golden serpents, their heads finally coming over his shoulders to rest on his

11

chest. The eyes of the embroidered serpents glittered with what would not possibly be life. He spoke.

"The man, Sitha."

The prisoners writhed in a frenzy to break their bonds, but the scaled henchman, muscles bulging like a blacksmith's, handled the man easily. In minutes the captive was spreadeagled atop a block of red-streaked black marble. A trough around the rim of the dark altar led to a spout above a large golden bowl. Sitha ripped the gag away and stepped back.

The bound man, a pale-skinned Ophirian, worked his mouth and spat. "Whoever you are, you'll get naught from me, spawn of the outer dark! I'll not beg! Do you hear? No plea will crack my teeth, dog! I will not. . . ."

Amanar heard nothing. He felt beneath his robe for the amulet, a golden serpent in the clutches of a silver hawk. That protected him, that and other things he had done, yet each time there was the realization of the power he faced. And controlled.

Those fools of Stygia, those who called themselves mages of the Black Ring, had so condescendingly allowed him to study at their feet, confident of his worshipful admiration. Until it was too late, none of them knew the contempt that festered in his heart. They prated of their power in the service of Set, Lord of the Dark, yet no man of them dared so much as lay a finger on the dread Book of Typhon. But he had dared.

He began to chant, and behind the altar a mist formed, red and golden, as a mist of flames. Beyond the mist blackness stretched into infinity. The Ophirian's tongue was stilled, and his teeth chattered in their place.

It was said that no human mind could comprehend the terrible knowledge contained in the book, or hold a single word of it without madness and death. Yet Amanar had learned. But a single page, it was true, before the numinous powers of it, wrenching at his mind, turning his bones to jelly, sent him grievously wounded and howling like a dog out of the city of Khemi into the desert. And in his madness, in that waterless waste beneath a burning sun, he had remembered that page still. Death could not come near him.

In the mists, from the mists, a shape coalesced. The Ophirian's eyes bulged in silence-stricken terror. The woman screamed into her gag. The golden head that reared above them in the swirling vapors—neither quite serpent nor lizard—was surrounded by a halo of a dozen tentacles longer than a man. The serpentine, golden-scaled body stretched back into the darkness, on beyond the reach of eye to see or mind to know. A bifurcate tongue flickered between fangs, and eyes holding the flames of all the furnaces that ever were regarded Amanar. Greedily, the mage thought, and fingered his amulet once more.

Across the sands he had stumbled, burning, drying, thirsting, remembering that page and unable to die. At last he came on Pteion the Accursed, fear-haunted ruins abandoned in the days of dark Acheron, before Stygia was aught but a stretch of sand. In the nameless, forgotten cavern beneath that city he had found Morath-Aminee, bound there for rebellion against Set when those who now called themselves men walked on all fours and rooted beneath stones for grubs. With his memories of that page—would they never stop burning at him?—he found the means to release the god-demon, the means to keep it in rein, however tenuously, and the means of his own protection. He had found power.

"Morath-Aminee," he half-chanted, half hissed. "O Eater of Souls, whose third name is death to hear, death to say, death to know, thy servant Amanar brings these offerings to thy sacrifice."

He held out his hand. Sitha placed a golden-hilted knife, its blade gilded, in his grasp. The Ophirian opened his mouth to scream, and gurgled horribly as Amanar slit his throat. At that instant the golden tentacles of the god-demon struck at the man on the altar, clutched him where he lay amid the spreading pool of his own blood. The tentacles avoided the proximity of Amanar.

"Eat, O Morath-Aminee," the mage chanted. He stared into the eyes of the sacrifice, waiting the proper moment.

Horror grew on the Ophirian's face as he realized he was dying. And yet he did not die. His heart pumped; his life blood poured from his ruined throat, the rubiate liquor flowing over ebon marble, channeled to the golden vessel at the foot of the altar for later necromancies. But he was not allowed to die.

Amanar heard in his mind the satisfied sibilation of the god-demon feeding. The Ophirian's pale eyes filled with desolation as the man realized what was being taken from him besides his life. The mage watched those eyes become lifeless though yet alive, empty windows on a soulless depth. With care he made a precise slit in the twitching chest. His hand poised above it, and he met the Ophirian's despairing gaze.

"Thank me for the release of death," he said.

The Ophirian's lips labored to form the words, but no sound emerged. Only horrendous bubbles in the diminishing flow of blood from the chasm that had been his throat.

Amanar smiled. His hand thrust into the slit, caught the pulsing heart, and ripped it free. It beat one last time as he held it before the Ophirian's eyes.

"Die," the mage said. The god-demon released its hold, and the husk on the altar slumped at last in death.

Sitha appeared beside the mage with a golden plate, on which Amanar placed the heart. That, too, had its uses in his magicks. He took the linen cloth the reptilian offered, and wiped his blood-stained hands. Sitha turned away.

"Amanar." The god-demon's susurration rolled against the walls. "Thou useth my sacrifice, soulless one, for thine own pleasure."

Amanar glanced hurriedly about him before answering. The woman writhed in her bonds on the edge of insanity. She heard nothing beyond the shrieks her gag choked back. Sitha continued out of the sacrificial chamber as if he had not heard. The S'tarra had little capacity to think for themselves, but they could obey orders. Sitha would place the heart in a golden bowl prepared beforehand with spells to keep its contents fresh. Only then would he be able to consider anything else, if his soulless mind were ever capable of considering anything.

The mage dropped his head on his chest and bowed in his most humble fashion. "O, great Morath-Aminee, I am but thy humble servant. Thy servant who freed thee from the bonds set upon thee by the Dark One." Gods and demons could not forget, not as men forget, but oft did they prefer not to remember debts in their dealings with men. The reminder could not be amiss.

A golden-scaled tentacle reached toward Amanar—it was all he could do not to flinch away—then jerked back as if from a great heat. "Thou wearest the amulet still."

"O Most High among the Powers and Dominions, this one is so insignificant beside thee that thou mightest destroy him without noticing such a speck in thy path. I wear this merely that thou mayst be aware of me, and spare me to thy service and greater glory."

"Serve me well, and in that day when Set is bound where I was bound, in that day when I rule the Outer Dark, I will give thee dominion over my herds, over those who call themselves men, and thou shalt bring the multitudes to my feeding."

"As thy word is, so shall it be, great Morath-Aminee." Amanar became aware that Sitha had returned with two other S'tarra. The necromancer flicked his hand in a summoning gesture, and the two scurried toward the bloodstained altar, dropping to all fours as they came near the black marble slab. Their eyes did not rise to the god-demon towering over them as, half-groveling, they unfastened the sacrifice and bore it away.

A different tap jerked Amanar around to stare at the tall cavern doors. No one dared disturb these ceremonies. The tap came again. He twitched as the voice of the god-demon hissed in his mind.

"Go, Amanar. This concerneth thee most vitally."

He glanced back at the great golden serpent-shape, rearing motionless above the black altar. The flame-filled eyes watched him with—what?— amusement? "Prepare the next sacrifice, Sitha."

The bound woman spasmed in ever greater frenzy as scaly hands lifted her from the tiled floor. Amanar hurried from the chamber.

A Turanian with a pointed beard stood eyeing the S'tarra nervously, his slight plumpness and loose yellow robes contrasting sharply with the empty red eyes and ring mail of the guards. The man craned to look beyond the mage into the sacrificial chamber, and Amanar closed the door firmly. He had few human servants who could be trusted beyond the Keep; it was not yet time for them to learn what they served.

"Why have you left Aghrapur, Tewfik?" he snapped.

The plump man put on a fawning smile and washed his hands in front of his chest. "It was not my fault, master, I beg you to understand that."

"What do you babble about, man?"

"That which you set me to watch, master. It is no longer in the strong-rooms of King Yildiz."

Amanar blanched. Tewfik, taking it for rage, cringed, and the S'tarra guardsmen stirred uneasily, but the thaumaturge was quaking inside. He gripped the Turanian's robes with iron fingers, pulling the man erect. "Where is it now? Speak, man, for your life!"

"Shadizar, master! I swear!"

Amanar glared at him and through him. Morath-Aminee had known the import of this message. The god-demon must know of what was now in Shadizar. A new hiding place must be found, but first he must secure within his power that which was gone. That which must be kept from Morath-Aminee at all costs. And to do that, he must risk bringing it within the very grasp of the god-demon. The risk! The risk!

He was not aware that he still carried the sacrificial knife until he slid it into the Turanian's ribs. He looked into the face that now stared open hate at him, and felt regret. Human servants were useful in so many ways that S'tarra could not be. Too useful to be thrown away casually.

The mage felt something thump against his chest and looked down. Jutting from his black robe was a knife hilt from which Tewfik's hand fell away. Contemptuously Amanar hurled the dying man from him. He plucked the knife free, held up its bloodless blade before the man on the stone floor, whose mouth was filling with his own blood.

"Fool," Amanar said. "You must kill my soul before mortal weapon can harm me."

He turned away. The guards' desire for fresh meat would dispose of what remained of Tewfik. If Amanar were to have the time he needed, Morath-Aminee must be kept satiated. More prisoners must be brought. More sacrifices for the Eater of Souls. He reentered the sacrificial chamber to attend to the first of these.

The purple-domed and many-spired city of Shadizar was known as 'the Wicked,' but the debauches of its high-chinned nobles, of their cruel-eyed wives and pearl-draped daughters, paled beside the everyday life of that part of the city known as the Desert. In those narrow, twisting streets and garbage-strewn alleys, haven of thief, kidnapper, murderer, and worse, the price of a body was silver, the price of a life copper, the price of a soul not worth speaking of.

The big youth lounging on the bed upstairs in the tavern of Abuletes, in the heart of the Desert, had no thought of those who might be coughing out their lives in the fetid squalor outside. His eyes, sapphire blue beneath a square-cut black mane, were on the olive-skinned woman across the small room, who was adjusting the gilded brass breastplates that displayed rather than concealed her swelling bilobate chest. The rest of her attire consisted of transparent pantaloons, slashed from waist to ankle, and a gilded girdle of no more than two fingers' breadth, slung low on her rounded hips. She wore four rings, green peridot and red almandine on her left hand, pale blue topaz and red-green alexandrite on her right.

"Do not say it, Conan," she said without looking at him.

"Say what?" he growled. If his unlined face proclaimed that he had seen fewer than twenty winters, his eyes at that moment said they had been winters of iron and blood. He tossed aside his fur covering with one massive hand and rose to dress, as always first seeing that his weapons were close to hand, the ancient broadsword in its worn shagreen sheath, the black-bladed Karpashian dagger that he strapped to his left forearm.

"I give to you freely what I sell to others. Can you not be satisfied with that?"

"There is no need for you to follow your profession, Semiramis. I am the best thief in Shadizar, in all Zamora." At her laugh, his knuckles whitened on his leather-wrapped sword hilt. He had more reason for his pride than she knew. Had he not slain wizards, destroyed liches, saved one throne and toppled another? What other of his years could say half so much? But he had never spoken of these things even to Semiramis, for fame was the beginning of the end for a thief.

"And for all your thievery," she chided, "what do you have? Every copper you steal drips from your fingers like water."

"Crom! Is that why you will not be mine alone? The money?"

"You're a fool!" she spat. Before he could say more, she flounced out of the room.

For a time he sat frowning at the bare wooden walls. Semiramis did not know half of his troubles in Shadizar. He was indeed the most successful thief in the city, and now his successes were beginning to rebound on him. The fat merchants and perfumed nobles whose dwellings he robbed were making up a reward to put an end to his depredations. Some of those self-same men had hired him upon occasion to retrieve an incriminating letter or a gift given indiscreetly to the wrong woman. What he knew of their secrets was likely as big a reason for the reward as his thefts. That, and their hot-eyed daughters, who found it delightfully wicked to dally with a muscular young barbarian.

With a grunt he got to his feet and slung a black Khauranian cloak edged in cloth-of-gold around his broad shoulders. These ruminations were gaining him nothing. He was a thief. He should be about it.

As he made his way down the rickety stair into the crowded common room, he ground his teeth. In the center of the room Semiramis sat on the lap of a mustachioed Kothian kidnapper in a striped cloak of many colors. Gold armlets encircled his biceps, and a gold hoop hung from one dark ear. The oily man's right hand gripped Semiramis' breasts; his left arm flexed as the other hand worked beneath the table. She wriggled seductively, and giggled as he whispered in her ear. Conan ignored the pair as he strode to the bar.

"Wine," he ordered, and dug into the leather purse at his belt for the necessary coppers. There were few enough remaining.

Fat Abuletes made the coins disappear, replacing them with a leathern jack of sour-smelling wine. His neck rose in grimy folds above the collar of a faded yellow tunic. His dark eyes, sunk in the suet of his face, could weigh a man's purse to the last copper at twenty paces. Instead of moving away, he remained, studying Conan from behind the fat, flat mask of his face.

The smells of the thin wine and half-burned meat from the kitchens warred with the effluvia wafted in from the streets whenever the door opened to let another patron in or out. It yet lacked three full glasses of night-fall, but the tables were filled with cutpurses, panderers and footpads. A busty courtesan in brass-belled ankle bracelets and two narrow strips of yellow silk hawked her wares with lascivious smiles.

Conan marked the locations of those who looked dangerous. A tur-banned Kezankian hillman licked his thin lips as he studied the prostitute, and two swarthy Iranistanis in loose, flowing red pantaloons and leather vests ogled her, as well. Blood might well be shed there. A Turanian coiner sat hunched over his mug, pointed beard waggling as he muttered to him-self. It was known in the Desert that he had been badly bested by a mark, and he was ready to assuage his humiliation with the three-foot Ibarri sword-knife at his hip. A third Iranistani, dressed like the first two but with a silver chain dangling on his bare chest, attended a fortuneteller turning her cards at a table against the far wall.

"What hold you, Conan," Abuletes said abruptly, "on the coming trou-bles?"

"What troubles?" Conan replied. His mind was not on the tavernkeeper's words. The soothsayer was no wrinkled hag, as such women were wont to be. Silken auburn hair showed at the edges of her voluminous brown cloak's hood, framing a heart-shaped face. Her emerald eyes had a slight tilt above high cheekbones. The cloak and the robe beneath were of rough wool, but her slender fingers on the K'far cards were delicate.

"Do you listen to nothing not connected to your thievery?" Abuletes grumbled. "These six months past no fewer than seven caravans bound for Turan, or coming from there, have disappeared without a trace. Tiridates has the army out after the Red Hawk, but they've never gotten a glimpse of that she-devil. Why should this time be any different? And when the soldiers return empty-handed, the merchants screaming for something to be done will force the king to crack down on us in the Desert."

"He has cracked down before," Conan laughed, "and nothing changes." The Iranistanis said something with a smirk. The soothsayer's green eyes looked daggers at him, but she continued to tell her cards. Conan thought the Iranistani had the same idea he did. If Semiramis wanted to flaunt her trade before him. . . . "What proof is there," he said, without taking his eyes from the pair across the room, "that the Red Hawk is responsible? Seven caravans would be a large bite for a bandit to chew."

Abuletes snorted. "Who else could it be? Kezankian hillmen never raid far from the mountains. That leaves the Red Hawk. And who knows how many men she has? Who knows anything of her, even what she looks like? I've heard she has five hundred rogues who obey her like hounds the huntsman."

Conan opened his mouth for an acid retort, and at that moment the situ-ation at the fortuneteller's table flared. The Iranistani laid a hand on her arm. She shook it off. He clutched at her cloak, whispering urgent words, hefting a clinking purse in his other hand.

"Find a boy!" she spat. Her backhand blow to his face cracked like a whip.

The Iranistani rocked back, his face livid. "Slut!" he howled, and a broad-bladed Turanian dagger appeared in his fist.

Conan crossed the room in two pantherish strides. His big hand clamped the bicep of the Iranistani's knife arm and lifted the man straight up out of his chair. The Iranistani's snarl changed to open-mouthed shock as he tried to slash at the big youth and his knife dropped from suddenly nerveless fingers. Conan's iron grip had shut off the blood to the man's arm.

With contemptuous ease, Conan hurled the man sprawling on the floor between the tables. "She doesn't want your attentions," he said.

"Whoreson dog!" the Iranistani howled. Left-handed, he snatched the Turanian coiner's Ibarri sword-knife and lunged at Conan.

Hooking his foot around the Iranistani's toppled chair, Conan swung it into the man's path. The Iranistani tumbled, springing up again even as he fell, but Conan's booted toe took him under the chin before he could rise above a crouch. He flipped backward to collapse at the feet of the coiner, who retrieved the sword-knife with a covetous glance at the Iranistani's purse.

Conan turned back to the pretty fortuneteller. He thought he saw a dagger disappearing beneath her capacious cloak. "As I saved you an unpleasantness," he said, "perhaps you will let me buy you some wine."

Her lip curled. "I needed no help from a barbar boy." Her eye flickered to his left, and he dove to his right. The scimitar wielded by one of the other Iranistanis bit into the table instead of his neck.

He tucked his shoulder under as he dove, rolling to his feet and whipping his broadsword free of its shagreen sheath in the same motion. The two Iranistanis who had been sitting alone faced him with scimitars in hand, well apart, knees slightly bent in the stance of experienced fighters. The tables around the three had emptied, but otherwise the denizens of the tavern took no notice. It was a rare day that at least one man did not give his death rattle on that sawdust-covered floor.

"Whelp whose mother never knew his father's name!" one of the long-nosed men snarled. "Think you to strike Hafim so and walk away? You will drink your own blood, spawn of a toad! You will—"

Conan saw no reason to listen to the man's rantings. Shouting a wild Cimmerian battle cry, he whirled his broadsword aloft and attacked. A contemptuous smile appeared on the dark visage of the nearer man, and he lunged to spit the muscular youth before the awkward-seeming overhand slash could land. Conan had no intention of making an attack that left him so open, though. Even as the Iranistani moved, Conan dropped to the right, crouching with his left leg straight out to the side. He could read death-knowledge in the man's dark bulging eyes. As the gleaming blue blade of the scimitar passed over his left shoulder his broadsword was pivoting, slashing through the leather jerkin, burying itself deep in the Iranistani's ribs.

Conan felt the blade bite bone; beyond the man choking on his own blood he saw the second Iranistani, teeth bared in a rictus, rushing at him with scimitar extended. He threw his shoulder into the pit of the dying man's stomach, straightening to lift the Iranistani and hurl him at his companion. The sword tearing free of the body held it up enough that it fell sprawling at the other man's racing feet. The second Iranistani leaped over his friend, curved blade swinging. Conan's slash beat the scimitar aside, and his backhand return ripped out the man's throat. Blood spilling down his dirty chest, the Iranistani tottered back with disbelieving eyes, pulling an empty table over when he fell.

Conan caught sight of Semiramis heading up the stair, one of the Kothian's big hands caressing a nearly bare buttock possessively as he followed. With a grimace, he wiped his blade clean on the baggy pantaloons of one of the dead men. Be damned to her, if her eyes had not shown her she already had a better man. He turned back to the table of the red-haired woman. It was empty. He cursed again, under his breath.

"This one's dead, too," Abuletes muttered. The fat tavern keeper knelt beside the first man Conan had confronted, his hands like plump spiders as they slipped the silver chain from about the dead man's neck. "You broke his neck. Hanuman's stones, Conan. That's three free-spenders you've done me out of. I've half a mind to tell you to take your custom elsewhere."

"Now you have it all," Conan said sourly, "and you don't have to give them any of your watered wine. But you can bring me a pitcher of your best. Kyroian. On them."

He settled at a table against the wall, thinking rough thoughts about women. At least the red-haired wench could have shown a little gratitude. He had saved her from a mauling, if nothing worse. And Semiramis. . . . Abuletes plonked down a rough earthenware pitcher in front of him and stretched out a grubby hand. Conan looked significantly at the last of the dead Iranistanis being hauled away by the two scruffy men who earned coppers fetching and carrying around the tavern. He had seen all three of the dead men's purses disappear beneath Abuletes' filthy apron. After a moment the tavern keeper shuffled his feet, wiped his fat hands on his apron, and left. Conan settled down to serious drinking.

he tables that had emptied during the fight refilled quickly. No
one had given more than a passing glance to the dead men as they
were removed; the level of shouted laughter and raucous talk had
never decreased. The half-naked courtesan briefly considered the breadth
of Conan's shoulder with lust-filled eyes, then passed on from his grim face.

His troubles, Conan decided by the time he had emptied four wooden
tankards of the sweet wine, would not be settled by the amounts he normally stole. Had he been a man of means the auburn-haired baggage would not
have gone. Semiramis would not have thought it so important to ply her
trade. But golden goblets lifted from the halls of fat merchants, pearl necklaces spirited from the very bedsides of sleek noblewomen, brought less
than a tenth their value from the fences in the Desert. And the art of saving
was not in him. Gambling and drinking took what remained from wenching. The only way to sufficient gain was one grand theft. But what? And
from where?

There was the palace, of course. King Tiridates had treasures beyond
counting. The king was a drunkard—he had been so since the days when
the evil mage Yara was the true power in Zamora—but in justice he should
willingly part with some portion of his wealth for the man who had brought
Yara and the Elephant Tower down. If he knew that man's deeds, and if he
were of a mind to part with anything to a barbarian thief. But the debt was
owed, to Conan's mind, and collecting on it—albeit without Tiridates'
knowledge or consent—would not be theft at all.

Then there was Larsha, the ancient, accursed ruins not far from Shadizar.
The origin of those toppled towers and time-eroded walls was shrouded in
the depths of time, but everyone agreed there was treasure there. And a
curse. A decade before, when Tiridates was still a vigorous king, he had sent
a company of the King's Own inside those walls in the full light of day. Not

one had returned, and the screams of their dying had so panicked the king's retinue and bodyguard that they had abandoned him. Tiridates had been forced to flee with them. If any had tried to penetrate that doom-filled city since, none had ever returned to speak of it.

Conan did not fear curses—had he not already proven himself a bane of mages?—as he did not fear to enter the very palace of the king. But which? To remove sufficient wealth from the palace would be as difficult as removing it from the accursed ruins. Which would give him the most for his labors?

He became aware of eyes on him and looked up. A dark, hook-nosed man wearing a purple head-cloth held by a golden fillet stood regarding him. A purple silk robe hung from the watcher's bony shoulders. He leaned on a shoulder-high staff of plain, polished wood, and, though he bore no other weapon and was plainly not of the Desert, there was no fear of robbery—or anything else—in his black eyes.

"You are Conan the Cimmerian," he said. It was not a question. "It is said you are the best thief in Shadizar."

"And who are you," Conan said warily, "to accuse an honest citizen of thievery? I am a bodyguard."

The man took a seat across from him without asking. He held his staff with one hand; Conan saw that he regarded it as a weapon. "I am Ankar, a merchant dealing in very special merchandise. I have need of the best thief in Shadizar."

With a confident smile Conan sipped his wine. He was on familiar ground, now. "And what special merchandise do you wish to acquire?"

"First know that the price I will pay is ten thousand pieces of gold."

Conan set his mug down before he slopped wine over his wrist. With ten thousand . . . by the Lord of the Mound, he would be no longer a thief, but a man with a need to guard against thieves. "What is it you wish stolen?" he said eagerly.

A tiny smile touched Ankar's thin lips. "So you are Conan the Thief. At least that is settled. Know you that Yildiz of Turan and Tiridates have concluded a treaty to stop the depredations against trade along their common border?"

"I may have heard, but there's no loot in treaties."

"Think you so? Then know that gifts were exchanged between the kings in token of this pact, which is to last for five years. To Tiridates Yildiz sent five dancing girls bearing a golden casket, on the lid of which are set five stones of amethyst, five of sapphire and five of topaz. Within the casket are five pendants, each containing a stone the like of which no man has ever seen."

Conan was tiring of the strange man's supercilious air. Ankar took him for a rude, untutored barbarian, and perhaps he was, but he was not a fool.

"You wish me to steal the pendants, not the casket," he said, and was pleased to see Ankar's eyes widen.

The self-named merchant took his staff with both hands. "Why do you say that, Cimmerian?" His voice was low and dark.

"The casket you describe could be duplicated for far less than what you offer. That leaves the pendants." He measured the other's age and added with a laugh, "Unless it's the dancing girls you want."

Ankar did not join in, continuing to watch Conan with hooded eyes. "You are not stupid—" He stopped abruptly.

Conan angrily shut off his laughter. Not stupid—for a barbarian. He would show this man a thing or three of barbarians. "Where are these pendants?" he growled. "If they're in the treasure room, I will need time for planning and—"

"Tiridates basks in the reflected glory of a more powerful monarch. The casket shows that Yildiz has concluded a treaty with him. It is displayed in the antechamber before his throne room, so that all who approach him may see."

"I will still need time," Conan said. "Ten days for preparations."

"Impossible! Make fewer preparations. Three days."

"Fewer preparations and you'll never see those pendants. And my head will decorate a pike above the West Gate. Eight days."

Ankar touched the tip of his tongue to thin lips. For the first time he appeared uncertain. His eyes clouded as if he had lost himself in his thoughts. "Fi . . . four days. Not a moment more."

"Five days," Conan insisted. "A moment less, and Tiridates will keep his pendants."

Ankar's eyes dimmed again. "Five days," he said finally.

"Done." Conan suppressed a grin. He meant to have those pendants in his hand that very night, but had he told this Ankar that, when he put the pendants in the man's hands, Ankar would think it nothing out of the ordinary. By negotiating for ten days and settling for five as the absolute minimum, he would be thought a miracle worker when he produced the pendants on the next morn. He had seen each reaction from men before. "There was mention of ten thousand gold pieces, Ankar."

The swarthy man produced a purse from beneath his robe and slid it halfway across the table. "Twenty now. A hundred more when you tell me your plan. The balance when you hand me the pendants."

"A small part beforehand for a payment of ten thousand," Conan grumbled, but inside he was not displeased at all. The twenty alone equalled his largest commission before this, and the rest would be in hand on the morrow.

He reached for the purse. Of a sudden Ankar's hand darted to cover his atop the gold-filled pouch, and he started. The man's hand was as cold as a corpse's.

"Hear me, Conan of Cimmeria," the dark man hissed. "If you betray me in this, you will pray long your head did in truth adorn a pike."

Conan tore his hand free from the other's bony grip. He had to restrain himself from working the hand, for those icy fingers had seemed to drain the warmth from his own. "I have agreed to do this thing," he said hotly. "I am not so civilized as to break the honor of my word."

For a moment he thought the hook-nosed man was going to sneer, and knew that if he did he would rip the man's throat out. Ankar contented himself with a sniff and a nod, though. "See that you remember your honor, Cimmerian." He rose and glided away before Conan could loose a retort.

Long after the dark man was gone the muscular youth sat scowling. It would serve the fool right if he kept the pendants, once they were in hand. But he had given his word. Still, the decision as to where to gain his wealth had been settled. He upended the pouch, spilling thick, milled-edge roundels of gold, stamped with Tiridates' head, into his palm, and his black mood was whisked away.

"Abuletes!" he roared. "Wine for everyone!" There would be time enough for frugality when he had the ten thousand.

The man who called himself Ankar strode out of the Desert, trailed to the very end of the twisting, odoriferous streets by human jackals. They, sensing something of the true nature of the man, never screwed their courage tight enough to come near him. He, in turn, spared them not a glance, for he could bend men's minds with his eye, drain the life from them with a touch of his hand. His true name was Imhep-Aton, and many who knew him shuddered when they said it.

At the house he had rented in Hafira, one of the better sections of Shadizar, the door was opened by a heavily muscled Shemite, as large as Conan, with a sword on his hip. A trader in rare gems—for as such he was known among the nobles of the city—needed a bodyguard. The Shemite cowered away from the bony necromancer, hastening to close and bolt the door behind him.

Imhep-Aton hurried into the house, then down, into the basement and the chambers beneath. He had chosen the house for those deep buried rooms. Some works were best done in the bowels of the earth, where no ray of sun ever found its way.

In the anteroom to his private chamber two lush young girls of sixteen summers fell on their knees at his entrance. They were naked but for golden chains at wrist and ankle, waist and neck, and their big, round eyes shone with lust and worshipful adoration. His will was theirs, the fulfillment of his slightest whim the greatest desire of their miserable lives. The spells that kept them so killed in a year or two, and that he found a pity, for it necessitated the constant acquisition of new subjects.

The girls groveled on their faces; he paused before passing into his inner chamber to lay his staff before the door. Instantly the wooden rod transmuted into a hooded viper that coiled and watched with cold, semi-intelligent eyes. Imhep-Aton had no fear of human intruders while his faithful myrmidion watched.

The inner room was barren for a mage's work-chamber—no piles of human bones to stoke unholy fires, no dessicated husks of mummies to be ground into noxious powders—but what little there was permeated the chamber with bone-chilling horror. At either end of a long table, thin, greasy plumes of smoke arose from two black candles, the tallow rendered from the body of a virgin strangled with her mother's hair and made woman after death by her father. Between them lay a book bound in human skin, a grimoire filled with secrets darker than any outside of Stygia itself and a glass, fluid-filled simulation of a human womb, within which floated the misshapen form of one unborn.

Before the table Imhep-Aton made arcane gestures, muttered incantations known to but a handful human. The homunculus twitched within the pellucid womb. Agony twisted its deformed face as the pitiful jaws creaked painfully open.

"Who calls?"

Despite the gurgling distortion of that hollow cry, there was an imperiousness to it that told Imhep-Aton who spoke across the countless miles from ancient Khemi, in Stygia, through another such monstrosity. Thoth-Amon, master mage of the Black Ring.

"It is I, Imhep-Aton. All is in readiness. Soon Amanar will be cast into the outer dark."

"Then Amanar still lives. And the One Whose Name May Not Be Spoken yet profanes the honor of Set. Remember your part, and your blame, and your fate, should you fail."

Sweat dampened Imhep-Aton's forehead. It had been he who brought Amanar into the Black Ring. He remembered once seeing a renegade priest given to Set in a dark chamber far beneath Khemi, and swallowed bile.

"I will not fail," he muttered, then forced strength into his words so the homunculus could hear and transmit. "I will not fail. That which I came to secure will be in my hands in five days. Amanar and the One Whose Name May Not Be Spoken will be delivered into the power of Set."

"That you are given this chance of redemption is not of my will. If you fail. . . ."

"There will be no failure. An ignorant barbarian thief who knows no more of reality than a gold coin will—"

The horrible, hollow voice from the twisted shape in the glass vessel cut him off. "I care naught for your methods. Set cares naught. Succeed, or pay."

The grotesque mouth snapped shut, and the homunculus curled tighter into a fetal ball. The communication was ended.

Imhep-Aton scrubbed damp palms down the front of his purple robe. Some measure of what had been sucked out of him these minutes past, he could regain at the expense of the two girls awaiting his desires. But they knew their place in the scheme of things, if not the brevity of that place. There was little to be gained from such. Not so the thief. The Cimmerian thought himself Imhep-Aton's equal, if not, from some strange barbarian perspective, his superior. The mere fact that he was alive would remind the mage of this time when he stank with fear-sweat. Once the pendants were safely in hand this Conan would find not gold, but death, as his payment.

IV

The alabaster walls of Tiridates' palace stood five times the height of a man, and atop them guardsmen of the King's Own marched sentry rounds in gilded half-armor and horsehair-crested helms. Within, when the sun was high, peacocks strutted among flowers from lands beyond the ken of man, the hours were struck on silver gongs, and silken maids danced for the pleasure of the drunkard king. Now, in the purple night, ivory towers with corbeled arches and golden-finialed domes pierced the sky in silent stillness.

Conan watched from the shadows around the plaza that surrounded the palace, counting the steps of guards as they moved toward each other, then away. His boots and cloak were in the sack slung at his side, muffling any clank of the tools of his trade. His sword was strapped across his back, the hilt rising above his right shoulder, and the Karpashian dagger was sheathed on his left forearm. He held a rope of black-dyed raw silk, on the end of which dangled a padded graponel.

As the guards before him met once more and turned to move apart, he broke from the shadows. His bare feet made almost no sound on the gray paving stones of the plaza. He began to swing the graponel as he ran. There would be little time before the guards reached the ends of their rounds and turned back. He reached the foot of the pale wall, and a heave of his massive arm sent the graponel skyward into the night. It caught with a muted click. Tugging once at the rope to test it, he swarmed up the wall as another man might climb a stair.

Wriggling flat onto the top of the wall, he stared at the graponel and heaved a sigh of relief. One point had barely caught the lip of the wall, and a scrape on the stone showed how it had slipped. A finger's breadth more. . . . But he had no time for these reflections. Hurriedly he pulled the sable rope up, and dropped into the garden below. He hit rolling, to absorb the fall, and came up in rustling bushes against the wall.

Above, the guards came closer, their footsteps thudding on the stone. Conan held his breath. If they noticed the scrape, an alarm would surely be raised. The guards came together, muttered words were exchanged, and they began to move apart. He waited until the sounds of their going had faded, then he was off, massive muscles working, in a loping stride past ferns that towered above his head and pale-flowered vines that rustled where there was no breeze.

Across the garden a peacock called, like the plaintive cry of a woman. Conan cursed whoever had wandered out to wake the bird from its roosting. Such noises were likely to draw the guards' attentions. He redoubled his pace. There was need to be inside before anyone came to check.

Experience had taught him that the higher he was above a ground-level entrance, the more likely anyone who saw him was to think he had a right there. If he were moving from a lower level to a higher, he might be challenged, but from a higher to a lower, never. An observer thought him servant or bodyguard returning from his master to his quarters below, and thought no more on it. It was thus his practice to enter any building at as high a level as he could. Now, as he ran, his eyes searched the carven white marble wall of the palace ahead, seeking those balconies that showed no light. Near the very roof of the palace, a hundred feet and more above the garden, he found the darkened balcony he sought.

The pale marble of the palace wall had been worked in the form of leafy vines, providing a hundred grips for fingers and toes. For one who had played on the cliffs of Cimmeria as a boy, it was as good as a path. As he swung his leg over the marble balustrade of the balcony, the peacock cried again, and this time its cry was cut off abruptly. Conan peered down to where the guardsmen made their rounds. Still they seemed to notice nothing amiss. But it would be well to get the pendants in hand and be away as quickly as possible. Whatever fool was wandering about—and perhaps silencing peacocks—must surely rouse the sentries given time.

He pushed quickly through the heavy damask curtains that screened the balcony and halfway across the darkened room before he realized his mistake. He was not alone. Breath caught in a canopied, gauze-hung bed, and someone stirred in the sheets.

The Karpashian dagger appeared in his fist as he gathered himself and sprang for the bed. Silken gauze as fine as spun cobwebs ripped away before him, and he grappled with the bed's occupant, his wild charge carrying them both onto the marble mosaic floor. Abruptly he became aware that the flesh he wrestled with, though firm, was yielding beneath his iron grip, and there was a sweet scent of flowery perfume. He tore away the silk sheets to see more clearly who it was that struggled so futilely against him.

First bared were long, shapely legs, kicking wildly, then rounded hips, a tiny waist, and finally a pretty face filled with dark, round eyes that stared at him fearfully above the fingers he locked instantly over her mouth. She wore a silver-mounted black stone that dangled between her small, shapely breasts, and beyond that was concealed only by dark, waist-long hair.

"Who are you, girl?" He loosened his grip to let her speak, but kept his hand poised in case she took it into her head to scream.

She swallowed, and a small, pink tongue licked her ripe lips. "I am called Velita, noble sir. I'm only a slave girl. Please do not hurt me."

"I won't hurt you." He cast a quick eye around the tapestry-draped bedchamber for something convenient to bind her with. She could not be left free to raise an alarm. It came to him that these were not the sleeping quarters of a slave girl. "What are you doing here, Velita? Are you meeting someone? The truth, now."

"No one, I swear." Her voice faltered, and her head dropped. "The king chose me out, but in the end he preferred a youth from Corinthia. I could not return to the zenana. I wish I were back in Aghrapur."

"Aghrapur! Are you one of the dancing girls sent by Yildiz?"

Her small head tossed angrily. "I was the best dancer at the court of Yildiz. He had no call to give me away." Suddenly she gasped. "You do not belong here! Are you a thief? Please! I will be yours if you free me from this catamite king."

Conan smiled. The idea had amusement value, this stealing of a dancing girl from the king's palace. Slight as she was, she would be no inconsiderable burden to carry over the palace wall, but he had pride of his youth and strength.

"I'll take you with me, Velita, but I have no desire to own slaves. I'll set you free to go where you will, and with a hundred pieces of gold, as well. This I swear by Crom, and by Bel, god of thieves." A generous gesture, he reflected, but he could well afford it. It would still leave nine thousand nine hundred for himself, after all.

Velita's lower lip trembled. "You aren't making sport of me, are you? Oh, to be free." Her slender arms snaked around him tightly. "I will serve you, I swear, and dance for you, and—"

For a moment he enjoyed the pleasant pressure of her firm breasts against his chest, then drew himself back to the matter at hand.

"Enough, girl. Help me obtain what I came for, and you need do no more. You know the pendants that came with you to Tiridates?"

"Surely. See, here is one." She pulled the silver chain from around her neck and thrust it into his hands.

He turned it over curiously. His time as a thief had given him some knowledge in the value of such things. The silver mounting and chain were of good workmanship, but plain. As for the stone. . . . An ebon oval as long as the top joint of his forefinger, it had the smooth feel of a pearl, but was not. Red flecks seemed to appear near the surface and dart into great depths. Abruptly he tore his gaze from the pendant.

"What are you doing with this, Velita? I was told they were displayed in a golden casket in the antechamber of the throne room."

"The casket is there, but Tiridates likes us to dance for him wearing them. We wear them this night."

Conan sat back on his heels, replacing his dagger in its sheath. "Can you fetch the other girls here, Velita?"

She shook her head. "Yasmeen and Susa are with officers of the guard, Consela with a steward, and Aramit with a counselor. As the king has little interest in women, the others take their pleasure. Does . . . does this mean you will not take me with you?"

"I said I would," he snapped. He hefted the pendant on his palm. Ankar would likely not pay any part of the ten thousand for one pendant, but to gather the other four from women scattered throughout the palace, each in the company of a man, was clearly impossible. Reluctantly he replaced the silver chain about her neck. "I will take you away, but I fear you must remain another night yet."

"Another night? If I must, I will. But why?"

"Tomorrow night at this hour I will come again to this room. You must gather the pendants here, with the other girls or without. I cannot carry more than one of you over the wall, but I'll not harm them, I promise."

Velita worried her lower lip with small, white teeth. "They care not, so long as their cage be gold," she muttered. "There's risk in what you ask."

"There is. If you cannot do it, say so. I'll take you away tonight, and get what I can for the single piece."

For a moment longer she knelt frowning among the tangled sheets. "You risk your life, I but a whipping. I will do it. What—"

He planted a hand over her mouth as the door of the darkened room opened. A mailed man entered, the red-dyed crest of a captain on his helm, blinking in the dimness. He was even taller than Conan, though perhaps a finger less broad of shoulder.

"Where are you, wench?" the captain chuckled, moving deeper into the room. Conan waited, letting him come closer. "I know you're here, you hot-bodied little vixen. A chamberlain saw you flee red-faced hence from our good king's chambers. You need a true man to assuage your—What!"

Conan launched himself at the large man as the other jumped back, clawing for his sword. One of the Cimmerian's big hands clutched the captain's sword wrist, the other seized his throat beneath a bearded chin. He could afford no outcry, not even such as the man might make after a dagger was lodged twixt his ribs.

Chest to chest the two big men stood, feet working for leverage on the mosaic arabesques of the floor. The guardsman's free hand clubbed against the back of Conan's neck, and again. The Cimmerian released his grip on the man's throat, throwing that arm around the Zamoran to hold him close. At the same instant he let go the sword wrist, snaked his hand under that arm and behind the other's shoulder to grab the bearded chin. His arms corded with the strain of forcing the helmeted head back. The tall soldier abandoned his attempt to reach his sword and suddenly grasped Conan's head with both his hands, twisting with all his might.

Conan's breath rasped in his throat, and the blood pounded in his ears. He could smell his own sweat, and that of the Zamoran. A growl built deep in his throat. He forced the man's head back. Back. Abruptly there was an audible snap, and the guardsman was a dead weight sagging on his chest.

Panting, Conan let the man fall. The helmeted head was at an impossible angle.

"You've killed him," Velita breathed. "You've . . . I recognize him. That's Mariates, a captain of the guard. When he's found here. . . ."

"He won't be," Conan answered.

Quickly he dragged the body out onto the balcony and dug his rope out of the sack at his side. It would stretch but halfway to the ground. Hooking the graponel over the stone balustrade at the side of the balcony, he let the dark rope fall.

"When I whistle, Velita, unloose this."

He bound the dead guardsman's wrists with the man's own swordbelt, and thrust his head and right arm through the loop they formed. When he straightened, the man dangled down his back like a sack. A heavy sack. He reminded himself of the ten thousand pieces of gold.

"What are you doing?" she asked. "And what's your name? I don't even know that."

"I'm making sure the body isn't found in this room." He stepped over the rail and checked the graponel again. It wouldn't do to have it slip here. Clad in naught but the pendant, Velita stood watching him, her big dark eyes tremulous. "I am Conan of Cimmeria," he said proudly, and let himself down the rope hand over hand.

Almost immediately he felt the strain in his massive arms and shoulders. He was strong, but the Zamoran was no feather, and a dead weight besides.

His bound wrists dug into Conan's throat, but there was no way to shift the burden while dangling half a hundred feet in the night air.

With a mountaineer's practiced eye he studied distances and angles, and stopped his descent in a stretch of the carven wall free of balconies. Thrusting with his powerful legs he pushed himself sideways, walking two steps along the wall, then swinging back beyond the point where he began. Then back the other way again. He stepped up the pace until he was running along the wall, swinging in an ever greater arc. At first the dead Zamoran slowed him, but then the extra weight added to his momentum, taking him closer to his goal, another balcony below and to the right of the first.

He was ten paces from the niveous stone rail. Then five. Three. And he realized he was increasing his arc too little on each swing now. He could not climb back up the rope—the guardsman's wrists were half-strangling him— nor could he continue to inch his way closer.

He swung back to his left and began his sideways run toward the balcony. It was the last time, he knew as he watched his goal materialize out of the dark. He must make it this time, or fall. Ten paces. Five. Three. Two. He was going to fall short. Desperately he thrust against the enchased marble wall, loosed one hand from the rope, stretched for the rail. His fingers caught precariously. And held. Straining, he hung between the rope and his tenuous grasp on the stone. The dangling body choked his burning breath in his throat. Shoulder joints cracking, he pulled himself nearer. And then he had a foot between the balusters. Still clutching the rope he pulled himself over the rail and collapsed on the cool marble, sucking at the night air.

It was an illusory haven, though. Quickly he freed himself from the Zamoran and bent back over the rail to whistle. The rope swung as the graponel fell free. He drew it up with grateful thanks that Velita had not been too terrified to remember, and stowed it in his sack. There was still Mariates to deal with.

Mariates' sword belt went back about the officer's waist. There was naught Conan could do about the abrasions on the man's wrists. On the side away from Velita's balcony, he rolled the dead man over the rail. From below came the crashing of broken branches. But no alarm.

Smiling, Conan used the cavern marble foliage to make his way to the ground. Evidence of Mariates' fall was plain in shattered boughs. The captain himself lay spreadeagled across an exotic shrub, the loss of which Conan thought the dilettante king might regret more than the loss of a soldier. And best of all, of the several balconies from which the man could have fallen, Velita's was not one.

Swiftly Conan made his way back through the garden. Once more the guards' paces were counted, and once more he went over the wall easily. As he reached the safety of the shadows around the plaza, he thought he heard a shout from behind, but he was not sure, and he did not linger to find out. Boots and cloak were on in moments, sword slung at his hip.

As he strode through pitchy streets at once broader and less odoriferous than those of the Desert, he thought that this might be almost his last return to that squalid district. After tomorrow night he would be beyond such places. From the direction of the palace, a gong sounded in the night.

Conan woke early the morning after his foray into the palace. He found the common room empty except for Abuletes, counting his night's take at the bar, and two skinny sweepers in rags. The fat tavernkeeper eyed Conan warily and put a protective arm about the stacked coins.

"Wine," Conan said, fishing out the necessary coppers. For all his celebration the night before there were still six of the dark man's gold coins in his purse. "I don't steal from friends," he added, when Abuletes drew the money down the bar after him in the crook of his arm.

"Friends! What friends? In the Desert, a brother in blood is no friend." Abuletes filled a rough earthenware mug from a tap in a keg and shoved it in front of Conan. "But perhaps you think to buy friends with the gold you were throwing about last night. Where did that come from, anyway? Had you aught to do with what happened at the palace in the night? No, that couldn't be. You were spending like Yildiz himself before ever it happened. You'd better watch that, showing your gold so free in the Desert."

The tavernkeeper would have gone on, but Conan cut him short. "Something happened at the palace?" He was careful to drink deep of the thin wine for punctuation, as if the question were casual.

"And you call a king's counselor dead something, plus others to the king's household and a dozen guardsmen besides, then it did."

"A dozen!"

"So I said, and so it was. Dead guardsmen at every hand, Yildiz's gifts to Tiridates taken, and never a one who saw a hair of those who did it. Never a one in all the palace." Abuletes rubbed his chins with a pudgy hand. "Though there's a tale about that a pair of the sentries saw a man running from the palace. A big man. Mayhap as big as you."

"Of course it was me," Conan snorted. "I leaped over the wall, then leaped back again with all that on my back. You did say all the gifts were taken, didn't you?" He emptied his mug and thumped it down before the stout man. "Again."

"Five gemstones, five dancing girls and a golden casket." Abuletes twisted the tap shut and replaced the mug on the bar. "Unless there's more than that, they took all. I'll admit you couldn't have done it. I admit it. But why are you so interested now? Answer me that."

"I'm a thief. Someone else has done the hard part on this. All I have to do is relieve him of his ill-gotten goods." Relieve whom, he wondered. Ankar had had no other plan beyond himself. Of that he was certain. That left guardsmen gone wrong, stolen away with the treasure and the slave girls after slaying their comrades, or slain themselves after letting someone else into the palace to do the theft.

Abuletes hawked and spat on a varicolored rag, and began to scrub the bartop. "Was me," he said absently, "I'd have naught to do with this. Those who did this thing aren't of the Desert. Those who rob kings aren't to be crossed. Necromancers, for all you know. There was no one seen, remember. Not a glimpse of a hair."

It could have been a mage, Conan thought, though why a mage, or anyone else, would go through the danger of stealing five dancing girls from the palace, he could not imagine. Too, magicians were not so thick on the ground as most men believed, and he was one who should know.

"You begin to sound worried for me, Abuletes. I thought you said there were no friends in the Desert."

"You spend freely," the tavernkeeper said sourly. "That's all there is. Don't think there's more. You stay out of this, whatever it is. Whoever's behind this is too big for the likes of you. You'll end with your throat cut, and I'll be out a customer."

"Perhaps you're right. Bel! I'm for a breath of air. This sitting around talking of other men's thefts gives me a pain in the belly."

He left the fat tapster muttering darkly to himself and found his way to the street. The air in the Desert was anything but fresh. The stench of rotting offal blended with the effluvia of human excrement and vomit. The paving stones, where they had not been ripped up to leave mudholes, were slick with slime. From the dim depths of an alley, barely wide enough for a man to enter, the victim of a robbery moaned for help. Or the bait for a robbery. Either was equally likely.

Conan strode the crooked streets of that thieves' district purposefully, though he was not himself sure of what that purpose was. A swindler with tarnished silver embroidery on his vest waved a greeting as he passed, and a whore, naked but for gilded brass bells and resting her feet in a doorway, smiled at the broadshouldered youth as she suddenly felt not so tired after all. Conan did not even notice them, nor the "blind" beggar in black rags, tapping his way down the street with a broken stick, who eased his dagger back under his soiled robes after a glance at the grim set of Conan's jaw, or the three who followed him through the winding streets, the edges of their headcloths drawn across their faces, white-knuckled hands gripping cudgels beneath their dingy cloaks, before the size of his arms and the length of his sword made them take another turning.

He tried telling himself that the pendants were beyond his reach now. He had naught beyond glimmers of suspicion who had taken them, no idea at all where they were. Still, ten thousand pieces of gold was not a thing a man gave up on easily. And there was Velita. A slave girl. She would be happy with any master who was kind to her. But he had promised, sworn, to free her. By Bel and by Crom he had sworn it. His oath, and ten thousand pieces of gold.

Suddenly he realized he was out of the Desert, near the Sign of the Bull Dancer, on the Street of the Silver Fish. A tree-lined sward of grass ran down the center of the broad avenue. Slave-borne sedan chairs vied in number with pedestrians, and there was not a beggar in sight. This place was far from the Desert, yet he had friends—or at least acquaintances—here. The tavern hoarding, a slender youth in a leathern girdle, vaulting between the needle horns of a great black bull, creaked in the breeze as he went in.

Taverns, Conan reflected as he searched for a certain face, were much alike, in the Desert or out. Rather than footpads and cutpurses, plump merchants in purple silk and green brocade occupied the tables, but only the methods of stealing were different. In place of a coiner was a slender man holding a pomander before his prominent nose. He did not make the money he passed, rather buying it through the back door of the king's mint. The panderers dressed like noblemen, in scarlet robes, with emeralds at their ears, and some of them were indeed noblemen, but they were panderers no less. The prostitutes wore gold instead of gilt, rubies instead of spessartine, but they were just as naked, and they sold the same wares.

Conan spotted the man he wanted, Ampartes, a merchant who cared little if the king's duties had been paid on the goods he bought, alone at a table against the wall. Whatever happened in Shadizar, Ampartes soon knew of it. The chair across the table from the plump merchant groaned in protest as Conan's bulk dropped into it, a sound not far from that which rose in Ampartes' throat. His oily cheek twitched as his dark eyes rolled to see who had noted the Cimmerian's arrival. He tugged at his short, pointed beard with a beringed hand.

"What are you doing here, Conan?" he hissed, and blanched as if in fear the name might have been overheard. "I have no need of . . . of your particular wares."

"But I have need of yours. Tell me of what happened in the city last night."

Ampartes' voice rose to a squeak.

"You . . . you mean the palace?"

"No," Conan said, and hid a smile at the relief on the merchant's face. He grabbed a pewter goblet from the tray of a passing serving girl, a hand's breadth strip of crimson silk low on her hips her only garb, and filled it from Ampartes' blue-glazed flagon. The girl gave him a coy smile, then tossed her blonde head with a snort and hurried on sulkily when he did not give her a second glance. "But anything else unusual. Anything at all."

For the next two hours the merchant babbled in his relief that Conan was not involving him in the palace theft. Conan learned that on the night before in Shadizar a dealer in rare wines had strangled his mistress on discovering her with his son, and a gem merchant's wife had put a dagger in her husband's ribs for no reason that anyone knew. A nobleman's niece had been taken by kidnappers, but those who knew said her ransom, to come from her inheritance, would pay her uncle's debts. Thieves had entered the homes of five merchants and two nobles. One noble had had even his sedan chair and the robes from his back taken on the High Vorlusian Way, and a slave dealer's weasand had been slit outside his own auction house, some said for the keys to his strongbox, others for not checking the source of his merchandise, thus selling an abducted noblewoman into Koth. A merchant of Akif, visiting a most specialized brothel called The House of the Lambs of Hebra, had. . . .

"Enough!" Conan's hand cracked on the tabletop. Ampartes stared at him open-mouthed. "What you've told me so far could happen on any night in Shadizar, and usually does. What occurred out of the ordinary? It doesn't have to do with gold, or theft. Just so it's strange."

"I don't understand what you want," the oily man muttered. "There's the matter of the pilgrims, but there's no profit there. I don't know why I waste my time with you."

"Pilgrims?" Conan said sharply. "What was unusual about these pilgrims?"

"In Mitra's name, why would you want to know about. . . ." Ampartes swallowed as Conan's steel blue eyes locked his. "Oh, very well. They were from Argos, far to the west, making a pilgrimage to a shrine in Vendhya, as far to the east."

"I need no lessons in geography," Conan growled. "I've heard of these lands. What did these pilgrims do that was out of the ordinary?"

"They left the city two full glasses before cock crow, that's what. Something about a vow not to be inside a city's walls at dawn, I understand. Now where's your profit in that?"

"Just you tell me what I want to hear, and let me worry about profit. What sort of men were these pilgrims?"

Ampartes threw him an exasperated look. "Zandru's Bells, man! Do you expect me to know more about a mere band of pilgrims than that they exist?"

"I expect," Conan said drily, "that on any given day you'll know which nobles lost how much at dice, who slept with whose wife, and how many times the king sneezed. The pilgrims? Rack your brains, Ampartes."

"I don't. . . ." The plump merchant grunted as Conan lay his left arm on the table. The forearm sheath was empty, and the Cimmerian's right hand was below the table's edge. "They were pilgrims. What more is there to say? Hooded men in coarse robes that showed not a hair of them. No better or worse mounted than most pilgrims. The bodies of five of their number who'd died on the way were packed in casks of wine on camels. Seems they'd made another vow, that all who started the pilgrimage would reach the shrine. Mitra, Conan, who can say much of pilgrims?"

Five bodies, Conan thought. Five dancing girls. "There were fighting men with these pilgrims? Armed men?"

Ampartes shook his head. "Not so much as a dagger in evidence, is what I heard. They told the sergeant at the Gate of the Three Swords that the spirit of their god would protect them. He said a good sword would do a better job, and wearing a soldier's boots wasn't enough."

"What about a soldier's boots?"

"For the love of . . . now I'm supposed to know about boots?" He spread his hands. "All right. All I know is one of them was wearing a pair of cavalryman's halfboots. His robe was caught on his stirrup leather so one showed." His tone became sarcastic. "Do you want to know what they looked like? Red, with some sort of serpent worked in the leather. Strange, that, but there it is. And that, Conan, is every last thing I know about those accursed pilgrims. Will you satisfy my curiosity now? What in the name of all the gods does a man like you want with pilgrims?"

"I'm seeking a religious experience," Conan replied, sheathing his dagger. He left the merchant laughing till tears ran down his fleshy cheeks.

As Conan hurried across Shadizar to the stable where his horse was kept, he knew he was right. Not only the five bodies in casks told him, but also the Gate of the Three Swords. That gate let out to the northeast, toward the caravan route that ran from Khesron through the Kezankian Mountains to Sultanapur. Vendhya might only be a name to him, but he knew it was reached by leaving through the Gate of the Black Throne and traveling southeast through Turan and beyond the Vilayet Sea. As soon as he could put saddle to horse, he would be off through the Gate of the Three Swords after Velita, the pendants, and his ten thousand pieces of gold.

VI

The man in field armor contrasted sharply with the others in Tiridates' private audience chamber. From greaves over his halfboots to ring mail and gorget, his armor was plain and dark, so as not to reflect light when on campaign. Even the horsehair crest on the helmet beneath his arm was russet rather than scarlet. He was Haranides, a captain of cavalry who had risen without patron or family connections. Now the hawk-nosed captain was wondering if the rise had been worth it.

Of the four others in the ivory-paneled room, only two were worthy of note. Tiridates, King of Zamora, slouched on the Minor Throne—its arms were golden hunting leopards in full bound, the back a peacock feathered in emeralds, rubies, sapphires and pearls—as if it were a tavern stool, a golden goblet dangling from one slack hand. His amethystine robe was rumpled and stained, his eyes but half-focused. With his free hand he idly caressed the arm of a slender blonde girl who knelt beside the throne in naught but perfume and a wide choker of pearls about her swanlike neck. On the other side of the throne a youth, equally blonde and slender and attired the same, sulked for his lack of attention.

The other man worth marking, perhaps more so than the king, stood three paces to the right of the throne. Graying and stooped, but with shrewd intelligence engraved on his wizened face, he wore a crimson robe slashed with gold, and the golden Seal of Zamora on its emeralded chain about his neck. His name was Aharesus, and the seal had fallen to him with the death of Malderes, the previous chief king's counselor, the night before.

"You know why you are summoned, captain?" Aharesus said.

"No, my lord Counselor," Haranides replied stiffly. The counselor watched him expectantly, until at last he went on. "I can suspect, of course. Perhaps it has to do with the events of last night?"

"Very good, captain. And do you have any glimmering why you, instead of some other?"

"No, my lord Counselor." And this time, in truth, he had not a flickering of an idea. He had returned to the city only shortly after dawn that very morning, coming back from duty on the Kothian border. A hard posting, but what could be expected for a man with no preferment?

"You are chosen because you were not in Shadizar this year past." Haranides blinked, and the counselor chuckled, a sound like dry twigs scraping together. "I see your surprise, captain, though you conceal it well. An admirable trait in a military man. As you were not in the city, you could not be part of any . . . plot, involving those on duty in the palace last night."

"Plot!" the captain exclaimed. "Pardon, my lord, but the King's Own has always been loyal to the throne."

"Loyalty to his fellows is another good trait for a military man, captain." The counselor's voice hardened. "Don't carry it too far. Those who had the duty last night are even now being put to the question."

Haranides felt sweat trickling down his ribs. He had no wish to join those men enjoying the attentions of the king's torturers. "My lord knows that I've always been a loyal soldier."

"I reviewed your record this morning," Aharesus said slowly. "Your return to the city at this juncture was like a stroke from Mitra. These are parlous times, captain."

"Their heads," the king barked abruptly. His head swung in a muddled arc between the captain and the counselor. Haranides was shocked to realize that he had forgotten the king was present. "I want their heads on pikes, Aharesus. Stole my . . . my tribute from Yildiz. Stole my dancing girls." Tiridates directed a bleary smile at the slave girl, then jerked his gaze back to Haranides. "You bring them back to me, do you hear? The girls, the pendants, the casket. And the heads. The heads." With a belch the king sagged back into a sodden lump. "More wine," he muttered. The blonde youth darted away and returned with a crystal vessel and a fawning smile.

The captain's sweating increased. It was no secret Tiridates was a drunkard, but being witness to it could do him no good.

"The insult to the honor of the king is, captain, paramount, of course," Aharesus said with a careful glance at the king, who had his face buried in the goblet of wine. "On a wider view, however, what must be considered is that the palace was entered and the Chief King's Counselor murdered."

"My lord counselor thinks that was the reason for it all, and the other just a screen?"

The Counselor gave him a shrewd look. "You've a brain, captain. You may have a future. Yes, it makes no sense otherwise. Some foreign power wished the Counselor dead for some purpose of their own. Perhaps Yildiz himself. He has dreams of an empire, and Malderes often thwarted those plans." Aharesus fingered the golden seal on his chest thoughtfully. "In any case, it's doubtful that Yildiz, or whoever is responsible, would send his own people into the very palace. One of those being questioned screamed the name of the Red Hawk before he died."

"She's just a bandit, my lord Counselor."

"And a man babbles when he's dying. But she's a bandit who will dare much for gold, and we have no other way to search. Until one of those being questioned loosens his tongue." The chill in his tone promised the questioning would continue until many tongues were loosened; Haranides shivered. "You, captain, will take two companies of cavalry and hound this Red Hawk. Run her to ground and bring her here in chains. We'll soon find if she had aught to do with this business."

Haranides took a deep breath. "My lord Counselor, I must have some idea of where to look. This woman brigand ranges the entire countryside." Incongruously, one of the slaves giggled. Tiridates had both fair heads clutched to his chest.

The stooped counselor flickered an eye at the king and pursed his lips briefly. "Before dawn this morning, captain, a party claiming to be pilgrims departed Shadizar by the Gate of the Three Swords. I believe these were the Red Hawk's men."

"I will ride within the hour, my lord Counselor," Haranides said with a bow. He suspected the guards at that gate were among those under the question. "With your permission, my lord Counselor? My King?"

"Find this jade, captain," Aharesus said, "and you will find yourself a patron as well."

He waved a bony hand in dismissal, but as the captain turned to go Tiridates lurched unsteadily to his feet, pushing the two pale-skinned slaves sprawling at his feet.

"Find my pendants!" the drunken King snarled. "Find my casket and my dancing girls! Find my gifts from Yildiz, captain, or I'll decorate a pike with your head! Now, go! Go!"

With a sour taste in his mouth, Haranides bowed once more and backed out of the audience chamber.

The garden of Imhep-Aton's rented dwelling was pleasant, a cool breeze rustling in the trees and stirring the bright-colored flowers, but the mage took no pleasure in it. He had had some idea that Conan could deliver the pendants before the five days he had bargained for—the necromancer had some knowledge of thieves, and the way their minds worked. But never had he expected the Cimmerian to revert to his barbarism and turn the palace into a charnel house. The chief king's counselor, in Set's name!

He cared not what Zamorans died, or how, but the fool had set the city on its ear with these murders. Now Imhep-Aton must worry that the thief would be run to earth before the prize was delivered into his bony hands.

The mage whirled as his muscular Shemite servant came into the garden, his lean face so twisted that the big man quailed.

"I did as you commanded, master. To the word."

"Then where is the Cimmerian?" The thaumaturge's voice was deceptively gentle. If this cretin had bungled as well. . . .

"Gone, master. He has not been seen at the tavern since this morning, early."

"Gone!"

The brawny Shemite half-raised his hands as if to shield himself from the other's anger. "So I was told, master. He sent a message to some wench at the tavern that he would be away some time, that he was riding to the northeast."

Imhep-Aton's scowl deepened. Northeast? There was nothing to the. . . . The caravan route from Khesron to Sultanapur. Could the barbarian be thinking of selling the pendants in the very country from which they came? Obviously he had decided to work for himself. But, Set, why the dancing girls? He shook his vulturine head angrily. The savage's reasons were of no account.

"Prepare horses and sumpter animals for the two of us at once," he commanded. "We ride to the northeast." The Cimmerian would pay for this betrayal.

VII

The Well of the Kings lay some days to the east and west of Shadizar, surrounded by huge, toppled slabs of black stone, worn by rain and wind. Some said they were the remains of a wall, but none knew when or by whom it could have been built, as none knew what kings had claimed the well.

Conan walked his horse between the slabs and into the stunted trees, to the well of rough stones, and dismounted. On the other side of the well, back under the trees, four swarthy men in dirty keffiyehs squatted, watching him with dark eyes that shifted greedily to his horse. He flipped back the edge of his Khauranian cloak so they could see his sword, and heaved on the hoist pole to lift a bucket of water from the depths. Other than his cloak, he was covered only by a breechclout, for he liked to travel unencumbered.

The four moved closer together, whispering darkly without looking away from him. One, the leader by the deference the others showed, wore rusting ring mail, his followers breastplates of boiled leather. All had ancient scimitars at their hips, the sort a decent weapons dealer sold for scrap. Behind them Conan could see a woman, naked and bound in a package, wrists and elbows secured behind her back, knees under her chin, heels drawn in tight to her buttocks. She raised her head, tossing back a mane of dark red hair, and stared at him in surprise, tilted green eyes above a dirty twist of cloth for a gag. The fortuneteller.

Conan emptied the bucket in a worn stone trough for his horse, and drew up another for himself. The last time he had helped this woman, she had shown not even the gratitude to warn him of the two Iranistanis' attack. Besides, he had Velita to find. He dashed water in his face, though it made little difference in the gritty heat, and upended the rest of the bucket over his head. The four men gabbled on.

So far he had tracked the pilgrims by questioning those passersby who would let an armed man of his size approach them. Enough had glimpsed something to keep him on this path, but in the last day he had seen only an old man who threw rocks and ran to hide in the thorn scrub, and a boy who had seen nothing.

"Have you fellows seen anything of pilgrims?" he said, levering up yet another bucket of water. "Hooded men on horseback, with camels?"

The leader's sharp nose twitched. "An we did, what's for us?"

"A few coppers, if you can tell me where they are." There was no reason to tempt this lot. After a day when he could be traveling away from the men he sought, he had no time to waste killing vultures. He put on a pleasant smile. "If I had silver or gold, I'd not be out chasing pilgrims. I'd be in Shadizar, drinking." He dried his hands on his cloak, just in case.

"What do you want with those pilgrims?" the sharp-nosed man wanted to know.

"That's my affair," Conan replied. "And theirs. Yours is the coppers, if you've seen them."

"Well, as to that, we have," sharp-nose said, dusting off his hands and getting up. He started toward Conan with his hand out. "Let's see the color of your coins."

Conan dug into the leather pouch at his belt with his right hand, and sharp-nose's grin turned nasty. A short dagger with a triangular blade appeared in his fist. Laughing wickedly, the other three pulled their scimitars and rushed forward to join the kill.

Without pausing a beat Conan snatched up the bucket left-handed and smashed it down on the man's head, blood and water flying in all directions. "No time!" he shouted. He plucked the dagger from its forearm sheath, and of a sudden its hilt was sticking from the throat of the foremost attacker. Even as it struck Conan was unlimbering his broadsword. "Bel strike you!" He leaped across the collapsing man, who was clutching the dagger in his throat with blood-covered hands. "I've no time!" A sweeping slash of the broad blade, and the third man's torso sank to the ground where his head was already spinning. "No time, curse you!" The last man had his scimitar raised high when Conan lunged with a two-handed grip and plunged his blade through leather breastplate, chest and backbone. Black eyes filmed over, and the man toppled to one side with his hands still raised above his head.

Conan put a foot on the leather armor and tugged his sword free, wiping it clean on the man's dingy keffiyeh before he sheathed it. The dagger was retrieved from its temporary home in a brigand's throat and cleaned in the same way. The woman watched him wide-eyed, starting away as much as her bonds allowed when he came near, but he only cut the cords and turned away, sheathing his dagger.

"If you don't have your own horse," he said, "you can have one of these vermin's. The rest are mine. You can have the weapons, if you want. They'll fetch something for your trouble." But not much, he thought. Still, he owed her nothing, and the horses, poor as they were likely to be, would be a help if he had to pursue those accursed pilgrims far.

The red-haired woman rubbed her wrists as she walked to the dead men, unashamed of her nakedness. She was an ivory-skinned callimastian delight, all curves and long legs and rounded places. There was a spring to her walk that made him wonder if she was a dancer. She picked up one of the scimitars, ran a contemptuous eye along its rust-pitted blade, and suddenly planted a bare foot solidly in the ribs of one of the dead men.

"Pig!" she spat.

Conan went about gathering the horses, five of them, one noticeably better than the rest, while she kicked and reviled each body in turn. Abruptly she whirled to face him, feet well apart, fist on rounded hip, scimitar swinging free. With her tousled hair in an auburn mane about her head, she had the air of a lioness brought to human form.

"They took me unawares," she announced.

"Of course," Conan said. "I suppose the black is yours? Best of the lot." He braided the reins of the other four, hairy plains animals two hands shorter at the shoulder than his own Turanian gray, and fastened them to his high-pommeled saddle. "Best for you would be to go straight back to Shadizar. It's dangerous out here for a woman alone. What possessed you to try it in the first place?"

She took a quick step toward him. "I said they took me unawares! They'd have died on my blade, else!"

"And I said of course. I can't take you back to the city. I seek men who took something that . . . that belongs to me."

A pantherine howl jerked him around, and he tumbled backwards between the horses just in time to avoid decapitation by her curved blade. "Derketo take you!" she howled, thrusting at him under a horse's belly. He rolled aside, and the blade gouged the packed earth where his head had been.

Scrambling on his back, he tried at once to avoid her steel and the hooves of the horses, now dancing excitedly as she moved swiftly around them trying to stab him. The roiling of them brought him suddenly looking out from under a shaggy belly at her as she pulled back her scimitar for yet another thrust. Desperately his legs uncoiled, propelling him out to tackle her around the knees. They went down in a heap together on the hard ground, and he found his arms full of female wildcat, clawing and kicking and trying to jerk her sword arm loose. Her soft curves padded her firm muscle, and she was no easy packet to hold.

"Have you gone mad, woman?" he shouted. For an answer she sank her teeth into his shoulder. "Crom!"

He hurled her away from him. She rolled across the ground and bounded to her feet. Still, he saw wonderingly, gripping the rusty sword.

"I need no man to protect me!" she spat. "I'm not some pampered concubine!"

"Who said you were?" he roared.

Then he had to jerk his sword free of its scabbard as she rushed at him with a howl of pure rage. Her green eyes burned, and her face was twisted with fury. He swung up his sword to block her downward slash. With a sharp snap the rusty scimitar broke, leaving her to stare in disbelief at the bladeless hilt in her hands.

Almost without a pause she hurled the useless hilt at his face and spun to dash for the dead men by the well. Their weapons still lay about them. Conan darted after her, and as she bent to snatch another scimitar, he swung the flat of his blade with all his strength at the tempting target thus offered. She lifted up on her toes with a strangled shriek as the steel paddle cracked against her rounded nates. Arms windmilling, she staggered forward, her foot slipping in a pool of blood, and screaming she plunged head-first over the crude stone wall of the well.

Conan dived as she went over; his big hand closed on flesh, and he was dragged to his armpits into the well by the weight of her. He discovered he was holding the red-haired wench by one ankle while she dangled over the depths. An interesting view, he thought.

"Derketo take you!" she howled. "Pull me up, you motherless whelp!"

"In Shadizar," he said conversationally, "I saved you a mauling. You called me a barbar boy, let a man near take my head off, and left without a word of thanks."

"Son of a diseased camel! Spawn of a bagnio! Pull me up!"

"Now here," he went on as if she had not spoken, "all I did was save you from rape, certainly, perhaps from being sold on the slave block. Or maybe they'd just have slit your throat once they were done with you." She wriggled violently, and he edged further over the rim to let her drop another foot. Her scream echoed up the stone cylinder. She froze into immobility.

"You had no thought of saving me," she rasped breathlessly. "You'd have ridden off to leave me if those dogs hadn't tried you."

"All the same, if I had ridden on, or if they'd killed me, you'd be wondering what you'd fetch at market."

"And you want a reward," she half wept. "Derketo curse you, you smelly barbar oaf!"

"That's the second time you've called me that," he said grimly. "What I want from you is an oath, by Derketo since you call on the goddess of love and death. An oath that you'll never again let an uncivil word pass your lips toward me, and that you'll never again raise a hand against me."

"Hairy lout! Dung-footed barbar! Do you think you can force me to—"

He cut her off. "My hand is getting sweaty. I wouldn't wait too long. You might slip." Silence answered him. "Or then again, I might grow tired of waiting."

"I will swear." Her voice was suddenly soft and sensuously yielding. "Pull me up, and I'll swear on my knees to anything you command."

"Swear first," he replied. "I'd hate to have to toss you back in. Besides, I like the view." He thought he heard the sound of a small fist smacking the stone wall of the well in frustration, and smiled.

"You untrusting ape," she snarled with all her old ferocity. "Very well. I swear, by Derketo, that I'll speak no uncivil word to you, nor raise a hand against you. I swear it. Are you satisfied?"

He hoisted her straight up out of the well, and let her drop on the hard ground with a thud and a grunt.

"You. . . ." She bit her lip and glared up at him from the ground. "You didn't have to be so rough," she said in a flat tone. Instead of answering, he unfastened his swordbelt, propping the scabbard against the well. "What . . . what are you doing?"

"You spoke of a reward." He stepped out of his breechclout. "Since I doubt a word of thanks will ever crack your teeth, I'm collecting my own reward."

"So you're nothing but a ravisher of women after all," she said bitterly.

"That was close to an uncivil word, wench. And no ravishment. All you need to do is say, 'stop,' and you'll leave this place as chaste as a virgin for all of me."

He lowered himself onto her, and though she beat at his shoulders with her fists and filled the air with vile curses the word 'stop' never once passed her lips, and soon her cries changed their nature, for she was a woman fully fledged, and he knew something of women.

After, he regained his clothes and his weapons while she rummaged among the dead men's things to cover herself. Her own garments, she said, had been ripped to shreds. He noted that this time she inspected the weapons carefully before selecting one, but he had no worries at turning his back on her even after she had belted it on. When she had been turning the air blue, not one of her curses had been directed at him. If she could keep her oath then, he was sure she would keep it now.

Once he had filled his goatskin waterbags, he swung into his saddle.

"Hold a moment," she called. "What's your name?" She had clothed herself in flowing pantaloons of bright yellow and an emerald tunic that was far too tight across the chest, though loose elsewhere. A braided gold cord held her auburn mane back from her face. He had seen her dig it out from the purse of one of the dead men.

"Conan," he said. "Conan of Cimmeria. And you?"

"My name is Karela," she said proudly, "of whatever land I happen to be standing on. Tell me, these pilgrims you seek, they have something of great value? I don't see you as a holy man, Conan of Cimmeria."

If he told her about the pendants, she would no doubt want to go with him. From the way she had handled her sword he was sure she could pull her weight, but even so he did not want her along. Let her get a sniff of ten thousand pieces of gold, and he would have to sleep with both eyes open, oath or no. He was sure of that, too.

"Valuable only to a man in Shadizar," he said casually. "A dancing girl who ran away with these pilgrims. Or maybe they stole her. Whatever, the man's besotted with her, and he'll pay five gold pieces to have her back."

"Not much for a ride in this country. There are harder bandits about than these dog stealers." She nodded to the bodies, where Conan had dragged them, well away from the water.

"I seek pilgrims, not bandits," he laughed. "They won't put up much fight. Farewell, Karela." He turned to ride away, but her next words made him draw rein.

"Don't you want to know where these pilgrims of yours are?"

He stared at her, and she looked back with green eyes innocently wide. "If you know where they are, why didn't you speak of it before? For that matter, why speak of it now? I can't see you volunteering help to me."

"Those jackals . . . made a fool of me." She grimaced, but the open look returned to her face quickly. "I was mad, Conan. I wanted to take it out on anyone. You saved my life, after all."

Conan nodded slowly. It was barely possible. And just as possible she would send him off chasing hares. But he had nothing else to go on besides picking a direction out of the air. "Where did you see them?"

"To the north. They were camped beyond some low hills. I'll show you." She vaulted easily into the saddle of her big black. "Well, do you want me to show you, or do you want to sit here all day?"

Short of dangling her down the well again, he could think no way of making her talk. He moved his black cloak to clear the leather-wrapped hilt of his sword, and motioned her to ride past. "You lead," he said.

"I know," she laughed as she dug her heels into her mount's ribs. "You like the view."

He did that, he thought wryly, but he intended to watch Karela with an eye to treachery. Trailing the robbers' horses, he rode after her.

VIII

For the rest of that day they rode north, across rolling countryside sparsely covered with low scrub. When they camped at nightfall, Conan said, "How much farther?"

Karela shrugged; her heavy round breasts shifted beneath the tight green tunic. "We'll reach it some time after dawn, if we break camp early."

She began to pile dry twigs from the scrub for a fire, but he scattered them. "No need to advertise our presence. What makes you think they'll still be there?"

Tucking flint and steel back in her pouch, she gave him an amused smile. "If they've gone, at least you'll be closer than you were. Who is this man in Shadizar who wants his slave girl back?"

"If we're riding early, we'd better turn in," he said, and she smiled again.

He wrapped himself in his cloak but did not sleep. Instead he watched her. She was wrapped in a blanket she had carried on her horse, and had her head pillowed on her high-pommeled saddle of tooled red leather. He would not have put it past her to try sneaking off with the horses in the night, but she seemed to settle right into sleep.

Purple twilight deepened to black night, and scudding clouds crossed stars like diamonds on velvet, but Conan kept his eyes open. A gibbous moon rose, and at its height the Cimmerian thought he felt eyes on him from the surrounding night. Easing his narrow-bladed dagger from its forearm sheath, he loosed the bronze brooch that held his cloak and snaked into the night on his belly. Thrice he circled the camp in silence, always feeling the eyes, but he saw no one, nor any sign that anyone had ever been there. And then, abruptly, the feeling was gone. Once more he crawled all the way around the camp, but there was still nothing. Disgusted with himself, he got up and walked back to his cloak. Karela still slept. Angrily he wrapped himself in the black wool. It was the woman. Waiting for her treachery was making him see and feel what just was not there.

While the sun was but a red rim shining above the horizon Karela woke, and they rode north again. Slowly the land changed, the low rollings becoming true hills. Conan was beginning to wonder what the men he sought would be doing so far to the north of the caravan route, when suddenly Karela kicked her horse into a gallop.

"There it is," she cried. "Just over those next hills."

Hurriedly he galloped after her. "Karela, come back! Karela!" She hurried on, disappearing around a hill. Fool woman, he thought. If the pilgrims were still there, she would have them roused.

As he rounded the hill, he slowed his mount to a walk. She was nowhere in sight, and he could no longer hear the sounds of her horse running.

"Conan!"

Conan's head whipped around at the shout. Karela sat her horse atop a hill to his right. "Crom, woman! What are you—"

"My name is Karela," she shouted. "The Red Hawk!"

She let out a shrill whistle, and suddenly mounted men in a motley collection of bright finery and mismatched armor were boiling through every gap in the hills. In a trice he was the center of a shoulder-to-shoulder ring of brigands. Carefully he folded his hands on the pommel of his saddle. So much as a twitch toward his sword would put iron-tipped quarrels through his body from the four crossbows he could see, and there might be more.

"Karela," he called, "is this the way you keep your oath?"

"I've said no uncivil word to you," she replied mockingly, "and I haven't raised my hand against you. Nor will I. I'm afraid the same can't be said of my men. Hordo!"

A burly, black-bearded man with a rough leather patch over his left eye forced his horse through the circle to confront Conan. A jagged scar ran from under the patch and disappeared in the thatch of his beard. That side of his mouth was drawn up in a permanent sneer. His ring mail had once belonged to a wealthy man—there were still traces of gilt left—and large gold hoops stretched his ears. A well-worn tulwar hung at his side.

"Conan, she called you," the big man said. "Well, I'm Hordo, the Red Hawk's lieutenant. And what I want to know, what we all want to know, is why we shouldn't cut your miserable throat right here."

"Karela was leading me," Conan began, and cut off as Hordo launched a fist the size of a small ham at him. The big man's single eye bulged as Conan caught his fist in mid-swing and stopped it dead.

For a moment the two strained, arm to arm, biceps bulging, then Hordo shouted, "Take him!" The ring of bandits closed in.

Dozens of hands clutched at Conan, tearing away his cloak, ripping loose his sword, pulling him from the saddle. But their very numbers hampered them somewhat, and he did not go easily. His dagger found a new home in ribs clothed in dirty yellow—in the press he never saw the face that went with them—a carelessly reached arm was broken at the elbow, and more than one face erupted in blood and broken teeth from his massive fists. The numbers were too many, though, and rough hands at last managed to bind his wrists behind him and link his ankles with a two-foot hobble of rawhide. Then they threw him to the stony ground, and those who had boots began to apply them to his ribs.

Finally Hordo chased them back with snarled threats, and bent to jerk Conan's head up by a fistful of hair. "We call her the Red Hawk," he spat. "You call her mistress, or my lady. But don't ever sully her name with your filthy mouth again. Not as you live."

"Why should he live at all?" snarled a weasel-faced man in dented half-armor and a guardsman's helmet with the crest gone. "Hepakiah's choking to death on his own blood from this one's dagger right now." He grimaced suddenly and spat out a tooth. "Cut his throat, and be done!"

With a grin Hordo produced a wavy-bladed Vendhyan dagger. "Seems Aberius has a good idea for a change."

Suddenly Karela forced her horse through the pack around Conan, her green cat-eyes glaring down at him. "Can't you think of something more interesting, Hordo?"

"Still keeping your oath?" Conan snarled. "Fine payment for saving you from the slave block, or worse." Hordo's fist smashed his head back into the ground.

"No man ever had to save the Red Hawk," her lieutenant growled. "She's better than any man, with sword or brains. See you remember it."

Karela laughed sweetly. "Of course I am, good Conan. If anything happens to you, it will be at the hands of these good men, not mine. Hordo, let's take him to camp. You can decide what to do with him at leisure."

The scar-faced man shouted orders, and quickly a rope was passed around Conan, under his arms. The bandits scrambled to their saddles, Hordo himself clutching the rope tied to Conan, and they started off at a trot, the horses' hooves spraying dirt and gravel in Conan's face.

Conan gritted his teeth as he was dragged. With his arms behind him, he was forced to skid along on his belly. Sharp rocks gashed his chest, and hardpacked clay scraped off patches of skin as large as his hand.

When the horses skidded to a halt, Conan spat out a mouthful of dirt and sucked in air. He ached in every muscle, and small trickles of blood still oozed from those scrapes that dust had not clotted. He was far from sure that whatever they had planned for him would be better than being dragged to death.

"Hordo," Karela exclaimed in delight, "you have my tent up."

She leaped from the saddle and darted into a red-striped pavilion. It was the only tent in the camp lying in a hollow between two tall, U-shaped hills. Rumpled bedrolls lay scattered around half-a-dozen burned-out fires. Some of the men ran to stir these up, while others dug out stone jars of *kil*, raw distilled wine, and passed them around with raucous laughter.

Conan rolled onto his side as Hordo dismounted beside him. "You're a bandit," the big Cimmerian panted. "How would you like a chance at a king's treasure?"

Hordo did not even look at him. "Get those stakes in," he shouted. "I want him pegged out now."

"Five pendants," Conan said, "and a jewel-encrusted casket. Gifts from Yildiz to Tiridates." He hated letting these men know what he was after—at best he would have a hard time remaining alive to claim a share of what he thought of as his own—but otherwise he might not live to collect even a share.

"Stir your stumps," the bearded outlaw shouted. "You can drink later."

"Ten thousand pieces of gold," Conan said. "That's what one man is willing to pay for the pendants alone. Someone else might pay more. And then there's the casket."

For the first time since arriving in the hollow Hordo turned to Conan, his one eye glaring. "The Red Hawk wants you dead. She's done good by us, so what she wants is what I want."

A score of bandits, laughing and already half-drunk, came to lift Conan and bear him to a cleared space where they had driven four stakes into the hard ground. Despite his struggles they were too many, and he soon found himself spread-eagled on his back, wet rawhide straps leading from his wrists and ankles to the stakes. The rawhide would shrink in the heat of the sun, stretching his joints to the breaking point.

"Why doesn't Hordo want you to have a chance at ten thousand pieces of gold?" Conan shouted. Every man but Hordo froze where he stood, the laughter dying in their throats.

With a curse the scar-faced brigand jumped forward. Conan tried to jerk his head aside, but lights flared before his eyes as the big man's foot caught him. "Shut your lying mouth!" Hordo snarled.

Aberius lifted his head to stare cold-eyed at the Red Hawk's lieutenant, a ferret confronting a mastiff. "What's he talking about, Hordo?"

Conan shook his head to clear it. "A king's treasure. That's what I'm talking about."

"You shut—" Hordo began, but Aberius cut him off.

"Let him talk," the pinch-faced brigand said dangerously, and other voices echoed him. Hordo glared about him, but said nothing.

Conan allowed himself a brief smile. A bit longer, and these cut-throats would turn him loose and bind Hordo and Karela in his place. But he did not intend to let them actually steal the pendants he had worked so hard for. "Five pendants," he said, "and a golden casket encrusted with gems were stolen from Tiridates' very palace not half a fortnight gone. I'm on the track of those trifles. One man's already offered me ten thousand pieces of gold for the pendants alone, but what one man offers another will top. The casket will bring as much again, or more."

The men encircling him licked their lips greedily, and shuffled closer. "What makes them worth so much?" Aberius asked shrewdly. "I never heard of pendants worth ten thousand gold pieces."

Conan managed a chuckle. "But these were gifts from King Yildiz to King Tiridates, gems that no man has ever seen before. And the same on the casket," he embroidered.

Abruptly Karela burst through the close-packed circle of men, and they edged back from the rage on her face. Gone were the makeshift garments she had acquired at the Well of the Kings. Silver filigreed breastplates of gold barely contained her ivory breasts, and a girdle of pearls a finger wide hung low on her hips. Red thigh boots covered her legs, and the tulwar at her side had a sapphire the size of a pigeon's egg on the pommel.

"The dog lies," she snarled. The men took another step back, but there was raw greed on their faces. "He seeks no gemstones, but a slave girl. He told me so himself. He's naught but a muscle-bound slave catcher for some besotted fool in Shadizar. Tell them you lie, Conan!"

"I speak the truth." Or some of it, he thought.

She whirled on him, knuckles white on the hilt of her sword. "Spawn of a maggot! Admit you lie, or I'll have you flayed alive."

"You've broken half your oath," he said calmly. "Uncivil words."

"Derketo take you!" With a howl of rage she planted the toe of one red boot solidly in his ribs. He could not contain a grunt of pain. "Think of something lingering, Hordo," she commanded. "He'll admit his lies soon enough then." Suddenly she spun on her heel, drawing her sword till a hand-breadth of razor-sharp blue steel showed above the worked leather scabbard. "Unless one of you has a mind to challenge my orders?"

A chorus of protests rose, and to Conan's amazement more than one gnarled and scarred face was filled with fear. With a satisfied nod Karela slammed the tulwar back into its sheath and strode away toward her tent. Men half-fell in their haste to get out of her way.

"The second part of your oath," Conan shouted after her. "You struck me. You're foresworn before Derketo. What vengeance will the goddess of love and death take on you, and on any who follow you?"

Her stride faltered for an instant, but she went on without turning. The doorflap of the red-striped pavilion was drawn behind her.

"You'll die easier, Conan," Hordo said, "if you watch your tongue. I've a mind to rip it out of you now, but some of the lads might want to hear if you babble more of this supposed treasure."

"You act like whipped curs around her," Conan said. "Have none of you ever thought for yourselves?"

Hordo shook his shaggy head. "I'll tell you a tale, and if you make me speak of it again I'll skewer your liver. From whence she came no one knows, but we found her wandering naked as a babe, and little more than one she was, in years, but with that sword she now wears clutched in her fist. He that led us then, Constanius by name, thought to have his sport with her, then sell her. He was the best of us with a sword, but she killed him like a fox killing a chicken, and when two who were close to him tried to take her, she killed them, too, and just as quick. Since then we've followed her. The looting she leads us to has always been good, and no man who did as he was told has ever been taken. She commands, and we obey, and we're satisfied."

Hordo went away then, and Conan listened to the others talking as they drank around the fires. Amid coarse laughter they discussed what sport would be had of him. Hot coals were much talked of, and the uses of burning splinters, and how much of a man's skin might be removed and yet leave him living.

The sun blazed higher and hotter. Conan's tongue swelled in his mouth with thirst, and his lips cracked and blackened. Sweat dried on his body till no more came, and the sun scored his flesh. Aberius and another fish-eyed rogue staggered over and amused themselves by pouring water on the ground beside his head, betting on how close they could come to his mouth without letting a drop fall where he could reach it. Even when the clear stream was so close he could feel the coolness of it on his cheek, Conan refused to turn his head toward it. He would not give them so much satisfaction.

In time the other man left, and Aberius squatted at Conan's head with the clay waterbottle cradled in his arms. "You'd kill for water, wouldn't you?" the weasel-faced man said softly. He glanced warily over his shoulder at the other bandits, still drinking and shouting of what tortures they would inflict on the big Cimmerian, then went on. "Tell me about this treasure, and I'll give you water."

"Ten—thousand—gold—pieces," Conan croaked. The words scraped like gravel across his dry tongue. Aberius licked his lips eagerly. "More. Where is this treasure? Tell me, and I'll convince the others to set you free."

"Free—first," Conan managed.

"Fool! The only way you'll get free at all is with my help. Now, tell me where to find—" He squawked suddenly as Hordo's big hand snatched him into the air by the scruff of his neck.

The one-eyed brigand shook the rat of a man, Aberius' feet dangling above the ground. "What are you doing?" Hordo demanded. "He's not for talking with."

"Just having a little sport," Aberius laughed weakly. "Just taunting him."

"Taunting," Hordo spat. He threw the smaller man sprawling in the dust. "It's more than taunting we'll do to him. You get back to the rest." He waited while Alberius scrambled, half-crawling, to where the other brigands watched laughing, then turned back to Conan. "Make peace with your gods, barbar. You'll have no time later."

Conan worked his mouth for enough moisture to get out a few painful words. "Letting her do you out of the gold, Hordo."

"You don't learn, do you, barbar?"

Conan had just time to see the booted foot coming, then the world seemed to explode.

IX

hen the Cimmerian regained consciousness, it was black night and the fires were burning low. A few brigands still squatted in muttered conversation, passing their stone jars of *kil*, but most were sprawled in drunken snoring. There was a light in the pavilion—Conan watched Karela's well-curved silhouette on the striped tent wall—but even as he watched it was extinguished.

The rawhide cords had tightened until they dug into his wrists. Feeling was almost gone from his hands. If he remained there much longer he would not be able to fight even were he to get free. His massive arms corded. There was no give to his bonds. Again he pulled, his body knotting down to the rippled-iron muscles of his stomach with the strain. Again. Again. Blood stained his wrists from the cutting rawhide, and wet the ground. Again he pulled. Again. And there was a slackness to the cord at his left wrist. No more than a fingers-breadth, but it was there.

Suddenly he froze. The feeling that had come in the camp with Karela, of eyes on him, was back. And more than back, for his senses told him the watcher was coming closer. Warily he looked around. The men by the low-burning fire had sunk into sodden mounds, making as much noise asleep as they had awake. The camp was still. Yet he could still feel those eyes approaching. His hackles rose, for he was sure the bearer of those watching eyes now stood over him, staring down, but there was nothing there.

Angrily he began to jerk at the rawhide binding his left wrist, harder and harder despite the quickened flow of blood and the burning pain that circled his wrist. If there was something standing above him—and he had seen enough in his life to know that there were many things not visible to the eye—he would not lie for it like a sheep at slaughter.

Rage fueled his muscles, and suddenly the stake tore free of the ground. Immediately he rolled to his right, clutching that cord in both hands and pulling with all his might. Slowly the second stake pulled out of the hard-packed earth.

Conan's bones creaked as he sat up. The lacerated flesh of his wrists had swollen to hide the cords. Diligently he worked to loose them, then freed his ankles. The craving in him for water was enough to send another man for the nearest waterbag, but he forced himself to work some suppleness back into his stiffened muscles before he moved. When he rose, if he was not at full strength he was nonetheless a formidable opponent.

In pantherine silence he moved among the sleeping men. It would have been easy for him to slay them where they lay, but killing drunken men in their stupor was not his way. He retrieved his sword and dagger and fastened them on. His red Turanian half-boots he found discarded by the coals of a burned-out fire. Of his cloak there was no sign, and he had no hope of recovering the coins from his purse. He would have to search every man there. Still, he thought as he stamped his feet to settle his boots, as soon as he could get to their horses he would be back on the trail of the pendants. He would take the precaution of scattering the rest of the mounts before he left. There was no need to leave the brigands able to pursue.

"Conan!" The shout rolled through the hollow as if launched from a dozen throats, but there was only one shape approaching the camp.

The Cimmerian cursed as bandits stirred from their sodden sleep and sat up. He was in their midst with no way out short of fighting, now. He drew his broadsword as a light appeared in Karela's striped tent.

"Conan! Where are the pendants?"

That booming voice stirred something in Conan's mind. He was sure he had heard it before. But the heavily muscled man approaching was unfamiliar. A spiked helmet covered the man's head, and a chain mail tunic descended to his knees. In his right hand he gripped a great double-bladed ax, in the other a round buckler.

"Who are you?" Conan called.

The brigands were all on their feet now, and Karela was before her pavilion with her jeweled tulwar in hand.

"I am Crato." The armored man came to a halt an arm's reach from Conan. Beneath his helm his eyes were glassy and unblinking. "I am the servant of Imhep-Aton. Where are the pendants you were to bring him?"

A chill ran down Conan's back. He knew the voice, now. It was the voice of Ankar.

From behind Conan the voice of Aberius rang out. "He was telling the truth. There are pendants."

"I don't have them, Ankar." Conan said. "I'm chasing the men who stole them, and a girl I made a promise to."

"You know too much," the big man muttered in Imhep-Aton's voice. "And you do not have the pendants. Your usefulness is at an end, Cimmerian."

With no more warning the ax leaped toward Conan. The Cimmerian jumped back, the razor steel drawing a fine red line across his chest. The possessed man recovered quickly and moved in, buckler held across his body, ax at the ready well to his side. If a sorcerer controlled the body, the man whose once it had been was an experienced ax fighter.

Conan danced back, broadsword flickering in snakelike thrusts. A slashing attack would leave him open, and that ax could cut a man half in two. Crato continued his slow advance, catching each sword thrust with his buckler. Watching those lifeless eyes was useless, Conan quickly realized. Instead he watched the massive shoulders for the involuntary movements that would foretell the big man's attacks.

The mailed right shoulder dipped fractionally, and Conan dropped to his heels as the ax whistled over his head. His broadsword darted out to stab through the mail at a thigh, then he was rolling away from the return ax-stroke to come once more erect facing his opponent. Blood ran down the ax-man's leg, but he came on.

Conan circled to the other's right, toward the ax. It would be more difficult for Crato to strike at him, thus. The ax slashed out in an awkward backhand blow. Conan swung, felt his blade bite through bone, and ax and severed hand fell together. On the instant Crato hurled his buckler at Conan's head and threw himself in a roll across the ground. Conan ducked, beat the round shield aside with his sword, but even as he recovered Crato was coming to his feet with the battle-ax in his left hand.

Blood pumped from the stump in regular spurts, and the man—or the sorcerer possessing him—seemed to know he was dying. Screaming, he rushed at the Cimmerian, ax slashing wildly. Conan caught the haft on his blade and smashed a knee into the other's midriff. The big Shemite staggered, but his great ax went up for another stroke. Conan's broadsword slashed into the man's shoulder, half-severing the ax arm. Crato sank to his knees, his mouth opening wide.

"Conan!" Imhep-Aton's voice screamed. "You will die!"

Conan's blade leaped forward once more, and the helmeted head rolled in the dust. "Not yet," the Cimmerian said grimly.

When he raised his gaze from the headless body on the ground Conan found the bandits had formed a ring around him. Some had swords in hand, others merely looked. Karela faced him with the curved blade of her tulwar bare. She glanced at the dead man, but kept her main attention on the big Cimmerian. Her gaze was oddly uncertain, her head tilted to watch him from the corner of her eye.

"Trying to leave us, Conan?" she said. "Whoever this Crato was, we owe him thanks for stopping you."

"The pendants!" someone called from among the gathered men. "The pendants are real."

"Who spoke?" Hordo demanded. The Red Hawk's bearded lieutenant lashed them with his eye, and some dropped their heads. "Whatever's real or isn't, the Red Hawk says this man deserves to die."

"Twenty thousand gold pieces sound very real to me," Aberius replied. "Too real to be hasty."

Hordo's jaw worked angrily. He started for the smaller man, and stopped with a surprised look at Karela as she laid her blade across his chest. She shook her head without speaking and took the sword away.

Conan eyed the woman, too, wondering what was in her head. Her face was unreadable, and she still did not look directly at him. He had no intention of sharing the pendants, but if her mind was changing on the matter he might yet leave that hollow between the hills without more fighting.

"They're real, all right," he said loudly. "A king's treasure, maybe worth more than twenty thousand." He had to pause to work enough moisture into his throat to speak, but he would not ask for water. The slightest sign of weakness now, and they could well decide to torture what he knew from him. "I can take you to the thieves. And mark you, men who steal from kings are likely to have other trinkets about." He turned slowly to catch each man's gaze in turn. "Rubies. Emeralds. Diamonds and pearls. Sacks bulging with gold coin." Avarice lit their eyes, and greed painted their faces.

"Gold, is it?" Hordo snorted. "And where are we to find all this wealth? In a palace, or a fortress, with stone walls and well-armed guards?"

"With the men I follow," Conan said. "Hooded men claiming to be pilgrims. They took five women when they stole the rest. Dancing girls from the court of Yildiz. One of these is mine, but the other four will no doubt he attracted to brave men with gold in their fists." Lecherous laughter rose, and one or two of the brigands swaggered posingly.

"Hooded men, you say?" Aberius said, frowning. "And five women?"

"Enough!" Hordo roared. "By the Black Throne of Erlik, don't you all see there are sorcerers in this? Did none of you look closely enough at this Crato to see he was possessed? Didn't you see his eyes, or listen to him speak? No mortal man has a voice like that, booming like thunder in the distance."

"He was mortal enough," muttered a thick-set man with a broad scar across his nose. "Conan's steel proved that."

"And what is sought by wizards," Conan said, "is doubly valuable. Did anyone ever hear of a wizard grasping for something that was not worth a king's crown?"

Hordo looked uncertainly at Karela, but she stood listening as if the talk had no connection to her. The one-eyed man muttered under his breath, then went on. "Where do we seek these hooded men? The country is wide. What direction do we ride? Conan himself has said he has no idea. He followed the Red Hawk thinking she'd lead him to them."

"I saw them," Aberius said, and stared about him defiantly as everyone turned to look at him. "I, and Hepekiah, and Alvar. Two days gone, riding to the east. A score of hooded men, and five bound women on camels. Speak, Alvar."

The thickset man with the scarred nose nodded heavily. "Aye, we saw them."

"They were too many for the three of us," Aberius went on hurriedly, "and when we came here to the meeting place, the Red Hawk had not yet come, so we didn't speak of it. You never let us make a move without her, Hordo." A mutter of angry assent rose.

Hordo glared, but there was satisfaction in his voice when he said, "Two days gone? They could be in Vendhya for all the good it does us."

The mutter grew in intensity, and Aberius took a step toward the huge, bearded man. "Why say you so? All here know I can track a lizard over stone, or a bird through the air. A two days' trail is a beaten path for me."

"And what of Hepekiah?" Hordo growled. "Have you forgotten the Cimmerian's blade in your friend's ribs?"

The weasel-faced man shrugged. "Gold buys new friends."

Hordo threw up his hands and turned to Karela. "You must speak. What are we to do? Does this Conan die, or not?"

The auburn-haired woman looked fully at Conan for the first time, her tilted green eyes cool and expressionless. "He's a good fighting man, and we may have need of such when we overtake these hooded men. Strike camp, and bring his horse."

Shouting excitedly and laughing, the bandits scattered. Hordo glared at the Cimmerian, then shook his head and stalked away. In an instant the camp was a stirred anthill, the pavilion going down, horses being saddled and blankets rolled. Conan stood looking at Karela, for she had not moved an inch, nor taken her eyes from his face.

"Who is this woman?" she said suddenly. Her voice was flat and expressionless. "The one you say is yours."

"A slave girl," he replied, "as I said."

Her face remained calm, but she sheathed her sword as if slamming it into his heart. "You trouble me, Conan of Cimmeria. See you do not come to trouble me too much." Spinning on her heel she marched toward the horses.

Conan sighed and looked to the east, where the red sun was just broaching the horizon. The night's dew had cleared the dust from the air, and it seemed he could see forever.

All he had to do now was find the hooded men, free Velita and take the pendants, all the while watching his back for a knife from some brigand who decided they had no need of him after all, and keeping an eye on Karela's mercurial temper. Then, of course, there was the matter of relieving the bandits of the pendants in turn, not to mention finding a new purchaser, for in Conan's eyes Crato's attack had finished his agreement with Ankar, or Imhep-Aton, or whatever his real name was. It was just his luck the man seemed to be a magician. But he had a tidy enough bundle without adding that worry to it. All he needed now, he thought, was the Zamoran army. He went in search of his cloak. And a water skin.

X

Puffs of dust lifted beneath the hooves of the column of Zamoran cavalry, a company strong, as they crossed rolling hills sparsely covered with low scrub. Their lance points and chain mail were blackened against reflecting the sun. They rode in a double line, round shields hanging ready to hand beside their saddles, with Haranides at their head, hard men, hand-picked by the captain, veterans of campaigning on the borders.

Haranides unconsciously shifted his buttocks on the hard leather of his saddle as he turned his head continually from side to side, watching, hoping, for a flash of light. With naught to go on but a direction, he had had to take a chance. Half his command was scattered in a line abreast on either side of him, and then only when both topped a hill. Every one of them had a metal mirror, and if any sign of a trail was found. . . .

He grimaced as his second in command, Aheranates, galloped up beside him from his place immediately before the column. A slender youth with smooth-shaven fine-featured face and big dark eyes more suited to flirting with a palace wench than looking on death, Aheranates had been foisted on him at the last minute. Ten years younger than Haranides, in two he would outrank him. His father, much in favor with the king, wanted his son to gain a touch of seasoning, and incidentally to share in the glory of bringing the Red Hawk before the king bound in chains.

"What do you want?" Haranides growled. If he succeeded on this mission, he would not need the good opinion of the youth's father. If he failed, the man could not save him from the king's threat.

"I've been wondering why we're not pursuing the Red Hawk," Aheranates said. Haranides looked at him, and he added, "Sir. Those were our orders, were they not? Sir?"

Haranides restrained his temper with no little effort. "And where would you pursue, lieutenant? In what direction? Or is it just that this isn't dashing enough for someone used to the glitter of parades in the capital?"

"Not the way I was taught to handle cavalry. Sir."

"And where in Sheol were you taught. . . ." A flash of light to the east caught his words in his throat. Once. Twice. Thrice. "Signal recall, lieutenant. By mirror," he added as the other pulled his horse around. "No need to let every running dog know we're out. And bring the company around."

"As you command. Sir."

For once Haranides did not notice the sarcasm. This had to be what he sought. By Mitra, it had to be. He could barely restrain himself from galloping ahead of his troop, but he forced himself to keep the march to a walk. The horses must be conserved if there was a pursuit close at hand, and he prayed there would be.

The men strung out to the east waited once they had passed on the signal, each man falling in behind the column as it reached him. Those beyond the man who first flashed his sighting would be riding west to join them. If this was a false alarm, Haranides thought. . . .

Then they topped another hill, and before them was a small knot of his men. As he rode closer another rider rejoined from the east. Haranides finally allowed himself to kick his mount into a gallop. One of the soldiers rode forward, touching his forehead respectfully.

"Sir, it looks to have been a camp, but there's. . . ."

Haranides waved him to silence. He could see what was unusual about this hollow between two hills. Black-winged vultures, their bald heads glistening red from their feeding, stood on the ground warily watching the quartet of jackals that had driven them from their feast.

"Wait here until I signal," Haranides commanded, and walked his horse down into the hollow. He counted the ash piles of ten burnt-out fires.

The jackals backed away from the mounted man, snarling, then snatched bones still bearing shreds of scarlet flesh and loped away. The vultures shifted their beady-eyed gaze from the jackals to Haranides. A half-eaten skull showed the thing on the ground had once been a man, but it could never have been proven by the scattered bones, cracked by the jackals' powerful jaws. Haranides looked up as Aheranates galloped down the hill.

"Mitra! What's that?"

"Proof there were bandits here, lieutenant. None else would leave a dead man for the scavengers."

"I'll bring the men down to search for—"

"You'll dismount ten men," Haranides said patiently, "and bring them down." He could afford to be patient, now. He was sure of it. "No need to grind what little we might find under the horses' hooves. And lieutenant? Tell off two men to bury that. See to it yourself."

Aheranates had been avoiding looking at the bloody bones. Now his face abruptly turned green. "Me? But—"

"Now, lieutenant. The Red Hawk, and your glory, are getting further away all the time."

The lieutenant stared open-mouthed, then swallowed and jerked his horse around. Haranides did not watch him go. The captain dismounted and slowly led his horse through the site of the camp. Around the remains of the fires was scruffed ground where men had slept. Perhaps fifty, he estimated. Well away from the fires were holes from the pegs and poles of a large tent. Four other holes, though, spaced in a large square, interested him more.

A short, bowlegged cavalryman trotted up and touched his sloping forehead. "Begging your pardon, sir, but the lieutenant said I was to tell you he found where they had their horses picketed." His voice became flatly noncommittal. "The lieutenant says to tell you there was maybe a hundred horses, sir."

Haranides looked to where two men were digging a hole in the hillside for the remains of the body. Aheranates apparently had decided he should search rather than oversee their work as ordered. "You've been twenty years and more in the cavalry, Resaro," the captain said. "How many horses would you say were on that picket line? If the lieutenant hadn't said a hundred, of course," he added when the man hesitated.

"Not to contradict the lieutenant, sir, but I'd say fifty-three. They didn't clear away the dung, and they kept the horses apart enough to keep the piles separate. Some would be sumpter animals, of course, sir."

"Very good, Resaro. Go back to the lieutenant and tell him I want. . . ." He stopped at the strained look on Resaro's face. "Is there something else you want to tell me?"

The stumpy man shifted awkwardly. "Well, sir, the lieutenant said we was mistaken, but Caresus and me, we found the way they went when they left here. They brushed their tracks some, but not enough. They went east, and a little north."

"You're sure of that?" Haranides said sharply.

"Yes, sir."

The captain nodded slowly. Toward the Kezankian Mountains, but not toward the caravan route through the mountains to Sultanapur. "Tell the lieutenant I want to see him, Resaro." The cavalryman touched his forehead and backed away. Haranides climbed the eastern hill to stare toward the Kenzankian Mountains, out of view beyond the horizon.

When Aheranates joined him, the lieutenant was carrying a stone unguent jar. "Found this down where the tent was," he said. "Someone had his leman along, seems."

Haranides took the jar. Empty, it still held the flowery fragrance of the perfume of Ophir. He tossed it back to Aheranates. "More like than not, your first souvenir of the Red Hawk."

The lieutenant gaped. "But how can you be certain this was the trull's camp? It could as easily be a . . . a caravan, wandered somewhat from the route. The man could have been left for some errand and been slain by wild animals. He could even have had no connection with those who camped here at all. He could have come after, and—"

"A man was staked out down there," Haranides said coldly. "'Tis my thought was the dead man. Secondly, no camels were here. Have you ever seen a caravan lacking camels, saving a slaver's? And there is no staking ground for a coffle. Thirdly, there was only one tent. A caravan of this size would have had half a score. And lastly, why have you lost your fervor for pursuing the Red Hawk? Can it be your thought that she has a hundred men with her? Fear not. There are fewer than fifty, though I grant you they may seem a hundred if it comes to steel."

"You have no right! Manerxes, my father, is—"

"Sir, lieutenant! Prepare the men to move out. Along that trail you thought not worth mentioning."

For a moment they stood eye to eye, Haranides coldly contemptuous, Aheranates quivering with rage. Abruptly the lieutenant tossed the unguent jar to the ground. "Yes, sir!" he grated, and turned on his heel to stalk down the hill.

Haranides bent to pick up the smooth stone jar. The flowery fragrance gave him a dim picture of the woman, one at odds with the coarse trollop with a sword he expected. But why was she riding toward the Kezankian Mountains? The answer to that could be of vital importance to him. Success, and Aharesus would smooth his path to the top. Failure, and the King's Counselor would give him not a thought as Tiridates had his head put over the West Gate. Placing the jar in his pouch, he went down to join his men.

XI

As the bandits climbed higher into the Kezankian Mountains, Conan stopped at every rise to look behind. Beyond the rolling foothills, on the plain they had left a day gone, something moved. Conan estimated the lead the brigands had, and wondered if it was enough.

"What are you staring at?" Hordo demanded, reigning in beside the Cimmerian. The outlaws were straggling up a sparsely treed mountainside toward a sheer-walled pass in the dark granite. Karela, as always, rode well in the lead, her gold-lined emerald cape flowing in the wind.

"Soldiers," Conan replied.

"Soldiers! Where?"

Conan pointed. A black snake of men inched toward the foothills, seeming to move through shimmering air rather than on solid ground. Only soldiers would maintain such discipline marching through those waterless approaches to the mountains. They were yet distant, but even as the two men watched the snake appeared to grow larger. On the plain the soldiers moved faster than the bandits in the mountains. The gap would close further.

"No matter," the one-eyed man muttered. "They'll not catch us up here."

"Dividing the loot, are you?" Aberius kicked his horse in the ribs, and the beast scrambled up beside the other two. "Best you wait till it's in our grasp. You might not be one of those left alive to. . . . What's that? Out there. Riders."

Others heard him and turned in their saddles to look. "Hillmen?" a hook-nosed Iranistani named Reza said hesitantly.

"Can't be," a bearded Kothian replied. His name was Talbor, and the tip of his nose had been bitten off. "Hillmen don't raid far from the mountains."

"And not so many together," Aberius agreed. His glower included both Conan and Hordo. "Soldiers, be they not? It's soldiers you've brought on us."

An excited gabble went up from the men gathered around them. "Soldiers!" "The army's on us!" "Our heads on pikes!" "A whole regiment!" "The King's Own!"

"Still your tongues!" Hordo shouted. "There's no more than two hundred, to my eye, and a day behind us, at that."

"'Tis still five to one against," Aberius said. "Or near enough as makes no difference."

"These mountains are not our place," Reza cried. "We be rats in a box."

"Ferrets in a woodpile," Hordo protested. "If this is not our own ground, still less is it theirs." The rest paid him no mind.

"We chase mists," Talbor shouted, rising in his stirrups to address the bandits who were gathering. "We ride into these accursed mountains after ghosts. It'll not stop till we find ourselves with our backs to a rock wall and Zamoran lances at our throats."

Aberius sawed his reins, and his horse pranced dangerously on the steeply sloping around. "Do you question my tracking, Talbor? The path we follow is the path taken by those I saw." He laid hand to his sword hilt.

"You threaten me, Aberius?" the Kothian growled. His fingers slid from his pommel toward the tulwar at his hip.

Karela spurred suddenly into their midst, her naked sword in hand. "I'll kill the first man to bare an inch of blade," she announced heatedly. Her cat-like eyes flicked each man in turn; both hurriedly removed their hands from their weapons. "Now tell me what has you at each other's throats like dancing girls in a zenana."

"The soldiers," Aberius began.

"These supposed pendants," Talbor started at the same instant.

"Soldiers!" Karela said. She jerked her head around, and seemed to breathe a sigh of relief when she spotted the distant line of men on the plain below. "Fear you soldiers so far away, Aberius?" she sneered. "What would you fear closer? An old woman with a stick?"

"I like not being followed by anyone," Aberius replied sulkily. "Or think you they follow us not?"

"I care not if they follow us or no," she flared. "You are the Red Hawk's men! An you follow me, you'll fear what I tell you to fear and naught else. Now all of you get up ahead. There's level ground there where we'll camp the night."

"There's a half a day yet we could travel," Hordo protested.

She rounded on him, green eyes flashing. "Did you not hear my command? I said we camp! You, Cimmerian, remain here."

Her one-eyed lieutenant grumbled, but turned his horse up the mountain, and the rest followed in sullen silence broken only by the creak of saddle leather and the slick of hooves on stone.

Conan watched the red-haired woman warily. She hefted her sword as if she had half a mind to drive it into him, then sheathed it. "Who is this girl, Conan? What is her name?"

"She's called Velita," he said. He had told her of Velita before, and knew she remembered the dancing girl's name. In time she would come to what she truly wanted to speak of. He twisted around for another look at the column of soldiers. "They gain ground on us, Karela. We should keep moving."

"We move when I say. And stop when I say. Do you think to play some game, Conan?"

He turned back to her. Her green eyes were clouded with emotion as she stared at him. What emotion he could not say. "I play no more games than you, Karela."

Her snort was eloquent. "Treasures taken from a king's palace, so you say, not to mention this baggage you claim to have promised her freedom. Why then do the thieves flee to these mountains, where none live but goats, and savages little better than goats?"

"I don't know," he admitted. "But it convinces me all the more they are the men I seek. Honest pilgrims do not journey to Vendhya by way of the heart of the Kezankian Mountains."

"Perhaps," she said, and shifted her gaze to the soldiers, far below. With a laugh she reared her big black to dance on its hind legs. "Fools. They'll not clip the Red Hawk's wings."

"It seems most likely they seek Tiridates' pendants, as we do," he said. "Much more so than that they seek you."

The red-haired woman glowered at him. "The Zamoran Army seeks me incessantly, Cimmerian. Of course, they'll never catch me. When their hunting becomes too troublesome, my men disperse to become guards on the very caravan routes we raid. The pay is high, for fear of the Red Hawk." Her sudden laugh was exultant.

To his amusement he realized she had been offended by his suggestion that the soldiers hunted other than her. "Your pardon, Karela. I should have remembered that taking seven caravans in six months would certainly rival even a theft from Tiridates' palace."

"I had naught to do with those," she said scornfully. "No creature from those caravans, man, horse, or camel, has even been seen again. When I take a caravan, those too old or ill-favored to fetch a price on the slave block are turned loose with food and water to find their way to the nearest city, albeit poorer than before."

"If not you, then who?"

"How should I know? The last caravan I took was a full eight months ago, and fat. When we left our celebrating in Arenjun it was to find the countryside too hot to hold us for those vanished caravans. I sent my men to their hiring, and these four months past have I been in Shadizar telling cards beneath the very noses of the King's Own." Her full mouth twisted. "I would be there still, if the risk of calling my band together once more had not seemed less than the odium of being eyed by men who thought to give me a tumble." Her glare seemed to include him and every other man in the world.

"Strange things are happening in the Kezankians," Conan said thoughtfully. "Perhaps those we follow have something to do with the vanished caravans."

"You make flight of fancy," she muttered, and he realized she was eyeing him oddly. "Come to my tent, Cimmerian. I would talk with you." She spurred away up the mountainside before he could speak.

Conan was about to follow when he became aware of being watched from the jagged mountains to the south. His first thought was of Kezankian hillmen, but then, as the hackles stood on the back of his neck, he knew it was the same invisible eyes he had felt that night with Karela, and again before Crato appeared. Imhep-Aton had followed him.

His massive shoulders squared, and he threw back his head. "I do not fear you, sorcerer!" he shouted. A hollow, ringing echo floated back to him. *Fear you, sorcerer!* Scowling, he spurred his horse up the mountain.

Karela's red-striped pavilion had been set up on a level patch of stony ground. Already the motley brigands had cook fires going, and were passing their stone jars of *kil*.

"What was that shouting?" Aberius called as Conan climbed down from his horse.

"Nothing," Conan said.

The weasel-faced man led a knot of ruffians down to face him warily. When he casually laid his hand on the leather-wrapped hilt of his sword, the memory of how he had used that sword against Crato was clear on those bearded, scarred and gnarled faces.

"Some of us have thought on these soldiers," Aberius said.

"You have thought," another muttered, but Aberius ignored him.

"And what have you thought?" Conan asked.

Aberius hesitated, looking to either side as if for support. There was scant to be found, but he went on. "Never before have we come into these mountains, excepting to hide a day. Here there is no room to scatter. We must go where the stone will let us go, not where we will. And this when five times our number of soldiers follow our backtrail."

"If you've lost your enthusiasm," Conan said, "leave. I'd as lief go on alone as not."

"Aye, and take the pendants alone," Aberius barked, "and the rest. You'd like it well for us to leave you."

Conan's sapphire eyes raked them scornfully. Even Aberius flinched under that lashing gaze. "Make up your minds. Fear the soldiers and run, or follow the pendants. One or the other. You cannot do both."

"And you bring us to where these soldiers can take us," Aberius began, "you'll not live—"

Conan cut him off. "You do as you will. On the morrow I ride after the pendants." He pushed through them. They muttered fretfully as he went.

He found himself wondering if it would be better for him if they stayed or went. They still had no right to the pendants, in his eyes, but now that they were in the mountains he could use Aberius' tracking ability, at least. The man could tell the mark a hoof made on stone from that made by a falling rock. That was always supposing the weasel-faced brigand did not decide to slip a knife between his ribs. The muscular young Cimmerian sighed heavily. What had started out to be a simple, if spectacular, theft, had grown as convoluted as a pit of snakes, and he had the uneasy feeling that he was not yet aware of all the twists and turns.

As he approached Karela's red-striped pavilion, with half its ropes tied to small boulders because the ground was too hard for driving pegs, Hordo suddenly stepped in front of him.

"Where do you think you're going?" the one-eyed bandit demanded.

Conan's temper had been shortened by knowing Imhep-Aton followed him, and by the encounter with Aberius. "Where I want to go," he growled, and pushed the scar-faced man from his path.

The startled brigand stumbled aside as Conan started past, then whirled, his broadsword coming out, at the whisper of steel leaving leather. Hordo's tulwar darted toward him. Conan beat the curved blade aside in the same motion as his draw, and the bearded man danced backward down the slope with surprising agility for one of his bulk. The scar that ran from under his rough leather eye-patch was livid.

"You have muscles, Cimmerian," he grated, "but no brains. You think above yourself."

Conan's laugh was short and mirthless. "Do you think I intend to displace you as lieutenant? I'm a thief, not a raider of caravans. But you do as you think you must." His broadsword was a heavy weapon, but he made it sing in interlocked figure eights about his head and to either side.

"Put up your blades!" came Karela's voice from behind him.

Without taking his gaze totally from Hordo, Conan took two quick steps to his left, turning so he could see both the bearded bandit and the red-haired woman. She stood in the entrance of the pavilion, her emerald cape drawn close to cover her from her neck to the ground. Her green-eyed gaze regarded them imperiously.

"He sought your tent," Hordo muttered.

"As I commanded him," she replied coldly. "You, at least, Hordo, should know I don't allow men of my band to draw weapons on each other. I'd have killed Aberius and Talbor for it. You two are more valuable. Shall I let each of you consider it the night with his hands and feet bound in the small of his back?"

Hordo seemed shaken by her anger. He sheathed his sword. "I was but trying to protect you," he protested.

The muscles along her jaw tightened. "Think you I need protection? Go, Hordo, before I forget the years you've served me well." The one-eyed man hesitated, cast a sharp glance at Conan, then stalked off toward the fires.

"You talk more like a queen than a bandit," Conan said finally, replacing his sword in its worn shagreen scabbard. She stared at him, but he met her gaze firmly.

"Others end at the headsman's block, or on the slave block, but none of mine has ever been taken, Conan. Because I demand discipline. Oh, not the foolishness soldiers call discipline, but any command I give must be obeyed at once. Any command. In this band the Red Hawk's word is law, and those who cannot accept that must leave or die."

"I am no hand at obedience," he said quietly.

"Come inside," she said, and disappeared through the entrance. Conan followed.

The ground inside the striped pavilion had been laid with fine, fringed Turanian carpets. A bed of glossy black furs, with silken pillows and soft, striped woolen blankets, lay against a side of the tent. A low, highly polished table was surrounded by large cushions. Gilded oil lamps illumined all.

"Close the flap," she said. Her mouth worked, and she added with obvious effort, "Please."

Conan unfastened the flap and let it drop across the entrance. He was wary of this strange mood Karela seemed to be in. "You should be more careful with Hordo. He's the only one of this lot who's loyal to you instead of to your success."

"Hordo is more a faithful hound than a man," she said.

"The more fool you for thinking so. He's the best man out there."

"He is no man, as I mean a man." Abruptly she threw back the emerald cape, letting it fall to the rugs, and Conan could not stop the gasp that rose in his throat.

Karela stood before him naked, soft auburn hair falling about her shoulders. A single strand of matched pearls hung low around the curve of her hips, glowing against the ivory skin of her sweetly rounded belly. Her heavy, round breasts were rouged, and the musky scent of perfume drifted from her as she stood with one knee slightly bent, shoulders back, hands behind her, in a pose at once offering and defiant.

He took a step toward her, and there was suddenly a dagger in her hand, its needle blade no wider than her finger but long enough and more to reach his heart. Her tilted green eyes never left his face. "You walk among my rogues like a wolf among a pack of dogs, Cimmerian. Even Hordo is but half wolf beside you. No man has ever called me his, for men come to believe the calling. If a woman must be a man's slave, then I'll be no woman. I'll walk behind no man, fawning for his favor and leaping to his command. I am the Red Hawk. I command. I!"

With great care he lifted the dagger from her fingers and tossed it aside. "You are a woman, Karela, whether you admit it or no. Does there have to be one to command between us? I knew the chains of slavery when I was but sixteen, and I have no desire to wish them on anyone." He lowered her to the furs.

"An you betray me," she whispered, "I'll put your head before my tent on a spear. I'll . . . ah, Derketo." For a time she made no sounds that came not unbidden to her lips.

XII

The private thaumaturgical chambers of Amanar were in the very top of the tallest tower of the keep, as far from the room of sacrifice as they could be and still remain within that dark fortress. He knew that Morath-Aminee was in no way limited to the columned room in the heart of the mountain, but distance yet gave an illusion of safety.

The walls of the circular stone room were lined with books bound in the skins of virgins, and light came from glass balls that hung from sconces glowing from a minor spell. There was no window, nor any opening save a single heavily barred, iron-bound door. The scent of incense hissing with colored flames on the coals of a bronze brazier warred with the odor of a noxious brew bubbling in a stone beaker above a fire stoked with human bones. On the tables, dried mummies waited to be powdered for philters, among carelessly scattered ewers of deadly venom and bundles of rare herbs and roots.

The necromancer himself stood watching the boiling brew, his attention rapt. The dark liquid began to froth higher. With but a moment's hesitation he removed the amulet from his neck. A chill climbed his backbone at being even so barely separated, but it was necessary. Before the black froth reached the rim of the beaker, he lowered the amulet by its chain until serpent and eagle alike were covered. The silver chain grew colder, bitter metal ice searing his preternaturally long fingers. The froth sank, but the black liquid bubbled even more fiercely. The stone of the beaker began to glow red.

> "Hand of a living man, powdered when dry
> Blood of an eagle, no more to fly
> Eye of the mongoose, tooth of the boar
> Heart of a virgin, soul of a whore
> Burn to their blackness, heat till they boil
> Dip in the periapt, confounding the roil."

Hands shaking with haste, Amanar removed the amulet. He wanted to wipe it dry on the instant and replace it about his neck, but this stage of the spell was critical. With long bronze tongs he lifted the stone beaker. Nearby, atop a white marble pedestal, was a small, clear crystal coffer, fragile seeming against even that smooth stone. Deliberately the mage tilted the tongs, pouring the boiling liquid over the gleaming box.

The words he muttered then were arcane, known only to him among the living. The scalding mixture struck the small coffer. The crystal shrieked as if it would shatter in ten thousand pieces. The liquid seemed to gather itself to fly away in steam. As if from a great distance, screams echoed in the room. Mongoose and boar. Virgin and whore. Abruptly there was silence. The noxious mix was gone, no drop of it remaining. The crystal walls of the coffer now contained gray clouds, shifting and swirling as if before a great wind.

Breathing heavily, Amanar set the beaker and tongs aside. Confidence was flowing back into him. The haven, however temporary, was prepared. He wiped the amulet clean, inspecting it minutely before placing it once more about his neck.

From below rose the dolorous tone of a great bronze gong. Smiling, the mage unbarred the door and took up the crystal coffer beneath his arm. The gong echoed hollowly again.

Amanar made his way directly to the alabaster-walled audience chamber, its domed ceiling held aloft by carven ivory columns as thick as a man's trunk. Behind his throne reared a great serpent of gold. The arms of the throne were hooded vipers of Koth, the legs adders of Vendhya, all of gold. As he surveyed the assemblage before him, the necromancer allowed no particle of his surprise to touch his face. The S'tarra he had expected knelt with heads bowed, while five young women he had definitely not expected, in gossamer silks, hands bound behind their backs, were forced to prostrate themselves before the throne.

Amanar sat, carefully holding the crystal coffer on his lap. "You have that which I sent you for?" he said.

Sitha stepped forward. "They brought this, master." The S'tarra Warden presented an ornate casket of worked gold, the lid set with gemstones.

The mage forced himself to move slowly, but still his fingers trembled as he opened the casket. One by one, four jewels the like of which no man had ever seen, mounted in pendants of silver or gold, were casually tossed on the mosaic floor. A blood-red pearl the size of a man's two thumbs. A diamond black as a raven's wing, and big as a hen's egg. A golden crystal heart that had come from the ground in that shape. A complex lattice of pale blue that could cut diamond. All were as nothing to him. His hand shook visibly as he removed the last, the most important. As long as the top joint of a man's finger, of midnight hue filled with red flecks that danced wildly as Amanar's palm cupped the stone, this was the pendant that must be kept from Morath-Aminee.

He waved the golden casket away. "Dispose of those trifles, Sitha." His S'tarra henchman bowed, and gathered the pendants.

Almost tenderly Amanar swathed the dark stone in silk, then laid it in the crystal coffer. When he replaced the lid, he breathed a sigh of relief. Safe, at last. Not even Morath-Aminee would be able to detect what was in there, for a time, at least. And before that could happen he would have found a new haven, far away, where the god-demon would never think to look.

Clutching the crystal box firmly, Amanar turned his attentions to the women lying before him with their faces pressed to the divers-colored tiles. They trembled, he noted with idle satisfaction.

"How came you by these women?" the mage demanded.

Surassa, who had led the foray, lifted a scaled head. The dark face was expressionless, the words sibilant. "Before Shadizar, master, we spoke the words you told us, and ate the powders, that the glamour might be on us, and none should see us enter."

"The women," Amanar said impatiently. "Not every last thing that happened." He sighed at the look of concentration that appeared in the S'tarra's red eyes. When they knew a thing by rote, it was difficult for them to separate one part.

"The palace, master," Surassa hissed finally. "We entered the palace of Tiridates unseen, but when we came to the place where that which you sent us to seek was to be, only the casket was to be found. Taking the casket, we searched then the palace. Questioning some, and slaying them for silence, we found the pendants about the necks of these women, and slew the men who were with them. Leaving then the palace, we found that, as you had warned us, the glamour had worn off. We donned the robes—"

"Silence," Amanar said, and the saurian creature's words ceased at once. For their limited intelligence he had commanded them to fetch the casket and all five pendants, fearing they might make a mistake in the pressure of the moment and bring the black diamond instead of that which he needed. Yet despite all his careful instructions they had managed to increase their risk of being caught by taking these women. Rage bubbled in him, made all the worse for knowing that punishing them would be like punishing dogs. They would accept whatever he did, and understand not a whit of why. The S'tarra, sensing something of his mood, shifted uneasily.

"Bring the women before me," the necromancer commanded.

Hastily the five women were pulled to their knees and the bare covering of their silks ripped away. With fearful eyes the kneeling, naked women watched Amanar rise. He walked thoughtfully down the line of them.

Severally and together, they were beautiful, and just as important to him, their dread was palpable.

He stopped before a pale blond with ivory satin skin. "Your name, girl?"

"Susa." He quirked an eyebrow, and she hastily added, "Master. I am called Susa, an it please you, master."

"You five are the dancing girls Yildiz sent to Tiridates?"

Her blue eyes were caught by his dark ones, growing more tremulous as he watched. "Yes, master," she quavered.

He stroked his chin and nodded. A king's dancing girls. Fitting for one who would come to rule the world. And when the last jot of amusement had been wrung from them, their puny souls could feed Morath-Aminee.

"Conan will free us," one of the girls suddenly burst out. "He will kill you."

Amanar walked slowly down the line to confront her. Slender and long of leg, her big, dark eyes stared defiance even as her supple body trembled. "And what is your name, girl?" His words were soft, but his tone brought a moan from her throat.

"Velita," she said at last.

He noted how her teeth had clamped lest she should say "master." There would be much pleasure in this one. "And who is this Conan who will rescue you?"

Velita merely trembled, but Surassa spoke. "Pardon, master, but there was one of that name spoken of in Shadizar. A thief who has grown troublesome."

"A thief!" Amanar laughed. "Well, little Velita. What shall I do about this rescue? Sitha, command the patrols, if they find this man Conan they are to bring me his skin. Not the man. Just the skin." Velita shrieked and crumpled forward to rest her sobbing head on her knees. Amanar laughed again. The other women watched him, terror-struck. But not enough, he thought. "Each night you will dance for me, all five of you. She who pleases me most will gain my bed for the night. The middle three will be whipped and sleep in chains. She who pleases me least . . ." he paused, feeling the anxiety grow " . . . will be given to Sitha. He is rough, but he knows still how to use a woman."

The kneeling women cast one horrified glance at the reptilian creature, now watching them avidly, and threw themselves prostrate, groveling, screaming, pleading. Amanar basked in the miasma of their terror. Surely this was what the god-demon felt when it consumed a soul. Stroking the crystal coffer and stroked by their shrieks, he strode from the chamber.

XIII

Conan eyed the ridge to the left of the narrow valley the bandits were traversing. There had been movement up there. Only a flicker, but his keen gaze had caught it. And there had been others.

He booted his horse forward along the winding trail to where Hordo rode. Karela was well to the front, fist on one red-booted thigh, surveying the mountainous countryside as if she headed an army rather than a motley band of two score brigands, snaking out behind her.

"We're being watched," Conan said as he came alongside the one-eyed bandit.

Hordo spat. "Think you I don't know that already?"

"Hillmen?"

"Of course." The lone eye frowned. "What else?"

"I don't know," Conan said. "But the one good chance I had, I saw a helmet, not a turban."

"The soldiers are still behind us," Hordo said thoughtfully. "Talbor and Thanades will let us know if they begin to close."

The two bandits had been ordered to trail behind, keeping the Zamoran cavalry in sight. Conan refrained from suggesting they might have become affrighted apart from the band and fled, or that Karela was holding the soldiers in too much contempt. "Whoever they are, we'd best hope they don't attack us here."

Hordo looked at the steep, scrub-covered slopes rising on either side of the trail and grimaced. "Mitra! Pray they're not strong enough, though a dozen good men. . . ." He trailed off as Aberius appeared on the trail ahead, whipping his horse steadily.

"That looks ill," Conan said. Hordo merely grunted, and the two rode forward to reach Karela as the weasel-faced bandit galloped up.

"Hillmen," Aberius panted. Greasy sweat dotted his face. "Six score, maybe seven. Camped athwart the trail ahead. And they're breaking camp."

There was no need to discuss the danger. Kezankian hillmen admitted allegiance to no one but themselves, though both Turan and Zamora had tried futilely to subdue them. The fierce tribesmen's way with strangers was simple, short and deadly. One not of his clan, even another hillman, was an enemy, and enemies were for killing.

"Coming this way?" Karela said quietly. At Aberius' anxious nod she cursed under her breath.

"And the soldiers behind," Hordo growled.

Karela's green eyes flashed at the bearded man. "Do you grow frightened with age, Hordo?"

"I've no desires to be between the sledge and the stone," Hordo replied, "and my age has naught to do with it."

"Watch you don't become an old woman," she sneered. "We'll leave the trail, and let the hillmen and the soldiers exhaust themselves on each other. Mayhap we'll have a good view from the ridge."

Conan laughed, and tensed as the red-haired woman rounded on him with her hand on her sword. If he was forced to disarm her—he did not think he could kill her, even to save his own life—he would certainly have to fight. Hordo as well. And likely the rest of the brigands, who had gathered a short distance down the rocky trail.

"Your idea of letting them fight among themselves is a good one," he said, "but if we try to take horses up these slopes we'll be at it still a week hence."

"You've a better plan, Cimmerian?" Her voice was sharp, but she had loosed her grip on her jeweled tulwar.

"I have. Most of the band will ride back along the trail and up one of the side canyons we've passed."

"Back toward the soldiers?" Hordo protested.

"The hillmen have trackers, too!" Aberius shrilled. "Once they pick up our trail, and they will, it's us that'll have to fight them, not the accursed Zamorans!"

"I trust there's more to your plan," Karela said softly. "If you turn out to be a fool after all. . . ." Her words trailed off, but there was a dangerous glint in her tilted eyes. Conan knew she would not forgive the shame of having taken a fool to her bed.

"I said most of the band," the big Cimmerian went on calmly. "I will take a few men forward to where the hillmen are."

Aberius' laugh was scathing, and frightened. "And defeat all seven score? Or perhaps you think your mild face and dulcet tones will turn their blades aside?"

"Be silent!" Karela commanded. She touched her full lips with her tongue before going on in a quieter voice. "If you're a fool, Conan, you're a brave one. Speak on."

"I'll attack the hillmen, all right," Conan said, "but as soon as they know I'm there, I'll be away, I'll lead them past where the rest have turned off the trail, straight to the soldiers. While they're fighting, I and who comes with me will slip away to rejoin you and the others."

"One or the other will have your guts for saddle ties," Aberius snorted.

"Then they'll have yours, too," Karela said, "And mine. For you and I will accompany him." The man's pinched face drew tighter, but he said nothing. Conan opened his mouth to protest; she cut him off. "I lead this band, Cimmerian, and I send no man to danger while I ride to safety. Accept that, or I'll have you tied across your saddle, and you can accompany the others."

A chuckle rumbled up from Conan's massive chest. "There's no sword I'd rather have beside me than yours. I only thought that without you there, those rogues might keep on riding right out of the mountains."

After a moment she joined his laughter. "Nay, Conan, for they know I'd pursue them to Gehanna, if they did. Besides, Hordo will keep my hounds in line. What's the matter with you, bearded one?"

Hordo stared at her with grim eyes. "Where the Red Hawk must bare her blade," he said flatly, "there ride I."

Conan waited for another blast of the red-haired bandit's temper, but instead she sat her horse staring at Hordo as if she had never seen him before. Finally she said, "Very well, though you're like to lose your other eye if you don't listen to me. Get the rest on their way."

The one-eyed man bared his teeth in a fierce grin and whirled his horse back down the trail.

"A good man," Conan said quickly.

Karela glared. "Do not upbraid me, Cimmerian."

The mass of brigands clattered down the twisting trail and were soon lost to sight. Hordo booted his horse back up to where Conan and the others waited.

"Think you the watchers will take a hand in this, Conan?" the bearded brigand asked.

"What watchers?" Karela demanded. Aberius let out a low moan.

Conan shook his head. "Men on the hillside, but not to concern us now, I think. If they numbered enough to interfere, we'd know it already."

"Hordo, you knew of this and didn't tell me?" Karela said angrily.

"Do we wait here talking," Conan asked, "or do we find the hillmen before they find us?"

For a reply Karela kicked her horse into a gallop up the trail.

"If her mind were not on you, Cimmerian," Hordo growled, "she'd not need to be told." He spurred after the Red Hawk.

Aberius looked as if he wanted to ride back after the other bandits, but Conan pointed ahead. "That's the way."

The weasel-faced brigand showed his teeth in a snarl, and reluctantly turned his horse after the other two. Conan rode in close behind, forcing him to a gallop.

As soon as they reached the others, Conan drew his sword and rested it across his muscular thighs. With thoughtful looks Karela and Hordo did the same. On that narrow trail, often snaking back on itself with screening escarpments of stone, they would be on the hillmen without warning. If the hillmen did not come on them the same way. Aberius lagged back, chewing his lip.

Abruptly they rounded a sharp bend, and were into the camp of the hillmen. There were no tents, but dark, hook-nosed men in turbans and dirty motley bent to strap bedrolls while others kicked dirt over the ashes of their fires. A thick, bow-legged man, his bare chest crossed by a belt that held his tulwar, saw them first, and an ululating cry broke from his throat. For a bare moment every man in the camp froze, then a shriek of "Kill them!" sent all rushing for their horses.

Conan pulled his horse around as soon as the shout rose. There was no need to do more to ensure being followed. "Back," he said, forcing his horse against those of Karela and Hordo. Aberius seemed to have broken free already. "Back, for your lives."

Karela sawed her reins, brought her horse around, and then all three were pounding back the way they had come. Conan kept an eye behind. For the twists of the trail he could see little, but what he saw told him the hillmen had been quicker to horse than he had hoped. The lead horseman, a burly man with his beard parted and curled like horns, flashed into and out of sight as the trail wound round boulders and rock walls. When they reached the soldiers, they must be far enough ahead to distinguish themselves from the fierce tribesmen, though not far enough to allow too many questions.

Conan looked ahead. Karela was stretching her black out as much as the trail would allow, and Hordo rode close behind her, using his quirt to urge greater speed from her mount. If Conan could buy them a tenth of a glass at one of these narrow places. . . . As the Cimmerian rode between two huge, round boulders, he abruptly pulled his horse around. A quick glance showed that neither of the others had noticed. A few moments, and he would catch up to them.

The fork-bearded hillman galloped between the boulders, raised a wavering battlecry, and Conan's blade clove turban and skull to his shoulders.

Even as the man fell from his saddle-pad, more turbanned warriors were forcing their way into the gap. Conan's sword rose and fell in murderous butchery, its steel length stained quickly red, blood running onto his arm and spattering across his chest.

Of a sudden he was aware of Karela, sword flashing, trying to force her way in beside him. Her red hair stood about her head like a mane, and battle light shone in her green eyes. Behind, Conan could hear Hordo calling for her to come back. Her curved blade took a hillman's throat, then another's slash cut one of her reins. A lance pinked her mount, and it reared, screaming and twisting, ripping the other rein from her hand.

"Take her, Hordo!" Conan cried. He brought the flat of his blade down across the rump of her great black horse, earning himself a bloody slash across his chest for his inattention to the hillmen. "Take her to safety, Hordo!"

The big, one-eyed brigand gathered in her dangling rein and spurred down the trail, pulling her horse behind. Conan heard her shouts fading. "Stop, Hordo! Derketo shrivel your eye and tongue! Stop this instant, Hordo! I command it! Hordo!"

Conan had no time to watch, though, for he was engaged again even as she shouted. The hillmen tried to force their way through by sheer weight of numbers, but only two men at a time would fit into the gap, and when more tried they fell before Conan's whirlwind blade. There were six men down beneath the prancing hooves, then seven. Eight. A horse stumbled on a body and reared. The savage cut Conan had intended for the hook-nosed rider half-severed the horse's neck. It fell kicking beneath the hooves of the next horse, and that one went down as well, its rider catapulting from the saddle to lose his turbanned head to the mighty Cimmerian's broadsword.

The rest of the swarthy riders fell back from that bloody passage, blocked now with dead to the height of a man. Raised tulwars and shouted threats of what would be done when Conan was taken told him they had not given up, though. He edged his horse back. Once he was gone they would clear away the dead, tumbling men and horses alike by the trail, and follow to avenge their honor. But he had gained the time he needed.

The Cimmerian pulled his horse around and booted it into a gallop. Behind him the blood-curdling cries still rose.

XIV

By the time Conan rejoined the other two, Karela was controlling her horse awkwardly with the single rein, and Hordo was assiduously avoiding her savage glare.

"Where's Aberius?" Conan said. There had been no sign of the man along the way.

Karela thrust a murderous look at the big Cimmerian, but there was no time to speak, for as he spoke they rounded a bend, and there ahead was the Zamoran cavalry column. The officer in the lead raised his hand to signal a halt as the three reached him. Some of the mailed men eyed Conan's bloody sword and loosened their own in their scabbards.

"Ho, my lord general," Conan said, bowing to the blocky, sunburnt officer. His armor showed more wear than any general's ever had, the Cimmerian thought, but flattery never hurt, and it could never be piled on too deeply. Though perhaps it might go better with the officer who joined them then, slender and handsome even beneath his dirt.

"Captain," the blocky officer said, "not general. Captain Haranides." Conan suddenly hoped the hillmen showed quickly. The dark eyes that regarded him from beneath that russet-crested helm were shrewd. "Who are you? And what are the lot of you doing in the Kezankians?"

"My name is Crato, noble captain," Conan said, "late guard on a caravan bound from Sultanapur, as was this man, Claudo by name. We had the misfortune to fall among hillmen. The lady is Vanya, daughter of Andiaz, a merchant of Turan who took passage with us. I fear that we three are all who survived. I also fear the hillmen are at our heels, for I looked back not long since and saw them on the trail behind."

"Merchant's daughter!" the young officer crowed. "With those bold eyes? If that wench is a merchant's daughter, I'm King of Turan." The captain's mouth tightened, but he kept silent. Conan could see him watching their reactions. "What say you, Crato? What price for an hour of the jade's time?"

Conan tensed, waiting for her to draw her sword, but she merely pulled herself haughtily erect. "Captain Haranides," she said coldly, "will you allow this man to speak so? My father may be dead, but I yet have relatives who have the ear of Yildiz. And in these months past I hear that your Tiridates wishes to be friends with King Yildiz." The captain still said nothing.

"Your pardon, noble sir," Conan said, "but the hillmen. . . ." Where were they, he wondered.

"I see no hillmen," the young officer said sharply. "And I've heard of no caravans since those seven that disappeared. More likely you're brigands yourselves, who had a falling out with the rest of your band. Perhaps being put to the question will loosen your tongues. The bastinado—"

"Easily, Aheranates," the captain said. Abruptly he wore a warm smile for the three. "Speak more easily. I'm sure these unfortunates will tell us all they know, if only. . . ." The smile froze on his face, then melted. "Sheol!" he thundered. "You've brought them straight to us!"

Conan looked over his shoulder and would have shouted for joy if he dared. The hillmen sat their horses in a startled knot not two hundred paces distant. But already the shock of seeing the soldiers was wearing off, and curved tulwars were being waved above turbanned heads. Ululating cries of defiance floated toward the cavalry.

"Shall we retreat?" Aheranates asked nervously.

"Fool!" the hook-nosed captain spat. "An we turn away, they'll be on our backs like vultures on dead meat. Pass the word—but quietly!—that I'll give no signal, but when I ride forward every man is to charge as if he had a lance up his backside. Move, lieutenant!" The slender officer licked his lips, then started down the column. Haranides turned a gimlet eye on Conan as he eased his sword. "I hope you can use that steel, big man, but in any case, you stay close to me. If we're alive when this is over, there are questions I want to ask."

"Of course, noble captain," Conan said, but Haranides was already spurring forward. Howling, the cavalry column poured after him up the trail. Screaming hillmen charged, and in an instant the two masses of men were locked in a maelstrom of flashing steel and blood.

Karela and Hordo turned away from the battle and rode for a narrow gorge that let off the trail. Conan hesitated, staring at the combat. Haranides might well have tried to kill him, had the captain known who he was, but this leading the man to his death suddenly festered inside the tall Cimmerian.

"Conan," Hordo called over his shoulder, "what are you waiting for? Ride before someone sees us going." The bearded ruffian continued to suit his actions to his words, following close behind his auburn-haired leader.

Reluctantly Conan rode after them. As they made their way up the sheer-walled cut in the dark granite, the sounds of killing seemed to follow them.

For a long time they rode in silence, till the battle noises had long since faded. The narrow passage opened into a canyon that meandered back to the east. Conan and Karela each rode locked in their own sour silence. Hordo looked from one to the other, frowning. Finally he spoke, with false jollity.

"You've a facile tongue, Conan. Why, you near had me believing my name was Claudo, for the bland look in those blue eyes of yours when you said it."

"A thief had best have a facile tongue," Conan grunted. "Or a bandit. And speaking of facile tongues, what happened to that snake Aberius? I have seen him not since before we met the hillmen."

Hordo forced a laugh with a worried glance at Karela, whose face looked like stormclouds on the horizon. "We encountered the craven well down the path. He said he was guarding our backtrail, to keep our retreat open."

Conan growled deep in his throat. "You should have slit the coward's throat."

"Nay. He has too many uses in him for that. I sent him to find the rest of the band, and to tell them to make camp. Can I but puzzle out how these canyons go, we'll be back to them soon."

"This is my band, Conan!" Karela suddenly snapped. "I command here! The Red Hawk!"

"Then if you think Aberius should escape his cowardice," Conan replied gruffly, "let him. But I'll not change my mind on it."

She tried to jerk her horse around to face him, but her single rein made the big black take a dancing sidestep instead. The auburn-haired bandit made a sound that in another woman Conan would have called a sob of frustration. But of course such was unlikely from her.

"You fool barbarian!" she cried. "What right had you to send me— me!—to safety? Giving my reins to this one-eyed buffoon! Whipping my horse as if I were some favored slave girl who must be kept from danger!"

"That's what you're angry about?" Conan said incredulously. "With but one rein left, you were easy meat for the next hillman's blade."

"You made that decision, did you? It was not yours to make. I choose when and where I fight, and how much risk I'll face. I!"

"You're the most ungrateful person at having your life saved that I've ever met," Conan grumbled.

Karela shook her fist at him, and her voice rose to an enraged howl. "I do not need you to save my life! I do not want you to save my life! Of all men, you least! Swear to me you will never again lift a hand to save my life or my freedom. Swear it, Cimmerian!"

"I swear it!" he answered hotly. "By Crom, I swear it!"

Karela nodded shortly and got her horse moving again with violent kicks and much tugging at her one rein. The bare brown rock through which they rode, layered in places with much faded colors, fitted Conan's mood well. Hordo dropped back to ride beside the muscular youth.

"Once I liked you not at all, Conan," the one-eyed man said in a voice that would not carry forward to Karela. "Now, I like you well, but still I say this. Leave us."

Conan cast a sour eye at him. "If there be leaving to do, you do it. And her, with the rest of her band. I have a seeking here, remember?"

"She'll not turn aside, despite hillmen, or soldiers, or demons themselves. That's the trouble, or what comes of it. That, and this oath, and a score of things more. Emotion rules her head, now, and not the other way round, as always before. I fear what this means."

"I did not ask for the oath," Conan replied. "If you think her temper runs away with her, speak to her, not me."

The bearded bandit's hands gripped his reins till his knuckles were white. "I do like you, Conan, but bring you harm to her, and I will carve you as a Kethan carves stone." He booted his horse ahead, and the three traveled once more in heavy silence.

Long shadows stretched across the mountain valleys by the time they found the bandit camp, among huge boulders at the base of a sheer cliff. Despite the crisp coldness of the air, the scattered fires were small, and placed among the boulders so as to lessen the chance of being seen. Karela's red-striped pavilion stood almost against the towering rock wall.

"I'll see you in my tent, Conan," the red-haired woman said. Without waiting for an answer, she galloped to the pavilion, gave her horse into a bandit's care, and disappeared inside.

As Conan dismounted, he found a knot of bandits gathering about Hordo and him. Aberius was among them, though not in the forefront.

"Ho, Aberius," the Cimmerian said. "I'm glad to see you well. I thought you might have been injured in holding the rail open for us." Some of the rough-faced men snickered. Aberius bared his teeth in what might have been meant to be a grin, but his eyes were those of a rat in a box. He said nothing.

"The hillmen are taken care of, then?" a Kothian with one ear asked, "And the soldiers?"

"Slitting each other's weasands," Hordo chuckled. "They're no more concern to us, not in this world."

"And I've no concern for the next," the Kothian laughed. Most of the others joined in. Conan noted Aberius did not.

"On the morrow, Aberius," Conan said, "you'll take up the trail again, and in a day or two we'll have the treasure."

The pinch-faced brigand had started at the sound of his name. Now he licked his lips before answering. "It cannot be. The trail is lost." He flinched as the other bandits turned to stare at him. "It's lost, I say."

"But only for the moment," Conan said. "Isn't that right? We'll go back to that valley where the hillmen were camped, and you'll pick it up again."

"I tell you it isn't so simple." Aberius shifted his shoulders and tugged nervously at his dented iron breastplate. "While on the trail I can tell a rock disturbed by a horse from one that merely fell. Now I'm away from the trail. If I go back, they'll both look the same."

"Fool!" someone snarled. "You've lost us the treasure."

"All this way for naught," another cried.

"Cut his throat!"

"Slit Aberius' gullet!"

Sweat beaded the man's narrow face. Hordo stepped forward quickly. "Hold, now! Hold! Can you track these men, Talbor? Alvar? Anyone?" Heads were shaken in reluctant denial. "Then open not your mouth against Aberius."

"I still say he is afeared," Talbor muttered. "That is why he cannot find the tracks again."

"I'm not affrighted of any man," Aberius said hotly. He licked his lips once more. "Of any man." There was a peculiar emphasis to the last word.

"Of what then?" Conan said. For a moment he thought Aberius would refuse to answer, then the man spoke in a rush.

"On the mountain slope, after we four rode forward, I saw a . . . a thing." His voice gained fervency as he spoke. "Like a snake, it was, yet like a man, too. It wore armor, and carried a sword, and flame shot from its mouth twice the length of a sword. As I watched it signaled for more of its kind to come forth. Had I not ridden to half-kill my horse, I'd be dead at those creatures' hands."

"If it had the flame," Conan muttered, "what need had it for the sword?" Some of the others began to murmur fearfully, though, and even those who were silent had unease on their faces.

"Why did you not speak of this before?" Hordo demanded.

"There was no need," Aberius replied. "I knew we would soon leave, since the tracks are lost. We must leave soon. Besides, I thought you would misbelieve me."

"There are strange things under the sky," Conan said. "I've seen some of them, myself. But I've never seen anything that could not be killed with cold steel." Or at least, very few, he amended to himself. "How many of these things did you actually see, Aberius?"

"Only the one," Aberius admitted with obvious reluctance. "But it summoned more, and I saw them moving beyond the rocks. There could have been a hundred, a thousand."

"Yet all in all," Hordo said, "you saw but one. There cannot be many of them, else we'd have heard before. A thing like that would be talked of."

"But," Aberius began.

"But nothing," Hordo barked. "We'll keep a wary eye for these creatures of yours, but on the morrow we see if you can tell a horse track from horse-moss."

"But I told you—"

"Unless you all want to give up the treasure," the one-eyed bandit went on as if the smaller man had not spoken. Loud objections went up on every side. "Then I'll talk to the Red Hawk, and at dawn we'll move. Now go get something into your bellies."

One by one the bandits drifted away to their fires. Aberius went last of all, casting a dark look at Conan as he went.

XV

While Hordo stumped off to the red-striped pavilion, Conan found a spot where he could sit with his back to a massive boulder and no one could come at him unseen. That look from Aberius had spoken of knives in the back. He got out his honing stone and broadsword and began to smooth the nicks made by hillmen's chain-mail. The sky became purple, and lurid red streamers filled the jagged western horizon. He was putting the finishing touches to his blade's edge when the one-eyed brigand stormed out of Karela's tent.

The bearded man stalked to within a few feet of Conan, obviously ill at ease. Hordo rubbed his bulbous nose, muttering under his breath. "A good habit, that," he said finally. "I've seen more than one good man die because an untended notch in his blade left him with a stump the next time it took a good blow."

Conan laid the broadsword across his thighs. "You didn't come to talk of swords. What does she say about tomorrow?"

"She wouldn't even listen to me." Hordo shook his bearded head. "Me, who's been with her from the first day, and she wouldn't listen."

"No matter. On the morrow, you turn back, and I go on. Perhaps she's right not to risk these snakemen on top of all else."

"Mitra! You don't understand. I never got to speak of the creatures, or of Aberius' denial he can find the trail again. She paced like a caged lioness, and would not let me say two words together." He tugged at his beard with both hands. "Too long have I been with her," he muttered, "to be sent on such an errand. Zandru, man, it's because you didn't come when she ordered that she's ready to bite heads off. And her temper worsens every minute you sit here."

Conan smiled briefly. "I told her once I was no hand at obedience."

"Mitra, Zandru, and nine or ten other gods whose names escape me at the moment." Hordo let out a long sigh and squatted with his thick arms crossed on his knees. "Another time I wouldn't mind wagering on which of you will win, but not when I might be shortened a head for being in the middle."

"There's no talk of winning or losing. I'm in no battle with her."

The side of the one-eyed man's mouth that was not drawn into a permanent sneer grimaced. "You're a man, and she's a woman. There's battle enough. Well, what happens, happens. But remember my warning. Harm her, and it's you will be shorter a head."

"Since she's angry with me, talk her into turning back. That will give you what you want. Her away from me." He did not add that it would also give him what he wanted, and relieve him of the necessity of stealing the pendants from the bandits.

"The temper she's in, 'tis more likely she'll order you staked out again, and begin again where first we were."

Conan touched his sword; his steel blue eyes were suddenly cold. "This time I'll collect my ferryman's fee, Hordo."

"Speak not of ferryman's fees," the other man muttered. "An she decides so . . . I'll get you away in the night. Bah! This talk of what will happen and what may happen is building towers of sand in the wind."

"Then let us talk on other things," Conan said with a laugh that did not touch his eyes. He believed the one-eyed brigand did indeed like him, but he would not trust his life to that where the need of going against Karela's commands was concerned. "Think you Aberius made these snakemen out of air, to cover his wanting to turn back?"

"He tells the truth with a face that shouts lie, yet this time I think he may actually have seen something. That's not to say it was what he says it was. Ah, I know not, Conan. Snakes that walk like men." The bearded bandit shivered. "I begin to grow old. This chasing after a king's treasure is beyond me. I'd settle for a good caravan with guards who have no wish to die."

"Than talk her into turning back. 'Tis almost full dark. I'll leave the camp tonight, and in the morning, with me gone, there will be no trouble in it."

"Much you know," Hordo snorted. "With the humor on her now, she'd order us to pursue, and slay any who would not."

The flap of the striped pavilion opened, and Karela emerged, her face almost hidden by the hood of a scarlet cloak that covered her to the ground. She moved purposefully toward the two men through the deepening purple twilight. The cookfires made small pools of light among the boulders.

Hordo got to his feet, dusting his hands nervously. "I . . . must see to the horses. Good luck to you, Conan." He hurried away, not looking in the direction of the approaching woman.

Conan picked up his sword again and bent to examine the blade. It must needs be sharp, but the razor-edge some men boasted of would split against chain mail and quickly leave naught but a metal club. He became aware of the lower edge of Karela's crimson cloak at the corner of his vision. He did not look up.

"Why did you not come to my tent?" she demanded abruptly.

"I had need to tend my sword." With a final examination of the edge, he stood and sheathed the sword. Her tilted green eyes glared up at him from within the shelter of her hood; his sapphire gaze met hers calmly.

"I commanded you to come to me! We have much to discuss."

"But I will not be commanded, Karela. I am not one of your faithful hounds."

Her gasp was loud. "You defy me? I should have known you would think to supplant me. Do not think simply because you share my bed—"

"Be not a fool, Karela." The big Cimmerian made an effort to keep a rein on his temper. "I have no designs on your band. Command your rogues, but do not try to command me."

"So long as you ride behind the Red Hawk—"

"I ride with you, and beside you, as you ride with and beside me. No more than that for either of us."

"Do not cut me off, you muscle-bound oaf!" Her shout rang through the camp, echoing from tall boulders and the looming cliff. Bandits at the cook fires, and currying horses, turned to stare. Even in the dimness Conan could see that her face had colored. She lowered her voice, but her tone was acid. "I thought that you were the man I sought, a man strong enough to be the Red Hawk's consort. Derketo blast your soul! You're naught but a street thief!"

He caught her swinging hand before it could strike his cheek, and held it easily despite her struggles. Her scarlet cloak gaped open, revealing that she wore nothing beneath. "Again you break your oath, Karela. Do you hold your goddess in such contempt as to believe she will not punish a foresworn oath?"

Abruptly the auburn-haired woman seemed to realize the spectacle they were making before her brigands. She gathered her cloak together with her free hand. "Release me," she said coolly. "Rot your soul, I will not say please."

Conan loosened his grip, but it was not her plea that caused him to do so. As she tore her wrist free the hairs on the back of his neck were rising in an unpleasantly familiar fashion. He stared through the now black sky at the mountains around them. The stars were glittering bright points, and the moon had not yet risen. The mountains were formless deepenings of the night's shadows.

"Imhep-Aton follows still," he said quietly.

"I may allow you some liberties in private, Conan," Karela grated, rubbing her wrist, "but never again in public are you to. . . . Imhep-Aton? That's the name the possessed man spoke, that night in the camp. The sorcerer's name."

Conan nodded. "It was he who spoke to me first of the pendants. If not for the man he sent to kill me that night, I'd have delivered them to him, once I had them, for the price agreed. Now he has no more claim on me, or on the pendants."

"How can you be sure it is him, and not a hillman, or just the weight of night in these mountains pressing on you?"

"I know," he said simply.

"But—" Abruptly she stared past him, green eyes going wide in shock, mouth dropping open.

Conan spun, broadsword leaving its scabbard as he turned to knock aside the thrust of a spear in the hands of a demon-like apparition. Red eyes glowed at him from a dark scaled face beneath a ridged helmet. A harsh cry hissed at him from a fanged mouth. The big Cimmerian allowed himself no time for surprise. His return blow from the parry opened the creature from crotch to neck, black blood bubbling forth as it fell.

Already that sibilant battle cry was going up around the camp. Men leaped to their feet around the fires, on the border of panic as scores of scaly-skinned warriors poured out of the night. Alvar stared, and screamed as a spear pierced him through the chest. A swarthy Iranistani turned to flee and had his spine severed by a massive battle-ax in claw-fingered hands. Bandits darted like rats searching for an escape.

"Fight, Crom blast you!" Conan shouted. "They can die, too!"

He ran toward the slaughter in the camp, looking for Karela. Almost at once he spotted her in the middle of the fighting. From somewhere she had acquired a tulwar, though not her jeweled blade. Her cloak now dangled, bunched, from her left hand as a snare to catch other's weapons, and she danced naked through the butchery, red hair streaming, a fury from the Outer Dark, her curved sword drinking ebon blood.

"Up, my hounds!" she screamed. "Fight, for your lives!" Roaring, Hordo dashed in behind her to take a spear in the thigh that had been meant for her back. The one-eyed brigand's blade sought his reptilian attacker's heart, and even as the creature was falling he tore the spear from his leg and waded into the fray, blood over his boot.

Before Conan loomed another of the scaled men, his back to the Cimmerian, his spear raised to transfix Aberius, who lay on the ground with bulging eyes, his gap-toothed mouth open in a scream. Battles are not duels. Conan slammed his sword through the creature's back to stand out a foot from its chest. While it still stood, death-shriek bubbling forth, he planted a booted foot on its agony-arched back to tug his blade free.

The saurian killer fell twitching across Aberius, who screamed again and wriggled free with a glare at Conan as if he wished the Cimmerian were in the scaled one's place. The weasel-faced bandit grabbed the dying creature's spear, and for a bare second the two men stared at one another. Then Aberius darted into the fighting, shouting, "The Red Hawk! For the Red Hawk!"

"Crom!" Conan bellowed, and plunged into the maelstrom. "Crom and steel!"

The battle became a kaleidoscoping nightmare for the Cimmerian, as all battles did for all warriors. Men battling scaled monsters flickered before him and were gone, still locked in their death struggles. The cloud of battles covered his mind, loosing the fury of his wild north country, and even those scaled snake-men who faced him knew fear before they died, fear at the battle light that glowed in his blue eyes, fear at the grim, wild laughter that broke from his lips even as he slew. He waded through them, broadsword working in murderous frenzy.

"Crom!" If these scaly demons were to pay his ferryman's fee, he would set it high. "Crom and steel!"

And then there were none left standing among the night-shrouded boulders save those of human kind. Conan's broad chest was splattered with inky blood, mixing with his own in more than one place. He looked about him wearily, the battle fury fading.

Reptilian bodies lay everywhere, some twitching still. And among them were no few of the bandits. Hordo hobbled from wounded brigand to wounded brigand, a red-stained rag twisted about his thigh, offering what aid he could do those who still could use it. Aberius sat hunched by a fire, leaning on his spear. Other bandits began to make their dazed way in from the darkness.

Karela strode across the charnel ground to the Cimmerian, the cloak discarded, tulwar still gripped firmly in her hand. He was relieved to note that none of the blood that smeared her round breasts was her own.

"It seems Aberius saw nothing after all," she said when she faced him. "At least we know now what you felt watching you. I could wish you had gotten your warning somewhat earlier."

Conan shook his head. It was no use explaining to her how he knew it had not been the gaze of these things he felt on him. "I wish I knew whence they—"

He broke off with a sudden oath, and bent to examine the boots of one of the dead creatures. They were worked in the pattern of an encircling serpent, its head seeming surrounded by rays. Hurriedly he went to another body, and still others. All wore the boots.

"What takes you, Conan?" Karela demanded. "Even if you need boots, surely you could never wear something that came from these."

"No," he replied. "Those who stole the pendants from Tiridates' palace wore boots worked with a serpent." He tugged one of the boots from a narrow foot and tossed it to her.

She stepped aside to let it fall with a grimace of distaste. "I've had my fill and more of those things. Conan, you can't believe these . . . these whatever they are, entered Shadizar and left, unhindered. The City Guard is blind, I'll grant, but not as blind as that."

"They wore hooded robes that covered them to their fingertips. And they left the city at night, when the guards on the gates are half asleep at best. They could have entered the night before and remained hidden until it was time to do their work at the palace."

"It could be as you say," Karela admitted reluctantly. "But what help that is to us, I cannot see."

Hordo limped up and stood glaring at Conan. "Two score men and four, Cimmerian. That's what I led into these accursed mountains on this mad quest of yours. Full fifteen are food for worms this night, and two more like not to last till dawn. Thank whatever odd gods you pray to, we took a pair of them alive. The amusement of putting them to the question will keep you from being staked out in their place. And I'll tell you, for all my liking, if they tried I'm not sure I'd stop them."

"Prisoners?" Karela said sharply. "I've little love for these creatures dead, none alive. Give them to the men now. Come dawn we'll be riding out of these mountains."

"We abandon the treasure, then?" The one-eyed bandit sounded more relieved than surprised. "Fare you well, then, Conan, for I see this will be the last night we spend in company."

Karela turned slowly to give the Cimmerian an unreadable look. "Do we part, then?"

Conan nodded reluctantly, and with a rueful glare at Hordo. He had not meant her to find out so soon. In fact, his plan had been to leave in the night, with one of the prisoners for a guide, and let her discover him gone come morning.

"I continue after the pendants," the Cimmerian said.

"And that girl," Karela said flatly.

"Company," Hordo muttered, before Conan could speak further.

Toward them marched those of the bandits who were able to walk, not one man without at least one bloody bandage, and every one with his weapon in hand. Aberius marched at their head, using his spear like a walking staff. The others wore purposeful looks on their faces, but only he had a spiteful smile. Ten paces from where Conan stood with Karela and Hordo, they stopped.

Hordo started forward angrily, but Karela put a hand on his arm. He stopped, but his glare promised reckonings another time. Karela faced the gathering calmly, hand on hip and sword point planted firmly on the ground.

"Not hurt too badly, eh, Aberius?" she said with a sudden smile. The weasel-faced man seemed taken aback. He had a scratch down his cheek, and a piece of rag about his left arm. "And you, Talbor," she went on before anyone could speak. "Not as hard a night's work as you've had. Remember when we took that slaver's caravan from Zamboula, only they'd doubled the guard for fear of those quarry slaves they had bound for Ketha? I mind carrying you away from that across my saddle, with an arrow through you, and—"

"That's of no matter now," Aberius snapped. Hordo lurched forward, snarling, but Karela stopped him with a gesture. Aberius seemed to relax at that, and his smile became more satisfied. "No matter at all, now," he repeated smugly.

"Then what is of matter?" she asked.

Aberius blinked. "Has the Red Hawk suddenly lost her vision?" A few of the men behind him laughed; the others looked grim. "More than a third of our number dead, and not a coin in anyone's purse to see for it. We were going to steal some pendants from a few pilgrims. Now we've followed them all the way into these accursed mountains, and might follow to Vendhya with naught to show for it. Hillmen. Soldiers. Now, demons. It's time to go back to the plains, back to what we know."

"I decide when to turn back!" Karela's voice was suddenly a whip, lashing them. "I took you from the mud, robbing wayfarers for a few coppers, and made you feared by every caravan that leaves Shadizar, or Zamboula, or Aghrapur itself! I found you scavengers, and made you men! I put gold in your purses, and the swagger in your walks that make men step wide of you and women wriggle close! I am the Red Hawk, and I say we go on, and take this treasure that was stolen from a king!"

"You've led us long," Aberius said. "Karela." The familiarity of the name brought a gasp from the red-haired woman, and a growl from Hordo. Suddenly she seemed only a woman. A naked woman. Aberius licked his lips. Lecherous lights appeared in the eyes of the men behind him.

Karela took a step back. Conan could read every emotion that fled across her face. Rage. Shame. Frustration. And finally the determination to sell her life dearly. She took a firmer grip on her tulwar. Hordo had unobtrusively slipped his blade from its sheath.

If he had half a brain, Conan told himself, he would slip away now. After all, he owed her nothing. There was the oath not to save her, too. Before the brigands knew what was happening, he could be gone into the night, with one of the prisoners to guide him to the pendants. And Velita. With a sigh, he stepped forward.

"I do not break my oath," he said softly, for Karela's ears alone. "It's my own life I'm saving." He walked down to confront Aberius and the rest with a friendly smile, though the casual-seeming way his hand rested on his sword hilt was deceptive.

"Do not think to join us, Conan," Aberius said. There was considerable satisfaction in his smile. "You stand with them."

"I thought we all stood together," the Cimmerian replied. "You do remember the reason we came, don't you? Treasure? A king's treasure?"

The narrow-faced bandit spat, barely missing Conan's boot. "That's well out of our reach, now. I'll never find that trail again."

Conan let his smile broaden. "There's no need. These creatures you've killed tonight wear boots with the same markings as those who stole the pendants and the rest from Tiridates' palace. You can rest assured they serve the same master."

"Demons," Aberius said incredulously. "The man wants us to fight demons for this treasure." A mutter of agreement rose from the others, but Conan spoke quickly on his heels.

"What demons? I see creatures with the skins of snakes, but no demons." Protests broke out; Conan did not allow them to form. "Whatever they look like, you killed them tonight." He caught each man's eye in turn. "You killed them. With steel, and courage. Do demons die from steel? And you've bound two of them. Did they mutter spells and make you disappear? Did they fly away when you put ropes on them?" He looked sideways at Aberius, and grinned widely. "Did they breathe flame at you?"

Laughter rippled through the brigands, and Aberius colored. "It matters not! It matters not, I tell you! I still cannot find the trail, and I've not heard a word from these monsters that any can understand."

"I said there's no need to find the trail again," Conan said. "At dawn we'll contrive to let these two escape. You can track them easily enough."

"They're both wounded," Aberius protested desperately. "Like as not, neither will last an hour."

"It's still a chance." Conan let his voice swell. "A chance for a king's treasure in gold and jewels. Who's for gold? Who's for the Red Hawk?" He risked unsheathing his sword and raising it overhead. "Gold! The Red Hawk!"

In an instant every man save Aberius was waving his weapon in the air. "Gold!" they bellowed. "Gold!" "The Red Hawk!" "Gold!"

Aberius twisted his thin mouth sourly. "Gold!" "Hawk!" His beady eyes glared murder at Conan.

"Good, then!" Conan shouted over their cries. "Off with you, to rest and drink! Till dawn!"

"Dawn!" they roared. "Gold!"

Conan waited until they were well on their way back to the fires, then returned to Karela. She stared at him as if stricken. He put out a hand to touch her, but she jerked her arm away and stalked toward her tent without a word. Conan stared after her in consternation.

"I said once you had a facile tongue," Hordo said, sheathing his sword. "You've more than that, Conan of Cimmeria. Belikes you'll be a general, someday. Mayhap even a king. If you live to get out of these mountains. If any of us do."

"What's the matter with her?" Conan demanded. "I told her I did this for me, not her. I did not break the oath she demanded."

"She thinks you try to supplant her," Hordo replied slowly. "As chief of the band."

"That's foolish!"

Hordo did not seem to hear. "I hope she does not yet realize that what was done tonight can never be undone. Mitra grant her time before she must know that."

"What are you muttering about, you one-eyed old ruffian?" Conan said. "Did one of those blows tonight addle your brains?"

"You do not see it either, do you?" The bearded man's voice was sad. "What has been shattered can be mended, but the cracks are always there, and those cracks will break again and again until there is no mending."

"Once there's gold in their purses, they'll be as loyal as they ever were. On the morrow, Hordo, we must bury these creatures as well as our own dead. There must be no vultures aloft to warn whoever sent them out."

"Of course." Hordo sighed. "Rest you well, Cimmerian, and pray you we live to rest another night."

"Rest you well, Hordo."

After the one-eyed bandit disappeared toward the camp fires, Conan peered toward Karela's pavilion, beneath the loom of the cliff. Her shadow moved on the striped walls. She was washing herself. Then the lamps were extinguished.

Muttering curses under his breath Conan found a cloak and wrapped himself in it beneath the shelter of a boulder. Rest you well, indeed. Women!

Imhep-Aton rose from his place on the mountainside above the bandit camp and turned into the darkness. When he reached a place where the shadows against the stone seemed to darken, he walked on, through the shadow-wall and into a large, well-lit cave. His mount and his packhorse were tethered at the rear of it. His blankets were spread by the fire where a rabbit roasted on a spit. Nearby sat the chest containing the necessities of his thaumaturgies.

The mage rubbed his eyes, then stretched, massaging the small of his back. One spell had been needed to gain the eyes of an eagle, a second to make the night into day to his sight, still a third to let him hear what was said in the camp. Maintaining all three at once had given him a pain that ran from his head all the way down his backbone.

Yet it was worth the discomfort. The fools thought they ruled where their horses' hooves trod. He wondered what they would think if they knew they were but dogs, to corner a bear and die holding its attention while he, the hunter, moved in for the kill.

Laughing, the necromancer bent to his supper.

XVI

Seated on his golden serpent throne, Amanar watched the four dancing girls flexing their sinuosities across the mosaic floor for his enjoyment. Naked but for golden bells at ankles and wrists, they spun and writhed with wild abandon, in the sweat of fear for his displeasure, the tinkle of the bells a counterpoint to the flutes of four human musicians who kept their eyes on their own feet. There were few human servants within the keep, and none ever raised their eyes from the ground.

Amanar luxuriated in the fear he felt emanating from the four women, enjoying that as much as he did the luscious curves they flaunted shamelessly before him. The fifth girl, golden-eyed Yasmeen, had been the first to find herself given screaming to Sitha—threats produced more fear if it was known they would be carried out—and she had somehow managed to cut her own throat with the huge S'tarra's sword.

It had been all the necromancer could do to keep her alive long enough to be sacrificed to Morath-Aminee, and there had been little pleasure for him in the haste of it. He had taken precautions to make certain there would be no repetition of the unfortunate incident. Through lidded eyes Amanar watched his possessions dance for his favor.

"Master?"

"Yes, Sitha?" the mage said without shifting his gaze. The heavily muscled S'tarra stood bowed at one side of the throne, but its scarlet eyes watched the dancing girls greedily.

"The map, master. It flashes."

Amanar uncoiled from the throne and strode out of the chamber with Sitha at his heels. The girls continued to dance. He had given no command to cease, and they dared not without it.

Close beside the throne chamber was a small room with only two furnishings. A silver mirror hung on one gray stone wall. Against the other a great sheet of clear crystal leaned on a polished wooden frame, etched with a map of the mountains surrounding the keep. In the crystal a flashing red light moved slowly along a valley, triggered by the wards Amanar had set. Lower animals would not set off the warning, nor would his S'tarra. Only men could do that.

Turning to the mirror Amanar muttered cryptic words and made cabalistic gestures that left a faint glow in the air. As the glow faded, the silver mirror grew clear as a window, a window that looked down from an eagle's height on men riding slowly along a mountain valley.

One of the men made a gesture, as if pointing to something on the ground. They were tracking. Amanar spoke further esoteric phrases, and the vision of the mirror raced ahead, seeking. Like a falcon sensing prey, the image stopped, then swooped. On a badly wounded S'tarra, stumbling, falling, rising to struggle forward again. Amanar returned the mirror to the mounted party that followed his servant.

Near thirty men, well armed, and one woman. The mage could not tell whether the woman or a heavily muscled youth with fierce blue eyes commanded. Amanar rubbed his chin thoughtfully with an over-long hand.

"The girl Velita, Sitha," he said. "Fetch her here immediately."

The big S'tarra bowed himself from the room, leaving Amanar to study the image in the mirror. S'tarra used their wounded, those too badly hurt to heal, as fresh meat. This one would not have been allowed to leave his patrol; therefore the patrol no longer existed. Since these men followed, it was likely they had destroyed the patrol, and that was no small feat. It was also unlikely that they followed to no purpose.

"The girl, master." Sitha appeared in the door grasping Velita by her hair so that the dark-eyed girl perforce must walk on the balls of her feet. Her hands hung passively at her sides, though, and she shivered in terror both of that which gripped her and of the man she faced.

"Let her down," Amanar commanded impatiently. "Girl, come here and look into this mirror. Now, girl!"

She stumbled forward—though with her grace it seemed more a step of her dancing—and gasped when she saw the images moving before her. For a moment the necromancer thought she would speak, but then her jaw tightened and she closed her eyes.

"You spoke a name once, girl," Amanar said. "A man who would rescue you. Conan. Is that man among these you see?" She did not move a muscle, or utter a sound. "I mean the man no harm, girl. Point him out to me, or I will have Sitha whip you."

A low moan rose in her throat, and she opened her large eyes long enough to roll them in terror at the huge S'tarra behind her. "I cannot," she whispered. Her body trembled, and tears streamed down her face in silent sobs, but she would speak no more.

Amanar made an exasperated noise. "Fool girl. All you do is delay me for a few moments. Take her, Sitha. Twenty strokes."

Fanged mouth open in a wide grin, the massive S'tarra gathered her hair once more in its fist, lifting her painfully as they left. Tears rolled down her face all the harder, yet still her sobs were soundless.

The mage studied the images further. She had actually answered his question, in part at least, though she likely thought she had protected the man. But she had named this Conan a thief, and thieves did not ride with more than a score of armed men at their backs.

From within his serpent-embroidered black robe he produced the things he needed for this simple task. A red chalk scribed a five-pointed star on the stone floor. From a pouch he poured a small mound of powder on each of the points. His left hand stretched forth, and from each fingertip a spark flew to flare the powders to blinding flame. Five thin streams of acrid red smoke rose toward the distant ceiling.

Amanar muttered words in a dead tongue, made a gesture with his left hand. The smoke was suddenly sucked back down onto the pentagram, swirling and billowing as if whipped by a great wind, yet confined to the five-pointed star. He spoke one further word, and with a sharp crack the smoke was gone. In its place was a hairless gray shape no higher than his knee. Vaguely ape-like in form, with sharply sloping forehead and knuckles brushing the stone floor, its shoulders bore bony wings covered with taut gray hide.

The creature chattered at him, baring fangs that seemed to fill half its simian face, and sprang for the mage. At the boundary of the pentagram it suddenly shrieked, and was thrown back in a shower of sparks to crumple in the center of the star. Unsteadily it rose, claws clicking on the stone. The bat-like wings quivered as if for flight. "Free!" it barked shrilly.

Amanar's lip curled in disgust and anger. He was far beyond dealing with these minor demons personally. That the girl had forced him to it was a humiliation he would assuage personally, to her great discomfort.

"Free!" the demon demanded again.

"Be silent, Zath!" the necromancer commanded. The gray form recoiled, and Amanar allowed himself a small smile. "Yes, I know your name. Zath! An you fail to do as I command, I'll use the power that gives me. Others of your kind have from time to time annoyed me, and have found themselves trapped in material bodies. Bodies of solid gold." Amanar threw back his head and laughed.

The ape-like creature shuddered. Its dead-white eyes watched the sorcerer malevolently from beneath bony eyebrow ridges, but it said, "Zath do what?"

"These two," Amanar said, touching the images of Conan and Karela. "Discover for me their names, and why they follow one of my S'tarra."

"How?" the demon shrilled.

"Play no games with me," Amanar snapped. "Think you I do not know? If you are close enough to an ordinary man to hear his speech, you can hear his thoughts as well. And you may as well stop trying me. You know it will not work."

The demon chattered his fangs angrily. "Zath goes." With a thunderous clap, it disappeared. A wind ruffled Amanar's robe as air rushed into the pentagram.

The sorcerer dusted his hands as though he had touched something demeaning, and turned back to the mirror. For a time the images rode on, then suddenly one of their number pointed aloft. Consternation swept across their faces. Crossbows were raised, bolts loosed at the sky.

A snap sounded in the chamber, and the apelike demon was back in the pentagram, flexing its wings and fondling a crossbow quarrel. "Try to kill Zath," it giggled, and added contemptuously, "With iron." The demon amused itself by poking the quarrel through its bony arm. The crossbow arrow left no wound.

"What of that which I sent you for?" Amanar demanded.

The demon glared at him a moment before speaking. "Big man named Conan. Woman named Karela, called Red Hawk. They come for pendants, for girl. Free!"

Amanar smiled at the images on the mirror, recovering now from their encounter with Zath and riding on. The lovely Velita's thief, and the famed Red Hawk at the same time, with her band. There were many uses to which such beings could be put.

"Ahead of these people," he said to the demon without taking his eyes from the mirror, "is one of my S'tarra. It is wounded, but yet lives. You may feed. Now, go." The necromancer's smile was far from pleasant.

The slopes of the twisting valley steepened and grew bleaker as the bandits rode. Conan eyed a thornbush, of which there were even fewer here than had been along the trail earlier. It was stunted and bent as if something in air or soil distorted the dark branches into an unwholesome simulacrum of the plant it had once been. All the scrub growth they passed grew more like that the further they went along the wounded snake-creature's trail.

"Fitting country," Hordo muttered just loud enough for Conan to hear. His lone eye watched Karela warily, where she rode at the column's head. "First snake-men, then that flying Mitra-alone-knows-what."

"It didn't hurt anyone," Conan said flatly, "and it went away." He was not about to say anything that might dissuade the others from turning back, but at the same time he could not entirely dispel his own sense of unease.

"It was hit," the one-eyed man went on. "Two bolts at least, but never a quiver out of it. 'Tis only luck the rest of these rogues didn't turn tail on the moment."

"Mayhap you should turn back, Hordo." He twisted in his saddle to peer down the line of mounted bandits straggled behind him on the winding valley floor. Greed drove them forward, but since the strange creature was seen flying above them, seeming to follow them, every man watched the gray skies and stony slopes with sullen eyes. From time to time a man would touch his bandaged wounds and look thoughtfully back the way they had come.

Conan shook his black-maned head at the bearded brigand. "If she says she has decided to turn back, they'll follow her gratefully; if she pushes on, they'll begin dropping away one by one."

"You of all men should know she'll not turn from this trail. Not so long as you go on."

Conan was spared answering by a loud hail from Aberius. The weasel-faced bandit had been riding ahead of them to track the wounded snake-creature. Now he sat his horse where the trail wound around a rock spire ahead, waving his arm over his head.

"Halloo!"

Karela galloped forward without a word.

"I hope he's lost the track," Hordo muttered. Conan booted his horse ahead. After a moment the one-eyed man followed.

The red-haired woman turned her horse aside as Conan rode up. He looked at what Aberius had been showing her. The reptilian creature they had been following lay sprawled on its back, dead, in the shadow of the stone spire. Its chain mail had been torn off, and its chest ripped open.

"Scavengers have been at it already," Hordo muttered. "It's too bad the other one crawled off somewhere to die." He did not sound as if he thought it too bad at all.

"No vultures in the sky," Conan said thoughtfully. "And never have I heard of jackals that rip out a heart and leave the rest."

Aberius' horse whinnied as he jerked at the reins. "Mitra! The Cimmerian's right. Who knows what slew him? Perhaps that foul thing that flew over us and took no mind of crossbow bolts." His beady eyes darted wildly, as if expecting the apparition to appear again, from behind a rock.

"Be silent, fool!" Karela snapped. "It died of the wounds it took last night, and your approach frightened a badger or some such off its feeding."

"It makes no matter," Aberius said slyly. "I can track this carrion no further."

The woman's green-eyed gaze was contemptuously amused. "Then I've no more need of you, have I? I'll wager I can find where it was going myself."

"It's time to leave these accursed mountains." The pinch-faced man swiveled his head to the other bandits, waiting down the trail. Enough fear of the Red Hawk remained to keep them back from her council.

Karela did not deign to acknowledge his whine. "Since loosing its bonds, the creature has kept a straight line. When the twists of the land took it aside, it found its way back again. We'll keep the same way."

"But—" Aberius swallowed the rest of his words as Hordo pushed his horse closer. Karela started ahead, ignoring them.

"An I hear any tales," the one-eyed man grated, "other than that you frighted some slinking vermin from this corpse, I'll see you cold carrion beside it." Conan caught his eye as he turned to follow Karela, and for a moment the bearded bandit looked abashed. "She needs one hound at least to remain faithful, Cimmerian. The way is forward, Aberius. Forward, you worthless rogues!" he bellowed. He met Conan's eyes again, then kicked his horse into a gallop.

For a time Conan sat his horse, watching the faces of the passing brigands as they came in view of the bloody, scaled corpse. Each recoiled, muttering or with an oath, as he rounded the spire and got a clear look at what lay there, but the greed in their eyes was undiminished. They rode on.

Muttering his own oath, Conan spurred after Karela and Hordo.

XVII

Haranides wearily raised his hand to signal a halt to the bedraggled column behind him. The site among the boulders at the face of the cliff had been a camp. An attempt had been made to hide the face, but a thin tendril of smoke still rose from ashes not covered well enough with dirt.

"Dismount the men, Aheranates," the captain commanded, wincing as he did so himself. A hillman's lance had left a gouge along his ribs that would be a long time in healing. "Take a party of ten and see if you can find which way they went without mucking up the tracks too badly."

The slender lieutenant—Haranides could not help wondering how he had come through the fight without a scratch—touched his forehead stiffly in salute. "Sir." He sawed at his reins to pull his horse around and began telling off the men.

Haranides sighed. He was not in good odor with the lieutenant, which meant he would not be in good odor with the lieutenant's father, which meant. . . . Odor. He fingered the polished stone jar in his pouch. The perfume had seemed familiar to him, but it was not until he was beating aside a hillman's curved sword that he remembered where he had smelled it before. And knew that the red-haired jade who had come to 'warn' him of the tribesmen was the Red Hawk.

The problem was that Aheranates, too, knew that he had had her in his grasp and let her slip away. Once the fighting was done and wounds were tended as well they could be in the field, Haranides had ordered them along the trail of the three.

"Sir?" Haranides looked up from his brown study to find Resaro knuckling his forehead. "The prisoner, sir?"

When the butchery was over they had found a hillman who had merely been stunned by a blow to the head. Now Haranides had great need to know what had brought such a body of tribesmen together. They normally formed much smaller bands for their raiding. It was necessary to know if he might find himself facing other forces as large. He grimaced in disgust. "Put him to the question, Resaro."

"Yes, sir. If the captain will pardon me for saying so, sir, that was a fine piece of work back there. The handful we didn't slice into dogmeat are likely still running."

"See to the prisoner," Haranides sighed. Resaro touched his forehead and went.

The man might think it fine work, the captain thought, and in the ordinary course of events it might have been considered so, but this was no ordinary patrol. Two hundred good cavalrymen had he led through the Gate to the Three Swords. After burying his dead, separating those too badly wounded to go on, and detaching enough healthy men to give the wounded a chance if they were attacked on their way out of the mountains, he had four score and three left. And he had neither the Red Hawk or Tiridates' trinkets in hand. In eyes of king and counselor it would be those lacks that damned him.

A choked scream rose from where Resaro had the hillman. "Mitra blast Tiridates and the Red Hawk both," the captain growled under his breath. He walked into what had been the bandit camp, examining the ground between the looming boulders as much to keep his mind off the hillman's moans as in hope of finding anything of importance.

Aheranates found him standing where the pavilion had been. "Would I could see what she saw from here," Haranides said without looking at the slender man. "There is a wrong feel to this place. What happened here?"

"A battle. Sir." A supercilious smile curled the lieutenant's mouth at for once being ahead of Haranides. "Or, at least, a fight, but it must have been a big one. Hillmen attacked the bandits in camp and cut them up badly. We no longer need worry about the Red Hawk. An she still lives, she's screaming over a torture-fire about now."

"A very complete picture," the captain said slowly. "Based on what?"

"Graves. One mass grave that must hold forty or more, and seventeen single graves. They're upslope, to the north there."

"Graves," Haranides repeated thoughtfully. The hill tribes never acted in concert. In their dialects the words for 'enemy' and 'one not of my clan' were the same. But if they had found some compelling reason. . . . "But who won, lieutenant?"

"What?"

The hook-nosed captain shook his head. "Learn something about those you chase. None of the hill tribes bury their victims, and they take their own dead back to their villages so their spirits won't have to wander among strangers. On the other hand, if the bandits won, why would they bury the hillman dead?"

"But the bandits wouldn't bury tribesmen," Aheranates protested.

"Exactly. So I suggest you take a few men and find out what's in those graves." It was Haranides' turn to smile, at the consternation on the lieutenant's face.

As the slender youth began to splutter about not being a graverobber, a bowlegged cavalryman ran to a panting halt before them. The edge of a blood-stained bandage showed under his helmet. "Captain," he said nervously. "Sir, there's something maybe you ought to see. It's. . . ." He swallowed convulsively. "You'd best see for yourself, sir."

Haranides frowned. He could not think of anything that would put one of these tough soldiers in this taking. "Lead the way, Narses."

The soldier swallowed again, and turned back the way he had come with obvious reluctance. Haranides noted as he followed that Aheranates was clinging to his heels. He supposed that to the lieutenant's mind, even something that made a seasoned campaigner turn green was better than opening day-old graves.

Near a thornbush springing from the crevice between two boulders a pair of soldiers stood, making an obvious effort not to look into the narrow opening. From chain mail and helmet to hook nose and bandy legs, they were like Narses, and like him, too, in the tightness around their eyes and the green tinge about their lips.

Narses stopped beside the two and pointed to the cleft. "In there, sir. Saw a trail of . . . of blood, sir, leading in, so I looked, and. . . ." He trailed off with a helpless shrug.

The blood trail was clear to be seen, dried black smears on the rock, and on the stony ground beneath the bush.

"Clear the brush away," Haranides ordered irritably. Likely the bandits, or the tribesmen, had tortured someone and tossed the body here for the ravens. He liked looking at the results of torture even less than he liked listening to it, and if the men's faces were any indication, this was a bad job of it. "Get a move on," he added as the men fiddled with their swords.

"Yes, sir," Narses said unhappily.

Swinging their swords like brush knives, to the accompaniment of grumbled curses as thorns found the chinks of their chain mail and broke off in the flesh, the bush was hacked to a stump and the limbs dragged clear of the crevice. Haranides put his foot on the stump and levered himself up to peer into the crevice. His breath caught in his throat.

He found himself staring straight into sightless, inhuman eyes in a leathery scaled face. The fanged mouth was frozen in rictus, seemingly sneering at him. One preternaturally long bony hand, a length of severed rope dangling from the wrist, clutched with clawed fingers at a sword gash in chain mail stained with dried blood. All of its wounds appeared to be from swords, he noted, or at least from the sorts of weapons men bore.

"But then, what self-respecting vulture would touch it," he muttered.

"What is it?" Aheranates demanded.

Haranides climbed down to let the lieutenant take his place. "Did you see anything else up this way?" the captain asked the three soldiers.

A shriek burst from Aheranates' mouth, and the slender young officer half tumbled back to the ground. He stared wildly at the captain, at the three soldiers, scrubbing his mouth with the back of his hand. "Mitra's Holies!" he whispered. "What is that?"

"Not a hillman," Haranides said drily. With a sob the lieutenant stumbled a few steps and bent double, retching. Haranides shook his head and turned back to the soldiers. "Did you find anything?"

"Yes, sir," Narses said. He seemed eager to talk about anything but what was in the crevice. "Horse tracks, sir. Maybe a score or more. Came from the camp down there, right past . . . past here, and went off that way, sir." He flung a hand to the south.

"Following?" the captain mused half to himself.

"We must go back," Aheranates panted suddenly. "We can't fight demons."

"This is the first demon I ever saw killed by a sword," Haranides said flatly. He was relieved to see the momentary panic in the three soldiers' eyes fade. "Get that thing down from there," he went on, turning their looks to pure disgust. "We'll see if our hillman friend knows what it is."

Grumbling under their breath, the bow-legged cavalrymen climbed awkwardly into the cranny and worked the stiffened body free. Haranides started back while they were still lifting it down.

The hillman was spreadeagled between pegs in the ground, surrounded by cavalrymen betting among themselves on whether or not he would open up at the next application. From the coals of a small fire projected the handles of half a dozen irons. The smell of scorched flesh and the blisters on the soles of the hillman's feet and on his dark, hairless chest told the use to which the irons had been put.

Resaro, squatting by the tribesman's side, thrust an iron carefully into the fire. "He isn't saying much so far, sir."

"Unbelieving dogs!" the hillman rasped. His black eyes glared at Haranides above a long, scraggly mustache that was almost as dark. "Sons of diseased camels! Your mothers defile themselves with sheep! Your fathers—"

Resaro casually backhanded him across the mouth. "Sorry, sir. Be a lot worse done to one of us in his village, but he seems to take it personally that we expect him to talk, instead of just killing him outright."

"Never will I talk!" the hillman growled. "Cut off my hands! I will not speak! Pluck out my eyes! I will not speak! Slice off—"

"Those all sound interesting," Haranides cut him off. "But I can think of something better." The black eyes watched him worriedly. "I'll wager the odds are good there's a hillman up there somewhere watching us right this minute. One of your lot, or another one. It doesn't matter. What do you think would happen if that man sees us turn you loose with smiles and pats on the back?"

"Kill me," the hillman hissed. "I will not talk."

Haranides laughed easily. "Oh, they'd kill you for us. A lot more slowly than we would, I suspect. But worst of all," his smile faded, "they'll curse your soul for a traitor. Your spirit will wander for all time, trapped between this world and the next. Alone. Except for other traitors. And demons." The hillman was silent, but unease painted his face. He was ready, Haranides thought. "Narses, bring that thing in here and show it to our guest."

The watching soldiers gasped and muttered charms as Narses and another carried the rigid corpse into the circle. Haranides kept his eyes on the hillman's face. The dark eyes slid away from the reptilian creature, then back again, abruptly so full of venom as to seem deadly.

"You know it, don't you?" the captain said quietly.

The hillman nodded reluctantly. His eyes were still murderous on Haranides. "It is called a S'tarra." His mouth twisted around the word, and he spat for punctuation. "Many of these thrice-accursed dung-eaters serve the evil one who dwells in the dark fortress to the south. Many men, and even women and children, disappear within those light-forsaken stone walls, and none are seen again. Not even their bodies to be borne away for the proper rites. Such abominations are not to be endured. So did we gather—" The thin-lipped mouth snapped shut; the tribesman resumed his glare.

"You lie," Haranides sneered. "You know not the truth, as your mother knew not your father. Hill dogs do not attack fortresses. You cower in fear of your women, and you would sell your children for a copper."

The dark face had become engorged with rage as Haranides spoke. "Loose me!" the tribesman howled. "Loose me, drinker of jackal's urine, and I will carve your manhood to prove mine!"

The captain laughed contemptuously. "With such numbers as you had, you could not have taken a mud hut held by an old woman and her granddaughter."

"Our strength was as the strength of thousands for the righteousness of our cause!" the dark man spat. "Each of us would have killed a score of the diseased demon-spawn!"

Haranides studied the hillman's anger-suffused eyes, and nodded to himself. That was as close as he was likely to get to confirmation that there were no more hillmen out. "You say they take people," he said finally. "Do valuables attract them? Gold? Gems?"

"No!" Aheranates burst out. Haranides rounded on him angrily, but the slender man babbled on. "We cannot pursue these . . . these monsters! Mitra! 'Twas the Red Hawk we were sent for, and if these creatures kill her, good and well enough!"

"Erlik take you, Aheranates!" the captain grated.

The hillman broke in. "I will guide you. And you ride to slay the scaled filth," he spat, "I will guide you faithfully." Anger had been washed from his face by some other emotion, but what emotion was impossible to say.

"By the Black Throne of Erlik!" Haranides growled. Seizing Aheranates' arm he pulled the young lieutenant away from the prying eyes of the men, behind a massive boulder. The captain glanced around to make certain none of the others had followed. When he spoke his voice was low and forceful. "I've put up with your insolence, with foolishness, slyness, and pettiness enough for ten girls in a zenana, but I'll not put up with cowardice. Especially not in front of the men."

"Cowardice!" Aheranates' slender frame quivered. "My father is Manerxes, who is friend to—"

"I care not if your father is Mitra! Hannuman's stones, man! Your fear is so strong it can be felt at ten paces. We were sent to return with the Red Hawk, not with a rumor that she might possibly be dead somewhere in the mountains."

"You mean to go on?"

Haranides gritted his teeth. The fool could make trouble for him once they returned to Shadizar. "For a time, lieutenant. We may overtake the bandits. And if they have been captured by these S'tarra, well the hilltribes may consider their keep a fortress, but if they thought to take it with fewer than ten score, it's possible eighty real soldiers can do the task. In any event, I won't turn back until I'm sure the Red Hawk and the king's playthings are beyond my grasp."

"You've gone mad." Aheranates' voice was cold and calm, his eyes glazed and half-focused. "I have no other choice. You cannot be allowed to kill us all." His hand darted for his sword.

In his shock Haranides was barely able to throw himself back away from the lieutenant's vicious slash. Aheranates' eyes were fixed; his breath came in pants. Haranides rolled aside, and the other's blade bit into the stony ground where his head had been. But now the captain had his own sword out. He lunged up from the ground, driving it under the younger man's ribs to thrust out behind his shoulder.

Aheranates stared down incredulously at the steel that transfixed him. "My father is Manerxes," he whispered. "He. . . ." A bubble of blood formed on his lips. As it broke, he fell.

Haranides got to his feet, cursing under his breath, and tugged his sword free of the body. He started at a footstep grating on the rock behind him. Resaro stepped up to look down at Aheranates' body.

"The fool," Haranides began, but Resaro cut him off.

"Your pardon for interrupting, sir, but I can see as you're distraught over the lieutenant's death, and I wouldn't want you to say something, in anguish, so to speak, that I shouldn't ought to hear."

"What are you saying?" the hook-nosed captain asked slowly.

Resaro's dark eyes met his levelly. "The lieutenant was a brave man, sir. Hid the terrible wounds he took against the hillmen till it was too late for him, but I expect he saved us all. His father will be proud of him." He fumbled a rag from beneath his tunic. "You'd best wipe your sword, sir. You must have dropped it and got some of the lieutenant's blood on it."

Haranides hesitated before accepting the cloth. "When we get back to Shadizar, come see me. I'll need a good sergeant in my next posting. Now get the hillman on a horse, and we'll see if we can find the Red Hawk."

"Yes, sir. And thank you, sir."

Resaro knuckled his forehead and disappeared, but Haranides stood looking at the lieutenant's corpse. Whatever slight chance he might have had of surviving a return to Shadizar without the Red Hawk *and* the Tiridates' trinkets had died with that foppish young idiot. With a muttered oath he went to join his men.

XVIII

onan's keen eyes swept the ridges as the bandit column wound its way along the floor of the narrow, twisting valley. Hordo was by his side, muttering unintelligibly beneath his breath, while Karela maintained her usual place ahead of them all. Her emerald cape was thrown back, and she rode with one fist planted jauntily on her hip. With the need for tracking past, Aberius was back with the rest of the brigands, riding strung out behind.

"She acts as if this is a parade," Hordo growled.

"It may be," Conan replied. He eased his broadsword in its worn shagreen sheath. His gaze still traversed the ridgelines, never stopping in any one place for long. "We have watchers, at least."

Hordo tensed, but he was too long in the trade of banditry to look around suddenly. He loosened his own blade. "Where are they?" he asked quietly.

"Both sides of the valley. I don't know how many."

"It won't take many in here," Hordo grumbled, eyeing the steep slopes. "I'll warn her."

"We both go," Conan said quickly. "Slowly, as if we're just riding forward to have a casual word." The one-eyed man nodded, and they kicked their mounts to a faster walk.

Karela looked around in surprise and irritation as they rode up on either side of her. Her mouth opened angrily.

"We're being followed," Hordo said before she could speak. "Along the ridges."

She glanced at Conan, then turned back to Hordo. "You're sure?"

"I'm sure," Conan said. Her back stiffened, and she faced forward again without speaking. He went on. "Half a glass past, I saw movement on the east ridge. I thought it was an animal, but now there are two to the east and three to the west, and they move together."

"Hannuman's stones," she muttered, still not looking at him. They rounded a bend in the trail, and whatever else she had to say was lost in a gasp.

In the center of the trail, only twenty paces from them, stood eight reptilian warriors like those they had killed, in chain mail and ridged helmets, bearing on their shoulders the four crossed poles of a bier. Atop the bier was a tall throne of intricately carved ivory, in which sat a man robed in scarlet. A white streak serpentined through his black hair. He held a long golden staff across his chest and bowed slightly without rising.

"I am called Amanar." His voice rang loudly against the precipitous slopes. "I welcome you, wayfarers."

Conan found he had his broadsword in hand, and noted from the corner of his eye that Karela and Hordo had their blades out as well. Amanar wore a smile, though it did not reach his strange, red-flecked black eyes, but the Cimmerian sensed evil there, evil beyond the scaled creatures that served him. There was nothing rational in his perception. It was a primitive intuition that came from bone and blood, and he trusted it all the more for that.

"Be not affrighted," Amanar intoned.

The sounds of sliding rock and gravel jerked Conan's gaze away from the man on the bier—he was shocked to realize the other had held his eyes thus—to find the abrupt rises to either side of the trail swarming with hundreds of the snake-men, many with javelins or crossbows. There were shouts from the bandits behind as they realized they were as good as surrounded.

"Rats in a barrel," Hordo growled. "Take a pull on the hellhorn for me, Conan, if you get to Gehanna first."

"What mean you by this?" Karela demanded loudly. "If you think to buy our lives cheaply—"

"You do not understand," the man on the bier interrupted smoothly. Conan thought he detected amusement. "The S'tarra are my servants. I greet what few strangers pass this way as I greet you, but betimes strangers are unscrupulous folk who think to use violence against me for all my friendliness. I find it best to remove all temptation by having my retainers near in sufficient numbers. Not that I suspect you, of course."

Conan was certain of the sarcasm in that last. "What kind of man is served by minions such as these scaled ones?" He suspected the answer, whether he got it or not, was that he had encountered another magician.

Instead of a reply from Amanar, Karela snapped, "You forget who commands here, Cimmerian!" Her green-eyed glare transferred to the man in the scarlet robes, lessening not a whit in intensity. "Still, Amanar, it is not a question out of place. Be you a sorcerer to be served by these monsters?"

Gasps rose from the bandits, and their mutterings increased. Conan winced, for he knew how dangerous it was to confront a mage too openly. But Amanar smiled as he might at rambunctious children.

"The S'tarra are not monsters," Amanar said. "They are the last remnants of a race that lived before man, and gentle of nature despite their outward appearances. Before I came the hillmen hunted them like animals, slaughtered them. No, you have naught to fear from them, nor from me, though some bands which do not serve me sometimes fail to distinguish between the hillmen who hate them and others of humankind."

"We met such a band," Karela said.

Conan looked at the red-haired bandit sharply, but he could not tell whether she believed the man, or whether she attempted some deeper game.

"Praise be to all the gods that you survived," Amanar said piously. "Let me offer you the shelter of my keep. Your retainers may camp outside the walls and feel safe. Pray say you will be my guests. I have few visitors, and there is something I would speak to you of, which I think you will find to your advantage."

Conan looked at the S'tarra arrayed on the slopes above and wondered wryly how many refused Amanar's invitations.

Karela did not hesitate. "I accept gratefully," she said.

Amanar smiled—once more it did not touch his eyes—bowed slightly to her, and clapped his hands. The eight S'tarra bearing his ivory throne turned carefully and started up the trail. Karela rode after him, and Conan and Hordo quickly followed her. On the slopes of the narrow valley the S'tarra kept alongside the bandits, moving over the slanted ground with lizardlike agility. Honor guard, Conan wondered, or simply guard?

"How much of what he says do you believe?" Hordo said softly.

Conan glanced at the throned man leading them—he had experience of the acuity of wizards' hearing. Amanar seemed to be ignoring them. "Not a word," he replied. "That—S'tarra, did he call it?—was headed here."

The one-eyed man frowned. "If we turn suddenly, we could be free of his minions before they had ought but a crossbow shot or two at us."

"Why?" Conan laughed softly. "We came for the pendants, and what else we might find. He takes us into his very keep, right to them."

"I never thought of that," Hordo said, joining Conan's quiet laughter.

Karela looked over her shoulder, her tilted green eyes unreadable. "Leave the thinking to me, old one," she said flatly. "That beard leeches your brain." An uncomfortable silence fell over them.

XIX

s the narrow, twisting gorge they had followed so long debouched into a broader valley, they saw the Keep of Amanar. Ebon towers reared into the sky, their rounded sides seeming to absorb the afternoon sun. Black ramparts, crenellated and sprouting bartizans, grew from the stone of the mountain. A ramp led to the barbican, topped by troughs for pouring boiling oil on those who approached unwarily. Not even a thornbush grew in the stony soil surrounding it all.

Amanar gestured to the wide expanse of the valley below the fortress. "Camp your men where you will. Then come you inside, and I will speak with you." His bier was carried swiftly up the ramp, leaving the bandits milling at its foot.

"Find a spot for my hounds, Hordo," Karela said, dismounting and handing him her reins. Conan climbed down as well. Her green eyes sparkled dangerously. "What do you think you're doing, Cimmerian?"

"I'm not one of your hounds," he replied levelly. He started up the ramp, noting the guard positions on the walls. It would not be an easy place for a thief to enter.

The Cimmerian tensed as running boots pounded up behind him. Karela eased her pace to a walk beside him, her heavy breathing coming more from anger, he suspected, than exertion. "Conan, you don't know what you're doing here. You're out of your depth."

"I need to see what's inside, Karela. These walls could hold off an army. I may yet have to scale them in the night if we're to gain the pendants. Unless Amanar and his scaly henchmen have frightened you out of it."

"I haven't said that, have I? And I won't have you accusing me of cowardice!"

They stopped before the lowered portcullis. From behind the heavy iron bars, a S'tarra peered at them with red eyes that seemed to glow slightly in the shadows of the gateway. Two more stepped from the arched doorway of the barbarian, pikes in hand.

"We are expected by Amanar," Conan said.

"*I* am expected," Karela said.

The S'tarra made a lifting gesture, and with a clanking of chain the grating began to rise. "Yes," it hissed. "The master said the two of you would come. Follow me." Turning on its heel, it trotted into the dark recesses of the fortress.

"How did he know we'd both come?" Karela said as they followed.

"I'm not the one out of my depth," Conan replied. Behind them the portcullis creaked shut. The muscular Cimmerian found himself hoping it would be as easy to get out as it had been to get in.

The granite-paved baileys of the fortress, the sable stone barracks and casemates, were as bleak as the exterior, but then the S'tarra led them through great iron-bound doors into the donjon, a massive obsidian cube topped by the tallest tower of the keep.

Conan found himself in a marble-walled hall with a floor mosaicked in rainbow arabesques. Silver sconces held golden dragon lamps, filling even the vaulted ceiling, carved with hippogriffs and unicorns, with lambent radiance. He nodded to himself with satisfaction. If Amanar lit his entry hall with such, he had wealth enough and more for Conan's needs. There was still the matter of Velita, though, and his oath to free her.

The S'tarra halted before tall doors of burnished brass, and knocked. The creature bent as if to listen, then, though Conan heard nothing, swung one weighty door open. The music of flutes and harps drifted out as the creature bowed, making a gesture for them to enter.

Conan strode in, Karela rushing so as not to seem to be following. He smiled at her, and she bared her teeth in return.

"Welcome," Amanar said. "Sit, please." He sat in an ornately carved chair beside a low ebony table, fondling his golden staff. Two similar chairs were arranged on the other side of the table.

The music came from four human musicians sitting cross-legged on cushions against the wall. They played softly, without looking at one another or raising their eyes from the floor. A woman appeared from behind a curtain with a silver tray holding wine. Her gaze, too, never left the costly carpets that covered the floor as she set the tray on the table, bowed to Amanar, and scurried silently from the room. Amanar seemed not to notice her. His red-flecked eyes were on Karela.

"I didn't know you had any human servants," Conan said. He sat on the edge of his chair, careful to leave his sword free.

Amanar swung his gaze to the Cimmerian, and Conan found himself hard-pressed not to look away. The scarlet flecks in the man's eyes tried to pull him into their inky depths. Conan gritted his teeth and stared back.

"Yes," Amanar said, "I have a few. Worthless things, totally useless unless they're under my eye. At times I have thought I might be better off if I simply gave them all to the hillmen." He spoke loudly, not seeming to care whether the musicians heard, but they played on without missing a beat.

"Why don't you use S'tarra servants, then?" Conan asked.

"They have limits. Yes, definite limits." The man with the odd white streak through his hair suddenly rubbed his hands together. "But come. Let us drink." No one moved to take one of the crystal goblets. "Do you yet distrust me?" There was a touch of mocking in his voice. "Then choose you any cup, and I will drink from it."

"This is ridiculous," Karela suddenly burst out, reaching for the wine.

Conan seized her wrist in an iron grip. "A sip from all three in turn," he said quietly. Amanar shrugged.

"Release me," Karela said quietly, but her words quivered with suppressed rage. Conan loosed his hold. For a moment she rubbed her wrist. "You've formed a bad habit of manhandling me," she said, and reached again for the goblet.

Amanar forestalled her by snatching the crystal cup from under her very fingers. "As your friend still mistrusts. . . ." Swiftly he sipped from each of the three goblets. "You see," he said as he set the last one back on the silver tray, "I do not die. Why should I bring you here to kill you, when I could have had the S'tarra bury you beneath boulders in the valley where we met?"

With an angry glare at Conan, Karela grabbed a goblet and drank, throwing her head back. Conan picked up another slowly, as Amanar took his. The fruity taste was a surprise. It was one of the heady wines of Aquilonia, costly so far from that western land.

"Besides," Amanar said quietly, "why should I wish harm to Conan, the thief of Cimmeria, and Karela, the Red Hawk?"

A scream burst from Karela. Conan bounded to his feet with a roar, crystal cup falling to the carpet as he drew his broadsword. Amanar made no move except to sway toward Karela, standing with her jeweled tulwar in hand, her head turning wildly as if seeking attackers. The dark man's heavy-lidded eyes half closed, and he inhaled deeply as if breathing in her perfume. The musicians played on unconcerned, eyes never lifting.

"Yes," Amanar murmured, leaning back in his chair. He appeared surprised to see Conan's sword. "Do you need that? There is only me, and I can hardly fight you with my staff." He extended the staff to tap Conan's blade. "Put it away and sit. You are in no danger."

"I'll stand," Conan said grimly, "until a few questions are answered."

"Conan was right," Karela whispered. "You're a sorcerer."

Amanar spread his hands. "I am what some men call a sorcerer, yes. I prefer to think of myself as a seeker of wisdom, wanting to bring the world a better way." He seemed pleased with that. "Yes. A better way."

"What do you want with us?" she said, taking a firmer grip on her curved sword. "Why did you bring us here?"

"I have a proposal to make to you. Both of you." The mage fingered his golden staff and smiled. Karela hesitated, then abruptly sheathed her blade and sat down.

"Before I put my sword up," Conan said, "tell me this. You know our names. What else do you know?"

Amanar seemed to consider before answering. "Quite incidentally to discovering your names, I discovered that you seek five dancing girls and five pendants. Searching further told me these were stolen from the palace of King Tiridates of Zamora. Why you seek them, most particularly why you seek them in the Kezankian Mountains, I do not know, however." His smile was bland, and Conan could see doubt spreading on Karela's face.

So much had already been revealed that the Cimmerian decided it could do little further harm to reveal a trifle more. "We came because the women and the gems were taken by S'tarra." He bridled at Amanar's answering laugh.

"Forgive me, Conan of Cimmerian, but the mere thought that S'tarra could enter Shadizar is ludicrous. The City Guard would kill them at sight, before they as much as reached the gates. Besides, my muscular friend, the S'tarra never leave the mountains. Never."

Conan answered in a flat voice. "Those who entered Tiridates' palace wore the boots the S'tarra wear, the boots worked with a serpent."

Amanar's laughter cut off abruptly, and his eyes lidded. Conan had the sudden impression of being regarded by a viper. "The boots," the sorcerer said at last, "are often taken by hillmen when they strip the S'tarra they have killed. I should imagine a caravan guard who killed a hillman during an attack and found a good pair of boots on him might take them. Who can say how far a pair of those boots might travel, or how many might be worn outside the mountains?" His voice was reasonable in the extreme, if devoid of color, but his black eyes challenged Conan to reject the explanation if he dared. The only sound in the room came from the musicians.

Karela abruptly broke the impasse. "Hannuman's stones, Conan. Would he have mentioned the gems in the first place if he had them?"

The young Cimmerian was suddenly aware of how foolish he must look. The musicians played their flutes and harps. Karela had retrieved her goblet from the carpet and poured more wine. Amanar sat with the long fingers of one hand casually caressing his golden staff. In the midst of this peaceful scene Conan stood sword in hand, balanced to fight on the instant.

"Crom!" he muttered, and slammed his blade into its sheath. He resumed his chair, ostentatiously sprawling back. "You spoke of a proposal, Amanar," he said sharply.

The mage nodded. "I offer you both . . . haven. When the City Watch searches too diligently for Conan the thief, when the Army of Zamora presses too hard against the Red Hawk, let them come here, where the hillmen keep the army away, and my fortress grants safety from the hillmen."

"From the kindness of your heart," Conan grunted.

Karela gave him a pointed look. "What would you require in return, Amanar? We have neither knowledge nor skills to be of use to a sorcerer."

"On the contrary," the mage replied. "The Red Hawk's fame is known from the Vilayet Sea to the Karpashian Mountains, and beyond. It is said that she would march her band into Gehanna, if she gave her word to do so, and that her rogues would follow. Conan is a thief of great skill, I am sure. From time to time I would ask you to perform certain . . . commissions for me." He smiled expansively. "There would, of course, be payment in gold, and I would in no way interfere with your, ah, professions."

Karela grinned wolfishly. "The caravan route to Sultanapur lies less than half a day to the south, does it not?"

"It does," Amanar laughed quietly. "And I'll not object if you should do business there. I may even have some for you myself. But make not your decision now. Rest, eat and drink. Tomorrow will be time enough, or the next day." He got to his feet, gesturing like a gracious host. "Come. Let me show you my keep."

Karela rose with alacrity. "Yes, I'd like very much to see it." Conan remained where he was.

"You may keep your sword," the mage said derisively, "if you yet feel the need of protection."

Conan sprang angrily to his feet. "Lead on, sorcerer."

Amanar looked at him searchingly, and the Cimmerian suddenly thought that he and Karela had been placed on the two ends of a merchant's balance scale. Finally the necromancer nodded and, using his golden rod as a walking staff, led them from the room. The musicians played on.

First the red-robed mage took them to the heights of the outer curtain wall, its sheer scarp dropping fifty feet to the mountain slope. Pike-bearing S'tarra sentries in chain-mail hauberks fell to their knees at Amanar's approach, but he did not deign to acknowledge the obeisance. From thence they went to the ebon parapet of the inner rampart, where S'tarra crossbowmen in bartizans could cut down any who managed to gain the outer wall. From the banquette catapults could hurl great stones. Atop the towers of the inner wall were ballistae, the arrows of which, as long as a man, could pierce through horse and rider together on the valley floor. Massive blocks of pitch-black stone had been piled to build barracks where dwelt S'tarra in their hundreds. The scaled ones knelt for the mage, and followed Conan and Karela with hungering rubiate eyes.

In the donjon itself, Amanar led them through floor after floor of many-columned rooms hung with cloth-of-gold and costly tapestries. Rare carpets covered mosaicked floors, and bore furnishings inlaid with nacreous mother-of-pearl and deep blue lapis-lazuli. Carven bowls of jasper and amber from far Khitai, great golden vases from Vendhya, set with glittering rubies and sapphires, silver ornaments adorned with golden chrysoberyl and crimson carnelian, all were scattered in profusion as if they were the merest of trinkets.

Human servants were few, and none that the Cimmerian saw ever raised his or her eyes from the floor as they sped by on their tasks. Amanar paid them less heed even than he did the S'tarra.

On the ground level of the donjon, as Amanar began to lead them to the door, Conan noticed an archway, its plain stonework at odds with the ornateness of all else they had seen within. The passage beyond seemed to slope down, leading back toward the mountain.

Conan nodded toward it. "That leads to your dungeons?"

"No!" Amanar said sharply. The black-eyed mage recovered his smile with an obvious effort. "That leads to the chambers where I carry out my ... researches. None but myself may enter there." The smile remained, but the eyes with the strange red flecks became flat and dangerous. "There are wards set which would be most deadly to one who made the attempt."

Karela laughed awkwardly. "I, for one, have no interest in seeing a magician's chambers."

Amanar shifted his dark gaze to the red-haired woman. "Perhaps, someday, I will take you down that passage. But not for a time yet, I think. Sitha will show you out."

Conan had to control a desire to reach for his sword as a S'tarra fully as large as he suddenly stepped from a side passage. He wondered if the mage had some means of communicating with his servants without words. Such a thing could be dangerous to a thief.

The big S'tarra gestured with a long, claw-tipped hand. "This way," it hissed. There was no subservience in its manner toward them, but rather a touch of arrogance in those red eyes.

Conan could feel the eyes of the sorcerer on his back as he followed the dark-eyed man's minion. At the portcullis Sitha gestured without speaking for the heavy iron grate to be raised. From within the barbican came the creak of the windlass. Clanking chains pulled the grate to chest height on

Karela. Sitha gestured abruptly, and the creak of the windlass ceased. The S'tarra's fanged mouth cracked in a mocking smile as it gestured for them to go.

"Do you not realize we are your master's guests?" Karela demanded hotly. "I'll—"

Conan grabbed her arm in his huge hand and pulled her protesting under the grate after him. It began to clank down at the very instant they were clear.

"Let's just be thankful to be out," Conan said, starting down the ramp. He saw Hordo waiting at the foot of it.

Karela strode angrily beside him, rubbing her arm. "You muscle-bound oaf! I'll not take much more of this from you. I intend to see that Amanar punishes that big lizard. These S'tarra must learn proper respect for us, else my hounds will constantly be goaded into fighting them. I might even carve that Sitha myself."

Conan looked at her in surprise. "You intend to accept this offer? The Red Hawk will wear this sorcerer's jesses and stoop at his command?"

"Have you no eyes, Conan? Five hundred of the scaled ones he commands, perhaps more. My hounds could not take this keep were they ten times their number, and I will not waste them against its walls in vain. On the other hand, if all the gold that you and I and all my pack have ever seen in our lives were heaped in one pile it would not equal the hundredth part of what I saw within."

"I've *seen* a lot of gold," Conan snorted. "How much of it stuck to my fingers, and how much of this would, is another matter. This Amanar prates of a better way for mankind, but I've never met a sorcerer who did not tread a black path. Think you what he will ask you to do for his payment."

"A safe haven," she snapped back, "close to the caravan route. No longer will I need to send my men off to hide as caravan guards when the army hunts us too closely. No longer must I play the fortuneteller while I wait to rejoin them. These things are worth much to me."

The Cimmerian snarled deep in his throat. "They mean naught to me. The Desert is haven enough. I came here to steal five pendants, not to serve a practitioner of the black arts."

They reached the bottom of the ramp, and Hordo looked from one to the other of them. "You two arguing again?" the one-eyed man growled. "What had this Amanar to say?"

The two ignored him, squaring off at one another.

Karela bit off her words. "He does not have the pendants. Remember, it was he who first mentioned them. And I saw no more than a handful of women among his servants, not one of whom looked to be your dancing girl."

"You talked of the pendants?" Hordo said incredulously.

Conan spared the bearded bandit not a glance. "You believe the man? A sorcerer? He'd have us think the mountains filled with tribes of S'tarra, whole nations of them, but that wounded one we followed was coming here. He knows of the pendants because his minions stole them."

"Sorcerer!" Hordo gasped. "The man's a sorcerer?"

Karela's green eyes flashed to the one-eyed man, the blaze in them so fierce that he took a step back. "Show me where you've camped my hounds," she snapped. "I'll see they're bedded properly." She stalked away without waiting for a reply.

Hordo blinked at Conan. "I'd best go after her. She's going the wrong way. We'll talk later." He darted after the red-haired woman.

Conan turned to look back up at the fortress. Dimly, through the grate of the portcullis, he could make out a shape, a S'tarra, watching him. Though he could distinguish no more than it was there, he knew it was Sitha. Fixing what he could remember of the keep's interior in his head, he went in search of the others.

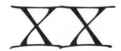

gibbous moon crept slowly over the valley of the Keep of Amanar while purple twilight yielded to the blackness of full night. And blackness it was, except about the fires where the bandits huddled well away from the keep, for the pale light of the moon seemed not to enter that maleficent vale.

"I've never seen a night like this," Hordo grumbled, tipping a stone jar of *kil* to his mouth.

Conan squatted across the fire from the one-eyed brigand. It was a larger blaze than he would have built, but Hordo as well as the others appeared to be trying to keep the night at bay.

"It is the place, and the man," the Cimmerian said, "not the night."

His eyes followed Karela for a moment, where she moved among the other fires stopping at each for a word, and a swallow of *kil*, and a laugh that more often than not sounded strained on the part of the men. She had decked herself in her finest, golden breastplates, emerald girdle, a crimson cape of silk and her scarlet thigh-boots. Conan wondered whether her attire was for the benefit of the others, or if she, too, felt the oppression of the darkness that pressed against their fires.

Hordo scrubbed his mouth with the back of his hand and tossed another dried dung-chip on the fire. "A sorcerer. To think we would ever serve such. She won't let me tell them, you know. That this Amanar's a mage, I mean." He added yet another chip to the blaze.

Conan edged back from the heat. "Soon or late, they'll find out." He checked the position of the moon, then laughed to himself. In that valley there might as well be no moon and sky full of rain clouds. A good night for a thief.

"More *kil*, Cimmerian? No? More for me, then." The one-eyed man turned the stone jar up and did not lower it until it was dry. "It'd take vats of this to comfort my bones this night. A mage. Aberius darts his eyes like a ferret. He'll bolt the first chance he sees. And Talbor says openly he'd ride out on the instant, could he find two coppers to steal."

"Why wait for the coppers?" Conan asked. "You like this thing as little as Aberius or Talbor. Why not ride out on the morrow?" It was in his mind that by dawn Amanar might not be so friendly toward the bandits. "You can persuade her if anyone can, and I think a night like this would be halfway to convincing her for you."

"You do not know her," Hordo muttered, avoiding the Cimmerian's blue-eyed gaze. "Once a thing is in her mind to do, she does it, and there's an end to it. And what she does, I do." He did not sound particularly happy about that last.

"I think I'll take a walk," Conan said, rising.

Hordo's lone eye stared at him incredulously. "A walk! Man, it's black as Ahriman's heart out there!"

"And it's hot as the gates of Gehanna here," Conan laughed. "If you build that fire any higher, you'll melt." He walked into the night before the other man could say more.

Once away from the pool of light cast by the fires—not far in that strange, malevolent night—he stopped to let his eyes adjust as best they could. By touch he checked the Karpashian dagger on his left forearm, and slung his sword across his back. He had no rope or grappel, but he did not think he would need either.

After a time he realized that he could see, in a fashion. The full moon, glowing blue-green in the sky, should have lit the night brightly. The thin, attenuated light that in truth existed flickered unnaturally. Objects could only be detected by gradations of blackness, and in that dark lambence all appeared to quiver and move.

Quickly he started toward the fortress, biting back a string of oaths as rocks turned beneath his feet on the slope and boulders loomed out of the black, often to be detected first by his outstretched hands. Then the wall of the keep reared before him, as if the black of the night had been concentrated and solidified.

The gargantuan stones of that wall seemed to form an unbroken vertical plane, yet were there finger- and toe-holds to be found by a man who knew where to look. Conan moved up that sheer escarpment heedless of the infinite darkness beneath him, and the rocks that would dash his life out if his grasp slipped.

Short of the top of the wall he stopped, clinging like a fly, massive body flattened tightly against the ebon stone. Above him the S'tarra sentries' boots grated closer, and past. In an instant he scrambled through the embrasure, across the parapet, and let himself down over the inner edge. The climb down into the other bailey was easier, for that side of the wall had not been designed with the intent of stopping anyone from scaling it.

His feet found the paving stones, and he squatted against the wall to get his bearings. Scattered lamps, brass serpents with wicks burning in their mouths, cast occasional pools of light within the fortress. The heavy iron-strapped gates letting into the inner bailey stood open, and apparently un-guarded. But that would be a dangerous assumption to make. He was choosing a spot to scale the inner rampart when a movement caught his eye.

From the shadows to his left down the wall a man darted across the bailey. As he passed through the meager light cast by a serpent lamp Conan recognized Talbor. So the man was not waiting to find his two coppers to steal. The Cimmerian only hoped the other raised no alarm to make his own task more difficult. Talbor ran straight to the open gate into the inner bailey and passed through.

Conan forced himself to wait. If Talbor was taken it would be no time for him to be halfway up the inner wall. No alarm was raised. Still he waited, and still there was no sound.

The Cimmerian uncoiled from his crouch and walked across the bailey, carefully avoiding the sparse pools of light from the serpent lamps. If glimpsed, he would be no more than another moving shadow, and it was rapid motion that drew the eye at night. He slowed, examining the gateway carefully. The guardpost was empty.

He went through the gate at the same slow walk and crossed the inner bailey. From the walls behind he could hear the tread of sentries' boots, their pace unchanging.

As he approached the huge cube of the donjon he chose his entry point. Best, because highest, would have been the single-black tower that rose into the darkness at one corner, but he had seen in the daylight that whatever mason had constructed it had been a master. He had been able to detect no slightest crack between the carefully fitted stones. It reminded him uncom-fortably of the Elephant Tower of the necromancer Yara, though that had glittered even in the dark where this seemed one with the night.

The walls of the donjon itself presented no such problem, though, and he quickly found himself squeezing with difficulty through an overly broad arrowslit on the top level. Once inside he swiftly drew his sword. A single oil lamp on the wall was lit; he began to examine his surroundings.

The purpose of the room he could not fathom. Its only furnishing, other than tapestries on the walls, seemed to be a single high-backed chair of carved ivory set before a gameboard, one hundred squares of alternating colors set in the floor. Pieces in the shapes of bizarre animals, each as high as his knee, were scattered about the board. He hefted one, and grunted in surprise. He had thought it gilded, but from its weight it had to be of solid gold. Could he depart with two or three of those, he would have no need of the pendants. Even one might do.

Regretfully he set the piece, a snarling, winged ape-creature back on the board. He must yet find Velita, and to attempt to do so burdened with that weight would be madness. With great care he cracked the door. The marble-walled hall was brightly lit by silver lamps. And empty. He slipped out.

As he moved along that corridor, its floor red-and-white marble lozenges in an intricate pattern, he realized that he moved through a strange silence. He had entered many great houses and palaces in the dead of night, and always there was some sound, however slight. Now he could have moved through a tomb in which no thing breathed. Indeed, as he cautiously examined room after room he saw no living thing. No S'tarra. No human servant. No Velita. He hurried his pace, and went down curving alabaster stairs to the next floor.

Through two more floors he searched, and the opulence he saw paled the golden figures to insignificance. A silver statue of a woman with sapphires for eyes, rubies for nipples and pearls for the nails of her fingers. A table encrusted with diamonds and emeralds till it cast back the light of silver lamps a hundredfold. A golden throne set with a king's ransom in black opals.

And then he was peering into a room, plain beside the others for merely being paneled in amber and ivory, peering at a pair of rounded female buttocks. Their owner knelt, naked, with her back to the door and her face pressed to the floor. The muscular youth found himself smiling at the view, and sternly drew his mind back to the matter at hand. She was the first living soul he had seen, and human rather than S'tarra.

One quick stride took him to the bent form; a big hand clasped over her mouth lifted her from the floor. And he was staring into Velita's large, liquid brown eyes.

"Come, girl," he said, loosing his hold, "I was beginning to think I'd never find you."

She threw her arms around him, pressing her soft breasts against his broad chest. "Conan! You did come. I never really believed, though I hoped and prayed. But it's too late. You must go away before Amanar returns." A shudder went through her slim form as she said the name.

"I swore to free you, didn't I?" he said gruffly. "Why are you kneeling here like this? I've seen no one else at all, neither S'tarra nor human."

"S'tarra are not allowed in the donjon when Amanar isn't here, and humans are locked in their quarters unless he desires them." She tilted her head up, and her voice dropped to a whisper. "I didn't betray you, Conan. Not even when Sitha whipped me. I would not tell Amanar who you are."

"It's over, Velita," he said.

She seemed not to hear. Tears trembled on her long lashes. "He became enraged. For my punishment several times a day, without warning, I am commanded to come to this room and kneel until I am told to leave. When I hear footsteps I never know if I am to be sent back to my mat, or if it is Amanar. Sometimes he merely stands, listening to me weep. I hate him for making me fear him so, and I hate myself for weeping, but I can't help it. Sometimes he beats me while I kneel, and if I move the punishment begins again."

"I'll kill him," Conan vowed grimly. "This I swear to you on pain of my life. Come, we'll find the pendants, and I'll take you away this night."

The lithesome naked girl shook her small head firmly. "I cannot go, Conan. I am spell-caught."

"Spell-caught!"

"Yes. Once I tried to escape, and my feet carried me to Amanar. Against my will I found myself telling him what I intended. Another time I tried to kill myself, but when the dagger point touched my breast my arms became like iron. I could not move them, even to set the knife down. When they found me Amanar made me beg before he would free me."

"There must be a way. I could carry you away." But he saw the flaw in that even as she laughed sadly.

"Am I to remain bound the rest of my life for fear of returning to his place? I don't know why I even tried to take my life," she sighed heavily. "I'm sure Amanar will kill me soon. Only Susa and I remain. The others have disappeared."

The big Cimmerian nodded. "Mages are not easily killed—this I know for truth—but once dead their spells die with them. Amanar's death will free you."

"Best you take the pendants and go," she said. "I can tell you where they are. Four are in the jeweled casket, in a room I can show you. The fifth, the one I wore, is in the chamber where he works his magics." She frowned and shook her head. "The others he tossed aside like offal. That one he wrapped in silk and laid in a crystal coffer."

The memory of the stone came back to Conan. A black oval the length of his finger joint, with red flecks that danced within. Suddenly he seized Velita's arms so hard that she cried out. "His eyes," he said urgently. "That stone is like his eyes. In some way it is linked to him. He'll free you rather than have it destroyed. We'll go down to his thaumaturgical chamber—"

"Down? His chamber is in the top of the tower above us. Please release me, Conan. My arms are growing numb."

Hastily he loosed his grip. "Then what lies at the end of that passage that seems to lead into the mountain?"

"I know not," she replied, "save that all are forbidden to enter it. His chamber is where I said. I've been taken to him there. Would the gods had made him like Tiridates," she added bitterly, "a lover of boys."

"Then we'll go up to his chamber," Conan said. She shook her head once more. "What's the matter now?" he asked.

"There is a spell on the stairway in the tower whenever he is out of the donjon. Truly he trusts no one, Conan. One of the human servants climbed that stair while Amanar was gone to meet you." She shivered and buried her face against his chest. "He screamed forever, it seemed, and none could get close even to end his misery."

He smoothed her hair awkwardly with a big hand. "Then I must enter the donjon when he is here. But if he isn't here now, Velita, where is he?"

"Why, in your camp of bandits. I heard him say that the night might affright them, so he has taken them rare wines and costly viands for a feasting."

Conan raised his hand helplessly. It seemed the gods conspired against him at every turn. "Velita, I must go back to the camp. If he suspects I'm here. . . ."

"I know," she said quietly. "I knew from the first you could not take me with you."

"Does not my standing here tell you my oath-sworn word is good? I will see Amanar dead, and you free."

"No!" she cried. "Amanar is too powerful. You'll die to no purpose. I release you from your oath, Conan. Leave these mountains and forget that I exist."

"You cannot release me from an oath sworn before gods," he said calmly, "and I will not release myself from one sworn on my life."

"Then you will die. Yet I do pray that somehow you will find a way. Please go now, Conan. I must await Amanar's return, and I don't want you to see me. . . ." The slender girl's head dropped, and her shoulders quivered with sobs.

"I swear!" Conan grated. Almost wishing to find himself face to face with the sorcerer, he strode from the room.

XXI

As Conan approached the bandit camp he was struck with the sounds of raucous laughter and drunken, off-key singing. Stumbling into the light he stared in amazement. The brigands were in full carouse. Hook-nosed Reza squatted with a whole roast in his hands, tearing at it with his teeth. Aberius staggered past, head tilted back and a crystal flagon upturned. Half the wine spilled down his chest, but the weasel-faced man laughed and tossed the costly vessel to shatter against the rocky ground. Hordo swung his tulwar in one hand, a golden goblet in the other, roaring an obscene song at the moon. Every man sang or laughed, ate or drank, as was his wont and his mood, belching and wiping greasy fingers on his robes, gulping down costly Aquilonian wines like the cheapest tavern swill.

Through the midst of the revelry Karela and Amanar approached Conan. She held a crystal goblet like a lady of high degree, but there was a stagger to her walk, and the mage had his long arm about her slim shoulder. Amanar had pushed back her scarlet cape so that his elongated fingers caressed her silken flesh in a possessive manner. Remembering Velita, Conan was both disgusted and offended, but he knew he must yet control his temper until the pendant was in his grasp.

"We wondered where you were," the red-haired woman said. "Look at this feast Amanar has brought us. This has cured the fit of sulking that had taken my hounds."

Amanar's dark eyes were unreadable. "There is little to see even in daylight, Conan of Cimmeria, and few men care to wander here in the night. What did you find to interest you in the darkness?"

"They built the fires too hot for my northern blood," Conan replied. He eyed the way those long fingers kneaded Karela's shoulder. "That's a shoulder, mage," he said with more heat than he had intended, "not a lot of bread dough."

Karela looked startled, and Amanar laughed. "The hot blood of youth. Just how old are you, Cimmerian?" He did not remove his hand.

"Not yet nineteen," Conan said proudly, but he was saddened to see the change in Karela's eyes. He had seen the same in other women's eyes, women who thought a man needed a certain number of years to be a man.

"Not yet nineteen!" Amanar choked on his own laughter. "Practically a beardless youth for all his muscles. The Red Hawk, the great robber of caravans, has robbed a cradle."

She shrugged off the mage's arm, her tilted green eyes glowing dangerously. "A barbar boy," she muttered. Then, in a louder voice, "I have considered your offer, Amanar. I accept."

"Excellent," the sorcerer said with a satisfied smile. He rubbed the side of his long face with the golden staff and regarded Conan. "And you, young Cimmerian who likes to wander in the dark? Despite your youth my offer to you yet holds, for I think there must be skill in those massive shoulders."

Conan managed to force a smile onto his lips. "I need to think longer. In a day or two, as you first spoke of, I will give you my answer."

Amanar nodded. "Very well, Cimmerian. In a day or two we shall see what your future will be." His red-flecked eyes turned to Karela with a caressing gaze that made Conan's flesh crawl. "You, my dear Karela, must come to the keep on the morrow. Without the young Cimmerian, of course, as he has not yet made up his mind. We must have a number of long private discussions concerning my plans for you."

Conan longed to smash his fist into that dark face but instead he said, "Perhaps you'll speak of some of those plans to us all. Knowing what they are might help me decide, and some of these others as well."

Karela's head had been turning between the two men with a comparing gaze, but at that she jerked rigidly erect. "My hounds go where I command, Cimmerian!"

A sudden silence fell, laughter and song all dying away. Conan looked around for the cause and found Sitha standing at the edge of the light, clutching a great double-bladed battle-ax across its broad chest. Red eyes glowed faintly as it surveyed the men around the fires, and they shifted uneasily, some loosening their weapons in their scabbards. The S'tarra's lipless mouth curled back from its fangs in what might have been meant for a smile. Or a sneer.

"Sitha!" Amanar said sharply.

Looking neither to left nor right, the S'tarra strode through the camp to kneel at Amanar's feet. At an impatient gesture Sitha rose and leaned close to whisper in its master's ear.

Conan could catch no sound of what was said, nor read anything on the mage's dark face, but Amanar's knuckles grew white on his golden staff, telling Conan the man found the news displeasing. Talbor, Conan thought. Amanar gestured for his minion to be silent.

"I must leave you," the mage said to Karela. "A matter requires my attention."

"Not trouble, I hope," she said.

"A small matter," Amanar replied, but his mouth was tight behind his close-cropped beard. "I will see you on the morrow, then. Rest well." He turned his attention to Conan. "Think well on your decision, Cimmerian. There are worse things than what I offer. Sitha." The sorcerer strode from the camp, his S'tarra minion at his heels.

With the departure of the scaled creature the noise level of the camp began to rise again quickly. Hordo staggered up to Conan and Karela.

"I do not like those things," the one-eyed brigand said unsteadily. He still held his bared tulwar and the now-empty golden goblet, and he swayed as he spoke. "When are we to leave this accursed valley and be about what we know? When are we for the caravan routes?"

"You're drunk, my old hound," Karela said affectionately. "Find yourself a place to sleep it off, and we'll talk in the morning."

"I entered the keep tonight," Conan said quietly.

Karela's green eyes locked with his sapphire gaze. "You fool!" she hissed. Hordo stared with his mouth open.

"He has the pendants," the Cimmerian went on, "and the women. At least, he has two of the women. The other three have disappeared. It's my belief he killed them."

"Killed slave girls?" Hordo said, scandalized. "What sort of man does a thing like that? Even a sorcerer. . . ."

"Keep your voice down," Karela snapped. "I told you not to bandy that word about until I gave you leave. And you, Conan. What's this nonsense you're babbling? If the women are gone, likely he sold them. Or was your precious Velita one of them?"

"She was not," Conan growled back. "And why should she still raise your hackles? You know there's nothing between us, though there seems to be quite a bit between you and Amanar, from the way he was fondling you."

"No!" Hordo protested, putting a hand on her shoulder. "Not Amanar. Not with you. I'll admit I thought better of you taking Conan to your bed, but—"

Face flaming, Karela cut him off sharply. "Be silent, you old fool! What I do, and with whom, is my business!" Her eyes flung green daggers at Conan, and she stalked away, snatching a flask from Aberius as she passed him.

Hordo shook his massive head. "Why did you not speak, Conan? Why did you not stop her?"

"She's a free woman," Conan said coldly. His pride was still pricked by the way she had accepted Amanar's arm about her. "I have no claim on her. Why didn't you stop her?"

"I'm too old to have my liver sliced out," Hordo snorted. "Your Velita was truly in the keep, then? I wonder you didn't take her, and the pendants, and ride from this place." He swept his curved sword in an arc that took in all the dark outside the firelight.

"She's spell-caught," Conan sighed, and told him how he had found Velita, and what she had said.

"So he lied to us," the bearded man said when Conan finished. "And if about the pendants and the women, about what else?"

"About everything. I had thought to tell her about what he's done with Velita, to show him for the man he is, but now I think she'd believe I made it up."

"And likely tell Amanar about it, to amuse him with your jealousy. Or what she'd see as jealousy," he added quickly as the big Cimmerian youth glared at him. "What am I to do, Conan? Even now I cannot abandon her."

Conan lifted his broadsword an inch free of its sheath and slammed it back again. "Keep your sword sharp, and your eye open." His steely gaze took in the motley rogues sprawled drunkenly around the fires. "And have these hounds of hers ready to move at an instant. Without letting her or Amanar discover it, of course."

"You don't ask much, do you, Cimmerian? What are you going to do?"

Conan peered through the darkness toward the fortress before answering. Even in that overpowering blackness those massive walls seemed blacker still. "Kill Amanar, free Velita, steal the pendants, and return to Shadizar, of course. Trifles like that."

"Trifles like that," Hordo groaned. "I need another drink."

"So do I," Conan said softly. The night weighed heavily on his broad shoulders. This valley would be a poor place to die.

The strange darkness lingered in the valley, resisting morning and fading to a gray dawn only after the blood-red sun stood well above the mountaintops. It was mid-morning before full daylight came, but Conan alone noticed in the bandit camp, for the others lay sprawled in drunken stupors. As the sun at last sucked the last canescence from the valley air, the Cimmerian made his way to the spring that bubbled from a cleft not far from the camp.

Scooping water in his cupped hands, he drank, and made a disgusted sound in his throat. Though cold, the water was flat and lifeless, like everything else in the barren and forboding rift. He contented himself with splashing it on his face, and settled to observe the valley.

On the battlements of the keep S'tarra moved, but nothing else stirred except vultures making slow circles in the distance. Conan wondered grimly how Velita had fared at Amanar's return. The sorcerer seemed not to know how far Conan's nocturnal peregrinations had taken him—at least, there was no sign of alarm, no squads of S'tarra sent for him—but that spoke not at all to her faring.

"Tonight," the muscular youth vowed.

Aberius, tottering up to fall on his knees beside the spring, glanced incuriously at him. The man's usual hostility seemed momentarily expelled by wine fumes. The weasel-faced bandit dashed a few handfuls of water over his head and staggered away to be replaced by Hordo, who threw himself at full length by the spring and plunged his head into the pool.

Just as Conan was about to go over and pull him out, the one-eyed man lifted his head and peered at the Cimmerian through dripping hair and beard. "Has this water no taste," he mumbled, "or did my tongue die last night?"

"Both," Conan chuckled. Hordo groaned and lowered his head once more to the water, but this time only far enough to drink. "Have you seen Talbor this morning, Hordo?"

"I've seen nothing this morning but the insides of my own eyelids. Let me decide in peace whether I desire to live or not."

"Talbor was inside the fortress last night, when I was."

Hordo lifted himself on his elbows, flipping water at his face with spatulate fingers. "Such a thing to tell a man with my head. Do you think that's why Amanar was summoned to the keep?"

Conan nodded. "Talbor's not in the camp. I checked at first light."

"He could have stolen what he wanted, taken a horse, and be halfway out of the Kezankians by now," the other man protested. "He's not as particular as you. He'd not insist on Tiridates' playpretties, and a dancing girl besides."

"You could be right," Conan said flatly.

"I know," Hordo sighed. "I don't believe it, either. So is he dead, or is he in the sorcerer's dungeon? And what do we tell her?"

"We wait to see what Amanar tells her. His S'tarra outnumber us at least twenty to one, and those are odds I bet small coins on."

He got to his feet as Sitha appeared at the portcullis and came down the black granite ramp. The tall S'tarra carried neither ax nor sword that Conan could see. It reached the bottom of the incline and set off at a brisk pace across the gray, boulder-strewn valley floor toward the bandit camp. Conan started down the rocky slope to meet it, and Hordo scrambled to his feet to follow.

When Conan walked into the camp, the scaled creature was the center of a ring of brigands. No weapons were in hand, he was relieved to see, but the human eyes there were far from friendly. And who could say of Sitha's?

Hordo pushed past Conan to confront the S'tarra. "What's this, then? Does your master send a message for us?"

"I come for myself," Sitha hissed. It stood half a head taller than the burly one-eyed bandit, taller even than Conan, and if there was no expression in those sanguine eyes there was certainly contempt in the sibilant voice. A padded gambeson and chainmail hauberk covered it to the knees, but it wore no helmet. "I am Sitha, Warden of the S'tarra, and I come to pit myself against you."

Aberius, behind Conan, laughed uneasily. "Without so much as a dagger?"

Sitha bared its fangs. "My master would not be pleased, an I slew you. We will pit strength at the stones."

"Stones?" Hordo said. "What stones?"

The S'tarra spun on its booted heel, motioning for them to follow. In a muttering file they did, down the valley away from the keep to a spot where boulders had been arranged to form a rough circle half a hundred paces across. The ground between had been smoothed and leveled, and in the center of the circle lay two rough spheres of dark granite. Conan estimated the smaller at twice the weight of a man, the larger at half again as much.

"Lift one of the stones," Sitha said. "Any one of you." It flashed bare fangs again, briefly. "Any two of you."

"Hordo!" someone called. "Hordo's strongest!"

Aberius eyed the stones, then Karela's one-eyed lieutenant. "Who'll wager?" he cried, his narrow face taking on a malicious smile. "Who thinks old Hordo can lift the small stone?"

"Old Hordo, is it?" Hordo spat.

He bent to the lesser of the huge stones as a babbling knot formed around Aberius to get their wagers marked. The burly man threw his arms about the stone, fitting his hands carefully to the undercurves, and heaved. The scar running from under his eye-patch whitened with strain, and his eye bulged. The round stone stirred. Abruptly his hands slipped, and he staggered back with an oath.

"Mitra!" the one-eyed brigand panted. "There's no way to get a good grip on the accursed thing." Chortling, Aberius collected his winnings.

"Your strongest cannot lift it," Sitha hissed. "Can two of you do it? Let any two try." His scathing glance took in Conan, but the Cimmerian said nothing.

Reza and another hawk-nosed Iranistani, named Banidr, pushed forward. Aberius began again to hawk his wagering. Those who had lost the first time were now quickest to press their coins at him.

Reza and Banidr conferred a moment, dark heads together, then squatted, one on either side of the stone. Pressing their forearms in under the lower curve of the stone sphere, each grasped the other's upper arm. Their closeness to the stone forced them into spraddle-legged stances. For a moment they rocked back and forth, counting together, then suddenly tried to heave themselves erect. Veins popped forth on their foreheads. The stone lifted. A finger breadth. A handwidth. Banidr cried out, and in an instant the stone had forced their arms apart, torn loose their grips, and thumped to the ground. Banidr fell back, clutching himself. Arguments broke out as to whether the two had lifted the stone far enough or not.

"This!" Sitha's shout riveted the bandits, drying their arguments in mid-word. "This I mean by lifting the stone!" The S'tarra bent over the large granite ball, locked its arms about it, and straightened as easily as if it had been a pebble. Gasps broke from the bandits as it started toward them; they parted before it. Five paces. Ten. Sitha let the stone fall with a crash, and turned back to the dumbstruck men. "That I mean by lifting." Peals of hissing laughter broke between its fangs.

"I'll have a try," Conan said.

The S'tarra's laughter slowed and stopped. Red eyes regarded Conan with open contempt. "You, human? Will you try to carry the stone back to its place, then?"

"No," the young Cimmerian said, and bent to the larger stone.

"Two to one he fails," Aberius cried. "Three to one!" Men eyed Conan's massive chest and shoulders, weighed the odds, and crowded around the weasel-faced man.

Conan squatted low to get his arms below the largest part of the big stone. As his fingers felt for purchase on the rough sphere, he found Sitha's frowning gaze on him.

With a sudden roar, the big Cimmerian heaved. His mighty thews corded, and his joints popped with the strain. The muscles of his broad back stood out in stark relief, and his massive arms knotted. Slowly he straightened, every fiber quivering as he came fully erect. His eyes met Sitha's once more, and snarling, the S'tarra took a backward step. With great effort Conan stepped forward, back bowed under the strain. He took another step.

"Conan," someone said softly, and another voice repeated, louder, "Conan!"

Teeth bared by lips drawn back in a rictus of effort, Conan went forward. Now his eyes were locked on the stone Sitha had carried.

Two more voices took up the cry. "Conan!" Five more. "Conan!" Ten. "Conan!" The shouts were flung back from the mountain slopes as a score of throats hurled forth their chant with his every step. "Conan! Conan! Conan!"

He came level with the other stone, took one step more, and let the great sphere fall with a thunderous thud that every man there felt in his feet. Conan's shoulder joints creaked as he straightened, looking at Sitha. "Will you try to take my stone back?"

Cheering bandits darted between a glowering Aberius, parting with all his former winnings and more, and Conan, some clasping his hand, others merely wanting to touch his arm. Sitha's hands twitched in front of its chest as if clutching for the thick haft of a battle-ax.

Of a sudden the bronzen tones of a great gong broke from the fortress and echoed down the valley. Sitha whirled at the first tone and broke into a run for the black keep. The gong pealed forth again, and again, its hollow resonance rolling against the mountains. Atop the ebon ramparts of the keep S'tarra ran.

"An attack?" Hordo said, bewildered. The bandits crowded in close behind the one-eyed man, their exuberance of moments before already dissipated. Some had drawn their swords.

Conan shook his head. "The portcullis is open, and I see no one near the ballistae or catapults. Whatever's happening, though. . ." He let his words trail off as Karela galloped up to face them, one fist on a scarlet thigh-boot.

"Are the lot of you responsible for this?" she demanded. "I heard all of you bellowing like oxen in a mire, then this infernal gong began." As she spoke the tolling ceased, though the ghost of it seemed yet to hang in the air.

"We know no more than you," Hordo replied.

"Then I'll find out what's happening," she said.

"Karela," Conan said, "do you not think it best to wait?"

Her green eyes raked him scornfully, and without a word she spun her horse and galloped toward the fortress. The big black's hooves rang on the black granite of the ramp, and after a moment's delay she was admitted.

Minutes later the portcullis opened once more. Sitha's massive form, helmeted and bearing the great battle-ax, galloped through the gate, followed by paired columns of mounted S'tarra. Conan counted lances as they streamed down the incline and pounded across the valley toward a gorge leading north.

"Three hundred," the Cimmerian said after the last S'tarra had disappeared. "More wayfarers, do you think?"

"So long as it's not us," Hordo replied.

Slowly the bandits returned to the cold ashes of their campfires, breaking into twos and threes to cast lots or dice. Aberius began maneuvering three clay cups and a pebble atop a flat rock, trying to entice back some of the silver he had lost. Conan settled with his back to a tilted needle of stone, where he could watch both the keep and the gorge into which Sitha had led the S'tarra. The day stretched long and flat, and except when Hordo brought him meat and cheese and a leather flagon of thin wine Conan did not change his position.

As the sanguinary sun sank on the western mountain peaks, the S'tarra returned, galloping from the same knife-sharp slash in the valley by which they had left.

"No casualties," Hordo said, coming up beside Conan as the S'tarra appeared.

Conan, once more counting lances, nodded. "But they took . . . something." Twenty riderless horses were roped together in the middle of the column, each bearing a long bundle strapped across it.

A spark of light in the east caught the Cimmerian's eye, a momentary glitter that flashed against the shadows of mountains already caught in twilight and was gone. It flashed again. Frowning, he studied the slopes around the valley. High above them, to the north, another spark flared and was gone.

"Think you Amanar knows the valley is watched?" Hordo asked.

"You use that eye," Conan said approvingly. The S'tarra rode up the long incline to the fortress, the portcullis creaking open to let them ride in without slowing. "I worry more about who does the watching."

The one-eyed brigand let out a long, low whistle between his teeth. "Who? Now that's a kettle of porridge to set your teeth on edge."

Conan knew the choices of who it could be—hillmen, the army, Zamoran or Turanian, or Imhep-Aton—but he was not certain which would be worst for him and for the bandits, or even if those two would be the same. Time ran short for him. "I mean to bring Velita out of the keep tonight, Hordo. It may mean trouble for you, but I must do it."

"I've half a memory of you saying as much last night," Hordo mused. Karela appeared, riding slowly down the ramp from the fortress. "Almost I wish you would, Cimmerian. 'Twould give the excuse to get her away from this place, away from the sorcerer."

Karela reached the bottom of the ramp and turned her big black toward the camp. She rode with one fist on her hip, her callimastian form swaying with the motion of the horse. The bloody sun was half obscured behind the peaks, now, yet enough remained to bathe her face in a golden glow.

"And if she will not go," Conan said, "you'll follow where she leads, be it a hillman's torture fire or Amanar's diabolic servitude."

"No more," Hordo replied sadly. "My last service to the Red Hawk, and it must be so, will be to tie her to her saddle and take her to safety." His voice hardened suddenly. "But it will be me, Conan. No other will raise a hand to her while Hordo yet lives. Not even you."

Conan met the fierce single-eyed gaze levelly. On the one hand, an oath not to lift a hand to save her; on the other, how could he stand and watch her die? It was a cleft stick that held his tongue.

Karela reined in before the two men, raising a hand to shield her eyes as she peered at the mountain-shrouded sun. "I had not realized I was so long with Amanar," she murmured, shifting her green eyes to them. "Why are you two glaring at each other like a pair of badgers? I thought you now were almost fraternal in your amity."

"We stand in concord, Hordo and I," Conan said. He stretched up his hand, and the other man grasped it, pulling him to his feet.

"We'll give them a good turn, eh, Cimmerian," Hordo said, "before we go under."

"We'll drink from golden goblets in Aghrapur yet," Conan replied soberly.

"What do you two babble about?" Karela demanded. "Gather my hounds, Hordo. I'll speak to them before that accursed dark comes on us."

With a quick nod Hordo darted ahead to assemble the bandits. Karela looked at Conan as if she wanted to speak, then the moment passed. There was much to say, he thought, but he would not speak first. He started after Hordo, and moments later heard her horse following slowly. She made no effort to catch up.

XXIII

Do you want gold?" Karela shouted. "Well, do you?"

She stood atop a boulder as high as a man's head, crimson-thigh-booted feet well apart, fists on hips, her hair an auburn mane. She was magnificent, Conan thought, from his place at the back of the semicircle of brigands who listened to her. Just looking at her was still enough to make his mouth grow dry.

"We want gold," Reza muttered. A few others echoed him. Most watched silently. Aberius had a thoughtful look in his beady eyes, making him look even more sly and malicious than usual. Hordo stood beside the flat-topped boulder, keeping a worried watch on the brigands and Karela both. The fires of the camp surrounded them, holding off the twilight.

"Do you like being chased into hiding by the army?" she cried.

"No!" half a dozen voices growled.

"Do you like spending half a year at guards' wages?"

"No!" a dozen shouted back at her.

"Well, do you know the caravan route is less than half a day south of here? Do you know that a caravan is coming along that route, bound for Sultanapur? Do you know that in three days time we'll take that caravan?"

Roars of approval broke from every throat. Except Aberius', Conan noted. While the others waved fists in the air, shouted and pounded each other on the shoulder, Aberius' look grew more thoughtful, more furtive.

"And the army won't hound us," she went on loudly, "because we'll come back here till they give up. The Zamoran Army are not men enough to follow where we go!"

The cheering went on. The bandits were too caught up in imagining the Zamorans less brave than they to think too closely on how brave they themselves were. Karela raised her hands above her head and basked in their adulation.

Hordo left his place by the boulder and came around to where Conan stood. "Once more, Cimmerian, she has us in the palm of her hand. You don't suppose this could. . . ."

Conan shrugged as the one-eyed man trailed off doubtfully. "You must do as you will." Hordo still looked uncertain. Conan sighed. He would not like seeing the burly bandit dead. Purple twilight was already giving way, night falling as if the inky air had jelled. The bandits around Karela continued their cheering. "I'll be away, now," the Cimmerian went on, "before they notice my going."

"Fare you well," Hordo said quietly.

Conan slipped into the caliginous night. Scudding clouds obscured the lustrous moon as he hurried along the stony slope. Before the full mantle of night enfolded that tenebrous vale, he wanted to be as close to the walls of the fortress as he could.

Abruptly he stopped, broadsword coming firmly into his hand. No sound had reached his ear, no glimmer of motion caught his eye, but senses he could not describe told him there was something ahead of him.

The darkness ahead seemed suddenly to split, fold and thicken, and there was an elongated shadow where there had been none. "How did you know?" came Imhep-Aton's low voice. "No matter. Truly now your usefulness is ended. Your pitiful efforts are futile, but as a rat scurrying beneath the feet of warrior in battle may cause him to trip and die, so may you discommode those greater than yourself."

The darkling shape moved toward Conan. He could see no weapon but an outstretched hand.

Of a sudden rock behind him grated beneath a boot. Conan dropped to a full squat, felt rather than saw a pike thrust pass above his head. Grasping his sword hilt with both hands he pivoted on his left foot, striking for where the pike-wielder must be. He felt the point of his blade bite through chain mail and flesh at the same moment that he saw his attacker's red eyes glowing in the night. The falling pike struck him on the shoulder, the rubiate glow faded, and he was tugging his sword free of a collapsing body.

Desperately Conan spun back, expecting at any moment to feel the sting of Imhep-Aton's steel, but before him he saw three shadowy shapes now, locked in combat. A sibilant shriek broke and was cut off, and one of the shadows fell. The other two fought on.

A cascade of small stones skittering down the slope heralded the arrival of more S'tarra. On the fortress walls torches began to move, and the great gong tolled into the dark. The portcullis began to clank noisily open.

Conan could see two pairs of glowing eyes now, approaching him slowly, well separated. Could the beings see in that dark, he wondered. Could they recognize him? He would not take the chance. The shining sanguinary eyes were located thusly, he calculated, so the pikes must be held so.

Silently, with a prayer to Bel, god of thieves, the Cimmerian sprang toward the closer S'tarra, his sword arcing down for where he hoped the pike was. With a solid chunk his blade bit into a wooden pike-haft. He kicked with the ball of his foot, and got a hissing grunt in reply. Reversing the swing of his broadsword, he spun it up and then down for the joining of neck and shoulder. The grunt became a scream.

Conan threw himself to one side as the second pike slashed along his ribs. The dying S'tarra grappled with him as it fell, pulling him to the ground. The other stood over him, triumph heightening the glow of its eyes. A howl burst from its fanged mouth as the Cimmerian's steel severed its leg at the knee, and the S'tarra fell beside the first. There was no time for precision. Like a cleaver Conan's blade split between those red eyes.

From the fortress pounding feet were drawing nearer. Quickly Conan jerked his sword free and ran into the night. The bandit camp had been roused as well. As he ran closer he could see them gathered at the edge of the light from their fires, peering toward the keep, where the gong still sounded. He circled around the camp and, cutting a piece from his breech-clout, wiped his sword and sheathed it before striding in.

The brigands' eyes were all toward the sounds of S'tarra approaching; none but Hordo saw him enter. Conan tossed the scrap of rag, stained with black blood, into a fire and snatched a cloak from his blankets to settle around his shoulders and hide the gash in his side.

"What happened?" Hordo whispered as Conan joined the others. "You're wounded!"

"I never reached the keep," Conan replied quietly. "S'tarra were waiting. And I discovered who watched from the mountain." He remembered the second light. "As least, I think I did. Later," he added as the other started to question him further. S'tarra were entering the camp, Sitha at their head.

The bandits backed away, muttering, as the reptilian creatures strode into the firelight. Only Karela stood her ground. Arms crossed beneath her round breasts, the red-haired woman confronted the massive bulk of Sitha. "Why do you come here?" she demanded.

"S'tarra have been slain this night," Sitha replied. Its crimson eyes ran arrogantly from her ankles to her face. "I will search your camp and question your men to see if any were involved." The bandits' muttering became angry; sword hilts were grasped.

"You may die trying," Karela said coldly. "I'll not have my camp searched by such as you. And if your master has questions, I'll answer them of him, but not of his cattle." She spat the last word, and Sitha quivered, claw-tipped hands working convulsively on the haft of the huge battle-ax.

"You may find," Sitha hissed malevolently, "that answering questions for my master is even less pleasant than answering them for me." It spun abruptly on its heel and stalked from the circle of light, followed by the rest of the S'tarra.

When the last of them disappeared into the dark, Karela turned to face the bandits. "If any of you were involved in this," she said sharply, "I'll have your ears." Without another word she strode through them and disappeared into her striped pavilion.

Hordo let out a long breath and pulled Conan aside. "Now what happened out there?" The brigands were breaking up into small knots, discussing the night's events in low voices. Aberius stood alone, watching Conan and Hordo.

"I slew three S'tarra," Conan said, "and Imhep-Aton slew two. Or was perhaps himself slain, but I don't believe that."

Hordo grunted. "He who sent the man Crato against you? A second sorcerer in this Mitra-forsaken valley is ill news indeed. I must tell her."

Conan grabbed the one-eyed man's arm. "Don't. She may well tell Amanar, and I do not think these two have any good will towards each other. Whatever comes between them may give you the chance to get her away from here."

"As with the hillmen and the soldiers," Hordo said slowly, "you will bring the two to combat while we slip away. But I think me being caught between two sorcerers may be worse than being caught between the others." He barked a short laugh. "I tell you again, Cimmerian, if you live, you'll be a general. Mayhap even a king. Men have risen from lower stations to become such."

"I have no desire to be a king," Conan laughed. "I'm a thief. And Imhep-Aton, at least, has no animosity toward you or Karela." Though the same, he reflected, could hardly be said of himself. "The keep is too much stirred for me to enter this night. I fear Velita must bear another day of Amanar. Come, let us find a bandage for my side and a flagon of wine."

Speaking quietly together the two men walked deeper into the bandit camp. Aberius watched them go, tugging at his lower lip in deep thought. Finally he nodded to himself and darted into the night.

XXIV

The sun, Conan estimated, stood well past the zenith. It was the day after his fight with the S'tarra, and Karela was once more closeted with Amanar for the entire morning. The bandits slept or drank or gambled, forgetting the ill of the night in the light of the sun. Conan sat cross-legged on the ground, honing his blade as he watched the black keep. To conceal his bandaged wound, he had donned a black tunic that covered him to below the hips. He lay the blade across his knees as a S'tarra approached.

"You are called Conan of Cimmeria?" the creature hissed.

"I am," Conan replied.

"She who is called Karela asks that you come to her."

There had been no further attempt to question the bandits about the occurrences in the night. Conan could not see how he might be connected with them now. He rose and sheathed his sword.

"Lead," he commanded.

The big Cimmerian tensed while passing through the gate, but the guards gave him no more than a flicker of their lifeless red eyes. In the donjon the S'tarra led him a way he did not know, to huge doors that Conan realized to his shock were of burnished gold. A great reptilian head was worked in each, surrounded by what appeared to be rays of light. The S'tarra struck a small silver gong hanging from the wall. Conan's neckhairs stirred at the great doors swung open with no human agency that he could see. The S'tarra gestured for him to enter.

With a firm tread Conan walked through the open doors; they swung shut almost on his heels with a thump of finality. The ceiling of the great room was a fluted dome, supported by massive columns of carved ivory. Across the mosaic floor Amanar sat on a throne made of golden serpents, while another burnished serpent reared behind it, great ruby eyes regarding all who approached. The mage's robe, too, was gold, seemingly of ten thousand scales that glittered in the light of golden lamps. Human musicians filed out by a side door as Conan entered. The only other present was Karela, standing beside Amanar's throne and drinking thirstily from a goblet.

She lowered the goblet in surprise at the sight of Conan. "What are you doing here?" she demanded. The chamber was cool, yet perspiration dampened her face, and her breath came quickly.

"I was told you sent for me," Conan said. Warily he placed a hand on his sword.

"I never sent for you," she said.

"I took the liberty," Amanar said, "of using your name, Karela, to ensure the man would come."

"Ensure he'd come?" Puzzled, Karela swung her green eyes from Conan to the mage. "Why would he not?"

Amanar pursed his lips and touched them with his golden staff. His eyes on Conan seemed amused. "This night past were five of my S'tarra slain."

Conan wondered from which direction the S'tarra would come. There could be a score of doors hidden behind those ivory columns.

"You think Conan did this killing?" Karela said. "I spoke to you of this matter this morning, and you said nothing."

"Sometimes," the dark sorcerer said, "it is best to wait, to let the guilty think they will escape. But I see you require proof." He swung his staff against a small crystal bell that stood in a silver stand beside the throne.

At the chime the door through which the musicians had departed opened again. Aberius hesitantly entered the chamber, his eyes darting from Conan to the throne, as if measuring the distance to each. He rubbed his palms on the front of his yellow tunic.

"Speak," Amanar commanded.

Aberius' pointed face twitched. He swallowed. "Last night, before the gong sounded, I saw this Conan of Cimmeria leave our camp." His beady black eyes avoided Karela. "This surprised me, for all of us think the darkness of the nights here strange, and none will go out in them. None other did, that night as before. Conan returned after the alarm, with a wound on his side. I'll warrant there's a bandage beneath that tunic."

"Why did you not come to me, Aberius?" Karela said angrily. Her piercing gaze shifted to the Cimmerian. "I said, Conan, that I'd have the ears of any man involved, and I—"

"I fear," Amanar interrupted smoothly, "that it is I who must set this man's punishment. It is me he has offended against. You, Aberius," he added in a sharper tone, "go now. The gold agreed upon will be given as you leave."

The weasel-faced bandit opened his mouth as if to speak, closed it again, then suddenly scurried from the room. The small door closed behind him.

"Why, Conan?" Karela asked softly. "Is that girl worth so much to you?" She squeezed her eyes shut and turned away. "I give him to you," she said.

Conan's blade slipped from its sheath with a rasping whisper. "You reckon without me," the Cimmerian said. "I give myself to no one."

Amanar rose, holding the golden staff across his chest like a scepter. "Extend your life, Cimmerian. Prostrate yourself and beg, and I may have mercy on you." He started forward at a slow walk.

"Dog of a sorcerer," Conan grated, "come no closer. I know your mage's tricks with powders that kill when breathed." The golden-robed man came on, neither speeding nor slowing. "I warn you," Conan said. "Die then!"

With the speed of a striking falcon the big Cimmerian youth lunged. Amanar's staff whipped up; hissing, a citron vapor was expelled from its tip. Conan held his breath and plunged through the cloud. His sword struck Amanar's chest, piercing to the hilt. For a bare moment Conan stood chest to chest and eye to eye with the mage. Then his muscles turned to water. He tried to cry out as he toppled to the mosaic floor, but there was no sound except the thud of his fall. His great chest labored for breath, and his every muscle twitched and trembled, but not at his command.

The sorcerer stood above him, viewing him with the same dispassion he might exhibit at a bird found dead in the keep. "A concentrated derivative from the pollen of the golden lotus of Khitai," he said in a conversational tone. A thin smile curled his lips cruelly. "It works by contact, not by breathing, my knowledgeable thief. The paralysis grows if no antidote is applied, deeper and deeper until life itself is paralyzed. I am told one feels oneself dying by inches."

"Amanar," Karela gasped, "the sword!" She stood by the throne, a trembling hand pressed to her lips.

The sorcerer looked at the sword as if he had forgotten it pierced his chest. Grasping the hilt he drew it from his body. The blade was unbloodied. He seemed pleased with her shock. "You see, my dear Karela? No mortal weapon can harm me." Contemptuously he dropped the sword almost touching Conan's hand.

The Cimmerian strained to reach the leather-wrapped hilt, but his arms responded only with drug-induced tremors.

Amanar emitted a blood-chilling laugh and casually moved the sword even closer with his foot, until the hilt touched Conan's twitching hand. "Even before Aberius betrayed you, Cimmerian, I suspected you in the slaying, though two of the dead displayed certain anomalies. You see, Velita betrayed you also." His dark laugh was like a saw on bone. "The *geas* I placed on her commanded her to tell me if you saw her, and she did, though she wept and begged me to kill her rather than let her speak." He laughed again.

Conan tried to curse, but produced only a grunt. The man would die, he vowed, if he had to return as a shade to do the deed.

The sorcerer's cold, lidded eyes regarded him thoughtfully. The red flecks in their black depths seemed to dance. "You rage, but do not yet fear," he said softly. "Still, where there is such great resistance, there must be great fear once the resistance is shattered. And you will be shattered, Cimmerian."

"Please," Karela said, "if he must die, then kill him, but do not torture him."

"As you wish," Amanar said smoothly. He returned to the throne and struck the crystal bell once more.

This time Sitha appeared from the small door through which Aberius had left. Four more S'tarra followed, bearing a litter. Roughly they lifted Conan onto the bare wood and fastened him with broad leather straps across his massive chest and thighs. As they were carrying him out Conan heard Amanar speak.

"There is much we must speak of, my dear Karela. Come closer."

The door swung shut.

XXV

As the litter was carried through the donjon, one mailed S'tarra at each corner and Sitha leading, Conan lay seemingly quiescent. For the moment struggle was futile, but he constantly attempted to clench his right hand. If he could make even that beginning. . . . The hand twitched of its own volition, but no more. He fought to keep breathing.

The litter was carried from a resplendent corridor through an archway and down rough stone stairs. The walls, at first worked smooth, became raw stone, a passage hacked from the living rock beneath the dark fortress. Those who went thither no longer had a care for mosaics or tapestries.

The crude corridor leveled. Sitha pounded a huge fist against an iron-strapped door of rough wood. The door opened, and to Conan's surprise, a human appeared, the first he had seen in the keep who did not keep his eyes on the ground.

The man was even shorter than Conan, but even more massive, heavy sloping muscles covered with thick layers of fat. Piggish eyes set deep in a round, bald head regarded Conan. "So, Sitha," he said in a surprisingly high-pitched voice, "you've brought Ort another guest."

"Stand aside, Ort," Sitha hissed. "You know what is to be done here. You waste time."

Shockingly, the fat man giggled. "You'd like to cut Ort's head off, wouldn't you Sitha, with that ax of yours? But Amanar needs Ort for his torturing. You S'tarra get carried away and leave dead meat when there's questions yet to be asked."

"This one is already meat," Sitha said contemptuously. Casually the S'tarra turned to smash a backhand blow to Conan's face. Ort giggled again.

Blood welled in Conan's mouth. Chest heaving, he fought to get painful words out. "Kill—you—Sitha," he gasped.

Ort blinked his tiny eyes in surprise. "He speaks? After the vapor? This one is strong."

"Strong," Sitha snarled. "Not as strong as I!" Its fist crashed into Conan's face, splitting his cheek. For a moment the S'tarra stood with fist upraised, fangs bared, then lowered its claw-tipped hand with an obvious effort. "Put him in his cell, Ort, before I forget the master's commands."

Giggling, Ort led the procession into the dungeons. Grim ironbound doors lined the rough stone walls. Before one Ort stopped, undoing a heavy iron lock with a key from his broad leather belt. "In here," he said. "There's another in there already, but I'm filling up."

Quickly, under Sitha's direction, the other S'tarra unstrapped Conan from the litter and carried him into the cell, a cubicle cut in the rock as crudely as the rest of the dungeon. As chains were being fastened to the Cimmerian's wrists and ankles he saw his fellow prisoner, chained in the same fashion to the far wall, and knew a second of shock. It was the Zamoran captain he had tricked into combat with the hillmen.

As the other S'tarra left, Sitha came to stand over Conan. "Were it left to me," it hissed angrily, "you would die now. But the master has use of you yet." From a pouch at its belt it took a vial and forced it between the Cimmerian's teeth. Bitter liquid flowed across his tongue. "Perhaps, Cimmerian, when the master has your soul, this time he will let me have what remains." With a sibilant laugh Sitha shoved the empty vial back into his pouch and strode from the cell. The thick door banged shut.

Conan could feel strength flowing slowly back into his limbs. Weakly he pushed himself to a sitting position and leaned against the cool stone of the cell wall.

The hook-nosed Zamoran captain watched him thoughtfully with dark eyes. There were long blisters on his arms, and others were visible on his chest where his tunic was ripped. "I am Haranides," he said finally. "Whom do I share these . . . accommodations with?"

"I am called Conan," the Cimmerian replied. He tested the chains that fastened his manacles to the wall. Three feet and more in length, the links of them were too thick for him to have burst even had he his full strength, and he was far from that as yet.

"Conan," Haranides murmured. "I've heard that name in Shadizar, thief. Would I had known you when we met last."

Conan shifted his full attention to the Zamoran. "You remember me, then, do you?"

"I'm not likely to forget a man with shoulders like a bull, especially when he brought me near ten score hillmen for a present."

"Did you indeed follow us, then? I would not have done it save for that."

"I followed you," Haranides replied bitterly. "Rather, I followed the Red Hawk and the trinkets she took from Tiridates. Or was it you, thief, who entered the palace and slew like a demon?"

"Not I," Conan said, "nor the Red Hawk. 'Twas S'tarra, the scaled ones, who did it, and we followed them as you followed us. But how came you to this pass, chained to the wall in Amanar's dungeon?"

"From continuing my pursuit of the red-haired wench when a wiser man would have returned to Shadizar and surrendered his head," the captain said. "Half a mountain of rock poured into the gorge by those things— S'tarra, you call them? No more than twenty of my men escaped. We had a hillman for a guide, but whether he led us into a trap, or perished beneath the stone, or even got away entirely, I know not."

"You got not those burns from falling rock."

Haranides examined his blisters ruefully. "Our jailor, a fellow named Ort, likes to entertain himself with a hot iron. He's surprisingly agile for one of his bulk. He'd strike and leap away, and in these," he rattled his chains, "neither could I attack nor escape him."

"If he comes again with his irons," Conan said eagerly, "perhaps in dodging from the one he will come close enough for the other to seize."

He pulled one of his chains to its fullest extent and measured with his eye. With a disgusted grunt he again slumped against the stone wall. There was room enough and more between him and the other man for Ort to leap and dodge as he would. The fat torturer could stand within a finger's breadth of either man with impunity. He realized the other man was frowning at him.

"It comes to me," Haranides said slowly, "that already I have told you more than I told Ort. How came you to be chained like an ox, Conan?"

"I misjudged the wiliness of a sorcerer," Conan replied curtly.

It rankled still, the ease with which he had been taken. He seemed to remember once calling himself a bane of wizards, yet Amanar had snared him like a three-years child. While Karela watched, too.

"Then you were in his service?" Haranides said.

Conan shook his head irritably. "No!"

"Perhaps you are in his service still, put in here to extract information more easily than good Ort."

"Are your brains moon-struck?" Conan bellowed, lunging to his feet. His chains left him paces short of the other man. At least, though, he had regained enough strength to stand. With a short laugh he sank back. "A cell is no place for a duel, and we can't reach each other besides. I'll ask you to watch your speaking, though. I serve no sorcerer."

"Perhaps," Haranides said, and he would say no more.

Conan made himself as comfortable as the bare stone floor and rough wall would permit. He had slept in worse conditions in the mountains as a boy, and of his own free will. This time he did not sleep, though, but rather set his mind to escape, and to the killing of Amanar, for that last he would do if his own life were extinguished in the same moment. But how to kill a man who could take a yard of steel through his chest and not even bleed? That was a weighty question, indeed.

Some men, he knew, had amulets which were atuned to them by magicks, so that the amulet could be used for good or ill against that man. The Eye of Erlik came to mind, which bauble had at last brought down the Khan of Zamboula, though not by its sorceries. That the pendant which Velita had worn nestled between her small breasts was a watch for Amanar's evil eyes was to the Cimmerian proof that it too was such an amulet. It could be used to kill Amanar, he was sure, if he but knew the way.

But first must come escape. He reviewed what he had seen since being carried to the dungeon, what Ort had said, what Haranides had told him, and a plan slowly formed. He settled to wait. The patience of the hunting leopard was in him. He was a mountain warrior of Cimmeria. At fifteen he had been one of the fierce Cimmerian horde that stormed the walls of Venarium and sacked that border city of Aquilonia. Even before that had he been allowed his place at the warriors' council fires, and since then he had traveled far, seen kingdoms and thrones totter, helped to steady some and topple others. He knew that nine parts of fighting was knowing when to wait, the tenth knowing when to strike. He would wait. For now. The hours passed.

At the rattle of a key in the massive iron lock Conan's muscles tensed. He forced them to relax. His full strength was returned, but care must be taken.

The door swung outward, and two S'tarra entered, dragging Hordo unconscious between them. Straight to the third set of chains they took him, and manacled him there. Without looking at either of the other two men they left, but the door did not close. Instead, Amanar came to stand in the opening. The golden robe had been replaced by one of dead black, encircled with embroidered golden serpents. The mage fingered something on his chest through the robe as he surveyed the cell with cold black eyes.

"A pity," he murmured, almost under his breath. "You three could be more use to me than all of the rest together, with the sole exception of Karela herself, yet you all must die."

"Will you imprison us all, then?" Conan said, jerking his head at Hordo. The one-eyed bandit stirred, and groaned.

Amanar looked at him as if truly realizing he were present for the first time. "No, Cimmerian. He meddled where he should not, as you did, as the man Talbor did. The others remain free. Until their usefulness ends."

Haranides' chains clinked as he shifted. "Mitra blast your filth-soaked soul," the captain grated.

The ebon-clad sorcerer seemed not to hear. His strange eyes remained on Conan's face. "Velita," he said in a near whisper, "the slave girl you came to free, awaits in my chamber of magicks. When I have used her one last time, she will die, and worse than die. For if death is horrible, Cimmerian, how much more horrible when no soul is left to survive beyond?"

The big Cimmerian could not stop his muscles from tensing.

Amanar's laugh curdled marrow in the bone. "Interesting, Cimmerian. You fear more for another than for yourself. Yes, interesting. That may prove useful." His hellborn laugh came again, and he was gone.

Haranides stared at the closed door. "He fouls the air by breathing," he spat.

"Twice now," Conan said softly, "have I heard the taking of a soul spoken of. Once I knew a man who could steal souls."

The captain made the sign of the horns, against evil. "How did you know such a man?"

"He stole my soul," Conan said simply.

Haranides laughed uncertainly, not sure if this were a joke. "And what did you do than?"

"I killed him, and took back my soul." The Cimmerian shivered. That reclaiming had not been easy. To risk the loss again, perhaps past reclaiming, was fearful beyond death. And the same would happen to Velita, and eventually to Karela, could he not prevent it.

Hordo groaned again, and sat up, sagging his broad back against the stone wall. At the clank of his chains he stared at his manacles, then closed his eye.

"What happened, Hordo?" Conan asked. "Amanar had you brought hence by S'tarra, saying you meddled. In what?"

Hordo's scarred face contracted as if he wished to cry. "She was gone so long from the camp," he said finally, "and you, that I became concerned. It was near dark, and the thought that she must either remain the night in this place or find her way to camp through that blackness. . . . At the gate they let me in, but reluctantly, and one of the scaled ones ran calling for Sitha. I found the chamber where thrice-accursed Amanar, may the worms feast long on him, sat on his throne of golden serpents." His one eye closed again, but he spoke on, more slowly. "Musicians played, men, though their eyes never left the floor. Those snake-skinned demon-spawn came, and beat me down with clubbed spears. The mage shouted for them to take me alive. Two of them I killed, before my senses went. Two, at least, I know."

He fell silent, and Conan prodded him. "Surely Amanar didn't have you imprisoned merely for entering his throne room?"

The bearded face contorted in a grimace of pain, and Hordo moaned through clenched teeth. "Karela!" he howled. "She danced for him, naked as any girl in a zenana, and with as wild an abandon! Karela danced naked for the pleasure of that. . . ." Sobs wracked his burly form, choking off his words.

The hackles stood on Conan's neck. "He will die, Hordo," he promised. "He will die."

"This Karela," Haranides said incredulously, "she is the Red Hawk?"

Redfaced, Hordo lunged to the full extent of his chains. "She was ensorceled!" he shouted. "She knew me not. Never once did she look at me, or cease her dancing. She was spell-caught."

"We know it," Conan said soothingly.

The one-eyed man glared at Haranides. "Who is this man, Conan?"

"Don't you recognize him?" the Cimmerian laughed. "Haranides, the Zamoran captain we introduced to the hillmen."

"A Zamoran officer!" Hordo snarled. "Can I get my hands free, at least I'll rid the world of one more soldier before I die."

"Think you so, rogue?" Haranides sneered. "I've killed five like you before breaking fast in the morning." The bandit and the captain locked murderous gazes.

"Forgetting your chains for the moment," Conan said conversationally, "do you intend to do Amanar's work for him?"

The glares shifted to him. "We're going to die anyway," Hordo growled.

"Die if you want," Conan said. "I intend to escape and let Amanar do the dying."

"How?" Haranides demanded.

The Cimmerian smiled wolfishly. "Wait," he said. "Rest." And despite their protests he settled down to sleep. His dreams were of strangling Amanar with the black pendant's chain.

XXVI

Karela woke and looked about her in confusion. She lay on a silk-draped couch, not in her pavilion, but in an opulent room hung with scarlet silken gauze. Silver bowls and ewers stood on a gilded table, and the finest Turanian carpet covered the floor. Sunlight streamed in through a narrow window. She was in Amanar's keep, she realized, and at the same moment realized she was naked.

"Derketo!" she muttered, sitting up quickly.

Her head spun. Had she taken too much wine the night before? For some reason she was sure she had spent a night inside the fortress. There was a vague memory of wild music, and a girl's sensual dancing. She put a hand to her forehead as if to wipe away perspiration, and jerked it back down with another oath. The room was cool; she was cool. Quickly she rose to search for her clothing.

Her golden breastplates and emerald girdle were carefully laid out on her scarlet cloak, atop a chest at the foot of the couch. Her crimson thigh-boots stood before the chest, and her jeweled tulwar leaned against it. She dressed swiftly.

"Who was that girl?" she muttered beneath her breath as she tugged the last boot on, pulling the soft red leather almost to the top of her thigh. The dance had been shamelessly abandoned, almost voraciously carnal.

But why should that be important, she wondered. More important was to see that she watched her drinking in the future. She did not trust Amanar enough to spend another night in that keep. Her cheeks flamed, only partly with anger. She was lucky she had not wakened in his bed. Not that he was not handsome, in a cruel fashion, and powerful, which had its own attractions, but that would be a matter of her own choosing.

The door opened, and Karela was on her feet, tulwar in hand, before she realized it. She looked in consternation at the girl who entered, head down, not looking at her, with a tall, wooden-handled silver pitcher on a tray. Why was she so jumpy, she thought, resheathing the curved blade. "I'm sorry, girl. I didn't mean to scare you."

"Hot water, mistress," the girl said in a toneless voice, "for your morning ablutions." Still without raising her eyes she set the tray on the table and turned to go. She seemed unaffected by being greeted with a sword.

"A minute," Karela said. The girl stopped. "Has anyone come asking for me at the portcullis? Hordo? A bearded man with an eye-patch?"

"Such a man was taken to the dungeons, mistress, this night past."

"The dungeons!" Karela yelped. "By the tits of Derketo, why?"

"It was said, mistress, that he was discovered attempting to free the man Conan, and also that he had many golden ornaments in a sack."

The red-haired woman drew a shuddering breath. She should have expected something of the kind, should have guarded against it. Hordo and Conan had become close—sword-brothers, the hillmen called it—and men, never truly sane in her opinion, were at their maddest in such relationships. Still, for her most loyal hound, she must do something.

"Where is your master, girl?"

"I do not know, mistress."

Karela frowned. There had been a slight hesitation before that answer. "Then show me to the dungeons. I want to speak to Hordo."

"Mistress, I . . . I cannot . . . my master. . . ." The girl stood staring at the floor.

Karela grabbed the girl's chin, twisting her face up. "Look at me. . . ."

Her breath caught in her throat. The girl might have been called beautiful, except that there was no single line of expression or emotion on her face. And her brown eyes were . . . empty was the only word Karela could think of. She pulled her hand away, and had to resist the desire to wipe it on something. The girl dropped her eyes again immediately on being released. She had made no slightest resistance then, and she stood waiting now.

"Girl," Karela said, making her tone threatening, "I am here, and your master is elsewhere. Now show me to the dungeons!"

The girl nodded hesitantly, and led the way from the room.

She had been on the topmost level of the keep, Karela discovered as they took curving marble stairs, seeming to hang suspended in air, down to the ground floor. In a small side corridor the girl stopped before a plain stone archway that led onto rough stone steps. She had not raised her eyes in the entire journey, and Karela did not really want her to.

"There, mistress," the girl said. "Down there. I am not permitted to descend."

Karela nodded. "Very well, girl. If trouble comes of this for you, I'll intercede with your master."

"The master will do as he will do," the girl replied in her toneless voice. Before Karela could speak again, she had scurried away and was gone around a corner.

Taking a deep breath, and with a firm grip on her sword, the red-haired bandit descended the stairs until she came to an iron-strapped door. On this she pounded with her sword hilt.

The door was opened by a huge, fat man in a stained yellow tunic. She presented her blade to his face before he could speak. At least this one did not stare at the ground, she thought, though perhaps he should to hide his face.

"The man, Hordo," she said. "Take me to where he is confined."

"But Amanar," the fat man began. Her sword point indented his neck and his piggy eyes bulged. "I'll take you to him," he stammered in a high-pitched voice, and added, "Mistress."

Blade against his backbone, she followed him down the crudely cut corridor. He fumbled with the keys at his belt, and unlocked one of the solid wooden doors.

"Over there," she ordered, gesturing with her sword. "Where I can see you. And do you move, I'll make a capon of you, if you're not one already."

Anger twisted his suety face, but he moved as she directed. She pulled open the door and stared at the three men inside. Conan, Hordo, and one who looked vaguely familiar to her. All three looked up as the door swung open.

"You came!" Hordo cried. "I knew you would!"

Her green eyes rested on the broad-shouldered Cimmerian. His gaze, like twinned blue agates, regarded her impassively. She was relieved to see he still lived, and angry that she was relieved. The hard planes of his un-lined face were handsome, it was true, and he was virile—her cheeks colored—but he was a fool. Why did he have to oppose Amanar? Why could he not forget that girl, Velita? Why?

"Why?" she said, and immediately pulled her gaze to Hordo. "Why did you do it, Hordo?"

The one-eyed bandit blinked at her in bewilderment. "Do what?"

"Steal from Amanar. Try to free this other fool." She jerked her head at Conan without looking at him again.

"I stole nothing," Hordo protested. "And I knew not that Conan was im-prisoned until I was chained beside him."

"Then you were brought here for no reason?" she said derisively. Hordo was silent.

"He," Conan began, but Hordo cut him off with a shout.

"No, Cimmerian!" He added, "Please?" and the word sounded as if it were carved from his vitals.

Karela looked at the two men in consternation. Their eyes met, and Conan nodded. "Well?" she demanded. Neither man spoke. Hordo would not meet her gaze. "Derketo take you, Hordo. I should have you flogged. Can I talk Amanar into releasing you, I may yet."

"Release us now," Hordo said quickly. "Ort has the keys. You can—"

"You!" she said sharply. "It's you I'll try to free. I have no interest in these others." She felt Conan's eyes on her, and could not look at him. "Besides, it may do you good to sit here and worry as whether or not I can talk Amanar into releasing you to me." She gestured to the fat jailer with her sword. "You! Close the door." She stepped back to keep him under her eye and blade as he moved to do so.

"Karela," Hordo shouted, "leave this place! Leave me! Take horse and—" The door banged shut to cut him off.

As the fat man turned from locking the massive door, she laid her curved blade against his fat neck. Her eyes were glittering emerald ice. "If I find you have not taken good care of him," she said coldly, "I'll carve that bulk away to see if there's a man inside." Contemptuously she turned her back and stalked from the dungeon.

By the time she reached the top of the rude stone stairs her brain was burning. Amanar had no right. Conan was one thing. Hordo quite another. She would maintain the discipline of her hounds, and she had no intention of letting the mage usurp her authority in this fashion. She strode through the ornate halls of the black donjon, still clutching her sword in her anger.

One of the S'tarra appeared before her, blinking in surprise at the weapon in her hand. "Where is Amanar?" she demanded.

It did not speak, but its red eyes twitched toward a plain arch. She remembered Amanar saying that the passage beyond led to his thaumaturgical chambers. In her present mood, bearding the sorcerer there was just what she sought. She turned for the arch.

With a hissed shout, the mailed S'tarra leaped for her, and jumped back just in time, so that her blade drew sparks across the chest of its hauberk.

"Follow," she growled, "and you'll never follow anything again."

Its rubiate eyes remained on her face, but it stood still as she backed down the sloping passage, lined with flickering torches set in plain iron sconces. The corridor was longer than she had suspected. The archway, and the S'tarra still standing there, had dwindled to mere specks by the time her back came up against a pair of tall wooden doors.

The doors were carved with a profusion of serpents in endless arabesques, as were the stone walls of the corridor, though this had not been so high up. She thought she might be under the very heart of the mountain. Pushing open one of the doors, she went in.

The room was a great circle, surrounded by shadowed columns. The floor was a mosaic of a strange golden serpent. On the far side of the room, Amanar whirled at her entrance. Sitha, crouching near the mage, half rose.

"You dare to enter here!" Amanar thundered.

"I dare anything," she snapped, "while you have Hordo chained . . ." What was beyond the black-robed sorcerer finally impressed itself on her. The red-streaked black marble altar. The slim blonde girl bound naked to it, rigid with terror. "By the black heart of Ahriman," Karela swore, "what is it you do here, mage?"

Instead of answering, the cold-eyed man traced a figure in the air, and the figure seemed to stand glowing as he traced, stirring some buried memory deep inside her. Behind her eyes she felt something break, like a twig snapping. She would teach him to play his magical tricks with her. She started for the dark man . . . and stared down in amazement at feet that would not move. They did not feel held, they had full sensation, but they would not move.

"What wizardry is this?" she demanded hoarsely. "Release me, Amanar, or—"

"Throw the sword aside," he commanded.

She stifled a scream as her arm obeyed, sending the jewel-hilted tulwar skittering across the mosaicked floor to ring against a column.

Amanar nodded in satisfaction. "Remove your garments, Karela."

"Fool," she began, and her green eyes started with horror as her slim fingers rose to the golden pin that held her scarlet cloak and undid it. The cloak slid from her shoulders to the floor. "I am the Red Hawk," she said. It was little more than a whisper, but her voice rose to a scream. "I am the Red Hawk!"

She could not stop watching with bulging eyes as her hands removed the golden breastplates from her heavy round breasts and casually dropped them, unfastened the emerald girdle that rode low on her flaring hips.

"Enough," Amanar said. "Leave the boots. I like the picture they present." She wanted to weep as her hands returned quiescent to her sides. "Beyond these walls," the black-robed man went on, "you are the Red Hawk. Inside them, you are . . . whatever I want you to be. I think from now on I will keep you thus when you are with me, aware of what is happening. Your fear is like the rarest of wines."

"Think you I'll return once I am free?" she spat. "Let me get a sword in my hand and my hounds about me, and I will tear this keep down about your head."

His laughter sent shivers along her bones. "When you leave these walls, you will remember what I tell you to remember. You will go believing that we conferred, on this matter or that. But when once again within this donjon, you will remember the true nature of things. The Red Hawk will grovel at my feet and crawl to serve my pleasure. You will hate it, but you will obey."

"I'll die first!" she shouted defiantly.

"That will not be permitted," he smiled coldly. "Now be silent." The words she was about to speak froze on her tongue. Amanar produced a knife with a gilded blade from beneath his robe and tested its edge with his thumb. "You will watch what occurs here. I do not think Susa will mind." The girl on the altar moaned. The sorcerer's red-flecked black eyes suddenly held Karela's gaze as a viper holds the gaze of a bird. She could feel those eyes reaching into the very depths of her. "You will watch," Amanar said softly, "and you will begin to learn the true meaning of fear." He turned back to the altar; his chant rose, cutting into her mind like a knife. Flaming mists began to form.

Karela's green eyes bulged as if they would start from her head. She would not scream, she told herself. Even if she had a voice she would not scream. But her flanks and the rounded slopes of her breasts were of a sudden slick with sweat, and in her mind there was gibbering terror.

XXVII

onan!" Haranides shouted. "Conan!" The three men still lay chained to the walls of the cell beneath Amanar's keep.

Conan opened one eye, where he lay curled as comfortably as he could manage on the stone. "I'm sleeping," he said, and closed it again.

The Cimmerian estimated that a full day and more had passed since Karela had come to their cell, though there had been no food and but three pannikins of stale water brought to their cell.

"Sleeping," Haranides grumbled. "When do we hear of this escape plan of yours?"

"The Red Hawk," Hordo said hopefully. "When she sets me free, I'll get the rest of you out. Even you, Zamoran."

Conan sat up, stretching until his shoulder joints cracked. "If she were coming, Hordo," he said. "she'd have been here long since."

"She may yet come," the one-eyed man muttered. "Mayhap she took my advice and rode away."

Conan said nothing. His best hope for Karela was that she had accepted Amanar's word for Hordo's crimes and was even then in the bandit camp, surrounded by the men she called her hounds.

"In any case," Haranides said, "we cannot put our hopes on her. Even if she gets you free, bearded one, you heard her say she'd do nothing for the Cimmerian and myself. I think me she is a woman of her word."

"Wait," Conan said. "The time will come."

A key rattled in the lock.

"'Tis Ort who's come," Haranides growled. "With his irons, no doubt."

"Ort?" Hordo said. "Who is—"

The heavy, iron-strapped cell door slammed open, and the fat jailor stood in the opening. Behind him was a brazier full of glowing coals, and

159

from the coals projected the wooden handles of irons, their metal ends already as bright red as the coals they nestled among.

"Who's to be first?" Ort giggled.

He snatched an iron from the fire and waved its fiery tip at them. Hordo put his back against the wall, teeth bared in a snarl. Haranides crouched, ready to spring in any direction, so far as his chains would let him. Conan did not move.

"You, captain?" Ort said. He feinted toward Haranides, who tensed. "Ort likes burning officers. Or you, one-eye?" Giggling, he waggled the glowing iron at Hordo. "Ort could give you another scar, burn out your other eye. And you, strong one," he said, turning his peg-eyed gaze on Conan, "think you to sit unconcerned?"

Suddenly Ort darted at the Cimmerian, red-hot iron flashing, and danced back. A long blister stood on Conan's shoulder. Awkwardly he raised one arm to cover his head, and huddled against the wall, half turning his back on the man with the burning iron. The other three men all stared at the big youth incredulously.

"Fight him!" Haranides shouted, and had to throw himself back to avoid a vicious slash of the iron that would have taken him across the face.

"Face him like a man, Conan," Hordo urged.

Cautiously Ort dashed again to strike and retreat, curiously agile on his feet. Conan groaned as a second blister grew across his shoulders, and pressed himself tighter to the stone.

"Why he is no man at all," Ort giggled. The nearly round jailor swaggered closer, to stand over Conan raising his blazing weapon.

A roar of battle rage broke from Conan's throat, and his mighty thews pushed him from his crouch. One hand seized Ort's bulk, pulling him closer; the other looped its chain about the jailor's neck, catching at the same time a desperately flung hand. Biceps bulging, he jerked the heavy iron chain tight, fat flesh bulging through the links. Ort's tiny eyes, too, bulged from that fat face, and his feet scrabbled desperately at the bare stone floor. The jailor had but one weapon, and he used it, stabbing again and again with the burning iron at the Cimmerian's broad back.

The stench of burning flesh rose as the fiery rod seared Conan's muscles, but he locked the pain from his mind. It did not exist. Only the man before him existed. Only the man whose eyes were staring from his fat face. Only the man he must kill. Ort's mouth opened in a futile attempt to breathe, or perhaps to scream. His tongue protruded through yellowed teeth. The chain had almost disappeared into the fat of his neck. The iron dropped, and breath rattled in Ort's throat and was silent. Conan put all his strength into one last heave, and there was the crack of a breaking neck.

Slowly he unwound the chain, freeing it with some difficulty, and let the heavy body fall.

"Mitra!" Haranides breathed. "Your back, Conan! I could not have stood it a tenth so long."

Wincing, Conan bent to pick up the iron. He ignored the dead man. To his mind all torturers should be treated so. "The means of our escape," he said, holding Ort's weapon up. Its metal was yet hot enough to burn, but the glow had faded.

Carefully Conan fit the length of the iron through a link of the chain a handsbreadth from the manacle on one wrist. He took a deep breath, then twisted, the iron one way, his wrist the other. The manacle cut into the just-healed wounds left from his being staked out by the bandits, and blood trickled over his hand. The other two men held their breath. With a sharp snap the chain broke.

Laughing, Conan held up his free wrist, the manacle still dangling a few inches of chain, and the iron. "I'd hoped the heat hadn't destroyed the temper of the metal. It would have broken instead of the chain, otherwise."

"You hoped," Hordo wheezed. "You hoped!" The bandit threw back his shaggy head and laughed. "You bet our freedom on a hope, Cimmerian, and you won."

As quickly as he could Conan broke the rest of his chains, and those of the other men. As soon as Hordo was free, the bearded man leaped to his feet. Conan seized his arm to stop him from rushing out.

"Hold hard," the Cimmerian said.

"The time is gone for holding hard," Hordo replied. "I go to see to the Red Hawk's safety."

"To see to her safety?" Conan asked. "Or to die by her side?"

"I seek the one, Cimmerian, but I'll settle for the other."

Conan growled deep in his throat. "I'll not settle for death on S'tarra pikes, and if you will you're useless to me. And to Karela. Haranides, how many of your men do you think still live? And will they fight?"

"Perhaps a score," the captain replied. "And to get out of these cells they'll fight Ahriman and Erlik both."

"Then take you the jailor's keys, and free them. If you can take and hold the barbican, we may live yet."

Haranides nodded. "I'll hold it. What will you be doing, Cimmerian?"

"Slaying Amanar," Conan replied. Haranides nodded gravely.

"What about me?" Hordo said. The other two had been ignoring him.

"Are you with us?" Conan asked. He barely waited for Hordo's nod before going on. "Rouse the bandits. Somehow you must get over the wall without being seen, and bring them up the ramp before the catapults can fire on them. You must kill S'tarra, you and Karela's hounds, and set as many fires as you can within the keep. Both you and Haranides must wait my signal to move, so we are all in position. When the top of the tallest tower in the keep begins to burn, then ride."

"I'll be ready," Hordo said. "It is taught that no plan of battle survives the first touch of battle. Let us hope ours is different."

"Fare you well, Haranides," Conan said; then he and Hordo were hurrying from the dungeon.

At the top of the stone stairs, as they entered the donjon itself, a S'tarra rounded the corner not two paces from them. Hordo's shoulder caught the creature in its mailed midriff, and Conan's balled fist broke its neck. Hurriedly Conan pressed the S'tarra's sword on Hordo, taking a broad-bladed dagger for himself. Then they, too, parted.

The way to Amanar's chamber atop the tower was easy to find, Conan thought. All one did was climb stairs until there were no more stairs to climb, sweeping marble arcs supported on air, polished ebon staircases wide enough to give passage to a score of men and massive enough to support an army.

And then there was only a winding stone stairway, curving around the wall of the tower with no rail to guard its inner drop. With his foot on the bottom step Conan paused, remembering Velita's tale of a spell-trap. Were Amanar not within the keep, Conan's next step could mean his bloody death by darkling sorceries. A slow death, he recalled. But if he did not go up, others would die at Amanar's hands even if he did not. He took a step, then a second and third before he could think, continuing to place one foot in front of another until he was at the top, staring at an iron-bound door.

A sigh of relief left him. Too, there was use in the knowledge that Amanar was within the keep. But this was not a way he cared to go about collecting information.

He opened the door and stepped into a room where evil soaked the walls, and the very air seemed heavy with sorcerous portent. Circular the room was, without windows and lined with books, but there was that about the pale leather of those fat tomes that made the Cimmerian want not to touch them. The tattered remains of mummies, parts of them ripped away, lay scattered across tables among a welter of beakers, flasks, tripods, and small braziers with their fires extinguished to cold ash. Jars of liquid held distorted things that might once have been parts of men. A dim light was cast over all by glass balls set in sconces around the walls that glowed with an eerie fire.

But Velita was not there. In truth, he admitted to himself, he had no longer expected her to be. He could, at least, avenge her.

Quickly he located the crystal coffer of which she had spoken. It sat in a place of honor, on a bronze tripod standing in the center of the room.

Carelessly he tossed the smoky lid aside to shatter on the stone floor, rummaged in the silken wrappings, and lifted out the silver-mounted black stone on its fine silver chain. Within the stone red flecks danced, just as in Amanar's eyes.

Tucking the pendant behind his wide leather belt he searched hurriedly for anything else that might be of use. He was ready to go when he suddenly saw his sword, lying among a litter of thaumaturgical devices on one of the tables. He reached for it . . . and stopped with his hand hovering above the hilt. Why had Amanar brought the sword to this peccant chamber? Conan had had experience of ensorceled swords, had seen one kill the man who grasped it at the command of another. What had Amanar done to his blade?

The door of the room banged open, and Sitha sauntered in, fanged mouth dropping open in surprise at seeing Conan. Conan's hand closed over the swordhilt in an instant and brought the blade to guard. At least, he thought with relief, it had not killed him so far.

"So, Cimmerian," Sitha said, "you have escaped." Almost casually it reached to a jumble of long, mostly unidentifiable objects, and produced a spear with a haft as thick as a man's wrist. The point was near a shortsword in length. "The master cannot punish me for killing you here, in this place."

"You must do the killing first," Conan said. And he must set a fire. Soon. He circled, trying to get the tables out from between them. Reach was the S'tarra's advantage. Sitha moved in the opposite direction, spear held warily.

Abruptly the bronze gong began to toll. Sitha's red eyes flickered away for just a moment; Conan bent, caught the edge of a long table with his shoulder, and heaved it over. Sitha leaped back as the heavy table crashed where his feet had been. Beakers of strange powder and flagons of multi-colored liquids shattered on the floor. Acrid fumes rose from their mixing. The tolling continued, and now could be heard the faint sounds of shouting from the walls. Could Haranides or Hordo have decided not to wait, he wondered.

"My master sent me hence for powders," Sitha hissed. "Powders he thinks will increase the fear in the sacrifice." On the last word he lunged, the spear point darting for Conan's head.

The Cimmerian's broadsword beat the thrust aside, and his riposte slashed open the creature's scaled chin. Sitha leaped back from the blow, putting an elongated hand to the bloody gash and letting out a string of vile oaths.

"You still don't seem to have killed me," Conan laughed.

Sitha's sibilant voice became low and grating. "The sacrifice, Cimmerian, is that girl you came to this valley for. Velita. I will watch your face before I kill you, knowing you know she dies."

A berserker rage rose in the Cimmerian. Velita alive. But to remain that way only if he got there in time. "Where is she, Sitha?"

"The chamber of sacrifice, human."

"Where's this chamber of sacrifice?" Conan demanded.

Sitha bared his fangs in a derisive laugh. With a roar Conan attacked. The berserker was on him. He jumped up, caught a foot on the edge of the over-turned table, and leaped down on the S'tarra's side. The spearpoint slashed his thigh while he was in midair, but his slashing sword, driven by the fury of a man who meant to kill or die, but to do it *now*, sliced through the haft. Conan screamed like a hunting beast as he attacked without pause, without thought for his own defense, without allowing time for Sitha to do else but stumble back in panic. His second cut, almost a continuation of the first, sev-ered the S'tarra's right arm. Black blood spurted; a shriek ripped through those fangs. The third blow bit into Sitha's thick neck, slicing through. Those red eyes glared at him, life still in them, for a bare moment as that head toppled from the mailed shoulders. Blood fountained, and the body fell.

Panting with reaction, Conan looked about him. There was still the fire to. . . . Where the arcane powders and liquids had mixed among shattered fragments of stone and crystal, yellow flames leapt up, emitting an acrid cloud. In seconds the fire had seized on the overturned table, igniting it as though the wood had been soaked in oil from a lamp.

Choking and coughing, Conan stumbled from the chamber. Behind him flames roared; air stirred already in the body of the tower, drifting upward. Soon that necromanical chamber would be a furnace, and the tower top would flare for the signal. The tollings of the bronze gong rolled forth. If the signal were still needed.

Quickly the Cimmerian found his way from the tower, to a room with a window overlooking the keep and the valley beyond. His jaw dropped. On the ramparts S'tarra scurried with their weapons like ants in a stirred hill, and to good reason, for the valley floor swarmed with near a thousand tur-banned hillmen, mounted and armed with lance and tulwar.

Where Haranides and Hordo were, Conan had no idea. Their plan was gone by the wayside, but he might still save Velita if he could find the sacri-ficial chamber. But where in the huge black keep to begin? Even the donjon alone would take a day to search room by room. A sudden thought struck him. A chance, a small, bare chance, for her.

Pantherine strides took him down alabaster halls and marble stairs, past startled S'tarra scurrying on appointed tasks and so afraid to stop him. Like a hawk he sped, straight to the plain stone arch and the sloping passage beyond that Amanar had falsely claimed led to his thaumaturgical chambers.

Conan ran down that passage leading into the very heart of the moun-tain, arms and legs pumping, deep muscled chest working like a bellows. Death rode in his steely blue eyes, and he cared not if it was his death so long as Amanar preceded him into the shadows.

The gray walls of the passage, lit by flickering torches, began to be carved with serpents, and then there were tall doors ahead, also carved with serpents in intricate arabesques. Conan flung the two doors wide and strode in.

Amanar stood in his black, serpent-embroidered robe, chanting before a black marble altar, on which lay Velita, naked and bound. Behind the altar a mist of lambent fire swirled; beyond the mist was an infinity of blackness. Conan stalked down the curving row of shadowed columns, his teeth bared in a silent snarl.

The dark sorcerer seemed to reach a resting place in his chant, for without looking around he said, "Bring it here, Sitha. Hurry!"

Conan had reached a point a dozen paces from the altar. From there he examined the evil mage with great care. The man had not his golden staff, but what had he in its place? "I am not Sitha," Conan said.

Amanar started convulsively, whirling to stare at Conan, who stood in the shadows of the columns. "Is that you, Cimmerian? How have you come. . . . No matter. Your soul will feed the Eater of Souls somewhat early, that is all." Velita peered past Amanar at Conan with dark eyes full of hope and desperation. The fiery mists thickened.

"Release the girl," Conan demanded. Amanar laughed. The Cimmerian dug the pendant from his belt, let it dangle from one massive finger by its chain. "I have this, mage!"

The cold-eyed sorcerer's laugh died. "You have nothing," he snapped. but he touched his lips with his tongue and glanced nervously at the constantly deepening mists. Something stirred in their depths. "Still, it might cause . . . difficulties. Give it to me, and I will—"

"It is his soul!" a voice boomed, seeming to come from every direction. Among the shadows along the columns on the far side of the chamber, one shadow suddenly split, folded, and thickened. And there before them stood Imhep-Aton.

The Stygian sorcerer wore a golden chaplet set with a square-cut emerald, and a severe black robe that fell to his ankles. He moved slowly toward Amanar and the altar.

"You," Amanar spat. "I should have known when those two S'tarra died without wounds that it was you."

"The pendant, Conan of Cimmeria," the Stygian said intently. "It contains Amanar's soul, to keep it safe from the Eater of Souls. Destroy the pendant, and you destroy Amanar."

Conan raised his hand to smash the black stone against a column. And the will was not there to make his arm move so. To no avail he strained, then let his arm down slowly.

Amanar's laugh came shrilly. "Fool! Think you I placed no protection in that which is so important to me? No one who touches or beholds the pendant can damage it in any way." Suddenly he drew himself up to his full height. "Slay him!" he shouted, each syllable a command.

Abruptly Conan became aware of what had coalesced in the mists above and behind the altar. A great golden serpent head reared there, surrounded by long tentacles like the rays of the sun. The auric-scaled body stretched into the blackness beyond the mists, and the ruby eyes that regarded Imhep-Aton were knowing.

The Stygian had time for one horrified look, and then the great serpent struck faster than a lightning bolt. Those long, golden tentacles seized the screaming man, lifted him high. The tentacles seemed but to hold, almost caressingly, but Imhep-Aton's shrieks welded Conans' joints and froze his marrow. The man sounded as if something irrevocably irretrievable were being ripped from him. Eater of Souls, Conan thought, and shuddered.

The tentacles shifted their grip, now encircling and entwining, covering Imhep-Aton from head to feet, tightening. His shrieks continued for a disturbingly long time, long after blood began to ooze between the tentacles like juice squeezed from a ripe fruit, long after there should have been no breath or lungs left to scream with. The bloody bundle was tossed aside, to strike the mosaic floor with a sound like a sack of wet cloth. Conan avoided looking at it. Instead, he concentrated on the pendant hanging from his fist.

"Thou commanded me," a voice hissed in Conan's head, and he knew it was the great serpent, god or demon, which mattered little at the moment, speaking to Amanar. "Thou growest above thyself."

Conan stared at the hand holding the pendant. The grim god of his Cimmerian northcountry, Crom, Lord of the Mound, gave a man only life and will. What he did with them, or failed to do, was up to him alone. Life and will.

"Thy servant begs thee to forgive him," Amanar said smoothly, but the smoothness slipped as the serpent's mind-talk went on.

"No, Amanar. Thou has passed thy time. Remove the amulet, and prostrate thyself for thy god's feeding."

Life and will. Will.

"No!" Amanar shouted. He clutched the chest of his black robe. "I wear the amulet still. You cannot touch me, Eater of Souls."

"Thou defieth me!" The serpent shape swayed toward Amanar, tentacles reaching, and recoiling.

Will. The soul pendant. Eater of Souls. Will.

"Crom!" Conan shouted, and convulsively he hurled the pendant toward the great serpent. Time seemed to flow like syrup, the pendant to float spinning in air.

A long scream burst from Amanar's throat. "Nooooo!"

The golden serpent head moved lazily, hungrily, the fanged mouth opening, bifurcate tongue flicking out to gather in the pendant, swallowing.

Despair drove Amanar's shriek up in pitch. Then another scream came, a hissing scream that sounded in the mind. On the altar Velita convulsed and went limp. Conan felt his bones turning to mush.

A bar of blue fire burst from the chest of the black-robed sorcerer, tearing his robe asunder, to connect him with the great golden god-demon. In unison their screams rose, Amanar's and Morath-Aminee's, higher, higher, drilling the brain, boring into bone and gristle. Then Amanar was a living statue of blue fire, but screaming still, and the great golden form of Morath-Aminee was awash with blue flame for all that length stretching into infinity. And that scream, too, continued, a sibilant shriek in the mind, wrenching at the soul.

The man's cry ended, and Conan looked up to find that Amanar was gone, leaving but a few greasy ashes and a small pool of molten metal. But Morath-Aminee still burned, and now the great blue flaming form thrashed in its agony. It thrashed, and the mountains trembled.

Cracks opened across the ceiling of the room, and the floor tilted and pitched like a ship in a storm at sea. Fighting to maintain his balance, Conan hurried to the black marble altar, beneath the very burning form of the god-demon in its death-throes. Velita was unconscious. Swiftly the Cimmerian cut her loose and, throwing her naked form across his shoulder, he ran. The ceiling of the sacrificial chamber thundered down as he ran clear, and dirt filled the air of the passage. The mountain shook still, ever more and more violently, twisting, yawing. Conan ran.

In the keep above, he found madness. Columns fell and dark towers toppled, long gaps were opened in the great outer wall, and in the midst of it all the S'tarra killed anything that moved, including each other.

The massive Cimmerian ran for the gate, his shimmering blade working its murderous havoc among those S'tarra which dared face him. Behind him Amanar's tower, flame roaring from its top as from a furnace, cracked down one side and fell into a thousand shards of obsidian stone. The ground shook like a mad thing as Conan fought to the gate.

The portcullis stood open, and as Conan started through, the lissome dancing girl still suspended across his broad shoulder, the barbican door burst open. Haranides hurried out, tulwar in hand and dark face bloodied, followed by half a dozen men in Zamoran armor.

"I held the gate for a time," he shouted above the din of earthquake and slaughter, "but then it was all we could do to keep from being shaken into jelly. At least the accursed lizards became too busy filling each other to pay us any mind. What madness has taken them?"

"No time!" Conan shouted back. "Run, before the mountain comes down on us."

They pounded down the ramp as the barbican and portcullis collapsed in a heap of rubble.

The floor of the valley was a charnel house, the ground soaked with blood and the moans of the dying filling the air. Savagely hacked S'tarra lay tangled with bleeding hillmen corpses in a hideous carpet, here and there dotted with the body of a bandit. From the mountains around, despite the trembling of the earth, the sounds of battle floated, as those who fled the horror of the keep and the valley fought still.

Conan saw Hordo near the bandit campsite, sitting beside Karela's crumpled red-striped pavilion as if nothing had happened. With Velita still dangling over his shoulder, the Cimmerian stopped before the one-eyed brigand. Haranides, having left his men a short distance back, stood to one side. Rock slides rumbled loudly as the earth still shook. But at least, Conan thought, the death screams of the god-demon had faded from his mind.

"Did you find her, Hordo?" he asked as quietly as the noise would allow. They were in the safest spot there, so far as the earthquake was concerned, well away from the danger of the mountain coming down on them.

"She's gone," Hordo replied sadly. "Dead, I don't know, gone."

"Will you search for her?"

Hordo shook his head. "After this shaking I could search for years and not find her if she was right under my nose. No, I'm for Turan, and a caravan guard's life, unless I can find an agreeable widow who owns a tavern. Come with me, Conan. I've about two coppers, but we can sell the girl and live off that for a while."

"Not this girl," Conan replied. "I promised to set her free, and I will."

"A strange oath," Haranides said, "but then you're a strange man, Cimmerian, though I like you for it. Look you, having decided there's no point to going back to Shadizar to lose my head, I, too, am going to Turan, with Resaro and such other few of my men as survived. Yildiz dreams of empire. He's hiring mercenaries. What I am trying to say is, join us."

"I cannot," Conan laughed, "for I'm neither soldier, nor guard, nor tavern keeper. I'm a thief." He studied his surroundings. Half of the black keep was covered beneath a mound ripped from the side of the mountains. The tremors had lessened too, till a man could stand with ease, and walk without too much difficulty. "And as I'm a thief," he finished, "I think it's time for me to steal some horses before the hillmen decide to return."

The reminder of the hillmen stirred them all to action. Quick farewells were said, and the three parted ways.

Epilogue

onan walked his mount back up the hill to where Velita sat her own horse, watching the caravan make ready to move below on the route to Sultanpur. This was the caravan that had been spoken of, the big caravan that would drive through despite those that had disappeared. It stretched out of sight along the winding path that led through the pass. Conan did not believe they would have any trouble at all.

"Your passage is booked," he told Velita. She was swathed in white cotton from head to foot. It was a cool way to dress for travel in the hot sun, and they had decided it was best she not advertise her beauty until she got to Sultanapur. "I gave the caravan master a gold piece extra to look after you, and a threat to find him later should anything untoward befall."

"I still don't understand how you have the money for my way," she said. "I seem to recall waking just enough to hear you tell a one-eyed man that you had no money."

"This," Conan said, pressing a purse into her hands, "I took from Amanar's chamber. Eighteen gold pieces left, after your passage. If I had told the others of it—and I didn't lie, Velita, I just didn't tell them—they'd likely have wanted a share. I'd have had to kill them to keep it for you, and I liked them too much for that."

"You are a strange man, Conan of Cimmeria," she said softly. She leaned forward to brush her lips delicately against his. Holding her breath, she waited.

Conan brought his hand down on her horse's rump with a loud slap. "Fare you well, Velita," he shouted as her horse galloped toward the caravan. "And I am likely a thrice-accursed idiot," he added to himself.

He turned his horse down the caravan, on the way that would lead him west out of the Kezankians into Zamora. He now had about enough coppers left for two jacks of sour wine when he got back to Abuletes.

"Conan!"

He pulled his horse around at the hail. It seemed to come from a slave coffle. The caravan contained sorts that would have formed their own if not for the fear of those caravans that had disappeared. As he rode closer, he began to laugh.

The slaver had arranged his male and female slaves separately, to avoid trouble. The women knelt naked in the slight shade of a long strip of cotton, linked to the coffle line by neck chains. And kneeling in the center of that line was Karela.

As he reined in before her, she leaped to her feet, her lightly sunburned breasts swaying. "Buy me out of here, Conan. We can go back and take what we want of Amanar's treasure. The hillmen will have gone by now, and I doubt they'll want anything of his."

Conan mentally counted the coppers in his purse again, and thought of an oath extracted not too many days before. Oaths were serious business. "How came you here, Karela? Hordo thought you dead."

"Then he's all right? Good. My tale is a strange one. I awoke in Amanar's keep, feeling as if I had had a monstrous nightmare, to find an earthquake shaking the mountains down, hillmen attacking and the S'tarra gone mad. It was almost as if my nightmare had come true."

"Not quite," Conan murmured. He was thankful she did not remember. At least she was spared that. "Speak on."

"I got a sword," she said, "though not mine. I couldn't find it. I regret losing that greatly, and I hope we find it when we go back. In any case, I fought my way out of the keep, through a break in the wall, but before I could reach the camp that fool sword broke. It wasn't good steel, Conan. I stole a horse then, but hillmen chased me south, away from the valley. I was almost to the caravan route before I lost them." She shook her head ruefully.

"But that doesn't explain how you ended up here," he said.

"Oh, I was paying so much heed to getting away from the hillmen that I forgot to mind where I was going. I rode right into half a dozen of this slaver's guards, and five minutes later I was tied across my own horse." She tried to manage a self-deprecating laugh, but it sounded strange and forced.

"In that case," Conan said, "any magistrate will free you on proof of identity, proof that you aren't actually a slave."

Her voice dropped, and she looked carefully at the women on either side of her to see if they listened. "Be not a fool, Conan! Prove who I am to a magistrate, and he'll send my head to Shadizar to decorate a pike. Now, Derketo take you, buy me free!"

To his surprise, she suddenly dropped back to her kneeling position. He looked around and found the reason: the approach of a plump man with thin, waxed mustaches and a gold ring in his left ear with a ruby the size of his little fingernail.

"Good morrow," the fellow said, bowing slightly to Conan. "I see you have chosen one of my prettiest. Kneel up, girl. Shoulders back. Shoulders back, I say." Red-faced and darting angry glances at Conan, Karela shifted to the required position. The plump man beamed as if she were a prime pupil.

"I know not," Conan said slowly.

Karela frowned in his direction, and the slave dealer suddenly ran a thoughtful eye over the Cimmerian's worn and ragged clothes. The plump man opened his mouth, then a second glance at the breadth of Conan's shoulders and the length of his sword made the slaver modify his words.

"In truth, the girl is quite new, and she'll be cheap. I maintain my reputation by selling nothing without letting the buyer know everything there is to know. Now, I've had this girl but two days, and already she has tried to escape twice and nearly had a guard's sword once." Conan was watching Karela from the corner of his eye. At this she straightened pridefully, almost into the pose the slave dealer had demanded. "On the other hand, all that was the first day." Karela's cheeks began to color. "A good switching after each, longer and harder each time, and she's been a model since." Her face was bright scarlet. "But I thought I should tell you the good and the bad."

"I appreciate that," Conan said. "What disposition do you intend to make of her in Sultanapur?" Her green eyes searched his face at that.

"A zenana," the slaver said promptly. "She's too pretty for the work market, too fine for a bordello, not fine enough for Yildiz, neither a singer nor a dancer, though she knows dances she denied knowing. So, a zenana to warm some stout merchant's bed, eh?" He laughed, but Conan did not join in.

"Conan," Karela said in a strangled whisper, "please."

"She knows you," the plump slaver said in surprise. "You'll want to buy her, then?"

"No," Conan said. Karela and the slaver stared at him in consternation.

"Have you been wasting my time?" the slaver demanded. "Do you even have the money for this girl?"

"I do," Conan answered hotly. He reflected that a lie to a slaver was not truly a lie, but now there was no way to let Karela know the entire truth of the matter. "But I swore an oath not to help this woman, not to raise a hand for her."

"No, Conan," Karela moaned. "Conan, no!"

"A strange oath," the slaver said, "but I understand such things. Still, with those breasts she'll fetch a fair price in Sultanapur."

"Conan!" Karela's green eyes pleaded, and her voice was a breathy gasp. "Conan, I release you from your oath."

"Some people," the Cimmerian said, "don't realize that an oath made before gods is particularly binding. It's even possible the breaking of such an oath is the true reason she finds herself kneeling in your coffle."

"Possibly," the slaver said vaguely, losing interest now that the chance of a sale was gone.

Karela reached out to pluck at Conan's stirrup leather. "You can't do this to me, Conan. Get me out of here. Get me out of here!"

Conan backed his horse away from the naked red-head. "Fare you well, Karela," he said regretfully. "Much do I wish that things could have ended better between us."

As he rode on down the caravan her voice rose behind him. "Derketo take you, you Cimmerian oaf! Come back and buy me! I release you! Conan, I release you! Derketo blast your eyes, Conan! Conan! Conan!"

As her cries and the caravan faded behind him, Conan sighed. Truly he did not like to see her left in chains. If he had had the money, or if there had not been the oath. . . . Still, he could not entirely suppress a small tinge of satisfaction. Perhaps she would learn that the proper response for a man saving her life was neither to have him pegged out on the ground nor to abandon him to a sorcerer's dungeon without so much as a glimmer of a protest. An he knew Karela, though, no zenana would hold her for long. Half a year or so, and the Red Hawk would be free to soar again.

As for himself, he thought, he was in as fine a position as a man could ask for. Four coppers in his pouch and the whole wide world in front of him. And there were always the haunted treasures of Larsha. With a laugh he kicked his horse into a trot for Shadizar.

Conan
the
Defender

Sunlight streaming through marble-arched windows illumined the tapestry-hung room. The servants, tongueless so that they could not speak of whom they saw in their master's house, had withdrawn, leaving five people to sip their wine in silence.

Cantaro Albanus, the host, studied his guests, toying idly with the heavy gold chain that hung across his scarlet tunic. The lone woman pretended to study the intricate weaving of the tapestries; the men concentrated on their winecups.

Midmorning, Albanus reflected, was exactly the time for such meetings, though it rubbed raw the nerves of his fellows. Traditionally such were held in the dark of night by desperate men huddled in secret chambers sealed to exclude so much as a moonbeam. Yet who would believe, who could even suspect that a gathering of Nemedia's finest in the bright light of day, in the very heart of the capital, could be intent on treason?

His lean-cheeked face darkened at the thought, and his black eyes became obsidian. With his hawk nose and the slashes of silver at the temples of his dark hair, he looked as if he should have been a general. He had indeed been a soldier, once, for a brief year. When he was but seventeen his father had obtained him a commission in the Golden Leopards, the bodyguard regiment of Nemedian Kings since time beyond memory. At his father's death he had resigned. Not for him working his way up the ladder of rank, no matter how swiftly aided by high birth. Not for one who by blood and temperament should be King. For him nothing could be treason.

"Lord Albanus," Barca Vegentius said suddenly, "we have heard much of the . . . special aid you bring to our . . . association. We have heard much, but thus far we have seen nothing." Large and square of face and body, the current Commander of the Golden Leopards pronounced his words carefully.

He thought to hide his origins by hiding the accents of the slums of Belverus, and was unaware that everyone knew his deception.

"Such careful words to express your doubts, Vegentius," Demetrio Amarianus said. The slender youth touched a perfumed pomander to his nose, but it could not hide the sneer that twisted his almost womanly mouth. "But then you always use careful words, don't you? We all know you are here only to—"

"Enough!" Albanus snapped.

Both Demetrio and Vegentius, whose face had been growing more purple by the second, subsided like well-trained animals at the crack of the trainer's whip. These squabbles were constant, and he tolerated them no more than he was forced to. Today he would not tolerate them at all.

"All of you," Albanus went on, "want something. You, Vegentius, want the generalship you feel King Garian has denied you. You, Demetrio, want the return of the estates Garian's father took from your grandfather. And you, Sephana. You want revenge against Garian because he told you he liked his women younger."

"As pleasantly stated as is your custom, Albanus," the lone woman said bitterly. Lady Sephana Galerianus' heart-shaped face was set with violet eyes and framed by a raven mane that hung below her shoulders. Her red silk robe was cut to show both the inner and outer slopes of her generous breasts, and slashed to expose her legs to the hip when she walked.

"And what do I want?" the fourth man in the room asked, and everyone started as if they had forgotten he was there.

It was quite easy to forget Constanto Melius, for the middle-aged noble was vagueness personified. Thinning hair and the pouches beneath his constantly blinking eyes were his most prominent features, and his intelligence and abilities matched the rest of him.

"You want your advice listened to," Albanus replied. "And so it shall be, when I am on the throne."

It would be listened to for as long as it took to order the man banished, the hawk-faced lord thought. Garian had made the mistake of rebuffing the fool, then leaving him free in the capital to foment trouble. Albanus would not make the same mistake.

"We seem to have passed by what Vegentius said," Sephana said abruptly, "but I, too, would like to see what help we can count on from you, Albanus. Demetrio and Vegentius provide information. Melius and I provide gold to buy disorders in the street, and to pay brigands to burn good grain. You keep your plans to yourself and tell us about the magicks that will make Garian give the throne to you, if we do these other things as well. I, too, want to see these magicks."

The others seemed somewhat abashed that she had brought the promised sorcery out into the open, but Albanus merely smiled.

Rising, he tugged a brocade bellpull on the wall before moving to a table at the end of the room, a table where a cloth covered certain objects. Cloth and objects alike Albanus had placed there with his own hands.

"Come," he told the others. Suddenly reluctant, they moved to join him slowly.

With a flourish he whisked the cloth aside, enjoying their starts. He knew that the things on that table—a statuette in sapphire, a sword with serpentine blade and quillons of ancient pattern, a few crystals and engraved gems—were, with one exception, practically useless. At least, he had found little use prescribed for them in the tomes he had so painfully deciphered. Items of power he kept elsewhere.

Ten years earlier, slaves on one of his estates north of Numalia had dug into a subterranean chamber. Luckily he had been there at the time, been there to recognize it as the storehouse of a sorcerer, been there to see that the luckless slaves were buried in that chamber once he had emptied it.

A year it had taken him just to discover how ancient that cache was, dating back to Acheron, that dark empire ruled by the vilest thaumaturgies and now three millenia and more gone in the dust. For all those years he had studied, eschewing a tutor for fear any sorcerer of ability would seize the hoard for his own. It had been a wise decision, for had he been known to be studying magicks he would surely have been caught up in Garian's purge of sorcerers from the capital. Garian. Thinking dark thoughts, Albanus lifted a small red crystal sphere from the table.

"I mistrust these things," Sephana said, shuddering. "Better we should rely on ways more natural. A subtle poison—"

"Would provoke a civil war for the succession," Albanus cut her off. "I don't want to tell you again that I have no intention of having to wrest the Dragon Throne from a half score of claimants. The throne will be given to me, as I have said."

"That," Vegentius grumbled, "I will believe when I see it."

Albanus motioned the others to silence as a serving girl entered. Blonde and pale of skin, she was no more than sixteen years of age. Her simple white tunic, embroidered about the hem with Albanus' house-mark, was slashed to show most of her small breasts and long legs. She knelt immediately on the marble floor, head bent.

"Her name is Omphale," the hawk-faced lord said.

The girl shifted at the mention of her name, but knew enough not to lift her head. She was but newly enslaved, sold for the debts of her father's shop, but some lessons were quickly learned.

Albanus held the red crystal at arm's length in his left hand, making an arcane gesture with his right as he intoned, *"An-naal naa-thaan Vas-ti no-entei!"*

A flickering spike of flame was suddenly suspended above the crystal, as long as a man's forearm and more solid than a flame should be. Within the pulsing red-and-yellow, two dark spots, uncomfortably like eyes, moved as if examining the room and its occupants. All moved back unconsciously except for Omphale, who cowered where she knelt, and Albanus.

"A fire elemental," Albanus said conversationally. Without changing his tone he added, "Kill Omphale!"

The blonde's mouth widened to scream, but before a sound emerged the elemental darted forward, swelling to envelop her. Jerkily she rose to her feet, twitching in the midst of an egg of flame that slowly opaqued to hide her. The fire hissed, and in the depths of the hiss was a thin shriek, as of a woman screaming in the distance. With the pop of a bursting bubble the flame disappeared, leaving behind a faint sickly sweet smell.

"Messy," Albanus mused, scuffing with a slippered foot at an oily black smudge on the marble floor where the girl had been.

The others' stares were stunned, as if he had transformed into the fabled dragon Xutharcan. Surprisingly, it was Melius who first regained his tongue.

"These devices, Albanus. Should we not have some of them as well as you?" His pouchy eyes blinked uncomfortably at the others' failure to speak. "As a token that we are all equals," he finished weakly.

Albanus smiled. Soon enough he would be able to show them how equal they were. "Of course," he said smoothly. "I've thought of that myself." He gestured to the table. "Choose, and I will tell you what powers your choice possesses." He slipped the red crystal into a pouch at his belt as he spoke.

Melius hesitated, reached out, and stopped with his hand just touching the sword. "What . . . what powers does this have?"

"It turns whoever wields it into a master swordsman." Having found that such was the extent of the blade's power, Albanus had researched no further. He had no interest in becoming a warrior-hero; he would be King, with such to do his bidding. "Take the blade, Melius. Or if you fear it, perhaps Vegentius. . . ." Albanus raised a questioning eyebrow at the square-faced soldier.

"I need no magicks to make me a bladesman," Vegentius sneered. But he made no move to choose something else, either. "Demetrio?" Albanus said. "Sephana?"

"I mislike sorcery," the slender young man replied, openly flinching away from the display on the table.

Sephana was made of sterner stuff, but she shook her head just as quickly. "If these sorceries can pull Garian from the Dragon Throne, 'tis well enough for me. And they can not. . . ." She met Albanus' gaze for a moment, then turned away.

"I'll take the sword," Melius said suddenly. He hefted the weapon, testing the balance, and laughed. "I have no such scruples as Vegentius about how I become a swordsman."

Albanus smiled blandly, but slowly his face hardened. "Now hear me," he intoned, fixing each of them in turn with an obsidian eye. "I have shown but a small sampling of the powers that will gain me the throne of Nemedia, and grant your own desires. Know that I will brook no deviation, no meddling that might interfere with my designs. Nothing will stand between me and the Dragon Crown. Nothing! Now go!"

They backed from his presence as if he already sat on the Dragon Throne.

I

The tall, muscular youth strode the streets of Belverus, monument-filled and marble-columned capital of Nemedia, with a wary eye and a hand close to the well-worn leather-wrapped hilt of his broadsword. His deep blue eyes and fur-trimmed cloak spoke of the north country. Belverus had seen many northern barbarians in better times, dazzled by the great city and easily separated from their silver or their pittance of gold—though often, not understanding the ways of civilization, they had to be hauled away by the black-cloaked City Guard, complaining that they had been duped. This man, however, though only twenty-two, walked with the confidence of one who had trod the paving stones of cities as great or greater, of Arenjun and Shadizar, called the Wicked; of Sultanapur and Aghrapur; even the fabled cities of far-off Khitai.

He walked the High Streets, in the Market District, not half a mile from the Royal Palace of Garian, King of Nemedia, yet he thought he might as well be in Hellgate, the city's thieves' district. The open-fronted shops had display tables out, and crowds moved among them pricing cloth from Ophir, wines from Argos, goods from Koth and Corinthia and even Turan. But the peddlers' carts rumbling over the paving stones carried little in the way of foodstuffs, and their prices made him wonder if he could afford to eat in the city for long.

Between the shops were huddled beggars, maimed or blind or both, their wailing for alms competing with the hawkers crying their wares. And every street corner had its knot of toughs, hard-eyed, roughly dressed men who fingered swordhilts, or openly sharpened daggers or weighed cudgels in their fists as their gazes followed a plump merchant scurrying by or a lissome shopkeeper's daughter darting through the crowd with nervous eyes. All that was missing were the prostitutes in their brass and copper bangles, sheer shifts cut to display their wares. Even the air had something of the cloying smell he associated with a dozen slums he had seen, a mixture of vomit, urine and excrement.

Suddenly a fruit cart crossing an intersection was surrounded by half-a-dozen ruffians in motley bits of finery mixed with rags. The skinny vendor stood silent, eyes down and care-worn face red, as they picked over his goods, taking a bite of this and a bite of that, then throwing both into the street. Stuffing the folds of their tunics with fruit, they started away, swaggering, insolent eyes daring anyone to speak. The well-dressed passersby acted as if the men were invisible.

"I don't suppose you'll pay," the vendor moaned without raising his eyes.

One of the bravos, an unshaven man wearing a soiled cloak embroidered with thread-of-gold over a ragged cotton tunic, smiled, showing the blackened stumps of his teeth. "Pay? Here's pay." His backhand blow split the skinny man's cheek, and the pushcart man collapsed sobbing across his barrow. With a grating laugh the bravo joined his fellows who had stopped to see the sport, and they shoved their way through the crowd of shoppers, who gave way with no more than a wordless mutter.

The muscular northern youth stopped a pace away from the pushcart. "Will you not call the City Guard?" he asked curiously.

The peddler pushed himself wearily erect. "Please. I have to feed my family. There are other carts."

"I steal not fruit, nor beat old men," the youth said stiffly. "My name is Conan. Will the City Guard not protect you?"

"The City Guard?" the old man laughed bitterly. "They stay in their barracks and protect themselves. I saw three of these scum hang a Guardsman by his heels and geld him. Thus *they* think of the City Guard." He wiped his hands shakily down the front of his tunic, suddenly realizing how visible he was talking to a barbarian in the middle of the intersection. "I have to go," he muttered. "I have to go." He bent to the handles of his pushcart without another glance at the young barbarian.

Conan watched him go with a pitying glance. He had come to Belverus to hire himself as a bodyguard or a soldier—he had been both, as well as a thief, a smuggler and a bandit—but whoever could hire his sword for protection in that city, it would unfortunately not be those who needed it most.

Some of the street-corner toughs had noticed his words with the peddler, and approached, thinking to have some fun with the outlander. As his gaze passed over them, though, cold as the mountain glaciers of his native Cimmeria, it came to them that death walked the streets of Belverus that day. There was easier prey elsewhere, they decided. In minutes the intersection was barren of thugs.

A few people looked at him gratefully, realizing he had made that one place safe for the moment. Conan shook his head, half angry with himself, half with them. He had come to hire his sword for gold, not to clear the streets of scum.

A scrap of parchment, carried by a vagrant breeze, fetched up against his boot. Idly he picked it up, read the words writ there in fine round hand.

King Garian sits on the Dragon Throne.
King Garian sits to his feast alone.
You sweat and toil for a scrap of bread,
And learn to walk the streets in dread.
He is not just, this King of ours,
May his reign be counted in hours.
Mitra save us from the Dragon Throne,
And the King who sits to his feast alone.

He let the scrap go with the breeze, joining still other scraps swirling down the street. He saw people lift one to read. Some let it drop, white-faced, or threw it away in anger, but some read and furtively tucked the bit of sedition into their pouches.

Belverus was a plum ripe for the plucking. He had seen the signs before, in other cities. Soon the furtiveness would be gone. Fists would be shaken openly at the Royal Palace. Stronger thrones had been toppled by less.

Suddenly a running man pushed past him with horror-stricken eyes, and on his heels came a woman, her mouth open in a soundless scream. A flock of children ran past shrieking unintelligibly.

Down the street more screams and cries rose, and the crowd suddenly stampeded toward the intersection. Their fear communicated itself, and without knowing why others joined the stream. With difficulty Conan forced his way to the side of the street, to a shop deserted by its owner. What could cause this, he wondered.

Then the torrent of people thinned and was gone, and Conan saw that the street they had fled was littered with bodies, few moving. Some had been trampled; others, further away, were lacking arms or heads. And striding down the center of the street was a man in a richly embroidered blue tunic, holding a sword with an odd, wavy blade that was encarmined for its entire length. A rope of spittle drooled from the corner of his mouth.

Conan put his hand to his sword, then firmly took it away. For gold, he reminded himself, not to avenge strangers on a madman. He turned to move deeper into the shadows.

At that instant a child broke from a shop directly in front of the madman, a girl no more than eight years old, wailing as she ran on flashing feet. With a roar the madman raised his sword and started after her.

"Erlik's Bowels and Bladder!" Conan swore. His broadsword came smoothly from its worn shagreen sheath as he stepped back into the intersection.

The child ran screaming past without slowing. The madman halted. Up close, despite his rich garb, thinning hair and pouches beneath his eyes gave him the look of a clerk. But those muddy brown eyes were glazed with madness, and the sounds he made were formless grunts. Flies buzzed about the fruit the bravos had scattered.

At least, Conan thought, the man had some reason left, enough not to run onto another's blade. "Hold there," he said. "I'm no running babe or shopkeeper to be hacked down from behind. Why don't you—"

Conan thought he heard a hungry, metallic whine. An animal scream broke from the man's throat, and he rushed forward, sword raised.

The Cimmerian brought his own blade up to parry, and with stunning speed the wavy sword changed direction. Conan leaped back; the tip of the other's steel slashed across his belly, slicing tunic and the light chain mail he wore beneath alike as if they were parchment. He moved back another step to gain room for his own attack, but the madman followed swiftly, bloody blade slashing and stabbing with a ferocity beyond belief. Slowly the muscular youth gave ground.

To his shock it came to him that he was fighting a defensive battle against the slight, almost nondescript man. His every move was to block some thrust instead of to attack. All of his speed and cunning were going into merely staying alive, and already he was bleeding from half a dozen minor wounds. It came to him that he might well die on that spot.

"By the Lord of the Mound, no!" he shouted. "Crom and steel!" But with the clash of the blades ringing in his ears he was forced back.

Abruptly Conan's foot came down on a half-eaten plum, and with a crash he went down, flat on his back, silver-flecked spots dancing before his eyes. Fighting for breath he watched the madman's wavy blade go back for the thrust that would end his life. But he would not die easily. From his depths he found the strength to roll aside as the other lunged. The bloody blade struck sparks from the paving stones where he had been. Frantically he continued to roll, coming to his feet with his back against a wall. The madman whirled to follow.

The air was filled with a whir as of angry hornets, and the madman suddenly resembled a feathered pincushion. Conan blinked. The City Guard had arrived at last, a black-cloaked score of archers. They stayed well back, drawing again, for transfixed though he was, the madman still stood. His mouth was a gash emitting a wordless howl of bloodlust, and he hurled his sword at the big Cimmerian.

Conan's blade had no more than a hand's span to travel to deflect the strange blade to clatter in the street. The Guardsmen loosed their arrows once more. Pierced through and through the madman toppled. For a brief moment as he fell, the look of madness faded to be replaced by one of unutterable horror. He hit the pavement dead. Slowly, weapons at the ready, the soldiers closed in on the corpse.

The big Cimmerian slammed his blade home in its sheath with a disgusted grunt. It was unnecessary even to wipe a speck of blood from it. The only blood shed had been his, and every one of those cuts, insignificant as each was, ached with the shame of it. The one attack he had managed to meet cleanly, the thrown sword, could have been met by a ten years' girl.

A Guardsman grabbed the dead man's shoulder and heaved him over onto his back, splintering half a dozen arrows on the stones of the street.

"Easy, Tulio," another growled. "Like as not our pay will be docked for those shafts. Why—"

"Black Erlik's Throne!" Tulio gasped. "It's Lord Melius!"

The knot of mailed men stepped back, leaving Tulio standing alone over the corpse. It was not well to be too near a dead noble, most especially if you had had a hand in killing him, and no matter what he had done. The King's Justice could take strange twists where nobles were concerned.

A livid scar across his broad nose visible beneath the nasal of his helmet, the Guardsmen's grizzled sergeant spat near the corpse. "There's naught to be done for it now. Tulio!" That Guardsman suddenly realized he was alone by the body and jumped, his eyes darting frantically. "Put your cloak over the . . . the noble lord," the sergeant went on. "Move, man!" Reluctantly Tulio complied. The sergeant told off more men. "Abydius, Crato, Jocor, Naso. Grab his arms and legs. Jump! Or do you want to stay here till the flies eat him?"

The four men shuffled forward, muttering as they lifted the body. The sergeant started up the street, and the bearers followed as quickly as they were able, the rest of the troop falling in behind. None gave a second look to Conan.

"Are you slowing that much, Cimmerian?" a gruff voice called.

Conan spun, his angry retort dying on his lips as he saw the bearded man leaning against a shop front. "I'm still faster than you, Hordo, you old robber of dogs."

Nearly as tall as Conan and broader, the bearded man straightened. A rough leather patch covered his left eye, and a scar running from beneath the leather down his cheek pulled that side of his mouth into a permanent sneer, though now the rest of it was bent to a grin. A heavy gold hoop swung from each ear, but if they tempted thieves the well-worn broadsword and dagger at his belt dissuaded them.

"Mayhap you are, Conan," he said. "But what are you doing in Nemedia, aside from taking a lesson on bladesmanship from a middle-aged noble? The last I saw of you, you were on your way to Aghrapur to soldier for King Yildiz."

Hordo was a friend, but he had not always been so. The first time they met, the one-eyed man and a pack of bandits had pegged Conan out on the Zamoran plains at the orders of Karela, a red-haired woman bandit known as the Red Hawk. Later they had ridden together to the Kezankian Mountains to try for treasure stolen by the sorcerer Amanar. From that they had escaped with naught but their lives. Twice more they had met, each time making a try at wealth, each time failing to gain more than enough for one grand carouse in the nearest fleshpots. Conan had to wonder if once again they would have a chance at gold.

"I did," Conan replied, "but I left the service of Turan a year gone and more."

"Trouble over a woman, I'll wager," Hordo chuckled, "knowing you."

Conan shrugged his massive shoulders. He always had trouble over women, it seemed. But then, what man did not?

"And what woman chased you from Sultanapur, Hordo? When last we parted you sat in your own inn with a plump Turanian wife, swearing never again to smuggle so much as a sweetmeat, nor set foot outside Sultanapur until you were carried out to your funeral pyre."

"It was Karela." The one-eyed man's voice was low with embarrassment. He tugged at his thick beard. "I could not give up trying to find word of her, and my wife could not cease nagging me to stop. She said I made a spectacle of myself. People talked, she said, laughed behind my back, said I was strange in the head. She would not have it said she married a man lacking all his brains. She would not stop, and I could not, so I said goodbye one day and never looked back."

"You still look for Karela?"

"She is not dead. I'm sure she lives." He grabbed Conan's arm, a pathetic urgency in his eyes. "I've heard never a whisper, but I'd know if she was dead. I'd know. Have you heard anything? Anything at all?"

Hordo's voice carried anguish. Conan knew that the Red Hawk had indeed survived their expedition into the Kezankians. But to tell Hordo would entail telling how last he saw her—naked and chained in a slave coffle on her way to the auction block. He could explain that he had had but a few coppers in his pouch, not even close to the price of a round-breasted, green-eyed slave in Turan. He could even mention the oath she had made him swear, that he would never lift a hand to save her. She was a woman of pride, Karela was. Or had been. For if Hordo had found no sign of her, it was more than likely the strap had broken her, and that she now danced for the pleasure of a dark-eyed master. And if he told the tale, he might well have to kill his old friend, the man who had always called himself Karela's faithful hound.

"The last I saw of her was in the Kezankians," he said truthfully, "but I'm sure she got out of the mountains alive. No pack of hillmen would have stood a chance against her with a sword in her hand."

Hordo nodded, sighing heavily.

People were venturing back into the street, staring at the bodies that still lay where they had been slain. Here and there a woman fell wailing across a dead husband or child.

Conan looked around for the sword the madman had been carrying. It lay before an open-fronted shop piled high with colorful bolts of cloth. The proprietor was gone, one of the dead or one of those staring at them. The Cimmerian picked up the sword, wiping the congealing blood from the serpentine blade on a bolt of yellow damask.

He hefted the weapon, getting the balance of it. The quillons were worked in a silver filigree that spoke of antiquity, and the ricasso was scribed with calligraphy that formed no words he had ever seen before. But whoever had made the weapon, he was a master. It seemed to become an extension of his arm. Nay, an extension of his mind. Still he could not help thinking of those it had just killed. Men. Women. Children. Struck from behind, or however they could be reached, as they fled. Slashed and hacked as they tried to crawl away. The images were vivid in his brain. He could almost smell their fear sweat and the blood.

He made a disgusted noise in his throat. A sword was a sword, no more. Steel had no guilt. Still, he would not keep it. Take it, yes—a sword was too valuable to be left behind—it would fetch a few silver pieces for his too-light purse.

"You're not keeping that?" Hordo sounded surprised. "The blade's tainted. Women and children." He spat and made the sign to ward off evil.

"Not too tainted to sell," Conan replied. On impulse he swung his fur-trimmed cloak from his shoulders and wrapped it around the sword. Its archaic pattern made it easily recognizable. Perhaps it would not be smart to carry it openly so soon after the death it had brought to Belverus.

"Are you that short of coin, man? I can let you have a little silver, an you need it."

"I've enough." Conan weighed his purse again in his mind. Four days, if he stayed at an inn. Two weeks if he slept in stables. "But how is it you're rich to the point of handing out silver? Have you taken back to the bandit trade, or is it smuggling again?"

"Hsst!" Hordo stepped closer, casting his lone eye about to see if any had heard. "Speak softly of smuggling," he said in a voice meant for the big

Cimmerian's ears alone. "The penalty now is slow impalement, and the crown pays a bounty for information that'd tempt your grandmother."

"Then why are you mixed in it?"

"I didn't say. . . ." The one-eyed man threw up his gnarled hands. "Hannuman's Stones! Yes, I'm in it. Have you no ear or eye that you don't know the prices in this city? The tariffs are more than the cost of the goods. A smuggler can make a fortune. If he lives."

"Maybe you need a partner?" Conan said suggestively.

Hordo hesitated. "'Tis not as it was in Sultanapur. Every cask of wine or length of silk that misses the King's Customs is brought in by one ring."

"For the whole of Nemedia?" Conan said incredulously.

"Aye. Been that way for more than two years, so I understand. I've only been here a year, myself. They're tight as a miser's fist about who they let in, and who they let know what. I get my orders from a man who gets his from somebody I've never seen, who likely gets his orders from somebody else." He shook his heavy head. "I'll try, but I make no promises."

"They can't be as tight as all that," Conan protested, "not if you're one of them after being here no more than a year."

Hordo chuckled and rubbed the side of his broad nose with a spatulate finger. "I'm a special case. I was in Koth, in a tavern in Khorshemish, because I'd heard a rumor . . . well, that's beside the point. Anyway, a fellow, Hassan, who works the Kothian end of the ring heard me asking questions. He had heard of the Red Hawk, admired her no end. When he found out I'd ridden with her, he offered me a job here in Belverus. I was about to the point of boiling my belt for soup, so I took it. If Hassan was here I could get you in in a fingersnap, but he stays in Koth."

"Strange," Conan mused, "that he wouldn't keep you there, too, since he admires the Red Hawk so. No matter. You do what you can. I'll make out."

"I'll try," Hordo said. He squinted at the sun, already well past its height, and shifted awkwardly. "Listen, there's something I have to do. The ring, you understand. I'd ask you along so we could swap lies, but they do not look kindly on people they don't know."

"We've plenty of time."

"Surely. Look you. Meet me at the Sign of the Gored Ox, on the Street of Regrets, just above Hellgate, half a glass or so after sunset." He laughed and clapped Conan on the shoulder. "We'll drink our way from one side of this city to the other."

"From top to bottom," Conan agreed.

As the one-eyed man left, Conan turned, the cloak-wrapped sword beneath his arm, and stopped. An ornate litter, scarlet-curtained, its frame and poles black and gold, stood a little way up the street, the crowd and even the toughs respectful enough to leave a cleared space about it. It was not the litter that arrested him—he had seen others in the streets, carrying fat merchants or sleek noblewomen—but as he had turned the curtain had twitched shut, leaving him with the bare impression of a woman swathed in gray veils till naught but her eyes showed. And he would have sworn, for all the briefness of that glimpse, that those eyes had been looking directly at him. Nay, not looking. Glaring.

Abruptly the front curtain of the litter moved, and apparently an order was passed, for the bearers set off swiftly up the street, away from the big Cimmerian.

Conan shook his head as he watched the litter disappear into the throng. 'Twas not a good way to begin in Belverus, imagining things. Aside from Hordo he knew no one. Taking a firmer grip on his cloak-wrapped bundle, he set out to wile away the time until his meeting with Hordo. He would learn what he could of this city wherein he hoped to forge some future for himself.

The Street of Regrets was the last street above Hellgate. It was the street where people hung on by their fingernails to keep from sliding down into the cauldron of the slum, people who knew despairingly that even if they managed to stay that one street above for their lives, their children would sink into the morass. A few had crawled there from Hellgate, stopping once they were safe above Crop-ear Alley, afraid to go further into a city they did not understand, ignoring the stench that told them how little distance they had come whenever the wind blew from the south. Those who truly escaped Hellgate did not stop on the Street of Regrets, not even for a day or an hour. But they were fewest of the few.

On such a street all folk desire to forget what lies ahead at the next turning, the next dawning, what lies behind on a thousand nights past. The Street of Regrets was a frantic, frenetic carnival. Corner musicians with lutes and zithers and flutes sent out frenzied music to compete with the laughter that filled the air, laughter raucous, drunken, hysterical, forced. Jugglers with balls and rings, clubs and flashing knives worked their art for the strumpets that strolled the street, half naked in brief silks, burnished brass bangles and stilted sandals, flaunting their wares for whoever had a coin. Their most lascivious wriggles and flagrant self-caresses, however, were offered to those well-dressed oglers from the Upper Town, standing out in the motley crowd as if they bore signs, come to witness what they thought was the depths of Hellgate depravity. And over it all floated the laughter.

The Sign of the Gored Ox was what Conan expected on such a street. At one end of a common room that reeked of stale wine was a small platform where three plumply rounded women in sheer yellow silk gyrated their hips and breasts to the sybaritic flutes. They were largely ignored by the men at the crowded tables, intent on drink or cards or dice. A brassy-haired trull, one strip of dark blue silk wrapped around and around her body in such a way as to leave much plump flesh bare, maintained a fixed smile as a fat Corinthian in striped robes stroked her as if attempting to calculate her price by the pound.

Another prostitute, her hair an impossible red, eyed the breadth of Conan's shoulders and adjusted the gilded halter that supported her large round breasts. She swayed toward him, wetting her full lips suggestively, then stopped with a disappointed frown when he shook his head. He could see Hordo nowhere in the drunken mass; there would be time to find women when they were together.

There was one woman in the tavern who stood out from the rest. Seated alone against the wall, her winecup untouched in front of her, she seemed to be the only one there watching the dancers. Long black hair swirled below her shoulders, and large, hazel eyes and bee-stung lips gave her a beauty that outshone any of the doxies by far. Yet she was not of the sisterhood of the night. That much was certain from the simple robe of white cotton that covered her from neck to ankles. It was as out of place as she, that robe, not gaudy or revealing enough for a denizen of the Street of Regrets, lacking the ornate embroideries and rich fabrics of the women of the Upper Town who came to sample wickedness by sweating beneath one who might be a murderer or worse.

Women came later, he reminded himself. Shifting the cloak-wrapped sword beneath his arm, he looked about for an empty table.

From what seemed rather a bundle of rags than a man, a bony hand reached out to pluck at his tunic. A thin, rasping voice emerged from a toothless mouth. "Ho, Cimmerian, where go you with that strange blade of murder?"

Conan felt the hair stir on the nape of his neck. The old man, too emaciated to be wrinkled, had a filthy rag tied across where his eyes should be. But even had he had eyes, how could he have known what was in the cloak? Or that Conan was from Cimmeria?

"What do you know of me, old man?" Conan asked. "And how do you know it, without sight?"

The old man cackled shrilly, touching the bandage across his eyes with a crooked stick he carried. "When the gods took these, they gave me other ways of seeing. As I do not see with eyes, I do not see what eyes see, but . . . other things."

"I've heard of such," Conan muttered. "And seen stranger still. What more can you tell me of myself?"

"Oh, much and much, young sir. You will know the love of many women, queens and peasant girls alike, and many between in station. You will live long, and gain a crown, and your death will be shrouded in legend."

"Bull dung!" Hordo grunted, thrusting his head past Conan's shoulder.

"I was wondering where you were," Conan said. "The old man knew I'm Cimmerian."

"An earful of your barbarous accent, and he made a lucky guess. Let's get a table and a pitcher of wine."

Conan shook his head. "I didn't speak, but he knew. Tell me, old man. What lies weeks ahead for me, instead of years?"

The blind man had been listening with a pained expression, tilting his head to catch their words. Now his toothless smile returned. "As for that," he said. He lifted his hand, thumb rubbing his fingertips, then abruptly flattened it, palm up. "I am a poor man, as you can see, young sir."

The big Cimmerian stuck two fingers into the pouch at his belt. It was light enough, filled more with copper than silver, and little enough of either, but he drew out a silver queenshead and dropped it on the old man's leathery palm.

Hordo sighed in exasperation. "I know a haruspex and three astrologers would charge half that together, and give you a better telling than you'll find in this place."

The old man's fingertips drifted lightly over the face of the coin. "A generous man," he murmured. The coin disappeared beneath his rags. "Give me your hand. The right one."

"A palmist with no eyes," Hordo laughed, but Conan stuck out his hand.

As swiftly as they had moved over the coin the old man's fingers traced the lines of the Cimmerian's hand, marking the callouses and old scars. He began to speak, and though his voice was still thin, the cackle was gone. There was strength, even power in it.

"Beware the woman of sapphires and gold. For her love of power she would seal your doom. Beware the woman of emeralds and ruby. For her love of you she would watch you die. Beware the man who seeks a throne. Beware the man whose soul is clay. Beware the gratitude of kings." To Conan his voice grew louder, but no one else looked up from a winecup as he broke into a sing-song chant. "Save a throne, save a king, kill a king, or die. Whatever comes, whatever is, mark well your time to fly."

"That's dour enough to sour new wine," Hordo muttered.

"And makes little sense, besides," Conan added. "Can you make it no plainer?"

The old man dropped Conan's hand with a shrug. "Could I say my prophecies plainer," he said drily, "I'd live in a palace instead of a pigsty in Hellgate."

Stick tapping, he hobbled toward the street, deftly avoiding tables and drunken revelers alike.

"But mark my words, Conan of Cimmeria," he called over his shoulder from the doorway. "My prophecies always tell true." And he disappeared into the feverish maelstrom outside.

"Old fool," Hordo grumbled. "If you want good advice, go to a licensed astrologer. None of these hedge-row charlatans."

"I never spoke my name," Conan said quietly.

Hordo blinked, and scrubbed his mouth with the back of his calloused hand. "I need a drink, Cimmerian."

The scarlet-haired strumpet was rising from a table, leading a burly Ophirian footpad toward the stairs that led above, where rooms were rented by the turn of the glass. Conan plopped down on a vacated stool, motioning Hordo to the other. As he laid the cloak-wrapped sword on the table, the one-eyed man grabbed the arm of a doe-eyed serving girl, her pale breasts and buttocks almost covered by two strips of green muslin.

"Wine," Hordo ordered. "The biggest pitcher you have. And two cups." Deftly she slipped from his grasp and sped away.

"Have you yet spoken to your friends of me?" Conan asked.

Hordo sighed heavily, shaking his head. "I spoke, but the answer was no. The work is light here, Conan, and the gold flows free, but I am reduced to taking orders from a man named Eranius, a fat bastard with a squint and a smell like a dungheap. This bag of slime lectured me—imagine you me, standing still for a lecture?—about trusting strangers in these dangerous times. Dangerous times. Bah!"

"'Tis no great matter," Conan said. Yet he had hoped to work again with this bearded bear of a man. There were good memories between them.

The serving girl returned, setting two leathern jacks and a rough clay pitcher half again the size of a man's head on the table. She filled the jacks and waited with her hand out.

Hordo rummaged out the coppers to pay, at the same time giving her a sly pinch. "Off with you, girl," he laughed, "before we decide we want more than you're willing to sell."

Rubbing her plump buttock she left, but with a steamy-eyed look at Conan that said she might not be averse to selling more were he buying.

"I told him you were no stranger," Hordo continued, "told him much of you, of our smuggling in Sultanapur. He'd not even listen. Told me you sounded a dangerous sort. Told me to stay away from you. Can you imagine him thinking I'd take an order like that?"

"I cannot," Conan agreed.

Suddenly the Cimmerian felt the ghost of a touch near his pouch. His big hand darted back, captured a slender wrist and hauled its owner before him.

Golden curls surrounded a face of child-like innocence set with guileless blue eyes, but the lush breasts straining a narrow strip of red silk named her profession, as did the girdle of copper coins low on her hips, from which hung panels of transparent red that barely covered the inner curves of her thighs before and the inner slopes of her rounded buttocks behind. Her fist above his entrapping hand was clenched tightly.

"There's a woman of sapphires and gold," Hordo laughed. "What's your price, girl?"

"Next time," Conan said to the girl, "don't try a man sober enough to notice how clumsy your touch is."

The girl put on a seductive smile like a mask. "You mistake me. I wanted to touch you. I'd not be expensive, for one as handsome as you, and the herbalist says I'm completely cured."

"Herbalist!" Hordo spluttered in his wine. "Get your hand off her, Conan! There's nine and twenty kinds of pox in this city, and if she's had one, she likely has the other twenty-eight yet."

"And tells me of it right away," Conan mused.

He increased the pressure of his grip slightly. Sweat popped out on her forehead; her generous mouth opened in a small cry, and her fingers unclenched to drop two silver coins into Conan's free hand. In a flash he pulled her close, her arm held behind her back, her full breasts crushed against his massive chest, her frightened, sky-blue eyes staring into his.

"The truth, girl," he said. "Are you thief, whore, or both? The truth, and I'll let you go free. The first hint of a lie, and I'll take you upstairs to get my money's worth."

She wet her lips slowly. "You'll truly let me go?" she whispered. Conan nodded, and her shuddering breath flattened her breasts pleasantly against his chest. "I am no doxy," she said at last.

Hordo grunted. "A thief, then. I'll still wager she has the pox, though."

"It's a dangerous game you play, girl," Conan said.

She tossed her blonde head defiantly. "Who notices one more strumpet among many? I take only a few coins from each, and each thinks he spent them in his cups. And once I mention the herbalist none want the wares they think I offer." Abruptly she brought her lips to within a breath of his. "I'm not a whore," she murmured, "but I could enjoy a night spent in your arms."

"Not a whore," Conan laughed, "but a thief. I know thieves. I'd wake with purse, and cloak, and sword, and mayhap even my boots gone." Her eyes flashed, the guilelessness disappearing for an instant in anger, and she writhed helplessly within the iron band of his arm. "Your luck is gone this night, girl. I sense it." Abruptly he released her. For a moment she stood in disbelief; then his open palm cracking across her buttocks lifted her onto her toes with a squeal that drew laughter from nearby tables. "On your way, girl," Conan said. "Your luck is gone."

"I go where I will," she replied angrily, and darted away, deeper into the tavern.

Dismissing her from his mind he turned back to his wine, drinking deep. Over the rim of the leathern jack his eyes met those of the girl who had seemed out of place. She was looking at him with what was clearly approval, though not invitation, just as clearly. And she was writing on a scrap of parchment. He would wager there were not a handful of women on that entire street who could read or write so much as their own names. Nor many men, for that matter.

"Not for us," Hordo said, noticing the direction of his gaze. "Whatever she is, she's no daughter of the streets dressed like that."

"I care not what she is," Conan said, not entirely truthfully. She was beautiful, and he was willing to admit his own weakness for beautiful women. "At the moment I care about finding employment before I can no longer afford any woman at all. I spent the day walking through the city. I saw many men with bodyguards. There's not so much gold in it as in smuggling, but I've done it before, and I likely will again."

Hordo nodded. "There's plenty enough of that sort of work. Every man who had a bodyguard a year ago has five now. Some of the fatter merchants, like Fabius Palian and Enaro Ostorian, have entire Free-Companies in their pay. There the real money is to be made, hiring out your own Free-Company."

"If you have the gold to raise it in the first place," Conan agreed. "I couldn't buy armor for one man, let alone a company."

The one-eyed man drew a finger through a puddle of wine on the table. "Since the trouble started, half of what we smuggle in is arms. Tariff on a good sword is more than the price used to be." He met Conan's gaze. "Unless I miscount, we could steal enough to outfit a company without anyone being the wiser."

"We, Hordo?"

"Hannuman's Stones, man! When they start telling me who my friends can be, I'm not much longer for smuggling."

"Then it's a matter of getting silver enough for enlistment bonuses. For, say, fifty men—"

"Gold," Hordo cut him off. "The going rate is a gold mark a man."

Conan whistled between his teeth. "It's not likely I'll see that much in one place. Unless you. . . ."

Hordo shook his head sadly. "You know me, Cimmerian. I like women, drink and dice too much for gold to stay long with me."

"Thief!" someone shouted. "We've caught a thief!"

Conan looked around to see the innocent-faced blonde struggling between a bulky, bearded man in a greasy blue tunic and a tall fellow with a weaselly look to his close-set eyes.

"Caught her with her hand in my purse!" the bearded man shouted.

Obscene comments rose amid the tavern's laughter.

"I told her her luck was gone," Conan muttered.

The blonde screamed as the bearded man ripped the strip of silk from her breasts, then tossed her up to the skinny man, who had climbed onto a table. Despite her struggles, he quickly tore away the rest of her flimsy garb and displayed her naked to the tavern.

The bearded man shook a dice cup over his head. "Who'll toss for a chance?" Men crowded round him. "Let us go," Conan said. "I don't want to watch this." He gathered up the cloak-wrapped sword and started for the street.

Hordo took one regretful look at the barely touched pitcher of wine, then followed.

At the door Conan caught the eye of the young woman in the plain cotton dress once more. She was staring at him again, but this time her face bore disapproval. What had he done, he wondered. Not that it mattered. He had more important concerns on his mind than women. Followed by Hordo, he ducked through the doorway.

Full dark was on the Street of Regrets, and the frenzy of its denizens had grown as if by motion they could warm themselves against the chill of night. Whores no longer strutted sensuously, but rather half-ran from potential patron to potential patron. Acrobats twisted and tumbled in defiance of gravity and broken bones as though for King Garian himself, receiving hollow, drunken laughter in payment, yet tumbling on.

Conan paused to watch a fire-juggler, his six blazing brands describing slow arcs above his bald head. A small ever-changing knot of people stood watching as well. Three came and two left even as the Cimmerian stopped. There were better shows that night on the street than a juggler. Conan fingered a copper out of his pouch and tossed it into the cap the quick-handed man had laid on the ground. There were only two in the cap to precede it. To Conan's surprise the juggler suddenly turned toward him, half-bowing as he kept the brands aloft, as if acknowledging a generous patron. As he straightened, he began to caper, legs kicking high, fiery batons spinning now so that it seemed his feet were always in the midst of the circles they described.

Hordo pulled at Conan's arm, drawing the muscular youth away down the street. "For a copper," the one-eyed man muttered disgustedly. "Time was, it'd have taken a silver piece to get that out of one of them. Maybe more."

"This city is gone mad," Conan said. "Never have I seen so many beggars this side of the Vilayet Sea. The poor are poorer, and more in number, than in any three other cities. Peddlers charge prices that would choke a Guild Merchant in Sultanapur, and wear faces like they were going bankrupt. More than half a silver queenshead for a pitcher of wine, but a juggler does his best trick for a copper. I haven't seen a soul who looks to care if tomorrow comes or no. What happens here?"

"What am I, Cimmerian? A scholar? A priest? 'Tis said the throne is cursed, that Garian is cursed by the gods."

Conan involuntarily made the sign against evil. Curses were nothing to fool with. Several people noticed and shied away from the big man. They had evil enough in their lives without being touched by the evil that troubled him.

"This curse," the big Cimmerian said after a time, "is it real? I mean, have the priests and astrologers spoken of it? Confirmed it?"

"I've heard nothing of that," Hordo admitted. "But it's spoken on every street corner. Everyone knows it."

"Hannuman's Stones," Conan snorted. "You know as well as I do that anything everyone knows is usually a lie. Is there any proof at all of a curse?"

"That there is, Cimmerian," Hordo said, poking a blunt finger at Conan for emphasis. "On the very day Garian ascended the Dragon Throne—the very day, mind you—a monster ran loose in the streets of Belverus. Killed better than a score of people. Looked like a man, if you made a man out of clay, then half melted him. Thing is, a lot of people who saw it said it looked something like Garian, too."

"A man made out of clay," Conan said softly, thinking of the blind man's prophecy.

"Pay no attention to that blind old fool," Hordo counseled. "Besides, the monster's dead. Wasn't those stay-in-the-barracks City Guards who did it, though. An old woman, frightened half out of her wits, threw an oil lamp at it. Covered it with burning oil. Left nothing but a pile of ash. The City Guard was going to take the old woman in, for 'questioning' they said, till her neighbors chased them off. Pelted them with chamber pots."

"Come," Conan said, turning down a narrow street.

Hordo hesitated. "You realize we're going into Hellgate?"

"We're being followed. Ever since the Gored Ox," Conan said. "I want to find out who. This way."

The street narrowed and twisted, and the laughter and the light of the Street of Regrets were quickly lost. The stench of offal and urine thickened. There was no paving here. The grate of their boots on gravel and the sounds of their own breathing were the loudest things to be heard. They moved through darkness, broken only occasionally by a pool of light from a window high enough for its owner to feel some safety.

"Talk," Conan said. "Anything. What kind of king is Garian?"

"Talk, he says," Hordo muttered. "Bel save us from you. . . ." He sighed heavily. "He's a king. What more is there? I hold no brief for any king. No more did you, last I saw you."

"Nor do I now. But talk. We're drunk, and too senseless to be silent, while walking Hellgate in the middle of the night." He eased his broadsword in its scabbard. A hint of light from a window far above glinted on his face; his eyes seemed to gleam in the dark like those of a forest animal. A hunting animal.

Hordo stumbled over something that made ripe squelching sounds beneath his boots. "Vara's Guts and Bones! Let me see. Garian. At least he got rid of the sorcerers. I like kings better than I do sorcerers."

"How did he do that?" Conan asked, but his ear was bent for sounds from behind rather than the answer. Was that a foot on gravel?

"Oh, three days after he took the throne he executed all the sorcerers still at court. Gethenius, his father, had had dozens of them in the palace. Garian told no one what he intended. Some few did leave, giving one excuse or another, but the rest. . . . Garian gave orders to the Golden Leopards three glasses past midnight. By dawn every sorcerer still in the palace had been dragged out of bed and beheaded. Those who fled were true sorcerers, Garian said, and could keep their wealth. These, who couldn't even discover he intended their deaths, were charlatans and parasites. He had their belongings distributed to the poor, even in Hellgate. Last good thing he's done."

"Interesting," Conan said absently. In the dark his keen eyes picked out one shadow from another. There was a crossing alley ahead. And behind? Yes. That was the mutter of someone who had stepped in whatever had fouled Hordo's boots. "Say on," he said. His blade whispered on leather as it eased from its sheath.

The one-eyed man lifted his eyebrow at what Conan had done, then he, too, drew his sword. Both men walked with steel swinging easily in their fists.

"That curse," Hordo continued conversationally. "Gethenius took ill a fortnight after the planting, and as soon as he took to his bed the rains stopped. It rained in Ophir. It rained in Aquilonia. But not in Nemedia. The sicker Gethenius got and the closer Garian came to the throne, the worse the drought grew. The day he took the throne the fields were dry as powdered bone. And they gave about as much harvest. Tell me that's not proof of a curse."

They reached the alley; Conan side-stepped into its shadows, motioning Hordo to go on. The burly one-eyed man shambled on into the dark ahead, his words fading slowly.

"With the crops gone, Garian bought grain in Aquilonia, and raised tariffs to pay for it. Fool brigands on the border starting burning the grain wagons, so he raises tariffs again to hire more guards for the wagons, and to buy more grain, which the fools on the border still burn. High tariffs make for good smuggling, but I'd just as soon he. . . ."

Conan waited, listening. Briefly he considered unwrapping the madman's blade, but he could still feel the taint to it, even through the cloak. He propped it behind him against the wall. The following footsteps came closer, hurrying, yet hesitant. But one set, he was sure now.

A slight, cloak-shrouded shape moved into the alley crossing, pausing in the dark, all its attention on Hordo's faintly receding footsteps. Conan took a quick step forward, left hand coming down on the figure's shoulder. Spinning the shape, he slammed it against the wall. Breath whooshed out of his opponent. Blade across the figure's throat, he dragged it down to the alley to a pool of light. His mouth fell open as he saw the other's face. It was the girl who had seemed so out of place at the Gored Ox.

There was fear in her large, hazel eyes, but when she spoke her voice was under control. "Do you intend killing me? I don't suppose killing a woman would be beyond you, since you abandon them with such ease."

"What are you talking about?" he rasped. "Are you working with footpads, girl?" He found it hard to believe she could be, but he had seen stranger things.

"Of course not," she replied. "I'm a poet. My name is Ariane. If you don't intend to cut my throat, could you take that sword away? Do you know what they were doing when I left? Do you have any idea?"

"Crom!" he muttered in confusion at her sudden torrent. Still, he lowered his blade.

She swallowed ostentatiously, and fixed him with a level gaze. "They were casting dice for who would have the first . . . turn with her. Every man there intended to take one. And in the meanwhile they were passing her about, beating her buttocks till they looked like ripe plums."

"The blonde thief," he exclaimed. "You're talking about the blonde thief. Do you mean to say you followed me into Hellgate just to tell me that?"

"I didn't know you were coming into Hellgate," she said angrily. "I do things on impulse. But what business is it of yours where I go? I'm not a slave. Certainly not yours. That poor girl. After you let her go I thought you had some sympathy for her, thought you might be different from the rest despite your rather violent appearance, but—"

"You knew she was a thief?" he broke in.

Her face turned defensive. "She has to live, too. I don't suppose you know about the things that drive people to become thieves, about being poor and hungry. Not you with your great sword, and your muscles, and—"

"Shut up!" he shouted, and immediately dropped his voice, taking a quick look up and down the alley. It was well not to attract attention in a place like Hellgate. When he looked back at her she was staring at him, open-mouthed. "I know about being poor," he said quietly, "about being hungry, and about being a thief. I was all of them before I was old enough to shave my face."

"I'm sorry," she said slowly, and he had the irritating feeling that it was as much for his youthful hunger as for what she had said.

"As for the girl. She threw away the chance I gave her. I told her her luck was gone, and it was, if I caught her, and you saw her."

"Maybe I should have spoken to her when I saw her," Ariane sighed.

Conan shook his head. "What kind of woman are you? A poet, you say. You sit in a tavern on the Street of Regrets, worrying about thieves. You dress like a shopkeeper's virgin daughter, and speak with the accents of a noblewoman. You chase me into Hellgate to upbraid me." He laughed, deep in his chest. "When Hordo returns we'll escort you back to the Street of Regrets, and may Mitra save the doxies and cut purses from you."

A dangerous light kindled in her eyes. "I *am* a poet, and a good one. And what's wrong with the way I dress? I suppose you'd rather I wore a few skimpy strips of silk and wriggled like—"

He clamped a hand over her mouth, not breathing while he listened. Her eyes were large and liquid on his face. It came again, that sound that had pricked his ear. The rasp of steel sliding from a sheath.

Shoving the girl further up the narrow confines of the dark alley, Conan spun just as the first man rushed him. The Cimmerian's blade slashed out his throat even while his sword was going up.

The first of the three following on his heels stumbled against the collapsing body, then shrieked as Conan's steel sought the juncture of shoulder and neck. From behind the men came a scream that ended in a gurgle, and a cry of "The Red Hawk!" told the Cimmerian youth that Hordo had joined the fray. The man facing Conan dropped into a guard position, nervously trying to see the combat behind him without taking his eyes from the massive youth.

Suddenly Conan shouted, shifting his shoulders as if he intended an overhand blow. His opponent's sword flashed up to block. Conan's lunge brought them face to face, the Cimmerian's blade projecting a foot through the other's back. He stared into the dying man's eyes, even in the darkness able to see the despair that came with the realization of death. Then only death was there. He tugged his blade free and wiped it on the dead man's cloak.

"Are you hurt, Conan?" Hordo called, stumbling past the bodies in the narrow alley.

"Just wiping my—" A foul odor filled Conan's nostrils. "Crom! What is that?"

"I slipped in something," Hordo replied sourly. "That's why I was so long getting back. Who's the wench?"

"I'm not a wench," Ariane said.

"Her name's Ariane," Conan said. He raised his eyebrows as he watched her slide a very efficient-looking little dagger inside her dress. "You didn't draw that against me, girl."

"I had it," she replied. "Perhaps I didn't think to need it with you. Are these friends of yours?"

"Footpads," he snorted.

Hordo straightened from examining one of the corpses. "Mayhap you ought to take a look, Conan. They're dressed well for Hellgate."

"Some of Hellgate's better citizens." The Cimmerian's nose wrinkled. "Hordo, as soon as we return Ariane to the Street of Regrets, you're going to find a bathhouse. That is, if you intend to keep drinking with me." Hordo muttered something under his breath.

"If it doesn't have to be a bathhouse," Ariane began, then stopped, chewing her full lower lip in indecision. Finally, she nodded. "It will be all right," she said to herself. "There's an inn called the Sign of Thestis, just off the Street of Regrets. It has baths. You can come as my guests, for the night at least."

"Thestis!" Hordo crowed. "Whoever heard of an inn called after the goddess of music and such?"

"I have," Ariane said with some asperity. "If you are invited, the bed, food and wine are free, though you're expected to contribute if you can. You'll understand when you see it. Well? Do you come, or do you stink until you can pay two silver pieces to a bathhouse?"

"Why?" Conan asked. "You sounded not so friendly a minute or two gone."

"You interest me," Ariane said simply.

Hordo snickered, and Conan suddenly wished the one-eyed man smelled just a little better, so he could get close enough to thump him. Hastily the Cimmerian gathered up the ancient sword in the cloak.

"Let's get out of here," he said, "before we attract more vermin."

Hurriedly they picked their way back out of Hellgate.

IV

Albanus angrily jerked the cord of his gold-embroidered dressing robe tight about his waist as he stalked into the carpeted ante-chamber of his sleeping apartments. Golden lamps cast a soft light on the walls, where basrelief depicted scenes from the life of Bragoras, the ancient, half-legendary King of Nemedia from whom Albanus claimed pure and unsullied descent through both his father and mother.

The hawk-faced lord had left orders to be called from his bed whenever the two men now awaiting him arrived. Neither Vegentius nor Demetrio appeared to have slept at all. The soldier's surcoat, worked with the Golden Leopard, was wrinkled and damp with sweat, while the eyes of the slender youth were haggard.

"What have you discovered?" Albanus demanded without preliminary.

Demetrio shrugged and sniffed at his ever-present pomander.

Vegentius stiffened in tired anger at the peremptory tone, and spoke harshly. "Nothing. The sword's gone. Let it be. We don't need it, and you've already gotten Melius killed, giving him the thing in the first place. Though, Mitra knows, the man is little enough loss."

"How was I to know the accursed blade would seize his mind?" Albanus broke out. Hands knotted to keep them from shaking, he managed to regain control. "The sword," he said in a somewhat calmer voice, "must be recovered. Another incident like today, another man going berserk with that blade in his hands, and Garian will know there's sorcery loose in Nemedia again. Even with his dislike of magicks he might well bring his own sorcerer to court, for protection. Do you think I'll so easily let my plans be thwarted?"

"Our plans," Demetrio reminded gently from behind his pomander.

Albanus smiled slightly, a curving of the lips, nothing more. "Our plans," he agreed. Then even that slight softness was gone. "The Guardsmen were put to the question, were they not, Vegentius? After all, they did kill Lord Melius."

Vegentius gave a short nod. "All except their sergeant, who disappeared from the barracks when my Golden Leopards came to make the arrests. 'Twas guilt sent him running, mark my words. He knows something."

"Most likely," Demetrio murmured, "he knew what methods of questioning would be used."

"Unless he took the sword," Albanus said. "What did they say of that under the question?"

"Little enough," Vegentius sighed. "For the most part they begged for mercy. All they knew was that they were ordered to stop a madman who was slaughtering people in the Market District. They found him fighting a northern barbarian and killed him. When they discovered they'd slain a lord, they were so terrified they had no thought for the sword. They didn't even bring in the barbarian."

"He was still alive?" Albanus said, surprised. "He must be a master swordsman."

Vegentius laughed disparagingly. "Melius barely knew one end of a blade from the other."

"The skill is in the blade," Albanus said. "Six masters of the sword were slain in the making of it, their blood used for quenching, their bones burned to heat it, the essence of their art infused into its metal."

"Slash and hack, that's all Vegentius knows." Demetrio's voice dripped mockery. "But the art of steel. . . ." His blade whipped from its sheath. Knees bent, he danced across the colorfully woven carpet, his sword working intricate figures in the air.

"That fancy work may be good enough for first-blood duels among the gently born," Vegentius sneered, "but 'tis a different matter in battle, when your life hangs on your blade."

"Enough!" Albanus snapped. "Both of you, enough!" He drew a ragged breath. One day he would let them fight, for his entertainment, then have the winner impaled. But now was not the time. Thirty years he had worked for this. Too much time, too much effort, too much humiliating terror to allow it all to be ruined now. "That barbarian may have taken the sword. Find him! Find that blade!"

"I've already started," the square-faced soldier said smugly. "I sent word to Taras. He'll have had his alley rats hunting all night."

"Good." Albanus rubbed his hands together, making a sound like dry parchment rustling. "And you, Demetrio. What have you been doing to find the blade?"

"Asking ten thousand questions," the slender noble replied wearily. "From the Street of Regrets to the House of a Thousand Orchids. I heard nothing. If Vegentius had thought to let me know of this barbarian it would have made my searching easier."

Vegentius examined his nails with a complacent smile. "Who'd have thought to look for you in the House of a Thousand Orchids? They provide only women to their customers."

Demetrio slammed his sword back into its sheath as if he were driving it into the soldier's heart. Before he could open his mouth, though, Albanus spoke.

"There's no time for this petty bickering. Find that sword. Steal it, buy it, I care not, but get it. And without attracting attention."

"And if its possessor has discovered its properties?" Demetrio asked.

"Then kill him," Albanus said smoothly. "Or her." He turned to go.

"One more thing," Vegentius said abruptly. "Taras wants to meet with you."

Albanus turned back to face them, his eyes black flints. "That scum dares? He should be licking the paving stones in gratitude for the gold he's given."

"He's afraid," Vegentius said. "Him and some of the others who know a little of what they really do. I can cow them, but even gold won't put their guts back unless they see you face to face and hear you tell them it all will happen as they've been told."

"Mitra blast them!" Albanus' eyes went to the bas-relief on the walls. Had Bragoras had to deal with such? "Very well. Arrange you a meeting in some out-of-the-way place."

"It will be done," the soldier replied.

Albanus smiled suddenly, the first genuine smile the others had ever seen on his face. "When I am on the throne, this Taras and his daggermen will be flayed alive in the Plaza of Kings. A good king should be seen to protect his people against such as they." He barked a laugh. "Now get you gone. When next I see you, bear a report of success."

He left with as little ceremony as he had come, for already he began to feel beyond the courtesies ordinary men offered one another. They were fools in any case, unable to realize that he saw them no differently than he saw Taras. Or that he would deal with them as harshly in the end. And if they would betray one king, they would betray another.

Inside his dimly lit bedchamber he strode impatiently to a large square sheet of transparent crystal hung on the wall. The thin crystal was undecorated save for odd markings around its outer edge, markings that lay entirely within the crystal. In the light from a single, small gold tripod lamp the markings were almost invisible, but from long practice Albanus' fingers touched the proper ones in the proper sequence, intoning words in a language three millennia dead.

As his finger lifted from the last, the crystal darkened to a deep silvery blue. Slowly pictures formed within it. In the crystal men moved and gestured, talking though no sound could be heard. Albanus gazed on Garian, who thought himself safe in the Royal Palace, conferring with long-bearded Sulpicius and bald Malaric, his two most trusted councelors.

The King was a tall man, heavily muscled still from a boyhood spent with the army, but now beginning to show a smooth layer of fat from half a year of inactivity on the throne. His square-jawed face with its deep-set dark eyes had lost some of the openness it had once had. Sitting on the throne was responsible for that change as well.

Albanus' hands moved around the rim of the crystal again, and Garian's face swelled until it filled the entire square.

"Why do you do that so often?"

The blonde who spoke watched him with sapphire cat eyes from the satin cushions of his bed. She stretched langorously, her skin gleaming like honeyed ivory in the dimness, her dancer's legs seeming even longer as she pointed her toes. Her large, pear-shaped breasts lifted as she arched her slender back. Albanus felt his throat thicken.

"Why do you not speak?" she asked, her voice all pure innocence.

Bitch, he thought. "It's as if he were here, Sularia, watching his mistress writhe and moan beneath me."

"Is that all I am to you?" Her tone was sultry now, caressing like warm oil. "A means of striking at Garian?"

"Yes," he said cruelly. "An he had a wife or a daughter, they would take their turns with you in my bed."

Her eyes drifted to the face in the crystal. "He has no time for a mistress, much less a wife. Of course, you are responsible for the many troubles that take his time. What would your fellows think, an they knew you took the risk of seducing the King's mistress to your bed?"

"Was it a risk?" His face hardened dangerously. "Are you a risk?"

She shifted in the cushions so that her head was toward him, her hips twisted to emphasize their curve against the smallness of her waist. "I am no risk," she said softly. "I wish only to serve you."

"Why?" he persisted. "At first I meant you only for my bed, but of your own will you began to spy in the palace, coming to kneel at my feet and whisper of who did what and who said what. Why?"

"Power," she breathed. "It is an ability I have, to sense power in men, to sense men who will have power. I am drawn to such men as a moth to the flame. I sense the power in you, greater than the power in Garian."

"You sense the power." His eyes lidded, and he spoke almost to himself. "I can feel the power inside, too. I've always felt it, known it was there. I was born to be king, to raise Nemedia to an empire. And you are the first other to realize it. Soon the people will take to the streets of Belverus with swords in hand to demand that Garian abdicate in my favor. Very soon. And on that day I will raise you to the nobility, Sularia. Lady Sularia."

"I thank my king."

Suddenly he unbelted his dressing robe and threw it off, turning so that the man in the crystal—if he were actually able to see from it—would have a clear view of the bed. "Come and worship your king," he commanded.

Mouth curving in a wet-lipped smile, she crawled to him.

As Conan made his way down to the common room at the Sign of Thestis the next morning, he wondered again if he had fallen into a nest of lunatics. Two lyres, four zithers, three flutes and six harps of assorted sizes were being played, but by musicians scattered about the room, and no two playing the same tune. One man stood declaiming verse to a wall with full gesticulations, as if performing for a wealthy patron. A dozen young men and women at a large table covered with bits of sculpture shouted over the music, telling one another in detail what was wrong with everyone else's work. Three men at the foot of the stairs also shouted at one another, all three simultaneously, about when morally reprehensible action was morally required. At least, that was what he thought they were shouting about. All the men and women in the room, none past their mid-twenties, were shouting about one thing or another.

He and Hordo had been made welcome the night before, after a fashion. There had been but a score of people in the inn then. If it was an inn. That was another thing the Cimmerian doubted. The lot of them had stared as if Ariane had brought back two Brythunian bears. And among that lot, with no more weapons than a few belt knives for cutting meat, perhaps they had seemed so.

While Hordo had gone out back to the baths—wooden tubs sitting on the dirt in a narrow court, not the marble palaces to cleanliness and indolence found elsewhere in the city—the odd youths had crowded around Conan, refilling his cup with cheap wine whenever it was in danger of becoming empty and prodding him to tell stories. And when Hordo returned they pressed him, too, for tales. Long into the night and the small hours of the morning, Conan and the one-eyed man had vied to top the other's last tale.

Those strange young men and women—artists, some said they were, others musicians, and still others philosophers—listened as if hearing of another world. Oft times those who called themselves philosophers made comments more than passing strange, not a one of which Conan had understood. It had taken him a while to realize that none of the others understood them either. Always there was a tick of silence punctuating each comment while the rest watched him who made it to see if they were supposed to nod solemnly at the pontification or laugh at the witticism. A time or two Conan had thought one of them was making fun of him, but he had done nothing. It would not have been proper to kill a man when he was not sure.

At the foot of the stairs he pushed past the philosophers—none of the three even noticed his passing—and stopped in astonishment. Ariane stood on a table in the corner of the room. Naked. She was slim, but her breasts were pleasantly full, her waist tiny above sweetly rounded hips.

He swung his cloak from his shoulders—the wavy-bladed sword was safely hidden in the tiny room he had been given for the night—and stalked across the room to thrust the garment up to her.

"Here, girl. You're not the sort for this kind of entertainment. If you need money, I've enough to feed both of us for a time."

For a moment she looked down at him, hands on hips and eyes unreadable, then astounded him by throwing back her head and laughing. His face reddened; he little enjoyed being laughed at. Instantly she dropped to her knees on the table, her face a picture of contrition. The way her breasts bounced within a handspan of his nose made his forehead suddenly grow beads of sweat.

"I'm sorry, Conan," she said softly, or what passed for softly in the din. "That may have been the nicest thing anyone has ever said to me. I shouldn't have laughed."

"If you want to exhibit yourself naked," he replied gruffly, "why not go to a tavern where there's a bit of money in it?"

"Do you see those people?" She pointed out three men and two women seated near the table, each with a piece of parchment fastened to a board and a bit of charcoal in hand, and each glaring impatiently at the girl and him. "I pose for them. They don't have the money to hire someone, so I do them a favor."

"Out in front of everybody?" he said incredulously.

"There isn't much room, Conan," she said, amusement plain in her voice. "Besides, everyone here is an artist of one sort or another. They do not even notice."

Eyeing her curves, he was willing to wager differently. But all he said was, "I suppose you can do what you want."

"You suppose right."

She waved to the people sketching and hopped down from the table, producing any number of interesting jiggles and bounces. He wished she would stop leaping about like that while she had her clothes off. It was all he could do not to throw her over his shoulder and take her back up to his room. Then he noticed a twinkle in her eye and a slight flush on her cheek. She knew the effect she had on him.

Deftly she took the cloak out of his hands and wrapped it chastely around her. "At the moment I would like to have some wine. With you." He looked at the cloak, raising an eyebrow questioningly, and she giggled. "It's different up there. There I'm posing. Down here I'm just naked. Come, there's a table emptying."

She darted away, and he followed, wondering what difference the distance from the table to the floor made, wondering if he would ever understand women. As he slid onto a stool across a small, rough-topped table from her, someone thrust a clay jug of wine and two battered metal cups in front of them, disappearing while Conan was still reaching for his pouch.

He shook his head. "'Tis the first tavern I've ever seen, where payment was not demanded before a cup was filled."

"Did not anyone explain last night?" she laughed.

"Perhaps they did. But there was more than a little wine being passed around."

"Did you really do all you talked about last night?" She leaned forward with interest, the top of the cloak gaping to expose the upper slopes of her cleavage. A part of his brain noted that that glimpse was almost as erotic as her fully exposed bosom had been. He wondered if she knew that and did it on purpose.

"Some of them," he answered cautiously. In truth he did not remember which stories he and Hordo had told. There had been *much* more than a little wine. He filled their cups from the clay jug.

"I thought so," she said in tones of satisfaction. "As to the money, you give what you can. Everyone staying here does, though some who only come in the day give nothing. Some of us receive money from our families, and of course we all put that in. They don't approve—the families that is—but they approve less of having us nearby to embarrass them. Whatever we have left over we use to distribute bread and salt to the hungry in Hellgate. It's little enough," she sighed, "but a starving man appreciates even a crumb."

"Some of these have families rich enough to give them money?" he said, looking around the room in disbelief. Suddenly her cultured accents were loud in his head.

"My father is a lord," she said defensively. She made it sound a crime, both being a lord and being the daughter of one.

"Then why do you live here, on the edge of Hellgate, and pose naked on tables? Can you not write poetry in your father's palace?"

"Oh, Conan," she sighed, "don't you understand that it's wrong for nobles to have gold and live in palaces while beggars starve in hovels?"

"Mayhap it is," Conan replied, "but I still like gold, though I've had little enough of it. As for the poor, were I rich, unless I misdoubt me I'd fill many a belly with what I spent."

"What other answer did you expect?" a lanky man said, pulling up a stool. His long face wore a perpetual scowl, made deeper by thick eyebrows that grew across the bridge of his nose. He scooped up Ariane's cup and drank half her wine.

"It is an honest answer, Stephano," Ariane said. Stephano snorted.

Conan remembered him now. The night before he had named himself a sculptor, and been free with his hands with Ariane. She had not seemed to mind then, but now she took back her winecup angrily.

"He is a generous man, Stephano, and I think me he'd be generous were he rich." She shifted her direct gaze back to Conan. "But can you not see that generosity is not enough? In Hellgate are those who lack the price of bread, while nobles sit safe in their palaces and fat merchants grow richer by the day. Garian is no just king. What must be done is clear."

"Ariane!" Stephano said sharply. "You tread dangerous ground. School your tongue."

"What leave have you to speak so to me?" Her voice grew more heated by the word. "Whatever is between us, I am none of your property."

"I have not named you so," he replied, matching heat for heat. "I ask but that you let yourself be guided by me. Speak not so to strangers."

Ariane tossed her pretty head contemptuously, her big eyes suddenly cold. "Art sure there is no part of jealousy in your words, Stephano? No intent to rid yourself of a rival?" The sculptor's face flamed red. "Stranger he may be," she continued remorselessly, "yet he is the kind of man we seek. A warrior. Have I not heard Taras speak so to you a hundred times? We must needs have fighters if—"

"Mitra's mercy!" Stephano groaned. "Have you mind at all for caution, Ariane? He is a northern barbarian who likely never knew his father and would sell his honor for a silver piece. Guard your tongue!"

With his left hand Conan slid his broadsword free of its scabbard, just enough so that the edge of the blade below the hilt rested against the side of the table. "When I was still a boy," he said in a flat voice, "I saw my father die with a blade in his hand. With that blade I killed the man who slew him. Care you to discuss it further?"

Stephano's eyes goggled at the sword, his scowl momentarily banished. He touched his lips with his tongue; his breath came in pants. "You see, Ariane? You see what kind of man he is?" His stool scraped on the floor as he rose. "Come away with me, Ariane. Leave this man now."

She held out her winecup to Conan. "May I have some more wine?" She did not look at Stephano, or acknowledge his presence. Conan filled the cup, and she drank.

Stephano looked at her uncertainly, then took a step backward. "Guard your tongue!" he hissed, and darted away, almost crashing into another table in his haste.

"Will you guard your tongue?" Conan asked quietly.

She peered into her wine a time before answering. "From the stories you told, your sword goes where the gold is. Do you choose only by who can pay the most gold?"

"No," he told her. "I've ridden away from gold rather than follow unjust orders." Sighing, he added truthfully, "But I do like gold."

Clutching his cloak about her, she rose. "Mayhap . . . mayhap we'll speak of it later. They wait for me to finish posing."

"Ariane," he began, but she cut him off.

"Stephano thinks he has a claim on me," she said quickly. "He has not." And she left almost as quickly as Stephano had.

Conan emptied his cup with a muttered curse, then turned to watch her drop his cloak and climb back to her pose on the table. After a moment her eyes shifted to him, then away, quickly. Again she met his gaze and tore hers away. Her rounded breasts rose and fell as her breathing became agitated. Spots of red appeared on her cheeks, growing, her face flushing hotter and hotter. Abruptly she uttered a small cry and leaped down, snatching up the cloak from the floor without looking again at Conan. She pulled the fur-trimmed garment about her as she ran, darting between the tables, feet flashing up the stairs.

The Cimmerian smiled complacently as he poured more wine from the clay jug. Perhaps things were not as bad as they seemed.

Hordo dropped onto the stool across the table, a frown creasing his eye. "Have you listened to what's said in this place?" he asked quietly. "Was there a Guardsman about, there'd be heads on pikes for sedition before many more dawns."

Conan looked casually to see if anyone was listening. "Or for rebellion?"

"This lot?" the one-eyed man snorted derisively. "They might as well march to the block and ask to have their heads chopped. Not that the city's not ripe for it, mind. But these have as much chance as a babe sucking a sugar-tit."

"But what if they had money? Gold to hire fighting men?"

Hordo raised his cup as Conan spoke; now he choked on the wine. "Where would this lot get gold? If one of them had a patron, you can wager your stones he'd not be living on the rim of Hellgate."

"Ariane's father is a lord," Conan said quietly. "And she told me some of the rest come of rich men, too."

The one-eyed man chose his words carefully. "Do you tell me they actually plan rebellion? Or think they do?"

"Stephano and Ariane, between them, as much as told me so."

"Then let us be gone from here. They may have some talents, but rebellion is not among them. If they met you last night and tell so much today, what have they told others? Remember, our heads can decorate pikes as easily as theirs."

Conan shook his head slowly, although Hordo was right, on the face of it. "I like it here," was all he said.

"You like a round-bottomed poet," Hordo said heatedly. "You'll die for a woman yet. Remember the blind soothsayer."

"I thought you said he was a fool," the Cimmerian laughed. "Drink, Hordo. Rest easy. We'll talk of our Free-Company."

"We've no gold yet that I can see," the other said sourly.

"I'll find the gold," Conan said with more confidence than he felt. He had no idea whence it might come. Still, it would be well to have his plans in order. A delay of days could mean the difference between being sought after and all who could afford such companies already having hired. "I'll find it. You say we can, ah, borrow weapons from the storehouses of the smuggling ring you serve. Are they serviceable? I've seen smuggled mail so eaten with rust it fell apart in a good rain, and blades that snapped at the first blow."

"Nay, Cimmerian. These are of good quality, and of any sort you want. Why, there are as many kinds of sword bundled in those storehouses as I've ever heard named. Tulwars from Vendhya, shamshirs from Iranistan, macheras in a dozen patterns from the Corinthian city-states. Fifty of this sort and a hundred of that. Enough to arm five thousand men."

"So many?" Conan murmured. "Why would they keep so much in their storehouses, and in such variety? There's no profit in storing swords."

"I bring what I'm told from the border to Belverus, and I'm paid for it in gold. I care not if they grow barley in the storehouses, so long as I get a fat purse each trip." Hordo tipped the jug over his cup; a few drops fell. "Wine!" he roared, a blast that brought dead silence to the room.

Everyone turned to stare in amazement at the two burly men. A slender girl in the same sort of plain neck-to-ankles cotton robe that Ariane wore approached hesitantly and placed another clay jug on the table. Hordo fumbled in the purse at his belt and tossed her a silver piece.

"The rest is for you, little one," Hordo said.

The girl stared at the coin, then laughed delightedly and dropped a mockingly deep curtsey before leaving. Conversation slowly resumed among those at the tables. The musicians struck up their various tunes, and the poet orated to the wall.

"Pretty serving girls," Hordo muttered as he refilled his battered metal cup, "but they dress like temple virgins."

Conan hid a smile. The one-eyed man had drunk deeply the night before. Well, he would discover soon enough that he did not have to pay for his wine. In the meantime, let him contribute for the both of them.

"Consider, Hordo. Such a motley collection of weapons is just the sort of thing these artists would put together."

"That again?" the other man grumbled. "In the first place, whoever runs the ring, I can't see him wanting Garian overthrown. Those fool tariffs might be starving the poor, but they make good profits for smuggling. In the second place. . . ." His face darkened, the scar below his patch standing out whitely. "In the second place, I've been through one rebellion with you. Or have you forgotten riding for the Venhyan border half a step in front of the headsman's sword?"

"I remember," Conan said. "I've said naught of joining their rebellion."

"Said naught, but thought much," Hordo growled. "You're a romantic fool, Cimmerian. Always were, likely always will be. Hannuman's Stones, man, you'll not mix me in another uprising. Keep your mind fixed on the gold for a Free-Company."

"I always keep my mind on gold," Conan replied. "Mayhap I think on it too much."

Hordo groaned, but Conan was saved having to say more by the appearance of the slender girl who had brought the wine jug. Tilting her head to one side, she favored the big Cimmerian with a look, half shyness, half invitation, that made the room suddenly too warm.

"What's your name, girl?" Hordo asked. "You're a pretty little bit. Get rid of that cotton shift, deck yourself with a little silk, and you could work in any tavern in Belverus."

She tossed her head, laughing gaily, silken brown hair rippling about her shoulders. "Thank you, kind sir, and for your generous contribution." Hordo frowned in uncomprehension. "My name is Kerin," she went on, her soft brown eyes shifting to Conan like a light-fingered caress. "And by those shoulders, you must be the Conan Ariane spoke of. I work in clay, though I hope to have my sculpture cast in bronze some day. Would you pose for me? I can't pay you, but perhaps. . . ." Her mouth softened, full lower lip dropping slightly, and her eyes left no doubt what sort of arrangement she wanted with the muscular barbarian.

Conan had barely listened after the mention of posing. An image flashed in his brain of Ariane, posing on the table, and he was uncomfortably aware of his face growing hot. Surely she did not mean. . . . She could not want. . . .

He swallowed hard and cleared his throat. "You mentioned Ariane. Did she send a message?"

"Why did she see you first?" Kerin sighed. "Yes, she did. She's waiting in your room. To tell you something very important, she said." She ended with a slight smirk.

Conan scraped back his stool.

"Girl," Hordo said as the Cimmerian rose, "what is this posing? I might well do it." Kerin slipped into the seat Conan had vacated.

All the way across the common room Conan waited for Hordo's outraged shout, but when he looked back from the foot of the stairs the one-eyed man was nodding slowly, a delighted grin on his face. Laughing, Conan ran up the stairs. It seemed his friend would receive more than good value for his silver piece.

Upstairs the narrow hall was lined with many doors, most crudely made, for the original chambers had been roughly partitioned into more. When Conan pushed open his own rude plank door, Ariane was standing below the small window high in the wall. His cloak was still wrapped tightly around her, her fists showing at the neck where she held it together. He closed the door behind him and leaned back against it.

"I pose," she said without preamble. Her eyes glinted with something he could not quite read. "I pose for my friends, who cannot hire models. I do it often, and never have I felt embarrassment. Never until today."

"I merely looked at you," he said quietly.

"You looked at me." She uttered a sound halfway between a laugh and a sob. "You looked at me, and I felt like one of those girls at the Gored Ox, wriggling to a flute for drooling men. Mitra blast your eyes! How dare you make me feel like that!"

"You are a woman," he said. "I looked at you as a man looking at a woman."

She closed her eyes and addressed the cracked ceiling. "Hama All-Mother, why must I be stirred by an untutored barbarian who thinks with his sword?" A smug smile grew on his face, to be quashed almost immediately by a glare from her large hazel eyes. "A man may take as many women as he wishes," she said fiercely. "I refuse to have less freedom than a man. If I choose to have but one man at a time to my mat, and have no other till he leaves or I do, that is my affair. Can you accept me as I am?"

"Did your mother never tell you a man likes to do the asking?" he laughed.

"Mitra blast your heart!" she snarled. "Why do I waste my time?" Muttering to herself she stalked toward the door, cloak flaring in her haste.

Conan reached out one massive arm, curling it around her waist beneath the cloak. She had time for one strangled squawk before he lifted her, the cloak floating to the floor, to crush her soft breasts against the hard expanse of his chest.

"Will you stay with me, Ariane?" he asked, looking into her startled eyes.

Before she could speak he tangled his free hand in her hair and brought her lips to his. Her small fists bruised themselves against his shoulders; her feet kicked futilely at his shins. Slowly her struggles subsided, and when a satisfied murmur sounded in her throat he released her hair. Panting, she let her head drop onto his broad chest.

"Why did you change your mind?" she managed after a time.

"I didn't change it," he replied. She looked up, startled, and he smiled. "Before you asked. This time I did the asking."

Laughing throatily, she let her head fall back. "Hama All-Mother," she cried, "will I never understand these strange creatures called men?"

He laid her gently on his sleeping mat, and for a long time thereafter only sounds passion-wrought passed her lips.

VI

The Street of Regrets in the morning hours fit well Conan's mood. The paving stones were littered with the tawdry refuse of the previous night's revelry; those few people to be seen were stumbling home bleary eyed and hollow faced. Conan kicked rubbish from his path as he strode along, and gave growl for growl to the stray dogs that scavenged among the leavings.

The ten nights past had been an idyll at the Sign of the Thestis, wrapped in Ariane's arms, her passions and appetites feeding his own even as they sated them. Stephano brooded much in jealousy and wine, yet the memory of the Cimmerian's anger kept his tongue between his teeth. Hordo, drawn by the attractions of the slender Kerin, had moved his few belongings from an inn three streets away, and of an evening they drank and told each other lies till the charms of Ariane and Kerin parted them. Those were the nights. Days were another matter.

Conan paused at the sound of running boots behind him, then continued on as Hordo joined him.

"Ill luck this morrow, too?" the one-eyed man asked, eyeing the Cimmerian's face.

Conan nodded shortly. "When I had defeated all three bodyguards now in his service, Lord Heranius offered three gold marks for me to take service as their chief, with two more every tenday."

"Ill luck?" Hordo exclaimed. "Mitra! That's twice the usual rate for bodyguards. I'm tempted to give up smuggling. At least there'd be no danger of the headsman's block."

"And I must swear bond-oath before the City Magistrates not to quit his service without leave for two years."

"Oh."

Conan's right fist cracked into the other palm with a sound like a club striking leather. A drunk, stumbling his way home, jumped a foot in the air and fell in a puddle of vomit. Conan did not notice.

"Everywhere it is the same," he grated, "Free-Companies or single blade-fee alike. All demand the bond-oath, and some require three years, if they do not require five."

"Before the bond-oaths," Hordo mused. "Some men changed masters every day, getting a silver piece more each time. Look you. Why not take service with whoever offers the most gold? This Lord Heranius, by the sound of it. When you're ready to go, if he won't release you, just go. An oath that makes a man a slave is no oath at all."

"And when I do, I must leave Belverus, perhaps all of Nemedia." He was silent for a time, his boots kicking broken clay wine-jars and soiled bits of abandoned clothing from his path. At last he said, "At first it was but talk, Hordo, this Free-Company that I would lead. Now it's more. I'll take no service until I ride at the head of my own company."

"It means so much to you?" Hordo said incredulously. He dodged a jar of slops thrown from a second-story window, hurling a curse at the thrower, already gone.

"It does," Conan said, ignoring the other's mutters about what had splashed on his boots. "In the final sum of it all, perhaps a man has no more than himself, naught but a strong right hand and the steel in it. And still, to rise, to make some mark in the world, a man must lead others. I was a thief, yet did I rise to command in the Army of Turan, and did well at it. I know not how far I may rise nor how far the path I follow may take me, yet do I intend to rise as high and go as far as my wits and a good sword will take me. I will have that Free-Company."

"When you do," the one-eyed man said drily, "be you certain they swear the bond-oath." They turned into the street that led to the Sign of Thestis.

As Conan laughed, three men stepped out to spread themselves across the narrow street, broadswords in hand. The sound of boots behind made Conan glance quickly over his shoulder. Two more armed men stood there, cutting off retreat. The Cimmerian's blade whispered from its worn shagreen scabbard; Hordo, sword flickering free, pivoted to face those behind.

"Stand aside," Conan called to the three. "Find you easier meat elsewhere."

"Naught was said of a second man," the one to Conan's left muttered, his thin, rat-like face twitching.

The man to the right, shaven dome gleaming in the morning sun, hefted his sword uneasily. "We cannot take one without the other."

"You'll find but your deaths here," Conan said. With his left hand he unfastened the bronze pin that held his cloak, doubling the furlined garment loosely over that arm.

The leader, for the tall man in the center with his closely cropped beard was clearly so, spoke for the first time. "Kill them," he said, and his blade thrust for Conan's belly.

With pantherine grace the muscular Cimmerian moved aside, his cloak tangling the tall man's blade while his right foot planted itself solidly in the fellow's crotch. In the same move Conan's sword beat aside a thrust of the shavenhead. Gagging, the leader attempted to straighten; but Conan pivoted, his left foot taking the bearded man on the side of the head, knocking him under the feet of onrushing ratface. Both went down in a heap.

The shaven-headed attacker hesitated, goggle-eyed at his companions on the ground, and died for it. Conan's slashing steel half-severed his throat. Bright red blood fountained as he went to his knees, then toppled onto his face in the muck of the street. Rat-face scrambled to his feet, and he tried a desperate overhead hack. Conan's blade rang against the other, bringing it into a sweeping downward circle, sliding his blade along his opponent's, thrusting it into the villain's chest.

A quick kick next to his blade freed the body to collapse alongside the other; and Conan spun to find the leader on his feet, his narrow, bearded face suffused with rage. He swung while the big Cimmerian was yet turning, staring with surprise as Conan dropped to a squat, buttocks on his heels. Conan's steel sliced a bloody line across his abdomen. The tall man screamed like a woman, dropping his sword as his frantic hands tried vainly to hold his intestines in. His eyes were glazed with death before he struck the filthy paving stones.

Conan looked for Hordo in time to see the one-eyed man's blade decapitate his second attacker. With the head still rolling across the pavement Hordo turned to glare at Conan, blood oozing from a gash on his sword arm and another, smaller, on his forehead.

"I'm too old for this, Cimmerian."

"You always say that." As he spoke, Conan bent to check the pouches of the men he had killed.

"It's true, I tell you," Hordo insisted. "If these hadn't been such fools as to talk and dither while we set ourselves, they might have chopped us to dog meat. As it was, my two nearly sliced my cods off. I'm too old, I say."

Conan straightened from the bodies with six new-minted gold marks. He bounced them on his palm. "Fools they may be, but they were sent after one of us. By somebody willing to pay ten gold marks for a death." He jerked his head at the two Hordo had killed. "You'll find each of them has a pair of these too."

Hordo muttered an oath and bent to the remaining bodies, straightening up with four fat coins. The one-eyed man closed his fist tightly on them. "Yon rat-face spoke of not expecting two. Mitra, who'd pay ten gold marks for either of us?"

A gangling boy shambled out of an alley not a dozen paces distant. At the sight of the bodies his jaw dropped open, and with a scream of pure terror he dashed away, his wail fading as he sped.

"Let us discuss it at the Thestis," Conan said, "before we gather an audience."

"With our luck," Hordo muttered, "this will be the one morning in half a year the City Guard has patrols out."

It was but a short distance down the twisting street to the inn, but obviously no one had heard the fighting. Only Kerin gave them a second glance when they walked in. In those morning hours there were few of the artists about, and none of the noise that would reverberate in the evening.

"Hordo," the slender girl said, "what happened to your arm?"

"I fell over a broken wine-jar," he replied sheepishly.

She gave him a sharp look and left, returning in a moment with a pile of clean rags and a jug of wine. Uncorking the wine, she began to pour it over the gash on Hordo's arm.

"No!" he shouted, snatching it from her hand.

An amused smile quirked her mouth. "It hurts not that much, Hordo."

"It hurts not at all," he growled. "But this is the proper way to use wine."

And he tipped the clay jug up to his mouth, with his free hand fending off her attempts to take it back. When finally he stopped for breath she jerked it away, pouring the little wine that remained over a cloth and dabbing at his forehead.

"Hold still, Hordo," she told him. "I will fetch you more wine later."

Across the common room Conan noticed a face strange to the inn. A handsome young man in a richly embroidered red velvet tunic sat at a table in a corner, talking to Graecus, a swarthy sculptor who spent considerable time in the company of Stephano.

After discovering that someone might want him dead, Conan was feeling suspicious of strangers. He touched Kerin's arm.

"That man," he said. "The one talking to Graecus. Who is he? He seems well dressed for an artist."

"Demetrio, an artist?" she snorted. "A catamite and a wastrel. They say he's a great wit, but I've never found him so. Betimes he likes to dazzle those among us who can be dazzled by his sort, when he is not rolling in the fleshpots."

"Think you it's him?" Hordo asked.

Conan shrugged. "Him, or anyone else."

"By Erebus, Cimmerian, I'm too old for this."

"What are you two talking about?" Kerin demanded. "No. I'd as lief not know." She rose, pulling Hordo behind her, a faun leading a bear. "That cut on your arm needs ointment. Wine-jar, indeed!"

"When I return," Hordo called over his shoulder to Conan, "we can begin looking for the men we want. Courtesy of our enemy, eh?"

"Done," Conan called back, rising. "And I'll fetch that sword. It should fetch a coin or two."

In his room abovestairs the Cimmerian pried up a loosened floor board and took out the serpentine blade. Light from the small window ran along the gleaming steel, and glinted on the silver work of the quillons. The feel of taint rose from it like a miasma.

As he straightened he wrapped his cloak, rent from the tall man's sword, about the blade. Even holding it in his bare hand made his stomach turn as the slaying of his first man had not.

When Conan returned to the common room, the man in the red velvet tunic was waiting at the foot of the stair, a pomander to his aquiline nose, his eyes lidded with languorous indolence, yet the Cimmerian noted that the hilt of his sword showed wear, and the hand that held the pomander had bladesman's calluses. Conan started past.

"A moment, please," the slender man said. "I am called Demetrio. I collect swords of ancient pattern, and I could not help but hear that you possess such a one, and wish to sell it."

"I remember nothing of calling it ancient," Conan replied. The man had a viperish quality the Cimmerian liked not. As if he could smile and clasp a hand, yet strike to the heart while doing so. Still, he found himself listening.

"Perhaps I but imagined you named it ancient," Demetrio said smoothly. "If it is not, I have no interest. But an it is, well might I buy." He eyed the cloak-wrapped bundle beneath the Cimmerian's arm. "You have it there?"

Conan reached into the cloak and drew forth the blade. "This is the sword," he said, and stopped as Demetrio jumped back, hand to his own sword. The Cimmerian flipped the sword over, proffering the hilt. "Perhaps you wish to try its heft?"

"No." The word was a shaky whisper. "I can see that I want it."

The flesh about Demetrio's mouth was tight and pale. The strange thought came to Conan that the slender man was afraid of the sword, but he dismissed the notion as foolish. He tossed the sword onto a nearby table. His hand felt dirty from holding it. And that was foolish too.

Demetrio swallowed, seeming to breathe more easily as he looked at the blade where it lay. "This sword," he said, not looking at the Cimmerian. "Has it any . . . properties? Any magicks?"

Conan shook his head. "None that I know." Such might add to the price he could demand, but any such claims would be easily disproved. "What will you give?"

"Three gold marks," Demetrio said promptly.

The big Cimmerian blinked. He had been thinking in terms of silver pieces. But if the sword had some value to this young man, it was time to bargain. "For a blade so ancient," he said, "Many collectors would pay twenty."

The slender man gave him a searching look. "I have not so much with me," he muttered.

Shocked, Conan wondered if the blade was that of some long-dead king; Demetrio had made not even a pretense of haggling. His practiced thief's eye priced the amethyst-studded gold bracelet on Demetrio's wrist at fifty gold marks, and a small ruby pin on his tunic at twice that. The man would be good for twenty marks, he thought.

"I would be willing to wait," Conan began, when Demetrio pulled the bracelet from his wrist and thrust it at him.

"Will you take that?" the fellow asked. "I would not risk another buying while I am gone to get coin. It is worth more than the twenty marks, I assure you. But add in that cloak, for I would not carry a bare blade in the streets."

"Cloak and blade are yours," the Cimmerian said, and quickly exchanged the fur-trimmed garment for the bracelet.

He felt a surge of joy as his fist closed over the amethyst-studded gold. No need to make do now with the few men ten gold pieces would hire. His Free-Company was literally in his grasp.

"I would ask you," he added, "why this blade has such worth. Is it perhaps the sword of an ancient king, or hero?"

Demetrio paused in the act of carefully wrapping the cloak about the sword. Carefully, Conan thought, and as gingerly as if it were a dangerous animal.

"How are you called?" the slender man asked.

"I am called Conan."

"You are right, Conan. This is the sword of an ancient king. In fact, you might say this is the sword of Bragoras." And he laughed as if he had said the funniest thing he had ever heard. Still laughing, he gathered up the sword and cloak and hurried into the street.

VII

lbanus paused at the door, the crude, fur-trimmed bundle beneath his arm out of place in the tapestry-hung room with its carpet-strewn marble floor. Sularia sat before a tall mirror, a golden silk robe about her creamy shoulders, a kneeling slave woman brushing the honey silk of her hair. Seeing his reflection Sularia let the robe drop, giving him a view of her generous breasts in the mirror.

The hawk-faced lord snapped his fingers. The slave looked around; at his gesture she bowed and fled on bare feet.

"You have brought me a gift?" Sularia said. "It is wrapped most strangely, an you have." She examined her face in the mirror, and lightly stroked rouge onto her cheeks with a brush of fur.

"This is not for you," he laughed. "'Tis the sword of Melius."

With a key that hung on a golden chain about his neck, he unlocked a large lacquered chest standing against the wall, turning the key first one way then the other in a precise pattern. Were that pattern not followed exactly, he had told Sularia, a cunningly contrived system of tubes and air-chambers would hurl poison darts into the face of the opener.

Albanus swung back the lid and, tossing aside the tattered cloak, carefully laid the sword in the place he had prepared for it. The tomes of ancient Acheron, bound in virgins' skin, were there, well layered in silk, and those most vital thaumaturgical implements from the cache. His fingers rested briefly on a bundle of scrolls and rolled canvases. Not yet of any magical significance, they still deserved their place in the chest, those sketches and paintings of Garian. In a place of honor, resting on a silken cushion atop a golden stand, was a crystal sphere of deepest blue within which silver flecks danced and glittered.

Letting her robe drift to the floor, Sularia came to stand naked beside him. Her tongue touched her lips in small flickers as she stared down at the sword. "It was that blade which slew so many? Is it not dangerous? Ought you not to destroy it?"

"It is too useful," he said. "Had I but known what I know now, never would I have put it in the hands of that fool Melius. 'Twas those runes on the blade led me at last to its secret, buried in the grimoires."

"But why did Melius slay as he did?"

"In the forging of this weapon, the essences of six masters of the sword were trapped within the steel." He let his fingers brush lightly along the blade, sensing the power that had been required for its making. Such power would be his, power beyond the ken of mortal minds, power far beyond that of earthly kings. "And in that entrapment did madness come." He reached down as if to lift the sword, but stopped with his hand clawed above the hilt. "Let the same hand grasp this hilt but three times to use this blade, and the mind that controls that hand will be ripped away, merging with the madness of those ancient masters of the sword. Escape. Slay, and escape. Slay. Slay!"

Ending on a shout, he looked at Sularia. Her mouth hung open, and she stared at his hand above the sword with open fear in her blue eyes.

"How often have you used the sword?" she whispered.

He laughed and took his hand away. Instead of the sword he picked up the crystal sphere, holding it delicately in his fingers, almost reverently, though he knew no power under heaven could so much as chip its seemingly fragile surface.

"You fear the sword?" he asked softly. His adamantine gaze seemed to pierce to the heart of the cobalt sphere. "Here is that which is to be feared, for by this is summoned and controlled a being—a demon? a god?—I know not, yet a being of such power that even the tomes of Acheron speak of it in whispers full of awe."

And he would be its master, master of more power than all the kings of all the nations of the world. His breath quickened at the thought. Never yet had he dared that summoning, for that act held dangers for he who summoned, dangers that master might find himself slave, a mortal plaything for an immortal monster with eternity to amuse itself. Yet, was he not descended of Bragoras, ancient hero-king who had slain the dragon Xutharcan and bound the demon Dargon in the depths of the Western Sea?

Almost unbidden, the words of summoning began to roll from his lips. *"Af-far mea-roth, Omini deas kaan, Eeth-far be-laan Opheah cristi. . . ."*

As the words came, the sky darkened above the city as though the sun had dimmed to twilight. Lightning cracked and forked across a cloudless sky, and, rumbling, the earth began to shake.

Albanus stumbled, looked around him in sudden panic at walls that quivered like cloth in the breeze. It was too soon for this. It was madness to have tried. And yet, he had not finished the incantation. There was a chance.

Hastily he returned the sphere, glowing now, to its cushion within the lac-quered chest. With great care he blanked his mind. There must be not even the merest thought of summoning. No thought at all. No thought.

Slowly the light in the crystal sphere faded, and the earth ceased to move. The lightnings faded and were gone. Light broke forth over the city as if at a new sunrise.

For a long time Albanus did not look at Sularia. Did she say one word, he thought grimly, but one word of the spectacle of fool he had made himself, he would gut her and strangle her with her own entrails. But one word. He turned to face her with a face dark as that beneath an executioner's hood.

Sularia stared at him with eyes filled with pure lust. "Such power," she whispered. "You are a man of such power, almost I fear me it might blind me to look on you." Her breath came in pants. "Is it thus you will destroy Garian?"

His spirit soared, and his pride. "Garian is not worthy of such," he sneered. "I will create a man, give him life with my two hands. So will I bring the usurper to his doom."

"You are so powerful as that?" she gasped.

He waved it away. "A mere trifle. Already have I done so, and this time the errors of the last will not be repeated." Abruptly he tangled his hand in her hair, forced her to the floor, forced her though she would have gone willingly and more than willingly. "Nothing stands in my way," he said as he lowered himself atop her. She cried out, and he heard in it the cries of the people acclaiming their king, their god.

Sephana raised herself from the cushions of her bed, her lushly rounded body sweat-oiled from love making. Her full breasts swayed with the motion.

The man in her bed, a lean young captain of the Golden Leopards, lifted himself unsteadily on one elbow. His dark eyes were worshipful as he gazed at her. "Are you a witch, Sephana? Each time I think that I will die from the pleasure. Each time I think that I've had all the ecstacy there is in the world. And each time you give more than I could dream of."

Sephana smiled contentedly. "And yet, Baetis, I think you tire of me."

"Never!" he said fervently. "You must believe me. You are Derketo come to earth."

"But you refuse me such a small favor."

"Sephana," he moaned, "you know not what you ask. My duty. . . ."

"A small favor," she said again, walking slowly back to the bed.

His eyes followed her hungrily. She was no slender girl, but a woman of curves, a callimastean and callipygian marvel to put hunger in any man's eyes. He reached for her, but she stepped back.

"A door left unlatched, Baetis," she said softly. "A passage left unguarded. Would you deny your king a surprise, the same delights you now enjoy?"

The young captain breathed heavily, and his eyes closed. "I, at least, must be there," he said at last.

"Of course," she said swiftly, and moved to kneel astride him. "Of course, Baetis, my love." Her smile was vulpine, the light in her violet eyes feral. Let Albanus make his long, drawn-out plans. She would strike while he still planned. It was a pity that Baetis had to die along with Garian. But that was in the future. Sighing contentedly, she gave herself over to pleasure.

VIII

The straw butts were each the size of a man's torso. Conan set the last of them in place, and swung into the saddle to gallop the hundred and fifty paces back to the men he and Hordo had gathered in the five days past. He wished the one-eyed man were with him, but Hordo was yet keeping his contacts with the smugglers, and he was seeing to the shifting of goods from a storehouse before the Kings Customs made a supposed surprise inspection. They could never tell, Hordo maintained, when those contacts might prove useful.

The Cimmerian reigned in his big Aquilonian black before the two score mounted men, holding up a short, heavy bow before the men. "This is a horse bow."

The bows had been a lucky find, for mounted archery was an art unknown in the west, and Conan counted on this skill to add to his Free-Company's appeal to patrons. The bows had been lying unstrung in the smugglers' storehouse, thought too short and of too heavy a draw to be wanted. Each of the forty now wore other acquisitions from the storehouse: metal jazeraint hauberks over padded tunics, and spiked helms. A round shield hung at each saddle, and a good Turanian scimitar, bearing the proof-mark of the Royal Foundry at Aghrapur, swung at each hip.

Conan hoped their armor was unfamiliar enough to Nemedia to give them a foreign flavor. Men usually believed that foreigners knew strange tricks of fighting. With the horse bows, they might believe correctly. As he and Hordo had chosen only men already possessing a horse—they had gold enough only for signing bonuses, not for buying horses—so had they chosen men who knew something of archery. But none knew mounted archery. That was why Conan had brought them to this clearing outside of Belverus.

"You're all accustomed to using a bow-ring on your thumb," he went on, "but when you fight mounted, you must be able to shift from bow to sword to lance and back, quickly. A bow-ring encumbers the grip."

"How do you draw the thing at all?" asked a grizzled man with a livid scar across his broad nose. He held the short bow out at arm's length and attempted to draw it. The cord moved no more than a handspan, producing laughter from some of the others.

The grizzled man's name was Machaon. Though he did not recognize Conan, the Cimmerian knew him for the sergeant who had commanded the City Guards in killing Lord Melius.

"Use a three-fingered grip on the cord," Conan said once the laughter had died, "and draw thusly."

The muscular Cimmerian notched an arrow and, placing the bowstring to his cheek, pushed the short, powerful bow out to draw it. As he did so, he pressed with his knees, bringing the war-trained black around. The straw butts seemed to swing before his eyes; he loosed. With a solid thud the shaft struck square in the center of the middle butt. A surprised murmur went up from the men.

"Thus is it done," Conan said.

"'Tis more than passing strange," a tall, hollow-cheeked man muttered, "this archery from horseback." His black eyes were sunken, and he looked as though he had been ravaged by disease, though those among the company who knew him said he had no sickness but a doleful spirit. "If it is a thing of use, why do we not see it among the armies of Nemedia or Aquilonia or any other civilized land?"

Conan was saved answering by Machaon.

"Open your mind, Narus," the grizzled man said, "and for once let not your mournful mood color what you see. Think you. We can appear, strike and be gone while foot-archers rush to plant their sharpened stakes against the charge they expect, while pikemen and ordinary infantry yet prepare to close ranks against the mounted attacks they know. Enemy cavalry will be but lowering their lances to countercharge when our arrows strike to their hearts. Put off your dolorous countenance, Narus, and smile at the surprise we will give our enemies."

Narus deliberately showed his teeth in a grin that made him look more the plague victim than ever. A ripple of laughter and obscene comment greeted his attempt.

"Machaon has seen the right of it," Conan announced. "I name him now as sergeant of this Free-Company."

A surprised and thoughtful look appeared on Machaon's scar-nosed face, and a murmur of approval rose from the rest. Even Narus seemed to think it a good choice, in his mournful way.

"Now," Conan continued, "let each man take a turn at the butts. First with the horse unmoving."

For three full turns of the glass the Cimmerian kept them at it, progressing to shooting with their mounts at a walk, thence to firing at the gallop. Every man knew horsemanship and the bow, if not together, and they made good advance. By that time's end, they did not use their horse bows so well as Turanian light cavalry, yet was their skill enough to surprise and shock any of these western lands. Machaon, to no one's surprise, and Narus, to everyone's, were the best after Conan.

After that time the Cimmerian led them back into Belverus, to one of the stables that lined the city's wall, where he had arranged for their horses to be tended. After each man had given his mount into the care of a stable slave he left to go his own way until the morrow, when Conan had commanded them to meet again at the stable, for such was the custom of Free-Companies when not in service. It was about that last that Machaon spoke as Conan was leaving.

"A moment, captain," the grizzled man said, catching Conan at the heavy wooden doors of the stable. Machaon had been handsome as a youth, but aside from the scar that cut across his broad nose his face was a map of his campaigns. On his left cheek was a small tattoo of a six-pointed star from Koth; three thin gold rings from Argos dangled from the lobe of his right ear, and his hair was cut short in front and long in back after the style of the Ophirian border.

"It would be well, captain, if you were to put the company into service soon. Though it's been but a few days since we swore the bond-oath yet have I heard some complain openly that we earn no gold, and speak of the ease of taking a second bond-oath using another name before another Magistrate."

"Let them know that we'll take service soon," Conan replied, though he wondered himself why he had approached none of the merchants who might wish to hire a Free-Company. "I see that I made a good choice for sergeant."

Machaon hesitated, then asked quietly, "Know you who I am?"

"I know who you are, but I care not who you were." Conan met the man's dark-eyed gaze until Machaon finally nodded.

"I'll see to the men, captain."

From the stable Conan made his way to the Sign of Thestis through streets that seemed to have twice as many beggars and three times as many toughs as a tenday past. No plump merchant or stern-faced noble now made his way in even the High Streets without a hard-eyed escort, and no slave-borne curtained litter, whether it contained a noble's sleek daughter or the hot-eyed courtesan who served him, traveled shorn of its bevy of armed and armored guardians. The City Guard were nowhere to be seen.

The Thestis when Conan entered was filling, as it always did of a midday, with youthful artists in search of a free meal from the inn's stewpot. Their arguments and musical instruments blended into a cacophony that the Cimmerian had learned to ignore.

He grabbed Kerin's arm as she rushed past, a clay wine-jug in each hand. "Has Hordo returned?" he asked.

She set one of the jugs down hard enough to crack it, ignoring the wine spreading across the table top and the yelps of those seated there. "He sent a message by a boy," she said coldly. "You are to meet him at the Sign of the Full Moon, on the Street of Regrets, a glass past the sun's zenith."

"Why there? Did he say why he does not come here?"

Kerin's eyes narrowed to slits, and she spoke through clenched teeth. "There was some mention of a dancer, with breasts. . . . Enough! If you would learn more, learn it from that miserable one-eyed goat!"

The Cimmerian suppressed a smile until she had flounced away. He hoped this dancer was all that Hordo thought, for the one-eyed man was surely going to pay for his pleasures when he again came in reach of Kerin.

He was trying to decide if he had time for a bowl of stew—it was assuredly better than that served on the Street of Regrets—before leaving to meet Hordo, when Ariane approached and put a small hand on his arm. He smiled, suddenly thinking of a better use for his time than a bowl of stew.

"Come up to my room," he said, slipping an arm around her. He pulled her close and tried out his best leer. "We could discuss poetry."

She tried to suppress a giggle, and almost succeeded. "If by poetry you mean what I think you mean, you want to do more than talk about it." Her smile faded, and her eyes searched his face. "There's something more important to speak of now, but I must have your oath never to repeat a word of what is said to you. You must swear."

"I do swear," he said slowly.

Abruptly he knew why he had not hired his Free-Company out. Without a doubt, a company in service to merchant or noble would be expected to support the throne in a rebellion. But he wanted no part of crushing Ariane and her friends. Most especially not Ariane.

"I've wondered," he went on, "when you would speak to me of this revolt of yours."

Ariane gasped. "You know," she whispered. Quickly she put her fingers on his lips to prevent him speaking. "Come with me."

He followed her through the tables into the back of the inn. There, in a small room, Stephano slouched scowling against the flaking wall, and Graecus, the stocky sculptor, straddled a bench, grinning. Leucas, a thin man with a big nose who called himself a philosopher, sat cross-legged on the floor chewing his lower lip.

"He knows," Ariane said as she closed the door, and they all jumped.

Conan casually put his hand to his sword hilt.

"He knows!" Stephano yelped. "I told you he was dangerous. I told you we should have nothing to do with him. This is not our part of it."

"Keep your voice down," Ariane said firmly. "Do you want to tell everyone in the inn?" He subsided sulkily, and she went on, addressing the others too. "It's true that recruiting men like Conan was not part of what we were supposed to do, but I've heard each one of you complain that you wanted to take a more direct part."

"At least you can write poetry taunting Garian," Graecus muttered. "All I can do is copy what you write and scatter it in the streets. I can't do a sculpture to rouse the people."

"King Garian sits on the Dragon Throne," Conan said suddenly. They all stared at him. "King Garian sits to his feast alone. I saw that one. Did you write it, Ariane?"

"Gallia's work," she said drily. "I write much better than that."

"This is all beside the point," Stephano shrilled. "We all know why you trust him, Ariane." He met Conan's icy blue stare and swallowed hard. "I think what we do is dangerous. We should leave hiring this sort of . . . this sort of man to Taras. He knows them. We don't."

"We know Conan," Ariane persisted. "And we all agreed—yes, you too, Stephano—that we should take a part in finding fighting men, whatever Taras says. With Conan we get not one, but forty."

"If they'll follow him," Graecus said.

"They will follow me wherever there is gold," Conan replied.

Graecus looked a little unsettled at that, and Stephano laughed mockingly, "Gold!"

"Fools!" Ariane taunted. "How many times have we talked of those who claimed that revolution should be kept pure, that only those who fought for the right reasons should be allowed to take part? How many of them went to the impaling stake for their purity?"

"Our cause is just," Stephano grated. "We taint it with gold."

Ariane shook her head wearily. "Time and again we have argued this. The time for such argument is long past, Stephano. How think you Taras gathers fighting men? With gold, Stephano. Gold!"

"And from the start did I oppose it," the lanky sculptor replied. "The people—"

"Would follow us and rise," she cut him off. "They would follow us and, none of us knowing aught of weapons or war, would be cut down."

"Our ideals," he muttered.

"Are not enough." She glared at each of her fellow conspirators in turn, and they shifted uneasily beneath her gaze. Of them all, Conan realized, the strongest will was housed within her sweet curves.

"What I want," Graecus announced, "is a chance to hold a sword in my hand. Conan, can I ride with you on the day?"

"I have not said I would join you," Conan replied slowly.

Ariane gasped, clutching her hands beneath her rounded breasts, her face a picture of dismay. Graecus sat open-mouthed.

"I told you he was not to be trusted," Stephano muttered.

"My men will follow me," the Cimmerian went on, "but not if I lead them only to the headsman's block or the impaling stake. I cannot join you without some idea of your chances of success, and to know that I must know your plans."

"He could betray us," Stephano said quickly.

"Be quiet, Stephano," Ariane said, but she studied the Cimmerian's face without speaking further.

"I am not civilized enough," Conan told her softly, "to betray my friends."

She nodded shakily. Stephano tried to cut her off, but she ignored him. "Taras hires warriors. He says that we need at least a thousand, but he will soon have that many. Our strength, though, is the people. Their anger is so great now, and their hunger, that they would pull Garian down with their bare hands, could they. Some know they will receive weapons. Others will follow. We have weapons for ten thousand, weapons smuggled across the border. Some no doubt by your friend, Hordo."

"*Ten* thousand?" Conan said, remembering Hordo's estimate of five.

"Ten," Graecus said. "I've seen them. Taras showed me a storehouse full."

And let him count them, too, Conan thought drily. "It takes a great deal of gold to arm ten thousand, even poorly. And more to hire a thousand already armed. You provided this gold?"

"Some part of it, yes," Ariane said defensively. "But, as you know, we earn no great amounts, and most of what we have from our . . . our other sources goes to this inn."

"There are some," Stephano said loftily, "who despite their wealth believe that we are right and Garian will destroy Nemedia. They furnish Taras with what is needed to acquire arms and men."

"Who are they?" Conan asked. "Will they support you openly, put their names behind you once you take to the streets?"

"Of course," Stephano said, but almost immediately his loftiness fell into uncertainty. "That is, I suppose they will. You see, they prefer to remain anonymous." He laughed shakily. "Why, not even any of us here has ever seen them. Their money goes directly to Taras."

"What Stephano means," Ariane said as the sculptor sank into silence, "is that they're affrighted we will fail, and fear to find themselves upon the headsman's block. 'Tis likely they think to manipulate us, and the revolution, to increase their own wealth and position. But if they do, they forget that we command the people. And a thousand armed men."

A thousand armed men who had taken gold from these mysterious benefactors, Conan thought wearily. "But what is your plan? Not just to rush into the streets handing swords out to the people?"

Graecus smiled broadly. "We are not such fools as you might think us, Conan. Those of us who distribute the bread in Hellgate have found men who can be trusted, marked out those who will follow when the word is given. These will receive the weapons. We will lead them to surround the Royal Palace, while Taras takes the thousand to seize the city gates and lay siege to the City Guard in their barracks."

"What of the Free-Companies, and the bodyguards?" Conan asked. "There must be three thousand such in the city, and those who have paid them will most certainly support the king."

"Yes," Ariane said, "but each will also keep his bodyguard close about him till he sees what happens. We can ignore them. If necessary, they can be rooted out later, one by one. A Free-Company of a hundred may be over-run by a thousand from the gutter to whom death is no more than an escape from hunger."

She looked ready to lead such an assault herself, small head erect, shoulders back outthrusting her breasts to strain the fabric of her shift, eyes alight with hazel fire. Conan knew her words were true. Men who welcomed death were fearsome opponents in the assault, though more easily dealt with in the long campaign. Whatever the outcome of this meeting, he must keep his company ready to move at all times with no more than an instant's warning.

What he said, though, was, "What of the army?"

It was Graecus again who answered. "The closest troops are a thousand at Heranium and two at Jeraculum. They would take five days to reach Belverus, once they have been commanded to march, but will be too few to do anything to effect while we hold the city gates. As to the forces on the Aquilonian border, they will still have to decide to abandon the border, worrying all the while of what Aquilonia will do."

"Ten days' march from the border for a sizeable force," Conan said thoughtfully. "Two days hard riding for a message to get there. So you can count on twelve days before you must face siege machinery and soldiers in numbers to assault the city walls. Perhaps it will be longer, but 'tis best to count on no more."

"You have an eye for such things," Graecus said approvingly. "We plan based on twelve days."

"And will have no need for them," Stephano pronounced with a dismissing wave of his hand. "Long before then, the downtrodden of the city will have risen to join us. A hundred thousand men will line the walls of the city, shoulder to shoulder. We will have called on Garian to abdicate—"

"Abdicate!" Conan shouted. The others started, staring at the walls as if they could see them listening. He went on in a lower tone. "You raise a rebellion, then call on Garian to abdicate? 'Tis madness. The Golden Leopards could hold the Royal Palace for half a year of siege, perhaps more. You have twelve days."

"'Tis none of my idea," Ariane said disgustedly. "From the first have I said we must sweep over the Palace in the first hour."

"And slaughter everyone there!" Stephano said. "Then we are no better than Garian, our beliefs and ideals so much rhetoric."

"I do not remember," Graceus said slowly, "who it was first suggested we demand that Garian abdicate. On first thought, perhaps it seems best to do as Ariane wishes, attack the Palace while the Golden Leopards yet believe it is no more than another disturbance in the streets. But we cannot totally abandon the very ideals for which we fight. Besides," he finished with a smile, as if he had found the solution, "it is well known that the hill on which the Royal Palace sits is riddled with a hundred passages, any one of which will take us inside its defenses."

"Everyone may know of these passages," Ariane said, her voice dripping acid, "but do you know where to find one of them? Just one?"

"We could dig," the stocky man suggested weakly. Ariane snorted, and he subsided.

Conan shook his head. "Garian will not abdicate. No king would. You will but waste time you do not have to waste."

"If he will not abdicate," Stephano said, "then the people will storm the Royal Palace and tear him to pieces with their bare hands for his crimes against them."

"The people," Conan said, staring at the dark-browed man as if he had never seen his like before. "You talk of preventing a slaughter that will tarnish your ideals. What of the thousands who will die taking the Palace? If they can?"

"We compromised our ideals by hiring swordsmen for gold," Stephano maintained stubbornly. "We cannot compromise them further. All who die will be martyrs to a just and glorious cause."

"When is this glorious day?" Conan asked sarcastically.

"As soon as Taras has gathered his thousand men," Graecus replied.

"In effect, then this Taras gives the word for your uprising?" Graecus nodded slowly, a suddenly doubtful look on his face, and Conan went on. "Then I must speak to Taras before I decide whether to join you."

Ariane's eyes grew wide. "You mean that you still may turn aside from us? After we have opened ourselves to you?"

"We have told him all!" Stephano cried, his voice growing more shrill by the word. "He can betray everything! We have given ourselves to this barbarian!"

His face suddenly hard, Conan gripped his sword with both hands, pulling it up so that the hilt was before his face. Stephano stumbled back with a shriek like a woman, and Graecus scrambled his feet. Ariane's face was pale, but she did not move.

"By this steel," Conan said, "and by Crom, Lord of the Mound, I swear that I will never betray you." His icy blue eyes found Ariane's and held them. "I will die first."

Ariane stepped forward, her face full of wonder, and placed a hesitant hand on the Cimmerian's cheek. "You are like no other man I have ever known," she whispered. Her voice firmed. "I believe him. We will arrange a meeting for him with Taras. Agreed, Stephano? Graecus?" The two sculptors nodded jerkily. "Leucas? Leucas!"

"What?" The skinny philosopher started as if he had been asleep. "Whatever you say, Ariane. I agree with you wholeheartedly." His eye lit on Conan's bared blade, and his head jerked back to thump against the wall. He remained like that, staring at the steel with horrified eyes.

"Philosophers," Ariane murmured laughingly.

"I must go," Conan said, returning his sword to its scabbard. "I must meet Hordo."

"I will see you tonight, then," Ariane said. Stephano suddenly looked as if his stomach pained him. "And, Conan," she added as he turned for the door, "I trust you with my life."

With her life, the Cimmerian thought as he left the inn. Yet was she involved to the heart in the conspiracy and uprising. It could succeed. If Taras had in fact the thousand trained and armed men he claimed. If the people rose, and followed, and did not flee when faced with the interlocked shields and steady tread of infantry, the armored charge of heavy cavalry and the roof-rending crash of monstrous siege engines. If the rebels in their pride could be convinced to let their ideals wait on victory and seize the Palace while the Golden Leopards yet stood unaware. Too many ifs. Her life was bound with a doomed cause. Yet in the pride of his youth Conan swore another oath, this to himself. While holding to his oath not to betray, he would save her life despite her.

IX

By one glass past midday the Street of Regrets had begun its revelry, though slowly, yet building for the climax of night. A hundred jugglers tossed balls, batons, rings, knives and flaming wands where a thousand soon would. A hundred strumpets, rouged, perfumed and bangled, lightly draped with brightly colored silks, postured where two thousand would strut at dark. Through them strolled scores of richly tunicked nobles and merchants, each convoyed by his sword-bearing man or pair, vanguard for the multitudes to follow. Litters in dozens, borne by well-muscled slaves, bounded by armored guards, carried sleek, hot-breathed women seeking in advance of their sisters the vices offered by the desperate. And among them all the beggars wheedled in their rags.

Conan, making his way down the street, indifferent to its sights and sounds, found himself laughing when at last he spied the Sign of the Full Moon. On a slab of wood hanging above the entrance was painted a naked woman, kneeling and bent, her back to the viewer, and her buttocks glowing as if reflecting the sun. This spoke of the raucous delights that Hordo would choose.

Suddenly one of the litters caught his eye, scarlet curtained, its black poles and framing worked with gold. Of a certainty it was the litter he had seen his first day in Belverus, the litter of the veiled woman who had looked at him so strangely. The scarlet curtain twitched aside, and once again he was looking into the eyes of the woman veiled in gray. Over that distance he could discern not even so much as their color, yet those tilted eyes were familiar to him. Hauntingly so; if he could but bring back the memory.

He shook his head. Memory and imagination played tricks. A hundred women he had known and a thousand he had not could have eyes exactly alike. He turned to enter the Full Moon.

From behind, sweeping over the murmur of the street, came a sound, a woman's laugh, half sob. He spun, an icy chill running up his spine. That laugh had seemed so familiar that he was almost sure if he opened his mouth a name would emerge to match it. But no woman was there, save the whores. The litter was swallowed up in the throng.

The Cimmerian eased sword and belt dagger in their sheaths, as if that easing would ease his mind. He was too much on edge for worry of Ariane, he told himself. It would do good to lose himself for a time with Hordo in drink and ogling of this fabulous dancer. He plunged into the Full Moon.

The common room of the Full Moon smelled of sour wine and stale perfume. The rough wooden tables were not more than a third filled at this hour, with men who hunched over their drinks, nursing their wine and their own dark fears together. Seven women danced to two shrill flutes and a zither, each carrying a strip of transparent red silk used now to cover the face, now to conceal bare breasts. From thin gilded girdles worn low on rounded hips depended curved brass plates that covered the juncture of their thighs, each plate marked with the price for which she who wore it could be enjoyed in the rooms above.

Though all the dancers were nicely curved, Conan saw none he believed would have excited Hordo's imagination the way the message indicated. Perhaps they had other dancers, he thought, who would appear later. As he took a table close to the narrow platform where the dancers writhed, a plump serving wench appeared at his elbow, a single twist of muslin about her hips.

"Wine," he said, and she darted away.

As he settled to enjoying the women on the stage he became aware of someone staring at him. Hesitantly the thin philosopher, Leucas, approached his table.

"I need . . . may I talk with you, Conan?"

The thin man looked about him nervously as he spoke, as though afraid of being overheard. The only other men not concentrating on their wine were three dark-skinned Kothians, their hair braided into metal rings and Karpashi daggers strapped to their forearms. They appeared to be arguing as to whether the dancers were worth the prices they bore. Still, Leucas half fell onto the stool across from Conan, leaning across the table and pitching his voice in an urgent whisper as if he expected someone to stop him, violently, at any second.

"I had to talk to you, Conan. I followed. Your sword. When I saw it, I knew. You're the one. You are the kind of man who can do this sort of thing. I . . . I am not. I'm just not a man of action." Sweat poured down his narrow face, though the tavern was shadowed and cool. "You do understand, don't you?"

"Not a word," Conan said.

Leucas squeezed his eyes shut, muttering under his breath, and when he opened them he seemed to have gotten a grip on himself. "You agree that Garian must be removed, do you not?"

"That's what you're planning," Conan replied noncommittally.

"But . . ." Leucas' voice rose alarmingly; he pulled it down with visible effort. "But that has to be changed, now. We can wait no longer. What happened these few days past. The sun darkening. The ground trembling. The gods have turned their faces from Nemedia. That was a sign, a warning that we must remove Garian before they remove him, and with him all of Belverus."

Conan's own god, Crom, Dark Lord of the Mound, gave a man life and will and nothing more. Conan had seen little evidence that other gods did any more. As for the darkened sky and the trembling ground, it was his opinion that someone in Belverus worked at sorcery, despite Garian's prohibitions. He had no love of such, but for once he was not involved, and he intended to remain that way.

All he said was, "You think your plans should be advanced, then? But why speak to me of it?"

"No, you don't understand. Not those plans. Something different. More immediate." The thin man's face had a sheen now, from the sweat that covered it, and his voice shook, though he kept it low. "We are to be introduced into the palace, you see. With knives. Garian must die. Immediately. But I cannot. I am not that sort of man. You are a man of violence. Take my place."

"I'm no assassin," Conan growled.

Leucas yelped, eyes darting frantically. "Keep your voice down," he almost sobbed. "You don't understand. You have to—"

"I understand what you ask," Conan said coldly. "Ask again and I'll give you my fist in your teeth." A sudden thought struck him. "Does Ariane know of this?"

"You must not tell her. You must not tell anyone. I should never have spoken to you." Abruptly Leucas stumbled to his feet. Backing away from the table, he made vague and futile gestures. "Consider it, Conan. Will you do that? Just consider it."

The Cimmerian made as if to rise, and with a yelp the philosopher scrambled away, almost diving into the street.

Conan's mouth twisted angrily. How dare the man consider him so, an assassin, a murderer? He had killed, surely, and likely would again, but because he had to, not because he had been paid to. But more important than his feelings was Ariane. Conan could see no way for a man like Leucas, smelling of fear-sweat, to enter the Royal Palace without being taken. And once given a whiff of hot irons and pincers, the philosopher would babble every name he knew back to his mother. The Cimmerian could escape if worse came to worst, but Ariane would be a fawn in a snare. Would Hordo appear, he decided, they would find Ariane, and he would warn her about Leucas.

Thinking of Hordo reminded him of his wine. Where could that serving girl be? Nowhere in sight, that was certain. In the entire tavern no one was moving except the dancers and the three Kothians, apparently ambling closer for a better inspection of the wares.

Conan started to rise to go in search of the girl, and as he did one of the Kothians suddenly shouted at him, "I told you she is my woman, barbar!"

With practiced moves the three crossed their wrists and drew their forearm daggers. The flutes ceased their play, and the dancers ran screaming as the Kothians plunged at the muscular Cimmerian, a blade in each fist.

One-handed, Conan heaved his table over to crash before them. "Fools," he shouted as he sprang to his feet, "you have the wrong man."

Two of the Kothians danced aside, but one fell, rolling to his knees before Conan, daggers stabbing. Conan sucked in his belly, and the blades skittered off his jazeraint hauberk, one to either side. Before the attacker could move, Conan's knee had smashed into his bony chin, splintering teeth in a spray of blood. Even as the man's blades fell from nerveless hands, and he followed them unconscious to the filthy floor, Conan's own steel was in his grasp, broadsword and belt dagger held low at the ready.

"You have the wrong man," he said again. The remaining two split, gliding in the feline crouch of experienced knife fighters. Noise picked up at the tables as men took wagers on the outcome. "I've never seen you before, nor your woman."

The two men continued to move, flanking the Cimmerian, blades held low for the thrust that would slip under the overlapping metal plates of his hauberk.

"You are he," one said, and when Conan's eyes flickered to him, the other attacked.

The Cimmerian had been expecting it, though. Even as his eyes shifted, so had his sword slashed. The attacking Kothian screamed, a fountain of blood where his right hand had been. Desperately clutching the stump of his wrist, the man staggered back, sinking to the floor with the front of his tunic staining deeper red with every spurt.

Conan spun back to face the third man, but that one was of no mind to continue the business. Dismay writ large on his dark face, he stared at his two fellows on the floor, one senseless and one bleeding to death.

The big Cimmerian pointed at him with his sword. "Now. You will tell me—"

Suddenly the door of the tavern was filled with City Guardsmen, a dozen of them, crowding through with swords in hand. The first one pointed at Conan. "There he is!" he shouted. In a mass the Guardsmen surged forward, plowing through onlookers and toppling tables in their haste.

"Crom!" Conan muttered. They looked to have no mind for asking who had begun the fighting, or why. Springing onto the narrow stage, he dashed for the door the dancers had used. It was latched.

"Take him!" a Guardsman howled. "Cut him down!" Bursting through the tavern's patrons—most of whom would gladly have gotten out of the way had they been given a chance—the Guardsmen rushed for the stage.

Conan took a quick step back and hurled himself against the rough wooden door, smashing through in a shower of splinters. Dancers, shrieking now again, huddled in the narrow passage, at the end of which he saw a doorway letting onto the outside. Hurriedly he forced his way through the scantily clad dancers. At the doorway he paused, then turned, waving his sword overhead, and roared, making the most horrible face he could. Screaming with renewed energy, the dancers stampeded back onto the stage. Shouts of consternation rose as the Guardsmen found themselves caught in a deluge of hysterical female flesh.

That should hold them, Conan thought. Sheathing his steel he hurried out into an alley behind the tavern. Little wider than his shoulders and twisting like a snake, it smelled of old vomit and human excrement. He chose a direction and started off through the buzzing flies.

Before he reached the first turning, a shout rose behind him. "There he goes!"

A glance over his shoulder confirmed that the Guardsmen were pouring into the alley. The gods must have tainted his luck, he thought, to send him the only Guardsmen in Belverus with a mind for duty. Perhaps they did not like women. Shouting and slipping in the filth, the black-cloaked squad rushed after him.

Conan set out at a run, keeping his balance as best he could, half falling against the walls at every twisting of the alley, his massive shoulders knocking more stucco from the flaking, mildewed buildings. Another alley serpentined across the one he followed; he dodged down it. Still another passage appeared, winding cramped between dark walls, and he turned into that. Behind the curses of his pursuit followed.

As he ran he realized that he was in a warren, a maze of ancient passages in an area surrounded by more normal roadways. The buildings seemed ready to topple and fill those passages with rubble, for though they had begun long years past with but single stories, as years and needs demanded more room that could not be got by building outward, extra rooms had been constructed atop the roofs, and more atop those, till they resembled nothing so much as haphazard stacks of stuccoed and gray-tiled boxes.

In such a region, running like a fox before hounds, it would be a matter of luck if he found his way to the outside before his pursuers seized him. And it seemed his luck was sour that day. But there was another option, for one who had been among the icy crags and cliffs of Cimmeria.

With a mighty leap he caught the edge of a roof, and swung himself up to lie flat on the slate tiles. The curses and shouts of the Guardsmen came closer, were below him, were moving off.

"He's up there!" a man shouted below. "I see his foot!"

"Erlik's Bowels and Bladder!" Conan muttered. His luck was not sour. Verily it had rotted.

As the Guardsmen struggled to climb, the Cimmerian darted across the slates, hoisted himself onto a higher level, scrambled over it and leaped to a lower roof. With a great crack the tiles gave way beneath his feet, and he plummeted into the room below.

Dazed, Conan struggled to his feet in a welter of broken slate. He was not alone, he realized. In the shadows against the far wall, face obscured, a large man in an expensive cloak of plain blue uttered a startled oath in the accents of the gutter. Another man, short beard circling a face pocked with the marks of some disease, stared in disbelief at Conan.

It was the third man, though, a gray cloak pulled over his scarlet tunic, who drew the eye. Hawk-faced and obsidian-eyed, his dark hair slashed at the temples with white, he looked born to command. And now he issued one. "Kill him," he said.

Crom, Conan thought, reaching for his sword. Did everyone in Belverus want him dead? The pock-faced man put hand to sword hilt.

"Down there!" came a shout from above. No muscle moved in the room save a twitching of the pock-faced man's cheek. "That hole in the roof! A silver piece to the man who first draws blood!"

Visage dark as death, the hawk-faced man raised a clawed hand, as if he could strike Conan across the breadth of the room. There were thuds above as men dropped to the roof. "No time," the hawk-faced one snarled.

Turning, he stalked from the room. The other two vanished behind him.

Conan had no mind either to greet the Guardsmen or to follow on the heels of those three. His eye lit on a tattered cloth, hung against the wall like a tapestry. As if it hid something. He jerked it aside to reveal a door. That let onto another room, full of dust and empty of else, but from there another door opened into a hall. As Conan closed that one softly behind him, he heard the thumps of men dropping through the hole in the roof.

For a wonder, after the maze of the alleys, the corridor ran straight to a street, and for its length the Cimmerian saw no one save one aging blowze who cracked a door and gave him a gap-toothed smile of invitation. Shuddering at the thought, he hurried on.

When he got back to the Thestis, the first person he saw was Hordo, scowling into a mug of wine. He dropped onto a stool across from him.

"Hordo, did you send a message telling me to meet you at the Sign of the Full Moon?"

"What? No." Hordo shook his head, without looking up from his mug. "Answer me this, Cimmerian. Do you understand any part of women? I walked in, told Kerin she had the prettiest eyes in Belverus, and she slapped my face and said she supposed I thought her breasts weren't big enough." He sighed mournfully. "And she won't say another word to me."

"Mayhap I can illumine your problem," Conan said, and in a low voice he told of the message purporting to come from the one-eyed man, and what had occurred at the Full Moon.

Hordo caught the import at once. "Then 'tis you they're after. Whoever 'they' are. Did the knifemen not take you, the Guardsmen were meant to."

"Aye," Conan said. "When the Guardsmen followed so doggedly, I knew their palms had been crossed with gold. But I still know not who did the crossing."

Hordo drew a line through a puddle of spilled wine with a spatulate finger. "Have you thought of leaving Belverus, Conan? We could ride south. Trouble brews in Ophir, too, and there's no dearth of hiring for Free-Companies. I tell you, this business of someone you know not seeking your death sits ill with me. I knew you should have heeded that blind soothsayer."

"You knew. . . ." Conan shook his head. "An I ride south, Hordo, I lose the company. Some would not leave the gold to be had here, and I have not the gold to pay the rest until we find service in Ophir. Besides, there are things I must attend to here first."

"Things? Conan, tell me you're not involving us in this . . . this hopeless children's revolt."

"Not exactly."

"Not exactly," Hordo said hollowly. "Tell me what it is you are doing. Exactly."

"Earn a little gold," Conan replied. "Discover who means to have me dead, and deal with them. Oh, and save Ariane from the headman's axe. You don't want Kerin's pretty head to fall, do you?"

"Perhaps not," the one-eyed man said grudgingly.

Looking around the room until he spotted Kerin, Conan waved for her to come to the table. She hesitated, then came over stiffly.

"Is Ariane here?" he asked her. The first part of saving her head was to let her know about Leucas, so she could stop him.

"She went out," Kerin said. She looked straight at the big Cimmerian as if Hordo did not exist. "She said she had to arrange a meeting for you."

"About that message this forenoon," Hordo said suddenly.

Casually Kerin leaned over and tipped his winemug into his lap. He leaped to his feet, cursing, as she left.

"Beheading's too good for her," he growled. "Since we've both been abandoned, as it seems, let us go to the Street of Regrets. I know a den of vice so iniquitous that whores blush to hear it mentioned."

"Not the Sign of the Full Moon, I trust," Conan laughed.

"Never a bit, Cimmerian." Hordo broke into song in a voice like a jackass in pain. "Oh, I knew a wench from Alcibies, her nipples were like rubies. Her hair was gold, but her rump was cold, and her. . . ." A sudden, shocked silence had descended on the common room. "You're not singing, Conan."

Laughing, Conan got to his feet, and roaring the truly obscene second verse they marched out to horrified gasps.

X

"A re you certain?" Albanus demanded. Golden lamps suspended on chains from the arched ceiling of the marble-columned hall cast shadows on the planes of his face, making him look the wolf he was fiercer cousin to.

Demetrio bristled sulkily, half at the doubting tone and half for having been made to wait on Albanus in the entry hall. "You wanted Sephana watched," he muttered. "I had her watched. And I'm certain. Would I have come in the night were I not?"

"Follow me," Albanus commanded, speaking as to a servant.

And he no more noticed the young catamite's pale lips and clenched fists than he would have those of a servant. Demetrio followed as commanded; that was all that was important. Albanus had slipped already into his persona of king. After all, it was now but a matter of days. His last essential acquisition had been made that very day.

The dark-eyed lord went directly to the chamber where he so often sported himself with Sularia, but the woman was not there now. He tugged the brocaded bell-pull on the wall in a particular fashion, then went straight to his writing desk.

"When?" he demanded, uncapping the silver inkpot. Taking quill and parchment before him, he scribbled furiously. "How long have I before she acts?"

"I was not privy to her planning," Demetrio answered with asperity. "Is it not enough that she gathers her myrmidons about her this night?"

"Fool!" Albanus grated.

With quick movements the hawk-faced lord sprinkled sand across the wet-inked parchment from a silver cellar, then lit the flames beneath a small bronze wax-pot. A slave entered, his short white tunic embroidered at the hem with Albanus' house-mark. Albanus ignored him, pouring off the sand and folding the parchment, sealing it with a drop of wax and his signet.

"Had all Sephana's conspirators come, Demetrios, when your watcher brought word to you?"

"When the third arrived, he came to me immediately. She would not have three of them together if she did not mean to strike tonight."

Cursing, Albanus handed the parchment to the slave. "Put this in the hands of Commander Vegentius within a quarter of a glass. On pain of your life. Go."

The slave bowed and all but ran from the room.

"If all have not yet come," Albanus said as soon as the slave had gone, "there may yet be time to stop her before she reaches the Palace." He hurried to the lacquered chest, unlocking it with the key that hung about his neck. "And stop her I will."

Demetrio eyed the chest and its contents uneasily. "How? Kill her?"

"You have not the stuff of kings in you," Albanus laughed. "There is a subtle art in shaping punishment to fit the crime and the criminal. Now stand aside and be silent."

The slender young noble needed no second warning. He buried his nose in his pomander—was it not said that all sorceries had great stenches associated with them?—and wished most fervently that he were elsewhere at that moment.

Carelessly sweeping a priceless bowl of Ghirgiz crystal from a table to shatter on the floor, Albanus laid in its place a round silver tray graven with an intricate pattern that pained the eye which tried to follow it. With hurried movements he pushed back the flowing sleeves of his deep blue tunic, opened a vial and traced a portion of that pattern in scarlet liquid, muttering incantations beneath his breath as he did. The liquid followed the precise lines worked in the silver, a closed rubiate intricacy that did not spread or alter.

A packet containing powdered hair from Sephana's head—her serving maids had been easily bribed to provide the gleanings of her brush—was emptied into a mortar wrought from the skull of a virgin. Certain other ingredients were minutely measured on burnished golden scales and added to the skull, the mixture then ground by a pestle made of an infant's thigh bone.

With this concoction he traced other lines of that scribing on the tray. Powder and liquid each formed a closed figure, yet though no part of one touched the other, some portions of each shape seemed to be within the other. But those portions were not always the same, and the eye that looked on them too long spun with nausea and dizziness.

For a bare moment Albanus paused, anticipating, savoring. There had been the matter of the droughts, but this was the first time that he had struck so at a human being. The power of it seemed to course through his veins, building like the pleasure of taking a woman. Every instant of prolonging made the pleasure greater. But he knew there was no time.

Spreading his arms he began to chant in a long-dead tongue, his voice invoking, commanding. Powder and liquid began to glow, and his words became more insistent.

Demetrio moved back as the arcane syllables pierced his brain, not stopping until he stood against the wall. He understood no single one of them, yet all had meaning in the depths of his soul, and the evil that he cherished there knew itself for a lighted spill beside a dark burning mountain. He would have screamed, but terror had him by the throat; his screams echoed in the sunless caverns of his mind.

Albanus' voice grew no louder, yet his words seemed to shake the walls. Tapestries stirred as if at an unseen, unfelt wind. The glow from the silver tray grew, brighter, ever brighter, till it sliced through closed eyelids like razors of fire. Then powder and liquid alike were no more, replaced by burning mist that still held the shape of that pattern and seemed more solid that those first substances had been.

A clap sounded in the room, as thunder, and the mist was gone, the graven silver surface clear. The glow lingered a moment longer, behind the eyes, then it, too, faded.

Albanus sighed heavily, and lowered his arms. "Done," he muttered. "'Tis done." His gaze rose to meet that of Demetrio; the slender young man shivered.

"My Lord Albanus," Demetrio said, long unattempted humility cloying in his throat, yet driven by his fear, "I would say again that I serve you to the best of my abilities, and that I wish no more than to see you take your rightful place on the Dragon Throne."

"You are a good servant?" Albanus said, his mouth curling with cruel amusement.

The young noble's face flushed with anger, but he stammered, "I am."

Albanus' voice was as smooth and as cutting as the surgeon's knife. "Then be silent until I have need for you to serve me again."

Demetrio's face went pale; Albanus noted it, but said nothing. The youth was beginning to learn his proper place in the scheme of things. He had his uses in gathering information. Perhaps, an he learned his place well enough, he could be allowed to live.

Carefully the cruel-eyed lord relocked the lacquered chest. "Come," he said, turning from the chest. "We have little time to meet the others."

He saw the question—what others?—trembling on Demetrio's lips. When it did not come, he allowed himself a smile. Such was the proper attitude toward a king, to accept what was given. How sweet it would be to have all of Nemedia so. And perhaps beyond Nemedia. Why should borders decided by others deter him?

In short order they had donned heavy cloaks against the night and left the palace. Four slaves carried torches, two before and two behind. Ten armed and armored guards, mail and leather creaking, surrounded Albanus as he made his way through the dark streets. That they surrounded Demetrio as well was incidental.

They saw no one, although scurrying feet could often be heard as footpads and others who lurked in the night hurried to be out of the way, and from time to time some glimmer of sound from the Street of Regrets came to them as the wind shifted. Elsewhere, those who could not afford to hire bodyguards slept ill at ease, praying that theirs would not be among the houses ravaged that night.

Then, as they approached Sephana's palace, where fluted marble columns rose behind the alabaster wall enclosing her garden, a procession of torches appeared down the street. Albanus stopped some distance from the palace gate, waiting in silence for a proper greeting.

"Is that you, Albanus?" came Vegentius' growl. "A foul night, and a foul thing to have to slit the throat of one of my own captains."

Albanus' mouth twisted. This one would not live, not an he were a hundred times as useful. He waited to speak until Vegentius and his followers, a score of Golden Leopards, their cloaks thrown back to give sword arms free play, half bearing torches, were close enough to be seen clearly.

"At least you managed to dispose of Baetis. Have you yet found the barbarian?"

"Taras has sent no word," the big soldier said. "'Tis likely, pursued as he was, that he's no more than a common thief or murderer. Naught to concern us."

Albanus favored him with a scornful glance. "Whatever disrupts a meeting like that concerns me. Why did the Guard pursue him so? Long time has passed ere they were known for such enthusiasm."

"This matter differs from that of Melius. I have no pretext to ask questions of the Guard."

"Make one," Albanus commanded. "And now force me this gate."

Vegentius spoke quietly to his men. Six of them moved quickly to the wall, dividing into two groups. In each trio two men linked hands to lift the third, who laid his cloak across the jagged shards of pottery set in the top of the wall and scrambled over to drop on the far side. From thence a startled cry was heard, then cut significantly short. With a rattle of stout bars being lifted, the gates swung open.

Albanus marched in, sparing not a glance for the guard who lay in the light spilling from the small gatehouse, surrounded by a spreading pool of blood.

Vegentius told off two more men to remain at the gate. The rest followed the hawk-faced lord through the landscape gardens to the palace itself, with its pale columns and intricately worked cornices, and up broad marble stairs to a spacious portico. Some ran to throw back the tall bronze-hung doors with a crash.

In the columned entry hall, half a dozen men started, and stared as soldiers rushed in to surround them with bared blades.

"Dispose of them," Albanus ordered without slowing. He went straight to the alabaster stairs, Demetrio trailing after.

Behind him men began shouting for mercy as they were herded away.

"No!" a skinny, big-nosed man screamed. "I would not have done it. I—" Vegentius' boot propelled him beyond hearing.

Albanus made his way to Sephana's bedchamber along halls he once had traversed for more carnal purposes. But not, he thought as he opened the door, for more pleasurable ones.

Demetrio followed him diffidently into the room, peering fearfully for the destruction the magick had wrought. There seemed to be none. Sephana lay on her bed, though to be sure she did not move or acknowledge their presence. She was naked, a robe of blue silk clutched in her hand as if she had been on the point of donning it when she decided instead to lie down. Albanus chuckled, a dry sound like the rattle of a poisonous serpent.

The slender youth crept forward. Her eyes were open; they seemed to have life, to see. He touched her arm, and gasped. It was as hard as stone.

"She still lives," Albanus said suddenly. "A living statue. She will not have to worry about losing her beauty with age now."

Demetrio shivered. "Would it not have been simpler to kill her?"

The hawk-faced lord gave him a glance that was all the more frightening for its seeming benevolence. "A king must think of object lessons. Who thinks of betraying me will think next on Sephana's fate and wonder at his own. Death is much more easily faced. Would you betray me now, Demetrio?"

Mouth suddenly too dry for words, the perfumed youth shook his head.

Vegentius entered the room laughing. "You should have heard their crying and begging. As if tears and pleas would stay our steel."

"They are disposed of, then?" Albanus said. "All who were under this roof? Servants and slaves as well?"

The big square-faced man drew a broad finger across his throat with a crude laugh. "In the cesspool. There was one—Leucas, he said his name was, as if it mattered—who wept like a woman and said it was not he, but one named Conan who was to do the deed. Anything to—What ails you, Albanus?"

The hawk-faced lord had gone pale. His eyes locked with those of Demetrio. "Conan. 'Twas the name of he from whom you bought the sword." Demetrio nodded, but Albanus, though looking at him, saw other things. He whispered, uttering his thoughts unaware. "Coincidence? Such is the work of the gods, and when they tangle the skeins of mens' fates so it is for cause. Such cause could be murderous of ambition. I dare not risk it."

"It cannot be the same man," Vegentius protested.

"Two with such a barbarous name?" Albanus retorted. "I think not. Find him." His obsidian glare drilled each man in turn, turning them to stone with its malignancy. "I want this Conan's head!"

XI

Conan poured another dipperful of water over his head and peered blearily about the courtyard behind the Thestis. The first thing his eye lit on was Ariane, arms crossed and a disapproving glint in her eye.

"If you must go off to strange taverns," she said firmly, "drinking and carousing through the small hours, you must expect your head to hurt."

"My head does not hurt," Conan replied, taking up a piece of rough toweling to scrub his face and hair dry. His face hidden, he winced into the toweling. He hoped fervently that she would not shout; if she did his skull would surely explode.

"I looked for you last night," she went on. "Your meeting with Taras is arranged, though he wished no part of it at first. You have little time now. I'll give you directions."

"You are not coming?"

She shook her head. "He was very angry at our having approached you. He says we know nothing of fighting men, of how to choose good from bad. After I told him about you, though, he changed his mind. At least, he will meet you and decide for himself. But the rest of us are not to come. That is to let us know he's angry."

"Mayhap." Conan tossed aside the toweling and hesitated, choosing his words. "I must speak to you of something. About Leucas. He is putting you in danger."

"Leucas?" she said incredulously. "What danger could he put me in?"

"On yesterday he came to me with some goat-brained talk of killing Garian, of assassination. An he tries that—"

"It's preposterous!" she broke in. "Leucas is the last of us ever to speak for any action, especially violent action. He cares for naught save his philosophy and women."

"Women!" the big Cimmerian laughed. "That skinny worm?"

"Yes, indeed, my muscular friend," she replied archly. "Why, he's accounted quite the lover by those women he's known."

"You among them?" he growled, his massive fists knotting.

For a moment she stared, then her eyes flared with anger. "You do not own me, Cimmerian. You have no leave to question me of what I did or did not do with Leucas or anyone else."

"What's this of Leucas?" Graecus said, ambling into the courtyard. "Have you seen him? Or heard where he is?"

"No," Ariane snapped, her face coloring. "And what call have you to skulk about like some spy?"

Graecus seemed to hear nothing beyond her denial. "He's not been seen since last night. Nor Stephano, either. When I heard his name mentioned. . . ." He laughed weakly. "Perhaps we could stand to lose a philosopher or three, but if they're taking sculptors this time as well. . . ." He laughed again, but his face was a sickly green.

Ariane was suddenly soothing. "They will return." She laid a concerned hand on the stocky man's shoulder. "Why, like as not they wasted the night in drink. Conan, here, did the same."

"Why should they not return?" Conan asked.

Ariane shot him a dagger look, but Graecus answered shakily. "Some months past some of our friends disappeared. Painters and sketchers, they were. But two were never seen again, their bodies found in a refuse heap beyond the city walls, where Golden Leopards had been seen to bury them. We think Garian wishes to frighten us into silence."

"It sounds not like the way of a king," Conan said, frowning. "They frighten with public executions and the like."

Graecus suddenly looked ready to vomit.

Ariane scowled at Conan. "Should you not be making ready to meet Taras?" Without waiting for an answer, she turned to Graecus, uttering soothing sounds and stroking his brow.

Disgruntled, Conan tugged on his padded under-tunic and jazeraint hauberk, muttering to himself on the peculiarities of Ariane. As he buckled his sword belt about him, she spoke again.

"Do you need to go so, as if armed for war?" Her tone was biting, her annoyance at him still high. "You'll not have to fight him."

"I have my reasons," Conan muttered.

Not for a sack of gold as big as a cask would he have told her that someone in the city was trying to kill him. In her present mood, she would think he was trying to shift her sympathy from Graecus to himself. Erlik take all women, he thought.

Setting his spiked helm on his head, he said coldly, "Give me your directions for finding this Taras." Her face as she gave them was just as cold.

The Street of the Smiths, whence Ariane's directions took him, was lined not only with the shops of swordsmiths and ironworkers, but also of smiths in gold, silver, copper, brass, tin and bronze. A cacophony of hammering blended with the cries of sellers to make the street a solid sheet of noise, reverberating from end to end. The Guilds made sure that a man who worked one metal did not work another, but so too did they hire the guards that patrolled the street. No bravos lurked on the Street of the Smiths, and shoppers strolled with an ease seen nowhere else in the city.

As he came closer to the place of the meeting—rooms reached by entering a narrow hall next to a coppersmith's shop and climbing the stairs at its end—the less he wished to enter it unprepared. He had no reason to foresee trouble, but too many times of late someone had tried to put a blade into him.

Short of the coppersmith's he began to dawdle, pausing here to heft a gleaming sword, there to finger a silver bowl hammered in an intricate pattern of leaves. But all the while he observed the building that housed the coppersmith with an eye honed by years as a thief.

A pair of Guild guards had stopped to watch him, where he stood before a silversmith's open-fronted shop. He raised the bowl he held to his ear and thumped it.

"Too much tin," he said, shaking his head and tossing the bowl back on the merchant's table. He strolled off pursued by the silversmith's frenzied imprecations, but the guards paid him no more mind.

Just beyond the coppersmith's was an alley, smelling as much of mold and old urine as any other in the city. Into this he slipped, hurrying down its narrow length. As he had hoped, damp air and mold had flaked away most of the mud plastered over the stones of the building.

A quick glance showed that no one was looking down the alley from the street. His fingers sought cracks amid the poorly dressed and poorly mortared stone. Another might have found such a climb impossible, most especially in heavy hauberk and boots, but to one of the Cimmerian mountains the wide chinks in the stone were as good as a highway. He scrambled up the side of the building so quickly that someone who had seen him standing on the ground and looked away for a moment might well have thought he had simply disappeared.

As he heaved himself onto the red clay tiles of the roof, a smile lit his face. Set in the roof was a skylight, a frame stretched with panes of fish-skin. It was, he was certain, situated above the room he sought.

Carefully, so as not to dislodge loose tiles—and perhaps send himself hurtling to the street below—he made his way to the skylight. The panes were clear enough to allow some light through, but not for seeing. It was the work of a moment with his belt dagger to make a slit, to which he put his eye.

The room below was narrow, and ill lit even with the skylight and two brass lamps on a table. In it four men stood, two with cocked crossbows in hands, watching the door through which he was supposed to walk.

The big Cimmerian shook his head, in anger and wonder at the same time. It was one thing to be wary of trouble where none was expected, another to find it waiting there.

"Is he coming, or not?" one of the men without a crossbow asked irritably. He had a deep scar across the top of his head, where someone had caught him a blow that should have killed him.

"He'll come," the other man with no crossbow replied. "The girl said she'd send him right to this room."

Conan froze. Ariane. Could she have sent him here to die?

"What will you tell her?" the horribly scarred man asked. "She has influence enough to cause trouble, Taras."

"That I hired him," Taras laughed, "and sent him out of the city to join the others she thinks I've hired. That should keep her quiet."

Lying on the roof, the big Cimmerian heaved a sigh of relief. Whatever Ariane had done, she had done unknowingly. Then the rest of what Taras had said penetrated. The others she thought he had hired. It was as he had feared. The young rebels were being duped. Conan had a great many questions for Taras. His broadsword slipped from its sheath, steel rasping on leather.

"Be you sure," Taras told the crossbowmen, "to fire the instant he steps into the room. These barbars die hard."

"Even now is he a dead man," one of the pair replied. The other laughed and patted his crossbow.

A wolfish grin came to Conan's face. It was time to see who would die in that room. Like silent death he rose, and leaped.

"Crom!" he roared as his feet tore through the skylight.

The men below had only time to start, then Conan's boots struck one of the crossbowmen squarely atop his head, bearing him to the floor with a crunch of snapping vertebrae. The second crossbowman desperately swung his weapon, trying to bring it to bear. Conan kept his balance with cat-like skill, and pivoted, dagger darting over the swinging crossbow to transfix the bowman's throat. With a gurgling scream he who had named the Cimmerian a dead man himself died, squeezing the trigger-lever as he did. Abruptly the scar-topped man, sword half drawn, coughed once and toppled, the crossbow quarrel projecting from his left eye.

Using the dagger as a handle Conan hurled the sagging body of the bowman at Taras, and as he did he recognized that pock-marked face. Taras had been at that other meeting he had interrupted by coming through the roof.

The pocked man staggered, clawing for his sword, as the corpse struck him. "You!" he gasped, getting his first clear look at the Cimmerian's face.

Snarling, Conan struck, his blade clanging against the hilt of the other's partially drawn sword. Taras shrieked, severed fingers dropping to the floor. And yet he was no man to go down easily. Even while blood flowed from his mutilated right hand, his left snatched his dagger from its sheath. With a cry of rage, he lunged.

It would have been easy for Conan to kill the man then, but he wanted answers more than he wanted Taras' death. Sidestepping Taras' lunge, he clubbed his fisted hilt against the back of the pock-faced man's neck. The lunge became a stumble, and, yelling, Taras fell over the scarred man's body and crashed to the floor. He twitched once, emitting a long sigh, and did not rise.

Cursing, Conan heaved the man onto his back. Taras' limp fingers slid away from his dagger, now embedded in his own chest. His sightless eyes stared at the Cimmerian.

"Erlik take you," Conan muttered. "I wanted you alive."

Wiping his blade on Taras' tunic, he returned the sword to its scabbard, thinking furiously all the while. The man was condemned out of his own mouth of duping the young rebels. Yet he had had that meeting with two who, by their clothing and bearing, were men of wealth and position. He had to assume that that meeting had a related purpose, and that someone did indeed intend to move against Garian, using Ariane and the rest as tools. And tools had a way of being broken and discarded once their use was done.

As Conan tugged his dagger from the crossbowman's throat, the door suddenly swung open. He crouched, dagger at the ready, and found himself staring across the corpse at Ariane and Graecus.

The stocky sculptor seemed to turn to stone as his bulging eyes swept the carnage. Ariane met Conan's gaze with a look of infinite sadness.

"I did not think Taras had the right to exclude us from this meeting," she said slowly. "I thought we should be here, to speak up for you, to. . . ." Her words trailed off in a weary sigh.

"They intended my death, Ariane," Conan said.

She glanced from the shattered skylight frame on the floor to the opening in the roof. "Which of them leapt from above, Conan? It seems clear that one entered that way. To kill. I wondered so when you armored yourself and would not tell me why. Wondered, and prayed I was wrong."

Why did the fool girl have to take everything wrongly, he thought angrily. "I listened at the skylight, Ariane, and entered that way. After I heard them speak of slaying me. Think you they had cocked crossbows to slay rats?" She looked at him, levelly but with eyes lacking hope or life. He drew a deep breath. "Hear me, Ariane. This man Taras has hired no armed men to aid your rebellion. I heard him say this. You must—"

"You killed them!" Graecus suddenly shouted. The stocky man's face was flushed, and he panted as if from great exertion. "It is as Stephano feared. Did you kill him also, and Leucas? Mean you to slay us all? You will not! You cannot! There are hundreds of us! We will slay you first!" Suddenly he glanced down the hall toward the stairs, and with a shrill cry dashed in the other direction. Ariane did not move.

Hordo appeared in the doorway, gazing briefly after the fleeing sculptor. His lone eye took in the bodies. "I returned to the Thestis in time to hear the girl and the other speak of following you. It looks well that I decided to follow them in turn."

Ariane stirred. "Will you murder me now, too, Conan?"

The Cimmerian rounded on her angrily. "Do you not know me well enough by now to know I would not harm you?"

"I thought I did," she said hollowly. Her eyes traveled from one corpse to the next, and she laughed hysterically. "I know nothing of you. Nothing!" Conan reached for her, but she shied away from his big hand. "I cannot fight you," she whispered, "but an you touch me, my dagger can yet seek my own heart."

He jerked back his hand as if it had been burnt. At last he said coldly, "Do not remain here o'erlong. Corpses attract scavengers, and those with two legs will see you as more booty." She did not look at him or make answer. "Come, Hordo," he growled. The one-eyed man followed him from the room.

In the street, those who saw Conan's dark face and the ice of his blue eyes stepped clear of his sweeping strides. Hordo hurried to keep up, asking once they were clear of the clangor of the Street of the Smiths, "What occurred in that room, Cimmerian, to turn the girl so against you?"

Conan's look at Hordo was deadly, but in swift, terse sentences he told of how he had gone there, of what he had heard and what deduced.

"I am too old for this," Hordo groaned. "Not only must we watch for Graecus and the others to put knives in our backs, but, not knowing who among the nobles and merchants is embraced in this, with whom can we take service? Where do we go now, Cimmerian?"

"To the only place left for us," Conan replied grimly. "The King."

XII

On the wide marble steps of the Temple of Mitra, a startled man dropped a cage of doves as the Free-Company made its way down the narrow, winding street. So surprised was he to see mounted and armed men in the Temple District that he watched them open-mouthed, not even noticing that his cage had broken and his intended sacrifices were beating aloft on white wings.

Hordo's saddle creaked as he leaned forward and whispered fiercely to Conan. "This is madness! 'Twill be luck if we are not met atop the hill by the whole of the Golden Leopards!"

Conan shook his head without answering. He knew full well that approaching the Royal Palace unannounced with two score armed men was far from the proper way to appeal for entry into the King's service. He knew, too, that there was no time for more usual methods, such as bribery, and that left only enlistment in the Nemedian army. Or this.

In truth, it was not the Golden Leopards who troubled him so much as the young rebels. Desperate, believing he had betrayed them or was on the way to do so, they might try almost anything. And these winding streets that climbed the hill to the Royal Palace were a prime place for ambush.

Those streets were a remnant of ancient times, for once in the dim past what would become the Royal Palace had been a hilltop fortress, about which a village had risen, a village which over the centuries had grown into Belverus. But long after the hilltop fortress had become the Royal Palace of Nemedia, long after the rude village huts had been replaced by columned temples of alabaster and marble and polished granite, the serpentine streets remained.

The Palace itself retained much of the fortress about it, although its battlements were now of lustrous white marble, and towers of porphyry and greenstone rose within. The portcullises were of iron beneath their gilt, and drawbridges spanned a drymoat bottomed with spikes. Round about it all a sward of grass, close cropped as if in a landscaped garden, yet holding not the smallest growth that might shelter a stealthy approach, separated the Palace from the Temple District that encircled the hill below.

At the edge of the greensward Conan halted the company. "Wait here," he commanded.

"Gladly," Hordo muttered.

Alone, Conan rode forward, his big black stallion prancing slightly. Two pikemen in golden cloaks guarded the drawbridge, and a man in the crested helmet of an officer stepped out from the barbican as the big Cimmerian drew rein.

"What seek you here?" the officer demanded. He eyed the rest of the Free-Company thoughtfully, but they were distant and few in number.

"I wish to enter my company in the service of King Garian," Conan replied. "I have trained them in a method of fighting new to Nemedia, and to the western world."

The officer smiled in mockery. "Never yet have I heard of a Free-Company without some supposedly secret art of war. What is yours?"

"I will demonstrate," Conan said. "It is better in the showing." Inwardly, he breathed a sigh of relief. His one real fear beyond reaching the Palace had been that they would not so much as listen.

"Very well," the officer said slowly, eyeing the rest of the company once more. "You alone may enter and demonstrate. But be you warned, an this secret is something every recruit in the Nemedian army is taught, as are most Free-Company tricks, you will be stripped and flogged from the gates to the foot of the hill for the edification of your company."

Conan touched boots to the big stallion's flanks. The horse pranced forward a step; the pikemen leveled their weapons and the officer looked wary. The Cimmerian allowed a cold smile to touch his mouth, but not his eyes. "'Tis nothing known to any Nemedian, though it may be taught to recruits."

The officer's mouth tightened at his tone. "I think others might like to see this, barbar." He stuck his head back into the gatehouse and muttered an order.

A golden-cloaked soldier emerged, gave Conan an appraising glance, and sped into the Palace. As Conan rode through the gate following the officer, other soldiers appeared from the barbican, some following behind. The Cimmerian wondered if they came to watch, or to guard that he did not take the Palace single-handed.

The Outer Court was paved in flagstone, four hundred paces in each direction, and surrounded by arcaded walks to the height of four stories.

Beyond those walks directly opposite the gate could be seen the towers that rose in the gardens of the Inner Court, and the Palace proper, wherein King Garian and his court lived.

The soldiers who had followed dropped back deferentially as a score of officers, led by one as large as Conan himself, appeared. The officer who had brought Conan in bowed as this big man came near.

"All honor to you, Commander Vegentius," he said. "I hoped this barbar might provide some entertainment."

"Yes, Tegha," Vegentius said absently, his eye on Conan. And a strangely wary eye, the Cimmerian thought. Abruptly the big officer said, "You, barbar. Know I you, or you me?" His hand tightened on his sword as he spoke.

Conan shook his head. "I know you not, Commander." Though, as he thought on it, this Vegentius did look familiar, but vaguely, as one seen but briefly. No matter, he thought. The memory would come, an it were important.

Vegentius seemed to relax as the Cimmerian spoke. Smiling vigorously, he said, "Let us have this demonstration. Tegha, get the barbar what he needs for it."

"I need a straw butt," Conan told the officer, "or some other mark."

Laughter rose among the officers as Tegha chose out two soldiers to fetch a butt.

"Archery," one of them laughed loudly. "I saw that bow at his saddle, but thought it for a child."

"Mayhap he shoots it with one hand," another replied.

Conan kept his silence as the comments grew more ribald, though his jaw tightened. Removing the short weapon from its lacquered saddlecase, he carefully checked the tension of the string.

"A harp," someone shouted. "He plays it like a harp."

Conan fingered through the forty arrows in the quiver strapped behind the cantle of his saddle, making sure once again that each fletching was sound.

"He must miss often, to carry so many shafts."

"Nay, he uses the feathers to tickle women. Take her ankle, you see, and turn her. . . ."

The laughing comments droned on, some measure of silence falling only when the soldiers returned with a straw butt.

"Set it there," Conan commanded, pointing to a spot some fifty paces away. The soldiers ran to comply, as eager as their superiors to see the barbarian's discomfiture.

"Not a great distance, barbar."

"But it's a child's bow."

Breathing deeply to calm himself, Conan rode away from the bunched officers, stopping when he was a full two hundred paces from the butt. Nocking a shaft, he paused. This demonstration must proceed perfectly, and for that his concentration must be on the target, not clouded by anger at the chattering baboons who called themselves officers.

"Why wait you, barbar?" Vegentius shouted. "Dismount and—"

With a wild cry Conan swung the bow up and fired. Even as the shaft thudded home in the butt he was putting boot to the stallion's flanks, galloping forward at full speed, sparks striking from the flagstones beneath the big black's drumming hooves, firing as quickly as he could nock arrow to bowstring, shouting the ululating warcry that oft had wrung fear from the warriors of Gunderland and Hyperborea and the Bossonian Marches.

Arrow after arrow sped straight to the butt. At a hundred paces distant he pressed with his knee, and the massive stallion broke faultlessly to the right. Conan fired again and again, mind and eye one with bow, with shaft, with target. Again his knees pressed, and the war-trained stallion pivoted, rearing and reversing his direction within his own length. Still Conan fired, thundering back the way he had come. When at last he put hand to rein there were four arrows left in the quiver behind his saddle, and he knew, did anyone count the feathered shafts that peppered the butt, they would number thirty and six.

He cantered back to the now silent officers.

"What sorcery is this?" Vegentius demanded. "Have your arrows been magicked, that they strike home while you careen like a madman?"

"No sorcery," Conan replied, laughing. For it was, indeed, his turn to laugh at the stunned expressions worn by the officers. "'Tis accounted a skill, though not a vast one, if a man can hit a running deer with a bow. This is but a step beyond. I myself had no knowledge at all of the bow when I was taught."

"Taught!" Tegha exclaimed, not noticing the glare Vegentius gave him. "Who? Where?"

"Far to the east," Conan said. "There the bow is the principal weapon of light cavalry. In Turan—"

"Whatever they do in these strange lands," Vegentius broke in harshly, "'tis of no matter here. We have no need of outlandish ways. A phalanx of good Nemedian infantry will clear any field, without this frippery of bowmen on horses."

Conan considered telling him what a few thousand mounted Turanian archers would do to that phalanx, but before he could speak another group approached, and the officers were all bowing low.

Leading this procession was a tall, square-faced man, the crown on his head, a golden dragon with ruby eyes and a great pearl clutched in its paws

CONAN THE DEFENDER   261

proclaiming him to be King Garian. Yet Conan had no eyes for the king, nor the counselors who surrounded him, nor the courtiers who trailed him, for there was among them a woman to seize the eye. A long-legged, full-breasted blonde, she was no gently born lady, not wearing transparent red silk held by pearl clasps at her shoulders and snugged about her slender waist by entwined ropes of pearls set in gold. But an she were someone's leman, he paid her not the attention he ought. For she returned Conan's stare, if not so openly as he, yet with a smoky heat that quickened his blood.

Conan saw that Garian was approaching him, and doffed his helm hoping the King had not seen the direction of his gaze.

"I saw your exhibition from the gallery," Garian said warmly, "and I have never seen the like." His brown eyes were friendly—which meant he had not noticed Conan's gaze—though not so open as the eyes of one who did not sit on a throne. "How are you called?"

"I am Conan," the Cimmerian replied. "Conan of Cimmeria." He did not see the blood drain from Vegentius' face.

"Do you come merely to entertain, Conan?"

"I come to enter your service," Conan said, "with my lieutenant and two score men trained to use the bow as I do."

"Most excellent," Garian said, clapping a hand against the stallion's shoulder. "Always have I had an interest in innovations of warfare. Why, from my childhood I as much as lived in the army camps. Now," a trace of bitterness crept into his voice, "I have not even time to practice with my sword."

"My King," Vegentius said deferentially, "this thing is no better than trickery, an entertainment, but of no use in war." As he spoke his eyes drifted to Conan. The Cimmerian thought, but could not believe, it was a look of hatred and fear.

"No, good Vegentius," Garian said, shaking his head. "Your advice is often sound on matters military, but this time you are wrong." Vegentius opened his mouth; Garian ignored him. "Hear me now, Conan of Cimmeria. An you enter my service, I will give each man of yours three gold marks, and three more each tenday. To yourself, ten gold marks, and another each day you serve me."

"It is meet," Conan said levelly. No merchant would have paid more than half so well.

Garian nodded. "It is done, then. But you must practice the sword with me for a full glass each day, for I see by the wear of your hilt that you have some knowledge of that weapon as well. Vegentius, see that Conan has quarters within the Palace, and let them be spacious."

In the way of kings, having issued his commands Garian strode away without further words, soldiers bowing as he left, courtiers and counselors trailing in his wake. The blonde went, too, but as she went her eyes played on Conan's face with furnace heat.

From the corner of his eye Conan saw Vegentius moving away. "Commander Vegentius," he called, "did not the King say my company was to be quartered?"

Vegentius almost snarled his reply. "The King said you were to receive quarters, barbar. He said naught of that rag-tag you call a company. Let them quarter in the gutter." And he, too, stalked away.

Some of Conan's euphoria left him. He could not run whining to Garian, asking that Vegentius be made to quarter his men. There were inns aplenty at the foot of the hill, but in even the cheapest of them, he would have to supplement the men's pay from his own purse. That would strain even his new-found resources. Yet it was not the worst of his worries. Why did Vegentius hate him? He must discover the answer before he was forced to kill the man. And he would have to keep the blonde from getting him beheaded. While enjoying her favors, if possible. But then, when had one born on a battlefield sought a life free of troubles?

Laughing, he rode to the gate to tell the others of their fortune.

XIII

The high domed ceiling of plain gray stone was well lit by cressets brass-hung about the bare walls, in which there was no window and but a single door, and that well guarded on the outside. Albanus would allow no slightest risk to that which the room housed. Even but gazing on it, he felt the power that would come to him from it. Centered in the room was a circular stone platform, no higher than a step from the floor, and on it sat a large rectangular block of peculiarly beige clay. It was that clay that would give Albanus the Dragon Throne.

"Lord Albanus, I demand again to know why I am brought here and imprisoned."

Albanus schooled his face to a smile before turning to the scowling, bushy-browed man who confronted him with fists clenched. "A misapprehension on the part of my guards, good Stephano. I but told them to fetch to me the great sculptor Stephano, and they overstepped themselves. I will have them flogged, I assure you."

Stephano waved that last away as unimportant, though Albanus noted he did not ask for the guards to be spared their promised flogging.

"You have heard of me?" the sculptor asked instead, his chest puffing.

"Of course," Albanus replied, hard put not to laugh. This man was read as easily as a page of large script. "'Tis why I want you to sculpt this statue for me. As you can see, your implements are all provided." He gestured a low table that held every sort of sculptor's tool.

"'Tis all wrong," Stephano said, with overbearing condescension. "Clay is used for small figures. Statues are of stone or bronze."

Albanus' lips retained their smile, but his eyes were frozen coals. "The clay is brought all the way from Khitai." He could think of no more distant land to serve as a source. "When fired, it has the hardness of bronze, yet is lighter than the damp clay. On the table are sketches of he whom the statue is to portray. Examine them."

Looking doubtfully at the block of clay, Stephano took up the parchments, unrolled them, and gasped, "Why, this is Garian!"

"Our gracious king," Albanus agreed unctuously, though he near choked on the words. "'Tis to be a present for him. A surprise."

"But how is the work to be clothed?" the sculptor asked, ruffling through the drawings. "In all of these is he naked."

"And so is the sculpture to be." Albanus forestalled the surprise on Stephano's face by adding, "Such is the custom of Khitai with statues of this clay. They are clothed in actual garments, this raiment being changed from time to time so that the figure is clothed always in the latest fashion." He was pleased with himself for that invention. He wondered if it might not be amusing to have a statue done so of himself once he ascended the throne.

Stephano laughed suddenly, a harsh sound like the scraping of slates. "And what would be done with a naked statue of Garian, were Garian no longer on the throne?"

"An unlikely event," Albanus said blandly.

Stephano looked startled, as if not realizing he had spoken aloud. "Of course. Of course." His face hardened, thick brows drawing down. "Yet why should I accept the offer of this commission, following as it does a night spent locked in your cellars?"

"A grievous error for which I have apologized. Shall we say a thousand gold marks?"

"I have no interest in gold," the sculptor sneered.

"To be distributed to the poor," Albanus continued smoothly. "I have heard much of the good charities you do in Hellgate." Stephano's face did not soften, but the hawk-faced lord saw the way. His voice became a mesmeric whisper. "Think of all the good that you could do with a thousand pieces of gold. Think of your fellows following you as you distribute it. I would wager none of them has ever had the hundredth part so much to give." Stephano nodded slowly, staring at the wall as if he saw a scene there. "How they would laud you, following in your steps with their praises. How great you would be in their eyes." Albanus fell silent, waiting.

Stephano seemed to stand straighter. Abruptly he shook himself and gave an embarrassed laugh. "Of a certainty, great good could come from so much gold. I was lost in thought of those I could help."

"Of course." The cruel-faced lord smiled, then his voice became brisker. "This must be a surprise to Garian. To that end, none may know that you are here. Food and drink will be brought to you. And women, should you desire.

Daily will you have leave of the gardens, an you remember your caution. Now get you to your labor, for time presses."

When Albanus left that room, he stood, trembling, between the guards who stood with bared swords to either side of the door. His stomach roiled with nausea. That he should have to treat one such as Stephano as near an equal! It was ill to be borne. Yet such could not be driven to their work by threat or even torture, as he had discovered to his regret, for the works they then produced were fatally flawed.

A deferential touch on the sleeve of his tunic brought him erect, teeth bared in a snarl.

The slave who had touched him cowered back, his head bent low. "Forgive me, master, but Commander Vegentius awaits, much exercised, and bids me beg your presence."

Albanus thrust the man aside and strode down the hall. He had every detail planned. Had the soldier contrived to foul some part of the scheme, he would geld him with his own hand.

Vegentius was in the columned entry hall, pacing, his face beaded with sweat. He began to speak as soon as Albanus appeared.

"Conan. The barbar who fought Melius and took his sword after. He whom Leucas named part of Sephana's plot. Now one of that name has caught Garian's eye, and taken service with him. And I recognize him; it is he who broke into our meeting with Taras. Four times has he tangled himself in our planning, Albanus, and I like it not. I like it not. 'Tis an ill omen."

"Do the gods join in my affairs?" Albanus whispered, not realizing that he spoke. "Do they think to contend with me?" Louder, he said, "Speak not of ill omens. This very morning a soothsayer told me that I would wear the Dragon Crown at my death. I had him slain, of course, to still his tongue. With such a prophecy of success, what omen can one barbarian be?"

The square-faced soldier bared a handspan of his blade. "Easily could I slay him. He is alone in the Palace, with none to guard his back."

"Fool!" Albanus grated. "A murder within the Palace, and Garian will think strongly to his safety. We do not need him on his guard."

Vegentius sneered. "His safety lies in my hand. One in three of the Golden Leopards answers to me, not to the Dragon Throne."

"And two in three do not. Nor does any part of my plan call for blades to be drawn within the walls of the Palace. I must be seen to save Nemedia from armed rabble rising in the streets."

"Then he is to live?" Vegentius blurted incredulously.

"Nay, he dies." Could this Conan be some weapon of the gods, lifted against him? No. He was destined to wear the Dragon Crown. He was born to be a king, and, with the power of the blue sphere, a living god. "Taras has been so commanded," he continued. "But make it known to him that the man must die well away from the Palace, in some place where his death may be placed to a drunken brawl."

"Taras seems to have vanished, Albanus."

"Then find him!" the cruel-eyed lord snapped irritably. "And remember, within the Palace walls let this barbarian be watched but inviolate. When he ventures out, slay him!"

XIV

S teel rang in the small courtyard as Conan blocked the descending
blade and smoothly moved back to a guard position. Sweat oiled
his massive chest, but his breathing was controlled, his eye firm,
his blade steady.

Garian circled to his left about the big Cimmerian. He also was stripped
to the waist, and but slightly smaller, though his muscles were covered by
the fat of recent inactivity. Sweat rolled down his sloping shoulders, and his
blade wavered, if but a hair's breadth.

"You are good, barbar," the king panted.

Conan said nothing, moving only enough to keep his face to the other
man. Fighting, even in practice, was not the time to talk.

"But you say little," the king continued, and as he spoke his sword darted
for the Cimmerian's middle.

Conan barely moved. His mighty wrists pivoted, his blade arced down
to clash against the king's, carrying it safely to one side. Instead of forcing
taking the other's blade further out of line, as was the favored tactic, Conan
dropped suddenly, squatting on his right leg with his left extended to the
side. His steel slid off the other blade, swung forward and stopped as it
touched Garian's stomach. Before the startled king could react, Conan
flowed back to his feet and to guard.

A disgusted expression on his face, Garian stepped back. "'Tis enough
for today," he said grimly, and strode away.

Conan picked up his tunic and began to wipe the sweat from his chest.

When Garian had disappeared through the arched courtyard gate,
Hordo stepped out from the shadows beneath a balcony, shaking his shaggy
head. "'Tis well he knew not that I was here, Cimmerian, else we both
might find ourselves in the dungeons beneath these stones. But then, kings
dislike being bested, even when there are no others to see."

"Did I accept defeat in practice, then soon defeat would find me when it was not practice."

"But still, man, could you not hold back a little? He is a king, after all. No need for us to be dismissed before we get as much of his gold as we can."

"I know no other way to fight, Hordo, save to win. How fare the men?"

"Well," Hordo replied, seating himself on a coping stone. "'Tis an easy life, drinking and wenching away their gold."

Conan pulled his tunic over his head and scabbarded his sword. "Have you seen any sign that Ariane and the others are ready to call their people into the streets?"

"Not a whisper," the one-eyed man sighed. "Conan, I do not say betray them—Kerin's shade would haunt me, an I did—but could we not at least say to Garian that we have heard talk of uprising? He'd give us much gold for such a warning, and there'd be no rising were he on his guard. I like not to think of Kerin and Ariane dying in the gutters, but so they will an they rise. I . . . I could not ride against them, Cimmerian."

"Nor I, Hordo. But rise they will, if Garian is on his guard or no, or I misread the fire in Ariane. To stop them we must find who uses them. That man who met with Taras could tell me much."

"I've given orders, as you said, to watch for a hawk-face man with white at his temples, but 'twill be a gift of the gods an we find him so."

Conan shook his head disgustedly. "I know. But we can do only what we can. Come. Let us to my chamber. I've good wine there."

Palaces far more opulent stood in Turan and Vendhya, but this one was no mean place. Many were the courtyards and gardens, some small, holding perhaps a marble fountain in the form of some fanciful beast, others large, in which rose alabaster towers with gilded corbeled arches and golden cupolas. Great obelisks rose to the sky, their sides covered with hieroglyphs and telling the legends of Nemedian kings for a thousand years and more.

While walking down a cool arcade beside a garden where peacocks cried and golden-feathered pheasants strutted, Conan suddenly stopped. Ahead, a woman swathed in gray veils had come out of a door and, seemingly not noticing them, was walking the other way. The Cimmerian was certain it was the woman he had twice seen in her litter. Now, he decided, was a good time to discover why she had looked at him with such hatred. But as he started forward, Hordo grabbed his arm, pulling him aside behind a column.

"I want to speak to that woman," Conan said. He spoke softly, for voices carried in those arcades. "She does not like me, of that I'm sure. And I have seen her before, without those veils. But where?"

"I, too, have seen her," Hordo replied in a hoarse whisper, "though not without the veils. She is called Lady Tiana, and 'tis said her face is scarred by some disease. She will not allow it to be seen."

"I'll not ask to see her face," Conan said impatiently.

"Listen to me," the one-eyed man pleaded. "Once I followed Eranius when he left us to get his orders. Always, I knew, he went to the Street of Regrets, each time to a different tavern. This time he left the city entire, and in a grove beyond the wall met this Lady Tiana."

"Then she is part of the smuggling," Conan said. "That may provide a lever, if she proves difficult about answering my questions."

"You do not understand, Cimmerian. I was not close enough to hear what was said, yet did I see Eranius all but grovel before her. He would not do so unless she were high, very high, in the ring. Bother her, and you may find ten score smugglers in this city, hard men all, seeking your head."

"Mayhap they do already." Assuredly someone did; why not a woman who seemed to hate him, for whatever reason? He shrugged off Hordo's hand. "She will be gone if I do not go now."

But Conan paused, for as the Lady Tiana reached the end of the arcade, the blonde who had accompanied Garian appeared before her. Sularia, he had learned her name was, and she was indeed Garian's mistress. The veiled woman moved to go past, but Sularia, in golden breastplates and a golden silk skirt no wider than a man's hand front or rear, sidestepped in front of her.

"All honor to you, Lady Tiana," Sularia said, a malicious smile playing over her sensual lips. "But why are you covered so on such a bright day? I know you would be lovely, could we but persuade you into bangles and silks."

The veiled woman's hand flashed out, cracking across Sularia's face in a backhand blow that sent the blonde crumpling to the ground. Conan was stunned at the blow; it had taken no common woman's strength.

Sularia stumbled to her feet, rage twisting her face into a mask. "How dare you strike me?" she spat. "I—"

"To your kennel, bitch!" a third woman snapped, appearing beside the other two. Tall and willowy, she was as beautiful as Sularia, but with silken black hair and imperious dark eyes in a haughty face. Her blue velvet robe, sewn with tiny pearls, made the blonde look a tavern girl.

"Speak not so to me, Lady Jelanna," Sularia answered angrily. "I am no servant, and soon. . . ." She stopped suddenly.

Jelanna's mouth curled in a sneer. "You are a slut, and soon enough Garian will decide so for himself. Now, get you gone before I summon a slave to whip you hence."

Sularia trembled from head to foot, her face venomous. With an inarticulate cry of rage, she sped away from the two women, past where Conan and Hordo stood behind the column.

Conan watched her go; when he turned back, Jelanna and Tiana were gone. Scowling, he leaned against the stone.

"In this place I could search a tenday and not find her," he growled. "I should have spoken straight off, instead of letting you draw me away like a frightened boy."

"Mitra, Conan, let us ride from this city." Hordo's single eye fixed the Cimmerian with entreaty. "Forget Lady Tiana. Forget Garian, and his gold. There's gold in Ophir, and when we take blade-fee there, at least we'll know who wants to kill us."

Conan shook his head. "Never have I run away from my enemies, Hordo. 'Tis a bad habit to form. Go you on to the taverns. I go to my chamber to think on how to find this Tiana. I'll find you later, and match you two drinks to one."

As the Cimmerian started away, Hordo called after him. "Always before you knew who your enemies were!"

But Conan walked on. A wise man did not leave an unknown enemy behind him, but rather sought that enemy out. Better to die than flee, for once flight began how could it end? The enemy would come at last, and victory or death would be decided then at a time and place of the foe's choosing. While there was yet life and will, the enemy must be sought.

Reaching his chamber, Conan put his hand to the door; it shifted at his touch. The latch had been drawn. Warily he drew his blade and stepped aside. With swordpoint he thrust the door open. It swung back to crash against the wall, but there was no other sound, no hint of movement within.

Snarling, the big Cimmerian threw himself through the open door in a long dive, tucking his shoulder under as he hit the floor to roll to his feet, sword at the ready.

Sularia sat up on his bed, crossing her long legs sensuously beneath her and clapping her hands with delight. "Horseman, bowman, swordsman, and now tumbler. What other tricks have you, barbarian?"

Keeping a tight rein on his anger, Conan closed the door. He was no man to enjoy making a fool of himself before a woman, most especially not a beautiful woman. When he turned back to her his eyes were blue glacier ice.

"Why are you here, woman?"

"How magnificent you are," she breathed, "with the sweat of combat still on you. You defeated him, didn't you? Garian could not stand against one such as you."

Hastily he searched the room, flipping aside each tapestry on the wall, putting his head out of the window to make sure no assassin clung to the copings. Even did he look under the bed, before her amused smile made him throw the coverlet back down with an oath.

"What do you look for, Conan? I have no husband to jump out accusing."

"You have a king," he growled. One look at her, golden breastplates barely containing her swelling orbs, narrow strips of golden silk tangled about her thighs, proved she could carry no weapon greater than a pin.

"A king who can talk of nothing but tariffs and grain and things even more boring." A sultry smile caressed her lips, and she let herself fall backward on the bed, breathing deep. "But you, barbarian, are not boring. I sense power in you, though afar as yet. Will you become a king, I wonder?"

Conan frowned. That sequence of words seemed to touch some deeply buried memory. Power. That he would be a king. He thrust it all from his mind. A fancy for children, no more.

He laid his sword across the bed above Sularia's head. It would be close to hand there, let come who would. The blonde twisted to gaze at the bare blade, wetting her lips as if its closeness excited her. Conan clutched the golden links that joined her breastplates in his fist and tore them from her. Her eyes darted back to him, the icy sapphire of his commanding the smoldering blue of hers.

"You have played a game with me, woman," he said softly. "Now 'tis my turn to play."

Neither of them saw the door move ajar, nor the woman in gray veils who stood there a time, watching them with eyes of emerald fire.

XV

As Conan walked through the Palace the next afternoon, Hordo ran to join him.

"'Tis well to see you, Cimmerian. I had some niggling fears when I did not meet you in the taverns last night."

"I found something else to do," Conan smiled.

Hurrying slaves thronged the corridors, keeping near the walls to leave the center free for strolling lords and ladies, of which there were some few in richly embroidered velvets and satins, hung about with gold chains and emeralds and rubies on necks and wrists and waists. Nobles gave the warrior pair curious looks, men haughtily disdainful, women thoughtful.

Hordo eyed them all suspiciously, then dropped his voice and leaned closer to Conan as they walked. "Mayhap you took time last night to reconsider what occurred yesterday. Even now Garian's torturers may be heating their irons. Let us to horse and away while we can."

"Cease this foolish prattle," Conan laughed. "Not two glasses ago I exercised at swords with Garian, and he said no ill word to me. In fact, he laughed often, except when his head was thumped."

The one-eyed man's stride faltered. "Cimmerian, you didn't. . . . Mitra! You do not crack the pate of a king!"

"I cracked no pate, Hordo. Garian's foot slipped on leaves blown by the breeze, and he struck his face with his own hilt in falling. A bruise, no more."

"What men like you and me account a bruise," Hordo said, raising a finger like one of the philosophers at the Thestis, "Kings account a mortal insult to dignity."

"I fear you are right," Conan sighed. "You do grow old."

"I am too," Hordo began, and snapped his mouth shut with a glare as he realized what the big Cimmerian had said.

Conan suppressed the laughter that wanted to escape at the look on the bearded man's face. Hordo might call himself old, but he was very ready to thump anyone else who named him so. Then the Cimmerian's mirth faded.

They had come on a courtyard in which a score of the Golden Leopards stood in a large circle about Vegentius, all including the Commander stripped to the waist. A small knot of nobles stood discreetly within an arcade on the far side, watching. Apart from them, but also among those columns so she should not seem to watch, was Sularia.

Vegentius turned within the circle, arms flexing over his head. "Who will be next?" he called to the men around him. "I've not worked up a sweat as yet." His bare chest was deep, his shoulders broad and covered with thick muscle. "Am I to get no exercise? You, Oaxis."

A man stepped forward, dropping into a crouch. As tall as Vegentius, he was not so heavily muscled, though no stripling. Vegentius laughed, crouching and circling. Oaxis circled with him, but not laughing.

Abruptly they rushed together, grappling, feet shuffling for position and leverage. Conan could see that the slighter man had knowledge, and agility. Even as the Cimmerian thought, Oaxis slipped an arm free, his fist streaking for Vegentius' corded stomach. Perhaps he remembered who it was he struck, for at the last instant the blow slowed, the impact bringing not even a grunt from the grinning Vegentius.

The bigger man was under no such restraints. His free hand axed into the side of Oaxis' neck with a sound like stone striking wood. Oaxis staggered and sagged, but Vegentius held him up yet a moment. Twice his fist rose and fell, clubbing the back of the other's neck. The first time Oaxis jerked, the second he hung limp. Vegentius released him to crumple in a heap on the flagstones.

"Who comes next?" the huge Commander of the Golden Leopards roared. "Is there none among you to give me a struggle?"

Two of the bare-chested soldiers ran out to drag their companion away. None of them seemed anxious to feel Vegentius' power. The big man continued turning, smiling his taunting smile, until he found himself facing Conan. There he stopped, his smile becoming grim.

"You, barbar. Will you try a fall, or has that northern cold frozen all the guts out of you?"

Conan's face tightened. He became aware of Sularia's gaze on him. The arrogance of a prideful man under the eyes of a beautiful woman spurred him. Unfastening his swordbelt, he handed it to Hordo. A murmur rose among the nobles; wagers began to be made.

"You've more courage than sense," the one-eyed man grumbled. "What gain you, an you defeat him, except a powerful enemy?"

"He is my enemy already," Conan replied, and added with a laugh, "One of them, at least."

The Cimmerian pulled his tunic over his head and, dropping it to the ground, approached the circle of men. The nobles measured the breadth of his shoulders, and the odds changed. Vegentius, sure that the barbarian's laughter had held some slur against him, waited with a snarl on his face. The soldiers moved back, widening the circle as Conan entered.

Abruptly Vegentius charged, arms outstretched to crush and destroy. Conan's massive fist slammed into the side of his head, jarring him to a halt. Crouching slightly, the Cimmerian dug his other fist under the big soldier's ribs, driving breath from him. Before Vegentius could recover Conan seized him by throat and belt, heaving him into the air, swinging the bulk of the man over his head to send him crashing to his back.

Awe grew in the eyes of the watching soldiers. Never had they seen Vegentius taken from his feet before. Among the nobles the odds changed again.

Conan waited, breathing easily, well balanced on his feet, while Vegentius staggered up, shock writ clear on his face. Then rage washed shock away.

"Barbar bastard!" the big soldier howled. "I spit on your mother's unmarked grave!" And he swung a blow that would have felled any normal man.

But Conan's face was painted now with rage, too. Eyes like icy, windswept death, too full of fury to allow thought of defense, he took the blow, and it rocked him to his heels. Yet in that same instant his fist splintered teeth in Vegentius' mouth. For long moments the two huge men stood toe to toe, giving and absorbing blows which would have been enough to destroy an ordinary man.

Then Conan took a step forward. And Vegentius took a step back. Desperation came on the soldier's face; on Conan's eyes was the cold glint of destruction. Back the Cimmerian forced the other. Back, fists pounding relentlessly, toward the arcade where an ever-growing crowd of nobles watched, dignity forgotten as they yelled excitedly. Then, with a mighty blow, he sent the brawny man staggering.

Struggling to remain on his feet, Vegentius stumbled back, nobles parting before him until he stopped at last against the wall in the shadows of the arcade. Straining, he pushed himself erect, tottered forward and fell at the edge of the arcade. One leg moved as if some part of his brain still fought to rise, and then he was still.

Cheering soldiers surrounded Conan, unheeding of their fallen Commander. Smiling nobles, men and women alike, rushed forward, trying to touch him diffidently, as they might reach to stroke a tiger.

Conan heard none of their praise. In that brief instant when Vegentius had stood within the shadows of the arcade, he had remembered where he had seen the man before. He pushed free of the adulation and acclaim, gathering his tunic and returning to Hordo.

"Do you remember," he asked the one-eyed man quietly, "what I told you of first seeing Taras, when I fell through the roof into his secret meeting, and the big man who stood in the shadows?"

Hordo's eye darted to Vegentius, now being lifted by his soldiers. The nobles were drifting away. "Him?" he said incredulously.

Conan nodded, and the bearded man whistled sourly.

"Cimmerian, I say again that we should ride for Ophir, just as soon as we can assemble the company."

"No, Hordo." Conan's eyes still held the icy grimness of the fight, and his face wore the look of a wolf on the hunt. "We have the enemy's trail, now. It's time to attack, not run."

"Mitra!" Hordo breathed. "An you get me killed with this foolishness, I'll haunt you. *Attack?*"

Before Conan could reply, a slave girl appeared, bending knee to the Cimmerian. "I am to bid you to King Garian with all haste."

The one-eyed man stiffened.

"Be at ease," Conan told him. "Was it my head the King sought, he'd not send a pretty set of ankles to fetch me." The slave girl suddenly eyed him with interest.

"I trust no one," Hordo grumbled, "until we find out who wants you dead. Or until we leave Nemedia far behind."

"I'll tell you when it is time to ride for the border," Conan laughed. "Lead on, girl." She darted away, and the Cimmerian followed.

King Garian waited in a room hung with weapons and trophies of the chase, but his mind was not on the hunt. Scrolls and sheets of parchment littered the many tables that dotted the room, and even the floor. As Conan entered, Garian hurled a scroll across the room with a sound of disgust. The bruise on his cheek stood out against the angry flush of his countenance.

"Never ask to be a king, Conan," were his first words.

Taken aback, Conan could only say. "And why not?"

Garian's bluff face was a picture of loathing as he swept his arms about to indicate all of the scrolls and parchments. "Think you these are the plans for some grand campaign? Some magnificent ceremony to honor my father's name and memory? Think you so?"

Conan shook his head. More times than one his life had been altered by the plans and strategies of one king or another, but he had never been party to those plannings. He eyed a parchment, lying almost at his feet. The sheet seemed covered with columns of numbers.

Garian stalked about the room lifting scrolls from tables, hurling them to the floor. "The city drains must be cleared or, so the Physicians' Guild claims, the miasmas will bring on a plague. It is recommended the ancient passages beneath the Palace be located and filled, to make the Palace more secure. Part of the city wall must be rebuilt. The army's pay is in arrears. Grain to be bought. Always more grain." He stopped, scowling at the spreading antlers of a great stag on the wall. "I took that in the wilderness on the Brythunian border. How I wish I were back there now."

"Can your counselors not deal with those things?" Conan asked.

The King laughed bitterly. "So they could, were it not for the gold. Gold, Conan. I am reduced to grubbing for it like a greedy merchant."

"The Treasury—"

"—is well nigh bare. The more grain I must buy in Ophir and Aquilonia, the higher the price goes, and I must try to replace an entire crop, with insane brigands burning those wagons that do not travel under army escort and many that do. Already have I ordered some ornaments to be melted, but even an I strip the Palace bare it would be barely enough."

"What will you do?" Conan asked. Always had he imagined the wealth of kings to be limitless. This was a new thing for him, that a king might have to worry about gold no less than he, if in greater amounts.

"Borrow," Garian replied. "A number of nobles and merchants have wealth to rival my own. Let them take a hand in preventing our nation from starving." He rooted among the parchments until he found one folded and sealed with the Dragon Seal of Nemedia. "You will carry this to Lord Cantaro Albanus. He is among the richest men in Nemedia, and so will be among the first to be asked to contribute." Face hardening, he handed the parchment to Conan and added, "Or be taxed if they will not lend."

The King motioned for Conan to go, but the big Cimmerian remained where he stood. It was a delicate thing he was about to do, but he was not a man used to delicacy, and he felt an unaccustomed awkwardness. Garian looked at him in obvious surprise that he did not leave.

"How well do you trust Vegentius?" Conan blurted finally.

"Well enough to retain him as Commander of the Royal Bodyguard," Garian replied. "Why ask such a question?"

Conan took a deep breath and began the tale he had planned on his way to this room. "Since coming here I have thought that I had seen Vegentius before. Today I remembered. I saw him in a tavern in the city in close converse with a man called Taras, one who has been known to say that some other would be better on the throne than you."

"A serious charge," Garian said slowly. "Vegentius has served me well, and my father before me for many years. I cannot think he means me harm."

"You are the king, yet one lesson of kingship I know. A man who wears a crown must be ever wary of others' ambitions."

Garian threw back his head and laughed. "A good swordsman you may be, Conan, but you must leave being king to me. I have somewhat more experience with wearing a crown than you. Now go. I would have that message to Lord Albanus quickly."

Inclining his head, Conan left. He hoped that he had planted some seed of suspicion, yet this fighting with words pleased him not at all. To face an enemy with steel was his way, and he hoped that it came soon.

XVI

When Conan reached the Palace gate, he found Hordo waiting with his horse. And twenty men, among them Machaon and Narus. The Cimmerian looked at Hordo questioningly, and the one-eyed man shrugged.

"I heard you were to carry a message to some lord," he told Conan. "Mitra! For all you know he could be the other man at that meeting with Taras. Or the one who wants you dead. Or both."

"You grow as suspicious as an old woman, Hordo," Conan said as he swung into the saddle.

Vegentius, battered but in full armor and red-crested helmet, appeared suddenly in the gate with half-a-score Golden Leopards at his heels. When his eyes fell on Conan's mounted men, he stopped, glaring. Abruptly he spun and, angrily pushing through the soldiers, stormed back into the Palace.

"Mayhap I am suspicious," Hordo said quietly, "but at least I've sense enough to remember that some of your enemies have faces we know. Besides, you'll find the city changed in the last few days."

As Conan led his twenty into the empty streets, the changes were evident. Here and there a dog with ribs protruding sniffed warily around a corner. Occasionally a man could be seen hurrying down a side street, as if pursued, though no one else was about. Windows were shuttered and doors were barred; no shop was open nor hawker's cry heard. A deathly silence hung palpable in the air.

"Soon after we rode to the Palace it began," Hordo muttered. He looked around and hunched his shoulders uneasily, as if riding among tombs. "First people abandoned the streets to the toughs, the beggars and the trulls. The last two went quickly enough, with none to give or buy, and the bravos had the city to themselves, terrorizing any who dared set foot out of doors. Yesterday, they disappeared too." He looked at Conan significantly. "All in the space of a glass."

"As if they had orders?"

The one-eyed man nodded. "Maybe Taras hired armed men after all. Of a sort."

"But not for the purpose Ariane believed." The big Cimmerian was silent for a time, staring at the seemingly deserted buildings. "What is the news of her?" he asked finally.

Hordo had no need to ask who he meant. "She's well. Twice I've been to the Thestis; the others look at me as they'd look at a leper come to their dinner. Kerin has taken up with Graecus."

Conan nodded without speaking, and they rode in silence to the gates of Albanus' palace. There Conan dismounted, pounding on the barred gate with his fist.

A flap no bigger than a man's hand opened in it, and a suspicious eye surveyed them. "What do you seek here? Who are you?"

"My name is Conan. Open the gate, man. I bear a message to your master from King Garian himself."

There was a moment's whispered conversation on the other side of the gate. Then came the rattle of a bar being drawn, and the gate opened enough for one man to pass.

"You can enter," the voice from inside called, "but not the others."

"Conan," Hordo began.

The Cimmerian quieted him with a gesture. "Rest easy, Hordo. I could not be safer in a woman's arms." He slipped through the opening.

As the gate closed behind him with a solid thud, Conan faced four men with drawn swords; another snugged the point of his blade under the Cimmerian's ribs from the side.

"Now, who are you?" rasped the swordsman who pricked Conan's tunic.

Wishing he had had sense enough to don his hauberk before leaving the Royal Palace, Conan turned his head enough to make out a narrow face with wide-set eyes and a nose with the tip gone. "I told you." He reached beneath his tunic, and froze as the sword point dug deeper. "I want only to show you the message. What trouble can I mean with a sword in my ribs?"

To himself, he thought that clip-nose stood too close. The man should never have touched blade to tunic unless he meant to thrust. One quick sweep of the arm would knock that sword aside, then clip-nose could be hurled at his fellow, and. . . . The big Cimmerian smiled, and the others shifted uneasily, wondering what he found to smile about.

"Let me see this message," clip-nose demanded.

From beneath his tunic Conan produced the folded parchment. Clip-nose reached, but he moved it beyond the man's grasp. "You can see the seal from there," he said. "It's meant for Lord Albanus, not you."

"'Tis the Dragon Seal, in truth," clip-nose muttered. His sword left Conan's ribs with obvious reluctance. "Follow me, then, and do not stray."

Conan shook his head as they started up the stone walk toward the palace proper, a massive structure of fluted columns, with a great gilded dome that hurled back the sun. Suspicion on the guards' part had been warranted, given the state of the city, but the surliness should have faded when they learned he was a Royal Messenger. That it had not spoke ill for Garian's plans. Often men absorbed the attitudes of their master without either man or master realizing.

In the many-columned entry hall, clip-nose conferred, well out of Conan's hearing, with a gray-bearded man whose tunic was emblazoned with Lord Albanus' house-mark backed by a great key. Clip-nose left, returning to his post at the gate, and the gray-bearded man approached Conan.

"I am Lord Albanus' chamberlain," he said, giving neither name nor courtesy. "Give me the message."

"I will place it in Lord Albanus' hands," Conan replied flatly.

He had no real reason not to give it to the chamberlain, for such a one was his master's agent in all things, yet he was irked. A messenger from the King should have been given chilled wine and damp towels to take the dust of the street from him.

The chamberlain's face tightened, and for a moment Conan thought the man would argue. Instead he said curtly, "Follow me," and led the Cimmerian up marble stairs to a small room. "Wait here," he commanded Conan, and left after casting an eye about as if cataloguing the room's contents against a light-fingered visitor.

It was no mean room for all its smallness. Tapestry-hung and marble-floored, its furnishings were inlaid with mother-of-pearl and lapis lazuli. An arch led onto a balcony overlooking a garden fountain. But still there were neither towels nor wine. It boded ill indeed for Garian, such insult to his messenger.

Muttering to himself, Conan walked to the balcony and looked down. Almost he cried out in surprise, slights forgotten for the moment. Stephano staggered drunkenly through the garden, half supported by two girls in skimpy silks.

The sculptor bent to dabble his fingers in the fountain and near fell in. "No water," he laughed at the girls, as they drew him back. "Want more wine, not water." Giggling together, they wound a shaky way from the fountain and into the exotic shrubs.

Someone cleared his throat behind Conan, and the Cimmerian spun.

A plump man of middling height stood there, one hand clutching his ill-fitting velvet tunic at the neck. "You have a message for me?" he said.

"Lord Albanus?" Conan said.

The plump man nodded shortly and thrust out his hand. Slowly Conan gave him the sealed parchment. The plump man's hand closed on it like a trap. "Now go," he said. "I have the message. Go!"

Conan went.

The gray-bearded chamberlain was waiting immediately outside to conduct him to the door, and there clip-nose waited with another man to escort him to the gate.

As he emerged, Hordo brought his horse forward, a relieved grin wreathing his scarred face. "Almost was I ready to come over that wall after you."

"I had no trouble," Conan said as he mounted. "I carried the King's message, remember. When next you see Ariane, tell her that Stephano is not dead, as she feared. He dwells within, sporting himself with serving girls."

"I mean to see her this day," Hordo replied. He stared at the gate thoughtfully. "'Tis odd he sent no message to his friends that he is well."

"Not so odd as a lord with broken nails and work-calloused hands," the Cimmerian said.

"A swordsman—"

"No, Hordo. I know work-wrought calluses when I see them. Still, 'tis none of our concern. Vegentius is, and this very night I mean to have private conversation with the good Commander." Grimly he rode from the gate, the others galloping in two columns behind.

Albanus thrust the plump man, now dressed in nought but a filthy breech-clout, to his knees, face to the marble floor.

"Well, Varius?" Albanus demanded of his chamberlain, his cruel face dark with impatience. He snatched the parchment, crumpled it in his fist. "Did he seem suspicious? Did he accept this dog as me?" He prodded the kneeling man with his foot. "Did he think you a lord, dog? What did he say?"

"He did, master." The plump man's voice was fearful, and he did not lift his face from the floor. "He asked only if I was Lord Albanus, then gave me the parchment and left."

Albanus growled. The gods toyed with him, to send this man whose death he sought beneath his very roof, where he could not touch the barbarian, lest suspicion be drawn straight to him, and where he must hide to escape recognition. Beneath his own roof! And on this, the first day of his triumph. His eye fell on the kneeling man, who trembled.

"Could you not have found someone more presentable to represent me, Varius? That even a barbarian should take this slug for me offends me."

"Forgive me, my lord," the chamberlain said, bowing even more deeply in apology. "There was little time, and a need to find one who would fit the tunic."

Albanus' mouth curled. "Burn that tunic. I'll not wear it again. And send this thing back to the kitchens. The sight of it disgusts me."

Varius made a slight gesture; the kneeling man scurried from the room, hardly rising higher than a crouch. "Will that be all, my lord?"

"No. Find that drunken idiot Stephano, and hasten him to the workroom. But sober him, first."

Albanus waved Varius from the room, and turned to the message from Garian. Curious as to what it could be, he split the seal.

Our Dear Lord Cantaro Albanus,
All honor to you. We summon you before the Dragon Throne that you may advise Us on matters near Our heart. As one who loves Us, and Nemedia, well, We know you will make haste.

GARIAN NEMEDIA PRIMUS

A feral gleam lit Albanus' black eyes as he wadded the parchment in clawed hands. "I will come to you soon enough," he whispered. "My love I will show with chains and hot irons till on your knees you will acknowledge me King. Albanus, First in Nemedia. You will beg for death at my hand."

Tossing the crumpled sheet aside, he strode to the workroom. The four guards before the door stiffened respectfully, but he swept past them without notice.

On the stone circle in the center of the room stood the clay figure of Garian, complete at last. Or almost, he thought, smiling. Perfect in every detail, just slightly larger than the living man—Stephano had made some quibble about that, saying it should be either exactly life size or of heroic proportions—it seemed to be striding forward, mouth open to utter some pronouncement. And it contained more of Garian than simply his looks. Arduously worked into that clay with complicated thaumaturgical rituals were Garian's hair and parings from his fingernails, his sweat, his blood, and his seed. All had been obtained by Sularia at the dark lord's command.

A huge kiln stood a short distance behind the stone platform, and a complicated series of wooden slides and levers designed to move the figure linked platform and kiln. Neither kiln nor slides were ever to be used, however. Albanus had allowed Stephano to construct them in order to allay the sculptor's suspicions before they arose.

Climbing onto the platform, Albanus began pushing the wooden apparatus off onto the floor. Unaccustomed as he was to even the smallest labor, yet he must needs do this. Stephano would have had to be chivied to it, his questions turned aside with carefully constructed lies, and Albanus had long since tired of allowing the sculptor to believe that his questions were worth answering, his vanities worth dignifying. Better to do the work himself.

Tossing the last lever from the platform, Albanus jumped to the floor, one hand out to steady himself against the kiln. With an oath he jerked it back from the kiln's rough surface. It was hot.

The door opened, and Stephano tottered in, green of face but much less under the sway of drink than he had been. "I want them all flogged," he muttered, scrubbing a hand across his mouth. "Do you know what your slaves did to me, with Varius giving the orders? They—"

"Fool!" Albanus thundered. "You fired the kiln! Have I not commanded you to do nothing here without my leave?"

"The figure is ready," Stephano protested. "It must be put in the kiln today, or it will crack rather than harden. Last night I—"

"Did you not hear my command that you were never to handle fire within this room? Think you I light these lamps with my own hands for the joy of doing a slave's work?"

"If the oils in that clay are so flammable," the sculptor muttered sullenly, "how can it stand being placed—"

"Be silent." The words were a soft hiss. Albanus' obsidian gaze clove Stephano's tongue to the roof of his mouth and rooted him to the spot as if it were a spike driven through him.

Disdainfully Albanus turned his back. Deftly he set out three small vials, a strip of parchment and a quill pen. Opening the first vial—it held a small quantity of Garian's blood, with the admixture of tinctures to keep it liquid—he dipped the pen and neatly wrote the King's name across the parchment. A sprinkling of powder from the second vial, and instantly the blood blackened and dried. The last container held Albanus' own blood, drawn only that morning. With that he wrote his own name in larger script, overlaying that of Garian. Again the powder dried the blood.

Next, murmuring incantations, Albanus folded the parchment strip in a precise pattern. Then he returned to the platform and placed the parchment into the open mouth of the clay figure.

Stephano, leaning now against the wall, giggled inanely. "I wondered why you wanted the mouth like that." At a look from Albanus he swallowed heavily and bit his tongue.

Producing chalks smuggled from Stygia, land of sorcerers far to the south, Albanus scribed an incomplete pentagram around the feet of the figure, star within pentagon within circle. Foul black candles went on the points where each broken shape touched the other two. Then, quickly, each candle was lit, the pentagram completed. He stepped back, arms spread wide, uttering the words of conjuring.

"Elonai me'roth sancti, Urd'vass teoheem. . . ."

The words of power rolled from his tongue, and the air seemed to thicken in silver shimmers. The flames of the unholy candles flared, sparking a seed of fear in the dark lord's mind. The flames. It could not happen again as last time. It could not. He banished the fear by main force. There could be no fear now, only power.

" . . . arallain Sa'm'di com'iel mort'rass. . . ."

The flames grew, but as they grew the room dimmed, as if they took light rather than gave it. Higher they flared, driven by the force of the dark lord's chant, overtowering the clay figure. Slowly, as though bent by some impossible and unfelt wind, the silent flames bent inward until the points of fire met above. From that meeting a bolt, as of lightning, struck down to the head of the statue, bathing it in glow unending, surrounding it in a haloed fire of the purest white that sucked all heat from the air.

Frost misting his breath, Albanus forced his voice to a roar. *"By the Unholy Powers of Three, I conjure thee! By blood and sweat and seed, vilified and attainted, I conjure thee! Arise, walk and obey, for I, Albanus, conjure thee!"*

As the last syllable left his mouth the flames were gone, leaving no trace of the candles behind. The figure stood, but now it was dried and cracked.

Albanus rubbed his hands together, and put them beneath his arms for warmth. If only it had all gone correctly this time. He glanced at Stephano, shivering against a wall that glinted from the myriad ice droplets that had coalesced from the air. Terror made the sculptor's eyes bulge. There was no point in delaying further. The hawk-faced man drew a deep breath.

"I command you, Garian, awake!" A piece of clay dropped from one arm to shatter on the stone. Albanus frowned. "Garian, I command you awake!"

The entire figure trembled; then crumbling, powdering clay was spilling to the platform. And what the figure had moulded, stood there, breathing and alive. A perfect duplicate of Garian, without blemish or fault. The simulacrum brushed dust from its shoulder, then stopped, eyeing Albanus quizzically.

"Who are you?" it said.

"I am Albanus," the dark lord replied. "Know you who you are?"

"Of course. I am Garian, King of Nemedia."

Albanus' smile was purest evil. "To your knees, Garian," he said softly. Unperturbed, the replica sank to its knees. Despite himself Albanus laughed, and the commands poured out for the sheer joy of seeing the image of the King obey. "Face to the floor! Grovel! Now up! Run in place! Faster! Faster!" The duplicate King ran. And ran.

Tears rolled down Albanus' cheeks, but his laughter faded as his eye lit on Stephano. Slowly the sculptor pushed himself erect from his crouch. Uncertainty and fear chased each other across his face.

"Be still, Garian," Albanus commanded, not loosing Stephano's gaze from his own. The simulacrum ceased running and stood quietly, breathing easily.

Stephano swallowed hard. "My . . . my work is done. I'll go now." He turned toward the door, flinching to a halt at the whipcrack of Albanus' voice.

"Your gold, Stephano. Surely you're not forgotten that." From beneath his tunic Albanus produced a short, thick cylinder, tightly wrapped in leather. He hefted it on his palm. "Fifty gold marks."

Cupidity warred with fear on Stephano's countenance. He licked his lips hesitantly. "The sum mentioned was a thousand."

"I am unclothed," the simulacrum said suddenly.

"Of course," Albanus said, seeming to answer them both.

From the floor he picked up a length of filthy rag that Stephano had used while sculpting, and with it carefully scrubbed away part of the pentagram. Many things, he knew, could happen to one attempting to enter a closed pentagram charged with magicks, and each was more horrible that the last. Stepping up onto the platform, he handed the rag to the simulacrum, which wrapped the cloth about its waist.

"This is but a first payment, Stephano," Albanus went on. "The rest will come to you later." He thrust the leather-wrapped cylinder into the simulacrum's hand. "Give this to Stephano." Leaning closer, he added whispered words.

Stephano shifted uneasily as the image of the King stepped down from the platform.

"So many times," Albanus murmured, "have I been forced to endure the babble that spills from your mouth."

The sculptor's eyes narrowed, darting from Albanus to the approaching figure, and he broke for the door.

With inhuman speed the simulacrum hurled itself forward. Before Stephano had gone a single step it was on him, a hand with the strength of stone seizing his throat. A scream tore from him as obdurate fingers dug into the muscles on either side of his jaw, forcing his mouth open. Futilely Stephano clawed at the hand that held him; his fingers might as well have scraped at hardened leather. With that single hand, as if the sculptor were but a child, the replica forced him to his knees. Too late Stephano saw the cylinder descending toward his mouth, and understood Albanus' words. Desperately he clutched the approaching wrist, but he could as easily have slowed a catapult's arm. Remorseless, the construct forced the gold deeper, and yet deeper, into the sculptor's mouth.

Choking rasps came from Stephano's throat as the simulacrum of Garian dropped him. Eyes staring from his head, face empurpling, the sculptor clawed helplessly at his throat. His back arched in his struggles till naught but head and drumming heels touched the floor.

Albanus watched the death throes dispassionately, and when the last twitching foot had stilled, he said softly, "Nine hundred fifty more will go with you to your unmarked grave. What I promise, I give." His shoulders shook with silent mirth. When the spasm had passed, he turned briskly to the likeness of Garian, still standing impassively over the body. "As for you, there is much to learn and little time. Tonight. . . ."

XVII

riane sat despondently, staring at nothing. Around her the common room of the Thestis murmured with intrigue. No musicians played, and men and women whispered as they huddled together over their tables. Reaching a decision, Ariane got to her feet and made her way through the tables to Graecus.

"I must talk to you, Graecus," she said quietly. That deathly silence had contaminated her also.

"Later," the stocky sculptor muttered without looking at her. To the others at his table he went on in a low, insistent voice. "I tell you, it matters not if Taras is dead. I know where the weapons are stored. In half a day I—"

Ariane felt some of her old fire rekindle. "Graecus!" In that room of whispers the sharp word sounded like a shout. Everyone at the table stared at her. "Has it not occurred to you," she continued, "that perhaps we are being betrayed?"

"Conan," Graecus began, but she cut him off.

"Not Conan."

"He killed Taras," a plump, pale-skinned brunette said. "You saw that yourself. And he's taken Garian's coin openly, now."

"Yes, Gallia," Ariane said patiently. "But if Conan had betrayed us, would not the Golden Leopards arrest us?" Silent stares answered her. "He has not betrayed us. Mayhap he spoke the truth about Taras. Perhaps there are no armed men waiting for us to lead the people into the streets. Perhaps we'll find we are no more than a stalking horse for some other's plan."

"By Erlik's Throne," Graecus grumbled, "you speak rubbish, Ariane."

"Perhaps I do," she sighed wearily, "but at least discuss it with me. Resolve my doubts, if you can. Do you truly have none at all?"

"Take your doubts back to your corner," Graecus told her. "While you sit doubting, we will pull Garian from his throne."

Gallia sniffed loudly. "What can you expect from one who spends so much time with that one-eyed ruffian?"

"Thank you, Gallia," Ariane said. She smiled for the first time since entering the room where Conan stood above Taras' body, and left the table to get her cloak. Graecus and the others stared at her as if she were mad.

Hordo was the answer to her problem, she realized. Not as one to talk to, of course. An she mentioned her doubts to him, he would gruffly tell her that Conan betrayed no one. Then he would pinch her bottom and try to inveigle his way into her bed. He had done all of those things already. But he had visited her earlier that afternoon, and had told her that Stephano lived, and was at the palace of Lord Albanus. The sculptor had had a good mind and a facile tongue before his jealousy of Conan soured him. Either he would dispel her doubts, convincing her of the big Cimmerian's guilt, or, convinced himself he would return with her to the Thestis to help her convince the rest. She wrapped her cloak about her and hurried into the street.

When she reached the Street of Regrets she began to rue her decision to leave the Thestis. That street, always alive with flash and tawdry glitter, lay bare to the wind that rolled pitiful remnants across the paving stones. A juggler's parti-colored cap. A silken scarf, soiled and torn. In the distance a dog howled, the sound echoing down other empty streets. Shivering, though not from the wind, Ariane quickened her pace.

By the time she reached Albanus' palace, she was running, though nothing pursued her but emptiness. Panting, she fell against the gate, her small fist pounding on the iron-bound planks. "Let me in!"

A suspicious eye regarded her through a small opening in the gate, swiveling both ways to see if she was accompanied.

"Mitra's mercy, let me in!"

The bars rattled aside, and the guard opened a crack barely wide enough for her to slip through.

Before she had taken a full step inside an arm seized her about the waist, swinging her into the air with crude laughter. She gasped as a hand squeezed her buttock roughly, and she looked down into a narrow face. The nose had the tip gone.

"A fine bit," he laughed. "Enough to keep us all warm, even in this wind." His half-score companions added their jocularity to his.

The mirth drained from his face as he felt the point of her short dagger prick him under the ear. "I am the Lady Ariane Pandarian," she hissed coldly. Mitra, how long had it been since she had used that name? "An Lord

Albanus leaves anything of you, I've no doubt my father will tend to the rest."

His hands left her as though scalded; her feet thumped to the ground. "Your pardon, my lady," he stammered. The rest stared with mouths open. "All honor to you. I did not mean. . . ."

"I will find my own way," she announced haughtily, and swept away while he was still attempting to fit together an apology.

Arrogance, she decided as she made her way up the flagstone walk, was her only hope, arriving at a lord's palace without servants or guards. When one of the great carven doors was opened by a gray-bearded man with a chamberlain's seal on his tunic, her large hazel eyes were adamantine.

"I am the Lady Ariane Pandarian," she announced. "Show me to the sculptor, Stephano Melliarus."

His jaw dropped, and he peered vaguely past her down the walk as if seeking her retinue. "Forgive me . . . my lady . . . but I . . . know no man named Stephano."

Brusquely she pushed by him into the columned entry-hall. "Show me to Lord Albanus," she commanded. Inside she quivered. Suppose Conan had been mistaken. What if Stephano were not there? Yet the thought of returning to those barren streets spurred her on.

The chamberlain's mouth worked, beard waggling, then he said faintly, "Follow me, please," adding, "my lady," as an afterthought.

The room in which he left her, while going "to inform Lord Albanus" of her presence, was spacious. The tapestries were brightly colored; flickering golden lamps cast a cheery glow after the gloom of the streets. But the pleasant surroundings did naught to stem her growing apprehension. What if she was seeking one who was not there, making a fool of herself before this lord who was a stranger to her? Bit by bit, her facade of arrogance melted. When Lord Albanus entered, the last vestiges of it were swept away by his stern gaze.

"You seek a man called Stephano," the hard-faced man said without preamble. "Why do you think he is here?"

She found herself wanting to wring her hands and instead clutched them tightly in her cloak, but she could not stop the torrent of words and worries. "I must talk to him. No one else will talk with me, and Taras is dead, and Conan says we are being betrayed, and. . . ." She managed a deep, shuddering breath. "Forgive me, Lord Albanus. If Stephano is not here, I will go."

Albanus' dark eyes had widened as she spoke. Now, he fumbled in a pouch at his belt, saying, "Wait. Have you ever seen the like of this?"

His fingers brought out a gemstone of almost fiery white; he muttered words she could not hear as he thrust it at her.

Despite herself, her eyes were drawn to the gem as iron to lodestone. Suddenly a pale beam sprang from the stone, bathing her face. Her breath came out in a grunt, as if she had been struck. Panic filled her. She must run. But all she could do was tremble, dancing helpless in that one spot as whiteness blotted out all her vision. Run, she screamed in the depths of her mind. Why, came the question. Panic dissolved. Will dissolved. The beam winked out, and she stood, breathing calmly, looking into the pale stone, now more fiery seeming than before.

"'Tis done," she heard Albanus murmur, "but how well?" In a louder voice he said, "Remove your garments, girl."

Some tiny corner of her being brought a flush to her cheek, but to the rest it seemed a reasonable command. Swiftly she dropped her cloak, undid the brooches that held her robes. They fell in a welter about her feet, and she stood, hands curled delicately on her rounded thighs, one knee slightly bent, waiting.

Albanus eyed her curved nudity and smiled mirthlessly. "If you obey that command so readily, you'll tell the truth an you die for it. Taras, girl. Is he in truth dead? How did he die?"

"Conan slew him," she replied calmly.

"Erlik take that accursed barbar!" the dark lord snarled. "No wonder Vegentius could not find Taras. And how am I to send orders...." His scowl lessened; he peered at her thoughtfully. "You are one of those foolish children who prate of rebellion at the Sign of Thestis, aren't you?"

Her answer was hesitant. "I am." His words seemed in some way wrong, yet the irritation was dimly felt and distant.

Albanus' fingers gripped her chin, lifting her head, and though they dug painfully into her cheeks she knew no urge to resist. Her large eyes met his obsidian gaze openly.

"When I wish the streets to fill with howling mobs," he said softly, "you will carry my words to the Thestis, saying exactly what I command and no more."

"I will," she said. Like the bite of a gnat, something called her to struggle, then faded.

He nodded. "Good. This Conan, now. What did he say to you of betrayal?"

"That Taras hired no armed men to aid us. That another used us for his own purposes."

"Did he name this other?" Albanus asked sharply.

She shook her head, feeling tired of talking, wanting to sleep.

"No matter," Albanus muttered. "I underestimated the barbar. He becomes more dangerous with every turn of the glass. Varius! A messenger to go to Commander Vegentius! Quickly, if you value your hide! Stand up straight, girl."

Ariane straightened obediently, and watched Albanus scribble a message on parchment. She wished only to sleep, but knew she could not until her master permitted. She accepted his will completely now; even the tiny pin-pricks of resistance fled.

XVIII

As the deep tone of a bronze gong sounded the first turn of the glass past full sundown, Conan uncoiled smoothly from his bed in the darkness of his room. Already he was prepared for his night's venture, in bare feet and tunic with a dagger at his belt. Sword and armor would hamper where he went.

On silent feet he moved to the window, climbed onto the stone lip, and twisted with catlike grace to find places for his fingers above. It was not a natural thing for men to look up, even when searching. Therefore the best way to go unobserved was to travel high. Scudding purple clouds crossed a gibbous moon, casting shadows that walked and danced. Conan became one with the shadows.

Even in that smooth-dressed stone, crevices and chinks were to be found by knowledgeable fingers and toes. Stone cornices and the rims of friezes made a pathway for him to the roof. With swift care he crossed its tiles, dropping on the far side to a rampart walk that bore no sentry, here in the heart of the Palace. Through an embrasure between man-high merlons he lowered himself to the roof of a colonnade three stories above the flag-stoned courtyard below.

Within the Palace behind him an alarm bell abruptly began to toll, and he froze there in the shifting shadows. Shouts carried to him, though he could make out no word. He frowned. To such an alarm Vegentius would surely be summoned. And yet the hue and cry was not general, for no sudden lights or tramp of marching men disturbed the outer part of the Palace. Eventually it would subside, and Vegentius would of a certainty return to his quarters. A lupine smile split the Cimmerian's face. He would return to find one waiting to ask questions, and demand answers.

Swiftly Conan hurried on, running along the roof, scaling another wall at its end with ease, then along the length of it uncaring of the dark below him, or the stones that waited if foot should slip or grip fail. Halting, he lay flat, swiveled his legs and hips over the edge, and climbed down the short distance to the window of Vegentius' sleeping chamber.

Dagger sliding from its sheath, the big Cimmerian entered the room like silent death. Some few brass lamps were lit, casting dim illumination there and in the outer chamber, yet both were empty, as he had feared. Grimly he settled himself by the door of the inner room to wait.

Long was that vigil, yet he kept it with the silent, unmoving patience of a hunting beast. Even when he heard the door of the outer chamber open, only his hand on the dagger moved, firming its grip. But the tread was of a single man. Conan flattened himself against the wall by the door as the footsteps came closer.

A tall shape entered the room, golden-cloaked and wearing the red-crested helmet of the Golden Leopards' commander. Conan's empty fist struck against the back of the man's neck, and with a groan the other fell, rolling onto his back. The Cimmerian stared in amazement. It was not Vegentius.

And then a howling horde in golden cloaks poured through the outer chamber to fall on him. Roaring, Conan fought. His dagger found a throat, and was torn from his grasp as the dying man fell. Teeth splintered and jaws broke beneath his hammer blows. One man he neatly hurled screaming through the window by which he had entered. Yet by sheer weight of numbers did they force him down. He found himself on his back, three men holding each arm and leg, though many of them spat blood. Writhing, he strained every thew, but he could only shift them, not gain freedom.

Vegentius, helmetless and wearing a look of great satisfaction, appeared in the doorway. "You can see that I was right," he said to someone still in the other chamber. "He intended to slay me first, so that if your death were discovered before he could flee, my absence in command might aid his escape."

Wrapped tightly in a cloak, his bruise standing out against the paleness of his cheeks, Garian stepped into the room. He stood gazing down at Conan in horrified wonder. "Even when I heard the others I could hardly believe," he whispered. A shudder went through him. "A score of times has he had me at the point of his blade."

"But then he would have surely been known as your assassin," Vegentius said smoothly.

"Liar!" Conan spat at the massive soldier. "I came here to force you to admit your own foul treachery."

Vegentius' face darkened, and he put a hand to his sword, but Garian stopped him with a gesture. The King moved closer to address the Cimmerian.

"Hear me, Conan. Before dusk began to fall this day, Vegentius arrested those who conspired with you. A man called Graecus. A woman, Gallia. Some three or four others. Do you deny knowing them, or that they plotted against my throne?"

Conan's brain roiled. Was Ariane among those taken? Yet to ask, naming her, was to give her into their hands if they did not have her. "Foolish youths," he said. "They talk, and will talk till they are gray and toothless, harming no one. Yet there are those who would use them." He cut off with a grunt as Vegentius' boot caught him under the ribs.

Garian waved the soldier back and spoke on. "Vegentius put these you call harmless to the question, and within two turns of the glass he had broken them. He brought them before me, those who could still speak, and from their mouths I heard them admit they plotted my murder, and that you are he who was to wield the blade."

"I am no murderer!" Conan protested, but Garian continued as if he had not spoken.

"The alarm was given; you were sought. And found lying in wait, dagger in hand. Your actions convict you."

"His head will adorn a pike before dawn," Vegentius said.

"No," Garian said softly. "I trusted this man." He wiped his hands on the edge of his cloak, as if ritually. His eyes were cold on Conan's face. "Long has it been since the ancient penalty for plotting to slay he who wears the Dragon Crown was last invoked. Let it be invoked now." Drawing his cloak about him, he turned his face from the Cimmerian and strode from the chamber.

Vegentius stared after him, then down at Conan. Abruptly he laughed, throwing back his head. "The ancient penalty, barbar. Fitting. To the dungeons with him!"

One of those holding Conan shifted. The Cimmerian saw a descending sword hilt, then saw no more.

XIX

lbanus smiled to himself as his sedan chair was borne through the night, up the winding streets that led through the Temple District to the Royal Palace. So close now, he was, to his inevitable triumph. He savored each step the bearers took, carrying him nearer his goal.

Ahead two torchbearers strode, and twenty guards surrounded him, though the streets were as empty as a tomb millenia old. Those truly important to him marched on either side of his chair, heavily cloaked and hooded, the woman and the man-shape. So close.

As the procession approached the gate of the Palace, Albanus uttered a command. His sedan chair was lowered to the ground. Even as the hawk-faced man climbed out, Vegentius crossed the drawbridge. Albanus looked at the guards and raised an inquiring brow.

"As planned," the soldier said quietly. "All men standing guard this night are loyal to me. My best."

"Good," Albanus said. "And Conan?"

"In the dungeons. Garian shouted so about invoking the ancient penalty that I could not kill him out of hand. The alarm had wakened others by then." His red-crested helmet bobbed as he spat disgustedly. "But he can go to the same unmarked grave as Garian."

The hawk-faced lord laughed softly. "No, Vegentius. I find the ancient ways a fitting end for this barbarian."

"Better to kill him straight out," Vegentius grumbled, but pursued it no further. Stooping, he attempted to look under the hood of the man-shape behind Albanus. "Does he truly look like—"

"Let us go," Albanus said, and strode forward, Ariane and the simulacrum at his heels. Vegentius could do naught but follow.

The dark lord hurried over the drawbridge exultantly, and into the Palace. Often had his feet trod these halls, yet now it was tread of possessor, of conqueror. When a shadow moved and resolved into Sularia, he stared at her with imperious fury.

"Why are you here, woman? I commanded you to remain in your apartments until I sent for you."

Her gaze met his without flinching, and even in the dim light the eager glow of her eyes was apparent. "I want to see him fall before you."

Albanus nodded slowly. There would be pleasure in that. "But make no sound," he warned. Shoulders back and head high, as a king in his own palace, he moved on.

Before the door to Garian's chambers four guards stood, stiffening at the party's approach.

Vegentius stepped forward. "He sleeps?" One of the four nodded. "Who else is within?"

He who had nodded spoke. "Only the serving girl, to bring him wine if he wakes."

"Slay her," Albanus said, and Vegentius started.

"You said you could make her remember nothing, Albanus. Questions may be asked if the girl disappears."

"The method can only be used on one person at a time," Albanus replied, fingers absently stroking the pouch that held the white gem. "Slay her."

Vegentius nodded to the guard who had spoken. The man slipped inside, returning in moments with a bloody blade to resume his post.

Albanus led the others in, sparing not a glance for the crumpled form of a woman lying across an overturned stool. The second room, Garian's sleeping chamber itself, was dim, the lamp wicks trimmed low. Garian lay on his bed amid rumpled blankets.

"Turn up the lamps, Sularia," Albanus commanded quietly. Not taking her eyes from the man in the bed, the blonde hastened to obey. To the two hooded figures, the lord said, "Remove your cloaks."

Vegentius gasped as the simulacrum obeyed. "'Tis Garian's very image!"

Sularia turned from a golden lamp, but her exclamation at the sight of the King's double was cut short, as, with narrowing eyes, her gaze caught Ariane. "Who is she?" the blonde demanded.

Ariane looked straight ahead, unmoving, until another command was given. The simulacrum peered about him curiously.

On the bed, Garian suddenly sat bolt upright. Growing more amazed by the instant, his eye jumped from Albanus to Sularia to Vegentius. "What," he began, but the words died. Mouth open, he stared at the duplicate of himself. Unperturbed, the simulacrum gazed back inquisitively.

Albanus felt like laughing. "Garian," he said mockingly, "this is he who will sit on the Dragon Throne for the last days of your line. For your usurping lineage now ends."

"Guards!" Garian shouted. From beneath his pillows a dagger appeared in his hand, and he leaped from the bed. "Guards!"

"Take him," Albanus ordered the simulacrum, "as I told you." Growing more amazed by the instant, his eye jumped from Albanus to Sularia to Vegentius.

The duplicate moved forward, and Garian's dagger struck with a fighter's speed. To be caught easily by an inhumanly powerful grip on Garian's wrist. Astonishment was replaced on his face by pain as those fingers tightened. The dagger fell from nerveless fingers.

Before that blade clattered on the floor, the simulacrum's other hand seized the true King by the throat, lifting him until his toes kicked frantically above a handspan of air. No sign of strain was on the construct's face as it watched that other like its own turn slowly purple. Garian's struggles weakened, then ceased. Casually the replica opened its hand and let the limp body fall.

Albanus hastened to bend over the King. Savage bruises empurpled his neck, and another darkened his cheek, though Albanus did not remember seeing the simulacrum strike. But the broad chest rose and fell, if faintly. Garian yet lived.

Vegentius, who had stood staring, sword half drawn, since the instant the duplicate moved, now slammed his blade home in its scabbard and cleared his throat. His eyes never left the simulacrum. "Should you not let him, it, kill him now?"

"I am King Garian," the creature said to Vegentius. The soldier muttered an oath.

"Be silent," Albanus commanded, straightening. "This," he prodded Garian's form with his foot, "will acknowledge my right to the throne before I let him die."

"But the danger," Vegentius protested. "He was to die now."

"Enough!" Albanus snapped. "Deliver him in chains to the dungeon beneath my palace. I'll hear no more on it."

Vegentius nodded reluctantly, and turned to go.

"And, Vegentius," the cruel-faced man added, "see that those who do this task are disposed of after. Fewer tongues to waggle loosely."

The big soldier stood rigidly in the door, then left without speaking. But he would do it, Albanus knew, even to his beloved Golden Leopards.

"Who is this woman?" Sularia asked again.

Albanus looked at her in amusement, wondering if there were room for two thoughts at once in that pretty head. All that had happened before her eyes, and it was Ariane that concerned her.

"Do not worry," he told her. "In the morning you will be proclaimed Lady Sularia. This," he touched Ariane's expressionless face, "is naught but a tool to build a path to the Dragon Throne. And tools are made to be discarded once used."

His gaze swung to Sularia, a reassuring smile on his face. Tools, he repeated to himself, are made to be discarded once used.

C onan awakened hanging spreadeagled in chains in the center of a
dungeon. At least, he assumed it was the center. Two tall tripod
lamps cast a yellow pool of light around him, but he could see no
walls in any direction. The chains that held his wrists disappeared into the
gloom above. Those holding his ankles were fastened to massive ringbolts
set in the rough stone blocks of the floor. His tunic was gone, he wore
naught but a breechclout.

Without real hope of escape he tensed every muscle, straining until
sweat popped out on his forehead, beaded his shoulders and rolled down
his broad chest. There was not slightest give in the chains. Nor in himself.
He had been stretched to the point of joints cracking.

Cloth rustled in the darkness, and he heard a man's voice.

"He is awake, my lady." There was a pause. "Very good, my lady."

Two men moved into the light, burly, shaven headed and bare chested.
One bore a burn across his hairless chest as if some victim had managed to
put hand to the hot iron intended for his own pain. The other was as heavily
pelted as an ape from the shoulders down, and wore a smile on his incongruously pleasant round face. Each man carried a coiled whip.

As they wordlessly took positions to either side of the Cimmerian, he
strained his eyes to penetrate the darkness. Who was this 'lady'? Who?

The first whip hissed through the air to crack against his chest. As it was
drawn back the other struck his thigh. Then the first was back, wrapping
around an ankle. There was no pattern to the blows, no way to anticipate
where the next would land, no way to steel the soul against pain like lines of
acid eating into the flesh.

The muscles of Conan's jaws were knots with the effort of not yelling.
He would not even open his mouth to suck in the lungfuls of air his great

body demanded in its agony. To open his mouth would be to make some noise, however slight, and from there it would be but a step to a yell, another to a scream. The woman watching from the darkness wanted him to scream. He would make no sound.

The two men continued until Conan hung as limply as the chains would allow, head down on his massive chest. Sweat turned to fire the welts that covered him from ankles to shoulders. Here and there blood oozed.

From the darkness he heard the clink of coins, and the same man's voice. "Very generous, my lady. We'll be just outside, an you need us." Then silence until hinges squealed rustily, stopping with the crash of a stout door closing.

Conan lifted his head.

Slowly a woman walked into the circle of light and stood watching him. The woman veiled in gray.

"You!" he rasped. "Are you the one who has been trying to kill me, then? Or are you the one who uses those fools at the Thestis, the one who put me here with lies?"

"I did try to have you killed," she said softly. Conan's eyes narrowed. That voice was so familiar. But whose? "I should have known there were no men in Nemedia capable of slaying you. Where you hang, though, is your own doing, though I joy to see it. I joy, Conan of Cimmeria."

"Who are you?" he demanded.

Her hand went to her face, pushed back the veils. No disease-ravaged skin was revealed, but creamy ivory beauty. Tilted emerald eyes regarded him above high cheekbones. An auburn mane framed her face in soft waves.

"Karela," he breathed. Almost he wondered if he saw a vision from pain. The Red Hawk, fierce bandit of the plain of Zamora and the Turanian steppes, in Belverus, masquerading as a woman of the nobility. It seemed impossible.

That beautiful face was impassive as she gazed at him, her voice tightly controlled. "Never again did I think to see you, Cimmerian. When I saw you that day in the Market District I thought I would die on the spot."

"And did you see Hordo?" he asked. "You must know he is here, still hoping to find you." He managed a wry smile. "Working with the smugglers you now command."

"So you have learned that much," she said wonderingly. "None but a fool ever accounted you stupid. Hordo surprised me almost as much as you did, turning up in Khorshemish while I was there. Still, I would not let him know who I am. He was the most faithful of my hounds, yet others were faithful, too, and even so remembered the gold on my head in Zamora and Turan. Think you I wear these veils for the pleasure of hiding?"

"It has been a long time, Karela," Conan said. "'Tis likely they've forgotten by now."

Her calm facade cracked. "The Red Hawk will never be forgotten!" Emerald eyes flaring, she faced him with fists on hips and feet apart. Almost he could see the jeweled tulwar at her hip as it had been.

"Now that you're no longer being the Lady Tiana," he said grimly, "why in Zandru's Nine Hells do you want me dead?"

"Why?" she screeched in furious astonishment. "Have you forgot so soon leaving me naked and chained, on my way to be sold to whatever man bid highest?"

"There was the matter of the oath you made me swear, Karela. Never to lift a hand to save—"

"Derketo blast you and your oaths, Cimmerian!"

"Besides which, I had four coppers in my pouch. Think you to have gone for so paltry a price?"

"You lie!" she spat. "I would not heel at your command, so you let me be sold!"

"I tell you—"

"Liar! Liar!"

Conan snarled wordlessly and clenched his teeth on any further explanation. He would not argue with her. Neither would he plead. That last he had never learned to do.

Pacing angrily, Karela hurled her words as if they were daggers, never looking at him directly. "I want you to know my humiliations, Cimmerian. Know them, and remember them, so the memory will be a blade to prick you constantly when you are in the mines, ever reminding you that when the King proclaims pardons for all who have served a certain time, I will be there to place gold in the proper hands so that one prisoner will be forgotten."

"I knew you would escape," Conan muttered. "As you obviously did."

Her emerald eyes squeezed shut for a moment, and when she opened them her tone was flat. "I was bought by a merchant named Haffiz, and placed in his zenana with two score other women. That very day did I escape. And that very day was I brought back and given the bastinado, the cane across the soles of my feet. I would not cry, but for ten days I could only hobble. The second time I was free for three days. On being returned, I was put to scrubbing pots in the kitchens."

Despite his position Conan chuckled. "A fool he was, to think to tame you so."

She turned to face him, and if her words were soft her eyes held murder. "The third time I was taken while still climbing the wall. I spat in Haffiz' face, told him to slay me, for he could never break me. Haffiz laughed. I thought I was a man, he said. I must be taught differently. Henceforth I was to be allowed no waking hour that I was not dressed as if about to be presented to a master's bed, in the sheerest silks and the finest fragrances, kohl on my eyelids and rouge on my lips and cheeks. I must learn to dance, to play instruments, to recite poetry. Failure in any of these, failure to be pleasing at all times, would be punished immediately. But, as I was like a young girl learning to be a woman, no punishment would I receive not suitable for a child. How he roared with laughter."

Conan threw back his head and roared as well. "A child!"

Raising a fist as if she wished it had strength to knock him senseless, Karela raged. "What do you know of it, fool? Having my buttocks turned up for the switch ten times a day. Spoons of ca'teen oil forced down my throat. A hundred more too shaming even to think on. Laugh, you barbar oaf! For a year was I forced to endure, and how I wish I could make you live a year in the mines for every day of it."

With an effort he managed to control his mirth. "I thought you would escape in half a year, perhaps less. But the Red Hawk turned to a thrush in a silver cage."

"Day and night was I watched," she protested. "And I did escape, with a sword in my hand."

"Because you tired of being sent to your bed with no supper?" Chuckles reverberated in his massive chest.

"Derketo blast your eyes!" Karela howled. She raced forward to pound her small fists against his great chest. "Erlik take you, you Cimmerian bastard! You . . . you. . . ." Abruptly she sagged, clutching him to keep from falling. Her cheek was pressed against his chest; he was astounded to see a tear at the corner of her eye. "I loved you," she whispered. "I loved you."

The muscular Cimmerian shook his head in wonderment. Did she act like this when she loved him, he could not imagine anyone surviving her hate.

Pushing herself away, she stepped back from him, refusing to acknowledge the tears that trembled on her long lashes. "There is no fear in you," she whispered. "You are not trembling. Nor will you think, 'if she suffered so, what will she make me suffer?'"

"I have no blame for what happened to you, Karela," he said quietly.

She did not seem to hear. "But if you have no fear, still you are a man." A strange smile played about her lips.

Abruptly her fingers went to the brooches that held her robes; in an instant the gray silk lay in a pool about her slender ankles. Gracefully she stepped from the robes. She was as he remembered, full breasts and rounded thighs, long legs and a tiny waist. Karela was a sensual delight for the male eye.

Slowly, on her toes, she spun, arms raised, head turning to let her silken tresses caress now creamy shoulders, now satin breasts. With a gentle sway to her hips she walked to him, stopping only when her breasts touched him, just below the ribs as he hung in the chains. Touching her full lower lip with her tongue and looking up at him through her lashes, she began in a sultry tone.

"When you are taken into the mines only death can bring you to the surface again. You will live your life in dank, foul air and the dim light of guttering torches. There are women there, if you want to call them women. Their hands are as calloused as any man's." Her fingers stroked across his iron-hard chest. "Their hair and skin are filth encrusted, their stench foul; their kisses. . . ."

Her slender arms stretched up, her hands hooked behind his neck, and she pulled herself up until her face was level with his.

"They have no sweet kisses such as this," she whispered, and pressed her lips to his. He met her kiss savagely, until at last she broke free with a whimper. Her emerald gaze was tremulous, his the blue of windswept northern skies. "You will never have a kiss like that again," she said breathlessly.

Abruptly she dropped to the stone floor and backed away, biting her full lower lip. There was sudden uncertainty in her green eyes. "Now I will be the only woman in your mind for the rest of your life," she said. "The only woman for the rest of your life." And, snatching her robes from the floor, she ran into the darkness. After a time he heard the door squeak open and clash shut.

She had not changed, he thought. She was still the Red Hawk, fierce and hot-blooded as any bird of prey. But if she thought he would go meekly to the mines, or whatever the ancient penalty Garian had spoken of, then she was also as wrong-headed as she had ever been.

Conan eyed his chains, but did not again attempt to break them. Among the lessons taught by the treacherous snow-covered crags of the Cimmerian mountains was this: when action was not possible, struggle only brought death sooner; waiting, conserving strength, brought the chance of survival. The Cimmerian hung in his chains with the patience of a hunting beast waiting for its prey to come closer.

XXI

Creaking, the chains that held Conan's arms began to rattle down, lowering him to the stone floor. He could not suppress a groan as his position shifted; he had no idea how many hours he had hung there. The pool of light and the dark beyond were unchanging, giving no sign of time's passage.

His feet touched the floor, and knees long strained gave way. The full length of his massive body collapsed on the stone. Straining, he tried to get his arms under him, but the blood had long since drained from them. They could only twitch numbly.

The two men who had wielded the whips hurried into the light and began removing the chains. His weakened struggles were useless as they manacled his hands behind him and linked his ankles with heavy iron chains. The man with the burn scar was as silent and expressionless as before, but hairy-chest, he with the oddly pleasant face, talked almost jovially.

"Almost did I think we'd let you hang another day, what with all the excitement of this one. Fasten that tighter," he added to the other. "He's dangerous, this one." The second man grunted and went on as he was, hammering a rivet into the iron band on Conan's left wrist.

"My men," the Cimmerian croaked. His throat felt dry as broken pottery shards.

"Oh, they were part of it," the round-faced man laughed deprecatingly. "Fought off the Golden Leopards sent to arrest them, they did, and disappeared. Might have been made much of, another time, but more has happened since dawn this day than since Garian took the throne. First the King banished all of his old councilors from the city on pain of death. Then he created the title High Councilor of Nemedia, with near the power of the King himself attached, and gave it to Lord Albanus, an evil-eyed man if ever I saw.

And to top that, he named his leman a lady. Can you imagine that blonde doxy a lady? But all those fine nobles walk wide of her, for they say she may be Queen, next. Then there were the riots. Get the rest of it, Struto."

The silent man grunted again and lumbered away.

Conan worked his mouth for moisture. "Riots?" he managed.

The round-faced man nodded. "All over the city." Looking about as if to see if anyone might overhear, he added in a whisper. "Shouting for Garian to abdicate, they were. Maybe that's why Garian got rid of the old councilors, hoping any change would satisfy them. Leastways, he didn't send the Golden Leopards out after them."

Ariane's people had finally moved, Conan thought. Perhaps they might even bring changes—indeed, it seemed as if they already had—but for better or for worse? He forced a question out, word by word. "Had—they—armed—men—with—them?"

"Thinking of your company again, eh? No, it's been naught but people of the streets, though a surprising number have swords and such, or so I hear. Struto! Move yourself!"

He with the burn scar returned, carrying a long pole that the two of them forced between Conan's arms and his back. Broad straps fastened about his thick upper arms held it in place. From a pouch at his belt, the round-faced one took a leather gag and shoved it between the Cimmerian's teeth, securing it behind his head.

"Time to take you before the King," he told Conan. "What they're going to do to you, likely you'd rather be in Lady Tiana's gentle care. Eh, Struto?" He shook with laughter; Struto stared impassively. "Well, barbarian, you have some small time to make peace with your gods. Let's go, Struto."

Grasping the ends of the pole, the two forced Conan to his feet. Half carrying, half pushing, they took him from the dungeon, up stairs of rough stone to the marble floors of the Palace. By the time they reached those ornate halls the Cimmerian had regained full use of his legs. Pridefully he shook off the support of the two, taking what short steps the chains at his ankles allowed.

Round-face looked at him and laughed. "Anxious to get it over with, eh?"

They let him shuffle as best he could, but retained their grip on the pole. A grim smile touched his lips. Did he wish to, he could sweep both men off their feet using the very pole with which they thought to control him. But he would still be chained and in the heart of the Palace. Patience. He concentrated on flexing his arms in their bonds to get full feeling back.

The corridors through which they passed seemed empty. The slaves were there, as always, scurrying close to the walls. But the nobles, sleek and elegant in silks and velvets, were missing. The three men made their way alone down the center of the passages.

As they turned into a broad hall, its high arched ceiling supported by pilasters, another procession approached them from ahead. Graecus, Gallia and three others from the Thestis stumbled along under the eyes of two guards. All five were gagged and had their hands roped behind them. At the sight of Conan, Graecus' eyes widened, and Gallia tried to shy away from the big Cimmerian.

One of their guards called out to the two with Conan, "This lot for the mines."

"Better than what this one gets," the round-faced man laughed.

Joining in his mirth, the guards prodded their charges on. The bedraggled young rebels hurried past, seeming as fearful of Conan as of their captors.

The Cimmerian ignored them. He did not hold them to account for the lies they had told against him. Few men and fewer women could hold out under the attentions of an expert torturer, and Vegentius would have found another way to imprison him, if not through them.

Before them at the end of the hall, great carven doors opened, swung wide by six golden-cloaked soldiers, and Conan passed into the throne room of Nemedia.

Double rows of slender fluted columns held a domed roof of alabaster aloft. Light from golden lamps dangling from the ceiling on silver chains glittered on polished marble walls. The floor was a vast mosaic depicting the entire history of Nemedia. Here was the explanation for the empty halls, for here the nobles had gathered in all their panoply, dark-eyed lords in robes of velvet with golden chains about their necks, sleek ladies coruscating with the gems that covered their silk-draped bodies. Through the center of them ran a broad path from the tall doors to the Dragon Throne. Its golden-horned head reared above the man seated there, and jeweled wings curved down to support his shoulders. On his head was the Dragon Crown.

Conan set his own pace down that path, though the two jailors tried to hurry him. He would not stumble in his chains for the amusement of this court. Before the throne he stood defiantly and stared into Garian's face. The men holding the pole tried to force him to his knees, but he remained erect. A murmur rose among the nobles. Rushing forward, guards beat at his back and legs with their spear butts until, despite all he could do, he was shoved to his knees.

Through it all, Garian's face had not changed expression. Now the man on the throne rose, pulling his robe of cloth-of-gold about him.

"This barbarian," he announced loudly, "we did take into our Palace honoring him with our attention. But we found that we nursed treachery at our bosom. Most foully our trust was betrayed, and. . . ."

He droned on, but Conan's attention was caught by the man standing slightly behind the Dragon Throne, one hand resting on it possessively while he nodded at the King's words like a teacher approving a pupil. The Seal of Nemedia hung on a golden chain about his neck, which marked him as the High Councilor of Nemedia, Lord Albanus. But Conan knew that cruel face, seen in the dark meeting with Taras and Vegentius. Did madness reign in Nemedia, the Cimmerian wondered.

" . . . So we pronounce the ancient penalty for his crime," the King intoned funereally.

That brought Conan's mind quickly back. There was on Garian's face none of the sadness he had shown when Conan was taken, only flat calm.

"When next the sun has dawned and risen to its zenith, let this would-be regicide be hurled to the wolves. Let the beast be torn by beasts."

As soon as the last word was spoken, Conan was pulled to his feet and hurried from the throne room. Not even the round-faced jailor spoke as the Cimmerian was returned to the dungeons, this time to a small cell, its stone floor strewn with filthy straw. The pole and the gag were removed, but not his chains. Another was added, linking that between his ankles to a ring set in the wall.

As soon as the two jailors were gone Conan began to explore his new prison. Lying full length on his belly, he could have reached the heavy wooden door were his hands not linked behind him, but there was nothing on which to get a grip even if his hands had been free. Nor did he truly believe he could break the stout iron hinges. The walls were rough stone, close set but with aged mortar crumbling. A man with tools might remove enough of them to escape. In a year or two. The rotting straw held nothing but a half-gnawed rat carcass. The Cimmerian could not help wondering whether the gnawing had been done by its fellows or by the last prisoner. Kicking it into a far corner, he hoped he would not long have to endure the smell.

No sooner had Conan settled himself with his back against the wall than a key rattled in the large iron lock, and the cell door creaked open. To his surprise Albanus entered, holding his black velvet robes carefully clear of the foul straw. Behind him the cloth-of-gold-clad form of the King stopped in the doorway. Garian's face turned this way and that, eyes curiously taking in the straw and the stone walls. He looked at Conan once, as if the big Cimmerian were just another fixture of the cell.

It was Albanus who spoke. "You know me, don't you?"

"You are Lord Albanus," Conan replied warily.

"You know me," the hawk-faced man said, as if confirming a suspicion. "I feared as much. 'Tis well I acted when I did."

Conan tensed. "You?" His eyes went to Garian's face. Why would this man make such an admission before the King?

"Expect no help from him," Albanus laughed. "For a time, barbar, you were a worry to me, but it seems in the end you are no weapon of the gods after all. The wolves will put an end to you, and the only real damage you have done me is being repaired by the girl you sent seeking the sculptor. No, in the sum of it, you are naught but a minor nuisance."

"Ariane," Conan said sharply. "What have you done with her?"

The obsidian-eyed lord laughed cruelly. "Come, King Garian. Let us leave this place."

"What have you done to Ariane?" Conan shouted as Albanus left. The King paused to look at him; he stared into Garian's face with as close to pleading as he could come. "Tell me what he has done. . . ."

The words died on his lips even as the other turned to go. The door creaked shut. Stunned, Conan leaned back against the stone wall.

Since that first entrance into the throne-room, he had felt some oddity in Garian but put it down to himself. No man sees things aright while hearing his own death sentence. But now he had noticed a small thing. There was no bruise on Garian's cheek. Garian was no man to cover such things with powder like a woman, and he had no court sorcerer to take away such blemishes with a quick spell and a burning candle. Nor had it had time to fade naturally. A small thing, yet it meant that he who had sat on the Dragon Throne and passed sentence on Conan was not Garian.

Mind whirling, the Cimmerian tried to make some sense of it. Albanus plotted rebellion, yet now was councilor to a King who was not Garian. But it had been Garian in Vegentius' apartments only the night before. Of that Conan was certain. He smelled the stench of sorcery as clearly as he did the rotting straw on which he sat.

Patience, he reminded himself. He could do nothing chained in a cell. Much would depend on whether he was freed of those bonds before he was thrown to the wolves. Even among wolves a great deal could be done by a man with hands free and will unfettered. This, Conan resolved, Albanus would learn to his regret.

Sularia lay face down on a toweled bench while the skilled hands of a slave woman worked fragrant oils into her back. Lady Sularia, she thought, stretching luxuriantly. So wonderful it had been standing among the lords and ladies in the throne room, rather than being crowded with the other lemans along the back wall. If her acceptance had been from fear, the smiles and greetings given her sickly and shamefaced, it only added to the pleasure, for those who spoke respectfully now had oft spoken as if she were a slave. And this did not have to be the end. If she could move from the mistresses' wall to stand with the nobles, why not from there to stand beside Albanus? Queen Sularia.

Smiling at the thought, she turned her head on her folded arms and regarded her maid, a plump gray-haired woman who was the only one in the Palace Sularia trusted. Or rather, the one she distrusted least.

"Does she still wait, Latona?" Sularia asked.

The gray-haired maid nodded briskly. "For two turns of the glass now, mistress. No one would dare disobey your summons."

The blonde nodded self-satisfied agreement without lifting her head. "Bring her in, Latona. Then busy yourself with my hair."

"Yes, mistress," Latona cackled, and hurried out. When she returned she escorted the Lady Jelanna.

The willowy noblewoman looked askance at Latona as the serving woman began to labor over her mistress' hair, while Sularia smiled like a cat at a dish of cream. Only when receiving an inferior would servants be retained so. Some of the arrogance had gone from Jelanna with her wait.

Enough remained, however, for her to demand at last, "Why have you summoned me here, Sularia?" Sularia raised a questioning eyebrow. After a moment Jelanna amended, "Lady Sularia." Her mouth was twisted as if at a foul taste.

"You grew from a child in this Palace, did you not?" the blonde began in a pleasant tone.

Jelanna's reply was curt. "I did."

"Playing hide and seek through the corridors. Gamboling in the courtyards, splashing in the fountains. Your every wish met as soon as it was made."

"Did you ask me here to speak of childhood?" Jelanna asked.

"I did not," Sularia said sharply. "I summoned. Know you Enaro Ostorian?"

If the imperiously beautiful woman was surprised by the question, she did not show it. "That repulsive little toad?" she sniffed. "I know of merchants, but I do not know them."

Sularia's feline smile returned. "He seeks a wife."

"Does he?"

"A young wife, of the nobility." Sularia saw the dart go home, and pressed to drive it deeper. "He thinks to marry the title he has not been able to buy. And of course he wants sons. Many sons. Garian," she added to the lie, "has asked me to suggest a suitable bride."

Jelanna licked her full lips uncertainly. "I wish, Lady Sularia," she said, a tremor in her voice, "to apologize if I have in any way offended you."

"Do you know the man Dario?" Sularia demanded. "The keeper of Garian's kennels?"

"No, my lady," Jelanna faltered.

"A foul man, I'm told, both in stenches and habits. The slave girls of the Palace hide from him, for his way with a woman is rough to the point of pain." Sularia paused, watching the horror grow on the imperious woman's face. "Think you, Jelanna, that one night with Dario is preferable to a lifetime with Ostorian?"

"You are mad," the slender woman managed. "I'll listen to no more. I go to my estates in the country, and if you were queen you could still choose which of Zandru's—"

"Four soldiers await without for you," Sularia said, riding over the other woman's words. "They will escort you to Dario, or to your wedding bed, and no place else."

The last shreds of haughtiness were washed from Jelanna's face by despair. "Please," she whispered. "I will grovel, an you wish it. Before the entire court on my knees will I beg your forgive—"

"Make your choice," Sularia purred, "else I will make it for you. Those soldiers can deliver you to Ostorian this day. With a note to let him know you think him a repulsive toad." Her voice and face hardened. "Choose!"

Jelanna swayed as if she would fall. "I . . . I will go to Dario," she wept.

For a moment Sularia savored the words she had waited for, counting hours. Then she spoke them. "Go, bitch, to your kennel!" As Jelanna ran from the room, peals of Sularia's laughter rang against the walls. How wonderful was power.

XXII

hen next the door of his cell opened, Conan at first thought that Albanus had decided to have him slain where he lay chained. Two men with drawn crossbows slipped through the open door and took positions covering him, one to either side of the cell.

As the Cimmerian gathered himself to make what fight of it he could, the round-faced jailor appeared in the door and spoke.

"The sun stands high, barbarian. 'Tis time to take you to the wolf pit. An you try to fight when Struto and I remove your chains, these two will put quarrels in your legs, and you'll be dragged to the pit. Well?"

Conan made an effort to appear sullen and reluctant. "Take the chains," he growled, glowering at the crossbowmen.

In spite of his words the two jailors kept clear of the crossbowmen's line of fire as they broke open his manacles with repeated blows of hammer on chisel. Did they think him a fool, he wondered. He might well be able to take both jailors and bowmen despite the way they were placed, yet he could hear measured steps approaching the cell, the sound of a middling body of men. Dying was not hard, but only a fool chose to die for naught.

Rubbing his wrists, Conan rose smoothly to his feet and let himself be herded from the cell. In the hall waited a full score of the Golden Leopards.

"Don't need so many," Struto said abruptly.

Conan blinked. He had thought the man without a tongue.

Struto's fellow jailor seemed only slightly less surprised at hearing him speak. The round-faced man stared before saying, "He near escaped from as many the night he was taken. You know I don't like prisoners escaping. I asked for twice as many. Move on, now. The King waits."

Half the soldiers went before him, and half behind, the jailors walking on either side. The crossbowmen brought up the rear, where they could get a shot at him did he run, in whatever direction. So they made their way up into the Palace and through corridors once more bare of nobles.

Conan strode in their midst as if they were an honor guard and he on his way to his coronation. There was no glimmer of escape in his mind. At the wolf pit would most certainly be the impostor Garian and Albanus. Under the circumstances, a man could do worse than die killing those two.

Their way led through the parts of the Palace familiar to the Cimmerian, and beyond. Polished marble and alabaster gave way to plain dressed granite, then to stone as rough as that of the dungeons. Lamps of gold and silver were replaced by torches in iron sconces.

The wolf pit was an ancient penalty indeed, and had, in fact, not been imposed since the time of Bragorus, nine centuries earlier. Nor had any come to this portion of the Palace at all in several centuries, to judge by its appearance. The halls showed signs of hasty cleaning, here a torn cobweb hanging from the ceiling, there dust left heaped against the wall. Conan wondered why Albanus had gone to all this trouble after replacing Garian with the impostor. And then they entered the circular chamber of the pit.

Though of the same rough stone, it was yet as marvelously wrought as any of the great alabaster rooms in the Palace. Like half of a sphere, its walls rose to a towering height unsupported by column or buttress. Below, a broad walk spotted with huge tripod lamps twice as tall as a man was crowded with the nobility of Nemedia, laughing gaily as men and women at a circus, pressing close about the waist-high stone wall that encircled the great pit.

A path to that wall cleared at their entrance, and the soldiers escorted Conan to it. Not waiting to be told, the Cimmerian leaped to the top of the wall and stood surveying those who had assembled to watch him die. Beneath his icy blue gaze they slowly fell silent, as they sensed that here was a man contemptuous of their titles and lineages. They were peacocks; he was an eagle.

Directly across the stone-floored pit from him stood the impostor King, Albanus to one side in robes of midnight blue, to the other Vegentius, his face still showing bruises beneath his red-crested helmet. Sularia was there as well, in scarlet silk and rubies, and Conan wondered why he had thought she would not attend.

Below the imposter was the man-high gate through which the wolves would be let into the pit. Conan saw no eager muzzles pressed between the bars of the gate, heard no hungry whines and growls. A complicated system of iron chains served to draw the gate aside. Perhaps he need not die.

Albanus touched the arm of the man wearing the Dragon Crown, and he began to speak. "We have gathered you—"

Conan's wild war cry rang from the rocky dome; shouts and screams ran through the nobles as, massive arms raised above his head, the Cimmerian hurled himself into the pit. Soldiers forced their way through the nobles to the wall; the crossbowmen took aim. About the straw-strewn pit Conan strode with all the cocky arrogance of youth that had never met defeat in equal combat, and in a few unequal. Albanus motioned, and the guards moved back.

"Fools!" Conan taunted the assemblage. "You who have not a man among you have come to see a man die. Well, must I be talked to death by that buffoon in the crown? Get on with it, unless your livers have shriveled and you have no stomach for killing." Angry cries answered him.

Albanus whispered to the impostor, who in turn said, "As he is so eager to die, loose the wolves."

"Loose the wolves," someone else shouted, relaying the command. "Hurry!" The gate slid smoothly back.

Conan did not wait for the first wolf to emerge. Before the astonished eyes of the court the Cimmerian ran into the tunnel, roaring his battle cry. Behind, in the pit, yelling nobles dropped over the wall to seize and slay the escaping barbarian who had denied their manhood.

In the dark of the tunnel Conan found himself suddenly in the midst of the snarling wolfpack. Razor teeth ripped at him. He matched them snarl for snarl, his fists hammers that broke bones and knocked beasts the size of a man sprawling. Seizing a growling throat in his hands he dashed the wolf's brains out against the low stone roof.

In the hellish cauldron of that tunnel, the wolves knew the kindred ferocity of the young giant who faced them. As Conan fought his way deeper into their pack, they began to slip past toward the pit, seeking easier meat. The noble lords' angry yells turned to screams as bloody wolves raced among them to slay.

Ahead of him Conan saw a light.

"Accursed wolves," a voice snarled from that direction. "You're to kill some fool barbar, not each—"

The man who spoke faltered as he saw Conan coming toward him. He stood with the iron-barred gate at his end of the tunnel half open, a spear in his hand. Instead of stepping back and slamming the gate shut, he thrust at the Cimmerian.

Conan grasped the spear with both hands and easily wrenched it from the other's grasp. Before the man could do more than gape the butt of his own spear smashed into his chest, hurling him back through the gate, Conan following close behind. The wolf-keeper scrambled to his feet, a curved blade the length of his forearm protruding from his fist, and lunged.

The spear reversed smoothly in the Cimmerian's big hands. He had not so much to thrust as to let the man run onto the point, spitting himself so that the whole blade of the spear stood out from his back. A cry of both pain and horrified disbelief wrenched from the wolf-keeper's throat.

"Your wolves will not kill this barbar," Conan growled, then realized that his words had been spoken to a dead man.

Letting spear and transfixed man fall, he closed the gate, thrust the heavy iron bar that fastened it into its brackets and shoved the latch pins home. It would take time to get that open from the other side, time for him to escape. Though, from the screams and snarls that yet echoed in the tunnel, it might be some while before the soldiers dealt with wolves and panicked nobles and reached that gate.

Little there was in that chamber to be of use to him. Crude rush torches guttered in rusty iron sconces on the walls, illuminating six large, iron-barred cages mounted on wheels. No weapons were in evidence excepting only the long, curved dagger, which Conan retrieved, and the spear. He left that lodged in the wolf-keeper's body; its length would make it a cumbersome weapon in the narrow confines of the old stone corridors. There was not even cloth to bind his gashes unless he tore from his own breechclout or from the filthy, and now blood-soaked, tunic on the corpse.

The wolf-keeper had, however, brought a clay jug of wine and a large spiced sausage on which to sup while his charges did their bloody work. On these Conan fell eagerly, ripping the sausage apart with his teeth and washing it down with long gulps of sour wine. He had had no food or drink since before his imprisonment. No doubt his jailors had deemed it a waste to feed one who was to die soon. Tossing the empty jug aside and popping the last bit of sausage into his mouth, the Cimmerian took one of the rush torches and set about finding his way out of the Palace.

It did not take him long to discover that those ancient corridors were a labyrinth, never straight, crossing and recrossing themselves and each other. He had no wonder in him that the secret passages beneath the Palace had been lost; it would be all men could do to keep track of these.

Suddenly, in crossing another pitch-dark hall, he realized that his footprints had mingled with others. Other fresh prints. He bent to examine them, and straightened with a curse. Both sets were his own. He had doubled back on himself, and could continue to do so until he starved.

Face grimly determined, he followed his own prints until he came to a forking of the passage. The trail in the dust went left. He went right. A short time later he found himself again staring at his own backtrail, but this time he did not pause to curse. Hurrying on to the next turning, he again took the opposite way to that he had taken before. And the next time. And the next.

Now the passages seemed to slope downward, but Conan pressed on regardless, even when he found himself burning a way through halls choked with cobwebs that crisped drily at the touch of the flame. Turning back held no more assurance of escape than going forward, only a greater chance of encountering the Golden Leopards.

Coming to a fork, the Cimmerian turned automatically right—he had taken the left at the last—and stopped. Far ahead of him was a dim glow, but it was no opening to the outside. Bobbing slightly, it was coming closer.

Hurriedly he turned back, ducked into the other side of the fork. On silent feet he ran twenty paces and hurled the torch ahead of him as far as it would go. The flames flared, fanned by the wind of the torch's flight, then winked out, leaving him in blackness.

Conan crouched, facing the direction of the fork, curved dagger at the ready. If those who approached went on, he would be without light but alive. If not. . . .

Diffuse light reached the fork, brightening slowly, resolving into two torch-bearing figures, swords in their free hands. The Cimmerian almost laughed. Hordo and Karela, but the Karela he had known long ago. Gone were the veils and gray robes of a Nemedian noblewomen, replaced by golden breastplates and a narrow girdle of gold and emeralds, worn low on her rounded hips, from which hung strips of pale green silk. A Turanian cape of emerald green encircled her shoulders.

"Hordo," Conan called, "had I known you were coming I wouldn't have drunk all the wine." Nonchalantly he strolled to meet them.

The two whirled, swords coming up, torches raised. From the other fork men in jazeraint hauberks crowded. Machaon, Narus, more familiar faces from his Free-Company, pushed into the light.

Hordo took in Conan's gashes, but did not speak of them. "'Tis not like you," he said gruffly, "to drink all the wine. Mayhap we could find some more, if we look."

Karela threw the one-eyed man a murderous look and shoved her torch into Machaon's hand. With gentle fingers she touched Conan's wounds, wincing at purpled flesh and dried blood.

"I knew you would change your mind," Conan said, reaching for her.

Her hand cracked across his face, and she stepped back smoothly with blade half raised. "I should throw you back to the wolves," she hissed.

From somewhere in the darkness beyond the armored men, a voice called unintelligibly. Another answered, both fading as the speakers moved further away.

"They hunt me," Conan said quietly. "An you know a way out of here, I suggest we take it. Else we must fight a few hundred Golden Leopards."

Muttering, Karela snatched back her torch and forced her way through the men of the Free-Company to disappear back up the other fork.

"She's the only one knows the way," Hordo said quickly. He hurried after her, and Conan followed. Machaon and the rest fell in behind, their booted feet grating in the dust of centuries.

"How did you get into the Palace?" Conan demanded of the one-eyed man as they half-trotted after the auburn-haired beauty. "And what made Karela decide to let you know who she was?"

"Mayhap I'd best begin at the beginning," Hordo puffed. "First thing that happened was, after you were arrested, a hundred Golden Leopards came for us, and—"

"I know about that," Conan said. "You got away. What then?"

"You heard about that, did you? I'm too old for this running, Cimmerian." Despite his heavy breathing, though, the bearded man kept pace easily. "I took the company to the Thestis. Hellgate is near the safest part of Belverus these days. Everybody who lives there is up in the High Streets waving a sword and shouting revolution. And maybe breaking into some rich man's house now and again."

"What else did you expect?" Conan laughed grimly. "They're poor, and have riches within their reach. But about Karela."

Hordo shook his shaggy head. "She walked into the Thestis this very morn. No, she strode in, looking as if she was ready for her hounds to follow her against a caravan of gold. From what you said, you knew she was here already, eh?"

"Not until I was in the dungeon," Conan replied. "I will explain later."

Suddenly Karela stopped, stretching on tiptoe to reach a rusty iron sconce. She seemed to be trying to twist it.

"Looks like where we came in," Hordo muttered softly. "Looks like twenty places we passed, too." Emerald eyes flashed at him scornfully, and he subsided.

Just as Conan was about to step forward to her aid, the sconce turned with a sharp click. A shot distance away on the same wall was another sconce, which Karela treated the same way. It swiveled, clicked, and there was a heavier thunk from deep within the wall. With a grate of machinery long unused, a section of stone wall as high as a man and twice as wide receded jerkily to reveal a descending flight of crude brick stairs.

"If you two can stop chattering like old women for a moment," Karela said bitingly, "follow me. And take care. Some of the bricks are crumbling. It would pain me for you to break your neck, Cimmerian. I reserve that pleasure for myself." And she darted down the steps.

Hordo shrugged uncomfortably. "I told you, she's the only one knows the way."

Conan nodded. "Follow me," he told Machaon, "and pass the word to watch for crumbling steps." The grizzled sergeant began muttering over his shoulder to those behind.

Taking a deep breath Conan followed Karela down the dark stairs, lit only by her torch, now only a glimmer far below. He did not actually believe that she would come just to lead him into a trap of her own devising rather than let him die at someone else's hands. But then, he did not entirely disbelieve it either.

At the bottom of the long stair, Karela waited impatiently. "Are they all in?" she demanded as soon as he entered the light of her torch. Without waiting for him to reply she called up the stair. "Is everyone clear of the entrance?"

There was some scraping of feet on stone, then a voice called back hoarsely, "We're clear, but I hear boots coming."

Calmly Karela placed both feet on one particular stone, which sank a finger's breadth beneath her weight. The grating of machinery sounded again.

"It's closing," the same man's voice shouted incredulously.

Karela's tilted eyes met Conan's. "Fools," she said, seeming to include all men, but most certainly him. With a quick, "Follow or stay, I care not," she started down a long tunnel, torchlight glinting off damp walls.

Even the air felt moldy, Conan thought as he set out after her.

"As I was saying," Hordo resumed, striding beside the Cimmerian, "she walked into the Thestis ready to take command. Wouldn't tell me where she'd been, or how she knew where I was. Threatened to put a scar down my other cheek if I did not stop asking questions."

His lone eye swiveled to Conan expectantly, but the big youth was watching Karela, wondering what was in her mind. Why had she come to rescue him? "And?" he said absently when he realized that Hordo had stopped talking.

The one-eyed man grunted sourly. "And nobody tells me anything," he grunted sourly. "She had a woman with her. You remember the Lady Jelanna? 'Twas her, but not so haughty this time. Bedraggled and haggard, she was, with bruises on her face and arms, and terrified to tears. 'She will not stop,' she kept moaning, 'not until I am broken.' And Karela kept soothing her and looking at the rest of us like it was us had done whatever had been done to this Jelanna."

"Crom," Conan muttered. "Do you have to be so long-winded? What does Jelanna have to do with anything?"

"Why, it was her told Karela how to find this passage. Lady Jelanna grew up in the Palace, it seems, playing hide-and-seek and such, as children do. Only sometimes they played in the old parts of the Palace, and she found three or four of the secret passages. She got out of the Palace by one herself. She was desperate to get out of the city, Cimmerian, so I told off two men to escort her to her estate in the country. Least I could do, and her showing us how to get in to you. I tell you true, I thought the next time I saw you we'd both be taking a pull at the Hellhorn."

"That still doesn't tell me why she would aid me," Conan said, with a jerk of his head at Karela to indicate which 'she' he meant.

Hardly were the words out of his mouth than the auburn-haired woman rounded on him. "The wolves were too good for you, you big Cimmerian oaf. If you are to be torn to pieces, I want to do it with my own hands. I want to hear you beg my forgiveness, you barbar bastard. I get first call at you, before that fool Garian."

Conan eyed her calmly, a slight smile on his lips. "Did you stop because you lost the way, Karela? I will take the lead, an you wish."

With a snarl she drew back her torch as if to strike him with it.

"There it is," Hordo shouted, pointing to a short flight of stairs, barely revealed by the light, that led up to the ceiling and stopped. Relief dripped from every word. "Come on, Cimmerian," he went on, herding Conan quickly past the furious-eyed woman. "We had trouble getting this back in place, in case anybody should take a look at the other side, but you and I should be able to lift it clear." In a fierce whisper he added, "Watch your tongue, man. She's been like a scalded cat ever since Machaon and those other fools told her they'd never heard of the Red Hawk."

Eyeing the fierce scowl with which Karela watched them, Conan managed to turn his laughter into a cough. "This other side," he said. "Where is it? If there's anyone there, will they be likely to fight?"

"Not a chance of it," Hordo laughed. "Now put your shoulder into it."

The stairs seemed to end in one large slab of stone. It was to this Hordo urged Conan to apply himself. When he did, the thick slab lifted. With Hordo's aid he slid it aside, then scrambled warily up. A heavy smell of incense filled the air. As the others followed with torches, Conan saw that he was in a windowless room filled with barrels and bales. Some of the bales were broken open to reveal incense sticks.

"A temple?" the Cimmerian asked in disbelief. "The passage comes out in the cellar of a temple?"

Hordo laughed and nodded. Motioning for silence, the one-eyed man climbed a wooden ladder fastened to one wall, and cautiously lifted a trapdoor. His head went up for a quick look, then he motioned the rest to follow and scrambled out himself.

Conan was quick to follow. He found himself in dim light from silver lamps, between a large rectangular block of marble and a towering, shadowed statue. With a start it came to him that he was between the altar stone and the idol of Erebus, a place where none but sanctified priests were allowed. But then, what was one death sentence more or less?

Quickly everyone found their way out of the cellar and, by way of narrow halls of pale marble, to a courtyard behind the temple. There two more of the Free-Company waited with the horses. And, Conan was glad to note, with hauberk, helm and scimitar for him. Hastily he armed himself properly.

"We can be beyond the city walls," Hordo said, swinging into his saddle, "before they think to look outside the Palace."

"We cannot leave yet," Conan said quietly. He settled his helm on his head and likewise mounted. "Ariane is in Albanus' hands."

"Yet another woman?" Karela said dangerously.

"She befriended Hordo and me," Conan said, "and as reward for it Albanus has her. I swore to see her safely out of this, and I will."

"You and your oaths," Karela muttered, but when he galloped out of the courtyard she was first of the company behind him.

XXIII

Isolated plumes of smoke rose into the bright afternoon sky above Belverus, marking houses of the wealthy that had been visited by revolutionary mobs. The sound of those mobs could be heard from time to time, borne on the breeze. It was a wordless, hungering snarl.

Once in that gallop across the city Conan saw one of those howling packs, some three of four score ragged men and women pounding at the locked doors and barred windows of a house with axes, swords, rocks, their bare hands. In the same instant that he saw them, they became aware of the Free-Company. A growl rippled through them, a sound that seemed impossible to come from a human throat, and like rats pouring from a sewer they threw themselves toward the mounted men. In their eyes was a hatred of any who had more than they, even if it was only armor. Many of the weapons they waved were bloodied.

"The bows will drive them back," Hordo shouted.

Conan was not so sure. There was desperation in those faces. "Ride," he commanded.

Galloping on, they quickly left the mob behind, yet even as it was disappearing from sight its members kept pursuing, their howls heard long after they could no longer be seen.

On reaching Albanus' palace, Conan did not pause. "Every third man stay with the horses," he commanded. "Everybody else over the wall. Bring your bows. Not you," he added, as Karela maneuvered her horse close to the wall.

"You do not command me, Cimmerian," she spat back. "I go where I please."

"Erlik take all hardheaded women," Conan muttered, but he said no more to her.

Standing on his saddle and taking a care where he placed his hands among the pottery shards, he hoisted himself to the top of the wall. As if they had trained for such a thing Hordo, Karela and four and twenty of the others smoothly followed. Below, half a score of men ran from the gate-house. They had only time to gape before arrows humming like hornets cut them down.

Conan dropped to the ground inside, his eyes blue ice, and ran past the bodies. He half heard the thuds of the others following, but he paid them no mind. Ariane filled his mind. His word had sent her to Albanus. Now his honor demanded he free her if it cost his own life.

With a single heave of his massive arm he threw back one of the tall doors of the palace. Before the crash of its striking the marble wall had finished reverberating in the columned hall, a helmeted man in the cloak of the Golden Leopards ran to face the young Cimmerian giant, sword in hand.

"Ariane," Conan shouted as he beat aside the soldier's attack. "Where are you, Ariane?" His blade half-severed the man's head; he kicked the falling body aside and hurried deeper into the palace. "Ariane!"

More Golden Leopards appeared now, and Conan threw himself at them in a frenzy, his wild battle cry ringing from the arched ceiling, his blade slashing and hacking as if possessed of a demon, or wielded by one. The soldiers fell back in confusion, leaving three of their number dead or dying, unsure of how to face this wildman of the barbarian northcountry. Then Hordo and the others were on them as well. The one-eyed man's fierce mien was matched by the ferocity of his attack. Karela danced among them, blade darting like a wasp, each time drawing back blooded.

Even as the last body fell, Conan was shouting to his men. "Spread out. Search every room, if need be. Find the girl called Ariane."

He himself strode through the halls like an avenging god. Servants and slaves took one look at the thundercloud of his face and fled. He let them go, seeking only one person. Then he saw another that interested him. The gray-bearded chamberlain tried to run, but Conan seized a fistful of the man's tunic and lifted him till only the other's toes touched the floor.

Conan's voice held the promise of death. "Where is the girl Ariane, chamberlain?"

"I . . . I know no girl—"

Conan's arm knotted, lifted the other clear of the floor. "The girl," he said softly.

Sweat beaded the chamberlain's face. "Lord Albanus," he gasped. "He took her to the Royal Palace."

With a groan the Cimmerian let the gray-bearded man drop. The chamberlain darted away; Conan let him go. The Palace. How could he get to her there? Could he return through the secret passage from the Temple of Erebus? He would spend the rest of his life wandering in the ancient labyrinth without ever finding his way into the newer Palace.

He heard footsteps behind him and turned to find Hordo bearing down on him, Machaon and Karela close behind.

"Machaon found someone in the dungeons," Hordo said quickly. "Not the girl. A man who looks like King Garian, and even claims he—"

"Show me," Conan said. Hope took life again within him.

The dungeons beneath Albanus' palace were much like any others, rough stone, heavy wooden doors on rusting hinges, a thick smell of stale urine and fear sweat. Still, when Conan looked into the cell to which Machaon led him, he smiled as if it were a fountained garden.

The ragged, dirty man chained to the wall stirred uncertainly. "Well, Conan," he said, "have you joined Albanus and Vegentius?"

"Derketo," Karela breathed. "He does look like Garian."

"He is Garian," Conan said. "That bruise on his cheek names him so."

Garian's chains clanked as he touched the bruise. He laughed shakily. "To be known by so little a thing."

"If this be Garian," Karela demanded, "then who sits on the Dragon Throne?"

"An impostor," Conan replied. "He has no bruise. Fetch me hammer and chisel. Quickly." Machaon disappeared to return in moments with the required items.

As Conan knelt to lay chisel to the first manacle at Garian's ankle, the King said, "You will be rewarded for this, barbarian. All that Albanus possesses will be yours when I regain the throne."

Conan did not speak. One mighty blow with the hammer split the riveted iron band open. He moved to the next.

"You must get me out of the city," Garian went on. "Once I reach the army, all will be well. I grew up in those camps. They will know me. I'll return at the head of ten thousand swords to tear Albanus from the Palace."

"And to start a civil war," Conan said. He freed the other ankle, again with a single blow. "The impostor looks much like you. Many will believe he is you, most especially since he speaks from the Dragon Throne. Perhaps even the army will not be as quick to believe as you think."

Hordo groaned. "No, Cimmerian. This is not our affair. Let us put the border behind us."

Neither Conan nor Garian paid him any mind. The King was silent until Conan had broken off the manacles from his wrists. Then he said quietly, "What do you suggest, Conan?"

"Re-enter the Palace," Conan said as though that were the easiest thing in the world. "Confront the imposter. Not all the Golden Leopards can be traitors. You can regain your throne without a sword being lifted outside the Palace walls." He did not think it politic to mention the mobs roaming the streets.

"A bold plan," Garian mused. "Yet most of the Golden Leopards are loyal to me. I overheard those who guarded me here talking. We will do it. I go to regain my throne, Cimmerian, but you have already gained my eternal gratitude." His regal manner was returning to him. He regarded his own filth with an amused smile. "But if I am to re-enter the Palace, I must wash and garb myself to look the King."

As Garian strode from the cell, shouting for hot water and clean robes, Conan frowned, wondering why the King's last words had been so disquieting. But there was no time to consider that now. There was Ariane to think of.

"Cimmerian," Karela said angrily, "if you think I will ride at your side back to the Palace, you are a bigger fool than I believe you. 'Tis a deathtrap."

"I have not asked you to go," he replied. "Often enough you've told me you go where you will."

Her scowl said that was neither the answer she expected nor the one she wanted.

"Hordo," the Cimmerian went on, "bring the men in from the street. Let all know where we go. Let those who will not follow go. I'll have no man ride with me this day against his will."

Hordo nodded and left. Behind Conan Karela uttered an inarticulate oath. Conan ignored her, his mind already occupied with the problem of gaining entry to the Palace and, more important to him than regaining Garian's throne, getting Ariane free.

When Conan strode from the palace with Garian, now resplendent in the best scarlet velvet he could find to fit him, the Cimmerian was not surprised to find all eight and thirty of his men mounted and waiting, even those who bore wounds from the past hour's fighting. He knew he had chosen good men. He was surprised though, to see Karela sitting her horse beside Hordo. Her green glare dared him to question her presence. He mounted without speaking. There were enough problems to be confronted that day without another argument with her.

"I am ready," Garian announced as he climbed into the saddle. He had a broadsword strapped on over his tunic.

"Let us ride," Conan commanded, and led the small band out of the palace grounds at a gallop.

XXIV

The approach to the Palace, up the winding streets to the top of the hill and across the greensward to the drawbridge, was made at a slow walk. Garian rode slightly to the front of Conan. A King should lead his army, he had said, even when it was a small one. Conan agreed, hoping the sight of Garian would make the guards hesitate enough to let them get inside.

At the drawbridge they dismounted, and the guards there indeed stared open-mouthed as Garian strode up to them.

"Do you recognize me?" Garian demanded.

Both nodded, and one said, "You are the King. But how did you leave the Palace? There was no call for an honor guard."

Conan breathed a sigh of relief. There were not Vegentius' men. The guards eyed those behind the King, most especially Karela, but kept their main attention on Garian.

"Do you think the King does not know the secret ways beneath this hill?" Garian smiled as if the thought were laughable. As the two guards began to smile as well, though, his face became grim. "Are you loyal men? Loyal to your King?"

The two stiffened as one, and both recited the oath of the Golden Leopards as if to remind Garian of it. "My sword follows he who wears the Dragon Crown. My flesh is a shield for the Dragon Throne. As the King commands, I obey, to the death."

Garian nodded. "Then know that there is a plot against the Dragon Throne, and its perpetrators are Lord Albanus and Commander Vegentius."

Conan put his hand to his sword as the soldiers started, but they merely stared at the King.

"What are we to do?" one of them asked finally.

"Take those who are in the barbican," Garian told them, "leaving only two to lower the portcullis and guard the gate, and go with them to your barracks. Rouse all who are there. Let your cry be, 'Death to Albanus and Vegentius!' Any who will not shout that are enemies of the Dragon Throne, even if they wear the golden cloak."

"Death to Albanus and Vegentius," one guard said, and the other repeated it.

When they had disappeared into the barbican, Garian sagged. "I did not think it would be this easy," he told Conan.

"It won't be," Conan assured him.

"I still think I should have told them of the imposter, Cimmerian."

Conan shook his head. "It would only confuse them. They'll find out after he's dead, if luck is with us." It mattered little to him when or how they found out, so long as there was enough confusion for his purposes. He eyed the door to the barbican. What took them so long?

Suddenly there was a cry from inside the stone gatehouse, cut abruptly short. One of those who had stood at the gate appeared in the door with a bloody blade in his fist. "There was one who would not say it," he said.

One by one those others who had been on guard slipped out, sword in hand. Each paused long enough to say to the King, "Death to Albanus and Vegentius," then trotted into the Palace.

"You see," Garian told Conan as they led the Free-Company through the gate. "It will be easy."

As the portcullis rattled down behind them, shouts rang out from the direction of the Golden Leopards' quarters, and the clash of swords. An alarm gong began to ring, then stopped with a suddenness that spoke of the death of him who had sounded it. The sounds of fighting spread.

"I want to find Albanus," Garian said. "And Vegentius."

Conan only nodded. He, too, wanted Albanus. Vegentius he would take if he came across him. He hurried on, the Free-Company deployed behind him. First he would try the throne room.

Abruptly two score golden-cloaked soldiers appeared ahead.

"For Garian!" Conan called, not slowing. "Death to Albanus and Vegentius!"

"Kill them!" came the reply. "For Vegentius!"

The two groups ran together roaring, swords swinging.

Conan ripped the throat from the first man he faced without even crossing swords, and then he was like a machine, blade rising and falling and rising again bloodier than before. The way was forward. He hacked his way through, like a peasant through a field of wheat, chopping and moving forward, leaving bloody human stubble behind.

And then he was clear of the melée. He did not pause to see how his companions fared against those who had survived his blade. The numbers were on the Free-Company's side, now, and he yet had to find Ariane. Of Garian he cared not one way or the other.

Straight to the throne room he ran. The guards that normally stood at the great carven doors were gone, drawn into the fighting that sounded now in every corridor. The door that usually was opened by three men, Conan pushed open unaided.

The great columned chamber stood empty, the Dragon Throne guarding it with a malignant glare.

The King's apartments, Conan thought. He set out still at a run, and those who faced him died. He no longer waited to call out the challenge. Any who wore the golden cloak and did not flee were the enemy. Few fled, and he regretted killing them only for the delay it caused him. Ariane. They slowed him finding Ariane.

Karela stalked the Palace halls like a panther. She was alone, now. After the first fight she had searched among the bodies for Conan, uncertain whether she wanted to find him or not. There had not been long to look, for other soldiers loyal to Vegentius had appeared, and the fighting that followed had carried all who still stood away from that spot. She had seen Garian laying about him, and Hordo desperately trying to fight his way to her side. The one-eyed man had been like death incarnate, yet she was glad he had not been able to follow. There was that she had to do of which her faithful hound would not approve.

Suddenly there was a man before her, blood from a scalp wound trickling down his too-handsome face. The sword in his hand was stained as well, and from the way he moved he knew how to use it.

"A wench with a sword," he laughed. "Best you throw it down and run, else I might think you intend to use it."

She recognized him then. "You run, Demetrio. I have no wish to soil my blade with your blood." She had no quarrel with him, but he stood between her and where she wanted to go.

His laugh turned into a snarl. "Bitch!" He lunged, expecting an easy kill.

With ease she beat aside his overconfident attack and slashed him across the chest with her riposte. Shaken, he leaped back. She followed, never allowing him to set himself for the attack again. Their blades flashed intricate silver patterns in the air between them, ringing almost continually. He was good, she admitted, but she was better. He died with a look of incredulous horror on his face.

Stepping over his body she hurried on, until at last she came to the chambers she sought. Carefully she pushed the door open with her blade.

Sularia, in the blue velvet robes of a noblewoman, faced her, frowning. "Who are you?" she demanded. "Some lord's leman? Don't you know enough not to enter my apartments without permission? Well, as you're here, what word of the fighting?" Her eye fell on the bloody sword in Karela's hand, and she gasped.

"You sent a friend of mine to the lowest of Zandru's Hells," Karela said quietly. With measured paces she stepped into the room. The blonde backed away before her.

"Who are you? I know none who are friends of your sort. Leave my chambers immediately, or I'll have you flogged."

Karela laughed grimly. "Jelanna would not know your sort, either, but you know of her. As for me, I do not expect you to recognize the Lady Tiana without her veils."

"You're mad!" Sularia said, a quaver in her voice. Her back was almost to the wall.

Karela let her sword drop as she continued her advance. "I need no sword for you," she said softly. "A sword is for an equal."

From beneath her robes Sularia drew a dagger, its blade as wide as a man's finger and no more than twice as long. "Fool," she laughed. "If you truly are Tiana, I'll give you reason to wear your veils." And she lunged for Karela's eyes.

The auburn-haired woman moved nothing but a single hand, which darted to close over the hand that held the dagger. Sularia's blue eyes widened in disbelief as her lunge was stopped by a grip made steel by long hours with a sword. Karela knotted her other hand in those blonde tresses, tight enough to force the woman to meet her hard emerald gaze. Slowly she twisted, forcing the dagger and the hand that held it alike to turn.

"Despite it all," she whispered to the blonde, "you might have lived had not you put your sluttish hands on him." With all her strength she drove the dagger home in Sularia's heart.

Letting the dead woman fall, Karela retrieved her sword and wiped the blade contemptuously on a wall hanging. There was still the Cimmerian.

Her mind whirling with a thousand thoughts of what she would do to him when she found him, she stalked from the room. Almost she had been ready to let him live, but Sularia had brought it all flooding back, all the thousand humiliations she had suffered because of him. That he had lain with such as Sularia was the worst humiliation of all, though when she questioned that strange thought her mind skittered away from answering.

Then, from a colonnaded gallery, she saw him in a courtyard below, lost in thought. No doubt he still wondered how to find this precious Ariane of his. Her beautiful face twisted in a savage snarl. From the corner of her eye she caught a movement below, and her breath suddenly would not come. Vegentius had entered the courtyard, and Conan had not moved. Slowly, like a murderer in the night, the big soldier, as big as Conan, crept forward, ensanguined sword upraised. His red-crested helmet and chain mail looked untouched, though that bloody blade was proof he had seen fighting. At any moment he would strike, and she would see Conan die. Tears ran down her face. Tears of joy, she told herself. It would give her much joy to see the Cimmerian meet his death. Much joy.

"Conan!" she screamed. "Behind you!"

Conan listened to the approaching footsteps, footsteps that grew less wary by the second. The Cimmerian's hand already rested on his sword hilt. He did not know who it was that crept toward him, save that by his actions he was an enemy. Whoever he was, a few steps more and the surpriser would be the one surprised. Just one step more.

"Conan!" a scream rang out. "Behind you!"

Cursing his lost advantage the Cimmerian threw himself forward, tucking his shoulder under as he hit the flagstones, drawing his scimitar as he rolled to his feet. He found himself facing a very surprised Vegentius.

A quick glance upward showed him the source of the shout, Karela, half hanging over the stone rail of a gallery two stories above the courtyard. He knew it had to be his imagination, yet in that brief look he could have sworn that she was crying. It did not matter, in any case. He must concern himself with the man he faced.

Vegentius wore a grin as if what was to come were the greatest wish of his life. "Long have I wanted to face you with steel, barbar," he said. His face yet bore the yellowing bruises of their last encounter.

"That is why you try to sneak up behind me?" Conan sneered.

"Die, barbar!" the big soldier thundered, launching a towering overhead blow with his sword.

Conan's blade rose to meet it with a clang, and immediately he moved from defense to offense. Almost without moving their feet the two men faced each other, blades ringing like hammer and anvil. But it was always Conan's blade that was the hammer, always he attacking, always Vegentius parrying, ever more desperately. It was time to end, the Cimmerian thought. With a mighty swing, he struck. Blood fountained from the headless trunk of the Commander of the Golden Leopards. As the body toppled, Conan was already turning to look for Karela. The gallery was empty.

Still, he could not suppress a complacent smile at the thought that she did not hate him as much as she pretended. Else why had she cried out?

He looked around as Hordo hurried into the courtyard.

"Vegentius?" the one-eyed man asked, looking at the headless body. "I saw Albanus," he went on when Conan nodded. "And Ariane and the imposter. But when I got to where I saw them, they were gone. I think they were headed for the old part of the Palace." He hesitated. "Have you seen Karela, Cimmerian? I can't find her, and I do not want to lose her again."

Conan pointed out the gallery where Karela had stood. "Find her if you can, Hordo. I've another woman to seek."

Hordo nodded, and the two men parted in opposite directions.

Conan wished the bearded man luck, though he suspected Karela had disappeared once more. But his own concern was still Ariane. He could not imagine why Albanus would go into the ancient portion of the Palace, unless it was to escape by way of one of the secret passages. If Jelanna knew some of them, it seemed reasonable that the hawk-faced lord might also. Yet the Cimmerian did not think he could find even the one he had escaped through, lost as it was in that maze of pitch-dark corridors. There was only the wolf pit to hope for. And hoping against hope Conan ran.

He thanked every god he could think of that he encountered no Golden Leopards as he sped through the Palace, into the rough stone corridor he remembered so well. He could afford not the slightest delay if he was to reach the wolf pit before Albanus departed. If Albanus had gone to the wolf pit. If Ariane was still alive. He refused to admit any of those ifs. They would be there. They had to be.

Almost to the pit, he heard Albanus' voice reverberating from that domed ceiling. The Cimmerian allowed himself one brief sigh of relief before entering the chamber, his eyes like blue steel.

"With this I will destroy them," Albanus was saying, caressing a blue crystal sphere in his hands as he spoke. The imposter stood beside him, and Ariane, staring unnaturally ahead, but the hawk-faced man appeared to speak only to himself. "With this I will unleash such power—"

Sorcery, Conan thought, yet it was too late to stop his advance. Albanus' dark eyes were on him already, and annoyingly seemed to see him as an irritation rather than a danger.

"Kill him, Garian," the nobleman said, and turned his attention back to the blue sphere. Ariane did not move or change expression.

Did the man truly think he was Garian, Conan wondered as the duplicate advanced. He noticed the sword the other carried, then, the same serpentine blade that he had sold to Demetrio what seemed like so long ago. That it was a sorceled weapon he no longer had any doubt, and his belief was confirmed when the blade was raised. A hungry, metallic whine sounded, the same he had thought he imagined when facing Melius.

Still he set himself. Death came when it would. No man could flee his appointed time.

The false Garian's blade blazed into motion, and Conan swung to block it. The shock of that meeting of blades nearly tore the Cimmerian's sword from his grip. There had been no such strength in Melius' blows. That force came not from any sorcery, but from the man wielding the blade, yet Conan refused to believe that anything human could have so much strength. The hair on the back of his neck rose. Nothing human. Warily he backed away, wondering what it was he faced.

Cupping the blue crystal, ignoring the two who faced each other not twenty paces from him, Albanus began to chant. *"Af-far mearoth, Omini deas kaan. . . ."*

Conan thought he felt a rumble from deep in the bowels of the earth, but he had no time to consider it. The creature with Garian's face stalked him, the wavy-bladed sword darting with preternatural speed. Conan no longer attempted to block it, only to deflect it, yet even the glancing blows he felt to his heels. Once the tip of that ensorceled blade opened a shallow gash in his cheek, sending a thin rivulet of blood trickling. The metallic whine sounded again, but louder, almost drowning out Albanus' chanting.

The creature swung again, a decapitating blow an it landed, but Conan leaped back. The blade smashed into the iron leg of one of the massive tripod lamps, shearing it in two. Slowly the lamp toppled, and Conan saw the first true expression on the creature's face. Terror, as it gazed at the fire in that falling lamp.

As if in mortal danger, the false Garian jumped back. Albanus' voice faltered, then resumed its incantation. The lamp crashed against the wall surrounding the pit, flaming oil pouring down into the pit. Dry straw crackled alight.

Conan risked a glance at the hawk-faced lord. Above Albanus' head something was forming. A darkness, a thickening of the air. The stones beneath the Cimmerian's feet shifted, and he thought he heard thunder.

There was no time for more than a glance, though, for the creature grasped one leg of the heavy lamp and heaved it into the now fire-filled pit as easily as a man might throw aside a stick of kindling. The ground trembled continuously now, the tremors growing stronger. From the corner of his eye Conan saw the dark amorphous shape above Albanus' head lift higher into the dome, grow more solid. The nobleman's chanting became louder, more insistent. The creature advanced on Conan.

"Run, Ariane!" the Cimmerian shouted, and steadied his feet against the now pitching floor. No man could flee his own death. "Run!"

She did not move, but the simulacrum continued its steady approach, sword lifting for a strike that would smash through the Cimmerian's blade and split the man in twain.

Desperately Conan leaped aside. The tremendous blow struck sparks from the floor where he had stood. In that instant, when the creature tottered off balance from the force of its own blow and the quaking of the earth, Conan struck. Every muscle from his heels up he put into that blow, blade slamming against the creature's side. It was like striking stone. Yet, added to the rest, it was enough, for just that one instant. The simulacrum fell.

Conan had seen the speed of the creature, and had no intention of giving it time to recover its feet. Before it struck the stone floor he had dropped his sword and seized the simulacrum by its swordbelt and its tunic. With a tremendous heave the massive Cimmerian lifted the creature into the air.

"Here's the fire you fear," he shouted, and hurled it over the wall.

As it fell, a scream ripped from its throat. The sword was hurled away as it twisted in an inhuman effort to find some salvation from the flames. As it struck the burning straw there was a whoosh, as of oil thrown on a fire, and flames engulfed the simulacrum, yet even as a statue of flame its horrible screams would not cease.

As Conan raised his eyes from the pit, they met those of Albanus. The dark lord's mouth struggled to form the words of his chant, but from his chest projected the blood-hungry sword that had been hurled with such inhuman strength. Beside him Ariane stirred. Sorcerous spells died with the sorcerer, and Albanus was dying.

Conan hurried to her side. As he took her hand, she looked at him dazedly. Albanus fought still to form words, but blood was filling his mouth.

As the Cimmerian turned to lead Ariane from the chamber, his gaze was drawn by what occupied the height of the dome. He had an impression of countless eyes, of tentacles without number. His own eyes refused to take it all in, his mind refused to accept what he saw. From whatever floated horribly above, a ray of light struck down, shattering the blue crystal. Albanus' eyes glazed in death as the fragments fell from his hand.

Thunder rumbled in the room, and Conan knew it for the laughter of a demon, or a god. The dark shape above gathered itself. Conan scooped up Ariane and ran, as that which was above smashed through the dome. Stones showered down, filling the wolf pit, and dust belched after him. Collapsing walls toppled still other walls. Spreading out in a wave of destruction from the wolf-pit, the ancient portions of the Palace crumbled in on themselves.

Conan was running on polished marble floors before he realized that that floor no longer tossed like a ship in a storm and rubble no longer pelted him. He stopped and looked back through the slowly clearing dust. The corridor behind him was filled from top to bottom with shattered debris, and he could see the sunset sky through a hole in a ceiling that had borne three stories above it. Yet, except for a few cracked walls, there seemed to be remarkably little destruction outside of the ancient parts of the Palace.

Ariane stirred in his arms, and he reluctantly set her down. She was a pleasant armful, even covered in dust and rock chips. Coughing, she stared around her. "Conan? Where did you come from? Is this the Royal Palace? What happened?"

"I'll explain later," the Cimmerian said. Or some of it, he thought with another look at the devastation behind them. "Let's find King Garian, Ariane. I've a reward coming."

XXV

S trolling down the hall of the palace that had once belong to Albanus—and had for two days now, by decree of King Garian, belonged to him—Conan paused to heft an ivory statuette. Intricately carved, it was light and would fetch a good price in almost any city. He added it to the sack he carried and moved on.

He reached the columned entry hall just as Hordo and Ariane came through the front doors, now standing open. "About time you came back," the Cimmerian said. "What is it like out there?"

Hordo shrugged. "City Guards and what Golden Leopards are left are patrolling the streets against looters. Not that many are left. Seems they thought that earthquake was the judgment of the gods against them. Then, too, some claim to have seen a demon hovering over the Royal Palace at the height of the earthquake." He gave an unconvincing laugh. "Strange what people see, is it not?"

"Strange indeed," Conan replied in what he hoped was a reassuring tone. Even if he managed to convince Hordo of what had occurred at the wolf pit, the one-eyed man would only moan about being too old for such any longer. "What about the Thestis?" he asked Ariane.

She sighed wearily, not looking at him. "The Thestis is done. Too many of us saw too much of what our fine talk leads to. Garian is releasing Graecus and the others from the mines, but I doubt we will be able to look any of the others in the face for a long time. I . . . I intend to leave Nemedia."

"Come with me to Ophir," Conan said.

"I go to Aquilonia with Hordo," she replied.

Conan stared. It was not that he objected to losing her to Hordo—well, a little, he admitted grudgingly, even to a friend—but after all, he had saved her life. What sort of gratitude was this?

She shifted defiantly under his gaze, and put an arm around the one-eyed man. "Hordo has a faithful heart, which is more than I can say for some other men. It may not be faithful to me, but it is still faithful. Besides, I told you long ago that I decide who shares my sleeping mat." Her voice held an exculpatory note; a tightness at her mouth said that she heard it, and refused to admit that she had anything to excuse.

Conan shook his head disgustedly. He remembered an ancient saying. Women and cats are never owned, they just visit for a time. At the moment he thought he would take the cat.

Then her destination, and Hordo's, penetrated. "Why Aquilonia?" Conan asked him.

The one-eyed man passed him a folded sheet of parchment and said, "I heard a rumor she went east. There's something in there for you, as well."

Conan opened the sheet and read.

Hordo, my most faithful hound,
When you receive this I will be gone from Nemedia with all my
goods and servants. Do not follow. I will not again be so pleased
to find you on my trail. Yet I wish you well. Tell the Cimmerian
I am not finished with him.

> *Karela*

Below the signature, in red ink, was the outline of a hawk.

"But you follow anyway," Conan said, handing back the sheet.

"Of course," Hordo replied. Carefully he tucked the letter into his pouch. "But why this talk of going to Ophir now? Garian will make you a lord, next."

"I remembered that blind soothsayer in the Gored Ox," the Cimmerian said.

"That old fool? I told you to see one of my astrologers."

"But he was right," Conan said quietly. "A woman of sapphires and gold. Sularia. A woman of emeralds and ruby. Karela. They'd both have watched me die, for exactly the reasons he named. The rest was right, as well. And do you remember how he ended?"

"How?" Hordo asked.

"Save a throne, save a king, kill a king or die. Whatever comes, whatever is, mark well your time to fly. He also said to beware the gratitude of kings. I'm taking him to heart, if a little late."

The one-eyed man snorted, looking about him at the marble columns and alabaster walls. "I see little enough to beware of in this gratitude."

"Kings are absolute rulers," Conan told him, "and feeling grateful makes them feel less absolute. On that I'll wager. And the best way to get rid of that feeling is to get rid of the man to whom he must be grateful. Do you see now?"

"You sound like a philosopher," Hordo grumbled.

Conan threw back his head and laughed. "All the gods forbid."

"Captain," Machaon said, entering from the back, "the company is mounted, every man with a sack of loot at his saddle. Though I never heard of a man ordering his own palace looted before."

Conan met Hordo's gaze levelly. "Take whatever you want, old friend, but do not tarry overlong." He held out his hand, and the other grasped it, a custom they had picked up in the east.

"Fare you well, Conan of Cimmeria," Hordo said gruffly. "Take a pull at the Hellhorn for me, an you get there before me."

"Fare you well, Hordo of Zamora. And you the same, if you're first."

The Cimmerian did not look again at Ariane as he strode from the hall. She had made her choice.

Behind the palace the Free-Company waited, the score that survived, mounted and armed. Conan swung into his saddle.

A strange end, he thought, riding away from proffered riches in this fashion. And two women, either of whom he would have been pleased to have ride with him, but neither of whom wanted him. That was a strange thing for him in itself. Still, he reminded himself, there would be women aplenty in Ophir, and the rumors of trouble meant there would be blade-fee for a Free-Company.

"We ride for Ophir," he commanded, and galloped out of the gates at the head of his company. He did not look back.

Conan
the
Unconquered

Prologue

Storm winds howling off the midnight-shrouded Vilayet Sea clawed at the granite-walled compound of the Cult of Doom. The compound gave the appearance of a small city, though there were no people on its streets at that hour. More than the storm and the lateness kept them fast in their beds, praying for sleep, though but a bare handful of them could have put a finger to the real reason, and those that could did not allow themselves to think on it. The gods uplift, and the gods destroy. But no one ever believes the gods will touch them.

The man who was now called Jhandar did not know if gods involved themselves in the affairs of mortals, or indeed if gods existed, but he did know there were Powers beneath the sky. There were indeed Powers, and one of those he had learned to use, even to control after a fashion. Gods he would leave to those asleep in the compound, those who called him their Great Lord.

Now he sat cross-legged in saffron robes before such a Power. The chamber was plain, its pearly marble walls smooth, its two arched entrances unadorned. Simple round columns held the dome that rose above the shallow pool, but ten paces across, that was the room's central feature. There was no ornamentation, for friezes or sculptures or ornate working of stone could not compete with that pool, and the Power within.

Water, it might seem at first glance, but it was not. It was sharply azure and flecked with argent phosphorescence. Jhandar meditated, basking in the radiance of Power, and the pool glowed silverblue, brighter and brighter until the chamber seemed lit with a thousand lamps. The surface of the pool bubbled and roiled, and mists rose, solidifying. But only so far. The mists formed a dome, as if a mirror image of the pool below, delineating the limits that contained the Power, both above and below. Within ultimate disorder was bound, Chaos itself confined. Once Jhandar had seen such a pool loosed from its bonds, and fervently did he wish never to see such again. But that would not happen here. Not now. Not ever.

Now he could feel the Power seeping into his very bones. It was time. Smoothly he rose and made his way through one of the archways, down a narrow passage lit by bronze lamps, bare feet padding on cool marble. He prided himself on his lack of ostentation, even to so small a thing as not wearing sandals. He, like the pool, needed no adornment.

The passage let into a circular sanctorum, its albescent walls worked in intricate arabesques, its high vaulted ceiling held aloft by fluted alabaster columns. Light came from golden cressets suspended aloft on silver chains. Massive bronze doors barred the chamber's main entrance, their surfaces within and without worked in a pattern of Chaos itself, by an artist under the influence of the Power, before madness and death had taken him. The Power was not for all.

The forty men gathered there, a fifth part of his Chosen, *did* need this show of splendor to reflect the glory of their cause. Yet the most important single item in that chamber, an altar set in the exact center of the circle formed by the room, was of unornamented black marble.

Two-score men turned silently as Jhandar entered, saffron robed and shaven of head as the laws of the cult demanded, just as it forbade its women to cut their tresses. Eager eyes watched him; ears strained to hear his words.

"I am come from the Pool of the Ultimate," he intoned, and a massive sigh arose, as if he had come from the presence of a god. Indeed, he suspected they considered it much the same, for though they believed they knew the purposes and meanings of the Cult, in truth they knew nothing.

Slowly Jhandar made his way to the black altar, and all eyes followed him, glowing with the honor of gazing on one they considered but a step removed from godhead himself. He did not think of himself so, for all his ambitions. Not quite.

Jhandar was a tall man, cleanly muscled but slender. Bland, smooth features combined with his shaven head to make his age indeterminate, though something in his dark brown eyes spoke of years beyond knowing. His ears were square, but set on his head in such a fashion that they seemed slightly pointed, giving him an other-worldly appearance. But it was the eyes that oft convinced others he was a sage ere he even opened his mouth. In fact he was not yet thirty.

He raised his arms above his head, letting the folds of his robes fall back. "Attend me!"

"We attend, Great Lord!" forty throats spoke as one.

"In the beginning was nothingness. All came from nothingness."

"And to nothingness must all return."

Jhandar allowed a slight smile to touch his thin mouth. That phrase, watchword of his followers, always amused him. To nothingness, indeed, all must return. Eventually. But not soon. At least, not him.

While he was yet a boy, known by the first of many names he would bear, fate had carried him beyond the Vilayet Sea, beyond even far Vendhya, to Khitai of near fable. There, at the feet of a learned thaumaturge, an aged man with long, wispy mustaches and a skin the color of luteous ivory, he had learned much. But a lifetime spent in the search for knowledge was not for him. In the end he had been forced to slay the old man to gain what he wanted, the mage's grimoire, his book of incantations and spells. Then, before he had mastered more than a handful, the murder was discovered, and he imprisoned. Yet he had known enough to free himself of that bare stone cell, though he had of necessity to flee Khitai. There had been other flights in his life, but those were long past. His errors had taught him. Now his way was forward, and upward, to heights without end.

"In the beginning all of totality was inchoate. Chaos ruled."

"Blessed be Holy Chaos," came the reply.

"The natural state of the universe was, and is, Chaos. But the gods appeared, themselves but children of Chaos, and forced order—unnatural, unholy order—upon the very Chaos from which they sprang." His voice caressed them, raised their fears, then soothed those fears, lifted their hopes and fanned their fervor. "And in that forcing they gave a foul gift to man, the impurity that forever bars the vast majority of humankind from attaining a higher order of consciousness, from becoming as gods. For it is from Chaos, from ultimate disorder, that gods come, and man has within him the taint of enforced order."

He paused then, spreading his arms as if to embrace them. Ecstasy lit their eyes as they waited for him to give the benediction they expected, and needed.

"Diligently," he said, "have you labored to rid yourselves of the impurities of this world. Your worldly goods you have cast aside. Pleasures of the flesh you have denied yourselves. Now," his voice rose to a thunder, "now you are the Chosen!"

"Blessed be Holy Chaos! We are the Chosen of Holy Chaos!"

"Let the woman Natryn be brought forth," Jhandar commanded.

From a cubicle where she had been kept waiting the Lady Natryn, wife of Lord Tariman, was led into the columned chamber. She did not look now the wife of one of the Seventeen Attendants, the advisors to King Yildiz of Turan. Naked, she stumbled in the hobble that confined her ankles, and would have fallen had not two of the Chosen roughly held her erect. Her wrists, fastened behind her with tight cords, lay on the swell of her buttocks. Her large brown eyes bulged in terror, and her lips worked frantically around a leather gag. Slender, yet full-breasted and well-rounded of hip, her body shone with the sweat of fear. No eyes there but Jhandar's looked on her as a woman, though, for the Chosen had forsaken such things.

"You have attempted to betray me, Natryn."

The naked woman shook at Jhandar's words as if pierced with needles. She had dabbled in the teachings of the cult as did many bored women of the nobility, but her husband made her different, and necessary to Jhandar's great plan. With his necromancies he had learned every dark and shameful corner of her life. Most noblewomen of Turan had secrets they would kill to hide, and she, with lovers and vices almost beyond listing, was no different. Natryn had wept at his revelations, and rebelled at his commands, but seemingly at the last she had accepted her duty to place certain pressures on her husband. Instead, the sorcerous watch he kept on her revealed that she intended to go to her husband, to reveal all and throw herself on his mercy. Jhandar had not slain her where she lay in the supposed safety of her chambers in her husband's palace, but had had her brought hither to serve her purpose in his grand design. It was death she feared, but he intended worse for her.

"Prepare her," the necromancer commanded.

The woman flung herself about futilely in the grasp of the men who fastened her by wrists and ankles to the black altar stone. The gag was removed; she licked fear-dried lips. "Mercy, Great Lord!" she pleaded. "Let me serve you!"

"You do," Jhandar replied.

From a tray of beaten gold proffered by one of the Chosen, the mage took a silver-bladed knife and lifted it high above the woman's body. His follower hastily set the tray on the floor by the altar and backed away. Natryn's screams blended with Jhandar's chant as he invoked the Power of Chaos. His words rang from the walls, though he did not shout; he had no wish to drown her wails. He could feel the Power flowing in him, flowing through him. Silvery-azure, a dome appeared, enveloping altar, sacrifice and necromancer. The Chosen fell to their knees, pressed their faces to the marble floor in awe. Jhandar's knife plunged down. Natryn convulsed and shrieked one last time as the blade stabbed to the hilt beneath her left breast.

Quickly Jhandar bent to take a large golden bowl from the tray. Blade and one quillon of that knife were hollow, so that a vivid scarlet stream of heart's blood spurted into the bowl. Swiftly the level rose. Then the flow slowed, stopped, and only a few drops fell to make carmine ripples.

Withdrawing the blade, Jhandar held knife and bowl aloft, calling on the Power in words of ice, calling on life that was not life, death that was not death. Still holding the bowl on high, he tilted it, pouring out Natryn's heart blood. That sanguinary stream fell, and faded into nothingness, and with it faded the glowing dome.

A smile of satisfaction on his face, Jhandar let the implements of his sorcery clatter to the floor. No longer did a wound mar Natryn's beauty. "Awake, Natryn," he commanded, undoing her bonds.

The eyes of the woman who had just been stabbed to the heart fluttered open, and she stared at Jhandar, her gaze filled with horror and emptiness. "I . . . I was dead," she whispered. "I stood before Erlik's Throne." Shivering, she huddled into a ball on the altar. "I am cold."

"Certainly you are cold," Jhandar told her cruelly. "No blood courses in your veins, for you are no longer alive. Neither are you dead. Rather you stand between, and are bound to utter obedience until true death finds you."

"No," she wept. "I will not—"

"Be silent," he said. Her protests died on the instant.

Jhandar turned back to his followers. The Chosen had dared now to raise their faces, and they watched him expectantly. "For what do you strike?" he demanded.

From beneath their robes the Chosen produced needle-sharp daggers, thrusting them into the air. "For disorder, confusion and anarchy, we strike!" they roared. "For Holy Chaos, we strike! To the death!"

"Then strike!" he commanded.

The daggers disappeared, and the Chosen filed from the chamber to seek those whose names Jhandar had earlier given them.

It was truly a pity, the necromancer thought, that the old mage no longer lived. How far his pupil had outstripped him, and how much greater yet that pupil was destined to become!

He snapped his fingers, and she who was now only partly Lady Natryn of Turan followed him meekly from the sacrificial chamber.

I

Many cities bore appellations, 'the Mighty' or 'the Wicked,' but Aghrapur, that great city of ivory towers and golden domes, seat of the throne of Turan and center of her citizens' world, had no need of such. The city's wickedness and might were so well known that an appellation would have been gilt laid upon gold.

One thousand and three goldsmiths were listed in the Guild Halls, twice so many smiths in silver, half again that number dealers in jewelry and rare gems. They, with a vast profusion of merchants in silks and perfumes, catered to hot-blooded, sloe-eyed noblewomen and sleek, sensuous courtesans who oft seemed more ennobled than their sisters of proper blood. Every vice could be had within Aghrapur's lofty alabaster walls, from the dream-powders and passion-mists peddled by oily men from Iranistan to the specialized brothels of the Street of Doves.

Turanian triremes ruled the cerulean expanse of the Vilayet Sea, and into Aghrapur's broad harbor dromonds brought the wealth of a dozen nations. The riches of another score found its way to the markets by caravan. Emeralds and apes, ivory and peacocks, whatever people wanted could be found, no matter whence it came. The stench of slavers from Khawarism was drowned in the wafted scent of oranges from Ophir, of myrrh and cloves from Vendhya, of attar of roses from Khauran and subtle perfumes from Zingara. Tall merchants from Argos strode the flagstones of her broad streets, and dark men from Shem. Fierce Ibars mountain tribesmen rubbed shoulders with Corinthian scholars, and Kothian mercenaries with traders from Keshan. It was said that no day passed in Aghrapur without the meeting of men, each of whom believed the other's land to be a fable.

The tall youth who strode those teeming streets with the grace of a hunting cat had no mind for the wonders of the city, however. Fingers curled lightly on the well-worn leather hilt of his broadsword, he passed marble palaces and fruit peddlers' carts with equal unconcern, a black-maned lion unimpressed by piles of stone. Yet if his agate-blue eyes were alert, there was yet travel weariness on his sun-bronzed face, and his scarlet-edged cloak was stained with sweat and dust. It had been a hard ride from Sultanapur, with little time before leaving for saying goodbye to friends or gathering possessions, if he was to avoid the headsman's axe. A small matter of smuggling, and some other assorted offenses against the King's peace.

He had come far since leaving the rugged northern crags of his native Cimmerian mountains, and not only in distance. Some few years he had spent as a thief, in Nemedia and Zamora and the Corinthian city-states, yet though his years still numbered fewer than twenty-five the desire had come on him to better himself. He had seen many beggars who had been thieves in their youth, but never had he seen a rich thief. The gold that came from stealing seemed to drip away like water through a sieve. He would find better for himself. The failure of his smuggling effort had not dimmed his ardor in the least. All things could be found in Aghrapur, or so it was said. At the moment he sought a tavern, the Blue Bull. Its name had been given him in haste as he left Sultanapur as a place where information could be gotten. Good information was always the key to success.

The sound of off-key music penetrated his thoughts, and he became aware of a strange procession approaching him down the thronging street. A wiry, dark-skinned sergeant of the Turanian army, in wide breeches and turban-wrapped spiral helmet, curved tulwar at his hip, was trailed by another soldier beating a drum and two others raggedly blowing flutes. Behind them came half a score more, bearing halberds and escorting, or guarding, a dozen young men in motley garb who seemed to be trying to march to the drum. The sergeant caught the big youth's glance and quickly stepped in front of him.

"The gods be with you. Now I can see that you are a man seeking—" The sergeant broke off with a grunt. "Mitra! Your eyes!"

"What's wrong with my eyes?" the muscular youth growled.

"Not a thing, friend," the sergeant replied, raising a hand apologetically. "But never did I see eyes the color of the sea before."

"Where I come from there are few with dark eyes."

"Ah. A far traveler come to seek adventure. And what better place to find it than in the army of King Yildiz of Turan? I am Alshaam. And how are you called?"

"Conan," the muscular youth replied. "But I've no interest in joining your army."

"But think you, Conan," the sergeant continued with oily persuasiveness, "how it will be to return from campaign with as much booty as you can carry, a hero and conqueror in the women's eyes. How they'll fall over you. Why, man, from the look of you, you were born for it."

"Why not try them?" Conan said, jerking his head toward a knot of Hyrkanian nomads in sheepskin coats and baggy trousers of coarse wool. They wore fur caps pulled tightly over grease-laced hair, and eyed everyone about them suspiciously. "They look as if they might want to be heroes," he laughed.

The sergeant spat sourly. "Not a half-weight of discipline in the lot of them. Odd to see them here. They generally don't like this side of the Vilayet Sea. But you, now. Think on it. Adventure, glory, loot, women. Why—"

Conan shook his head. "I've no desire to be a soldier."

"Mayhap if we had a drink together? No?" The sergeant sighed. "Well, I've a quota to fill. King Yildiz means to build his army larger, and when an army's big enough, it's used. You mark my words, there will be loot to throw away." He motioned to the other soldiers. "Let us be on our way."

"A moment," Conan said. "Can you tell me where to find the tavern called the Blue Bull?"

The soldier grimaced. "A dive on the Street of the Lotus Dreamers, near the harbor. They'll cut your throat for your boots as like as not. Try the Sign of the Impatient Virgin, on the Street of Coins. The wine is cheap and the girls are clean. And if you change your mind, seek me out. Alshaam, sergeant in the regiment of General Mundara Khan."

Conan stepped aside to let the procession pass, the recruits once more attempting unsuccessfully to march to the drum. As he turned from watching the soldiers go he found himself about to trample into another cortege, this a score in saffron robes, the men with shaven heads, the women with braids swinging below their buttocks, their leader beating a tambourine. Chanting softly, they walked as if they saw neither him nor anyone else. Caught off balance, he stumbled awkwardly aside, straight into the midst of the Hyrkanian nomads.

Muttered imprecations rose as thick as the rank smell of their greased hair, and black eyes glared at him as dark leathery hands were laid to the hilts of curved sword-knives. Conan grasped his own sword hilt, certain that he was in for a fight. The Hyrkanian's eyes swung from him to follow the saffron-robed procession continuing down the crowded street. Conan stared in amazement as the nomads ignored him and hurried after the yellow-robed marchers.

Shaking his head, Conan went on his way. No one had ever said that Aghrapur was not a city of strangeness, he thought.

Yet, as he approached the harbor, it was in his mind that for all its oddities the city was not so very different from the others he had seen. Behind him were the palaces of the wealthy, the shops of merchants, and the bustle of prosperous citizens. Here dried mud stucco cracked from the brick of decaying buildings, occupied for all their decay. The peddlers offered fruits too bruised or spoiled to be sold elsewhere, and the hawkers' shiny wares were gilded brass, if indeed there was even any gilding. Beggars here were omnipresent, whining in their rags to the sailors swaggering by. The strumpets numbered almost as many as the beggars, in transparent silks that emphasized rather than concealed swelling breasts and rounded buttocks, wearing peridot masquerading as emeralds and carbuncle passing for ruby. Salt, tar, spices, and rotting offal gave off a thick miasma that permeated everything. The pleadings of beggars, the solicitations of harlots, and the cries of hawkers hung in the air like a solid sheet.

Above the cacophony Conan heard a girl's voice shout, "If you will be patient, there will be enough to go around."

Curious, he looked toward the sound, but could see only a milling crowd of beggars in front of a rotting building, all seeming to press toward the same goal. Whatever, or whoever, that goal was, it was against the stone wall of the building. More beggars ran to join the seething crowd, and a few of the doxies joined in, elbowing their way to the front. Suddenly, above the very forefront of the throng, a girl appeared, as if she had stepped up onto a bench.

"Be patient," she cried. "I will give you what I have." In her arms she carried an engraved and florentined casket, almost as large as she could manage. Its top was open, revealing a tangled mass of jewelry. One by one she removed pieces and passed them down to eagerly reaching hands. Greedy cries were raised for more.

Conan shook his head. This girl was no denizen of the harbor. Her robes of cream-colored silk were expensively embroidered with thread-of-gold, and cut neither to reveal nor emphasize her voluptuous curves, though they could not conceal them from the Cimmerian's discerning eye. She wore no kohl or rouge, as the strumpets did, yet she was lovely. Waist-length raven hair framed an oval face with skin the color of dark ivory and melting brown eyes. He wondered what madness had brought her here.

"Mine," a voice shouted from the shoving mass of mendicants and doxies, and another voice cried, "I want mine!"

The girl's face showed consternation. "Be patient. Please."

"More!"

"Now!"

Three men with the forked queues of sailors, attracted by the shouting, began to push their way through the growing knot of people toward the girl. Beggars, their greed vanquishing their usual ingratiating manner, pushed back. Muttered curses were exchanged, then loud obscenities, and the mood of the crowd darkened and turned angry. A sailor's horny fist sent a ragged, gap-toothed beggar sprawling. Screams went up from the strumpets, and wrathful cries from the beggars.

Conan knew he should go on. This was none of his affair, and he had yet to find the Blue Bull. This matter would resolve itself very well without him. Then why, he asked himself, was he not moving?

At that instant a pair of bony, sore-covered hands reached up and jerked the casket from the girl's arms. She stared helplessly as a swirling fight broke out, the casket jerked from one set of hands to another, its contents spilling to the paving stones to be squabbled over by men and women with clawed fingers. Filth-caked beggars snarled with avaricious rage; silk-clad harlots, their faces twisted with hideous rapacity, raked each other with long, painted nails and rolled on the street, legs flashing nakedly.

Suddenly one of the sailors, a scar across his broad nose disappearing beneath the patch that covered his right eye, leaped up onto the bench beside the girl. "This is what I want," he roared. And sweeping her into his arms, he tossed her to his waiting comrades.

"Erlik take all fool women," Conan muttered.

The roil of beggars and harlots, lost in their greed, ignored the massive young Cimmerian as he moved through them like a hunting beast. Scar-face and his companions, a lanky Kothian with a gimlet eye and a sharp-nosed Iranistani, whose dirty red-striped head cloth hid all but the tips of his queues, were too busy with the girl to notice his approach. She yelped and wriggled futilely at their pawings. Her flailing hands made no impression on shoulders and chests hardened by the rigors of stormy, violent Vilayet Sea. The sailors' cheap striped tunics were filthy with fish oils and tar, and an odor hung about them of sour, over-spiced ship's cooking.

Conan's big hand seized the scruff of the Kothian's neck and half hurled him into the scuffle near the casket. The Iranistani's nose crunched and spurted blood beneath his fist, and a back-hand blow sent Scarface to join his friends on the filthy stones of the street.

"Find another woman," the Cimmerian growled. "There are doxies enough about."

The girl stared at him wide-eyed, as if she was not sure if he was a rescuer or not.

"I'll carve your liver and lights," Scarface spat, "and feed what's left to the fish." He scrambled to his feet, a curved Khawarismi dagger in his fist.

The other two closed in beside him, likewise clutching curved daggers. The man in the headcloth was content to glare threateningly, ruining it somewhat by scrubbing with his free hand at the blood that ran from his broken nose down over his mouth. The Kothian, however, wanted to taunt his intended victim. He tossed his dagger from hand to hand, a menacing grin on his thin mouth.

"We'll peel your hide, barbar," he sneered, "and hang it in the rigging. You'll scream a long time before we let you—"

Among the lessons Conan had learned in his life was that when it was time to fight, it was well to fight, not talk. His broadsword left its worn shagreen scabbard in a draw that continued into an upward swing. The Kothian's eyes bulged, and he fumbled for the blade that was at that moment in mid-toss. Then the first fingerlength of the broadsword clove through his jaw, and up between his eyes. The dagger clattered to the paving stones, and its owner's body fell atop.

The other two were not men to waste time over a dead companion. Such did not long survive on the sea. Even as the lanky man was falling, they rushed at the big youth. The Iranistani's blade gashed along Conan's forearm, but he slammed a kick into the dark man's midsection that sent him sprawling. Scarface dropped to a crouch, his dagger streaking up toward Conan's ribs. Conan sucked in his stomach, felt the dagger slice through his tunic and draw a thin, burning line across his midriff. Then his own blade was descending. Scarface screamed as steel cut into the joining of his neck and shoulder and continued two handspans deeper. He dropped his dagger to paw weakly at the broadsword, though life was already draining from him. Conan kicked the body free—for it was a corpse before it struck the pavement—and spun to face the third sailor.

The Iranistani had gotten to his feet yet again, but instead of attacking he stood staring at the bodies of his friends. Suddenly he turned and ran up the street. "Murder!" he howled as he ran, heedless of the bloody dagger he was waving. "Murder!" The harlots and mendicants who had so recently been lost in their fighting scattered like leaves before a high wind.

Hastily Conan wiped his blade on Scarface's tunic and sheathed it. There were a few things worse than to be caught by the City Guard standing over a corpse. Most especially in Turan, where the Guard had a habit of following arrest with torture until the prisoner confessed. Conan grabbed the girl's arm and joined the exodus, dragging her behind him.

"You killed them," she said incredulously. She ran as if unsure whether to drag her heels or not. "They'd have run away, an you threatened them."

"Mayhap I should have let them have you," he replied. "They would have ridden you like a post horse. Now be silent and run!"

Down side streets he pulled her, startling drunks staggering from seafarers' taverns, down cross-alleys smelling of stale urine and rotting offal. As soon as they had put some distance between themselves and the bodies, he slowed to a walk—running people were too well noticed—but yet kept moving. He wanted a *very* goodly distance between himself and the Guardsmen who would be drawn to the corpses like flies. He dodged between high-wheeled pushcarts, carrying goods from harbor warehouses deeper into the city. The girl trailed reluctantly at his heels, following only because his big hand engulfed her slender wrist as securely as an iron manacle.

Finally he turned into a narrow alley, pushing the girl in ahead of him, and stopped to watch his back-path. There was no way that the Guard could have followed him, but his height and his eyes made him stand out, even in a city the size of Aghrapur.

"I thank you for your assistance," the girl said suddenly in a tone at once haughty and cool. She moved toward the entrance of the alley. "I must be going now."

He put out an arm to bar her way. Her breasts pressed pleasurably against the hardness of his forearm, and she backed hastily away, blushing in confusion.

"Not just yet," he told her.

"Please," she said without meeting his eye. There was a quaver in her voice. "I . . . I am a maiden. My father will reward you well if you return me to him in the same . . . condition." The redness in her cheeks deepened.

Conan chuckled deep in his throat. "It's not your virtue I want, girl. Just the answers to a question or three."

To his surprise her eyes dropped. "I suppose I should be glad," she said bitterly, "that even killers prefer slender, willowy women. I know I am a cow. My father has often told me I was made to bear many sons and . . . and to nurse all of them," she finished weakly, coloring yet again.

Her father was a fool, Conan thought, eyeing her curves. She was a woman made for more than bearing sons, though he did not doubt that whoever she was wed to would find the task of giving them to her a pleasurable one.

"Don't be silly," he told her gruffly. "You'd give joy to any man."

"I would?" she breathed wonderingly. Her liquid eyes caressed his face, innocently, he was certain. "How," she asked falteringly, "is a post horse ridden?"

He had to think to remember why she asked, and then he could barely suppress a smile. "Long and hard," he said, "with little time for rest, if any."

She went scarlet to the neck of her silken robe, and he chuckled. The girl blushed easily, and prettily.

"What is your name, little one?"

"Yasbet. My father calls me Yasbet." She looked past him to the street beyond, where pushcarts rumbled by. "Do you think the casket, at least, would be there if we went back? It belonged to my mother, and Fatima will be furious at its loss. More furious than for the jewels, though she'll be mad enough at those."

He shook his head. "That casket has changed hands at least twice by now, for money or blood. And the jewels as well. Who is Fatima?"

"My amah," she replied, then gasped and glared at him as if he had tricked her into revealing the fact.

"Your amah!" Conan brayed with laughter. "Are you not a little old to have a nursemaid?"

"My father does not think so," Yasbet replied in a sullen voice. "He thinks I must have an amah until I am given to my husband. It is none of my liking. Fatima thinks I am still five years of age, and father sides with her decisions always." Her eyes closed and her voice sank to a weary whisper. She spoke as if no longer realizing she spoke aloud. "I shall be locked in my room for this, at the least. I shall be lucky if Fatima does not. . . ." Her words drifted off with a wince, and her hands stole back to cover her buttocks protectively.

"You deserve it," Conan said harshly.

Yasbet started, eyes wide and flushing furiously. "Deserve what? What do you mean? Did I say something?"

"You deserve to have an amah, girl. After this I shouldn't be surprised if your father takes two or three of them in service." He smiled inwardly at the relief on her face now. In truth, he thought she deserved a spanking as well, but saying so would be no way to gain satisfaction for his curiosity. "Now tell me, Yasbet. What were you doing alone on a street like that, giving your jewels to beggars? It was madness, girl."

"It was not madness," she protested. "I wanted to do something significant, something on my own. You have no idea what my life is like. Every moment waking or sleeping is ruled and watched by Fatima. I am allowed to make not the smallest decision governing my own life. I had to climb over the garden wall to leave without Fatima's permission."

"But giving jewels to beggars and strumpets?"

"The . . . the women were not part of my plan. I wanted to help the poor, and who can be poorer than beggars?" Her face firmed angrily. "My father will know I am no longer a child. I do not regret giving up the pretties he believes mean so much to me. It is noble to help the poor."

"Perhaps he'll hire six amahs," Conan muttered. "Girl, did it never occur to you that you might be hurt? If you had to help someone, why not ask among your own servants? Surely they know of people in need? Then you could have sold a few of your jewels for money to help."

Yasbet snorted. "Even if all the servants were not in league with Fatima, where would I find a dealer in gems who would give me true value? More likely he would simply pretend to deal with me while he sent for my father! And *he* would no doubt send Fatima to bring me home. That humiliation I can do without, thank you."

"Gem dealers would recognize you," he said incredulously, "and know who your father is? Who is he? King Yildiz?"

Suddenly wary, she eyed him like a fawn on the edge of flight. "You will not take me back to him, will you?"

"And why should I not? You are not fit to walk the streets without a keeper, girl."

"But then I'll never keep him from discovering what happened today." She shuddered. "Or Fatima."

Wetting her lips with the tip of her tongue, she moved closer. "Just listen to me for a moment. Please? I—"

Abruptly she darted past him into the street.

"Come back here, you fool girl," he roared, racing after her.

She dashed almost under the wheels of a heavy, crate-filled cart, and was immediately hidden from view. Two more carts pressed close behind. There was no room to squeeze between them. He ran to get ahead of the carts and to the other side of the street. When he got there, Yasbet was nowhere in sight. A potter's apprentice was setting out his master's crockery before their shop. A rug dealer unrolled his wares before his. Sailors and harlots strolled in and out of a tavern. But of the girl there was no sign.

"Fool girl," he muttered.

Just then the tavern sign, painted crudely, creaked in the breeze and caught his eye. The Blue Bull. All that had happened, and he had come right to it. Aghrapur was going to be a lucky city. Giving his swordbelt a hitch and settling his cloak about his broad shoulders, he sauntered into the stone-fronted inn.

II

The interior of the Blue Bull was poorly lit by guttering rush torches stuck in crude black iron sconces on the stone walls. A dozen men, hunched over their mugs, sat scattered among the tables that dotted the slate floor, which was swept surprisingly clean for a tavern of that class. Three sailors took turns flinging their daggers at a heart crudely painted on a slab of wood and hung on a wall. The rough stones around the slab were pocked from ten thousand near misses. A pair of strumpets, one with multi-hued beads braided in her hair, the other wearing a tall wig in a bright shade of red, circulated among the patrons quietly hawking the wares they displayed in diaphanous silk. Serving girls, their muslin covering little more than the harlots' garb, scurried about with pitchers and mugs. An odor of sour wine and stale ale, common to all such places, competed with the stench of the street.

When he saw the innkeeper, a stout, bald man scrubbing the bar with a bit of rag, Conan understood the cleanliness of the floors. He knew the man, Ferian by name. This Ferian had a passion for cleanliness uncommon among men of his profession. It was said he had fled from Belverus, in Nemedia, after killing a man who vomited on the floor of his tavern. But as a source of information he had always been unsurpassed. Unless he had changed his ways he would know all the news in Aghrapur, not only the gossip of the streets.

Ferian smiled as Conan leaned an elbow on the bar, though his small black eyes remained watchful, and he did not cease his wiping. "Hannuman's Stones, Cimmerian," he said quietly. "They say all roads lead to Aghrapur—at least, they say it in Aghrapur—and seeing you walk in here, I believe it. A year more, and all of Shadizar will be here."

"Who else from Shadizar is in the city?" Conan asked.

"Rufo, the Kothian coiner. Old Sharak, the astrologer. And Emilio, too."

"Emilio!" Conan exclaimed. Emilio the Corinthian had been the best thief in Zamora, next to Conan. "He always swore he'd never leave Shadizar."

Ferian chuckled, a dry sound to come from one so plump. "And before that he swore he would never leave Corinthia, but he left both for the same reason—he was found in the wrong woman's bed. Her husband was after him, but her mother wanted him even more. Seems he'd been bedding her as well, and lifting bits of her jewelry. The older wench hired a bevy of knifemen to see that Emilio would have nothing to offer another woman. I hear he left the city disguised as an old woman and did not stop sweating for half a year. Ask him about it, an you want to see a man turn seven colors at once, the while swallowing his tongue. He's upstairs with one of the girls now, though likely too drunk to do either of them any good."

"Then they'll be there till the morrow," Conan laughed, "for he'll never admit to failure." He laid two coppers on the bar. "Have you any Khorajan ale? My throat is dusty."

"Do I have Khorajan ale?" Ferian said, rummaging under the bar. "I have wines and ales you have never heard of. Why, I have wines and ales *I* have never heard of." He drew out a dusty clay crock, filled a leathern jack, and made the coppers disappear as he pushed the mug in front of Conan. "Khorajan ale. How stand affairs in the Gilded Bitch of the Vilayet? You had to leave in a hurry, did you?"

Conan covered his surprise by drinking deeply on the dark, bitter ale, and wiped white froth from his mouth with the back of his hand before he spoke. "How knew you I have been in Sultanapur? And why think you I left hurriedly?"

"You were seen there these ten days gone," Ferian smirked, "by Zefran the Slaver, who came through here on his way back to Khawarism." It was the tavernkeeper's major fault that he liked to let men know how much he knew of what they had been about. One day it would gain him a knife between his ribs. "As for the rest, I know naught save that you stand there with the dust of hard riding on you, and you were never the one to travel for pleasure. Now, what can you tell me?"

Conan drank again, pretending to think on what he could tell. The fat man was known to trade knowledge for knowledge, and Conan had one piece of it he knew was not yet in Aghrapur, unless someone had grown wings to fly it there ahead of him.

"The smuggling is much abated in Sultanapur," the Cimmerian said finally. "The Brotherhood of the Coast is in disarray. They sweat in the shadows, and stir not from their dwellings. 'Twill be months before so much as a bale of silk passes through that city without the customs paid."

Ferian grunted noncommittally, but his eyes lit. Before the sun next rose, men who would try to fill the void in Sultanapur would pay him well.

"And what can you tell me of Aghrapur?"

"Nothing," Ferian replied flatly.

Conan stared. It was not the tapster's way to give less than value. His scrupulousness was part and parcel of his reputation. "Do you doubt the worth of what I've told you?"

"'Tis not that, Cimmerian." The tavernkeeper sounded faintly embarrassed. "Oh, I can tell you what you can learn for yourself in a day's listening in the street. Yildiz casts his eyes beyond the border, and builds the army accordingly. The Cult of Doom gains new members every day. The—"

"The Cult of Doom!" Conan exclaimed. "What in Mitra's name is that?"

Ferian grimaced. "A foolishness, is what it is. They're all over the streets, in their saffron robes, the men with shaven heads."

"I saw some dressed so," Conan said, "chanting to a tambourine."

"'Twas them. But there's naught to them, despite the name. They preach that all men are doomed, and building up earthly treasures is futile." He snorted and scrubbed at his piggish nose with a fat hand. "As for earthly treasure, the cult itself has built up quite a store. All who join give whatever they possess to the Cult. Some young sons and daughters of wealthy merchants, and even of nobles, have given quite a bit. Not to mention an army of rich widows. There've been petitions to the throne about it, from relatives and such, but the cult pays its taxes on time, which is more than can be said of the temples. And it gives generous gifts to the proper officials, though that is not well known." He brightened. "They have a compound, almost a small city, some small distance north, on the coast. Could I find where within their treasures are kept . . . well, you are skillful enough to make your fortune in a single night."

"I'm a thief no more," Conan said. Ferian's face fell. "What else can you tell me of the city?"

The fat man sighed heavily. "These days I know less than the harlots, whose customers sometimes talk in their sleep. In these three months past, two thirds of those who have given me bits and pieces, servants of nobles and of those high in the Merchant's Guild, have been murdered. What you have told me is the best piece of intelligence I have had in a month. I owe you," he added reluctantly. He was not one to enjoy indebtedness. "The first thing I hear that you might use to advantage, I will place in your hands."

"And I will hear it before anyone else? Let us say two days before?"

"Two days! As well as a year. Knowledge spoils faster than milk under a hot sun."

"Two days," Conan said firmly.

"Two days, then," the other man muttered.

Conan smiled. Breaking his word was not among Ferian's faults. But this matter of the murders, now. . . . "It seems beyond mere chance that so many of your informants should die in so short a time."

"No, friend Conan." To the Cimmerian's surprise, Ferian refilled his mug without asking payment. That was not like him. Perhaps he hoped to pay off his debt in free drink, Conan thought. "Many more have died than those who had a connection to me. There is a plague of murder on Aghrapur. More killings in these three months than in the whole year before. Were it not for the sorts who die, I might think some plot was afoot, but who would plot against servants and Palace Guards and the like? 'Tis the hand of chance playing fickle tricks, no more."

"Conan!" came a shout from the stairs at the rear of the common room. The big Cimmerian looked around.

Emilio stood on the bottom step with his arm around a slender girl in gauds of brass and carnelian and a long, narrow strip of red silk wound about her in such a way as almost to conceal her breasts and hips. She half supported him as he swayed drunkenly, which was no easy task. He was a big man, as tall as Conan, though not so heavily muscled. He was handsome of face, with eyes almost too large for a man. His eyes and his profile, he would tell anyone who would listen, drew women as honey drew flies.

"Greetings, Emilio," Conan called back. "No longer dressing as an old woman, I see." To Ferian he added, "We'll talk later." Taking his mug, he strolled to the staircase.

Emilio sent the girl on her way with a swat across her pert rump, and eyed Conan woozily. "Who told you that tale? Ferian, I'll wager. Fat old sack of offal. Not true, I tell you. Not true. I simply left Zamora to seek rich—" he paused to belch "—richer pastures. You're just the man I want to see, Cimmerian."

Conan could sense an offer of cooperation coming. "We no longer follow the same trade, Emilio," he said.

Emilio did not seem to hear. He grabbed the arm of a passing serving girl, ogling her generous breasts as he did. "Wine, girl. You hear?" She nodded and sped off, deftly avoiding his attempted pinch; he tottered and nearly fell. Still staggering, he managed to fall onto a stool at an empty table and gestured drunkenly toward another. "Sit, Conan. Sit, man. Wine'll be here before you know it."

"Never before have I seen you so drunk," Conan said as he took the stool. "Are you celebrating, or drowning sorrows?"

The other man's eyes had drifted half shut. "Do you know," he said dreamily, "that a blonde is worth her weight in rubies here? These Turanian men will kill to have a fair-haired mistress. Does she have blue eyes, they'll kill their mothers for her."

"Have you turned to slaving, then, Emilio? I thought better of you."

Instead of answering, the other man rambled on.

"They have more heat in them than other women. I think it's the hair. Gods put color in a woman's hair, they must have to take some of her heat to do it. Stands to reason. Davinia, now, she's hotter than forge-fire. That fat general can't take care of her. Too much army business." Emilio's snicker was at once besotted and lascivious. Conan decided to let him run out of wind. "So I take care of her. But she wants things. I tell her she doesn't need any necklace, beautiful as she is, but she says a sorcerer laid a spell on it for a queen. Centuries gone this happened, she claims. Woman wears it, and she's irresistible. Thirteen rubies, she says, each as big as the first joint of a man's thumb, each set on a moonstone-crusted seashell in gold. Now that's worth stealing." He snickered and leaned toward Conan, leering. "Thought she'd pay me for it with her body. Set her straight on that. I already have her body. Hundred gold pieces, I told her. Gold, like her hair. Softest ever I tangled my hand in. Softest skin, too. Buttery and sleek."

The serving girl returned to set a mug and wine-jar on the table, and stood waiting. Conan made no move to pay. *He* had no hundred gold pieces coming to him. The girl poked Emilio in the ribs with her fist. He grunted, and stared at her blearily.

"One of you pays for the wine," she said, "or I take it back."

"No way to treat a good customer," Emilio muttered, but he rooted in his pouch until he came up with the coins. When she had gone he stared at the Cimmerian across the table. "Conan! Where did you come from? Thought I saw you. It's well you are here. We have a chance to work together again, as we used to."

"We never worked together," Conan said levelly, "And I thieve no more."

"Nonsense. Now listen you close. North of the city a short distance is an enclosure containing much wealth. I have a commission to steal a—to steal something from there. Come with me; you could steal enough to keep you for half a year."

"Is this enclosure by any chance the compound of the Cult of Doom?"

Emilio rocked back on his seat. "I thought you were fresh come to the city. Look you, those seven who supposedly entered the compound and were never seen again were Turanians. These local thieves have no skill, not like us. They'd last not a day in Shadizar or Arenjun. Besides, I think me they did not go to the compound at all. They hid, or died, or left the city, and men made up this story. People will do that, to make a place they do not know, or do not like, seem fearful."

Conan said nothing.

Ignoring his mug, Emilio swept up the clay wine-jar, not lowering it until it was nearly drained. He leaned across the table, pleading in his voice. "I know exactly where the—the treasure is to be found. On the east side of the compound is a garden containing a single tower, atop which is a room where jewelry and rarities are kept. Those fools go there to look at them. The display is supposed to show them how worthless gold and gems are. You see, I know all about it. I've asked questions, hundreds of them."

"If you've asked so many questions, think you that no one knows what you intend? Give it over, Emilio."

A fur-capped Hyrkanian stepped up to the table, the rancid odor of his lank, greased hair overpowering the smells of the tavern. A scar led from the missing lower lobe of his left ear to the corner of his mouth, pulling that side of his face into a half-smile. From the corner of his eye the Cimmerian saw four more watching from across the room. He could not swear to it, but he thought he had encountered these five earlier in the day.

The Hyrkanian at the table spared only a glance to Conan. His attention was on Emilio. "You are Emilio the Corinthian," he said gutturally. "I would talk with you."

"Go away," Emilio said without looking at him. "I know no Emilio the Corinthian. Listen to me, Conan. I would be willing to give you half what I get for the necklace. Twenty pieces of gold."

Conan almost laughed. Dead drunk Emilio might be, but he still thought to cheat his hoped-for partner.

"I would talk with you," the Hyrkanian said again.

"And I said go away!" Emilio shouted, his face suddenly suffusing with red. Snatching the wine-jar, he leaped to his feet and smashed it across the Hyrkanian's head. With the last dregs of the wine rolling down his face, the scarred nomad collapsed in a welter of clay fragments.

"Crom!" Conan muttered; a deluge of rank-smelling men in fur caps was descending on them.

Conan pivoted on his buttocks, his foot rising to meet a hurtling nomad in the stomach. With a gagging gasp the man stopped dead, black eyes goggling as he bent double. The Cimmerian's massive fist crashed against the side of his head, and he crumpled to the floor.

Emilio was wallowing on the floor beneath two of the Hyrkanians. Conan seized one by the back of his sheepskin coat and pulled him off of the Corinthian thief. The nomad spun, a dagger in his streaking hand. Surprise crossed his face as his wrist slapped into Conan's hand. The Cimmerian's huge fist traveled no more than three handspans, but the fur-capped nomad's bootheels lifted from the floor, and then he collapsed beside his fellow.

Conan scanned the room for the fifth Hyrkanian, but could not find the remaining nomad anywhere. Emilio was getting shakily to his feet while examining a bloody gash on his shoulder. Ferian was heading back toward the bar, carrying a heavy bungstarter. Another instant and Conan saw a pair of booted feet stretched out from behind a table. "You get them out of here," Ferian shouted as he reached the bar and thrust the heavy mallet out of sight. "You dirtied my floor, now you clean it. Get them out of here, I say!"

Conan seized one of the unconscious men by the heels. "Come on, Emilio," he said, "unless you want to fight Ferian this time."

The Corinthian merely grunted, but he grabbed another of the nomads. Together they dragged the unconscious men into the street, shadowed with night, now, and left them lying against the front of the rug dealer's shop.

As they laid out the last of the sleeping men—Conan had checked each to make sure he still breathed—Emilio stared up at the waxing pearlescent moon and shivered.

"I've an evil feeling about this, Conan," he said. "I wish you would come with me."

"You come with me," Conan replied. "Back inside where we'll drink some more of Ferian's wine, and perhaps try our luck with the girls."

"You go, Conan. I—" Emilio shook his head. "You go." And he staggered off into the night.

"Emilio!" Conan called, but only the wind answered, whispering down shadowed streets. Muttering to himself, the Cimmerian returned to the tavern.

hen Conan came down to the common room of the Blue Bull the next morning, the wench with the beads in her hair accompanied him, clutching his arm to her breast, firm and round through its thin silk covering, letting her swaying hip bump into his thigh at every step.

Brushing her lips against his massive shoulder, she looked up at him smokily through her lashes. "Tonight?" She bit her lip and added, "For you, half price."

"Perhaps, Zasha," he said, though even at half price his purse would not stand many nights of her. And those accursed beads had quickly gotten to be an irritation. "Now be off with you. I've business." She danced away with a saucy laugh and a saucier roll of her hips. Mayhap his purse could stand *one* more night.

The tavern was almost empty at that early hour. Two men with sailors' queues tried to kill the pain of the past night's drink with still more drink, while morosely fingering nearly flat purses. A lone strumpet, her worknight done at last and her blue silks damp with sweat, sat in a corner with her eyes closed, rubbing her feet.

At the bar Ferian filled a mug with Khorajan ale before he was asked.

"Has aught of worth come to your ear?" Conan asked as he wrapped one big hand around the leathern jack. He was not hopeful, since the fat tavern-keeper had once more failed to demand payment.

"Last night," the stout man said, concentrating on the rag with which he rubbed the wood of the bar, "it was revealed that Temba of Kassali, a dealer in gems who stands high in the Merchant's Guild, has been featuring Hammaram Temple Virgins at his orgies, with the result that fourteen former virgins and five priestesses have disappeared from the Temple, likely into a slaver's kennels. Temba will no doubt be ordered to give a large gift to the Temple. Last night also twenty-odd murders took place, that I have heard of so far, and probably twice so many that have not reached my ears. Also, the five daughters of Lord Barash were found by their father entertaining the grooms of his stable and have been packed off into the Cloisters of Vara, as has the Princess Esmira, or so 'tis rumored."

"I said of worth," the Cimmerian cut off. "What care I for the virgins or princesses? Of worth!"

Ferian gave a half-hearted laugh and studied his bit of scrub cloth. "The last is interesting, at least. Esmira is the daughter of Prince Roshmanli, closest to Yildiz's ear of the Seventeen Attendants. In a city of sluts she is said to be a virgin of purest innocence, yet she is being sent away to scrub floors and sleep on a hard mat until a husband can be found." Suddenly he slammed his fist down on the bar and spat. The spittle landed on the wood, but he seemed not to see it. "Mitra's Mercies, Cimmerian, what expect you? Its been but one night since I told you I know nothing. Am I a sorcerer to conjure knowledge where there was none? An you want answers from the skies, ask old Sharak over there. He—" Suddenly his eye lit on the gobule of spit. With a strangled cry he scrubbed at it as if it would contaminate the wood.

Conan looked about for the astrologer he had known in Shadizar. The bent old man, wearing what seemed to be the same frayed and patched brown tunic he had worn in Shadizar, was lowering himself creakily to a stool near the door. His white hair was thinner than ever, and as always he leaned on a long blackwood staff, which he claimed was a staff of power, though no one had ever seen any magicks performed with it. Wispy mustaches hung below his thin mouth and narrow chin, and he clutched a rat's-nest of scrolls in his bony fingers.

Ferian gave the bar one more scrub and eyed it suspiciously. "I like not this owing, Cimmerian," he muttered.

"I like not being owed." Conan's icy blue eyes peered into the fulvous ale. "After a time I begin to think I will not be repaid, and I like that even less."

"I pay my debts," the other protested. "I'm a fair man. 'Tis known from Shahpur to Shadizar. From Kuthchemes to—"

"Then pay me."

"Black Erlik's Throne, man! What you told me may be worth no more than the wind blowing in the streets!"

Conan spoke as quietly as a knife leaving its scabbard. "Do you call me a liar, Ferian?"

Ferian blinked and swallowed hard. Of a sudden, the Cimmerian seemed to fill his vision. And he remembered with a sickly sinking of his stomach that among the muscular youth's more uncivilized traits was a deadly touchiness about his word.

"No, Conan," he laughed shakily. "Of a certainty not. You misunderstand. I meant just that I do not know its value. Nothing more than that."

"An you got no gold for that information last night," Conan laughed scornfully, "I'll become a priest of Azura."

Ferian scowled, muttered under his breath, and finally said, "Mayhap I have some slight idea of its worth."

A smile showed the big Cimmerian's strong white teeth. The tavern keeper shifted uncomfortably.

"An you know its worth, Ferian, we can set some other payment than what was first agreed."

"Other payment?" Despite his plump cheeks the innkeeper suddenly wore a look of rat-like suspicion. "What other payment?" Conan took a long pull of ale to let him steep. "What other payment, Cimmerian?"

"Lodgings, to begin."

"Lodgings!" Ferian gaped like a fish in surprise and relief. "Is that all? Of course. You can have room for . . . for ten days."

"A fair man," Conan murmured sardonically "Your best room. Not the sty I slept in last night."

The fat man snickered greasily. "Unless I misread me the look on Zasha's face, you did little sleeping." He cleared his throat heavily at the look on Conan's face. "Very well. The best room."

"And not for ten days. For a month."

"A month!"

"And some small information."

"This is in place of the information!" Ferian howled.

"Information," Conan said firmly. "I'll not ask to be the only one to get it, as we first spoke of, but for that month you must keep me informed, and betimes."

"I have not even agreed to the month!"

"Oh, yes. Food and drink must be included. I have hearty appetites," he laughed. Tipping up his mug, he emptied it down his throat. "I'll have more of that Khorajan."

Ferian clutched at his shiny scalp as if wishing he had hair to pull out by the roots. "Do you want anything else? This tavern? My mistress? I have a daughter somewhere—in Zamora, I think. Do you want me to find her and bring her to your bed?"

"Is she pretty?" Conan asked. He paused as if considering, then shook his head. "No, the lodgings and the rest will be enough." Ferian sputtered, his beady eyes bulging in his fat face. "Of course," the Cimmerian continued, "you could continue in my debt. You do understand I'd just want the right piece of information, do you not? 'Twas good value I gave, and I'll expect the same in return. It would be well if you found it quickly." A growl had entered his voice, and his face had slowly darkened. "You know we barbars are not so understanding as you civilized men. Why, if a tenday or two passed with you silent, I might think you wished to take advantage of me. Such would make me angry. I might even—" His big hands abruptly clutched the bar as if he intended to vault it.

Ferian's mouth worked for a moment before he managed to shout "No!" and seized Conan's hand in his. "Done," he cried. "It's done. The month and the rest. Done!"

"Done," Conan said.

The fat innkeeper stared at him. "A month," he moaned. "My serving wenches will spend the whole time in your bed. You keep your hands off them, Cimmerian, or I'll get not a lick of work from the lot of them. You've taken advantage of me. Of my good nature."

"I knew not that you had one, Ferian. Mayhap if you take a physic it will go away."

"Mitra be thanked that most of you Cimmerians like your god-forsaken frozen wastes. Did any more of your accursed blue-eyed devils come south, you would own the world."

"Be not so sour," Conan said chidingly. "I'll wager you got twenty times so much for what I told you as what my staying here will cost."

Ferian grunted. "Just keep your hands off my serving wenches, Cimmerian. Go away. Am I to make up what you cost me, I cannot stand here all day talking to you. Go talk to Sharak."

The young Cimmerian laughed, scooping up his mug of dark ale. "At least he can tell me what the stars say." When he left the bar, Ferian was still sputtering over that.

The astrologer peered at Conan dimly as he approached the table where the old man sat; then a smile creased his thin features. The skin of his visage was stretched taut over his skull. "I thought I saw you, Conan, but these eyes. . . . I am no longer the man I was twenty years ago, or even ten. Sit. I wish that I could offer you a goblet of wine, but my purse is as flat as was my wife's chest. May the gods guard her bones," he added in the careless way of a man who has said a thing so many times that he no longer hears the words.

"No matter, Sharak. I will buy the wine."

But as Conan turned to signal, one of the wenches bustled to the table and set a steaming bowl of lentil stew, a chunk of coarse bread and a pannikin of wine before the astrologer. The food set out, she turned questioningly toward the muscular youth. Abruptly her dark, tilted eyes went wide with shock, and she leaped into the air, emitting a strangled squawk. Sharak

began to cackle. The wench glared at the aged man then, rubbing one buttock fitfully, darted away.

Sharak's crowing melded into a fit of coughing, which he controlled with
difficulty. "It never does," he said when he could speak, "to let them start
thinking you're too old to be dangerous."

Conan threw back his black-maned head and roared with laughter.
"You'll never get old," he managed finally.

"I'm a dotard," Sharak said, digging a horn spoon into the stew. "Ferian
says so, and I begin to think he is right. He gives me a bowl of stew twice a
day, else I would eat only what I scavenge in the garbage, as many must in
age. He is almost my only patron, as well. In return for the stew I read his
stars. Every day I read them, and a more boring tale they could not tell."

"But why no patrons? You read the stars as a scribe reads marks on parchment. Never once did you tell me wrong, though your telling was at divers
times none too clear to me."

"'Tis these Turanians," the old man snorted. "Ill was the day I journeyed
here. Half the stars they name wrongly, and they make other errors.
Important errors. Those fools in this city who call themselves astrologers had the gall to charge me with unorthodoxy before the Guild. 'Twas
no more than luck I did not end at the stake. The end result is the same,
though. Without the Guild's imprimatur, I would be arrested if I opened a
shop. The few who deal with me are outlanders, and they come merely
because I will tell their stars for a mug of wine or a loaf of bread instead of
the silver piece the others charge. Did I have a silver piece, I would return to
Zamora on the instant." With a rueful grunt he returned to spooning the
stew into his mouth.

Conan was silent a moment. Slowly he dug into his pouch and drew out a
silver piece, sliding it across the rough boards. "'Tell my horoscope, Sharak."

The gaunt old man froze with his spoon half raised to his face. He
peered at the coin, blinking then at Conan. "Why?"

"I would know what this city holds for me," the young Cimmerian said
gruffly. "I hold you better than any Guildsman of Aghrapur, and so worth at
least the footing they demand. Besides," he lied, "my purse is heavy with
coin."

Sharak hesitated, then nodded. Without touching the coin, he fumbled
through his scrolls with his left hand, all the while absently licking traces of
stew from the fingers of his right. When those scrolls he wanted were spread
out atop the table; he produced a wax tablet from beneath his patched tunic.
The side of a stylus scraped the wax smooth. Nose almost touching the
parchments, he began to copy arcane symbols with deft strokes.

"Do you not need to know when I was born, and such?" Conan asked.

"I remember the details of your natal chart," the other replied with his eyes on the parchment, "as if it were drawn on the insides of my eyelids. A magnificent chart. Unbelievable. Hmm. Mitra's Chariot is in retrograde."

"Magnificent? You have never told me of any magnificence before."

Sighing, Sharak swiveled his head to gaze at the big youth. "Unbelievable, I called it as well, and you would not believe did I tell you. Then you did not believe anything else I told you, either, and I could do you no good. Therefore I do not tell you. Now, will you allow me to do what you have paid me for?" He did not wait for a reply before turning his eyes back to the scrolls. "Aha. The Bloodstar enters the House of the Scorpion this very night. Significant."

Conan shook his head and quaffed deeply on his ale. Was Sharak attempting to inflate his payment? Perhaps the habit of trying to do so was too deeply ingrained to lose.

He busied himself with drinking. The common room was beginning to fill, with queued sailors and half-naked trulls for the most part. The wenches were the most interesting, by far. One, short, round-breasted and large-eyed in her girdle of coins and gilded wristlets and torque, made him think of Yasbet. He wished he could be certain she was safe at home. No, in truth he wished her in his bed upstairs, but, failing that, it was best if she were at home, whatever her greeting from Fatima. Could he find her again, it would of a certainty brighten his days in Aghrapur. Let Emilio talk of his blonde—what was her name? Davinia?—as if she were the exotic these Turanians thought her. In his own opinion it was women with large eyes who had the fires smoldering within, even when they did not know it themselves. Why—

"I am done," Sharak said.

Conan blinked, pulled from his reverie. "What?" He looked at the wax tablet, now covered with scribbled symbols. "What does it say?"

"It is unclear," the old astrologer replied, tugging at one of his thin mustaches with bony fingers. "There are aspects of great opportunity and great danger. See, the Horse and the Lion are in conjunction in the House of Dramath, while the Three Virgins are—"

"Sharak, I would not know the House of Dramath from the house of a rugmaker. What does it mean?"

"What does it mean?" Sharak mimicked. "Always 'what does it mean?' No one wants to know the truly interesting part, the details of how. . . Oh, very well. First of all: there is a need to go back in order to go forward. To become what you will become, you must become again what you once were."

"That's little help," Conan muttered. "I have been many things."

"But this is most important. This branching here, indicates that if you fail to do so, you will never leave Aghrapur alive. You have already set events in motion."

The air in the tavern seemed suddenly chill. Conan wished the old man had not been right so often before. "How can I have set events in motion? I've been here barely a day."

"And spoken to no one? Done nothing?"

Conan breathed heavily. "Does it speak of gold?"

"Gold will come into your hands, but it does not seem to be important, and there is danger attached."

"Gold is always important, and there is always danger attached. What of women?"

"Ah, youth," Sharak murmured caustically. "You will soon be entangled with women—two, it seems here—but there is danger there as well."

"Women are always at least as dangerous as gold," Conan replied, laughing.

"One is dark of hair, and one pale-haired."

The Cimmerian's laughter faded abruptly. Pale haired? Emilio's Davinia? No! That would almost certainly mean aiding Emilio in his theft, and that had been left behind. But he was to 'become what he had been.' He forced the thought away. He was done with thieving. The astrologer's reading must mean something else.

"What more?" he asked harshly.

"'Tis not my fault if you like it not, Conan. I merely read what is writ in the stars."

"What more, I said!"

Sharak sighed heavily. "You cannot blame me if. . . . There is danger here connected in some fashion to a journey. This configuration," he pointed to a row of strangely bent symbols scribed in the wax, "indicates a journey over water, but these over here indicate land. It is unclear."

"'Tis all unclear, an you ask me of it." Conan muttered.

"It becomes less clear. For instance, here the color yellow is indicated as of great importance."

"The gold—"

"—is of small import, no matter your feeling on it. And there is more danger tied to this than to the gold."

The big Cimmerian ground his teeth audibly. "There is danger to breathing, to hear you tell it."

"I can well believe it so, to look at this chart. As to the rest, the number thirteen and the color red are of some significance, and are linked. Additionally, this alignment of the Monkey and the Viper indicates the need of acting quickly and decisively. Hesitate, and the moment will be lost to you. And that will mean your death."

"What will come, will come, old man," Conan snapped. "I'll not be affrighted by stars, gods or demons."

Sharak scowled, then pushed the silver piece back across the table. "If my reading is so distasteful to you, I cannot take payment."

The muscular youth's anger dropped to a simmer instantly. "'Tis no blame of yours whether I like the reading you give or no. You take the money, and I'll take your advice."

"I am four score and two-years of age," the astrologer said, suddenly diffident, "and never in all that time have I had an adventure." He gripped his knobbly staff, leaning against the table. "There is power in this, Cimmerian. I could be of aid."

Conan hid a smile. "I've no doubt of it, Sharak. An I need such help, I will call on you, have no fear. There is one thing you might do for me now. Know you where I might find Emilio at this hour?"

"That cankerous boaster?" Sharak said disdainfully. "He frequents many places of ill repute, each worse than the last." He reeled off the names of a dozen taverns and as many brothels and gaming halls. "I could help you look for him, if you really think he's needed, though what use he could be I do not know."

"When you finish supping you can search the hells."

"I would rather search the brothels," the old man leered.

"The hells," Conan laughed, getting to his feet. Sharak returned grumbling to his stew.

As he turned toward the door, the Cimmerian's eyes met those of a man just entering, hard black eyes in a hard black face beneath the turban-wrapped spiral helmet of the Turanian army. Of middling height, he moved with the confidence of a larger man. The striping on his tunic marked him as a sergeant. Ferian hurried, frowning, to meet the dark man. Soldiers were not usually habitués of the Blue Bull.

"I am seeking a man called Emilio the Corinthian," the sergeant said to Ferian.

Conan walked out without waiting for the innkeeper's reply. It had nothing to do with him. He hoped.

IV

onan entered the seventh tavern with never so much as a wobble of his step, despite the quantity of wine and ale he had ingested. The large number of wenches lolling about the dim, dank common room, roughed and be-ringed, their silks casually disarrayed, told him that a brothel occupied the upper floors of the squat stone building. Among the long tables and narrow trestle-boards crowding the slate floor, sailors rubbed shoulders with journeymen of the guilds. Scattered through the room were others whose languid countenances and oiled mustaches named them high-born no less than their silk tunics embroidered in gold and silver. Their smooth fingers played as free with the strumpets as did the sailors' callused hands.

The Cimmerian elbowed a place at the bar and tossed two coppers on the boards. "Wine," he commanded.

The barkeeper gave him a rough clay mug, filled to the brim with sour-smelling liquid, and scooped up the coins. The man was wiry and snake-faced, with heavy-lidded, suspicious eyes and a tight, narrow mouth. He would not be one to answer questions freely. Another drinker called, and the tapster moved off, wiping his hands on a filthy apron that dangled about his spindly shanks.

Conan took a swallow from his mug and grimaced. The wine was thin, and tasted as sour as it smelled.

As he eyed the common room, a strangely garbed doxy caught his gaze. Sleek and sinuous, she had climbed upon a trestle-board to dance for half a dozen sailors who pawed her with raucous shouts, running their hands up her long legs. Her oiled breasts were bare, and for garb she wore but a single strip of silk, no wider than a man's hand, run through a narrow gilded girdle worn low on the roundness of her hips, to fall to her ankles before and behind. The strangeness was that an opaque veil covered her from just below her hot, dark eyes to her chin. The sisterhood of the streets might paint their faces heavily, but they never covered them, for few men would take well to the discovery that their purchase was less fair of visage than they had believed. But not only was this woman veiled, he now saw no less than three others so equipped.

Conan caught the tavernkeeper's tunic sleeve as he passed again. "I've never seen veiled strumpets before. Do they cover the marks of the pox?"

"New come to Aghrapur, are you?" the man said, a slight smile touching his thin mouth.

"A short time past. But these women?"

"'Tis rumored," the other smirked, "that some women highly born, bored with husbands whose vigor has left them, amuse themselves by disporting as common trulls, wearing veils so those same husbands, who frequent the brothels as oft as any other men, will not recognize them. As I say, 'tis but a rumor, yet what man will pass the chance to have a lord's wife beneath him for a silver piece?"

"Not likely," Conan snorted. "There would be murder done when one of those lords discovered that the doxy he'd bought was his own wife."

"Nay. Nay. The others flock about them, but not the lordlings. What man would risk the shame of knowing his wife had been bought?"

It was true, Conan saw. Each veiled woman was the center of a knot of sailors or dockworkers or tradesman, but the nobles ignored them, looking the other way rather than acknowledge their existence.

"Try one," the snake-faced man urged. "One silver piece, and you can see for yourself if she moves beneath you like a noblewoman."

Conan drank deeply, as if considering. Had he been interested in dalliance, it was in his mind that better value would come from an honest strumpet than from a nobly-born woman pretending to be such. The tapster had none of the fripperies of the panderer about him—he did not sniff a perfumed pomander or wear more jewelry than any three wenches—but no doubt he took some part of what was earned on the mats above the common room. He might talk more easily if he thought Conan a potential patron. The Cimmerian lowered his mug.

"It's a thing to think on," he chuckled, eyeing a girl nearby. A true daughter of the mats, this one, in an orange-dyed wig with her face as bare as her wiggling buttocks. "But I seek a friend who was supposed to meet me. I understand he frequents this place betimes."

The tavernkeeper drew back half a step, and his voice cooled noticeably. "Look around you. An he is here, you will see him. Otherwise. . . ." He shrugged and turned to walk away, but Conan reached across the bar and caught his arm, putting on a smile he hoped was friendly. "I do not see him, but I still must needs find him. He is called Emilio the Corinthian. For the man who can tell me where to find him, I could spare the price of one of these wenches for the night." If Sharak was correct—and he always was—Conan *had* to find Emilio, and what word he had thus far garnered was neither copious nor good.

The tapster's face became even more snake-like, but his lidded eyes had flickered at Emilio's name. "Few men must pay for the whereabouts of a friend. Mayhap this fellow—Emilio, did you say his name is?—is no friend of yours. Mayhap he does not wish to meet you. Ashra! Come rid me of this pale-eyed fool!"

"I can prove to you that I know him. He is—"

A massive hand landed on the Cimmerian's broad shoulder, and a guttural voice growled, "Out with you!"

Conan turned his head enough to look coldly at the wide hand, its knuckles sunken and scarred. His icy azure gaze traveled back along a hairy arm as big around as most men's legs. And up. This Ashra stood head and shoulders taller even than Conan himself, and was half again as broad with no bit of fat on him. For all the scarring of his hands, the huge man's broad-nosed face was unmarked. Conan thought few could reach high enough to strike it.

He attempted to keep his tone reasonable. Fighting seldom brought information. "I seek a man this skinny one knows, not trouble. Now unhand me and—"

For an answer the big man jerked at Conan's shoulder. Sighing, the Cimmerian let himself be spun, but the smile on Ashra's face lasted only until Conan's fist hooked into his side with a loud crack of splintering ribs. Shouting drinkers scrambled out of the way of the two massive men. Conan's other fist slammed into the tall man, and again he felt ribs break beneath his blow.

With a roar Ashra seized the Cimmerian's head in both of his huge hands and lifted Conan clear of the floor, squeezing as if to crush the skull he held, but a wolfish battle-light shone in Conan's eyes. He forced his arms between Ashra's and gripped the other's head in turn, one hand atop it, the other beneath the heavy chin. Slowly he twisted, and slowly the bull neck gave. Panting, Ashra suddenly loosed his hold, yet managed to seize Conan about the chest before he could fall. Hands locked, he strained to snap the Cimmerian's spine.

The smile on Conan's face was enough to chill the blood. In the time it took three grains of sand to fall in the glass, he knew, he could break Ashra's neck, yet a killing would of a certainty gag the tapster's mouth. Abruptly he released his grip. Ashra laughed, thinking he had the victory. Conan raised his hands high, then smashed them, palms flat, across the other's ears.

Ashra screamed and staggered back, dropping the Cimmerian to clutch at his bleeding ears. Conan bored after him, slamming massive fists to the ribs he had already broken, then a third blow to the huge man's heart. Ashra's eyes glazed, and his knees bent, but he would not fall. Once more Conan struck. That never-struck nose fountained blood, and Ashra slowly turned, toppling into a table that splintered beneath him. Once the prostrate man stirred as if to rise, then was still.

A murmuring crowd gathered around the fallen man. Two men grabbed his ankles, grunting as they dragged the massive weight away. More than one wench eyed Conan warmly, licking her lips and putting an extra sway in her walk, among them those with veiled faces. He ignored them and turned back to the business at hand, to the tapster.

The snake-faced innkeeper stood behind the bar wearing an expression almost as stunned as Ashra's. A bung-starter dangled forgotten in his hand.

Conan took the heavy mallet from the slack grip and held it up before the man's eyes, fists touching in the middle of the thick handle. The muscles of his arms and shoulders knotted and bunched; there was a sharp crack, and he let the two pieces fall to the bar.

The tavernkeeper licked his thin lips. He stared at Conan as if at a wonderment. "Never before have I seen the man Ashra could not break in two with his bare hands," he said slowly. "But then, even he couldn't have. . . ." His gaze dropped to the broken mallet, and he swallowed hard. "Have you a mind to employment? The job held by that sack of flesh they're hauling off is open. A silver piece a day, plus a room, food, drink, and your choice of any wench who has not a customer. My name is Manilik. How are you called?"

"I am no hauler of tosspots," Conan said flatly. "Now tell me what you know of Emilio."

Manilik hesitated, then gave a strained laugh. "Mayhap you do know him. I'm careful of my tongue, you see. Talk when you shouldn't, and you're apt to lose your tongue. I don't waggle mine."

"Waggle it now. About Emilio."

"But that is the problem, stranger. Oh, I know of Emilio," he said quickly, as Conan's massive fist knotted atop the bar, "but I know little. And I've not seen him these three days past."

"Three days," Conan muttered despondently. Thus far he had found many who knew Emilio, but none who had seen the Corinthian these three days past. "That boasting idiot is likely gazing into a mirror or rolling with that hot-blooded Davinia of his," he growled.

"Davinia?" Manilik sounded startled. "If you know of her, perhaps you truly *do* know. . . ." He trailed off with a nervous laugh under Conan's icy eyes.

"What do *you* know of Davinia, Manilik?"

The innkeeper shivered, so quietly was that question asked. It seemed to him the quiet of the tomb, mayhap of *his* tomb an he answered not quickly. Words bubbled from him as water from a spring.

"General Mundara Khan's mistress, bar-, ah, stranger, and a dangerous woman for the likes of Emilio, not just for who it is that keeps her, but for her ambition. 'Tis said lemans have bodies, but not names. This Davinia's name is known, though. Not two years gone, she appeared in Aghrapur on the arm of an ivory trader from Punt. The trader left, and she remained. In the house of a minor gem merchant. Since then she's managed to change her leash from one hand to another with great dexterity. A rug merchant of moderate wealth, the third richest ship owner in the city, and now Mundara Khan, a cousin of King Yildiz himself, who would be a prince had his mother not been a concubine."

The flow of talk slowed, then stopped. Greed and fear warred on Manilik's face, and his mouth was twisted with the pain of giving away what he might, another time, have sold.

Conan laughed disparagingly and lied. "Can you not tell me more than is known on every street corner? Why, I've heard strumpets resting their feet wager on whether the next bed Davinia graces will be that of Yildiz." He searched for a way to erase the doubt that still creased the tavernkeeper's face. "Next," he said, "you'll tell me that as she chooses her patrons only to improve herself, she must risk leaving her master's bed for her own pleasures." How else to explain Emilio, and this Davinia so clearly a woman intent on rising?

Manilik blinked. "I had no idea so much was so widely known. It being so, there are those who will want to collect what the Corinthian owes before Mundara Khan has him gelded and flayed. He had better have the gold he has bragged of, or he'll not live to suffer the general's mercies."

"He mentioned gold, did he?" Conan prompted.

"Yes, he. . . ." The heavy-lidded eyes opened wide. "Mean you to say it's a lie? Four or five days, he claimed, and he would have gold dripping from his fingers. An you *are* a friend of the Corinthian, warn him clear most particularly of one Narxes, a Zamoran. His patience with Emilio's excuses is gone, and his way with a knife will leave your friend weeping that he is not dead. Narxes likes well to make examples for others who might fail to pay what they owe. Best you tell him to keep quiet about my warning, though. I've no wish for the Zamoran to come after me before Emilio finishes him."

"I will tell him," Conan said drily. Manilik was licking his narrow lips, avarice personified. As soon as he could, the tavernkeeper would have a messenger off to this Narxes. Whether it was Narxes or Emilio who survived, Manilik would claim it was his warning that tipped the balance. But Conan did not mean to add to the Corinthian thief's troubles. "So far as I know, the gold will be his, as he claims."

The innkeeper shrugged. "If you say it, then I believe it, stranger." But his voice carried a total lack of conviction.

Conan left with a wry smile, but just outside he stopped and leaned against the doorjamb. The lowering sun was a bloody ball on the rooftops. Moments later a slender, dark-haired serving wench darted from the inn, pulling a cloak of coarse brown wool about her. He caught the girl's arm, pulling her aside. The wench stared up at him, dark eyes wide and mouth hanging open.

"You are the one Manilik is sending to Narxes," he said.

She straightened defiantly—she came no higher than Conan's chest—and glared. "I'll tell you naught. Loose me."

Releasing his grip, he half pushed her toward the street. "Go then. Never before have I seen anyone run to have her throat slit."

The girl hesitated, rubbing her arm and eyeing the passing carts rumbling over the cobblestones. Sailors and tradesmen thronged between the high-wheeled vehicles. A quick dash and she could be lost among them. Instead she said, "Why should Narxes wish to harm me? I've never had a copper to wager at his tables. The likes of me'd never get past the door."

"You mean you don't know?" Conan said incredulously. "That alters matters."

"Know what? What matters?"

"I heard Manilik say he was sending a girl to Narxes for. . . ." He let his voice trail off, shaking his head. "No, it's no use. Better you do not know. You couldn't escape, anyway."

She laughed shakily. "You're trying to frighten me. I am just to tell Narxes that Manilik has word for him. What did you hear?" Conan was silent, frowning as if in thought, until she stepped closer and laid a trembling hand on his arm. "You must tell me! Please?"

"Not that it will do you any good," Conan said, feigning reluctance. "Narxes will find you no matter how far you run."

"My parents have a farm far from the city. He'd never find me there. Tell me!"

"Narxes had been selling young girls to the Cult of Doom for sacrifices," he lied, and invented some detail. "You'll be strapped to an altar, and when your throat is cut the blood will be gathered in a chalice, then—"

"No!" She staggered back, one hand to her mouth. Her face had a greenish cast, as if she were about to be sick. "I've never heard that the Cult of Doom makes such sacrifices. Besides, the use of freeborn for sacrifices is forbidden by law."

"How will anyone ever know, once you're safely dead and your body tossed to the sea?" He shrugged. "But if you do not believe me, then seek out Narxes. Perhaps he will explain it to you on your way to the compound of the Cult."

"What am I to do?" she moaned, taking quick steps first in one direction then another. "I have no money, nothing but what I stand in. How am I to get to my parents' farm?" Sighing, Conan dug a fistful of coppers from his pouch. Emilio would repay him, or he would know the reason why. "Here, girl. This will see you there."

"Thank you. Thank you." Half-sobbing, she snatched the coins from his outstretched hand and ran.

Not even a kiss for gratitude, Conan thought grumpily as he watched her disappear down the teeming street. But with luck Manilik would not discover for at least a day that his plans had gone awry. A day to find Emilio without worrying about finding him dead. The story he had concocted for the girl had sounded even more convincing than he had hoped. With a satisfied smile he started down the street.

In the dimnesses that foreshadowed dusk he did not notice the shaven-headed man in saffron robes, standing in the mouth of an alley beside the inn he had just left, a man who watched his going with interest.

Ʋ

Night filled the ivory-walled compound of the Cult of Doom. No dimmest flicker of light showed, for those of the Cult rose, worked, ate and slept only by command. No coppers were wasted on tapers. In an inner room, though, where Jhandar met with those who followed him most faithfully, bronze lion lamps illumined walls of alabaster bas-relief and floors mosaicked in a thousand colors.

The forty saffron-robed men who waited beneath the high vaulted ceiling knelt as Jhandar entered, each touching a dagger to his forehead. "Blessed be Holy Chaos," they intoned. "Blessed be disorder, confusion, and anarchy."

"Blessed be Holy Chaos," the mage replied perfunctorily. He was, as always, robed as they.

He eyed the lacquered tray of emerald and gold that had been placed on a small tripod table before the waiting men. His hands moved above the two-score small, stone bottles on the tray, fingers waving like questing snakes' tongues, as if they could sense the freshness of the blood within those stoppered containers.

One of the men shifted. "The kills were all made within the specified hours, Great Lord."

Jhandar acknowledged him only with an irritated flick of an eyelid. Of course those killed had died as he had commanded, at the hour he had commanded. Those who knelt before him did not know why the deaths must occur so, nor even why they must collect the blood while their victims' hearts still beat. They believed that they knew a great deal, but what they knew was how to obey. For Jhandar's purposes, that was enough.

"Go," the necromancer commanded. "Food and drink await you. Then sleep. Go."

"Blessed be Holy Chaos," they chanted and, rising, filed slowly from the room.

Jhandar waited until the heavy bronze door had clanged shut behind them before speaking again. "Che Fan," he said. "Suitai. Attend me."

Two men, tall, lean, and robed in black, appeared as if materializing from air. It would have taken a quick eye to see the turning panel of stone in the wall from behind which they had stepped. But then, even a quick eye would have stared so at the men as to miss everything else. Even in Aghrapur, they were unusual. Their black eyes seemed to slant, and their skin was the color of parchment left in the sun till it yellowed, yet so smooth that it gave no hint of age. Like as twins they were, though, the man called Che Fan was perhaps a fingerbreadth the taller. By birth and training they were assassins, able to kill with no more than the touch of a hand.

Suitai took the tray, while Che Fan hurried to open a small wooden door, lacquered and polished to mirror brightness. Jhandar swept through, followed by the two men. The passage beyond was narrow, brightly lit by gold lamps dangling from wall sconces, and empty. The shaven-headed mage kept his tame killers out of sight, for there might be those who would know them for what they were. Even the Chosen saw them but rarely.

The narrow corridor led to a chamber in the center of which was a large circle of bare dirt, with dead sterility. Great fluted columns supported the domed alabaster ceiling, and surrounding the barren earth were thirteen square pillars truncated at waist height.

As he had done many times before, Suitai began setting out the stone bottles on the hard-packed dirt. He made four groups of five, each group forming a cross.

"Great Lord." Che Fan spoke in a hoarse whisper. "We follow as you command, yet our existence is empty."

Jhandar looked at him in surprise. The two assassins never spoke unless spoken to. "Would you prefer to be where I found you?" he asked harshly.

Che Fan recoiled. He and Suitai had been walled up alive within the Khitan fortress where Jhandar had been imprisoned. Accidentally the necromancer had freed them in his own escape, and they had sworn to follow him. He was not certain they believed he could actually return them to their slow death in Khitai, but they seemed to.

"No, Great Lord," the Khitan said finally. "But we beg, Suitai and I, that we be allowed to use our talents in your service. Not since. . . ." His voice trailed off. Suitai glanced up from placing the last of the bottles, then studiously avoided looking at either of the other two men again.

Jhandar's face darkened. To speak of the distant past was one thing, to speak of the near past another. He disliked being reminded of failure and ignominy. Effort went into keeping his voice normal, but it still came out like the grate of steel on rock. "Fool! Your *talents*, as you call them, destroy the essence of the man, as you well know. There is naught left for me to summon when you kill. When I need your abilities again, *if* I need them again, I will command you. Unless you wish to step within the circle and be commanded now?"

Suitai stumbled hurriedly from the patch of dirt. "No, Great Lord," Che Fan replied hastily. "I beg forgiveness for my presumption." As one, the two assassins bowed low.

Jhandar left them so for a moment, then spoke. "Rise. In the days ahead there will be labors to sate even your desires. Now get you gone until I call again. I have my own labors to perform."

As they bowed their way from his presence, he put them from his awareness. There were more important matters which needed all of his attention.

From beneath his robes he produced a piece of black chalk. Atop four of the pillars, equidistantly spaced about the circle, he marked the ancient Khitan ideograms for the four seasons, chanting as he did in a language not even he understood, though he well understood the effect of the words. Next were drawn the ideograms for the four humors, then the four elements, and all the while he intoned the primordial spells. But one of the short, square pillars remained. He drew the symbol for life, then quickly, over it, the symbol of death.

A chill rose in the air, till his words came in puffs of white, and his voice took on a hollow aspect, as though he called from a vast deep. Mist roiled over the circle of earth, blue and flecked with silver, like the mist above the Pool of the Ultimate, yet pale and transparent. The hairs on Jhandar's arms and legs stirred and rose. He could feel the Power flowing through him, curling around his bones.

In the center of the mist light flashed, argent and azure lightning. In silence the air of the chamber quivered, as to a monstrous clap of thunder. Within the circle every stone jar shattered into numberless grains of dust, and the parched dirt drank blood. The tenuous vapors above began to glow.

Never ceasing his incantation, Jhandar sought within himself for the root of the Power that coursed his veins, seized on it, bent it to his bidding. With every fiber of his being he willed a summoning, he commanded a summoning, he *forced* a summoning.

Blood-clotted earth cracked and broke, and a hand reached up from the crack to claw at the surface, a hand withered and twisted, its nails like claws, its skin a mottled moldy gray-green. In another blood-soaked place the ground split, and monstrously deformed hands dug upward, outward. Then another, and another. A slavering panting beat its way up from below the surface. Inexorably drawn by Jhandar's chant, they dug their way from the bowels of the earth, stumpy misshapen creatures bearing little resemblance to humankind, for all they were the summoned corporeal manifestations of the essences of murdered men and women. There were no distinctions now between male and female. Neuter all, they were, with hairless mottled skin stretched tightly over domed skulls whose opalescent eyes had seen the grave from inside. Their lipless mouths emitted a cacophony of howls and lamentations.

Jhandar stopped his chant, reluctantly felt the Power pour from him like water from a ewer. As the Power went, so did the mist within the circle. The ravening creatures turned to him, seeming to see him for the first time, their cries rising.

"Be silent!" he shouted, and all sound was gone as if cut off with a knife.

He it was who had summoned; they could not but obey, though some glared at him with hellborn fury. Some few always did.

"Hear you my words. Each of you will return to the house that you served in life." A low moan rose and was stilled. "There, in incorporeal form, you will watch, and listen. What your former masters and mistresses do not want known, you will tell to me when I summon you again. Nothing else will you do unless I command." That last was necessary, he had learned, though there was little they could do without being told to.

"I hear," came the muttering moans, "and obey."

"Then by the blood and earth and Power of Chaos by which I summoned you, begone."

With a crack of inrushing air the twisted shapes disappeared.

Jhandar smiled when he left the chamber. Already he knew more of the secrets of Turan than any ten other men. Already, with a whisper in the proper ear of what the owner of that ear would die to keep secret, he influenced decisions at the highest levels. Nay, he *made* those decisions. Soon the throne itself would bow to his will. He would not demand that his position as true ruler of Turan be made known to all. That he ruled would be enough. First Turan, then perhaps Zamora, and then. . . .

"Great Lord."

Reverie broken, Jhandar glared at the shaven-headed man who had accosted him in a main corridor of his palatial quarters. Lamps of gold and silver, made from melted-down jewelry provided by new members of the Cult, cast glittering lights from walls worked in porphyry and amber.

"Why do you disturb me, Zephran?" he demanded. Not even the Chosen were allowed to approach him unbidden.

"Forgive me, Great Lord," Zephran answered, bowing low, "but I had a most distressing encounter in the city near dusk."

"Distressing encounter? What are you blathering about? I have no time for foolishness."

"It was a barbarian, Great Lord, who spoke of sacrifices within the Cult, of the altar and the use of blood."

Jhandar clutched his robes in white-knuckled fists. "Hyrkanian? He was Hyrkanian?"

"Nay, Great Lord."

"He must have been."

"Nay, Great Lord. His skin was pale where not bronzed by the sun, and his eyes were most strange, as blue as the sea."

Jhandar sagged against the wall. In Hyrkania, across the Vilayet Sea, he had first founded the Cult, first created and confined a Pool of Chaos. He would have welded the scattered Hyrkanian tribes of fierce horsemen into a single force that moved at his word. He would have launched such a wave of warriors as would have washed over Turan and Zamora and all to the West until it came to the sea. He would have. . . .

But the spirit manifestations had not been properly controlled. They had managed to communicate to the living what occurred within the compound he was building, and the tribesmen had ridden against him, slaughtering his followers. Only by loosing the Power, turning a part of the Hyrkanian steppes into a hell, had he himself managed to escape. They believed in blood vengeance, those Hyrkanians. Deep within him was the seed of fear, fear that they would follow him across the sea. Ridiculous, he knew, yet he could not rid himself of it.

"Great Lord," Zephran said diffidently. "I do not understand why filthy Hyrkanians should concern you. The few I have seen in—"

"You understand nothing," Jhandar snarled. "This barbarian. You killed him?"

Zephran shifted uneasily. "Great Lord, I . . . I lost him in the night and the crowd among the taverns near the harbor."

"Fool! Roust your fellows from their beds! Find that barbarian! He must die! No! Bring him to me. I must find out how many others know. Well, what are you waiting for! Go, fool! Go!"

Zephran ran, leaving Jhandar staring at nothing. Not again, the necromancer thought. He would not fail again. He would pull the world down in ruins if need be, but he would not fail.

VI

Conan descended to the common room of the Blue Bull taking each step with care. He did not truly believe that his head would crack if he took a misstep, but he saw no reason to take a chance. The night before had turned into a seemingly endless procession of tavern after tavern, of tankard after tankard. And all he had gotten for his trouble was a head like a barrel.

He spotted Sharak, digging eagerly into a bowl of stew, and winced at the old man's enthusiasm. With a sigh he dropped onto a bench at the astrologer's table.

"Do you have to be so vigorous about that, Sharak?" the Cimmerian muttered. "It's enough to turn a man's stomach."

"The secret is clean living," Sharak cackled gleefully. "I live properly, so I never have to worry about a head full of wine fumes. Or seldom, at least. And it brings me luck. Last night, asking about for Emilio, I discovered that the strumpets of this city fancy Zamoran astrology. And do you know why?"

"What did you find out about Emilio, Sharak?"

"Because it's foreign. They think anything imported must be better. Of course, some of them want to pay in other coin than gold or silver." He cackled again. "I spent the night in the arms of a wench with the most marvelous—"

"Sharak. Emilio?"

The gaunt old man sighed. "If *you* wanted to boast a bit, I wouldn't stop you. Oh, very well. Not that I discovered much. No one has seen him for at least two nights. Three different people, though—two of them trulls—told me Emilio claimed he would come into a great deal of gold yesterday. Perhaps someone did him in for it."

"I'd back Emilio against any man in this city," Conan replied, "with swords, knives or bare hands." But there was no enthusiasm in his voice. He was sure now that Emilio was dead, had died while trying to steal the necklace. And while dead drunk, at that. "I should have gone with him," he muttered.

"Gone where?" Sharak asked. "No matter. More than one was counting on his having this gold. I myself heard the gamester Narxes make such dire threats against Emilio as to put me off eating." He shoveled more stew into his mouth. "Then there's Nafar the Panderer, and a Kothian moneylender named Fentras, and even a Turanian soldier, a sergeant, looking for him. As he still lives, he's left Aghrapur, and wisely so."

"Emilio intended to steal from the compound of the Cult of Doom, Sharak. I think me he tried two nights past."

"Then he is dead," Sharak sighed. "That place has acquired a bad name among the Brotherhood of the Shadows. Some thieves say 'tis doom even to think of stealing from them."

"He meant to steal a necklace of thirteen rubies for a woman with blonde hair. He wanted me to aid him."

The old astrologer tossed his spoon into the bowl of stew. "Mayhap your chart . . ." he said slowly. "These eyes are old, Conan. 'Tis possible what I saw was merely an effect of your association with Emilio."

"And it's possible men can fly without magic," Conan laughed ruefully. "No, old friend. Never have I known you to make a mistake in your star-reading. The meaning was clear. I must enter that compound and steal the necklace."

Conan's bench creaked as a man suddenly dropped onto it beside him. "And I must go with you," he said. Conan looked at him. It was the hard-eyed, black-skinned Turanian army sergeant he had seen asking after Emilio. "I am called Akeba," the sergeant added.

The big Cimmerian let his hand rest lightly on the worn leather hilt of his broadsword. "'Tis a bad habit, listening to other men's conversation," he said with dangerous quietness.

"I care not if you steal every last pin from the cult," Akeba said. His hands rested on the table, and he seemed to take no notice of Conan's sword. "'Twas rumored this Emilio did not fear to enter that place, but I heard you say he is dead. I have need to enter the compound, and need of a man to guard my back, a man who does not fear the cult. If you go there, I will go with you."

Sharak cleared his throat. "Pray tell us why a sergeant of the Turanian army would want to enter that compound in secret."

"My daughter, Zorelle." Akeba's face twisted momentarily with pain. "She was taken by this Mitra-accursed cult. Or joined, I know not which.

They will not allow me to speak to her, but I have seen her once, at a distance. She no longer looks as she did before falling into their hands. Her face is cold, and she does not smile. Zorelle wore a smile always. I will bring her out of there."

"Your daughter," Conan snorted. "I must needs go with stealth. The stealth of two men is the tenth part that of one. Add the need to drag a weeping girl along. . . ." He snorted again.

"How will you steal so much as a drink of water if I summon my men to arrest you?" Akeba demanded.

Conan's fist tightened on his sword hilt. "You will summon no one from your grave," he growled. Akeba reached for his own blade, and the two men began to rise.

"Be not fools!" Sharak said sharply. "You, Akeba, will never see your daughter again if your skull is cloven in this tavern. And Conan, you know the dangers of what you intend. Could not another sword be of use?"

"Not that of a blundering soldier," Conan replied. His eyes were locked with those of the Turanian, blue and black alike as hard as iron. "His feet are made for marching, not the quiet of thieving."

"Three years," Akeba said, "I was a scout against the Ibarri mountain-tribes, yet I still have my life and my manhood. From the size of you, *you* look to be quiet as a bull."

"A scout?" the Cimmerian said thoughtfully. The man had some skill at quietness, then. Perhaps Sharak had a point. It was all too possible that he *could* use another blade. Besides, killing a soldier would make it near impossible for him to remain in Aghrapur.

Conan lowered himself slowly back to the bench, and Akeba followed. For a moment their eyes remained locked; then, as at a signal, each loosed his grip on his sword.

"Now that is settled," Sharak said, "there is the matter of oaths to bind us all together in this enterprise."

"Us?" Akeba said with a questioning look.

Conan shook his head. "I still do not know if this soldier is coming with me or not, but I *do* know that you are not. Find yourself a wench who wants her stars read. I can recommend one here, if you mind not a head full of beads."

"Who will watch your horses," Sharak asked simply, "while you two heroes are being heroic inside the compound? Besides, Conan, I told you I've never had an adventure. At my age, this may be my last chance. And I do have this." He brandished his walking staff. "It could be useful."

Akeba frowned. "It's a stick." He looked at Conan.

"The thing has magical powers," the Cimmerian said, and dropped his eyelid.

After a moment the dark man smiled faintly. "As you say." His face grew serious. "As to the compound, I would have this thing done quickly."

"Tonight," Conan said. "I, too, want it done."

"The oaths," Sharak chimed in. "Let us not forget the oaths."

The three men put their heads together.

VII

eaving Sharak beneath a tree to mind the horses, Conan and Akeba set out through the night in a crouching run for the alabaster-walled compound of the Cult of Doom. Within those walls ivory towers thrust into the night, and golden-finialed purple domes were one with the dark amethystine sky. Scudding clouds cast shifting moon-lit shadows, and the two men were but two shades in the night. A thousand paces distant, the Vilayet Sea beat itself to white froth against the rocky shore.

At the base of the wall they quickly unlimbered the coiled ropes they carried across their shoulders. Twin grapnels, well padded with cloth, hurtled into the air, caught atop the wall with muffled clatters.

Massive arms and shoulders drew Conan upward with the agility of a great ape. At the top of the wall he paused, feeling along that hard, smooth surface. Akeba scrambled up beside him and, without pausing to check the top of the wall, clambered over. Conan's dismay that the other had done so—it was the error of a greenling thief—was tempered by the fact that there were no shards of pottery and broken stone set in the wall to rip the flesh of the unwary.

Conan pulled himself over the wall and, holding his grapnel well out to one side, let himself fall. He took the shock of the drop by tucking a shoulder under and rolling, coming to his feet smoothly. He was in a landscaped garden, exotic shrubs and trees seemingly given life by the moving shadows. Akeba was hastily coiling his rope.

"Remember," Conan said, "we meet at the base of the tallest tower in the compound."

"I remember," Akeba muttered.

There had been more than a little discussion over which man's task was to be carried out first. Akeba feared that, in stealing the necklace, Conan might rouse guards, while Conan was sure the sergeant's daughter could not be rescued without raising an alarm. The women's quarters were certain to be guarded, while Emilio had intimated that the necklace was unguarded. It had been Sharak who effected a compromise: Conan would go after the necklace while Akeba located the women's quarters. Then they would meet and together solve the problem of getting Zorelle out. Agreement had been more reluctant on Akeba's part than on Conan's. The Cimmerian was not certain he needed a companion on this venture, for all Sharak's urging.

With a last doubtful glance at the Turanian, Conan hurried away, his pantherine stride carrying him swiftly through the night. He remembered well Emilio's description of the necklace's location. The topmost chamber of the lone tower in a garden on the east side of the compound. They had entered over the east wall, and looming out of the night ahead was a tower, square and tall. He slowed to a walk, approaching it with silent care. A short distance away he stopped. There was enough light from the moon, barely, with which to see.

Of smooth greenstone, surrounded by a walk of dark tiles some seven or eight paces in width, the tower had no openings save an arch at ground level and a balcony around its top. The onion-dome roof glittered beneath the moon as if set with gems.

It was the lack of guards that worried the Cimmerian. True, the avowed purpose of the tower room was to teach the Cult's disciples the worthlessness of wealth, but nothing in Conan's near twenty years led him to believe than any sane man would leave wealth unwatched and unprotected by iron bars and locks.

The tower walls were polished, offering no crevices for fingers or toes, not even those of one familiar with the sheer cliffs of Cimmeria. He looked down. The tiles of the walk were scribed in an unusual pattern of tiny cross-hatches. Any one of them could be the trigger to a trap, letting onto pits filled with Kothian vipers or the deadly spiders of the Turanian steppes.

He had seen such before. Yet the place for that sort of device was before the archway. There a marble-laid path led toward the tower, stopping at the edge of the tiles. Kneeling, he examined the joining and smiled. The marble slab stood two fingerwidths higher than the tiles, and its lip was shiny, as if something were often rubbed against it. And from that low angle he could see two lines of wear, spaced at the width of the marble, stretching toward the tower arch. Here was located the trap—it did not matter what it was—and something was laid atop these tiles to make a way for the members of the cult to enter the tower. So much, he thought, for the worthlessness of wealth.

Cocking an ear for sounds elsewhere in the compound, he strode down the marble walk away from the tower, counting his steps. Silence. At least Akeba had raised no alarm as yet. At forty paces he turned around. The tower he could see dimly, but the arch that would be his target was no more than a smudge at its base. Hastily he refastened his sword belt around his chest and over one shoulder, so the nubby leather sheath hung down his back. It would not do to have the blade tangle in his feet at the wrong time.

With a deep breath he began to run, legs driving, broad chest heaving like a bellows in the effort for speed and more speed. The width of tiles was clear, then the archway. Almost on the instant he felt the edge of the marble beneath his boot and sprang, flying through the night air. With a thump his toes landed just inside the arch. He tottered on the edge of toppling back, fingers scrabbling for the rim of the archway. For an infinite moment he hung poised to drop into the trap. Then, slowly, he drew himself into the tower.

Laughing softly, he drew his sword and moved deeper inside. Try to keep a Cimmerian out, he thought.

On the ground level of the tower were several rooms, but the doors to all of them were locked. Still, what he wanted was above, and a spiraling stone stair led up from a central antechamber. Sword questing ahead, he climbed careful step by careful step. The first trap did not mean there were not others. Without incident, though, he came to the top of the stair and to the chamber atop the tower.

Hammered silver on the domed roof reflected and magnified the moonlight, turning it into palely useful illumination that filtered into the chamber. Half-a-dozen archways, worked in delicate filigree, let onto the narrow-railed balcony. Open cabinets, lacquered over gilded scrollwork, stood scattered about the mosaicked floor, displaying priceless jewels on velvet cushions. A crown of rubies and pearls, fit for any king. A single emerald as big as a man's fist. A score of finger-long matched sapphires, carved in erotic figures. More and more till the eyes of a mendicant priest oath-sworn to poverty would have lit with greed.

And there was the necklace, with its thirteen flawless rubies glowing darkly in the silvery light. Conan appraised it with a practiced eye before slipping it into his pouch. Perhaps it *would* make the woman who wore it irresistible to men, but then, most women seemed to believe gems of great-enough cost would do that, magic or no. This Davinia would get a bargain for her hundred gold pieces, in any case. His gaze ran around the room once more. Here was treasure worth ten thousand gold pieces. Ten times ten thousand. Ferian had been right; he could carry enough from this place to make him a rich man.

With difficulty but no regret, he put the thought firmly aside. He had turned from thieving, and what he did this night made no difference in that. But if he looted this chamber of all he could carry, he knew it would not be so easy to leave that life again. And he did not doubt that whatever gold he got for these things would last no longer than the gold he had received for other thefts. Such coin never stayed long.

"I hoped you would not come."

Conan spun, sword raised, then lowered it with a grin. "Emilio! I thought you were dead, man. You can have this Mitra-accursed necklace, and be welcome to it."

The tall Corinthian came the rest of the way up the stairs into the tower-top chamber. He had sword and dagger in hand. "'Tis a fit punishment, do you not think, guarding forever that which I intended to steal?"

Hair stirred on the back of Conan's neck. "You are ensorceled?"

"I am dead," Emilio replied, and lunged.

Conan dodged aside, and the other's blade passed him to shatter the treasure-laden shelves of a cabinet. Snake-like, Emilio whirled after him, but he circled to keep cabinets between them.

"What foolishness is this you speak?" he demanded. "I see a man before me, not a shade."

Emilio's laugh was hollow. "I was commanded to kill all who came to this tower in the night, but naught was said against speaking." He continued to move in slow deadliness; Conan moved the other way, keeping a lacquered cabinet between them. "I was taken in this very chamber, with the necklace in my hand. So near did I come. For my pains a hollow poniard was thrust into my chest. I watched my heart's blood pump into a bowl, Cimmerian."

"Crom," Conan muttered, tightening his grip on his sword. To kill a friend was ill, even one spell-caught and commanded to slay, yet to kill was better than to die at that friend's hands.

"Jhandar, whom they call Great Lord, took life from me," Emilio continued, neither speeding nor slowing his advance. "Having taken it, he forced some part of it back into this body that once was mine." His face twisted quizzically. "And this creature that once was Emilio the Corinthian must obey. It must . . . obey."

Abruptly Emilio's foot lashed out against the lacquered cabinet. In a crash of snapping wood it toppled toward the young Cimmerian. Conan leaped back, and Emilio charged, boots splintering delicate workmanship, carelessly scattering priceless gems.

Conan's blade flashed upward, striking sparks from the other's descending steel. Dagger darting to slide beneath Conan's ribs, the Corinthian's wrist slapped into his hand and was seized in an iron grip. Locked chest to chest they staggered out onto the balcony. Conan's knee rose, smashing into Emilio's crotch, but the reanimated corpse merely grunted. Risking freeing the Corinthian's sword, Conan struck with his hilt into Emilio's face. Now the other man fell back. Conan's blade slashed the front of his old friend's tunic, and Emilio leaped back again. Abruptly the backs of his legs struck the railing, and for an instant he hung there, arms waving desperately for balance. And then he was gone, without a cry. A sickening thud came from below.

Swallowing hard, Conan stepped to the rail and looked toward a ground that seemed all flitting shadows. He could make out no detail, but that Emilio had lived through the fall—if, indeed, he had lived before he fell—was beyond his belief. It was ill to kill a friend, no matter the need. There would be no luck in it.

Resheathing his sword, he hurried down the stairs. At the archway he stopped. Emilio's body lay sprawled just outside, and its fall had triggered the trap. From the archway to the marble path, thin metal spikes the length of a man's forearm had thrust up through the tiles. Four of them transfixed the Corinthian.

"Take a pull on the Hellhorn for me," Conan muttered.

But there was still Akeba to meet, and no time for mourning. Quickly he picked his way between the spikes and set out at a dead run for the landmark they had chosen, the tallest tower in the compound, its high golden dome well visible even by moonlight.

Abruptly a woman's scream pierced the night, and was cut off just as suddenly. With an oath Conan drew his sword and redoubled his speed. That cry had come from the direction of the gold-topped tower.

Deep in the compound a gong sounded its brazen alarm, then a second and a third. Distant shouts rose, and torches flared to life.

Conan dashed into the shadows at the base of the tower, and stopped to stare in amazement. Akeba was there, holding a slender sable-skinned beauty in saffron robes, one arm pinning her arms, his free hand covering her mouth. Large dark eyes glared fiercely at him from above the soldier's fingers.

"This is your daughter?" Conan asked, and Akeba nodded, an excited smile splitting his face.

"Zorelle. I could not believe my luck. She was fetching water to the women's quarters. No one saw me."

The shouts had grown louder, and the torches now seemed to rival the stars in number.

"That does not seem to matter, at the moment," Conan said drily. "It will be no easy task to remove ourselves from this place, much less a girl who doesn't seem to want to go."

"I am taking her out of here," the Turanian replied, his voice hard.

"I did not suggest otherwise." He would not leave any woman to the mercies of Emilio's destroyer. "But we must . . . hsst!" He motioned for silence.

An atavistic instinct rooted deep inside the Cimmerian shouted that he was being watched by inimical eyes, eyes that drew closer by the moment. But his own gaze saw nothing but deceptively shifting shadows. No. One shadow resolved itself into a man in black robes. Even after Conan was certain, though, he found it difficult to keep his eyes on that dim figure. There was something about it that seemed to prevent the eye from focusing on it. The hairs on his neck rose. There was sorcery of a kind here, sorcery most foul and unnatural throughout this place.

"Mitra!" Akeba swore suddenly, jerking his hand from his daughter's mouth. "She bit me!"

Twisting in his loosened grasp, she raked at his face with her nails. At the distinct disadvantage of struggling with his own daughter, he attempted to keep his grip on her while avoiding being blinded. Under the circumstances it was an unequal fight. In an instant she was free and running. And screaming.

"Help! Outsiders! They are trying to take me! Help!"

"Zorelle!" Akeba shouted, and ran after her.

"Zandru's Hells!" Conan shouted, and followed.

Of a sudden the black-robed man was before the girl. Gasping, she recoiled.

The strange figure's hand reached out, perhaps to brush against her face. Her words stopped on the instant, and she dropped as if her bones had melted.

"Zorelle!" The scream from Akeba held all the anguish that could be wrung from a man's throat.

Primitive instinct, primed now, reared again in Conan. Diving, he caught Akeba about the waist and pulled him to the ground. The air hummed as if a thousand hornets had been loosed. Arrows sliced through the space where they had stood, toward the man in black. And before Conan's astounded gaze the man, hands darting like lightning, knocked two shafts aside, seized two more from the air, then seemed to slide between the rest and disappear.

Close behind their arrows came half-a-score Hyrkanians, waving short horn bows and curved yataghans as they ran. Two veered toward Conan and Akeba, but another shouted gutturally, "No! Leave them! 'Tis Baalsham we want!" The squat Hyrkanians ran on into the night.

Shaking his head, Conan got slowly to his feet. He had no notion what was happening, and was, in fact, not sure that he wanted to know. Best he got on about his business and left the rest to those already involved. Screams had been added to the shouts in the distance, and the pounding of hundreds of panic-stricken feet. Fire stained the sky as a building exploded in flame.

Akeba crawled on hands and knees to his daughter. Cradling her in his arms, he rocked back and forth, tears streaming down his flat cheeks. "She is dead, Cimmerian," he whispered. "He but touched her, yet she. . . ."

"Bring your daughter," Conan told him, "and let us go. We have no part in what else happens here this night."

The Turanian lowered Zorelle carefully, drew his tulwar and examined the blade. "I have blood to avenge, a man to kill." His voice was quiet, but hard.

"Revenge takes a cool head and a cold heart," Conan replied. "Yours are both filled with heat. Remain, and you will die, and likely never see the man who killed her."

Akeba twisted to face the Cimmerian, his black eyes coals in a furnace. "I want blood, barbar," he said hoarsely. "If need be, I will begin with yours."

"Will you leave Zorelle for the worms and the ravens, then?"

Akeba squeezed his eyes shut and sucked in a long, hissing breath. Slowly he returned his blade to its sheath and, stooping, gathered his daughter in his arms. When he straightened his face and voice were without expression. "Let us be gone from this accursed place, Cimmerian."

A score of saffron-robed men and women appeared out of the dark and fled past as if terror driven. None glanced at the two men, one holding a girl's body in his arms.

Twice more as they headed for the wall they saw clusters of cult members, running mindlessly. Behind them the shouts and screams had become a solid wave of sound. Two fires now licked at the sky.

They ran into the bushes near where they had crossed the wall, and, like a covey of quail, cult members burst from hiding. Some fled shrieking; others tried to dash past the two men, almost trampling them.

Conan cuffed a pair of shaven-headed men aside and shouted, "Go Akeba! Take her on!" He knocked another man sprawling, seized a woman to toss her aside . . . and stopped. It was Yasbet.

"You!" she shouted.

Without pausing, Conan threw her over his shoulder and scrambled on, scattering the few who remained to try to hinder him. Yasbet's feet fluttered in futile kicking, and her small fists pounded at his broad back.

"Let me down!" she screamed. "You have no right! Loose me!" They reached the wall; he let her down. She stared at him with the haughtiness of a dowager queen. "I will forget this if you go now. And for the kindness you did me earlier, I'll not tell—" She broke off with a shriek as he bent to cut a strip from her robe with his dagger. In a trice her hands were bound behind her, and before she could more than begin another protest he added a gag and a hobble between her ankles.

Akeba had taken care of the grapnels. Two ropes dangled from the top of the wall. "Who is she?" he asked, jerking his head toward Yasbet.

"Another wench who should not be left to this cult," Conan replied. "Climb up. I'll attend to your daughter so you can draw her after you."

The Turanian hesitated, then said, "The live girl first. There may not be time for both." Without waiting for a reply he scrambled up one of the ropes.

Despite her struggles, Conan fastened the end of the rope about Yasbet beneath her arms. In moments her muffled squeals were rising into the air. Hurriedly he did the same to Zorelle's body with the other rope. As he was pulled up, he waited, watching and listening for Hyrkanians, for cult members, for almost anything, considering the madness of the night. He listened and waited. And waited. Akeba had to climb down on the outside, he knew, and free one of the girls before he could return atop the wall and lower a rope to Conan, but it seemed to be taking a very long time.

The rope end slapped the wall in front of his face, and he could not stop a sigh of relief. At the top of the wall he found himself face to face with Akeba. "For a time there," he said, "I almost thought you'd left me."

"For a time," Akeba replied flatly, "on the ground outside with my daughter, I almost did."

Conan nodded, and said only, "Let us go while we can."

Dropping to the ground they picked up the women—Conan Yasbet and Akeba Zorelle—and ran for Sharak and the horses. The cacophony of conflict still rose within the compound behind them.

VIII

The red glare of fire in the night glinted on Jhandar's face as he turned from the window. The shouts of initiates carrying water to fight the blazes rang through the compound, but one building, at least, was too far gone in flame to be saved.

"Well?" he demanded.

Che Fan and Suitai exchanged glances before the first-named spoke. "They were Hyrkanians, Great Lord."

The three men stood in the antechamber to Jhandar's apartments. The austerity of decoration that the necromancer invoked for his garb was continued here. Low, unadorned couches dotted the floor that was, if marble, at least plain and bare of rugs, as the walls were bare of tapestries and hangings.

"I know they were Hyrkanians!" Jhandar snarled. "I could hear them shouting, 'Death to Baalsham!' Never did I think to hear that name again."

"No, Great Lord."

"How many were there?"

"Two score, Great Lord. Perhaps three."

"Three score," Jhandar whispered. "And how many yet live?"

"No more than a handful, Great Lord," Che Fan replied. "Well over a score perished."

"Then perhaps a score still live to haunt me," Jhandar said pensively. "They must be found. There will be work for the two of you, then, you may be sure."

"Great Lord," Suitai said, "there were others in the compound tonight. Not Hyrkanians. One wore the helmet of a Turanian soldier. The other was a tall man, pale of skin."

"A barbarian?" Jhandar asked sharply. "With blue eyes?"

"Blue eyes?" Suitai asked incredulously, then recovered himself. "It was dark, Great Lord, and with the fighting I could not draw near enough to see.

But they robbed the Tower of Contemplation, taking the necklace of thirteen rubies and slaying the thief you set there as guard." He hesitated. "And they killed one of the initiates, Great Lord. The girl Zorelle."

The necromancer made a dismissive gesture. He had marked the girl for his bed, in time, but her life or death was unimportant. But the necklace, now. The thief had come for that same bit of jewelry. There had to be a link there.

"Wait here," he snarled.

Carefully shutting doors behind him, he made his way to the column-lined outer hall, where waited half a score of the Chosen, Zephran among them. They thought they stood as his bodyguard, though either of the Khitan assassins could have killed all ten without effort. They bowed as he appeared. He motioned to Zephran, who approached, bowing again.

"Go to the Tower of Contemplation," Jhandar commanded. "There you will find the body of the one I set to guard that place. Bring the body to the Chamber of Summoning."

"At once, Great Lord." But Zephran did not move. He wished to ingratiate himself with the Great Lord Jhandar. "It was the Hyrkanians, Great Lord. Those I spoke to you about, I have no doubt."

Jhandar's cheek twitched, but otherwise his face was expressionless. "You knew there were Hyrkanians in Aghrapur?" he said quietly.

"Yes, Great Lord." Sweat broke out on Zephran's forehead. Suddenly he was no longer certain it had been a good idea to speak. "Those . . . those I spoke to you of. Surely you remember, Great Lord?"

"Bring the body," Jhandar replied.

Zephran bowed low. When he straightened the necromancer was gone.

In his antechamber Jhandar massaged his temples as he paced, momentarily ignoring the Khitans. The fool had known of the Hyrkanians and yet said nothing! Of course, he had set no watch for them, warned none of the Chosen to report their appearance. To guard against them was to expect them to come, and did he expect them to come, then they would. It was the way of such things. The proof was in himself. He had not been able to destroy his own belief that they would appear. And they had come.

Carefully Jhandar gathered the powders and implements he would need. Dawn was but a few hours distant, now, and in the light of the sun he had few abilities beyond those of other mortals. He could not call on the Power at all while the sun shone. He could not summon the spirit manifestations then, though commands previously given still held, of course. Perhaps he should summon them now, set them to find the Hyrkanians. No. What he intended would sap much of his strength, could it be done at all. He was not certain he would be physically able to perform both rituals, and what he intended was more important. He knew something of the Hyrkanians, nothing of the tall barbarian. The unknown threat was always more dangerous than the known.

He motioned the Khitans to follow. A sliding stone panel in the wall let into a secret passage, dim and narrow, that led down to the chamber containing the circle of barren earth. The Chamber of Summoning.

Quickly the corpse was brought to him there, as if Zephran thought to mitigate his transgressions with haste, and arranged by the Khitans under Jhandar's direction, spreadeagled in the center of the circle. At a word the Chosen withdrew, while the mage studied on what he was about. He had never done the like before, and he knew no rituals to guide him. There was no blood to manifest the spirit of the man; there had been no blood in that body since its first death. After that there had been a tenuous connection between that spirit and the body, a connection enforced by his magic, but the second death, at the tower, had severed even that. Still, what he intended must be attempted.

While the Khitans watched Jhandar chose three pillars, spaced equidistantly around the circle. On the first he chalked the ideogram for death, and over it that for life. On the second, the ideogram for infinity covered that of nullity. And on the last, order covered chaos.

Spreading his arms, he began to chant, words with meanings lost in the mists of time ringing from the walls. Almost immediately he could feel the surge of Power, and the near uncontrollability of it. His choice of symbols formed a dissonance, and if inchoate Power could know fury, then there was fury in the Power that flowed through Jhandar's bones.

Silver-flecked blue mist coalesced within the circle, roiling, swirling away from the posts he had marked. He willed it not to be so, and felt the resistance ripping at his marrow. Agony most torturous and exquisite. It would be as he willed. It would be. Through a red haze of pain he chanted.

Slowly the mists shifted toward, rather than away from, those three truncated pillars, touching them, then rushing toward them. Suddenly there was a snap, as from a spark leaping from a fingertip on a cold morning, but ten thousand times louder, and bars of silver-blue light, as bright as the sun, linked the posts. Chaos, forced into a triangle, the perfect shape, three sides, three points—three, the perfect number of power. Perfect order forced on ultimate disorder. Anathema, and anathema redoubled. And from that anathema, from that perversion of Chaos, welled such Power that Jhandar felt at any moment he would rise and float in the air. Sweat rolled down his body, plastering his saffron robes to his back and chest.

"You who called yourself Emilio the Corinthian," Jhandar intoned. "I summon you back to this clay that was you. By the powers of Chaos enchained, and the powers of three, I summon you. I summon you. I summon you."

The triangle of light flared, and within the circle the head of Emilio's corpse rolled to one side. The mouth worked raggedly. "Noooo!" it moaned.

Jhandar smiled. "Speak, I command you! Speak, and speak true! You came to steal a necklace of rubies?"

"Yes." The word was a pain-filled hiss.

"Why?"

"For . . . Da-vin-ia."

"For a woman? Who is she?"

"Mis-tress . . . of . . . Mun-da-ra . . . Khan."

The mage frowned. He had tried for some time to 'obtain' one of General Mundara Khan's servants, so far without success. The man stood but a short distance from the throne. Could he be taking an interest in Jhandar, as the necromancer took in him? Impossible.

"Do you know a tall barbarian?" he demanded. "A man with pale skin and blue eyes who would also try to steal that necklace."

"Co-nan," came the moaned reply. The head of the corpse twitched and moved.

Jhandar felt excitement rising in him. "Where can I find this Conan?"

"Noooo!" The head rolled again, and one arm jerked.

"Speak, I command!" The triangle of chaotic light grew brighter, but no sound came from the body.

"Speak!" Brighter.

"Speak!" Brighter.

"Speak! I command you to speak!" Brighter, and brighter still.

"I . . . am . . . a maaan!"

As the wail came, the light suddenly flared, crackling like lightning and wildfire together. Jhandar staggered back, hands thrown up to shield his eyes. Then the light was gone, and the Power, and the body. Only a wisp of oily black smoke drifting toward the ceiling remained.

"Freeee. . . ." The lone, thin word dissipated with the smoke, and naught remained of Emilio the Corinthian.

Weariness rolled into Jhandar's bones as the Power left. Despite himself, he sagged and nearly fell. There would be no summoning of spirit manifestations this night. That meant a full day must pass before he could send those incorporeal minions searching for the Hyrkanians, and for the barbarian. Conan. A strange name. But there was the woman, Davinia. There could be use in her, both for finding the barbarian and beyond. General Mundara Khan's mistress.

With a tired hand he motioned the Khitans to help him to his chambers.

IX

The palace of Mundara Khan was of gray marble and granite, relieved by ornate gardens from which rose towers of ivory and porphyry, while alabaster domes whitely threw back the sun. The guards who stood before its gates with drawn tulwars were more ceremonial than otherwise, for an attack on the residence of the great General Mundara Khan was as unlikely as one on the Royal Palace of King Yildiz. But the guards were numerous enough to cause trouble, especially if a handsome young man should announce that he had come to see the general's mistress.

Conan had no intention of entering by a guarded gate, though. Finding a tall, spreading tree near the garden wall, well out of the guards' sight, he pulled himself up into its thick branches. One, as thick as his leg, ran straight toward the garden, but it was cut cleanly, a bit higher than the wall but well short of it. The top of *this* wall was indeed set with razor shards of obsidian. Within the garden, slate walks and paths of red brick wound through the landscaping, and in the garden's center was a small round outbuilding of citron marble, cupolaed and columned, gossamer hangings stirring in the breeze at its windows and archways.

Arms held out to either side for balance, he ran along the limb, leaped, and dropped lightly inside the garden.

Moving carefully, eyes watchful for guards or servants, he hurried to the yellow structure. It was of two stories, the ground level walled about entirely with gauze-hung archways. Within those arches, the glazed white tiles of the floor were covered with silken pillows and rare Azerjani rugs. Face down on a couch in the center of the room lay a woman, her pale, generous curves completely bare save for the long golden hair that spilled across her shoulders. Above her a wheel of white ostrich plumes revolved near the ceiling, a strap of leather disappearing through a hole above.

Conan swore to himself. A servant must be occupying the floor above, to turn the crank that in turn rotated the plumes. Still, he would not turn back. His calloused hand moved aside delicate hangings, and he entered.

For a time he stood enjoying his view of her, a woman of satiny rounded places. "Be not alarmed, Davinia," he said at last.

With a yelp of surprise the blonde rolled from the couch, long legs flashing, and snatched up a length of pale blue silk that she clutched across her breasts. The nearly transparent silk covered her ineffectually to the ankles.

"Who are you?" she demanded furiously. High cheekbones gave her face a vulpine cast.

"I am called Conan. I come in the place of Emilio the Corinthian."

Fury fading into consternation, she wet her full lips hesitantly. "I know no one of that name. If you come from Mundara Khan, tell him his suspicions are—"

"Then you do not know this, either," Conan said, fishing the ruby necklace from his pouch and dangling its gold-mounted length from his fingertips. He chuckled to watch her face change again, deep blue eyes widening in shock, mouth working wordlessly.

"How . . . ," she fumbled. "Where. . . ." Her voice dropped to a whisper. "Where is Emilio?"

"Dead," he said harshly.

She seemed neither surprised nor dismayed. "Did you kill him?"

"No," he replied with only partial untruth. Emilio's true death had come before their meeting in the tower. "But he is dead, and I have brought you the necklace you want."

"And what do you wish in return?" Her voice was suddenly warm honey, and her arm holding the strip of blue had lowered until pink nipples peered at him, seeming nestled in the silk. He did not think it an accident.

Smiling inside, Conan replied, "Emilio spoke of one hundred pieces of gold."

"Gold." Her tinkling laughter dismissed gold as trivial. Rounded hips swaying, she moved closer. Then, suddenly, she was pressed tightly against his chest. In some fashion the silk had disappeared. "There are many things of more interest to a man like you than gold," she breathed, snaking an arm around his neck. "Of much more interest."

"What of he who turns the fan?" he asked.

"He has no tongue to tell what he hears," she murmured. "And no one will enter without being commanded, except Renda, my tirewoman, who is faithful to me."

"Mundara Khan?"

"Is far from the city for two nights. Can you only ask questions, barbarian?"

She tried to pull his head down for a kiss, but he lifted her, kissing her instead of being kissed. When she moaned softly deep in her throat, he let her drop.

"What," she began as her heels thudded to the floor, but he spun her about, and his hard palm flattened her buttocks. With a shrill squeal she tumbled head over heels among the cushions, long, bare legs windmilling in the air.

"The gold first, Davinia," he laughed.

Struggling to her knees, she threw a cushion at his head. "Gold?" she spat. "I'll summon the guards and—"

"—And never see the necklace again," he finished for her. She frowned fretfully. "Either I will escape, taking it with me, or the guards will take me, and the necklace, to Mundara Khan. He will be interested to find his leman is receiving jewelry from such as me. You did say he was suspicious, did you not?"

"Erlik blast your eyes!" Her eyes were blue fire, but he met them coolly.

"The gold, Davinia."

She glared at him a time longer, then, muttering to herself, crawled over the cushions. Carefully keeping her back to him she lifted a tile set in the floor and rummaged beneath.

She need not have bothered, he thought. With the view he had as she knelt there, he would not have looked away to survey the treasure rooms of King Yildiz.

Finally she replaced the tile and turned to toss a bulging purse before him. It clanked heavily when it hit the floor. "There," she snarled. "Leave the necklace and go."

That was an end to it. Or *almost*, he thought. He had the gold—the amount did not matter—the tellings of Sharak's star-charts had been fulfilled. But the woman had thought to use him, as she had tried to use Emilio. She had threatened him. The pride that only a young man knows drove him now.

"Count it," he demanded. She stared at him in disbelief, but he thrust a finger at the purse. "Count it. It would pain me, and you, to discover you'd given me short weight."

"May the worms consume your manhood," she cried, but she made her way to the purse and emptied it, rondels of gold ringing and spinning on the white tiles. "One. Two. Three. . . ." As she counted each coin she thrust it back into the small sack, as viciously as though each coin was a dagger that she was driving into his heart. Her acid eyes remained on his face. ". . . . One hundred," she said at last. Tying the cords at the mouth of the purse, she hurled it at him.

He caught the gold-filled bag easily in one hand, and tossed the necklace to her. She clutched it to her breasts and backed away, still on her knees, eyeing him warily.

He saw no shimmers of magic when she touched the necklace, but by all the gods she was a bit of flesh to dry a man's mouth and thicken his throat.

He weighed the purse in his hand. "To feel this," he said, "no one would suspect that you counted five coins twice."

"It is . . . possible I made an error," she said, still moving away. "An it is so, I'll give you the five gold pieces more."

Conan dropped the purse on the floor, unbuckled his sword belt and let it fall atop the gold.

"What are you doing?" she asked doubtfully.

"'Tis a heavy price to pay for a wench," he replied, "but as you do not want to pay what you agreed, I'll take the rest in your stock in trade."

A strangled squawk rose from her throat, and she tried to scramble away. He caught her easily, scooping her up in his muscular arms. She attempted to fend him off, but he pulled her to him as easily as if she had not tried at all. Her hands were caught inside the circle of his arms, her full breasts flattened against his broad chest.

"Think you," she gasped, "that I'll lie with you after what has passed here? After you've struck me, called me strumpet, manhandled me. . . ." Her angry words gave way to protesting splutters.

"Mundara Khan is old," Conan said softly. He trailed one finger down her spine to the swell that began her buttocks. "And fat." He brought the finger up to toy with a strand of golden hair that lay on her cheek. "And he often leaves you alone, as now." She sighed, and softened against him. Blue eyes peered into blue eyes, and he said quietly, "Speak, and I will go. Do you want me to go?"

Wordlessly she shook her head.

Smiling, Conan laid her on the couch.

X

onan was still smiling when he strolled into the Blue Bull much later in the day. Davinia had been *very* lonely indeed. He knew it was madness to dally with the mistress of a general, but he knew his own weakness where women were concerned, too. He was beginning to hope the army took Mundara Khan from Aghrapur often.

The common room was half-filled with the usual crowd of sailors, laborers and cutpurses. Sharak and Akeba shared a table in one corner, conversing with their heads close together, but instead of joining them, Conan went to the bar.

Ferian greeted him with a scowl, and began scrubbing the bar top even faster than before. "I've nothing for you yet, Cimmerian. And I want you to get that wench out of here."

"Is she still secured in my room?" Conan demanded. Yasbet had become no more reasonable about being rescued for finding herself in a waterfront tavern.

"She's there," the innkeeper said sourly, "but I'd sacrifice in every temple in the city if she disappeared. She near screamed the roof off not a glass gone. Thank all the gods she's been quiet since. That's no trull or doxie, Cimmerian. Men are impaled for holding her sort against their will."

"I'll see to her," Conan replied in a soothing tone. "You keep your eyes and ears open."

He hurried upstairs, listening to what suddenly seemed an ominous silence from his room. The latch-cord on his door was still tied tightly to a stout stick. A man might break the cord and lift the latch inside, but for Yasbet it should have been as good as an iron lock. Unless she had managed to wriggle through the window. Surely that small opening was too narrow even for her, but. . . . Muttering oaths beneath his breath, Conan unfastened the cord and rushed in.

A clay mug, hurled by Yasbet's hand, shattered against the door beside his head. He ducked beneath the pewter basin that followed and caught her around the waist. It was difficult to ignore what a pleasant armful she made, even while her small fists pounded at his head and shoulders. He caught her wrists, forcing them behind her back and holding them there with one hand.

"What's gotten into you, girl? Did that cult addle your wits?"

"Addle my . . . !" She quivered with suppressed anger. "They thought I had worth. And they treated me well. You brought me here bound across a horse and imprisoned me without so much as word. Then you went off to see that strumpet."

"Strumpet? What are you talking about?"

"Davinia." She growled the name. "Isn't that what she's called? That old man—Sharak?—came up to try to quiet me. He told me you'd gone to see this . . . woman. And you have the same smug look on your face that my father wears when he's just visited his zenana."

Mentally Conan called down several afflictions, all of them painful, on Sharak's head. Aloud he said, "Why should you care if I visit twenty women? Twice now I've saved your fool life, but there's naught between us."

"I did not say there was," she said stoutly, but her shoulders sagged. Cautiously he released her wrists, and she sat down dejectedly on the roughly built bed, no more than straw ticking covered with a coarse blanket, with her hands folded in her lap. "You saved my life once," she muttered. "Perhaps. But this other was naught but kidnap."

"You did not see what I saw in that place, Yasbet. There was sorcery there, and evil."

"Sorcery!" She frowned at him, then shook her head. "No, you lie to try to stop me from returning."

He muttered under his breath, then asked, "How did you end up with them? When you ran away from me I thought you were going home." He grinned in spite of himself. "You were going to climb over the garden wall."

"I did," she muttered, not meeting his eye. "Fatima caught me atop the wall and locked me in my room." She shifted her seat uncomfortably, and the remnants of an unpleasant memory flitted across her face.

Conan was suddenly willing to wager that locking her in her room was not all that the amah had done. Barely suppressing his chuckle, he said, "But that's no reason to run away to something like this cult."

"What do you know of it?" she demanded. "Women labor on an equal footing with men there, and can rise equally, as well. There are no rich or poor in the cult, either."

"But the cult itself is rich enough," he said drily. "I've seen some of its treasures."

"Because you went there to steal!"

"And I saw a man ensorceled to his death."

"Lies!" she cried, covering her ears with her palms. "You'll not stop me returning."

"I'll leave that to your father. You're going back to him if I have to leave you at his door bound hand and foot."

"You don't even know who he is," she said, and he had the impression that she just stopped herself from sticking her tongue out at him.

"I'll find out," he said with an air of finality.

As he got to his feet she caught his wrist in both of her hands. Her eyes were large with pleading. "Please, Conan, don't send me back to my father. He . . . he has said I am to be married. I know the man. I will be a wife, yes, honored and respected. And locked in his zenana with fifty other women."

He shook his head sympathetically, but said only, "Better that than the cult, girl."

He expected her to make a break for the door as he left, but she remained sitting on the bed. Retying the latch cord, he returned to the common room. Akeba and Sharak barely looked up when he took a stool at their table.

" . . . And so I tell you," Sharak said, tapping the table with a bony finger for emphasis, "that any attempt at direct confrontation will be disaster."

"What are you two carrying on about?" Conan asked.

"How we are to attack the Cult of Doom," Akeba replied shortly. His eyes bore the grim memory of the night before. "There must be a way to bring this Jhandar down." His face twisted with distaste. "I am told they call him Great Lord, as if he were a king."

"And the Khitan, of course," Sharak added. "But Jhandar—he is leader of the cult—must have given the man orders. His sort do not kill for pleasure, as a rule."

Conan was more than a little bewildered. "Khitan? His sort? You seem to have learned a great deal in the short time I've been gone."

"'Twas not such a short time," Sharak leered. "How was she?" At the look on Conan's face he hastily cleared his throat. "Yes. The Khitan. From Akeba's description of the man who . . . well, I'm sure he was from Khitai, and a member of what is called the Brotherhood of the Way. These men are assassins of great skill." A frown added new creases to his face. "But I still cannot understand what part the Hyrkanians played."

"I've never heard of any such Brotherhood," Conan said. "In truth, I no more than half believe Khitai exists."

"They were strange to me, also," Akeba said, "but the old man insists they are real. Whatever he is, though, I will kill him."

"Oh, they're real, all right," Sharak said. "By the time your years number twice what they do now, you'll begin to learn that more exists beneath the sky than you conceive in your wildest flights of fancy or darkest nightmares. The two of you must be careful with this Khitan. They of the Brotherhood of the Way are well versed in the most subtle poisons, and can slay with no more than a touch."

"That I believe," Akeba said hoarsely, "for I saw it." He tilted up his mug and did not lower it till it was dry.

"You, especially, must take care, Conan," the astrologer went on. "I know well how hot your head can be, and that fever can kill you. This assassin—"

Conan shook his head. "This matter of revenge is Akeba's, not mine."

Sharak squawked a protest. "But, Conan! Khitan assassins, revenge, Hyrkanians, and the gods alone know what else! How can we turn our backs on such an adventure?"

"You speak of learning," Conan told him. "You've still to learn that adventure means an empty belly, a cold place to sleep, and men wanting to put a dagger in your ribs. I find enough of that simply trying to live, without seeking for it."

"He is right," Akeba said, laying a hand on the old man's arm. "I lost a daughter to the Gravedigger's Guild this morn. I have reason to seek vengeance, but he has none."

"I still think it a poor reason to stand aside," Sharak grumbled.

Conan shared a smile with Akeba over the old man's head. In many ways Sharak qualified as a sage, but in some he was far younger than the Cimmerian.

"For now," Conan said, "I think what we must do is drink." Nothing would ever make Akeba forget, but at least the memory could be dulled until protecting scars had time to form. "Ferian!" he bellowed. "A pitcher of wine! No, a bucket!"

The innkeeper served them himself, a pitcher of deep red Solvanian in each hand and a mug for Conan under his arm. "I have no buckets," he said drily.

"This will do," Conan said, filling the mugs all around. "And take something up to my room for the girl to eat."

"Her food is extra," Ferian reminded him. Conan thought of the gold weighting his belt, and smiled. "You'll be paid." The tapster left, muttering to himself, and Conan turned his attention to the astrologer. "You, Sharak," he said sharply.

Sharak spluttered into his wine. "Me? What? I said nothing."

"You said too much," the Cimmerian said. "Why did you tell Yasbet I was going to see Davinia? And what *did* you tell her, anyway?"

"Nothing," the old man protested. "I was trying to quiet her yelling—
you said not to gag her—and I thought if she knew you were with another
woman she wouldn't be afraid you were going to ravish her. That's what
women are always afraid of. Erlik take it, Cimmerian, what was wrong with
that?"

"Just that she's jealous," Conan replied. "I've talked to her but twice and
never laid a hand on her, but she's jealous."

"Never laid a hand on her? You tied her like a sack of linen," Akeba said.

"It must be his charm," Sharak added, his face impossibly straight.

"'Tis funny enough for you two," Conan said darkly, "but I was near
brained with my own washbasin. She. . . ."

As rude laughter drowned Conan's next words, Ferian ran panting up to
the table.

"She's gone, Cimmerian!" the tavernkeeper gasped. "I swear by Mitra and
Dagon I don't believe she could squeeze through that window, but she did."

Conan sprang to his feet. "She cannot have been gone long. Akeba,
Sharak, will you help me look?"

Akeba nodded and rose, but Sharak grimaced. "An you don't want her,
Cimmerian, why not leave her for someone who does?"

Without bothering to reply Conan turned to go, Akeba with him. Sharak
followed hastily, hobbling with his staff.

Once in the street, the three men separated, and for near a turn of the
glass Conan found nothing but frustration. Hawkers of cheap perfumes
and peddlers of brass hairpins, fruit vendors, potters, street urchins—none
had seen a girl, so tall, large-breasted and beautiful, wearing saffron robes
and possibly running. All he found were blank looks and shaken heads. No
few of the strumpets suggested that he could find what he was looking for
with them, and some men cackled that they might keep the girl themselves,
did they find her, but their laughter faded to nervous sweating under his icy
blue gaze.

As he returned to the stone-fronted tavern, he met Akeba and Sharak. At
the Turanian's questioning glance he shook his head.

"Then she's done with," the astrologer said. "My throat needs cool wine
to soothe it after all the people I've questioned. I'll wager Ferian has given
our Solvanian to someone else."

The pitchers remained on the table where they had left them, but Conan
did not join in the drinking. Yasbet was not done with, not to his mind. He
found it strange that that should be so, but it was. Davinia was a woman to
make a man's blood boil; Yasbet had heated his no more than any other
pretty wench he saw in passing. But he had saved her life, twice, for all her
denials. In his belief that made him responsible for her. Then too, she

needed him to protect her. He was not blind to the attractions she had for a man.

He became aware of a Hyrkanian approaching the table, stooped and bowed of leg, his rancid smell preceding him. His coarse woolen trousers and sheepskin coat were even filthier than was usual for the nomads, if such was possible. Two paces short of them he stopped, his long skinny nose twitching as if prehensile and his black eyes on the Cimmerian. "We have your woman," he said gutturally, then straightened in alarm at the blaze of rage that lit Conan's face.

Conan was on his feet with broadsword half-drawn before he himself realized that he had moved.

Akeba grasped his arm. Not the sword arm; he was too old a campaigner for that. "Hear him out before you kill him," he urged.

"Talk!" Conan's voice grated like steel on bone.

"Tamur wants to talk with you," the Hyrkanian began slowly, but his words came faster as he went. "You fought with some of us, though, and Tamur does not think you will talk with us, so we take your woman until you talk. You will talk?"

"I'll talk," Conan growled. "And if she's been harmed, I'll kill, too. Now take me to her."

"Tonight," was the thick reply.

"Now!"

"One turn of the glass after the sun sets, someone will come for you." The Hyrkanian eyed Akeba and Sharak. "For you alone."

The last length of Conan's blade rasped from its worn shagreen sheath.

"No, Conan," Sharak urged. "Kill him, and you may never find her again."

"They would send another," Conan said, but after a moment he tossed his sword on the table. "Leave me before I change my mind," he told the nomad, and, scooping up one of the wine pitchers, tilted back his head in an effort to drain it. The Hyrkanian eyed him doubtfully, then trotted from the tavern.

XI

Davinia stretched luxuriously as gray-haired Renda's fingers worked perfumed oils into the smooth muscles of her back. There was magic in the plump woman's hands, and the blonde woman needed it. The big barbarian had been more than she bargained for. And he had intimated that he would return. He had not named time but that he would return was certain. Her knowledge of men told her so. Though it was but a few turns of the glass since Conan had left her, a tingling frisson of anticipation rippled through her at the thought of long hours more in his massive arms. To which gods, she wondered, should she offer sacrifices to keep Mundara Khan from the city longer?

A tap at the door of Davinia's tapestry-hung dressing chamber drew Renda's hands from her shoulders. With a petulant sigh, the sleek blonde waited impatiently until her tiring woman returned.

"Mistress," Renda said quietly, "there is a man to see you."

Careless of her nakedness, Davinia sat up. "The barbarian?" She confided everything in her tiring woman. Almost everything. Surely Conan would not dare enter through the gates and have himself announced, yet simply imagining the risk of it excited her more than she would have believed possible.

"No, mistress. It is Jhandar, Great Lord of the Cult of Doom."

Davinia blinked in surprise. She was dimly aware of the existence of the cult, though she did not concern herself unduly with matters of religion. Why would a cult leader come to her? Perhaps he would be amusing.

"A robe, Renda," she commanded, rising.

"Mistress, may I be so bold—"

"You may not. A robe."

She held out her arms as Renda fastened about her a red silken garment. Opaque, she noted. Renda always had more thought for her public reputation—and thus her safety—than did she.

Davinia made a grand entrance into the chamber where Jhandar waited. Slaves drew open the tall, ornately carved doors for her to sweep through. As the doors were closed she posed, one foot behind the other, one knee slightly bent, shoulders back. The man half-reclined on a couch among the columns. For just an instant her pose lasted, then she continued her advance, seeming to ignore the man while in fact she studied him. He no longer reclined, but rather sat on the edge of the couch.

"You are . . . different than I expected," he said hoarsely.

She permitted herself a brief smile, still not looking directly at him. Exactly the effect she had tried for.

He was not an unhandsome man, this Jhandar, she thought. The shaven head, however, rather spoiled his looks. And those ears gave him an unpleasantly animalistic countenance.

For the first time she faced him fully, lips carefully dampened with her tongue, eyes on his in an adoring caress. She wanted to giggle as she watched his breath quicken. Men were so easily manipulated. Except, perhaps, the barbarian. She hastily pushed aside the intruding thought. Carefully, she made sure of a breathy tone.

"You wish to see me . . . Jhandar, is it not?"

"Yes," he said slowly. Visibly he caught hold of himself. His breath still came rapidly, but there was a degree of control in his eyes. A degree. "Have you enjoyed the necklace, Davinia?"

"Necklace?"

"The ruby necklace. The one stolen from me only last night."

His voice was calm, so conversational that it took a moment for the meaning of his words to enter her. Shock raced through her. She wondered if her eyes were bulging. The necklace. How could she have been so stupid as not to make the connection the moment Jhandar was announced? It was that accursed barbarian. She seemed able to concentrate on little other than him.

"I have no idea of what you speak," she said, and was amazed at the steadiness of her voice. Inside she had turned to jelly.

"I wonder what Mundara Khan will say when he knows you have a stolen necklace. Perhaps he will inquire, forcefully, into who gave such a thing to his mistress."

"I bought—" She bit her tongue. He had flustered her. It was not supposed to happen that way. It was she who disconcerted men.

"I know that Emilio was your lover," he said quietly. "Has Conan taken his place there, too?"

"What do you want?" she whispered. Desperately she wished for a miracle to save her, to take him away.

"One piece of information," he replied. "Where may I find the barbarian called Conan?"

"I don't know," she lied automatically. The admission already made was one too many.

"A pity." He bit off the words, sending a shiver through her. "A very great pity."

Davinia searched for a way to deflect him from his purpose. All that passed through her mind, echoing and re-echoing, was 'a very great pity.'

"You may keep the necklace," he said suddenly.

She stared at him in surprise. He did not have complete control of himself still, she saw. He had continually to lick dry lips, and his eyes drank her in as a man in the desert drank water. "Thank you. I—"

"Wear it for me."

"Of course," she said. There was still a chance.

She left the room as regally as she had entered, but once outside, before the slaves had even closed the doors, she ran—despite the fact that to be languid at all times was one mark of a properly cared-for mistress.

Renda, arranging the pillows on Davinia's bed, leaped, as her mistress dashed into the chamber. "Mistress, you startled me!"

"Tell me what you know of this Jhandar," Davinia panted, as she dropped to her knees and began rooting in her jewel chest. "Quickly. Hurry!"

"Little is known, mistress," the plump tirewoman said hesitantly. "The cult professes—"

"Not that, Renda!" Tossing bits of jewelry left and right, she came up with the stolen necklace clutched in her fist. Despite herself, she breathed a sigh of relief. "Mitra be thanked. Tell me what the servants and slaves know, what their masters will not know for half a year more. Tell me!"

"Mistress, what has he. . . ." She broke off at Davinia's glare. "Jhandar is a powerful man in Turan, mistress. So it is whispered among the servants. And 'tis said he grows more powerful by the day. Some say the increase in the army was begun by him, by his telling certain men, who in turn convinced the king, that it should be so. Of course, it is well known that King Yildiz has long dreamed of empire. He would not have taken a great deal of telling."

"Still," Davinia murmured, "it is a display of power." Mundara Khan had never swayed the king for all his blood connections to the throne. "How does he accomplish it?"

"All men have secrets, mistress. Jhandar makes it his business to learn their secrets. To keep their secrets, most men will agree to any suggestion Jhandar makes." She paused. "Many believe he is a sorcerer. And the cult does have immense wealth."

"How immense?"

"It may rival that of King Yildiz."

A look of intense practicality firmed Davinia's face. This situation, which had seemed so frightening, might yet be turned to her advantage. "Fetch me a cloak," she commanded. "Quickly."

When she returned to Jhandar, surprise was plain on his countenance. A cloak of the fine scarlet wool swathed her from her neck to the ground.

"I do not understand," he said, anger mounting in his voice. "Where is the necklace?"

"I wear it for you." She opened the cloak, revealing the rubies caressing the upper slopes of her breasts. And save for the necklace, her sleek body was nude.

Only for an instant she held the cloak so. Even as he gasped, she pulled it closed. But then, rising on her toes, she spun so that her hips flashed whitely beneath flaring crimson. Around the room she danced, offering him brief tantalizing glimpses, but never so revealing as the first.

She finished on her knees before him, the scarlet cloth lowered to bare pale shoulders and the rubies nestled in her sweat-slick cleavage. Masking her triumph with care, she met his gaze. His face was flushed with desire. And now for the extra stroke.

"The man Conan," she said, "told me that he stays at the Blue Bull on the Street of the Lotus Dreamers, near the harbor."

For a moment he stared at her, uncomprehending; then he lurched to his feet. "I have him," he muttered excitedly. "An the Hyrkanians are found. . . ." All expression fled from his face as he regarded her. "Men have no use for lemans who lie," he said.

She replied with a smile. "A mistress owes absolute truth and obedience to her master." Or at least, she thought, a mistress should make him believe he had those things. "But you are not my master. Yet."

"I will take you with me," he said thickly, but she shook her head.

"The guards would never let me go. There is an old gate at the rear of the palace, however, unused and unguarded. I will be there with my serving woman one turn of the glass past dark tonight."

"Tonight. I will have men there to meet you." Abruptly he pulled her to her feet, kissing her brutally.

But not so well as Conan, she thought as he left. It was a pity the barbarian was to die. She had no doubt that was what Jhandar intended. But Jhandar was a step into her future; Conan was of the past. As she did with all things past, she put him out of her mind as if he had never existed.

XII

The common room of the Blue Bull grew crowded as the appointed hour drew near, raucous with the laughter of doxies and drunken men. Conan neither laughed nor drank, but rather sat watching the door with his two friends.

"When will the man come?" Sharak demanded of the air. "Surely the hour has passed."

Neither Conan nor Akeba answered, keeping their eyes fastened to the doorway. The Cimmerian's hand on his sword hilt tightened moment by long moment till, startlingly, his knuckles cracked.

The old astrologer flinched at the sound. "What adventure is this, sitting and waiting for Mitra knows how long while—"

"He is here," Akeba said quietly, but Conan was already getting to his feet.

The long-nosed Hyrkanian stood in the doorway beckoning to Conan, casting worried glances out into the night.

"Good luck be with you, Cimmerian," Akeba said quietly.

"And with you," Conan replied.

As he strode across the common room, he could hear the astrologer's querulous voice. "Why this talk of luck? They but wish to talk."

He did not listen for Akeba's answer, if answer there was. More than one man taken to a meeting in the night had never left it alive.

"Lead on," he told the Hyrkanian, and with one more suspicious look up and down the street the nomad did so.

Twilight had gone, and full night was upon the city. A pale moon hung like a silver coin placed low above the horizon. Music and laughter drifted from a score of taverns as they passed through yellow pools of light spilling from their doors, and occasionally they heard shouts of a fight over women or dice.

"Where are you taking me?" Conan asked.

The Hyrkanian did not answer. He chose turnings seemingly at random, and always he cast a wary eye behind.

"My friends will not follow," Conan told him. "I agreed to come alone."

"It is not your friends I fear," the Hyrkanian muttered, then tightened his jaws and looked sharply at the muscular youth. Thereafter he would not speak again.

Conan wondered briefly who or what it was the man *did* fear, but his own attention was split between watching for the ambush he might be entering and unraveling the twists and turns through which he was taken. When the fur-capped man motioned him through a darkened doorway and up a flight of wooden stairs, he was confident—and surprised—that for all the round-about way they had gone the Blue Bull was almost due north, no more than two streets away. It was well to be oriented in case the meeting came to a fight after all.

"You go first," Conan said. Expressionless, the nomad complied. Loose steps creaked alarmingly beneath his tread. Conan eased his sword in its scabbard, and mounted after him.

At the top of the stairs a door let into a room lit by two guttering tallow lamps set on a rickety table. The rancid smell of grease filled the room. Including his guide, half a score sheepskin-coated Hyrkanians watched him warily, though none put hand to weapon. One Conan recognized, the man with the scar across his cheek, he over whose head Emilio had broken the wine jar.

"I am called Tamur," Scarface said. "You are Conan?" With his guttural accent he mangled the name badly.

"I am Conan," the young Cimmerian agreed shortly. "Where is the woman?"

Tamur gestured, and two of the others opened a large chest sitting against a wall. They lifted out Yasbet, bound in a neat package and gagged with a twisted rag. Her saffron robes were mud-stained and torn, and dried tracks of tears traced through the dust on her cheeks.

"I warned this one," Conan grated. "If she is hurt, I'll—"

"No, no," Tamur cut in. "Her garments were so when we took her, behind the inn where you sleep. Had we ravaged your woman, would we show her to you so and yet expect you to talk with us?"

It was possible. Conan remembered the narrowness of the window through which she had had to wriggle. "Loose her feet."

Producing a short, curved dagger, one of the nomads cut the ropes at Yasbet's ankles. She tried to stand and, with a gag-muffled moan, sat on the lid of the chest in which she had been confined. The Hyrkanian looked questioningly at Conan, and motioned with the knife to her still-bound wrists, and her gag, but the muscular youth shook his head. Based on past experience he would not risk what she might say or do if freed. She gave him an odd look, but, surprisingly, remained still.

"You were recognized in the enclosure of Baalsham," Tamur said.

"Baalsham?" Conan said. "Who is Baalsham?"

"You know him as Jhandar. What his true name is, who can say?" Tamur sighed. "It will be easier if I begin at the beginning."

He gave quick orders, and a flagon of cheap wine and two rough clay mugs were produced. Tamur sat on one side of the table, Conan on the other. The Cimmerian noted that the other nomads were careful not to move behind him and ostentatiously kept their hands far from swords. It was a puzzlement. Hyrkanians were an arrogant and touchy people, by all accounts little given to avoiding trouble in the best of circumstances.

He accepted a mug of wine from Tamur, then forgot to drink as he listened.

"Five years gone," the scar-faced nomad began, "the man we call Baalsham appeared among us, he and the two strange men with yellow skins. He performed some small magicks, enough to be accepted among the tribal shamans, and began to preach much as he does here, of chaos and inevitable doom. Among the young men his teachings caught hold, for he called the western nations evil and said it was the destiny of the Hyrkanian people once more to ride west of the Vilayet Sea. And this time we were to sweep the land clean."

"A man of ambitions," Conan muttered. "But failed ambitions, it seems."

"By the thickness of a fingernail. Not only did Baalsham gather about him young warriors numbering in the thousands, but he began to have strange influence in the Councils of the Elders. Then creatures were seen in the night—like demons, or the twisted forms of men—and we learned from them that they were spirits of murdered men, men of our blood and friendship, conjured by Baalsham and bound to obey him. Their spying was the source of his powers in the Councils."

Yasbet made a loud sound of denial through her gag, and shook her head violently, but the men ignored her.

"I've seen his sorcery," Conan said, "black and foul. How was he driven out? I assume he did not leave of his own accord."

"In a single night," Tamur replied, "ten tribes rose against him. The very spirits that had warned us, shackled by his will, fought us, as did the young warriors who followed him." He touched the scar on his cheek. "This I had from my own brother. The young warriors—our brothers, our sons, our cousins—died to the last man, and even the maidens fought to the death. In the end our greater numbers carried the victory. Baalsham fled, and with his fleeing the spirits disappeared before our eyes. To avoid bloodshed among the tribes, the Councils decreed that no man could claim blood right for the death of one who had followed Baalsham. Their names were not to be spoken. They had never existed. But some of us could not forget that we had been forced to spill the same blood that flows in our own veins. When traders brought rumors of the man called Jhandar and the Cult of Doom, we knew him for Baalsham. Two score and ten crossed the sea to seek our forbidden vengeance. Last night we failed, and now we number but nineteen." He fell silent.

Conan frowned. "An interesting tale, but why have you told it to me?"

The nomad's face twisted with reluctance. "Because we need your help," he said slowly.

"My help?" Conan exclaimed.

Tamar hurried on. "When the palace Baalsham was building was overrun, powers beyond the mind were loosed. The very ground melted and flowed like water. That place is now called the Blasted Lands. For three days and three nights the shamans labored to contain that evil. When they had constructed barriers of magic, the boundaries of the Blasted Lands were marked, and a taboo laid. No one of the blood may pass those markers and live. There must be devices of sorcery within, devices that could be turned against Baalsham. He could not have taken all when he fled. But no Hyrkanian may go to bring them out. No Hyrkanian." He looked at the big Cimmerian with intensity.

"I am done with Jhandar," Conan said.

"But is he done with you, Conan? Baalsham's enmity does not wither with time."

Conan snorted. "What care I for his enmity? He does not know who I am or where I am to be found. Let his enmity eat at him like foxes."

"You know little of him," Tamur said insistently. "He—"

With a loud crack the floorboards by Conan's feet splintered, and a twisted gray-green hand reached through the opening to grasp his ankle.

"The spirits have come!" one of the nomads cried, eyes bulging, and Yasbet began to scream through her gag. The other men drew weapons, shouting in confusion.

Conan scrambled to his feet, trying to pull his leg free, but those leathery fingers held with preternatural strength. Another deformed hand broke through the boards, reaching for him, but his sword leaped from its sheath and arched down. One hand dropped to the floor; the other still gripped him. But at least, he thought, steel would slice them.

With his sword point he pried the fingers loose from his ankle. Even as that hand fell free, though, the head of the creature, with pointed ears and dead, haunted eyes above a lipless gash of a mouth, smashed up through the floor in a shower of splintered wood. Handless arms stretched out to the hands lying on the floor. The mold-colored flesh seemed to flow, and the hands were once more attached to the arms. The creature began to tear its way up into the room, ripping the sturdy floor apart as if its boards were rotted.

Suddenly another set of hands smashed through a wall, seizing a screaming Hyrkanian, tearing at his flesh. Conan struck off the head of the first creature, but it continued to scramble into the room even while its head spun glaring on the floor. A third head broke through the floor, and a hand followed to seize Yasbet's leg. With a shriek, she fainted.

Conan caught her as she fell, cutting her free of the creature that held her. There was naught to do in that room but die.

"Flee!" he shouted. "Get out!"

Tossing Yasbet over his shoulder like a sack of meal, he scrambled out the window to drop to the street below.

Struggling Hyrkanians fought to follow. Screams from that suddenly hellish room rose to a crescendo, pursuing the big Cimmerian as he ran with his burden. As abruptly as it had begun, the screaming ceased. Conan looked back, but he could see nothing in the blackness.

A low moan broke from Yasbet, stirring on his shoulder. Remembering the tenacity of the hand ground and bent to feel along her leg. His fingers encountered the lump of leathery skin and sinew; it writhed at his touch. With an oath he tore it from her flesh and hurled it into the night.

Yasbet groaned, and opened her eyes. "I . . . I had a nightmare," she whispered.

"'Twas no dream," he muttered. His eyes searched the dark for pursuit. "But it is done." He hoped.

"But those demons . . . you mean that they were real?" Sobs welled up in her. "Where did they come from? Why? Oh, Mitra, protect us," she wailed.

Clamping a hand over her mouth, he growled, "Quiet yourself, girl. Were I to wager on it, I'd stack my coin on Jhandar's name. And if you continue screeching like a fishwife, his minions will find us. We may not escape so easily again." Cautiously he took his hand away; she scrambled to her feet, staring at him.

"I do not believe you," she said. "Or those smelly Hyrkanians." But she did not raise her voice again.

"There is evil in the man," he said quietly. "I've seen the foulest necromancy from him, and I doubt not this is more of his black art."

"It cannot be. The cult—"

"Hsst!"

The thump of many feet sounded down the street. Pulling Yasbet deeper into the shadows, Conan waited with blade at the ready. Dim figures appeared, moving slowly from the way he had come. The smell of old grease drifted to him.

"Tamur?" he called softly.

There were mutters of startlement, and the flash of bare blades in the dark. Then one figure came closer. "Conan?"

"Yes," the Cimmerian replied. "How many escaped?"

"Thirteen," Tamur sighed. "The rest were torn to pieces. You must come with us, now. Those were Baalsham's spirit creatures. He will find you eventually, and when he does. . . ."

Conan felt Yasbet shiver. "He cannot find me," he said. "He does not even know who to look for."

Suddenly another Hyrkanian spoke. "A fire," he said. "To the north. A big fire."

Conan glanced in that direction, a deathly chill in his bones. It *was* a big fire, and unless he had lost his way entirely the Blue Bull was in the center of it. Without another word he ran, pulling Yasbet behind him. He heard the nomads following, but he cared not if they came or stayed.

The street of the Lotus Dreamers was packed with people staring at the conflagration. Flames from four structures whipped at the night, and reflected crimson glints from watching faces. One, the furthest gone, was the Blue Bull. Someone had formed a chain of buckets to the nearest cistern, Ferian among them, but it was clear that some goodly part of the district would be destroyed before the blaze was contained, most likely by pulling down buildings to surround the fire and letting it burn itself out.

As Conan pushed through the crowd of onlookers, a voice drifted to him.

"I hit it with the staff, and it disappeared in a cloud of black smoke. I told you the staff had magical powers."

Smiling for what seemed the first time in days, Conan made his way toward that voice. He found Akeba and Sharak, faces smudged with smoke, sitting with their backs against the front of a potter's shop.

"You are returned," Sharak said when he saw the big Cimmerian. "And with the wench. To think we believed it was you who would be in danger this night. I killed one of the demons."

"Demons?" Conan asked sharply.

Akeba nodded. "So they seemed to be. They burst through the walls and even the floors, tearing apart anyone who got in their way." He hesitated. "They seemed to be hunting for someone who was not there."

"Me," Conan said grimly.

Yasbet gasped. "It cannot be." The men paid her no mind.

"I said that he would find you," Tamur said, appearing at Conan's side. "Now you have no choice but to go to Hyrkania."

"Hyrkania!" Sharak exclaimed.

Regretfully Conan nodded agreement. He was committed, now. He must destroy Jhandar or die.

XIII

In the gray early morning Conan made his way down the stone
quay, already busy with lascars and cargo, to the vessel that had
been described to him. *Foam Dancer* seemed out of place among
the heavy-hulled roundships and large dromonds. Fewer than twenty paces
in length, she was rigged with a single lateen sail and pierced for fifteen
oars a side in single banks. Her sternpost curved up and forward to assume
the same angle as her narrow stem, giving her the very image of agility. He
had seen her like before, in Sultanapur, small ships designed to beach
where the King's Custom was unlikely to be found. They claimed to be
fishing vessels, to the last one, these smugglers, and over this one, as over
every smuggler he had seen, hung a foul odor of old fish and stale ship's
cooking.

He walked up the gangplank with a wary eye, for the crews of such vessels invariably had a strong dislike for strangers. Two sun-blackened and
queued seamen, stripped to the waist, watched him with dark unblinking
eyes as he stepped down onto the deck.

"Where is your captain?" he began, when a surreptitious step behind
made him whirl.

His hand darted out to catch a dagger-wielding arm, and he found himself staring into a sharp-nosed face beneath a dirty red-striped head scarf. It
was the Iranistani whose companions he had been forced to kill his first day
in Aghrapur. And if he was a crew member, then as like as not the other two
had been as well. The Iranistani opened his mouth, but Conan did not wait
to hear what he had to say. Grabbing the man's belt with his free hand,
Conan took a running step and threw him screaming over the rail into the
harbor. Sharp-nose hit the garbage-strewn water with a thunderous splash
and, beating the water furiously, set out away from the ship without a backward glance.

"Hannuman's Stones!" roared a bull-necked man, climbing onto the deck from below. Bald except for a thin black fringe, he wore a full beard fanning across his broad chest. His beady eyes lit on Conan. "Are you the cause of all the shouting up here?"

"Are you the captain?" Conan asked.

"I am. Muktar, by name. Now what in the name of Erlik's Throne is this all about?"

"I came aboard to hire your ship," Conan said levelly, "and one of your crew tried to put a dagger in my back. I threw him into the harbor."

"You threw him into the. . . ." The captain's bellow trailed off, and then went on in a quieter, if suspicious tone. "You want to hire *Foam Dancer*? For what?"

"A trading voyage to Hyrkania."

"A trader! You?" Muktar roared with laughter, slapping his stout thighs.

Conan ground his teeth, waiting for the man to finish. The night before he, Akeba and Tamur had settled on the trading story. Never a trusting people, the Hyrkanians had become less tolerant of strangers since Jhandar, but traders were still permitted. Conan thought wryly of Davinia's gold. When the cost of trade goods, necessary for the disguise, was added to the hiring of this vessel, there would not be enough left for a good night of drinking.

At last Muktar's mirth ran its course. His belly shook a last time, and cupidity lit his eyes. "Well, the fishing has been very good of late. I don't think I could give it up for so long for less than say, fifty gold pieces."

"Twenty," Conan countered.

"Out of the question. You've already cost me a crewman. He didn't drown, did he? An he did, the authorities will make me haul him out of the harbor and pay for his burial. Forty gold pieces, and I consider it cheap."

Conan sighed. He had little time to waste. If Tamur was right, they had to be gone from Aghrapur by nightfall. "I'll split the difference with you," he offered. "Thirty gold pieces, and that is my final offer. If you do not like it, I'll find another vessel."

"There isn't another in port can put you ashore on a Hyrkanian beach," the captain sneered.

"Tomorrow, or the next day, or the next, there will be." Conan shrugged unconcernedly.

"Very well," Muktar muttered sourly. "Thirty gold pieces."

"Done," Conan said, heading for the side. "We sail as soon as the goods are aboard. The tides will not matter to this shallow draft."

"I thought there was no hurry," the bearded man protested.

"Nor is there," Conan said smoothly. "Neither is there any need to waste time." Inside, he wondered if they would get everything done. There simply *was* no time to waste.

"Speak on," Jhandar commanded, and paced the bare marble floor of his antechamber while he listened.

"Yes, Great Lord," the young man said, bowing. "A man was found in one of the harbor taverns, an Iranistani who claimed to have fought one who must be the man Conan. This Iranistani was a sailor on a smuggler, *Foam Dancer*, and it seems that this ship sailed only a few hours past bearing among its passengers a number of Hyrkanians, a huge blue-eyed barbarian, and a girl matching the description of the initiate who disappeared the night of the Hyrkanians' attack." He paused, awaiting praise for having ferreted out so much so quickly.

"The destination, fool," Jhandar demanded. "Where was the ship bound?"

"Why, Hyrkania, or so it is said, Great Lord."

Jhandar squeezed his eyes shut, massaging his temples with his fingers. "And you did not think this important enough to tell me without being asked?"

"But, Great Lord," the disciple faltered, "since they have fled . . . that is. . . ."

"Whatever you discover, you will tell me," the necromancer snapped. "It is not for you to decide what is important and what is not. Is there aught else you have omitted?"

"No, Great Lord. Nothing."

"Then leave me!"

The shaven-headed young man backed from Jhandar's presence, but the mage had already dismissed him from his mind. He who had once been known as Baalsham moved to a window. From there he could see Davinia reclining in the shade of a tree in the gardens below, a slave stirring a breeze for her with a fan of white ostrich plumes. He had never known a woman like her before. She was disturbing. And fascinating.

"I but listen at corners, Great Lord," Che Fan said behind him, "yet I know that already there is talk because she is not treated as the rest."

Jhandar suppressed a start and glanced over his shoulder at the two Khitans. Never in all the years they had followed him had he gotten used to the silence with which they moved. "If wagging tongues cannot be kept still," he said, "I will see that there are no tongues to wag."

Che Fan bowed. "Forgive me, Great Lord, if I spoke out of my place."

"There are more important matters afoot," Jhandar said. "The barbarian has sailed for Hyrkania. He would not have done so were he merely fleeing. Therefore he must be seeking something, some weapon, to use against me."

"But there is nothing, Great Lord," Suitai protested. "All was destroyed."

"Are you certain of that?" Jhandar asked drily. "Certain enough to risk all of my plans? I am not. I intend to secure the fastest galley in Aghrapur, and the two of you will sail on the next tide. Kill this Conan, and bring me whatever it is he seeks."

"As you command, Great Lord," the Khitans murmured together.

All would be well, Jhandar told himself. He had come too far to fail now. Too far.

XIV

Gray seas rolled under *Foam Dancer*'s pitching bow, and a mist of foam carried across her deck. The triangular sail stood taut against the sky, where a pale yellow sun had sunk halfway from zenith to western horizon. At the stern a seaman, shorter than Conan but broader, leaned his not inconsiderable weight against the steering oar, but the rest of the crew for the most part lay sprawled among the bales of trade goods.

Conan stood easily, one hand gripping a stay. He was no sailor, but his time among the smugglers of Sultanapur had at least taught his stomach to weather the constant motion of a ship.

Akeba was not so fortunate. He straightened from bending over the rail—as he had done often since the vessel left Aghrapur—and said thickly, "A horse does not move so. Does it never stop?"

"Never," Conan said. But at a groan from the other he relented. "Sometimes it will be less, and in any case you will become used to it. Look at the Hyrkanians. They've made but a single voyage, yet show no illness."

Tamur and the other nomads squatted some distance in front of the single tail mast, their quiet murmurs melding with the creak of timbers and cording. They passed among themselves clay wine jugs and chunks of ripe white cheese, barely interrupting their talk to fill their mouths.

"I do not want to look at them," Akeba said, biting off each word. "I swear before Mitra that I know not which smells worse, rotted fish or mare's milk cheese."

Nearby, in the waist of the ship, a few of the sailors listened to Sharak. " . . . Thus did I strike with my staff of power," he gestured violently with his walking staff, "slaying three of the demons in the Blue Bull. Great were their lamentations and cries for mercy, but for such foul-hearted creatures

421

as they I would know no mercy. Many more would I have transmuted to harmless smoke, blown away on the breeze, but they fled before me, back to their infernal regions, casting balls of fire to hinder my pursuit, as I...."

"Did he truly manage to harm one of the creatures?" Conan asked Akeba. "He has boasted of that staff for years, but never have I seen more from it than support for a tired back."

"I know not," Akeba said. He was making a visible effort to ignore his stomach, but his dark face bore a greenish pallor. "I saw him at the first, leaping about like a Farthii fire-dancer and flailing with his stick at whatever moved, then not again till we had fled to the street. Of the fire, however, I do know. 'Twas Ferian. He threw a lamp at one of the demons, harming the creature not at all, but scattering burning oil across a wall."

"And burned down his own tavern," Conan chuckled. "How it will pain him to build anew, though I little doubt he has the gold to do it ten times over."

Muktar, making his way aft from the necessary—a plank held out from the bow on a frame—paused by Conan. His beady eyes rolled to the sky, then to the Cimmerian's face. "Fog," he said, then chewed his thought a moment before adding, "by sunset. The Vilayet is treacherous." Clamping his mouth shut as though he had said more than he intended, he moved on toward the stern in a walk that would have seemed rolling on land, but here exactly compensated for the motion of the deck.

Conan grimly watched him go. "The further we sail from Aghrapur, the less he talks and the less I trust him."

"He wants the other half of his gold that you hold back. Besides, with the Hyrkanians we outnumber his crew."

Mention of the gold was unfortunate. After he paid the captain, Conan would have exactly eight pieces of gold in his pouch. In other times it would have seemed a tidy sum, but not so soon after having had a hundred. He found himself hoping to make a profit on the trade goods, and yet thoughts of profits and trading left a taste in his mouth as if he had been eating the Hyrkanians' ripest cheese.

"Mayhap," he said sourly. "Yet he would feed us to the fish and return to his smuggling, were he able. He— What's the matter, man?"

Eyes bulging, Akeba swallowed rapidly, and with force. "Feed us to—" With a groan he doubled over the rail again, retching loudly and emptily. There was naught left in him to come up.

Yasbet came hurrying from the stern, casting frowns over her shoulder as she picked her way quickly among coiled ropes and wicker hampers or provisions. "I do not like this Captain Muktar," she announced to Conan. "He leers at me as if he would see me naked on a slave block."

Conan had declared her saffron robe unsuited for a sea voyage, and she had shown no reluctance to rid herself of that reminder of the cult. Now she wore a short leather jerkin, laced halfway up the front, over a gray wool tunic, with trousers of the same material and knee-high red boots. It was a man's garb, but the way the coarse wool clung to her form left no doubt there was a woman inside.

"You've no need to fear," Conan said firmly. Perhaps he should have a talk with Muktar in private. With his fists. And the captain was not the only one. His icy gaze caught the leering glances of a dozen sailors directed at her.

"I've no fear of anything so long as you are with me," she said, and innocently pressed a full breast against his arm. At least, he thought it was innocently. "But what is the matter with Akeba, Conan?" She herself had showed no effects from the roughest seas.

"He's ill."

"I am so sorry. Perhaps if I brought him some soup?"

"Erlik take the woman," Akeba moaned faintly.

"I think not just now," Conan laughed. Taking Yasbet's arm he led her away from the heaving form on the rail and seated her on an upturned keg before him. His face was serious now.

"Why look you so glum, Conan?" she asked.

"An there is trouble," he said quietly, "here or ashore, stay close to me, or to Akeba if you cannot get to me. Sick or not, he'll protect you. Does the worst come, Sharak will help you escape. He is no fighter, but no man lives so long as he without learning to survive."

A small frown creased her forehead. When he was done, she exclaimed, "Why do you speak as if you might not be with me?"

"No man knows what comes, girl, and I would see you safe."

"I thought so," she said with a warmth and happiness he did not understand. "I wished it to be so."

"As a last resort, trust Tamur, but only if there is no other way." He thought the nomad was the best of the lot, the least likely to betray a trust, but it was best not to test him too far. As the ancient saying held, he who took a Hyrkanian friend should pay his burial fee beforetime. "Put no trust in any of the rest, though, not even if it means you must find your way alone."

"But you will be here to protect me," she smiled. "I know it."

Conan growled, at a loss to make her listen. By bringing her along, for all he had done it for the best, he had exposed her to danger as great as Jhandar's, if different in kind. How could he bring that home to her? If only she were capable of her own protection. Her own. . . .

Rummaging in the bales of trade goods, the Cimmerian dug out a Nemedian sica, its short blade unsharpened. The Hyrkanian nomads liked proof that a sword came to them fresh from the forge, such proof as would be given by watching the first edge put on blunt steel.

He flipped the shortsword in the air, catching it by the blade, and thrust the hilt at Yasbet. She stared at it wonderingly.

"Take it, girl," he said.

Hesitantly she put a hand to the leather-wrapped hilt. He released his grip, and she gasped, almost dropping the weapon. "'Tis heavy," she said, half-laughing.

"You've likely worn heavier necklaces, girl. You'll be used to the weight in your hand before we reach Hyrkania."

"Used to it?"

Her yelp of consternation brought chortles and hoots from three nearby sailors. The Hyrkanians looked up, still eating; Tamur's face split into an open grin.

Conan ignored them as best he could, firmly putting down the thought of hurling one or two over the side as a lesson for the others. "The broadsword is too heavy," he said, glowering at the girl. "Tulwar and yataghan are lighter, but there is no time to teach the use of either before we land. And learn the blade you will."

She stared at him silently with wide, liquid eyes, clutching the sword to her breasts with both hands.

Raucous laughter rolled down the deck, and Muktar followed close behind the sound of his merriment. "A woman! You intend to teach a woman the sword?"

Conan bit back an oath, and contented himself with growling, "Anyone can learn the sword."

"Will you teach children next? This one," Muktar crowed to his crew, "will teach sheep to conquer the world." Their mirth rose with his, and their comments became ribald.

Conan ground his teeth, his anger flashing to the heat of a blade in the smith-fire. This fat, lecherous ape called itself a man? "A gold piece says in the tenth part of a glass I can teach her to defeat any of these goats who follow you!"

Muktar tugged at his beard, the smile now twisting his mouth into an emblem of hatred. "A gold piece?" he sneered. "I'd wager five on the ship's cook."

"Five," Conan snapped. "Done!"

"Talk to her, then, barbar." The captain's voice was suddenly oily and treacherous. "Talk to the wench, and we'll see if she can uphold your boasting."

Already Conan was wishing his words unsaid, but the gods, as usual in such cases, did not listen. He drew Yasbet aside and adjusted her hands on the sword hilt.

"Hold it so, girl." Her hand was unresisting—and gripped with as much strength as bread dough, or so it seemed to him. She had not taken her eyes from his face. "Mitra blast your hide, girl," he growled. "Clasp the hilt as you would a hand."

"You truly believe that I can do this," she said suddenly. There was wonder in her voice, and on her face. "You believe that I can learn to use a sword. And defeat a man."

"I'd not have wagered on you, else," he muttered, then sighed. "I have known women who handled a blade as well as any man, and better than most. 'Tis not a weapon of brute muscle, as is an axe. The need is for endurance, and agility and quickness of hand. Only a fool denies a woman can be agile, or quick."

"But—to defeat a man!" she breathed. "I have never even held a sword before." Abruptly she frowned at the blade. "This will not cut. Swords are supposed to cut. Even I know that."

Conan mouthed a silent prayer. "I chose it for that reason, for practice. Now it will serve you better than another. The point can still draw blood, but you'll not kill this sailor by accident, so I'll not have to kill Muktar."

"I see," she said, nodding happily. Her face firmed, and she started past him, but he seized her arm.

"Not yet, wench," he laughed softly. "First listen. These smugglers are deadly with a knife, especially in the dark, but they are no warriors in the daylight." He paused for that to sink in, then added. "That being so, were this a true fight, he would likely kill you in the space of three breaths."

Dismay painted her face. "Then how—"

"By remembering that you can run. By encouraging his contempt for you, and using it."

"I will not," she protested hotly. "I have as much pride as any man, including you."

"But no skill, as yet. You must win by trickery, and by surprise, for now. Skill will come later. Strike only when he is off balance. At all other times, run. Throw whatever comes to hand, at his head or at his feet, but never at his sword for those objects he will easily knock aside. Let him think that you are panicked. Scream if you wish, but do not let the screaming seize you."

"I will not scream," she said sullenly.

He suppressed a smile. "It would but make him easier to defeat, for he would see you the more as a woman and the less as an opponent."

"But the sword. What do I do with the sword?"

"Beat him with it," he said, and laughed at her look of complete uncomprehension. "Think of the sword as a stick, girl," Understanding dawned on her features; she hefted the sica with both hands like a club. "And forget not to poke him" he added. "Such as these usually think only to hack forgetting a sword has a point. You remember it, and you'll win."

"How long will you talk to the wench?" Muktar shouted. "Your minutes are gone. An you talk long enough, perhaps Bayan will grow old, and even your jade can defeat him."

Beside the bearded sea captain stood a wiry man of middle height, his sun-darkened torso stripped to the waist. With his bare tulwar he drew gleaming circles of steel, first to one side then the other, a tight smile showing yellowed teeth.

Conan's heart sank. He had hoped Muktar would indeed choose his fat ship's cook, or one of the bigger men of the crew, so as to intimidate Yasbet with her opponent's sheer size. Thus Yasbet's agility would count for more. Even if it meant eating his words, he could not allow her to be hurt. A bitter taste on his tongue, he opened his mouth to end it.

Yasbet strode out to meet the seaman before Conan could speak, shortsword gripped in her two small hands. She fixed the man with a defiant glare. "Bayan, are you called?" she sneered. "From the look of you, it should be Baya, for you have about you a womanish air."

Conan stood with his mouth still open, staring at her. Had the wench gone mad?

Bayan's dark eyes seemed about to pop from his narrow head. "I will make you beg me to prove my manhood to you," he snarled.

"Muktar!" Conan called. Yasbet looked at him, pleading in her eyes, and despite himself he changed what he had been about to say. "This is but a demonstration, Muktar. No more. Does he harm her, you'll die a heartbeat after he does."

The bearded man jerked his head in a reluctant nod. Leaning close to Bayan he began whispering with low urgency.

The wiry sailor refused to listen. Raising his curved blade on high, he leaped toward Yasbet, a snarling grimace on his face and a terrible ululating cry rising from his mouth.

Conan put a hand to his sword hilt.

Bayan landed before her without striking, though, and it was immediately obvious that he thought to frighten her into immediate surrender. His grimace became a gloating smile.

Yasbet's face paled, but with a shout of her own she thrust the sword into the seaman's midsection. The unsharpened blade could not penetrate far, but the point was enough to start a narrow stream of blood, and the force of the blow bulged Bayan's eyes.

He gagged and staggered, but she did not rest. Clumsily, but swiftly, she brought the blunted blade down like a club on the shoulder of his sword arm. Bayan's scream was not of his choosing, this time. His blade dropped from a hand suddenly useless. Before the tulwar struck the deck Yasbet caught him a glancing blow on the side of the head, splitting his scalp to the bone. With a groan Bayan sank to his knees.

Conan watched in amazement as the wiry sailor tried desperately to crawl away. Yasbet pursued him across the deck, beating at his shoulders and back with the edgeless steel. Yelping, Bayan found himself against the rail. At one and the same time he tried to curl himself into a ball and claw his way through the wood to safety.

"Surrender!" Yasbet demanded, standing above him like a fury. She stabbed at Bayan's buttocks, drawing a howl and a stain of red on his dirty once-white trousers.

Hand on his dagger, Muktar started toward her, a growl rising in his throat. Suddenly Conan's blade was a shining barrier before the captain's eyes.

"She won, did she not?" the young Cimmerian asked softly. "And you owe me five gold pieces. Or shall I shave your beard at the shoulders?"

Another shriek came from Bayan; the other buttock of his trousers bore a spreading red patch as well, now.

"She won," Muktar muttered. He flinched as Conan caressed his beard with the broadsword, then almost shouted, "The wench won!"

"See that this goes no further," Conan said warningly. He got a reluctant nod in reply. When the Cimmerian thrust out his palm, the gold coins were counted into it with even greater reluctance.

"I won!" Yasbet shouted. Waving her shortsword above her head, she capered gaily about the deck. "I won!"

Conan sheathed his blade and swept her into the air, swinging her in a circle. "Did I not say that you would?"

"You did!" she laughed. "Oh, you did! On my oath, I will believe anything that you tell me from this moment. Anything."

He started to lower her feet to the deck, but her arms wove about his neck, and in some fashion he found himself kissing her. A pleasant armful, indeed, he thought. Soft round breasts flattened against his broad chest.

Abruptly he pulled her loose and set her firmly on the deck. "Practice, girl. There's a mort of practice to be done before I grind an edge on that blade for you. And you did not fight as I told you. I should take a switch to you for that. You could have been hurt."

"But, Conan," she protested, her face falling.

"Place your feet so," he said, demonstrating, "for balance. Do it, girl!"

Sullenly she complied, and he began to show her the exercises in the use of the short blade. That was the problem, he thought grimly, about setting out to protect a wench. Sooner or later you found yourself protecting her from you.

XV

S quatting easily on his heels against the pitching of the ship as it breasted long swells, Conan watched Yasbet work her blunted blade against a leather-wrapped bale of cloaks and tunics. Despite a freshening wind, sweat rolled down her face, but already she had gone ten times as long as she had managed the first day. She still wore her mannish garb, but had left off the woolen tunic, complaining that the coarse fabric scratched. The full curves of her breasts swelled at the lacings of her jerkin, threatening to burst the rawhide cords at her every exertion.

Sword arm dropping wearily, she looked at him with artistic pleading in her eyes. "Please, Conan, let me retire to my tent." That tent, no more than a rough structure of grimy canvas, had been his idea, both to keep her from the constant wetting of sudden squalls and to shelter her sleep from lustful eyes. "Please? Already I will be sore."

"There's plenty of liniment," he said gruffly.

"It smells. And it stings. Besides, I cannot rub it on my back. Perhaps if you—"

"Enough rest," he said, motioning her back to the bale.

"Slaver," she muttered, but her shortsword resumed its whacking against leather.

Well over half their voyage was done. The coast of Hyrkania was now a dark line on the eastern horizon, though they had yet a way north to sail. Every day since placing the sica in her hands he had forced Yasbet to practice, exercising from gray dawn to purple dusk. He had dragged her from her blankets, poured buckets of water over her head when she whined of the midday heat, and threatened keelhauling when she begged to stop her work. He had tended and bandaged blisters on her small hands, as well, and to his surprise those blisters seemed at once a mark of pride to her and a spur.

Akeba dropped down beside him, eyeing Yasbet with respect. "She learns. Can you teach so well, and to a woman, there is need of you in the army, to train the many recruits we take of late."

"She has no ideas of swordplay to unlearn," Conan replied. "Also, she does exactly as I say."

"Exactly?" Akeba laughed, lifting an eyebrow. At the look on Conan's face he pulled his countenance into an expression of exaggerated blandness.

"Does your stomach still trouble you?" the youthful Cimmerian asked hopefully.

"My head and my legs now ignore the pitching," Akeba replied with a fixed grin.

Conan gave him a doubtful look. "Then perhaps you would like some well-aged mussels. Muktar has a keg of the ripest—"

"No, thank you, Conan," the Turanian said in haste, a certain tautness around his mouth. As though eager to change the subject, he added, "I have not noticed Bayan about today. You did not drop him over the side, did you?"

The Cimmerian's mouth tightened. "I overheard him discussing his plans for Yasbet, and I spoke to him about it."

"In friendly fashion, I trust. 'Tis you who mutters that these sea rats would welcome an excuse to slit our throats."

"In friendly fashion," Conan agreed. "He is nursing his bruises in his blankets this day."

"Good," the Turanian said grimly. "She is of an age with Zorelle."

"A tasty morsel, that girl," Sharak said, sitting down on Conan's other side. "Were I but twenty years younger I would take her from you, Cimmerian."

Yasbet's sword clanged on the deck, drawing all three men's eyes. She glared at them furiously. "I am no trained ape or dancing bear that you three may squat like farm louts and be entertained by me!"

She stalked away, then back to snatch up the sica—her eyes daring them to speak, as she did—and marched down the deck to disappear within her small tent before the mast.

"Your wench begins to develop a temper, Conan," Sharak said, staring after her. "Perhaps you have made a mistake in teaching her to use a weapon."

Akeba nodded with mock gravity. "She is no longer the shy and retiring maiden that once she was, Cimmerian, thanks to you. Of course, I realize that she is no longer a maiden at all, also thanks to you, but at least you could gentle her before she begins challenging us all to mortal combat."

"How can you talk so?" Conan protested. "But moments gone you likened her to your own daughter."

"Aye," Akeba said gravely, his laughter gone. "I was much concerned with Zorelle's virtue while she lived. I see things differently now. Now she is dead, I hope that she had what joy she could of her life."

"I have not touched her," Conan muttered reluctantly, and bridled at their disbelieving stares. "I rescued her. She's innocent and alone, with none to protect her but me. Mitra's Mercies! As well ask a huntsman to pen a gazelle fawn and slay it there for sport."

Sharak hooted with laughter. "The tiger and the gazelle. But which of you is which? Which hunter, which prey? The wench has you marked, Cimmerian."

"'Tis true," Akeba said. He essayed a slight smile. "The girl is among those aboard this vessel who think her your wench. Zandru's Nine Hells, do you think to be a holyman?"

"I may let the pair of you swim the rest of the way," Conan growled. "I tell you. . . ." His words trailed off as Muktar loomed over the three men.

The bull-necked man tugged at his beard, spread fan-shaped across his chest, and eyed Conan with speculation. "We are followed," he said finally. "A galley."

Conan rose smoothly to his feet and strode to the stern, Akeba and Sharak scrambling in his wake. Muktar followed more slowly.

"I see nothing but water," the Turanian sergeant complained, shading his eyes. Sharak muttered agreement, squinting furiously.

Conan saw the follower, though, seeming no more than a chip on the water in the distance, but with the faint sweep of motion at its sides that told of long oars straining for speed.

"Pirates?" Conan asked. Although there were many such on the Vilayet Sea, he did not truly believe those who followed were numbered among them.

Muktar shrugged. "Perhaps." He did not sound as if he believed it either.

"What else could they be?" Akeba demanded.

Muktar glanced sideways at Conan, but did not speak.

"I still see nothing," Sharak put in.

"How soon before they come up on us?" Conan said.

"Near dark," Muktar replied. He looked at the gray-green water, its long swells feathering whitely in the wind, then peered at the sky, where pale gray clouds were layered against the afternoon blue. "We may have a storm before, though. The Vilayet is a treacherous bitch."

The Cimmerian's eyes locked on the approaching ship, one huge fist thumping the rail as he thought. How to fight the battle that must come, and win? How?

"If we have a storm," the old astrologer said, "then we will hide from them in it."

"If it comes," Conan told him.

"I have counted their oarstroke," Muktar said abruptly, "and they will kill slaves if they do not slacken it. Yet I do not believe they will. No one cares enough about Hyrkanians to chase them with such vigor. And *Foam Dancer* is a small ship, not a dromond loaded to the gunnels with ivory and spices. It must be you three, or the wench. Have you the crown of Turan hidden in your bales? Is your jade a princess stolen from her father? Why do they follow so?"

"We are traders," Conan said levelly. "And you have been paid to carry us to Hyrkania and back to Turan."

"I've gotten no coin for the last."

"You will get your gold. Unless you let pirates take our trade goods. And your ship. Then all you'll receive is a slaver's manacles, an you survive."

Motioning the others to follow, the big Cimmerian left Muktar muttering into his beard and peering at the ship behind.

In the waist of the ship Conan took a place by the rail where he, too, could watch the galley. It seemed larger, now. Tamur joined them.

"It follows us," Conan said quietly.

"Baalsham," the Hyrkanian snarled at the same instant that Akeba, nodding, said, "Jhandar."

Sharak shook his staff at the galley with surprising fierceness. "Let him send his demons. I am ready for them."

Tamur's dark eyes shone. "This time we will carve him as a haunch of beef if he has a thousand demons."

Conan met Akeba's gaze. It seemed more likely that those on *Foam Dancer* would be meat on a spit.

"How many men does such a vessel carry?" the Turanian asked. "I know little of naval matters."

Conan's own knowledge of the sea was limited to his short time with the smugglers in Sultanapur, but he had been pursued by such vessels before. "There are two banks of oars to a side, but the oar-slaves will not be used to fight. A vessel of that size might carry five score besides the crew."

There was a moment of silence, broken only by the rigging lines humming in the rising wind. Then Sharak said hollowly, "So many? This adventuring begins to seem ill-suited for a man of my years."

"By the One-Father, I shall die happy," Tamur said, "an I know Baalsham goes with me into the long night."

Akeba shook his head bleakly. "He will not be on this ship. Such men send others to do their killing. But at least we shall find blood enough to pay our ferryman's fee, eh, Cimmerian?"

"It will be a glorious fight in which to die," Tamur agreed.

"I do not intend to die yet," the Cimmerian said grimly.

"The storm," Sharak said, his words holding a new excitement. "The storm will hide us." The clouds were thicker now, and darker, obscuring the lowering sun.

"Mayhap," Conan replied. "But we will not depend on that."

The god of the icy peaks and wind-ravaged crags of Conan's Cimmerian homeland was Crom, Dark Lord of the Mound, who gave a man life and will, and nothing more. It was given to each man to carry his own fate in his hands and his heart and his head.

Conan strode aft to Muktar, who still stood gazing at the galley. The bronze glint of its ram could be seen plainly now, knifing through gray swells. "Will they reach us before night falls?" Conan asked the captain. "Or before the storm breaks?"

"The storm may never break," Muktar muttered. "On the Vilayet lightning may come from a sky where the sun was bright an instant before, or clouds may darken for days, then lift without a drop of rain. Do you lose me my ship, Cimmerian, I'll see your corpse."

"It was in my mind you were a sea captain," Conan taunted, "not an old woman wanting only to play with her grandchildren." He waited for Muktar's neck to swell with anger and his face empurple, then went on. "Listen. We may all be saved. For as long as we are able, we must run before them. Then. . . ."

As Conan spoke the dark color slowly left Muktar's face. Once he blanched, and tried to stop the Cimmerian's flow of words, but Conan would not pause for the other's objections. He pressed on, and after a time Muktar began to listen intently, then to nod.

"It may work," he said finally. "By Dagon's Golden Tail, it may just work. See to your nomads, Cimmerian." Whirling with more agility that would have seemed possible, the bulky captain roared, "To me, you whoreson dogs! To me, and listen to how I'll save your worthless hides still another time!"

"What in Mitra's name is that all about?" Akeba asked when Conan was back at the rail.

As Muktar's voice rose and fell in waves, haranguing the crew in the stern, Conan told his companions what he planned.

A grin appeared on Sharak's thin face, and he broke into a little dance. "We have them. We have them. What a grand adventure!"

Tamur's smile was wolfish. "Whether we escape or die, this will be a thing to be told around the campfires. Come, Turanian, and show us if any remnant of Hyrkanian blood remains in you." With a wry shake of his head Akeba followed Tamur to join the other nomads.

It was done then, Conan thought. Nothing remained but . . . Yasbet. Even as her name came into his head, she was there before him. Her soft round eyes caressed his face.

"I heard," she said. "Where is my place in this?"

"I will make you a place in the midst of the bales," he told her, "where you will be safe. From archers or slingers, at least."

"I will not hide." Her eyes flashed, suddenly no longer soft. "You've taught me much, but not to be a coward!"

"You'll hide if I must bind you hand and foot. But if it comes to that, I promise you'll not sit without wincing for a tenday. Give me your sword," he added abruptly.

"My sword? No!"

She clutched the hilt protectively, but he snatched the blade from her and started down the deck. She followed in silence, hurt, tear-filled eyes seeming to fill her face.

In front of the mast the ship's grindstone, where the crew sharpened axes and swords alike, was fastened securely to the planking. Working the foot treadle, Conan set the edge of the blunt sica to the spinning stone. Sparks showered from the metal. With his free hand he dripped oil from a clay jug onto the wheel. The heat must not grow too great, or the temper of the blade would be ruined.

Yasbet scrubbed a hand across her cheek, damp with tears. "I thought that you meant to . . . that you. . . ."

"You are no woman warrior," he said gruffly. "Not in these few days. But you may have need to defend yourself, an the worst comes."

"Then you will not make me," she began, but he quelled her with an icy glance. The blood of battle was rising in him, driving out what small softness he had within. When steel was bared, the slightest remnant of gentleness could slay the one who bore it. Fiery sparks fountained from steel that was no harder than him who sharpened it.

XVI

bout *Foam Dancer*'s deck men rushed, readying the parts of Conan's plan. The clouds darkened above as if dusk had come two turns of the glass before its time, and wind strummed the rigging like a lute, yet no moisture fell on the deck save spume from waves shattering on the bow.

Bit by bit the galley closed the distance, a deadly bronze-beaked centipede skittering across the water, seemingly unimpeded by the rising waves through which *Foam Dancer* now labored, wallowing heavily from trough to trough. *Foam Dancer* seemed a sluggish water beetle, waiting to die.

"They busy themselves in the bows!" Muktar bellowed suddenly.

Conan finished tying the line around Yasbet's waist where she lay between stacked bales, themselves lashed firmly to the deck. "You've no fear of being washed overboard now," he told her, "no matter how violent the storm becomes."

"It's the catapult!" Muktar cried.

Conan started to turn away, but Yasbet seized his hand, pressing her lips to his callused palm. "I shall be waiting for you," she murmured, "when the battle is done." She tugged his hand lower, and he found his fingers inside her leather jerkin, a swelling breast nestled in his hand.

With an oath he pulled his hand free, though not without reluctance. "There is no time for that now," he said roughly. Did she not realize how difficult it was for him already, he wondered, protecting a wench he longed to ravish?

"They prepare to fire!" Muktar shouted, and Conan put Yasbet from his mind.

"Now!" the young Cimmerian cried. "Cut!"

In the stern Muktar raced to the steering oar, roughly shoving aside the burly steersman to seize the thick wooden shaft himself. In the bow two scruffy smugglers drew curved swords and chopped. Lines parted with loud snaps, and the bundles of extra sailcloth Conan had put over the side were loosed. The sleek vessel leaped forward, all but jumping from wave-top to wave-top.

Almost beneath her stern a stone fell, half-a-man-weight of granite, raising a fountain that drenched Muktar.

"Now, Muktar!" Conan shouted. Snatching an oilskin bag, he ran aft. "I said now! The rest of you watch the pots!"

The deck was dotted with scores of covered clay pots, scavenged from every corner of the ship. Some hissed as foaming water swirled around them and ran across the planking.

Cursing at the top of his lungs, Muktar heaved at the steersman's oar, its massive thickness bowing from the strain. Slowly *Foam Dancer* responded, coming around. The crew dashed to run out long sweeps, stroking and backing desperately to aid the turn.

This was the point that had made Muktar's face pale when Conan told him of it. Turned broadside to the line of waves, the vessel heeled over, further, further, till her rail lay nearly on the surface. Faces twisted with fear, the smugglers worked their oars with feverish intensity. Akeba, Sharak, and the Hyrkanians scrambled to keep the clay containers from toppling or washing over the side. For a froth-peaked gray mountain of water now rolled over the rail, till it seemed that men waded in shallows.

Among those laboring men Conan's eyes suddenly lit on Yasbet, free of her bonds, struggling among the rest of the pots. His curses were borne away by the wind, and there was no time to do anything about her.

Sluggishly but certainly *Foam Dancer*'s bow came into the waves, and the vessel lifted. She did not ride easily, as she had before—there was likely water enough below decks to float a launch—but still she crested that first wave and raced on. Back toward the galley.

On the other ship, the catapult arm stood upright. If another stone had been launched, the splash of its fall had been lost in the rough seas. On the galley's decks, seeing their intended prey turn back on them, men raced about like ants in a crushed anthill. But not so many men as Conan had feared, unless they kept others below. Most of those he could make out wore the twinned queues of sailors.

"We've lost half the pots!" Akeba shouted over the howling wind. "Gone into the sea!"

"Then ready what we have!" Conan bellowed back. "In full haste!" The Hyrkanians took up oilskin sacks, like that Conan carried.

Those on the other ship, apparently believing their quarry intended to come to grips, had now provided themselves with weapons. Swords, spears and axes bristled along the galley's rail. In its bow, men labored to winch down the catapult's arm for another shot, but too late, Conan knew; *Foam Dancer* was now too close.

Undoing the strings that held the mouth of his sack, Conan drew out its dry contents: a quiver of arrows, each with rags tied behind the head, and a short, recurved bow. Near him a Hyrkanian, already holding his bow, knocked the top from a clay crock. Within coals glowed dully, hissing from the spray that fell inside the container. A few quick puffs fanned them to crackling flame, and into that fire Conan thrust an arrow. The cloth tied to it burst into flame.

In one swift motion the big Cimmerian turned, nocked, drew and released. The fire arrow flew straight up to the galley, lodging in a mast. His was the signal. A shower of fire arrows followed, peppering the galley.

Conan fired again and again as the two ships drew closer. Though now the galley tried to veer away, *Foam Dancer* gave chase. On the galley men rushed with buckets of sand to extinguish points of flame, but two blossomed for each that died. Tendrils of fire snaked up tarred ropes, and a great square sail was suddenly aflame, the conflagration whipped by shrieking wind.

"Closer!" Conan called to Muktar. "Close under the stern!"

The bull-necked man muttered, but *Foam Dancer* curved away from her pursuit, crossing the galley's wake a short spear-throw from its stern.

Hastily Conan capped the pot of coals, edging it into the oilskin bag with ginger respect for its blistering heat. Once the sack whirled about his head, twice, and then it arced toward the galley, dropping to its deck unnoticed by men frantically cutting away the flaming sail.

"The oil!" Conan shouted even as the sack fell. He seized another jar, this with its lid sealed in place with pitch, and threw it to smash aboard the galley. "Quickly, before the distance widens!"

More sealed pots flew toward the other vessel. Half fell into tossing water, but the rest landed on the galley's stern. The two ships diverged, but now the galley's burning sail was over the side, and her men were turning to *Foam Dancer*.

Conan pounded his fist on the rail. "Where is it?" he muttered. "Why has nothing—"

Flame exploded in the stern of the galley as spreading oil at last reached the coals that had burned out of the sack. Screams rose from the galley, and wild cheers from the men of *Foam Dancer*.

In that instant the rains came at last, a solid sheet of water that cut off all vision of the other ship. Wind that had howled now raged like a mad beast, and Muktar's vessel reeled to the hammer blows of waves that towered above her mast.

"Keep us sailing north!" Conan shouted. He had to put his mouth close to Muktar's ear to be heard, even so.

Straining at the steering oar, the bearded man shook his head. "You do not sail a storm of the Vilayet!" he bellowed. "You survive it!"

And then the wind rose, ripping away even shouted words as they left the mouth, and talk was impossible.

The wind did not abate, nor did the furious waves. Gray mountains of water, their peaks whipped to violent white spray, hurled themselves at *Foam Dancer* as if the gods themselves, angered by her name, would prove that she could not dance with their displeasure. Those who had dared to pit this cockleshell against the unleashed might of the Vilayet could do naught but cling and wait.

After an endless age, the rains began to slacken and, at last, were gone. The wind that flogged choppy waves to whitecaps became no more than stiff, and whipped away the clouds to reveal a bright gibbous moon hung in a black velvet sky, its pale light half changing day for night. There was neither sight nor hint of the galley.

"The fire consumed it," Sharak gloated. "Or the storm."

"Perhaps," Conan answered doubtfully. An the fire had not been well caught, the storm would have extinguished it. And if *Foam Dancer* could ride that tempest, then the galley, if well handled, could have too. To Muktar, who had returned the steering oar to the steersman, he said, "Find the coast. We must find how far we've gone astray."

"By dawn," the bearded man announced confidently. He seemed to feel that the battle with the sea had been his alone; the victory had put even more swagger into his walk.

Yasbet, approaching, laid a hand on Conan's arm. "I must speak with you," she said softly.

"And I with you," he replied grimly. "What in Mitra's name did you mean by—"

But she was walking away, motioning for him to follow, stepping carefully among the night-shrouded shapes of men who had collapsed where they stood from exhaustion. Growling fearsome oaths under his breath, Conan stalked after her. She disappeared into the pale shadow of her sagging tent, its heavy fabric hanging low from the pounding of the storm. Furiously jerking aside the flap, he ducked inside, and had to kneel for lack of headroom.

"Why did you leave where I put you?" he demanded. "And how? I made that knot too firm for your fingers to pick. You could have been killed, you fool wench! And you told me you'd stay there. Promised it!"

She faced his anger, if not calmly at least unflinchingly. "Indeed your fingers wove a strong knot, but the sharp blade you gave me cut it nicely. As to why, you have taught me to defend myself. How could I do that lashed like a bundle for the laundress? And I did *not* promise. I said I would be waiting for you when the battle was done. Did I not better that? I came to find you."

"I remember a promise!" he thundered. "And you broke it!"

Disconcertingly, she smiled and said quietly, "Your cloak is wet through." Delicate fingers unfastened the bronze pin that held the garment, and soft arms snaked about his neck as she pushed the cloak from his shoulders. Sensuous lips brushed the line of his jaw, his ear.

"Stop that," he growled, pushing her away. "You'll not distract me from my purpose. Had I a switch to hand, you would think yourself better off in your amah's grasp."

With an exasperated sigh she leaned on one arm, frowning at him. "But you have no switch," she said. As he stared in amazement, she undid the laces of her jerkin and drew it over her head. Full, rounded breasts swung free, shimmering satin flesh that dried his throat. "Still," she went on, "your hand is hard, and your arm strong. I have no doubt it will suffice for your— purpose, did you call it?" Boots and trousers joined the jerkin. Twisting on her knees to face away from him, she pressed her face to the deck.

Conan swallowed hard. Those lush buttocks of honeyed ivory would have brought sweat to the face of a statue, and he was all too painfully aware at that moment that he was flesh and blood. "Cover yourself, girl," he said hoarsely, "and stop this game. 'Tis dangerous, for I am no girl's toy."

"And I play no game," she said, kneeling erect again, her knees touching his. She made no move toward her garments. "I know that all aboard this vessel think I am your . . . your leman." Her cheeks pinkened; that, more than her nudity, made him groan and squeeze his eyes shut. A brief look of triumph flitted across her face. "Have I not complained to you before," she said fiercely, "about protecting me when I did not want to be protected?"

Unclenching white-knuckled fists, he pulled her to him; she gasped as she was crushed against his chest. "The toying is done, wench," he growled. "Say go, and I will go. But if you do not. . . ." He toppled them both to the deck, her softness a cushion under him, his agate blue eyes gazing into hers with unblinking intensity.

"I am no girl," she breathed, "but a woman. Stay." She wore a triumphant smile openly now.

Conan thought it strange, that smile, but she was indeed a woman, and his mind did not long remain on smiles.

XVII

From a rocky headland covered with twisted, stunted scrub, waves crashing at its base, Conan peered inland, watching for Tamur's return. The nomad had claimed that he would have horses for them all in three or four turns of the glass, but he had left at dawn, and the sun sat low in its journey toward the western horizon.

On a short stretch of muddy sand north of the headland *Foam Dancer* lay drawn up, heeling over slightly on her keel. An anchor had been carried up the beach to dunes covered with tall, sparse brown grass, its long cable holding the vessel against the waves that tugged at her stern. Cooking fires dotted the sand between the ship and the dunes. Yasbet's tent had been pitched well away from the blankets of the Hyrkanians and the sailors, scattered among their piles of driftwood.

As Conan turned back to his scanning, a plume of dust inland and to the south caught his eye. It could be Tamur, with the horses, or it could be . . . who? He wished he knew more about this land. At least the sentry he had set atop the highest of the dunes could see the dust, too. He glanced in that direction and bit back an oath. The man was gone! The dust was closer, horses plain at its base. Tamur? Or some other?

Making an effort to appear casual, he walked up the headland to where a steep downward slope led to the beach, dotted with wind-sculpted trees, their gnarled roots barely finding a grip in the rocky soil. Between the dunes and the plain lay thickets of such growth. He half-slid down that slope, still making an effort to show no haste.

At the fires he leaned over Akeba, who sat cross-legged before a fire, honing his sword. "Horsemen approach," he said quietly. "I know not if it is Tamur or others. But the sentry is nowhere to be seen."

Stiffening, the Turanian slid his honing stone into his pouch and his curved blade into its scabbard. He had removed his distinctive tunic and spiral helmet, for the Turanian army was little loved on this side of the Vila-yet. "I will take a walk in the dunes. You can see to matters here?" Conan nodded, and Akeba, taking up a spade as if answering a call of nature, strolled toward the dunes.

"Yasbet!" Conan called, and she appeared at the flap of her tent. He mo-tioned her to come to him.

She made a great show of buckling on her sword belt and adjusting its fit on her hips before making her way slowly across the sand. As soon as she was in arm's reach of him, he grabbed her shoulders and firmly sat her down in the protection of a large driftwood bole.

"Stay there," he said when she made to rise. Turning to the others, scat-tered among the campfires, he said, as quietly as he could and still be heard, "None of you move." Some turned their faces to him curiously, and Muk-tar got to his feet. "I said, don't move!" Conan snapped. Such was the tone of command in his voice that the bearded captain obeyed. Conan went on quickly. "Horsemen will be here any moment. I know not who. Be still!" A Hyrkanian drew back the hand he had stretch forth for his bow, and a sailor, who had risen with a look of running on his face, froze. "Besides this, the sen-try has disappeared. Someone may be watching us. Choose your place of cover and when I give the word—not yet!—seize your weapons and be ready. Now!"

In an instant the beach seemed to become deserted as men rolled behind piles of driftwood. Conan snatched a bow and quiver, and dropped behind the bole with Yasbet. He raised himself enough to barely look over it, searching the dunes.

"Why did you see to my safety before telling the others?" Yasbet de-manded crossly. "All my life I have been wrapped in swaddling. I will be coddled no longer."

"Are you the hero in a saga, then?" Was that the drumming of hooves he heard? Where in Zandru's Nine Hells was Akeba? "Are you impervious to steel and proof against arrows?"

"A heroine," she replied. "I will be a heroine, not a hero."

Conan snorted. "Sagas are fine for telling before a fire of a cold night, or for entertaining children, but we are made of flesh and blood. Steel can draw blood, and arrows pierce the flesh. Do I ever see you attempting to be a hero—or a heroine—you'll think your bottom has suddenly become a drum. Be still, now."

Without taking his eyes from the dunes he felt the arrows in his quiver, checking the fletching.

"Will we die then, Conan, on this pitiful beach?" she asked.

"Of course not," he said quickly. "I'll take you back to Aghrapur and put pearls around your neck, if I don't return you to Fatima for a stubborn wench first." Of a certainty the sound of galloping horses was closer.

For a long moment she seemed to consider that. Then suddenly she shouted, "Conan of Cimmeria is my lover, and I his! I glory in sharing his blankets!"

Conan stared at her. "Crom, girl! I told you to be still!"

"If I am to die, I want the world to know what we share."

As Conan opened his mouth, the drumming abruptly became a thunder, and scores of horses burst over the dunes, spraying muddy sand beneath their hooves, roiling in a great circle on the beach. Conan nocked an arrow, then hesitated when he saw that many of the horses had no riders. Tamur appeared out of the shifting mass of riders.

"Do not loose!" Conan shouted, striding out to meet the Hyrkanian, who swung down from his horse as Conan approached. "Erlik take you, Tamur! You could have ended wearing more feathers than a goose, riding in that way."

"Did not Andar tell you who we were?" The scarred Hyrkanian said, frowning. "I saw you set him to watch."

"He was relieving himself," Akeba said disgustedly, joining them, "and did not bother to set another in his place." He was trailed by a narrow-jawed Hyrkanian, greased mustaches framing his mouth and chin.

Tamur glared at the man, who shrugged and said, "What is there to watch for, Tamur? These scavenging dung-rollers?" Andar jerked his head at the mounted men, who sat their small, shaggy horses in a loose circle about those they herded.

"You did not keep watch as you were told," Tamur grated. He turned and called to the other Hyrkanians, "Does any here stand for this one?" None answered.

Alarm flashed onto Andar's face, and he grabbed for his yataghan. Tamur spun back to the mustached man, his blade flashing from its scabbard, striking. Andar fell, sword half-drawn, his nearly severed neck spurting blood into the sand.

Tamur kicked the still-jerking body. "Take this defiler of his mother's womb into the dunes and leave him with the offal he thought was more important than keeping watch."

Two of the Hyrkanians seized the dead man by his ankles and dragged him away. None of the others so much as twitched an eyebrow. Behind him Conan could hear Yasbet retching.

"At least you got the horses," Conan said.

"They look more like sheep," Akeba muttered.

Tamur gave the Turanian a pained look. "Perhaps, but they are the best mounts to be found on the coast. Hark you now, Conan. These horse traders tell me they have seen other strangers. Give them what they ask for the mounts, and they will tell what they know."

"What they ask," Conan said drily. "They would not be blood kin of yours, would they, Tamur?"

The Hyrkanian looked astonished. "You are an outlander, Cimmerian, and ignorant, so I will not kill you. They are the scavengers and dung-rollers Andar named them, living by digging roots and robbing the nests of sea-birds. From time to time they loot a ship driven ashore by a storm." He thrust his blade into the sand to clean away Andar's blood. "They are no better than savages. Come, I will take you to their leader."

The men on the shaggy horses were a ragged lot, their sheepskin coats motheaten, their striped tunics threadbare and even filthier than when they were worn by seamen whose luckless vessels had ended on this coast. The leader was a stringy, weather-beaten man with one suspicious, darting eye and a sunken socket where the other had been. About his neck he wore a necklace of amethysts, half the gilding worn from the brass. It seemed one of those ships had carried a trull.

"This is Baotan," Tamur said, gesturing to the one-eyed man. "Baotan, this is Conan, a trader known in far lands and a warrior feared by many."

Baotan grunted and shifted his eye to Conan. "You want my horses, trader? For each horse, five blankets, a sword and an axe, plus a knife, a cloak, and five pieces of silver."

"Too much," Conan said.

Tamur groaned. For Conan's ear alone, he muttered, "Forget the trad-ing, Cimmerian. 'Tis the means to destroy Baalsham we seek."

Conan ignored him. Poor traders were little respected, and a lack of re-spect would mean poor information, if not outright lies. "For every two horses, one blanket and one sword."

Baotan showed the stumps of yellowed teeth in a grin, and climbed down from his horse. "We talk," he said.

The talk, Baotan and Conan squatting by one of the campfires, was more leisurely than Conan would have liked, yet he had to maintain his pose as a trader. Tamur produced clay jugs of sour Hyrkanian beer and lumps of mare's milk cheese. The beer made Baotan's eyes light up, but the one-eyed man gave ground grudgingly, and often stopped bargaining entirely to talk of the weather or some incident in his camp.

At last, though, the bargain was struck. The sky was beginning to darken; men dragged in more driftwood to pile on the fires. For the pack horses they needed, one sword and one blanket. For the animals they would ride, one axe and one blanket. Plus a knife for every man with Baotan and two pieces of gold for the stringy man himself.

"Done," Conan said.

Baotan nodded and began to produce items from beneath his coat. A pouch. A small pair of tongs. What appeared to be a copy of a bull's horn, half-sized and molded in clay. Before Conan's astonished gaze, Baotan stuffed herbs from the pouch into the clay horn. With the tongs, the one-eyed man deftly plucked a coal from the fire and used it to puff the herbs to a smoldering burn. Conan's jaw dropped as the man drew deeply on the horn, inhaling the pungent smoke. Tilting back his head, Baotan expelled the smoke in a long stream toward the sky, then offered the horn to Conan.

Tamur leaned close to speak in his ear. "'Tis the way they seal a bargain. You must do the same. I told you they were savages."

Conan was prepared to believe it. Doubtfully he took the clay horn. The smoldering herbs smelled like a fire in a rubbish heap. Putting it to his mouth, he inhaled, and barely suppressed a grimace. It tasted even worse than it smelled, and felt hot enough to blister his tongue. Fighting an urge to gag, he blew a stream of smoke toward the sky.

"They mix powdered dung with the herbs," Tamur said, grinning, "to insure even burning."

From across the fire Akeba laughed. "Would you like some aged mussels, Cimmerian?" he called, near to rolling on the sand.

Conan ground his teeth and handed the clay horn back to Baotan, who stuck the horn in his mouth and began to emit small puffs of smoke. The Cimmerian shook his head. He had seen many strange customs since leaving the mountains of his homeland, but, sorcery aside, this was certainly the strangest.

When his mouth no longer felt as if he were attempting to eat a coal from the fire—though the taste yet remained—Conan said, "Have you seen any other strangers on the coast? You understand that I must be concerned with other traders."

"Strangers," Baotan said through teeth clenched around the clay horn, "but no traders." Each word came out accompanied by a puff of smoke. "They bought horses, too. No trade goods. Silver." He grinned suddenly. "They paid too much."

"Not traders," Conan said, pretending to muse. "That is strange indeed."

"Strangers are strangers. Their boat was much charred at the back, and some of them suffered from burns."

The galley. It had survived both fire and storm after all. "Perhaps we might help these men," Conan said. "How far off are they, and in which direction?"

Baotan waved a hand to the south. "Half a day. Maybe a day."

Far enough that they might not know *Foam Dancer* had also survived. But if that was so, why the horses? Perhaps there *was* something here that Jhandar feared. Conan felt excitement rising.

"Use our campfires this night," he said to Baotan. "Akeba, Tamur, we ride at first light."

Yasbet appeared from the dark to nestle her hip against Conan's shoulder. "It grows cold," she said. "Will you warm me?" Ribald laughter rose from the listening men, but, oddly, a glare from her silenced them, even Tamur and Baotan.

"That I will," Conan said, and as he rose flipped her squealing over his shoulder.

Her squeals had turned to laughter by the time they reached her tent. "Put me down, Conan," she managed between giggles. "'Tis unseemly."

Suddenly the hair on the back of his neck rose, and he whirled, staring into the dark, at the headland.

"Are you trying to make me dizzy, Conan? What is it?"

Imaginings, he told himself. Naught but imaginings. The galley and those it carried were far to the south, sure *Foam Dancer* and all aboard had perished in the storm.

"'Tis nothing, wench," he growled. She squealed with laughter as he ducked into the tent.

Che Fan rose slowly from the shadows where he had dropped, and peered at the beach below, dotted with campfires. There was no more to learn by watching. The barbarian was abed for the night. He made his way across the headland and down the far slope, gliding surefooted over the rough ground, a wraith in the night.

Suitai was waiting at their small fire—well shielded by scrub growth— along with the six they had chosen from the uninjured to accompany them. The men huddled silently on the far side of the fire from the Khitans. They had seen just enough on the voyage to guess that the two black-robed men carried a sort of deadliness they had never before encountered. Thus they feared greatly, and wisely, although still ignorant.

"What did you see?" Suitai asked. He sipped at a steaming decoction of herbs.

Che Fan squatted by the fire, filling a cup with the same bitter liquid as he spoke. "They are there. And they have obtained horses from that dung-beetle Baotan."

"Then let us go down and kill them," Suitai said. "It may be more diffcult if we must find them again." The six who had accompanied them from the galley shifted uneasily, but the Khitans did not appear to notice.

"Not until they have found what they came to seek," Che Fan replied. "The Great Lord will not be pleased if we return with naught but word of their deaths." He paused. "We must be careful of the barbarian called Conan."

"He is but a man," Suitai said, "and will die as easily as any other."

Che Fan nodded slowly, uncertain why he had spoken such a thing aloud. And yet. . . . In his boyhood had he learned the art of appearing invisible, of hiding in the shadow of a leaf and becoming one with the night, but there was that about the muscular barbarian's gaze that seemed to penetrate all such subterfuge. That was nonsense, he told himself. He was of the Brothers of the Way, and this Conan *was* but a man. He would die as easily as any other. Yet . . . the doubts remained.

XVIII

Tugging his cloak closer about him against the brisk wind, Conan twisted on his sheepskin saddle pad to look behind for the hundredth time since dawn. Short-grassed plain and rolling hills, so sparsely grown with a single stunted tree was a startlement, revealed no sign of pursuit. Disgruntled, he faced front. The pale yellow sun, giving little warmth in the chill air, rose ahead of them toward its zenith. The Vilayet lay two nights behind. No matter what his eyes told him, deeper instinct said that someone followed, and that instinct had kept him alive at times when more civilized senses failed.

The party rode well bunched, half of the Hyrkanians leading strings of pack horses, cursing. The small beasts, seeming little larger than the hampers and bales lashed to their pack saddles, tried to turn their tails into the wind whenever they found slack in the lead ropes. The men not so encumbered kept hands near weapons and eyes swiveling in constant watch. It was not unknown for travelers to be attacked on the plains of Hyrkania. Traders were usually immune, but more than one had lost his head.

Tamur galloped his shaggy horse between Conan and Akeba. "Soon we shall be at the Blasted Lands."

"You have been saying that since we left the sea," Conan grumbled. His temper was not improved by the way his feet dangled on either side of his diminutive mount.

"A few more hills, Cimmerian. But a few more. And you must be ready to play the trader. One of the tribes is sure to be camped nearby. Each takes its turn guarding the Blasted Lands."

"You've said that as well."

"I hope we find a village soon," Yasbet said through clenched teeth. She half stood in her stirrups then, seeing the amusement that flitted across the men's faces, sat again hastily, wincing.

Conan managed to keep a straight face. "There is liniment in one of the packs," he offered. It was not his first time to do so.

"No," she said brusquely, the same answer she had given to his other offers. "I need no coddling."

"'Tis not coddling," he snapped, exasperated. "Anyone may use liniment for a sore . . . muscle."

"Let him rub some on," Sharak chortled. The astrologer clung to his horse awkwardly, like a stick figure placed on a pony by children. "Or if not him, wench, then let me."

"Still your tongue, old man," Akeba said, grinning. "I see you ride none too easily yourself, and I may take it in mind to coat you with so much liniment that you run ahead of us the rest of the way."

"You have done well, woman," Tamur said suddenly, surprising everyone. "I thought we would have to tie you across your saddle before the sun was high, but you have the determination of a Hyrkanian."

"I thank you," she told him, glaring at the Cimmerian. "I was not allow . . . that is, I have never ridden before. I walked, or was carried in a palanquin." She eased herself on her saddle pad and muttered an oath. Sharak cackled until he broke into a fit of coughing. "I will use the liniment this night," Yasbet said stiffly, "though I am not certain the cure won't be worse than the disease."

"Good," Conan said, "else by tomorrow you'll not be able to walk, much less—" He broke off as they topped a rise. Spread before them was a great arc of yurts. More than a thousand of the domed felt structures dotted the rolling plain like gray mushrooms. "There's the encampment you predicted, Tamur. I suppose 'tis time for us to begin acting the part of traders."

"Wait. This could be ill," the nomad said. "There are perhaps four tribes camped here, not one. Among so many there may well be one who remembers that we swore vengeance on Baalsham despite the ban. Do they realize we have brought you here to break the taboo on the Blasted Lands. . . ." A murmur rose from the other Hyrkanians.

From the tents two score of fur-capped horsemen galloped toward them, lance points glittering in the rising sun.

"It is too late to turn back now." Conan kicked his mount forward. "Follow me, and remember to look like traders."

"For violating a taboo," Tamur said, trailing after the Cimmerian, "a man is flayed alive, and kept so for days while other parts important to a man are removed slowly. Burning slivers are thrust into his flesh."

"Flayed?" Sharak said hollowly. "Other parts? Burning slivers? Perhaps we could turn back after all?"

Yet he followed as well, as did the others, Yasbet riding with shoulders back and hand on sword hilt, Akeba in an apparently casual slouch above the cased bow strapped ahead of his saddle pad. The rest of the Hyrkanians came more slowly, muttering, but they came.

Tamur raised his sword hand in greeting—and no doubt to show that he did not intend to draw the weapon—as they approached the other horsemen. "I see you. I am called Tamur, and am returned to my people from across the sea, bringing with me this trader, who is called Conan."

"I see you," the leader of the mounted nomads said, lifting his right hand. Squat and dark, mustaches thick with grease dangling below his chin, he eyed Conan suspiciously from beneath the fur cap pulled down to his shaggy brows. "I am called Zutan. It is late in the year for traders."

Conan put on a broad smile. "Then there will be no others to compete with me."

Zutan stared at him, expressionless, for a long moment. Then, wheeling his horse, he motioned them to follow.

The riders from the encampment spread out in two lines, one to either side of Conan and his party, escorting them—or guarding them, perhaps—into the midst of the yurts, to a large open space in the center of the crescent. People gathered around them, men in fur caps and thick sheepskin coats, women in long woolen dresses, dyed in a rainbow of colors, with hooded fur cloaks held close about them. Those males who had reached an age to be called men were uniformly surrounded by the rankness of rancid grease, and those of middle years or beyond were so weathered and leather-skinned as to make their ages all but impossible to tell. The women, however, were another matter. There were toothless crones among them, and wrinkled hags, but one and all they seemed *clean*. Many of the younger women were pretty enough for any zenana. They moved lithely to the tinkle of ankle bells beneath their skirts, and more than one set of dark, kohled eyes followed the young giant above full, smiling lips.

Sternly Conan forced himself to ignore the women. He had come for a means to destroy Jhandar, not to disport himself with nomad wenches. Nor would the need to kill father, brother, husband or lover help him. Nor would trouble with Yasbet.

As he swung down from his wooly mount, Conan leaned close to Tamur and spoke softly. "Why do the women not grease their hair also?"

Tamur looked shocked. "'Tis a thing for men, Cimmerian." He shook his head. "Hark you. I have meant to speak on this to you for some time. Many traders adopt this custom while among us. It would aid your disguise to be seen to do so. Perhaps you could grow a mustache as well? And this washing you insist on is a womanly thing. It saps the strength."

"I will think on these things," Conan said. He noticed Akeba, a wry smile on his dark face, peering at him over his horse.

"Long mustaches," the Turanian said. "And mayhap a beard like that of Muktar."

Conan growled, but before he could reply a sharp cry broke from Yasbet. He spun to see her half fall from her saddle-pad in attempting to dismount. Darting, he caught her before she collapsed completely to the ground.

"What ails you, wench?"

"My legs, Conan," she moaned. "They will not support me. And my . . . my. . . ." Her face reddened. "My . . . muscles are sore," she whispered.

"Liniment," he said, and she moaned again. The crowd about them stirred. Hastily he lifted her back to her feet and put her hands on her sheepskin saddle-pad. "Hold to that. You must keep your feet a moment longer." Half-sobbing, she tangled her hands in the thick wool; he turned immediately from her to more pressing matters.

Zutan pushed his way to the forefront of those watching. Four squat, bow-legged elders followed him, and the murmurs of the onlookers were stilled. "I present to you," Zutan intoned, "the trader called Co-nan. Know, Co-nan, that you are presented to the chiefs of the four tribes here assembled, to Olotan, to Arenzar, to Zoan, to Sibuyan. Know that you are presented to men who answer only to the Great King. Know this, and tremble."

It was near impossible to tell the age of any man above five-and-twenty in those tribes, but these men had surely each amassed three times so many years, if not four. Their faces were gullied rather than wrinkled, and had the color and texture of a boot left ten years in the desert sun. The hair that straggled from under their filthy fur caps was as white as bleached parchment, beneath a coating of grease, and their mustaches, just as pale, were long and thin. One had no teeth at all, muttering through his gums, while the other three showed blackened stumps when they opened their mouths. Yet the eight black eyes that peered at him were hard and clear, and there was no tremor in the bony hands that rested lightly on the hilts of their yataghans.

Conan raised his right hand in the greeting Tamur had used. What did traders say at these times, he wondered. Whatever he said, though, it had best come fast. Zutan was beginning to tug at his mustache impatiently. "I see you. I am honored to be presented to you. I will trade fairly with your people."

The four stared at him unblinkingly. Zutan's tugging at his mustache became more agitated.

What else was he supposed to say, Conan thought. Or do? Suddenly he turned his back on the chiefs and hurried back among the pack animals. Mutters sounded among the tribesmen, and the Hyrkanians who held the guide-ropes eyed him with frowns. Hastily he unroped a wicker hamper and drew out four tulwars, their hilts ivory and ebony. The blades had been worked with beeswax and acid into scenes of men hunting with bows from horseback, with silver rubbed across the etchings hammered till the argentine metal shone. Conan had raised a storm when he found the blades among the trade goods—he was still of a mind that Tamur had meant them for himself and his friends—but they had already been paid for. Now he was glad of them.

As the Cimmerian returned, two swords in each huge fist, Tamur groaned, "Not those, northerner. Some other blades. Not those."

Conan reached the four chiefs and, after a moment, awkwardly sketched a bow. "Accept these, ah, humble gifts as a, ah, token of my admiration."

Dark eyes sparked avariciously, and the blades were snatched as if the squat men expected them to be withdrawn. The etched steel was fingered; for a time Conan was ignored. At last the chief nearest him—Conan thought he was the one called Sibuyan—looked up. "You may trade here," he said. Without another word the four turned away, still fingering their new swords.

Akeba put a hand on Conan's arm. "Come, Cimmerian. We traders must display our wares."

"Then display them. I must see to Yasbet."

As he returned to her, Conan ignored the bustle of hampers being lifted from pack saddles, of pots and knives, swords and cloaks being spread for eager eyes. The throng pressed close, many calling offers of furs, or ivory, or gold as soon as items appeared. Some of Tamur's followers began gathering the horses.

Yasbet had sagged to her hands and knees on the hard-packed ground beside her mount. Muttering an oath Conan stripped off his cloak and spread it on the ground. When he had her lying on it, face down, he removed the sheepskin saddle-pad from her horse and put it beneath her head.

"Are you all right?" he asked. "Can you stand at all?"

"I do not need to be wrapped in swaddling," she replied between clenched teeth.

"Hannuman's Stones, wench! I do not swaddle you. You must be able to ride when it is time to go."

She sighed, not looking at him. "I can neither stand nor ride. I cannot even sit." She laughed mirthlessly.

"It is possible we may have to leave suddenly," he said slowly. "It may be needful to tie you across a saddle. And again I do not mean to mock you by that."

"I know," she said quietly. Suddenly she grasped his hand and pulled it to her lips. "You have not only my body," she murmured, "but my heart and soul. I love you, Conan of Cimmeria."

Brusquely he pulled his hand away and stood. "I must see to the others," he muttered. "You will be all right here? It may be some time before your tent can be put up."

"I am comfortable."

Her words were so soft he barely heard them. With a quick nod he strode to where the trade goods were displayed. Why did women always have to speak of love, he wondered. The most calloused trull would do it, given a fingerbreadth of encouragement, and other women took even less. Then they expected a man to act like a giddy boy with his first hair on his chin. Or worse, like a poet or a bard.

He glanced back at Yasbet. Her face was buried in the sheepskin, and her shoulders shook as if she cried. No doubt her rump pained her. Growling wordlessly under his breath, he joined his fellows acting the trader.

Sharak bounced from nomad to nomad, always gesticulating, here offering lumps of beeswax, there pewter cups from Khauran or combs of tortoise shell from Zamboula or lengths of Vendhyan silk. Akeba was more sedate in his demonstrations of the weapons, tulwars bearing the stamp of the Royal Arsenal of Turan, glaives from far Aquilonia, and even khetens, broadbladed battleaxes from Stygia. Tamur and his men, on the other hand, squatted to one side, passing among themselves clay jars of the ale they had gotten from men of the tribes.

Conan walked among the goods, stopping from time to time to listen to Akeba or Sharak bargain, nodding as if he agreed with what was being done. A merchant who had two men to do the actual peddling surely was not expected to do more.

The trading was brisk, but Conan was soon thinking more of quenching his thirst with a crock of ale than of his playacting. It was then that he noticed the woman.

Past her middle years, she was yet a beauty, tall and well-breasted, with large dark eyes and full red lips. Her fur-trimmed blue cloak was of fine wool, and her kirtle of green was slashed with panels of blue silk. Her necklace of intricate links was gold, not gilded brass; the brooch that held her cloak was a large emerald; and the bracelets at her wrists were of matched amethysts. And she had no eye for the perfumes or gilded trinkets that Sharak bartered away. Her gaze never left the muscular Cimmerian. An interested gaze.

Conan judged her to be the woman of a wealthy man, perhaps even of a chief. That made her just the sort of woman he should avoid, even more so than the other women of the tribe. He made sure there was nothing in his expression that she could read as invitation, and turned away to make a show of studying the goods laid out on a nearby blanket.

"You are young to be a trader," a deep female voice said behind him.

He turned to find himself face to face with the woman who had been watching him. "I am old enough," he said in a flat tone. His youth was a touchy point with him, especially with women.

Her smile was half mocking, half . . . something more. "But you are still young."

"A man must begin at some age. Do you wish to trade for something?"

"I would think you would be demonstrating the swords and spears to the men, youngling." Her gaze caressed the breadth of his shoulders, trailed like fingers across the tunic strained by the muscles of his deep chest.

"Perhaps kohl for your eyes." He snatched a small blue-glazed jar from the blanket and held it out to her. His eyes searched the crowd for a man taking an unfriendly interest in their conversation. This woman would have men after her when she was a grandmother.

"From the way that sword sits on your hip, I would name you, not merchant, but . . ." she put a finger to her lips as if in thought " . . . warrior."

"I am a trader," he said emphatically. "If not kohl, perhaps perfume?"

"Nothing," she said, amusement in her eyes. "For now, at least. Later I will have something from you." She turned away, then stopped to look at him over her shoulder. "And that *is* perfume. Trader." Her laughter, low and musical, hung in the air after she had disappeared into the crowd.

With a sudden sharp crack the small jar shattered in Conan's grip.

"Erlik take all women," he muttered, brushing shards of glazed pottery from his hand. There was nothing to be done about the smell of jasmine that hung about him in a cloud.

Grumbling, he resumed his pacing among the trade goods. Occasionally a man would glance at him in surprise, nose wrinkling, or a woman would eye him and smile. Each time he hurried furiously elsewhere, muttering ever more sulphurous oaths under his breath. A bath, he decided. When their camp was set he would bathe, and Mitra blast all the Hyrkanians if they thought it unmanly.

XIX

T hroughout the day the trading continued briskly, goods from the west for goods looted from eastern caravans. As twilight empurpled the air Zutan returned. The bargaining tribespeople began to trail away at his appearance.

"I will show you to your sleeping place," the greasy-mustached Hyrkanian said. "Come." And he stalked off in the rolling walk of one more used to the back of a horse than to his own feet.

Conan set the others to repacking the trade goods, then scooped Yasbet into his arms. She was in an exhausted sleep so deep that she barely stirred as he carried her after Zutan, to a spot a full three hundred paces from the yurts.

"You sleep here," the nomad said. "It would be dangerous to leave your fires after dark. The guards do not know you. You might be injured." That thought apparently caused no pain in his heart. Traders might be necessary, his expression said, but they warranted neither the hospitality of shelter nor trust.

Conan ignored him—it was better than killing him, though less satisfying—and commanded Yasbet's tent to be erected. As soon as the stakes were driven and the ropes drawn taut, he carried her inside. She gave but a sleepy murmur as he removed her garments and wrapped her in blankets.

Perhaps sleep would help her, he thought. His nose twitched at the scent of jasmine that was beginning to fill the tent. Sleep would not help him.

When he went outside, Zutan was gone. The sky grew blacker by the moment, and fires of dried dung cast small pools of light. The yurts could have been half a world away, for their lamps and fires were all inside, and the encampment of the tribes was lost in the dark. The horses had been tied to a picket line, near which the hampers of trade goods were shadowy mounds.

Straight to those mounds Conan went, rummaging through them until he found a lump of harsh soap. Thrusting it into his belt pouch, he hefted two water bags in each hand and stalked into the night. When he returned an odor of lye came from him, and it was all he could do to stop his teeth from chattering in the chill wind that whipped across the plain.

Settling crosslegged beside the fire where a kettle of thick stew bubbled, he accepted a horn spoon and a clay bowl filled to the brim.

"I am not certain that lye improves on jasmine," Akeba said, sniffing the air pointedly.

"A fine scent, jasmine," Sharak cackled. "You are a little large for a dancing girl, Cimmerian, but I do believe it became you more than your new choice." Tamur choked on stew and laughter.

Conan raised his right hand, slowly curling it into a massive fist until his knuckles cracked. "I smell nothing." He looked challengingly at each of the other three in turn. "Does anyone else?"

Chuckling, Akeba spread his hands and shook his head.

"All this washing is bad for you," Tamur said, then added quickly as Conan made to rise, "But I smell naught. You are a violent man, Cimmerian, to act so over a jest among friends."

"We will talk of other things," Conan said flatly.

Silence reigned for a moment before Sharak spoke up. "Trade. We'll talk of trade. Conan, it is no wonder merchants are men of wealth. What we bargained for today will bring at least three hundred pieces of gold in Aghrapur, yet a full two-thirds of the trade goods remain. Mayhap we should give up adventuring and become traders in truth. I have never been rich. I think I would find it pleasing."

"We are here for more important matters than gold," Conan growled. He set aside his bowl; his hunger had left him. "Know you that we have been followed since the coast?"

Tamur looked up sharply. "Baotan? I thought he had an eye for more than he received for the horses."

"Not Baotan," Conan replied.

"You looked back often," Akeba said thoughtfully, "but said nothing. And I saw no one."

Conan shook his head, choosing his words with care. "Nor did I see anyone. Still, someone was following. Or something. There was a feel . . . not human about it."

Sharak laughed shakily. "An Jhandar, or Baalsham, or whatever he chooses to call himself, has come after us to these wastes, I will think on journeying to Khitai. Or further, if there is any place further."

"Baalsham is a man," Tamur said nervously. He eyed the surrounding darkness and edged closer to the fire, dropping his voice. "But the spirits— if he has sent dead men after us. . . ."

A footstep sounded beyond the small pool of light from the fire, and Conan found himself on his feet, broadsword in hand. He was somewhat mollified to see that the others had drawn weapons as well. Even the old astrologer was shakily holding his staff out like a spear.

Zutan stepped into the light and stopped, staring at the bared steel.

Conan sheathed his blade with a grunt. "It is dangerous to leave your fires in the dark," he said.

The Hyrkanian's mustache twitched violently, but all he said was, "Samarra will see you now, Co-nan."

"Samarra!" Tamur's voice was a dry speak. "She is here?"

"Who is this Samarra?" Conan demanded. "Mayhap I do not wish to see her."

"No, Conan," Tamur said insistently. "You must. Samarra is a powerful shamaness. *Very* powerful."

"A shamaness," Sharak snorted. "Women should not be allowed to meddle in such matters."

"Hold your tongue, old man," Tamur snapped, "else you may find your manhood turned to dust, or your bones to water. She is powerful, I say." He had turned his back to Zutan and was grimacing vigorously at Conan.

The young Cimmerian eyed him doubtfully, wondering if Tamur's fear of this woman was enough to unhinge him. "Why does Samarra wish to see me?" he asked.

"Samarra does not give reasons," Zutan replied. "She summons, and those she summons come. Even chiefs."

"I will go to her," Conan said.

Tamur's groan was loud as Conan followed Zutan into the dark.

They walked to the yurts in silence. The nomad would not deign to converse with a trader, and Conan had his own thoughts to occupy him. Why did this Samarra wish to speak with him? Her sorcerous arts could have told her the true reason for his presence in Hyrkania, but only if she had purposely sought it out. In his experience of such things nothing was found unsought, and nothing was sought casually. Knowledge had its price when gained by thaumaturgical means, and though he had met sorcery and magic in many forms, never had he known it used to satisfy mere curiosity.

Had this Samarra been a man he could have first explained, then, an that did not work, slain the fellow. But it was not in him to kill a woman.

Lost in the workings of his mind, Conan started when the other halted before a huge yurt and motioned him to enter. The structure of felt stretched on wooden frames was at least twenty paces across, fit for a chief. But then, he told himself, a shamaness who could summon chiefs would certainly live as well as they. Without another glance at Zutan, he pushed open the flap and went in.

He found himself in a large chamber within the yurt, its "walls" brocaded hangings. The ground was covered by Kasmiri carpets in a riot of colors, dotted with cushions of silk. Gilded lamps hung on golden chains from the wooden frames of the roof, and a charcoal fire in a large bronze brazier provided warmth against the chill outside.

So much he had time to note, then his eyes popped as eight girls burst from behind the hangings. From lithe to full-bodied they ranged, and their skins from a paleness that spoke of Aquilonia to Hyrkanian brownness to the yellow of well-aged ivory. Gilded bells tinkled at their ankles as they ran giggling to surround him; such was the whole of their costume.

His vision seemed filled by rounded breasts and buttocks as they urged him to a place on the cushions before the brazier. A scent of roses hung about them.

No sooner was he seated than two darted away to return with damp cloths to wipe his face and hands. Another set a chased silver tray of dates and dried apricots by his side, while a fourth poured wine from a crystal flagon into a goblet of beaten gold.

The music of flutes and zithers filled the chamber; the remaining girls had taken up the instruments and, seating themselves cross-legged, played. The four who had served him began to dance.

"Where is Samarra?" he asked. "Well? Answer me! Where is she?" The music soared, and the dancers with it, but none spoke.

He picked up the goblet, but put it down again untouched. Strong powders could be put in wine; he wagered that this shamaness knew of them. Best he neither eat nor drink till he was gone from Samarra's dwelling place. And best he not eye the girls too closely, either. Mayhap the shamaness had a reason for wishing his attention occupied. He kept a close watch on the hangings, and a hand on his sword.

But despite his intentions he found his eyes drifting back to the dancing girls. Graceful as gazelles they leaped, legs striding wide on air, then rolled to the carpets, hips thrusting in abandon. Sweat beaded his forehead, and he wondered if perhaps the fire in the brazier made the yurt too hot. Did this Samarra remain away much longer, he might forget himself. Even though they would not talk, these girls might be willing to disport themselves with a young northerner.

A single sharp clap sounded above the music. Immediately the girls left off playing and dancing, and dashed behind the hangings. The grin that had begun on Conan's face faded, and his hand returned to his sword as he sprang to his feet. The hangings parted, and the woman who had taunted him earlier appeared. The cloak was gone now, and long hair as black as night hung in soft waves about her shoulders. Her long kirtle clung to her curves.

"I prefer the dancing of young men," she said, "but I did not think you would share my taste."

"You?" Conan said incredulously. "You are Samarra?"

She gave a throaty laugh. "You are disappointed that I am not an aged crone, with a beak of a nose and warts? I prefer to remain as I am for as long as the arts of woman and magic combined can keep me so." Her hands smoothed the bosom of her kirtle, pulling it tight over full round breasts. "Some say I am still beautiful." Delicately wetting her lips, she moved closer. "Do you think so?"

The woman had no need of sorcery for distraction, Conan thought. The musk of her perfume seemed to snare his brain. With no more than what was known to every woman she had his blood inflamed, his throat thick with desire. "Why did you send for me?" he rasped.

Her dark eyes caressed his face more sensuously than hands might have done, slid lingeringly across his broad shoulders and massive chest. Her nostrils flared. "You washed the scent away," she said, a touch of mocking disappointment in her tone. "Hyrkanian women are used to men who smell of sweat and horse and grease. That scent would have gained you many favorable looks. But even so you are an exotic, with your muscles and your size and that pale skin. And those eyes." Her slender fingers stopped a hair's breath from his face, tracing along his cheek. "The color of the sky," she whispered, "and as changeable. The spring sky after a rain, the sky of a fall morning. And when you are angry, a sky of thunder and storms. An exotic giant. You could have your pick of half the women in this encampment, perhaps three or four at a time, if such is your taste."

Angrily he wrapped an arm about her, lifting her from the ground, crushing her softness against his chest. His free hand tangled in her hair, and the blue eyes that stared into hers did indeed have much of the storm in them. "Taunting me is a dangerous game," he said, "even for a sorceress."

She stared back unperturbed, a secretive smile dancing on her lips. "When do you mean to enter the Blasted Lands, outlander?"

Involuntarily his grip tightened, wringing a gasp from her. There was naught of the sky in his gaze now, but rather ice and steel. "It is a foolish time to reveal your sorceries, woman."

"I am at your mercy." With a sigh that smacked of contentment she wriggled to a more comfortable position, shifting her breasts disturbingly against his hard chest. "You could break my neck merely by flexing your arm, or snap my spine like a twig. I can certainly perform no magic held as

I am. Perhaps I have made myself helpless before your strength to prove that I mean you no harm."

"I think you are as helpless as a tigress," he said wryly. Abruptly he set her heels on the carpets; there was a tinge of disappointment in her eyes as she patted her hair back into place. "Speak on, woman. What suspicions caused you to bend your magic to the reason of my coming?"

"No magic except that of the mind," she laughed. "You came in company with Tamur and others who I know crossed the Vilayet to find and slay Baalsham. I know well the horror of those days, for I was one of those who laid the wards that contain what lies within the Blasted Lands."

Conan realized why Tamur had been agitated at hearing her name. "Perhaps I, wishing to trade in Hyrkania, merely took Tamur into service."

"No, Conan. Tamur has many faults, but he, and the others, swore oaths to defy the ban on Baalsham's memory and avenge their blood. That they returned with you merely means that they think to find success in the Blasted Lands. Though their oaths led them to defiance, they know that violating the taboo means death for one of Hyrkanian blood, and so sought another to do the deed."

"Then why am I not fighting for my life against your warriors?"

She answered slowly, her voice tense, as if her words held import below the surface. As if there was danger in them for her, danger that she must carefully avoid. "When the barriers were erected, I alone among the shamans believed that they were not enough. I spoke for pursuing Baalsham and destroying him, for surely if he managed to establish his evil elsewhere it would eventually return to haunt us. The others, fearing another confrontation with him, forced me—" She stopped abruptly.

"Forced you to what?" he growled. "Swear oaths? What?"

"Yes," she said, nodding eagerly. "Both oath and *geas*. Do I break that oath, I will find myself the next dawn scrubbing pots in the yurt of a most repulsive man, unable to magic the pain from a sore tooth or think beyond a desire to obey. Many take it ill that there is a line of women who use the powers, and they would as soon see it end with me." Again her words halted, but her eyes begged him to question further.

"What holds your tongue, woman? What oath did you swear?"

"It took long enough to bring you to it," she sighed, tightness draining visibly from her face. "Firstly, I can speak to no one of the oaths unless asked, and no Hyrkanian but another who, like me, sits Guardian on the Blasted Lands would ask. Betimes one or another of them likes to taunt me with it."

"So you must trick me into asking," Conan muttered.

"Exactly. For the rest, I can aid no Hyrkanian to enter the Blasted Lands or act against Baalsham, nor can I seek out any man to do those things."

A broad smile spread over his features. "But if a man who is not a Hyrkanian seeks you out. . . ."

". . . Then I can help him. But he must be the right man, outlander. I will not risk failure." Her mouth twisted as at a foul taste. "Anator, the repulsive toad of whom I spoke, waits for me to fall into his hands. Death I would risk, but not a life with him till I am old and shriveled."

"But you will help me?" he asked, frowning.

"If you are the right man. I must consult the Fire that Burns Backwards in Time. And I must have a lock of your hair for that."

In spite of himself, he took a step back. Hair, spittle, nail parings, anything that came from the body could be used in thaumaturgies that bound the one from whom they came.

"Do you think I need magicks to bind you?" Samarra laughed, and swayed her hips exaggeratedly.

"Take it, then," he said. But a grimace crossed his face as she deftly cut a few strands from his temple with a small golden knife.

Swiftly then she opened a series of small chests against a hanging, removing her paraphernalia. The hair was ground in a small hand-mill, then mixed in an unadorned ivory bowl with the contents of half a score of vials—powders of violent hue and powerful stench, liquids that seethed and bubbled—and stirred with a rod of bone. Setting up a small golden brazier on a tripod, Samarra filled it with ashes, smoothing them with the bone rod. Chanting words unintelligible to Conan, she poured the contents of the bowl onto the dead ash, and set the bowl aside.

Her voice rose, not in volume, but in pitch, till it pierced his ears like red-hot needles. Strange flames rose from the ash, blue flames, not flickering like ordinary fire, but rolling slowly like waves of a lazy sea. Higher that unnatural fire rose with Samarra's words, to the reach of a man's arm. Unblinking she stared into its depths as she spoke the incantations. A rime of frost formed on the outside of the golden dish that held the flames.

The other fires in the chamber, the flickering lamps and blazing charcoal, sank low, as if overawed, or drained. The Cimmerian realized that his fingernails were digging into his palms. With an oath he unclenched his fists. He had seen sorcery before, sorcery directed at him with deadly intent. He would not be affrighted by this.

Abruptly Samarra's chanting stopped. Conan blinked as he looked into the golden dish; half-burned pieces of wood now nestled among ash that was less than it had been. Then Samarra set a golden lid atop the brazier, closing off the blue fire.

For a long time she stared at the brazier before turning to him. "An you enter the Blasted Lands, scores will die," she said bleakly, "among them perhaps Baalsham. And perhaps you, as well. Your bones may feed the twisted beasts that dwell trapped in that accursed place."

"Perhaps?" he said. "What means of divining is this? Even Sharak does not so hedge his star-readings about."

"The fire shows the many things which can be. Men choose which *will* be by their decisions. What is, is like a line, but at every decision that line branches, in two directions or ten, and each of those will also branch until numbers beyond counting are reached. I will tell you this: if you enter, you, or Baalsham, or both, will stare Erlik's minions in the eyes. But if you do not, you will surely die. A hundred lines I examined, hoping to find an escape for you, and a hundred times I saw you die, each time more horribly than the last. And if you do not enter, not only will you die. Tens upon tens of thousands will perish fighting the spread of Baalsham's evil, and every day hundreds more will walk willingly to their deaths for his necromancies. Kings and queens will crawl on their bellies to worship at his feet, and such a darkness will cover the earth as has not been seen these many thousands of years, not since the attainted days of foul Acheron."

Conan laughed mirthlessly. "Then it seems I must try to save the world, whether I will or no." His blade leaped into his hand; he tested the edge carefully. "If I must wager my life, the odds will grow no better for waiting. I will go to these Blasted Lands now."

"No," she said sharply. He opened his mouth, but she hurried on. "Night is best, it is true, but not this night. Think of the girl with you. When you have done this thing, you must go immediately, for others sit Guardian besides me, and they will soon know what has been done. But she cannot stand, much less sit a saddle."

"Then I'll tie her across it," he answered roughly. Already the battle rage was rising in him. If he was to die this night, he would not die easily.

"But if you let me bring her here, I can cure her sore flesh in a day. She will be able to ride by tomorrow night." Samarra smiled. "Many women have asked me to take the pain from a smarting rump, but this will be the first time I have used my powers for so low a purpose."

"The longer I wait, the greater the chance that someone else will remember Tamur."

"But you still cannot enter the Blasted Lands without any help. The barrier of the Outer Circle will slay only those of Hyrkanian blood, but that of the Inner Circle, where you must go if you are to find what you seek, will destroy anything that lives. I must give you special powders to spread, and teach you incantations, if you are to survive."

"Then give them to me," he demanded.

Instead she untied her silk sash and tossed it aside. "No Hyrkanian man," she said, staring him in the eye, "will look at a shamaness as a woman. I have slaves, young men, full of vigor, but full of fear, too." She began to undo the silver pins that held her garment. "They touch me because I command it, but they do so as if I might shatter, afraid of hurting or angering. Until you put your hands on me, no man in my entire life has touched me as a woman, who will not break for a little roughness in a caress. I can wait no longer." The long kirtle slid to the carpets and she stood in lush nudity, all ripe curves and womanly softness. Feet apart she faced him, defiance in her eyes, fists on the swelling of her hips, shoulders thrown back so that her breasts seemed even fuller. "There is a price for my aid. If that makes me a harlot, well, that is something I have never experienced. And I want to experience everything that a man and a woman can do to each other. Everything, Conan."

Conan let his sword fall to the ground. Battle rage had changed to a different sort of fire in his blood. "Tomorrow night will be time enough," he said hoarsely, and pulled her into his embrace.

XX

arly the next morning Conan sent a message to Akeba that the Turanian was to see to the trading that day. Soon after, Yasbet was brought to the shamaness's yurt on a litter borne by two of Samarra's muscular young male slaves. Samarra scrambled red-faced to her feet, hastily pulling a silk robe around her nudity. The slaves glared at Conan with covert jealousy.

"Conan, why am I here?" Yasbet almost wept. Lying face down on the litter, she winced at every movement. "I hurt, Conan."

"Your pain will soon be gone," he told her gently. "Samarra will see to you."

Still blushing furiously, the shamaness led the litter-bearers to another part of the yurt. Half a turn of the glass later she returned, with high color yet in her cheeks. Conan lay sprawled on the silken cushions, occupying himself with a flagon of wine.

"I gave her a sleeping potion as well," she said. "The spell took her pain away immediately, but she needs rest, and it is best if that does not come from magic. If I relieved her fatigue so, she would repay it ten times over, later. The powers always demand repayment."

All the while she spoke she remained across the chamber from him, rubbing her hands together as if in nervousness. He motioned her to him. "Come Sit, Samarra. Do not make me play host under your roof."

For a moment she hesitated, then knelt gracefully beside him. "Everything, I said," she murmured ruefully, "but I did not mean to have my own slaves enter while I lay naked in a stupor of lust. Not to mention the woman of the man I am lying with. I feel strange to have your lover but a few paces away."

Her ardor had surprised Conan in its fierceness. "What she does not know will not harm her," he said, tugging her robe from a smooth shoulder.

She slapped his hand away. "Is that all women are to you? A tumble for the night, and no more?"

"Women are music and beauty and delight made flesh." He reached for her again. She shrugged him away, and he sighed. So much for poetry, even when it was true. "Someday I will find a woman to wed, perhaps. Until then, I love all women, but I'll not pretend to any that she is more to me than she really is. Now, are you ready to remove that robe?"

"You know not your own vigor," she protested. Attempting to stretch, she stopped with a wince. "I am near as much in need of aid for sore muscles as that poor girl."

"In that case, I might as well return to Akeba and the others," he said, getting to his feet.

"No," she cried. Ripping the robe from her, she scrambled on her knees to throw her arms around his legs. "Please, Conan. Stay. I . . . I will keep you here by brute force, if I must."

"Brute force?" he chuckled.

She gave a determined nod. Laughing, he let her topple him to the pillows.

By two glasses after sunfall he was ready to go. Briefly he looked in on Yasbet. She slept naturally now; the potion had worn off. He brushed her cheek with his fingers, and she smiled without waking.

When he returned to the large chamber Samarra had donned her kirtle, and put on a somber mien as well. "You have the powder?" she demanded. "You must take care not to lose it."

"It is here," he replied, touching the pouch that hung from his belt along with sword and dagger. Within were two small leather bags containing carefully measured powders that would weaken the barrier of the Inner Circle enough for him to pass it, one portion for entering and one for leaving.

"The incantation. You remember the incantation?"

"I remember. Do not worry so."

He tried to put his arms around her, but she stepped back out of his embrace, her face a mask. "The gods be with you, Conan." She swallowed, and whispered, "And with all of us."

There was more help in steel than in gods, Conan thought as he went into the night. The moon hung bright in a cloudless sky, bathing the countryside in pale light, filling the camp with shadows. It seemed a place of the dead, that camp. No one was about, and even the guard dogs huddled close to the yurts, only lifting their heads to whine fretfully as he passed. He gathered his cloak against the chill of the wind, and against a chill that was not of the wind.

Akeba, Sharak and Tamur were waiting, as they had agreed, east of the crescent of yurts. The rest of the Hyrkanians remained in their small camp, so that it should not be found empty. The horses remained in camp as well; the sound of hooves in the night might attract unwanted attention.

Tamur peered beyond Conan nervously and whispered, "She did not come with you, did she?"

"No," Conan said. Tamur heaved a heavy sigh of relief. "Let's do this and be done," he went on. "Tamur, you lead."

Hesitantly, the Hyrkanian started to the east. Akeba followed, horsebow in hand and arrow nocked, to one side of Conan. Sharak labored on the other, leaning on his staff and muttering about the footing despite the bright moonlight.

"Tamur almost did not come," Akeba said quietly, "so afraid is he of Samarra. Did he hate Jhandar one iota less, he would have ridden for the coast, instead."

"But he does hate Jhandar," Conan replied. "He will lead us true."

"I wonder you have energy for this night, Conan," Sharak snickered, "after a day and a night with this witch-woman. I saw little of her, not nearly so much as you," he paused to cackle shrilly, "but I'd say she was a woman to sap a man's strength."

"Watch your step, old man," the big Cimmerian said drily. "I've not seen you read your own stars of late. This could be the night you break your neck."

"Mitra!" Sharak swore, stumbled, and almost fell. "I have not," he went on in a shaken voice. "Not since Aghrapur. The excitement, and the adventure, and the. . . ." He stumbled, peered at the sky and muttered, "The brightness of the moon blinds me. I cannot tell one star from another."

They traveled without words, then, following the dim shape of Tamur until abruptly the Hyrkanian stopped. "There," he said, pointing to two tall shadows ahead. "Those are the marks of the barrier. I can go no closer."

Samarra had described the shadowy objects as well as telling Conan what she knew of what lay beyond them. Around the perimeter of the Outer Circle huge pillars of crude stone had been set, thrice the height of a man and four times as thick. To pass those stelae meant death for one of Hyrkanian blood.

"There is no need for me to accompany you, Conan," Sharak said. "My eyes. I would be more hindrance than help. No, I must remain here and learn what I can of our prospects from the stars." He suddenly clutched the arm of a surprised Tamur, and though the Hyrkanian tried to shake himself free, Sharak clung tightly, pulling on the other man. "Can you tell one star from another, Hyrkanian? No matter. I will tell you what to look for. Come." The two moved off to the side, Tamur still jerking futilely at his arm.

"I, at least, will come with you," Akeba said, but Conan shook his head.

"Samarra told me that any who enters other than myself will die." She had said no such thing, but what she did say convinced him that two men, or fifty, would have no better chances of survival than one, and perhaps less.

"Oh. Then I will await your return, Cimmerian. You are an odd fellow, but I like you. Fare you well."

Conan clapped the slighter man on the shoulder. "Take a pull at the Hellhorn, an you get there before me, Akeba."

"What? 'Tis a strange thing to say."

"Other countries, other customs," Conan said. "It is a way of saying fare you well." His amusement faded abruptly as he eyed the stone pillars. It was time to be on with it. His blade slid from its scabbard, steel rasping on leather.

"Strange, indeed, you pale-eyed barbarians," Akeba said. "Well, you take a pull at the . . . whatever it was you said."

But Conan was already moving forward. Without pausing, the Cimmerian strode by the crude pillars, sword at the ready. As he did, a tingle passed through his body, as if nails and teeth had all been dragged across slate at once. The greatest tingle was at his waist, beneath the pouch at his belt. Samarra had warned him of this, and told him to ignore it, but he fumbled for the two smaller sacks anyway. Both were intact.

There was no growth of any kind, not even the tough grass that covered the plains of Hyrkania. The ground was smooth, yet ridged, as if it had flowed then hardened in waves. He had seen such before, where fissures had opened and the bowels of the earth had spewed forth molten rock. The moonlight here was tinged with the xanthous color of flesh gone to mold. Shadows moved furtively in that nacreous light, though no clouds crossed the moon.

Had he been the hero of a saga, he thought, he would seek out those creatures and hack his way to the Inner Circle. But the heroes of sagas always had the luck of ten men, and used it all. He went on, deeper into the Blasted Lands, moving with pantherine grace, yet carefully, as if avoiding seeking eyes. That eyes were there, or something that sensed movement, he was certain. Strange slitherings sounded from the rocks around him, and clickings, as of chitinous claws on stone. Once he did indeed see eyes, three unblinking red orbs, set close together, peering at him from the dark beside a boulder, swiveling to follow his passage. He quickened his pace. The sound of scraping claws came closer, and more quickly. A piping hiss rose, behind and either side, like the hunting cry of a pack.

Abruptly there was silence. Did the shadow creatures attack in silence, he wondered, or had they ceased their pursuit? And if they had, why? What could lie ahead that would frighten. . . . ? The answer came as he skidded to a halt, a bare pace from a pillar marking the deadly Inner Circle.

Despite himself he let out a long breath. But he still lived, and perhaps fear of the barrier would hold whatever followed at bay for a time longer. Behind he heard the hissing begin again. Hastily he pulled one leather sack from his pouch and sprinkled the scintillating powder in a long line by the stone pillar. With great care he spoke the words Samarra had taught him, and a shimmering appeared in the air above the line, as wide as a man's outstretched arms and reaching nearly as high as the stone marker. Within that shimmer the barrier was weakened, not destroyed, so Samarra said. A strong man could survive passing through it. So she said.

The scraping claws were louder, and the hissing. Whatever made those sounds was almost to him. Taking a deep breath, he leaped. The hisses rose to a scream of frustrated hunger, and then he struck the shimmer. Every muscle in his body knotted and convulsed in agony. Back arched, he was hurled into the Inner Circle.

Head spinning, he staggered to his feet. Somehow he had retained his sword. If that was a weakened barrier, he thought, he wanted no part of it at full strength. He checked his pouch again. The second sack was still safe.

Whatever had hunted him had gone, sucked back into those writhing shades outside the Inner Circle. The shimmer in the barrier yet held, but by the time he could count to one hundred the force of its protection would be gone. That second portion of the powder was his only way of crossing the barrier again, unless he went now. Turning his back on the shimmer, he went deeper into that twisted country.

Blasted Lands they were indeed. Here hills were split by gaping fissures, or stood in tortured remnants as if parts had been vaporized. Fumaroles bubbled and steamed, and the air was heavy with the stench of a decay so old that only sorcery could have kept it from disappearing long since. Foul vapors drifted in sheets, like noxious clouds hugging the ground; they left a feel of dampness and filth on the skin they touched.

Samarra had told him where Jhandar's unfinished palace had stood on that day when nightmares were loosed. What he might find there she could not say—the forces unleashed had been more than even the shamans could face—but it was the only place she could suggest for his search. In the midst of these hills the land had been leveled for the palace. Ahead he saw the hills end. It must be the location.

He hurried forward, around a sheer cliff where half a hill had disappeared, out onto the great leveled space . . . and stopped, shoulders sagging in defeat.

Before him marble steps led up to a portico of massive, broken columns. Beyond, where the palace should have stood, a huge pit opened into the depths, a pit that pulsed with red light and echoed with the bubbling of boiling rock far below.

There could be nothing there, he told himself. And yet there must be. Samarra had foretold that his entry into the Blasted Lands would bring at least the chance of Jhandar's destruction. Somewhere within that blighted region something must exist that could be used against the necromancer. He had to find it.

A slavering roar spun him around, an involuntary, "Crom!" wrenched from his lips.

Facing him was a creature twice the height of a man, its gangrenous flesh dripping phosphorescent slime. A single rubiate eye set in the middle of its head watched him with a horrifying glimmer of intelligence, but with hunger as well. And that gaping fanged maw, the curving needle claws that tipped its fingers, told what it chose to eat.

Even as the creature faced him, Conan acted. Waving his sword, he screamed as if about to attack. The beast reared back to take his charge, and Conan darted for the cliff. A being of such size could not be his equal at scaling sheer heights, he thought.

Thrusting his blade into its scabbard as he ran, he reached the cliff and climbed without slowing, fingers searching out crevices and holds with a speed he had never matched before. Chances he would have eschewed if men had pursued him he now took as a matter of course, hooking his fingernails in cracks he could not even see, planting his feet on stone that crumbled at his weight, yet moving with such desperate quickness that he was gone before its crumbling was complete. Catching the top of the cliff, he heaved himself over, lay with chest heaving.

A slime-covered, clawed hand slammed down a handsbreadth from his head. Cursing, Conan rolled to his feet, blade whispering into his grip. Its eye above the rim of the cliff, the beast saw him and roared, clawing with its free hand for him instead of securing its hold. Burnished steel blazed an arc through the air, severing the hand that held the ground. With a scream like all the fiends of the pit the beast toppled back, and down, into the fetid mists. The crash of its fall sent a shiver through the cliff that Conan could feel through his boots.

The clawed hand, faintly glowing, still lay where he had severed it. Glowing slime oozed from it like blood. He was relieved, after the sendings in Aghrapur, to see that it did not so much as twitch by itself. With the tip of his sword he flipped it into the vapors below.

Even through the clouded gloom Conan could yet see the broken pillars of Jhandar's palace; from his vantage point they were outlined in the fiery glow from the pit. No use could he see in returning there, however. His search must lead elsewhere. He started down the steep slope that backed the cliff, leaping to cross the fissures that slashed and re-slashed the terrain, dodging among boulders, crazed with a thousand lines like ill-mended pottery, abruptly lost in fetid gray curtains of drifting mist then as suddenly revealed again.

Stone clattered against stone behind him, toward the top of the precipitous slope. Weighing the broadsword in his hand, Conan peered back, attempting in vain to pierce the sheets of fog. He *could* have missed seeing some small creature on the clifftop in the mists. A thud, as of heavy body falling, drifted down to him. He could *not* have missed something large enough to. . . . Then the one-eyed beast was rushing at him out of the vapors, clawed hand and the stump of its severed wrist both raised to strike.

Conan leaped back. And found himself falling into a gaping fissure. Twisting like a great cat he caught the rock rim, slammed against it supported only by a forearm. Dislodged stone rattled into the depths of the broad crack, the sound dwindling away without striking bottom, as if the drop went on forever.

The beast was moving too fast to stop. With a roar of frustrated rage it leaped for the far side of the fissure, its lone red eye glaring at the big Cimmerian. Awkwardly Conan thrust up at the creature with his broadsword as it passed over him. Snarling, the beast curled into a ball to avoid the blade, hit heavily on the other side of the wide crack, and went rolling down the steep slope, its cries of fury ripping through the fog.

Hurriedly Conan pulled himself out of the fissure. Silence descended abruptly, but he took that for no sign of the beast's demise. Not now.

As if to confirm his dire suspicions came the sound of scrabbling claws and hungry panting. The creature yet survived, and was climbing toward him.

Being above on the slope might give him slight advantage—perhaps— but the young Cimmerian had not come to this hellish place to slay monsters. He began to run down the length of the crevice, cursing under his breath at every stone that turned beneath his boot and clattered downhill. Sheer distance from where the thing had last seen him would be his safeguard. At least, it would be so long as the beast did not hear him and follow. Had he half the luck of those ill-begotten heroes of the thrice-accursed sagas, the creature would make bootless search of the hill while he completed his own quest.

Halting, he pricked his ears for sounds of the one-eyed beast . . . and heard it still directly below him, but nearer now. Black Erlik's Bowels and Bladder! He wished he had half a score of those feckless spinners of tales there with him, to see what trials men of flesh and bone faced when confronted with the monsters so easily despatched with words in a market square. He would have fed two or three of them to the beast, feet first.

An he was forced to face the creature—and he could see no other way— the time and the place were as any others. Did he continue to run, the facing would merely be at another place, perhaps when he had run himself to exhaustion. Mayhap it would be off balance for a moment, leaping across the fissure from down slope. If he attacked then. . . . At that moment he noticed that the fissure he had followed had dwindled to a handspan crack.

For a moment the Cimmerian was too angry even to curse. For a simple lack of keeping his eyes open he had placed himself in worse danger. The great beast was no more than fifty paces straight down the slope, with only the steepness to slow it and naught between it and. . . . Straight down the slope. He peered toward the climbing beast. Its red eye was visible, glowing, as was the pale, leprous phosphorescence of its body; and it was making better going of the shattered hillside than any human could have. It seemed to move with the speed and tenacity of a leopard.

Conan knew he needed a long headstart on the creature if he was to escape it long enough to carry out his search; still, the merest breath of a chance had come to his brain, as fresh air in the foulness about him.

He cast about hurriedly for what he needed, and found it but ten paces away, a shadowy bulk near as tall as he, but seeming squat for its thickness, obscured by a curtain of fog that clung rather than drifted. Quickly his eyes sought the beast. Some forty paces below, the glowing mass edged sideways until it was once more directly below the Cimmerian. Forty paces. Conan waited.

The slavering beast clawed its way nearer, nearer. Thirty-five paces. Thirty. Conan could hear its rasping pant now. Ravenous hunger was in it as well, and in that sanguinary eye was something else, a pure desire to kill divorced from the need for meat. The hairs on the back of his neck stirred. Twenty-five paces. Twenty. Conan drifted back, through the sheet of filthy gray mist behind him. Screaming with rage, not to be denied, the creature quickened its climb.

Knees bent, Conan set his broad back to the uphill side of the boulder he had chosen and heaved. Shrieks of primordial rage echoed over the hills. The Cimmerian's every thew strained, great muscles corded and knotted till they seemed carved from some more obdurate substance than the stone with which he fought. The boulder shifted a fingerwidth. The howls came closer. In moments the foul creature would be upon him. The sweat of effort at the limits of human ability rolled down Conan's face and chest. The great stone moved again. And then it was rolling free.

Conan spun in time to see the boulder strike the now narrow crack in the hillside, bound into the air, and catch the monstrous creature full in the chest. Even as the beast was borne backward down the slope, screaming and clawing at the massive stone as if it were a living enemy, Conan set off at a dead run diagonally down the hill, leaping crevices with reckless disregard for the dangers of falling, racing toward the barrier.

He did not intend to leave the Inner Circle yet, but neither did he believe the boulder would slay the one-eyed beast. He would not believe that being *could* die until he had seen it dead. Or perhaps it already was; he had seen stranger things. But in the Outer Circle, the unseen things with claws had feared to approach the barrier. Could he reach those deadly wards before the one-eyed creature freed itself, it was possible the monstrous being would not search for him there.

Through curtains of noxious mist Conan ran like a ghostly panther past pools of bubbling, steaming mud and geysers that sprayed boiling fountains into the night. The columns marking the barrier appeared ahead in the sickly sallow moonlight.

In a silent rush the one-eyed beast hurtled from the fog, lunging for Conan. Desperately the Cimmerian threw himself aside; scythe-like claws ripped across the front of his tunic, slashing it to tatters. He rolled to his feet, broadsword at the ready, facing the towering creature. Rumbling growls sounded deep in the beast's throat as it edged toward him. It had learned respect for the steel that had taken its hand.

Blood trickled down Conan's chest from four deep gashes, but that was not what concerned him at the moment, nor even the fangs that hungered for his flesh. Fumbling at his belt with his free hand, he swallowed hard. The pouch was gone, torn away by those dagger claws, and with it the powder he needed to cross the barrier. With the thought his eyes drifted toward the marking columns . . . and there, at the base of a rough-hewn monolith, lay the pouch and his hope of escape.

Slowly, keeping the point of his sword directed at the glowing beast, Conan began to edge sideways toward the crude pillar. The creature hesitated, and a twisted intelligence shone in its eye as it, too, saw the pouch. As if divining the importance of what lay within, the slime-covered giant darted to stand over the small leather sack, almost touching the deadly barrier. Its fanged mouth twisted in what seemed almost a mocking smile.

Thus for the beast fearing the barrier, Conan thought. An it could reason so, it would not leave the pouch for him to find, even did he manage to lead it away. It seemed that Erlik was enfolding his Cloak of Unending Night about him, yet a man was not meant to accept his own death meekly.

"Crom!" Conan roared and attacked. "Crom and steel!"

Fangs bared in a snarl the creature dashed to meet him, but Conan did not mean to come to grips with the foul beast. At the last instant he dropped into a crouch, still moving, blade slashing across a belly of deathly argentine flesh covered with glowing slime, and ducked beneath slicing claws that struck only his cloak. For an instant Conan was snubbed short, then cloth ripped, and he was beyond the beast with the tatters of the garment dangling down his back.

Barely slowing, Conan bent to snatch his pouch from the ground, pivoted on one foot, and raced down the line of barrier stones. Stones grated close behind, and the Cimmerian whirled, broadsword striking at a clawed hand descending toward his head. Three cruel-tipped fingers fell, severed, but the mutilated hand slammed into Conan, driving him dazed to his knees.

Then he was enveloped in adamantine arms, being drawn toward the great flesh-rending teeth. Only Conan's sword arm was free of the unyielding grip, and with it he thrust his blade into that fanged mouth, the point knifing through flesh, grating on bone, bursting through the back of the beast's great head.

The creature snarled and snapped at the blade, trying with unabated fury to reach the Cimmerian, the stench of its breath flowing into Conan's nostrils. Like the iron bands of a torture device those huge arms tightened, till Conan thought his spine would snap. No longer could he feel his legs, or his trapped hand. He did not even know if he still held the pouch that contained his sole hope of leaving the Blasted Lands. All he could do was fight with his last measure of strength to keep that ravenous mouth from his throat.

Suddenly there was a greater worry than the beast in Conan's mind. Over the creature's shoulder he could see the marking pillars; its struggles were carrying them closer to that deadly shield. And closer. At least he would die with sword in hand, and not alone. Uncertainty flickered in the beast's blood-red eye as grim laughter burst from Conan's mouth. Contact with the barrier.

Pain ripped through the Cimmerian, pain such as he had never known. Skin flayed from muscle, muscle torn from bone, bone ground to powder and the whole thrown into molten metal, then the torturous cycle began again. And again. And. . . .

Conan found himself on the ground, on hands and knees, every muscle quivering with the effort of not falling flat on his face. Through blurred eyes he saw that he still clutched his pouch in a death-grip. He still had his means of escape from the Inner Circle, and in some fashion he had survived touching the barrier, but one thought dominated his swirling brain, the desperate need to regain his feet, to be ready to face the monster's next attack. His broadsword lay before him. Lurching forward, he grabbed the worn leather hilt, and almost let the blade fall. The leather was cracked and blistering hot.

Abruptly sound crashed in on him, crackling and hissing like a thousand chained lightning bolts, and Conan realized that he had been deaf. Shakily he scrambled to his feet . . . and stood staring.

The beast lay across the barrier, twitching as scintillating arcs of power rose from one part of its body to strike another. Flames in a hundred hues lanced from the already blacking hulk.

A grin began on the Cimmerian's face, and died as he stared at the barrier. He was no longer within the Inner Circle. How he had survived crossing the barrier—perhaps the monstrous vitality of the beast had absorbed the greater part of the deadly force, partially shielding him—did not matter. What mattered was that he had but enough of the required powder to cross that boundary once. Did he enter again, he would never leave.

In silence he turned his back on the still-jerking body of the beast, on the Inner Circle, a dark light in his eyes that boded ill.

XXI

keba and the others were huddled around a tiny fire when Conan strode out of the Blasted Lands, wiping glittering black blood from his blade with the shredded remnants of his cloak. The Cimmerian announced his presence by tossing the bloody rag into the fire, where it flared and gave off thick, acrid smoke.

All three men leaped, and Sharak wrinkled his nose. "Phhaw! What Erlik-begotten stench is that?"

"We will return to the yurts," Conan said, slamming his sword home in its shagreen sheath, "but only briefly, I must get Samarra's help to reenter the Inner Circle."

"Then you found nothing," Akeba said thoughtfully. He eyed the dried blood on Conan's tattered tunic, the pouch crudely tied to his swordbelt, as he added, "Are you certain you want to go back, Cimmerian? What occurred in there?"

Tamur spoke. "No!" Everyone looked at him; he scrubbed at his mouth with the back of his hand before speaking further. "It is a taboo place. Do not speak of what happened within the barriers. It is taboo."

"Nonsense," Sharak snorted. "No harm can there be merely in the hearing. Speak on, Conan."

But the Cimmerian was of no mind to waste time in talk. The night was half gone. With a curt, "Follow me," he started off into the night. The others kicked dirt over the fire and hurried after.

As soon as they arrived at Samarra's yurt, Conan motioned the rest to wait and ducked inside.

The interior was dark; not so much as a single lamp was lit, and the big charcoal fire was coal ash. Strange, Conan thought. Samarra, at least, would have remained awake to hear what he had found. Then the unnatural silence of the yurt struck him. There was a hollow emptiness that denied the presence of life. His broadsword eased into his hand almost of its own accord.

He started across the carpets, picking his way among the scattered cushions. Suddenly his foot struck something firmer than a cushion, yet yielding. With a sinking of his stomach, he knelt; his fingers felt along a woman's contours, the skin clammily cold.

"Conan! Look out!" Akeba shouted from the entrance.

Conan threw himself into a diving roll, striking something that bounced away with a clatter of brass, and came up in a wary crouch with his sword at the ready. Just as he picked out the shadow of what could have been a man, something hummed from the entrance and struck it. Stiffly the dim shape toppled to the ground with a thud.

"It's a man," Akeba said uncertainly. "At least, I *think* it's a man. But it did not fall as a man falls."

Conan felt around him for what he had knocked over. It was a lamp, with only half the oil spilled. Fumbling flint and steel from his pouch, he lit the wick. The lamp cast its light on the body he had stumbled over.

Samarra lay on her back, dead eyes staring up at the roof of the yurt. Blended determination and resignation were frozen on her features.

"She knew," Conan murmured. "She said if I entered the Blasted Lands many would die."

With a sigh he moved the light to the shape that had fallen so strangely. Akeba's arrow stood out from the neck of a yellow-skinned man in black robes, his almond eyes wide with disbelief. Conan prodded the body with his sword, and started in surprise. The corpse was as hard as stone.

"At least she took her murderer with her," Conan growled. "And avenged your Zorelle."

"'Tis not he, though he is very like," Akeba said. "I will remember to my tomb the face of the man who killed my daughter, and this is not he."

Conan shifted the light again, back to Samarra. "I could have saved her," he said sadly, though he had no idea of how. "Had she told me . . . Yasbet!"

Leaping to his feet, he searched furiously through the other curtained compartments of the yurt. The structure was a charnel house. Slaves, male and female alike, lay in tangled heaps of cold flesh. None bore a wound, any more than did Samarra, but the face of each was twisted in horror. Nowhere did he find Yasbet.

When he returned to Akeba, Conan was sick to his stomach. *Many would die if he entered the Blasted Lands.* Samarra had said there were many branchings of the future. Could she not have found one to avoid this?

"Jhandar sent more than this one to follow us," he told the Turanian. "Yasbet is gone, and the others are dead. All of them."

Before Akeba could speak, Tamur stuck his head into the yurt. "There are stirrings. . . ." His eyes lit on Samarra's body in the pool of lamp light. "Kaavan One-Father protect us! This is the cause! We will all be gelded, flayed alive, impaled—"

"What are you talking about?" Conan demanded. "The cause of what?"

"The yurts of the other shamans," Tamur replied excitedly. "Men are gathering there, even though none like to venture into the night this close to the Blasted Lands."

Akeba grunted. "They must have sensed the death of one of their own."

"But they'll not find us standing over the bodies," Conan said, pinching the lamp wick between his fingers. The dark seemed deeper once that small light was gone. He started for the door flap.

Outside, Sharak leaned on his staff and peered toward the distant torches that were beginning to move toward Samarra's yurt. The mutters of the men carrying those lights made a constant, angry hum. The old astrologer jumped when Conan touched his shoulder. "Do we return to the Blasted Lands, Conan, we must do it now. This lot will take it unkindly, our wandering their camp at night."

"Yasbet is gone," Conan told him quietly, "taken or slain. Samarra is dead." Sharak gasped. Conan turned away, and Sharak, after one quick glance at the approaching torches, fell silently in behind the others.

As four shadows they made they made their way between the dark yurts, out onto the plain, and hurried toward their camp, ignoring as best they could the rising tumult behind them. Then a great shout rose, a cry of rage from a hundred throats.

Akeba quickened his pace to come abreast of Conan. "They have found her," the Turanian said, "but may not think we slew her."

"We are strangers," Conan laughed mirthlessly. "What would your soldiers do if a princess of Aghrapur were murdered, and there were outlanders close to hand?"

The Turanian sucked air between his teeth. "Mitra send us time to get to our horses."

With no more words the four men broke into a run, Conan and Akeba covering the ground with distance-eating strides. Tamur ran awkwardly, but with surprising speed. Even Sharak kept up, wheezing and puffing, and finding breath to complain of his years.

"Awake!" Tamur cried as they ran into their dark camp. The fires had burned low. "To your horses!" Nomads rolled instantly from their blankets, booted and clothed, seized their weapons, and stared at him blankly. "We must flee!" Tamur shouted to them. "We stand outside the laws!" Leaping as if pricked, they darted for the horses. Tamur turned to Conan, shaking his head. "We shall not escape. We ride reedy coastal stock. Those who pursue will be astride war mounts. Our animals will drop before dawn, while theirs can maintain a steady pace all the way to the sea."

"The pack horses," Conan said. "Will they carry men?"

Tamur nodded. "But we have enough mounts for everyone."

"What if," Conan said slowly, "when our horses are about to fall, we change to horses that, if tired somewhat from running, have at least not carried a man? And when those are ready to fall. . . ." He looked at the others questioningly. He had heard of this in a tavern, and tavern tales were not always overly filled with truth. "We have several extra mounts for each man. Even these war mounts cannot outrun them all, can they?"

"It could work," Tamur breathed. "Kaavan One-Father watch over us, it could work."

Akeba nodded. "I should have thought of that. I've heard this is done on the southern frontier."

"But the trade goods," Sharak complained. "You'll not abandon—"

"Will you die for them?" Conan cut him off, and ran for the hobbled pack horses. The others followed at his heels, the old astrologer last and slowest.

The nomads wasted no time once Conan's idea was explained to them, hastily fumbling in the dark with bridles, finishing just as roaring horsemen burst from among the Hyrkanian yurts. Conan wasted but a single moment in thought of the gold from their trading, and the greater part of his own gold, hidden in a bale of tanned hides, then he scrambled onto his mount with the others, lashing it into a desperate gallop. Death rode on their heels.

As they entered the tall, scrub-covered sand dunes on the coast, four men rode double, and no spare horses were left. The sweat-lathered mounts formed a straggling line, but no man pressed his horse for fear of the animal's collapse. In the sky before them the sun hung low; the two-days' journey had consumed less than one with the impetus of saving their lives.

Conan's shaggy mount staggered under him, but he could hear the crash of waves ahead. "How much lead do we have?" he asked Akeba.

"Perhaps two turns of the glass, perhaps less," the Turanian replied.

"They held their animals back, Cimmerian, when they saw they would not overtake us easily," Tamur added. His breath came in pants almost as heavy as those of his mount. He labored the beast with his quirt, but without real force. "Ours will not last much longer, but theirs will be near fresh when they come up on us."

"They'll come up on empty sand," Conan laughed, urging his shaggy horse to the top of a dune, "for we've reached the ship." Words and laughter trailed away as he stared at the beach beyond. The sand was empty, with only the cold remains of fires to show he had come to the right place. Far out on the water a shape could be seen, a hint of triangularity speaking of *Foam Dancer's* lateen sail.

"I never trusted that slime-spawn Muktar," Akeba muttered. "The horses are played out, Conan, and we're little better. This stretch of muddy sand is no fit place to die, if any place is fit, but 'tis time to think of taking a few enemies with us into the long night. What say you, Cimmerian?"

Conan, wrestling with his own thoughts, said nothing. So far he had come in his quest for a means to destroy Jhandar, and what had come of it? Samarra dead, and all her slaves. Yasbet taken by Jhandar's henchmen. Even in small matters the gods had turned their faces from him. The trade goods for which he had spent his hundred pieces of gold—and hard-earned gold it was, too, for the slaying of a friend, even one ensorceled to kill— were abandoned. Of the gold but two pieces nestled in his pouch with flint, steel, Samarra's pouch and a bit of dried meat. And now he had fallen short by no more than half a turn of the glass. Muktar had not even waited to discover that Conan lacked the coin to pay for his return voyage. Though, under the circumstances, a show of steel would have disposed of that quibble.

"Are you listening?" Akeba demanded of him. "Let us circle back on our trail to the start of the dunes. We can surprise them, and with rest we may give a good account of ourselves." Muttering rose among the Hyrkanians.

Still Conan did not speak. Instead he chewed on a thought. Yasbet taken by Jhandar's henchmen. There was something of importance there, could he but see it. A faint voice within him said that it was urgent he did see it.

"Let us die as men," Tamur said, though his tone was hesitant, "not struggling futilely, like dungbeetles seized by ants." Some few of his fellows murmured approval; the rest twitched their reins fretfully and cast anxious backward glances, but kept silent.

The Turanian's black eyes flicked the nomad scornfully; Tamur looked away. "No one who calls himself a man dies meekly," Akeba said.

"They are of our blood," Tamur muttered, and the soldier snorted.

"Mitra's Mercies! This talk of blood has never stayed one Hyrkanian's steel from another's throat that I have seen. It'll not stay the hands of those who follow us. Have you forgotten what they will do to those they take alive? Gelded. Flayed alive. Impaled. You told us so. And you hinted at worse, if there can *be* worse."

Tamur flinched, licking his lips and avoiding Akeba's gaze. Now he burst out, "We stand outside the law!" A mournful sigh breathed from the other nomads. Tamur rushed breathlessly on. "We are no longer shielded by the laws of our people. For us to slay even one of those sent by the shamans would be to foul and condemn our own spirits, to face an eternity of doom."

"But you didn't kill Samarra," Akeba protested. "Surely your god knows that. Conan, talk to this fool."

But the Cimmerian ignored all of them. The barest glimmerings of hope flickered in him.

"We will face the One-Father having broken no law," Tamur shouted.

"Erlik take your laws! You were willing to disobey the edict against revenging yourself on Jhandar." Akeba's thin mouth twisted in a sneer. "I think you are simply ready to surrender. You are all dogs! Craven women whining for an easy death!"

Tamur recoiled, hand going to the hilt of his yataghan. "Kaavan understands revenge. You Turanians, whose women have watered your blood for a thousand years with the seed of western weaklings, understand nothing. I will not teach you!"

Steel slid from scabbards, and was arrested half-drawn by Conan's abrupt, "The ship! We will use the ship."

Akeba stared at him. Some of the Hyrkanians moved their horses back. Madmen were touched by the gods; slaying one, even in self-defense, was a sure path to ill luck.

Sharak, clinging tiredly to his mount with one hand and his staff with the other, peered ostentatiously after *Foam Dancer*. The vessel was but a mote, now. "Are we to become fish, then?" he asked.

"The galley," Conan said, his exasperation clear at their stupidity. "How much before us could Jhandar's henchmen have left the camp? And they had no reason to ride as we did, for no one was pursuing them. Their galley may still be waiting for them. We can rescue Yasbet and use it to cross the sea again."

"I'd not wager a copper on it," Akeba said. "Most likely the galley is already at sea."

"Are the odds better if you remain here?" Conan asked drily. Akeba looked doubtful. He ran an eye over the others; half the nomads still watched him warily. Sharak seemed lost in thought. "I'll not wait here meekly to be slaughtered," Conan announced. "You do what you will." Turning his horse to the south, he booted it into a semblance of a trot.

Before he had gone a hundred paces Sharak caught up to him, using his staff like a switch to chivy his shaggy mount along. "A fine adventure," the astrologer said, a fixed grin on his parchment face. "Do we take prisoners when we reach the galley? In the sagas heroes never take prisoners."

Akeba joined them in a gallop; his horse staggered as he reined back to their pace. "Money is one thing," the Turanian said. "My life I'm willing to wager on long odds."

Conan smiled without looking at either of them, a smile touched with grimness. More hooves pounded the sand behind him. He did not look around to see how many others had joined. One or all, it would be enough. It had to be. With cold eyes he led them south.

XXII

One horse sank to its knees, refusing to go on, as they passed the first headland, and another fell dead before they were long out of sight of the first. Thick scrub grew here in patches too large to ride around. There were no paths except those forced by the horses.

Conan grimaced as yet another man mounted double. Their pace was slower than walking. Keeping their strength was important if they were to face the galley's crew, or Jhandar's henchmen, but the horses were at the end of theirs. And time was important as well. They must reach the ship before Yasbet's captors did, or at least before they sailed, and before the pursuing Hyrkanians overtook them. The nomads would have little difficulty following their tracks down the coast.

Reaching a decision, he dismounted. The others stared as he removed his horse's crude rope bridle and began to walk. Sharak pressed his own mount forward and dropped off beside the big Cimmerian.

"Conan," Akeba called after him, "what—"

But Conan strode on; the rest could follow or not, as they chose. He would not spend precious moments in convincing them. With the old astrologer struggling to keep up he plunged ahead. Neither spoke. Breath now was to be saved for walking.

Where the horses had struggled to pass there were spaces where a man might go more easily. Akeba and the Hyrkanians were soon lost to sight, had either chosen to look back. Neither did.

There was no smooth highway for them, though. Even when the sandy ground was level, their boots sank to the ankles, and rocks lay ready to turn underfoot and throw the unwary into thornbushes boasting black, finger-long spikes, that would rip flesh like talons.

But then the ground was seldom level, except for occasional stretches of muddy beach, pounded by angry waves. For every beach there were a pair of headlands to be descended on one side and scaled on the other, with steep hills between, and deep gullies between those. Increasingly the land became almost vertical, up or down. One hundred paces forward took five hundred steps to travel, or one thousand. The horses would have been useless.

Of course, Conan reasoned, sweat rolling down his face, grit in his hair and eyes and mouth, he could move inland to the edge of the plain. But then he would not know when he reached the beach where the galley lay. He would not let himself consider the possibility that it might no longer be there. Too, on the plain they would leave even clearer traces of his passage for their hunter, and most of the time gained by traveling there thus would be lost in struggling to the beaches when they were sighted.

A crashing in the thick brush behind them brought Conan's sword into his hand. Cursing, Akeba stumbled into sight, his dark face coated with sweat and dust.

"Two more horses died," the Turanian said without preamble, "and another went lame. Tamur is right behind me. He'll catch up if you wait. The others were arguing about whether to abandon the remaining horses when I left, but they'll follow as well, sooner or later."

"There is no time to wait." Resheathing his blade, Conan started off again.

Sharak, who had no breath for speaking, followed, and after a moment Akeba did as well.

Three men, the young Cimmerian thought, since Tamur would be joining them. Three and a half, an he counted Sharak; the old astrologer would be worth no more than half Akeba or Tamur in a fight, if that much. Mayhap some of the other nomads would catch up in time, but they could not be counted on. Three and a half, then.

As Tamur joined them, plucking thorns from his arm and muttering curses fit to curl a sailor's hair, fat raindrops splattered against the back of Conan's neck. The Cimmerian peered up in surprise at thick, angrily purple clouds. His eyes had been of necessity locked to the ground; he had not noticed their gathering.

Quickly the sprinkling became a deluge, a hail of heavy pounding drops. A wind rose, ripping down the coast, tearing at the twisted scrub growth, howling higher and higher till it rang in the ears and dirt hung in the air to mix with the rain, splashing the four men with rivulets of mud. Nearby, a thick-rooted thornbush, survivor of many storms, tore lose from the ground, tangled briefly in the branches around it, and was whipped away.

Tamur put his mouth close to Conan's ear and shouted. "It is the Wrath of Kaavan! We must take shelter and pray!"

"'Tis but a storm!" the Cimmerian shouted back. "You faced worse on *Foam Dancer*!"

"No! This is no ordinary storm! It is the Wrath of Kaavan!" The Hyrkanian's face was a frozen mask, fear warring plainly with his manhood. "It comes with no warning, and when it does, men die! Horses are lifted whole into the air, and yurts, with all in them, to be found smashed to the ground far distant, or never to be seen again! We must shelter for our lives!"

The wind was indeed rising, even yet, shaking the thickets till it seemed the scrub was trying to tear itself free and flee. Driven raindrops struck like pebbles flung from slings.

Akeba, half-supporting Sharak, raised his voice against the thundering wind and rain. "We must take shelter, Cimmerian! The old man is nearly done! He'll not last out this storm if we don't!"

Pushing away from the Turanian, Sharak held himself erect with his staff. His straggly white hair was plastered wetly to his skull, "If you are done, soldier, say so. I am not!"

Conan eyed the old man regretfully. Sharak was clinging to his staff as to a lifeline. The other two, for all they were younger and hardier, were not in greatly better condition. Akeba's black face was lined with weariness, and Tamur, his fur cap a sodden mass hanging about his ears, swayed when the wind struck him fully. Yet there was Yasbet.

"How many of your nomads followed, Tamur?" he asked finally. "Will they catch up if we wait?"

"All followed," Tamur replied, "but Hyrkanians do not travel in the Wrath of Kaavan. It is death, Cimmerian."

"Jhandar's henchmen are not Hyrkanian," he shouted against the wind. "They will travel. The storm will hold the galley. We must reach it before the wind does and they put to sea. They, and Yasbet, will surely be aboard by then. If you will not go with me, then I go alone."

For a long moment there was no sound except the storm, then Akeba said, "Without that ship I may never get Jhandar."

Tamur's shoulders heaved in a sigh, silent in the storm. "Baalsham. Almost, with being declared outlaw, did I forget Baalsham. Kaavan understands revenge."

Sharak turned southward, stumping along leaning heavily on his staff. Conan and Akeba each grabbed one of the old man's arms to help him over the rough ground, and though he grumbled he did not attempt to pull free. Slowly they moved on.

Raging, the storm battered the coast. Stunted, wind-sculpted trees and great thornbushes swayed and leaned. Rain lashed them, and grit scoured through the air as if in a desert sandstorm. The wind that drove all before it drowned all sound in a demonic cacophony, till no man could hear the blood pounding in his own ears, or even his own thoughts.

It was because of that unceasing noise that Conan looked back often, watching for pursuit. Tamur might claim that no Hyrkanian would venture abroad in the Wrath of Kaavan, but it was the Cimmerian's experience that men did what they had to and let gods sort out the rights and wrongs later. So it was that he saw his party had grown by one in number, then by two more, and by a fourth. Rain-soaked and wind-ravaged, the grease washing from their lank hair and the filth from their sheepskin coats, the rest of Tamur's followers staggered out of the storm to join them, faces wreathed in joyous relief at the sight of the others. What had driven them to struggle through the storm—desire for revenge on Jhandar, fear of their pursuers, or terror of facing the Wrath of Kaavan alone? Conan did not care. Their numbers meant a better chance of rescuing Yasbet and taking the galley. With a stony face that boded ill for those he sought, the huge Cimmerian struggled on into the storm.

It was while they were scaling the slope of a thrusting headland, a straggling file of men clinging with their fingernails against being hurled into the sea, that the wind and rain abruptly died. Above the dark clouds roiled, and waves still crashed against cliff and beach, but comparative silence filled the unnaturally still air.

"'Tis done," Conan called to those below, "and we've survived. Not even the wrath of a god can stop us."

But for all his exuberant air, he began to climb faster. With the storm done the galley could sail. Tamur cried out something, but Conan climbed even faster. Scrambling atop the headland, he darted across, and almost let out a shout of joy. Below a steep drop was a length of beach, and drawn up on it was the galley.

Immediately he dropped to his belly, to avoid watching eyes from below, and wriggled to the edge of the drop. The vessel's twin masts were dismounted and firmly lashed on frames running fore and aft. No doubt they had had time to do little more before the storm broke on them. Two lines inland to anchors in the dunes, to hold the ship against the action of the waves, and the galley had been winched well up the beach, yet those waves had climbed the sand as well, and still clawed at the vessel's sides. Charred planks at the stern, and the blackened stumps of railing, spoke of their first meeting.

As each of the others reached the top of the headland they threw themselves to the ground beside Conan, until a line of men stretched along the rim, peering at the ship below.

"May I roast in Zandru's Hells, Cimmerian," Akeba breathed, "but I did not think we'd do it. The end of the storm and the ship, just as you said."

"The Wrath of Kaavan is not spent," Tamur said. "That is what I was trying to tell you."

Conan rolled onto one elbow, wondering if the nomad's wits had been pounded loose by the storm. "There is no rain, no wind. Where then is the storm?"

Tamur shook his head wearily. "You do not understand, outlander. This is called Kaavan's Mercy, a time to pray for the dead, and for your life. Soon the rain will come again, as suddenly as it left, and the wind will blow, but this time it will come from the other direction. The shamans say—"

"Erlik take your shamans," Akeba muttered. The nomads stirred, but were too tired to do more than curse. "If he speaks the truth, Cimmerian, we're finished. Without rest, a troupe of dancing girls could defeat us, but how can we rest? If we don't take that ship before this accursed Wrath of Kaavan returns. . . ." He slumped, chin on his arms, peering at the galley.

"We rest," Conan said. Drawing back from the edge, Conan crawled to Sharak. The aged astrologer lay like a sack of sodden rags, but he levered himself onto his back when Conan stopped beside him. "Lie easy," the Cimmerian told him. "We'll stay here a time."

"Not on my account," Sharak rasped. He would have gotten to his feet had Conan not pressed him back. "This adventuring is a wet business, but my courage has not washed away. The girl, Conan. We must see to her. And to Jhandar."

"We will, Sharak."

The old man subsided, and Conan turned to face Akeba and Tamur, who had followed him from the rim. The other nomads watched from where they lay.

"What is this talk of waiting?" the Turanian demanded. "Seizing that galley is our only hope."

"So it is," Conan agreed, "but not until the storm comes again."

Tamur gasped. "Attack in the face of the Wrath of Kaavan! Madness!"

"The storm will cover our approach," Conan explained patiently. "We must take the crew by surprise if we are to capture them."

"Capture them?" Tamur said incredulously. "They have served Baalsham. We will cut their throats."

"Can you sail a ship?" Conan asked.

"Ships! I am a Hyrkanian. What care I for. . . ." A poleaxed expression spread over the nomad's face, and he sank into barely audible curses.

In quick words Conan outlined his plan. "Tell the others," he finished, and left them squatting there.

Crawling back to the rim, he lowered himself full-length on the hard, wet ground, where he could watch the ship. The vessel could not sail until the storm had passed. With the patience of a great cat watching a herd of antelope draw closer, he waited.

The rain returned first, a pelting of large drops that grew to a roaring downpour, and the wind followed close behind. From the south it screamed, as Tamur had predicted, raging with such fury that in moments it was hard to believe it had ever diminished.

Wordlessly, for words were no longer possible, Conan led them down from the height, each man gripping the belt of the man ahead, stumbling over uneven ground, struggling against the wind with grim purposefulness. He did not draw his sword; this would be a matter for bare hands. Unhesitatingly Conan made his way across the sand, through blinding rain. Abruptly his outstretched hand touched wood. The side of the ship. A rope lashing in the wind struck his arm; he seized the line before it could whip away from him, and climbed, drawing himself up hand over hand. As he scrambled over the rail onto the forepart of the galley he felt the rope quiver. Akeba was starting up.

Quickly Conan's eyes searched the deck. Through the solid curtain of rain washing across the vessel, he could see naught but dim shapes, and none looked to be a man, yet it was his fear that even in the height of the storm a watch was kept.

Akeba thumped to the deck beside him, and Conan started aft with the Turanian close behind. He knew the rest would follow. They had nowhere else to go.

A hatch covered the companionway leading down into the vessel. Conan exchanged a glance with Akeba, hunched against the driving rain. The Turanian nodded. With a heave of his arm Conan threw the hatchcover back and leaped, roaring, down the ladder.

There were four men, obviously ship's officers, in the snug, lantern-lit cabin, swilling wine. Goblets crashed to the deck as Conan landed in their midst. Men leaped to their feet; hands went to sword hilts. But Conan had landed moving. His fist smashed behind an ear, sending its owner to the deck atop his goblet. A nose crunched beneath a backhand blow of the other fist, and his boot caught a third man in the belly while he still attempted to come fully erect.

Now his sword came out, its point stopping a fingerbreadth from the beaked nose of the fourth man. The emerald at his ear and the thick gold chain about his neck named him captain of the vessel as surely as their twin queues named all four sailors of the Vilayet. The slab-cheeked captain froze with his blade half drawn.

"I do not need all of you," Conan snarled. "'Tis your choice."

Hesitatingly licking his lips, the captain surveyed his fellows. Two did not stir, while the third was attempting to heave his guts up on the deck. "You'll not get away with this," he said shakily. "My crew will hand your hearts in the rigging." But he slowly and carefully moved his hand from his weapon.

"Why you needed me," Akeba grumbled from a seat on the next-to-bottom rung of the ladder, "I don't see at all."

"There might have been five," Conan replied with a smile that made the captain shiver. "Get Sharak, Akeba. It's warm in here. And see how the others are doing." With a sigh the soldier clattered back up the ladder into the storm. Conan turned his full attention on the captain. "When are those who hired you returning?"

"I'm a trader here on my own—" Conan's blade touched the captain's upper lip; the man went cross-eyed staring at it. He swallowed, and tried to move his head back, but Conan kept a light pressure with the edged steel. "They didn't tell me," the sailor said hastily. "They said I was to wait until they returned, however long it might be. I was of no mind to argue." His face paled, and he clamped his lips tight, as if afraid to say more.

While Conan wondered why the galley's passengers had affected the captain so, Akeba and Tamur scrambled down the ladder, drawing the hatch shut on the storm behind them. The Turanian half-carried Sharak, whom he settled on a bench, filling a goblet of wine for him. The astrologer mumbled thanks and buried his face in the drink. Tamur remained near the ladder, wiping his dagger on his sheepskin coat.

Conan's eyes lit on that dagger, and he had to bite his tongue to keep from cursing. Putting a hand on the captain's chest, he casually pushed the man back down in his seat. "I told you we need these sailors, Tamur. How many did you kill?"

"Two, Cimmerian," the nomad protested, spreading his hands. "Two only. And one carved a trifle. But they resisted. My people watch the rest." A full dozen remain."

"Fists and hilts, I said," Conan snarled. He had to turn away lest he say too much. "How do you feel, Sharak?"

"Much refreshed," the astrologer said, and he did seem to be sitting straighter, though he, like all of them, dripped pools of water. "Yasbet is not here?"

Conan shook his head. "But we shall be waiting when she is brought."

"Then for Jhandar," Sharak said, and Conan echoed, "Then for Jhandar."

"They resisted," Tamur said again, in injured tones. "There are enough left to do what they must." No one spoke, or even looked at him. After a moment he went on. "I went down to the rowing benches, Conan, to see if any of them were hiding among the slaves, and who do you think I found? That fellow from the other ship. What is he called? Bayan. That is it. Chained to a bench with the rest." Throwing back his head, the nomad laughed as if it were the funniest story he had ever heard.

Conan's brow knitted in a frown. Bayan here? And in chains? "Bring him here, Tamur," he snapped. "Now!" His tone was such that the Hyrkanian jumped for the ladder immediately. "Tie these others, Akeba," Conan went on, "so we do not have to worry about them." With his sword he motioned the captain to lie down on the deck; fuming, the hook-nosed seaman complied.

By the time the four ship's officers, two still unconscious, were bound hand and foot, Tamur had returned with Bayan. Other than chains, the wiry sailor from *Foam Dancer* wore only welts and a filthy twist of rag. He stood head down, shivering wetly from his passage through the storm, watching Conan from the corner of his eye.

The big Cimmerian straddled a bench, holding his sword before him so that ripples of lantern light ran along the blade. "How came you here, Bayan?"

"I wandered from the ship," Bayan muttered, "and these scum captured me. There's a code among sailors, but they chained me to an oar," he raised his head long enough to spit at the tied figure of the captain, "and whipped me when I protested."

"What happened at *Foam Dancer*? You didn't just wander away." The wiry man shifted his feet with a clank of iron links, but said nothing. "You'll talk if I have to let Akeba heat his irons for you." The Turanian blinked, then grimaced fiercely; Bayan wet his lips. "And you'll tell the truth," Conan went on. "The old man is a soothsayer. He can tell when you lie." He lifted his sword as if studying the edge. "For the first lie, a hand. Then a foot. Then. . . . How many lies can you stand? Three? Four? Of a certainty no more."

Bayan met that glacial blue gaze; then words tumbled out of him as fast as he could force them. "A man came to the ship, a man with yellow skin and eyes to freeze your heart in your chest. Had your . . . the woman with him. Offered a hundred pieces of gold for fast passage back to Aghrapur. Said this ship was damaged, and he knew *Foam Dancer* was faster. Didn't even bother to deny trying to sink us. Muktar was tired of waiting for you, and when this one appeared with the woman, well, it was plain you were dead, or it seemed plain, and it looked easy enough to take the woman and the gold, and—"

"Slow down!" Conan commanded sharply. "Yasbet is unharmed?"

Bayan swallowed hard. "I . . . I know not. Before Mitra and Dagon I swear that I raised no hand against her. She was alive when I left. Muktar gave a signal, you see, and Tewfik and Marantes and I went at the stranger with our daggers, but he killed them before a man could blink. He just touched them, and they were dead. And then, then he demanded Muktar slit my throat." He made a sound, half laughter, half weeping. "Evidence of future good faith, he called it. And that fat spawn of a diseased goat was going to do it! I saw it on his face, and I ran. I hope he's drowned in this accursed storm. I pray he and *Foam Dancer* are both at the bottom of the sea."

"An ill-chosen prayer," Conan said between clenched teeth. "Yasbet is on that vessel." With a despairing wail Bayan sank groveling to his knees. "Put him back where he was," Conan spat. Tamur jerked the wiry seaman to his feet; the Cimmerian watched them go. "Is this galley too damaged to sail?" he demanded of the captain.

The hook-nosed man had lain with his mouth open, listening while Bayan talked. Now he snorted. "Only a dirt-eater would think so. Once this storm is gone, give me half a day for repairs and I'll sail her anywhere on the Vilayet, in any weather."

"The repairs you need, you'll make at sea," Conan said levelly. "And we sail as soon as the storm abates enough for us to get off this beach without being smashed to splinters." The captain opened his mouth, and Conan laid his blade against the seaman's throat. "Or mayhap one of these other three would like to be captain."

The captain's eyes bulged, and his mouth worked. Finally he said, "I'll do it. 'Tis likely we'll all of us drown, but I'll do it."

Conan nodded. He had expected no other decision. Yasbet was being carried closer to Jhandar by the moment. The storm drumming against the hull seemed to echo the sorcerer's name. Jhandar. This time they would meet face to face, he and Jhandar, and one of them would die. One or both. Jhandar.

XXIII

Jhandar, lounging on cushions of multicolored silk spread beside a fountain within a walled garden, watched Davinia exclaiming over his latest gifts to her, yet his thoughts were elsewhere. Three days more and, as matters stood, all his plans would come to naught. Could the wench not sense the worry in him?

"They are beautiful," Davinia said, stretching arms encircled by emerald bracelets above her head. Another time he would have felt sweat popping out on his forehead. Her brief, golden silks left the inner slopes of her rounded breasts bare, and her girdle, two fingerwidths of sapphires and garnets hung with the bright feathers of rare tropic birds, sat low on the swelling of her hips. Sultry eyes caressed him. "I will have to think of a way to show my gratitude," she purred.

He acknowledged her only with a casual wave of his hand. In three days Yildiz, that fat fool, would meet with his advisors to decide where to use the army he had built. Of the Seventeen Attendants, eight would speak for empire, for war with Zamora. Only eight, and Jhandar knew that Yildiz merely counted the number of those who supported or opposed, rather than actually weighing the advice given. Jhandar needed one more to speak for war. One of the nine other. Who could have believed the nine lived lives which, if not completely blameless, still gave him no lever to use against them? One more he needed, yet all the nine would speak for peace, for reducing the numbers of the army. Short of gaining Yildiz's own ear, he had done all that could be done, yet three days would see a year's work undone.

It would take even longer to repair matters. He must first arrange the assassination of an Attendant, perhaps more than one if his efforts to guide the selection of the new Attendant failed. Then it would take time to build the army again. If things were otherwise, three days could see the beginnings of an empire that would be his in all but name. Kings would journey to him, kneel at his feet to hear his commands. Instead, he would have to begin again, wait even longer for that he had awaited so long.

And that wait added another risk. What had the man Conan sought in Hyrkania? What had he found that might be used against the Power? Why did Che Fan not return with the barbarian's head in a basket?

"You will let me have them, Jhandar?"

"Of course," he said absently, then pulled himself from his grim ruminations. "Have what?"

"The slaves." There was petulance in Davinia's voice, a thing he had noticed more often of late. "Haven't you been listening?"

"Certainly I've been listening. But tell me about these slaves again."

"Four of them," she said, moving to stand straddle-legged beside him. Now he could feel sweat on his face. Sunlight surrounded her with a nimbus, a woman of golden silk, glowing hot. "Well-muscled young men, of course," she went on. "Two of blackest hue, and two as pale as snow. The one pair I will dress in pearls and rubies, the other in onyx and emeralds. They will be as a frame for me. To make me more beautiful for you," she added hastily.

"What need have you for slave boys?" he growled. "You have slaves in plenty to do your bidding. And that old hag, Renda, to whom you spend so much time whispering."

"Why, to bear my palanquin," she laughed, tinkling musical notes. Fluidly she sank to her knees, bending till her breasts pressed against his chest. Her lips brushed the line of his jaw. "Surely my Great Lord would not deny my bearers. My Great Lord, who it is my greatest pleasure to serve. In every way."

"I can deny you nothing," he said thickly. "You may have the slaves."

In her eyes he caught a fleeting glimpse of greed satisfied, and the moment soured for him. She would leave him did she ever find one who could give her more. He meant to be sure there could never be such a one, but still. . . . He could bind her to him with the golden bowl and her heart's blood. None who saw or talked with her would ever know she did not in truth live. But he would know.

Someone cleared his throat diffidently. Scowling, Jhandar sat up. Zephran stood on the marble path, bowing deeply over folded hands, eyes carefully averted from Davinia.

"What is it?" Jhandar demanded angrily.

"Suitai is returned, Great Lord," his shaven-headed myrmidion replied.

Instantly Jhandar's anger was gone, along with his thoughts of Davinia. Careless of his dignity, he scrambled to his feet. "Lead," he commanded.

Dimly he noted that Davinia followed as well, but matters not of the flesh dominated his mind once more.

Suitai waited in Jhandar's private audience chamber, its bronze lion lamps unlit at this hour. A large sack lay on the mosaicked floor at the Khitan's feet.

"Where is Che Fan?" Jhandar demanded as he entered.

"Perished, Great Lord," Suitai replied, and Jhandar hesitated in his stride.

Despite his knowledge to the contrary, Jhandar had begun to think in some corners of his mind that the two assassins were indestructible. It was difficult to imagine what could slay one of them.

"How?" he said shortly.

"The barbarian enlisted the aid of a Hyrkanian witch-woman, Great Lord. She, also, died."

That smile meant that Suitai had been her killer, Jhandar thought briefly, without interest. "And the barbarian?"

"Conan is dead as well, Great Lord."

Jhandar nodded slowly, feeling a strange relief. This Conan had been but a straw in the wind after all, catching the eye as it flashed by, yet unimportant. Suitai's smile had faded at the mention of the barbarian, no doubt because Che Fan had actually slain the fellow. At times he thought that Suitai's thirst for blood would eventually prove a liability. Now he had no time for such petty worries.

"The crew of the galley was disposed of as I commanded. Suitai? I wish no links between myself and Hyrkania." Not until he was able to control that region the shamans had blasted, thus containing whatever might be of danger to him within. Not until his power was secure in Turan.

The tall Khitan hesitated. "The galley was damaged, Great Lord, and could not put to sea. I left its crew waiting for me. Without doubt the coastal tribes have attended to them by now. Instead I hired the vessel the barbarian used, and came ashore well north of the city."

"And the crew of this ship?"

"Dead, Great Lord. I slew them, and guided the ship to the beach myself." An unreadable expression flickered across the assassin's normally impassive face, and Jhandar eyed him sharply. Suitai shifted uneasily beneath that gaze, then went on slowly. "The captain, Great Lord, a fat man called Muktar, leaped into the sea, surely to drown. I have no doubt of it."

"You have no doubt of a great many things, Suitai." Jhandar's voice was silky, yet dripped venom like a scorpion's tail.

Sweat appeared on Suitai's brow. The mage had a deadly lack of patience with those who did not perform exactly as he commanded. Hurriedly the Khitan bent to the large sack at his feet.

"I brought you this gift, Great Lord." The lashings of the sack came loose, and he spilled a girl out onto the mosaicked floor, wrists bound to elbows behind her back, legs doubled tightly against her breasts, the thin cords that held her cutting deeply into her naked flesh. She grunted angrily into her gag as she tumbled onto the floor, and attempted to fight her bonds, but only her toes and fingers wriggled. "The girl the barbarian stole from the compound, Great Lord," Suitai announced with satisfaction.

Jhandar snorted. "Don't think to make up for your shortcomings. What is one girl more or less to—"

"Why, it's Esmira," Davinia broke in.

The necromancer scowled irritably. He had forgotten that she had followed him. "That's not her name. She is called. . . ." It took a moment, though he did remember marking the wench for his bed, long ago it seemed. ". . . Yasbet. That's it. Now return to the garden, Davinia. I have matters to discuss here that do not concern you."

Instead the lithe blonde squatted on her heels by the bound girl, using both hands to twist the struggling wench's gagged face around for a better look. "I tell you this is the Princess Esmira, Prince Roshmanli's daughter."

Jhandar's mouth was suddenly dry. "Are you certain? The rumors say the princess if cloistered."

She gave him a withering look that would have elicited instant and painful punishment for anyone else. From her, at this moment, he ignored it. The prince was Yildiz's closest advisor among the Attendants, of the nine, a man who seduced no woman with a husband and gambled only with his own gold. Yet it was said his daughter was his weakness, that he would do anything to shelter her from the world. For the safety of his Esmira, would Roshmanli send Turan to war? He had had men slain for casting their eyes upon her. If handled carefully, it could be done.

Then his eyes fell on Davinia, smiling smugly as he examined the bound girl, and a new thought came to him.

He pulled the blonde to her feet. "You say you want only to serve me. Do you speak the truth?"

"To you," she replied slowly, "I speak only truth."

"Then this night there will be a ceremony. In that ceremony you will plunge a dagger into the heart of this girl." He gazed deeply into her eyes, searching for hesitation, for vacillation. There was none.

"As my Great Lord commands me," Davinia said smoothly.

Jhandar felt the urge to throw back his head and laugh wildly. She had taken the first step. Once she had wielded the knife, she would be bound to him more firmly than with iron chains. And by the same stroke he would gain the ninth voice among the King's Attendants. All of his dreams were taking shape. Empire and the woman. He would have it all.

XXIV

Dark seas rolled beneath the galley's ram, phosphorescence dancing on her bow wave, as the measured sweep of three score oars drew it on. Ahead in the night the darker mass of the Turanian coast was marked by white-breaking waves glinting beneath the pale, cloud-chased moon.

Echoes of those crashing breakers rolled across the waters to Conan. He stood in the stern of the galley, where he could keep close watch on both captain and steersman. Already they had attempted to take the ship other than as he directed—perhaps into the harbor at Aghrapur, so that he and the rest could be seized as pirates—and only the scanty knowledge he had gained with the smugglers had thus far thwarted them. The rest of the vessel's crew, sullen and disarmed, worked under the watchful eyes of Akeba, Tamur, and the nomads. Sharak clung to the lines that supported the foremast, and gazed on the heavens, seeking the configurations that would tell their fates that night.

Conan cared not what the stars foretold. Their destinies would be as they would be, for he would not alter what he intended by so much as a hair. "There," he said, pointing ahead. "Beach there."

"There's nothing there," the captain protested.

"There," Conan repeated. "'Tis close enough to where we're going. I'd think you would be glad to see our backs, wherever we wanted to be put ashore."

Grumbling, the slab-cheeked captain spoke to his steersman, and the galley shifted a point to larboard, toward the stretch of land at which the big Cimmerian had pointed.

With scanty information had Conan made his choice. The distant glow of lamps from Aghrapur to the south. A glimpse at the stars. Instinct. Perhaps, he thought, that last had played the most important part. He *knew* that on that shore stood the compound of the Cult of Doom, Yasbet's place of imprisonment, and Jhandar, the man he must kill even if he died himself.

Sand grated beneath the galley's keel. The vessel lurched, heeled, was driven further forward by the motion of long sweeps. Finally motion ceased; the deck tilted only slightly.

"It's done," the hook-nosed captain announced, anger warring with satisfaction on his face. "You can leave my vessel, now, and I'll give burnt offerings to Dagon when you're gone."

"Akeba!" Conan called. On receiving an answering hail he turned back to the captain. "I advise you to go south along the coast, you and your crew. I do not know what will happen here this night, but I fear powers will be unbound. One place I have seen where such bonds were cut; there nightmares walked, and some would count death a blessing."

"Sorcery?" The word was a hiss of indrawn breath in the captain's mouth, changing to shaky, blustering laughter. "An sorceries are to be loosed, I have no fears of being caught in them. I will be clear of the beach before you, and I will go south as fast as whips can drive my oar-sl—" Hatch covers crashing open amidships cut him off, and the clatter of men scrambling on deck, whipscarred, half-naked men falling over themselves in their eagerness to dash to the rail and drop to the surf below. The hook-nosed man's eyes bulged as he stared at them. "You've loosed the oar slaves! You fool! What—" He spun back to Conan, and found himself facing the Cimmerian's blade.

"Three score oars," Conan said quietly, "and two men chained to each. I have no love for chains on men, for I've worn them around my own neck. Normally I do not concern myself with freeing slaves. I cannot strike off all the chains in the world, or in Turan, or even in a single city, and if I could, men would find ways to put them back again before they had a chance to grow dusty. Still, the world may end this night, and the men who have brought me to my fate deserve their freedom, as they and all the rest of us may be dead before dawn. You had best get over the side, captain. Your own life may depend on how fast you can leave this place."

The hook-nosed captain glared at him, face growing purple. "Steal my slaves, then order me off my own vessel? Rambis!" He bit it off as he stared at the vacant spot by the steering oar. Conan had seen the man slip quietly over the railing as he spoke.

Discovery of the defection took what was left of the captain's backbone. With a strangled yelp he leaped into the sea.

Sheathing his sword, Conan turned to join his companions, and found himself facing some two dozen filthy galley slaves, gathered in a different knot amidships. Akeba and the Hyrkanians watched them warily.

A tall man with a long, tangled black beard and the scars of many flog-gings stepped forward, ducking his head. "Your pardon, lord. I am called Akman. It is you who has freed us? We would follow you."

"I'm no lord," Conan said. "Be off with you while you have time, and be grateful you do not follow me. I draw my sword against a powerful sorcerer, and there is dying to be done this night." A handful of the former slaves melted into the darkness, splashes sounding their departure.

"Still there are those of us who would follow you, lord," Akman said. "For one who has lived as a dead man, to die as a free man is a greater boon than could be expected from the gods."

"Stop calling me lord," Conan growled. Akman bowed again, and the other rowers behind him. Shaking his head, Conan sighed. "Find weapons, then, and make peace with your gods. Akeba! Tamur! Sharak!"

Without waiting to see what the freed slaves would do, the big Cim-merian put a hand to the railing and vaulted into waist-deep seas that broke against his broad back and sent foam over his shoulders. The named men followed as he waded to shore, a stretch of driftwood-covered sand where moon-shadows stirred.

"They'll be more hindrance than help, those slaves," Sharak grumbled, attempting to wring seawater from his robes without dropping his staff. "This is a matter for fighting men."

"And you are the stoutest of them all," Akeba laughed, clapping the old astrologer on the shoulder and almost knocking him down. His laughter sounded wild and grim, the laughter of a man who would laugh in the face of the dark gods and was doing so now. "And you, Cimmerian. Why so somber? Even if we die we will drag Jhandar before Erlik's Black Throne behind us."

"And if Jhandar looses the magicks that he did when he was defeated before?" Conan said. "There are no shamans to contain them here."

They stared at him, Akeba's false mirth fading. Sharak held a corner of his robes in two hands, his dampness forgotten, and Conan thought he heard Tamur mutter a prayer.

Then the men from the galley were clambering up the beach, the half score who had not succumbed to fear or good sense, led by Akman with a boarding pike in his calloused hands. The Hyrkanian nomads came too, cursing at the wet as they waded through the surf. A strange army, the Cimmerian thought, with which to save the world.

He turned from the sea. They followed, a file of desperate men snaking into the Turanian night.

*   *   *

"Must I actually put a knife in her heart?"

Davinia's question jangled in Jhandar's mind, which had been almost settled for his period of meditation. "Do you regret your decision?" he demanded. In his thoughts, he commanded her: have no regrets. Murder a princess in sorcerous rites. Be bound to me by ties stronger than iron.

"No regrets, my Great Lord," she said slowly, toying with the feathers of her girdle. When she lifted her gaze to his her sapphire eyes were clear and untroubled. "She has lived a useless life. At least her death will be to some purpose."

Despite himself he could not stop the testing. "And if I said there was no purpose? Just her death?" Her frown almost stopped his heart.

"No purpose? I do not like getting blood on my hands." She tossed her blonde mane petulantly. "The feel of it will not wash away for days. I will not do it if there is no purpose."

"There is a purpose," he said hastily, "which I cannot tell you until the proper time." And to forestall questions he hurried from the room.

His nerves burned with how close he had come to dissuading her. Almost, he thought, there would be no joy in achieving all his ambitions without her. Some rational corner of his mind told him the thought was lust-soaked madness. The fruition of his plans would hold her to him, for where would she then find one of greater power or wealth? With the taking of Yasbet—if she chose to call herself so, so he would think of her—all would be in place. His power in Turan would be complete. But Davinia. . . .

He was still struggling with himself when he settled in the simple chamber, before the Pool of the Ultimate. That would not do. He must be empty of emotion for the Power to fill him. Carefully he focused on his dreams. War and turmoil would fill the nations, disorder hastened by his ever-growing band of the Chosen. Only he would be able to call a halt to it. Kings would kneel to him. Slowly the pool began to glow.

From the branches of the tree, Conan studied the compound of the Cult of Doom. Ivory domes gleamed in the dappled moonlight, and purple spires thrust into the sky, but no hint of light showed within those high marble walls, and no one stirred. The Cimmerian climbed back down to the ground, to the men waiting there.

"Remember," he said, addressing himself mainly to the former galley slaves, "any man with a weapon must be slain, for they will not surrender." The Hyrkanians nodded somberly; they knew this well.

"But the black-robed one with the yellow skin is mine," Akeba reminded them. Time and again on the short march he had reiterated his right to vengeance for his daughter.

"The black-robe is yours," Akman said nervously. "I but wish you could take the demons as well."

Sharak shook his staff, gripping it with both hands as if it were a lifeline. "I will handle the demons," he said. "Bring them to me." A wind from the sea moaned in the treetops as if in answer, and he subsided into mutters.

"Let us be on with it," Tamur said, fidgeting—whether with eagerness or nervousness, Conan could not tell.

"Stay together," the Cimmerian said by way of a last instruction. "Those who become separated will be easy prey." With that he led them down to the towering white wall.

Grapnels taken from the galley swung into the air, clattered atop the wall and took hold. Men swarmed up ropes like ants and dropped within.

Once inside the compound Conan barely noticed the men following him, weapons in hand, falling back on either side so that he was the point of an arrow. His own blade came into his hand. Jhandar. Ignoring other buildings, Conan strode toward the largest structure of the compound, an alabaster palace of golden onion-domes and columned porticos and towers of porphyry. Jhandar would be there in his palace. Jhandar and Yasbet, if she still lived. But first Jhandar, for there could be no true safety for Yasbet until the necromancer was dead.

Suddenly there was a saffron-robed man before him, staring in astonishment at the intruders. Producing a dagger, he screamed, "In the name of Holy Chaos, die!"

A fool to waste time with shouts, Conan thought, wrenching his blade free so the man's body could fall. And in Crom's name, what god was this Chaos?

But the noise produced another shaven-headed man, this with a spear that he thrust at Conan, sounding the same cry. The Cimmerian grasped the shaft to guide the point clear of his body; the point of his broadsword ended the strange shout in a gurgle of blood.

Then hundreds of saffron-robed men and women were rushing into the open. At first they seemed only curious, then those nearest Conan saw the bodies and screamed. In an instant panic seized them by the throat, and they became a boiling mass, seeking only escape, yet almost overwhelming those they feared in a tide of numbers.

Forgetting his own instructions to stay together, Conan began to force his way through the pack of struggling flesh, toward the palace. Jhandar, was the only thought in his head. Jhandar.

"Great Lord, the compound is under attack."

Jhandar stirred fretfully in his communion with the Power. It took a moment for him to pull his eyes from the glowing pool and focus them on Suitai, standing ill at ease in the unnatural glow that filled the chamber.

"What? Why are you disturbing me here, Suitai? You know it is forbidden."

"Yes, Great Lord. But the attack. . . ."

That time the word got through to Jhandar. "Attack? The army?" Had disaster come on him yet again?

"No, Great Lord. I know not who they are, or how many. The entire compound is in an uproar. It is impossible to count their numbers. I slew one; he was filthy and half-naked, and bore the welts of a lash."

"A slave?" Jhandar asked querulously. It was hard to think, with his mind attuned to the communion and that communion not fully completed. "Take the Chosen and dispose of these interlopers, whoever they are. Then restore order to the compound."

"All of the Chosen, Great Lord?"

"Yes, all of them," the necromancer replied irritably. Could the man not do as he was told? He must settle his mind, complete his absorption of the Power.

"Then you will delay the ceremony, Great Lord?"

Jhandar blinked, found his gaze drifting to the Pool of the Ultimate, and jerked it back. "Delay? Of course not. Think you I need those fools' rapturous gazes to perform the rite?" Desperately he fought to stop his head spinning, to think clearly. "Take the Chosen as I commanded you. I will myself bring the girl to the Chamber of Sacrifice and do what is necessary. Go!"

Bowing, the black-robed Khitan sped away, glad to be gone from the presence of that which was bound in that room.

Jhandar shook his head and peered into the pool. Glowing mists filled the limits of the wards, an unearthly dome that seemed to draw him into its depths. Angrily he pushed that feeling aside, though he could not rid himself of it. He was tired, that was all. There was no need to complete the communion, he decided. Disturbed as he was, completion might take until dawn, and he had no time to wait. The girl must be his tonight. As it was the Power flowed along his bones, coursed in his veins. He would perform the rite now.

Gathering his robes about him, he left to fetch Yasbet and Davinia to the Chamber of Sacrifice.

XXV

arily, sword at the ready, Conan moved along one wall of a palace corridor, with no eye for rich tapestries or ancient vases of rare Khitan porcelain. Akeba stalked along the other, tulwar in hand. As a pair of wolfhounds they hunted.

The Cimmerian did not know where the others were. From time to time the clash of steel and the cries of dying men sounded from outside, or echoed down the halls from other parts of the palace. Who won and who died he could not tell, and at that moment he did not care. He sought Jhandar, and instinct told him he drew closer with every step.

Silent as death three saffron-robed men hurtled from a side corridor, scimitars slashing.

Conan caught a blade on his broadsword, sweeping it toward the wall and up. As his own blade came parallel to the floor he slipped it off the other in a slashing blow that half-severed his opponent's head. Flashing swiftly on, his sword axed into the second man's head a heartbeat before Akeba's steel buried itself in the man's ribs. Twice-slain, the body fell atop that of he who had faced the Turanian at the first attack.

"You work well," Akeba grunted, wiping his blade on a corpse's robe. "You should think of the army if we live to leave this. . ." His words trailed off as both men became aware of a new presence in the corridor. The black-robed Khitan assassin.

Unhurriedly he moved toward them, with the casual confidence of a great beast that knows its kill is assured. His hands were empty of weapons, but Conan remembered well the dead in Samarra's yurt, with no wound on any but looks of horror on every face, and Zorelle, dead from a touch.

Conan firmed his grip on the worn leather hilt of his broadsword, but as he stepped forward Akeba laid a hand on his arm. The soldier's voice was as cold as frozen iron. "He is mine. By right of blood, he is mine."

Reluctantly Conan gave way, and the Turanian moved forward alone. Of necessity the big Cimmerian waited to watch his friend do battle. Jhandar was still uppermost in his mind, but the way to him led deeper into the palace, past the murderously maneuvering pair before him.

The Khitan smiled; his hand struck like a serpent, and, like a mongoose, Akeba was not there. The assassin flowed from the path of the soldier's flashing steel, yet the smile was gone from his face. Like malefic dancers the two men moved, lightning blade against fatal touch, each aware of the other's deadliness, each intent on slaying. Abruptly the Khitan deciphered the pattern of Akeba's moves; the malevolent hand darted for the soldier's throat. Desperately Akeba blocked the blow, and it struck instead his sword arm. Crying out, the Turanian staggered back, tulwar falling, arm dangling, clawing with his good hand for his dagger. The assassin paused to laugh before closing for the kill.

"Crom!" Conan roared, and leapt.

Only the Khitan's unnatural suppleness saved him from the blade that struck where he had been. Smiling again, he motioned the Cimmerian to come to him, if he dared.

"I promised to let you kill him," Conan said to Akeba, without taking his eyes from the black-robed man, "not the other way around."

The Turanian barked a painful laugh. He clutched his dagger in one hand, but the other twitched helplessly at his side and only the tapestry-covered wall kept him from falling. "As you've interfered," he said between clenched teeth, "then you must kill him for me, Cimmerian."

"Yes," the assassin hissed. "Kill me, barbarian."

Without warning, Conan lunged, blade thrusting for the black-robed one's belly, but the killer seemed to glide backward, stopping just beyond the sword's point.

"You must do better, barbar. Che Fan was wrong. You are just another man. I do not think you truly entered the Blasted Lands, but even if you did, you survived only by luck. I, Suitai, will put an end to you here. Come to me and find your death."

As the tall man spoke Conan moved slowly forward, sliding his feet along the marble floor so that he was at no time unbalanced. His sword he held low before him, point flickering from side to side like the tongue of a viper, light from the burnished brass lamps on the walls glittering along the steel, and though the Khitan spoke confidently, he kept an eye on that blade.

Abruptly, as the assassin finished his speech, Conan tossed his sword from right hand to left, and Suitai's gaze followed involuntarily. In that instant the Cimmerian jerked a tapestry from the wall to envelop the other man. Even as the hanging tangled about the Khitan's head and chest Conan lunged after, steel ripping through cloth and flesh, grating on bone.

Slowly the assassin heaved aside the portion of the tapestry that covered his head. With glazing eyes he stared in disbelief at the blade standing out from his chest, the dark blood that spread to stain his robes.

"Not my death," Conan told him. "Yours."

The Khitan tried to speak, but blood welled from his mouth, and he toppled, dead as he struck the marble floor. Conan tugged his blade free, cleaning it on the tapestry as he might had it been thrust into offal.

"I give you thanks, my friend," Akeba said, pushing unsteadily away from the wall. His face gleamed with the sweat of pain, and his arm still dangled at his side, but he managed to stand erect as he looked on the corpse of his daughter's murderer. "But now you have hunting of your own to do."

"Jhandar," Conan said, and without another word he was moving forward again.

Like a great hunting cat he strode through halls lit by glittering brass lamps, but bare of life. The gods smiled on those who did not meet him in those passages, for he would not now have slowed to see if they bore weapons or not. His blood burned for Jhandar's death. Any who hindered or slowed him now would perish in a pool of their own blood.

Then great bronze doors stood before him, doors scribed with a pattern that seemed to have no pattern, that rejected the eye's attempt to focus on it. Setting hands against those massive metal slabs, muscles cording with strain, he forced the portals open. Sword at the ready, he went through.

In an instant the horror of that great circular chamber engraved itself on his brain. Yasbet lay chained and gagged on a black altar, to one side of her Davinia, knife upraised to plunge into the bound girl's heart, to the other Jhandar, an arcane chant rising from his mouth to pierce the air. Over the entire blood-chilling tableau a shimmering silvery-azure dome was forming.

"No!" Conan shouted.

Yet even as he dashed forward he knew he would not reach them before that knife had done its terrible work. He fumbled for his dagger. Davinia froze at his cry. Jhandar's incantation died as he spun to confront the man who had dared interrupt the rite; the glow disappeared as his words ceased. Desperately Conan hurled his dagger—toward Davinia, for she still held her gleaming blade poised above Yasbet—but Jhandar turning, moved between them. The mage screamed as the needle-sharp steel sliced into his arm.

Clutching his wound, blood dripping between his fingers, Jhandar turned a frightful glare on Conan. "By the blood and earth and Powers of Chaos I summon you," he intoned. "Destroy this barbarian?" Davinia shrank back, as if she would have fled had she dared.

The floor trembled, and Conan skidded to a halt as chunks of marble erupted almost beneath his feet. Leather-skinned and fanged, a sending such as those he had faced before clawed its way clear of dirt and stone. With a wild roar, the Cimmerian brought his blade down with all his might in an overhead blow, slicing through the demoniac skull to the shoulders. Yet, unbleeding and undying, it struggled to reach him, and he must needs chop and chop again, hacking the monstrous thing apart. Even then its fragments twitched in unabated fury. More creatures tore through stone between him and the altar, and still more to either side of him, snarling in bloodlust. As a man might reap hay Conan worked his sword, steel rising and falling tirelessly. Severed limbs and heads and chunks of obscene flesh littered the floor, yet there were more, always more, ripping passage from the bowels of the earth. Cut off from Yasbet and the altar, it was but a matter of time before he was overwhelmed by sheer numbers.

A smile, pained, yet tinged with satisfaction at the Cimmerian's coming doom, appeared on Jhandar's face. "So Suitai lied," he rasped. "I will settle with him for it. But now, barbar, pause a moment in your exertions, if you can, to watch the fate of this woman, Esmira. Davinia! Attend the rite as I commanded you, woman!"

Terror twisting her face, Davinia raised the silver-bladed dagger once more. Her eyes bulged when they strayed to the deformed creatures battling Conan, but her hand was steady. Jhandar began again his invocation of the Power.

Raging, Conan tried to clear a path to the altar with his sword, but for each diabolic attacker he hewed to the floor, it seemed that two more appeared.

There was a commotion behind the Cimmerian, and a saffron-robed man staggered into his view, blood streaming down his face, weakly attempting to lift his sword. After him followed Sharak. Conan was so amazed that he hesitated with sword raised, staring. In that momentary respite the creatures tightened their circle about him, and he was forced to redouble his efforts to stop their advance.

Sharak's staff cracked down on his opponent's head; blood splattered from that shaven skull, and its owner fell, his sword sliding across the floor to stop against the altar. Irritably Jhandar looked over his shoulder, but did not stop his chant.

Conan lopped off a fang-mouthed head and kicked the headless body, now clawing blindly, into the path of another creature. His sword took an arm, then a leg, sliced away half of a skull, but he knew his sands had almost run out. There were just too many.

Abruptly Sharak was capering beside him, waving his staff wildly.

"Be gone from here," Conan shouted. "You are too old to—"

Sharak's staff thumped a leathery skull, and the creature screamed. At the altar Jhandar jerked as if he had felt the blow. Even the other beings froze as sparks ran along the struck creature's blue-gray skin. With a clap, as of thunder, it was gone, leaving only oily, black smoke that drifted upward.

"I told you it had power!" the old astrologer cried wildly. He struck out again; more greasy smoke rose toward the vaulted ceiling.

Now those hell-born backed warily from Conan and Sharak, rolling fearsome red eyes at Jhandar. For that moment at least, the way to the altar was clear, and Conan dashed for the black stone.

For but a heartbeat Jhandar faced that charge, then howled, "There are Powers you have not seen in your nightmares! Now face them!" and darted across the floor and down a small arched passage. With his departure the creatures, yet whole, seemingly freed of his command, vanished also.

Indecision racked Conan. For all he had sworn the necromancer would be dealt with first, Yasbet lay chained before him, with Davinia. . . .

As his gaze fell on her, the lithesome blonde backed away, wetting her lips nervously. "I heard you had sailed away, Conan," she said, then quickly abandoned that line as his face did not soften. "I was forced, Conan. Jhandar is a sorcerer, and forced me to this." She held the dagger low in the thumb-and-forefinger grip of one who knew how to gut a man, but she did not move toward Conan.

One eye on Davinia, Conan stepped up to the altar. Yasbet writhed in her chains. Four times his blade rang against her bonds, and steel conquered iron.

Ripping the gag from her mouth, Yasbet scrambled from the altar and plucked the dead Cult member's sword from the floor. Her hair lay wildly on her shoulders and breasts; she looked a naked goddess of battles. "I will deal with this. . . ." Words failed her as she glared at Davinia.

"Fool wench," Conan snapped. "I did not free you to see you stabbed!"

"'Tis a Cimmerian fool I see," Sharak called. He still leaped about like a puppeteer's stick figure, disposing with his staff of the portions of creatures that littered the chamber floor. "The necromancer must be slain, or all this is for naught!"

The old man spoke true, Conan knew. With a last look at Yasbet, closing grimly in on a snarling Davinia, he turned into the small passage Jhandar had taken.

It was not long, that narrow corridor. Almost immediately he saw a glow ahead; the same silver blue that had shone about the altar, yet a thousand times brighter. Quickening his pace, he burst into a small, unadorned chamber. In its center, surrounded by plain columns, a huge bubble of roiling mist burned and pulsed. Barely, through the brightness, Conan could make out Jhandar beyond the pool, arms outspread, his voice echoing like a bronze bell in words beyond understanding. Yet it was the brilliantly shining mass that held his eye, and hammered at him as it did. From those pulsating mists radiated, neither good nor evil, but the antithesis of being, beating at his mind, threatening to shatter all that was in him into a thousand fragments.

Pale images, washed out by the blinding glow, moved at the edge of his vision, then resolved themselves into two of the leather-skinned beings from the grave, sidling toward him along the wall as if they feared that shining. He knew that he must deal with the creatures and reach Jhandar, reach him quickly, before he completed whatever sorceries he was embarked upon, yet within the Cimmerian there was struggle. Never had he given in while he had strength or means to resist, but a thought strange to him now crept into his mind. Surrender. The mist was overpowering. Then, as if the words were a spark, rage flared in him. As a boy in the icy mountains of Cimmeria he had seen men, caught in an avalanche, hacking at towering waves of snow and dirt as they were swept away, refusing to accept the thing that killed them. He would not surrender. *He—would—not—surrender!*

A wordless scream of primal rage burst from Conan's throat. He spun, swinging his sword like an axe. Head and trunk of the foremost creature toppled, sliced cleanly from its hips and legs. Jhandar, rang in the Cimmerian's brain, and he was moving even as his steel broke free of that unnatural flesh.

But such a creature could not be slain like a mortal. The upper portion twisted as it fell, seized Conan about the legs, and together they crashed to the stone floor. Jagged teeth slashed Conan's thigh, yet in the beserker rage that gripped him he was as much beast as that he fought. His fisted hilt smashed into the creature's skull, again and again, till he pounded naught but slimy pulp. Yet those mindless arms gripped him still.

And Jhandar's chant continued unabated, as if he were too enmeshed in the Power to even be aware of another's presence.

Claws clattering on marble warned the Cimmerian that the second creature drew near. Wildly, half-blinded by the ever-brightening glow, Conan struck out. His blade caught but an ankle, yet the thing stumbled, flailed for balance . . . and fell shrieking against the shining dome. Lightnings arced and crackled, and the creature was gone.

The way to Jhandar was open. Grim determination limning his icy eyes, Conan crawled. Animal fury burned in his brain. Now the sorcerer would die, if he had to rip out his throat with bared teeth. Yet in a small, sane corner of his mind there was despair. Jhandar's ringing incantation was rising to a crescendo. The necromancer's foul work would be done before Conan reached him. Powers of darkness would be loosed on the land.

Something about the way the last beast had disappeared tugged at him. It reminded him of . . . what? The barrier to the Blasted Lands. Feverishly he dug into his pouch—it had to be there!—and drew out the small leather bag of powder Samarra had given him. Almost did he laugh. If nightmares were loosed to walk, still this time Jhandar would not escape. Undoing the rawhide strings that held the bag closed, he carefully tossed it ahead of him, toward the oblivious, chanting sorcerer. On the very edge of the burning dome the bag fell, open, contents spilling broadly. It had to be enough.

"Your vengeance, Samarra," Conan murmured, and slowly, coldly, spoke the words the shamaness had taught him. As the last syllable was pronounced, a shimmer sprang into being above the powder.

Jhandar's words of incantation faltered. For a brief moment he stared at the shimmer. Then he screamed. "No! Not yet! Not till I am gone!"

Through that shimmer, that weakened area of the wards that held the Pool of the Ultimate, flowed *something*. The mind could not encompass it, the eye refused to see it. Silver flecks danced in air that was too azure. No more did it seem, yet an ever-deepening channel was etched into the marble floor as it came from the pool. It touched pillars about the circumference of the pool; abruptly half pillars dangled in the air. The ceiling creaked. It washed against a wall, and stones ceased to exist. The wall and part of the ceiling above collapsed. The rubble fell into that inexorable tide of nonexistence, and was not.

Some measure of sanity returned to Conan in the face of that horror. Part of *it* moved toward him, now. Desperately he sliced with his broadsword at the undying arms that gripped his legs.

Jhandar turned to run, but as he ran the fringes of that flowing *thing* touched him. Only the fringes, the outer mists, yet full-throated he screamed, like a woman put to torture or a soul damned. Saffron robes melted like dew, and on his legs flesh disappeared at every touch of that mist. Bone gleamed whitely, and he fell shrieking to match the cries of all the victims he had ever laid on his black altar.

With a groan the far end of the chamber collapsed into vapor, though with less sound than Jhandar's screams. Conan redoubled his efforts, hacking at the tough flesh. The last sinew was severed; the unnatural grip was gone.

As the Cimmerian rolled to his feet and dove for the entrance passage, the invisible silver-flecked tide washed over the spot where he had been. Ignoring his gashed thigh, Conan ran, the sounds of Jhandar shrieking to the gods for mercy echoing in his ears.

When the Cimmerian reached the altar chamber, Sharak was peering down the passage. From a safe distance. "What was that screaming?" the astrologer asked, then added thoughtfully, "It's stopped."

"Jhandar's dead," Conan said, looking for Yasbet. He found her slicing the dead cult member's robes into some sort of garment, using the very dagger Davinia had intended for her heart. The blonde knelt fearfully nearby, bruised but unbloodied, gagged with the remnants of her own golden silks. A strip of the same material bound her hands; another circled her neck as a leash, with the end firmly in Yasbet's grasp.

Suddenly the earth moved. The floor heaved, twisted, and sagged toward the chamber from which Conan had fled.

"It's eating its way into the bowels of the earth," he muttered.

Sharak eyed him quizzically. "It? What? Nothing could—"

Again the ground danced, but this time it did not stop. Lamps crashed from the ceiling, splattering patches of burning oil. Dust rose, beaten into the air by the quivering of the floor, a floor that was tilting more with every heartbeat.

"No time," Conan shouted, grabbing Yasbet's hand. "Run!" And he suited his actions to his words, drawing Yasbet behind him, and perforce Davinia, for the dark-eyed woman would not loosen her grip on the blonde's leash. With surprising swiftness Sharak followed.

Down crumbling halls they ran, past flame-filled rooms, priceless rugs and rare tapestries the fuel. Dust filled the air, and shards of stone from collapsing ceilings.

Then they were outside, into the night, but there was no safety. The rumblings of the ground filled the air as if Erlik himself walked the face of the earth, making it tremble beneath his footsteps. Great trees toppled like weeds, and tall spires fell thunderously in ruin.

Here there were people, hundreds of them, fleeing in all directions, fur-capped Hyrkanians mixed with saffron-robed cult members. But safety did not always come with flight. Ahead of him, Conan saw a rift open in the earth beneath the very feet of four running men, three with shaven heads, one in a bulky sheepskin coat. When the Cimmerian reached the spot the ground had closed again, sealing all four in a common tomb.

Other fissures were opening as well, great crevasses that did not close. A tower tilted slowly, shaking with the earth, and slid whole into a great chasm that widened and lengthened even as Conan looked.

At the wall there was no need to climb. Great lengths of it had fallen into rubble. Over those piled stones they scrambled. Conan would not let them slow. Memories of the Blasted Lands drove him on, away from the compound, into the forest surrounding, further and further, till even his great muscles quivered with effort and he half-carried and half-dragged Yasbet and Davinia.

With shocking abruptness the land was still. Dead silence hung in the air. A new sound began, a hissing roar, building.

Hanging onto a tree, Sharak looked a question at Conan.

"The sea," Conan panted. The women stirred tiredly in his encircling grasp. "The fissures have reached the sea."

Behind them the sable sky turned crimson. With a roar, fiery magma erupted, scarlet fountains mixed with roaring geysers of steam as the sea sought the bowels of the earth. The air stirred, became a zephyr, a gale, a whirlwind rushing in to battle with the ultimate void.

Conan tried to hold the women against the force of that wind, but the strength of it grew seemingly without end. One moment he was standing, the next he was down, his hold on the women gone, clutching the ground lest he be sucked back toward the holocaust. Dirt, leaves, branches, even stones, filled the air in a hail.

"Hold on!" he tried to shout to them, but the fury of the wind drove the words back in his teeth.

Then the earth began to heave again. The Cimmerian had only an instant to see a broken branch flying toward him, and then his head seemed to explode into blackness.

Epilogue

onan woke to daylight. The flat coastal forest had become rolling hills, covered with a tangle of uprooted trees. Yasbet. Scrambling to his feet, he began to pick his way among trees tossed like jack-straws, calling her name without reply. Then, as he topped a hill, he fell silent in amazement.

The hills were not the only change that had been wrought upon the land. A bay now cut into the land, its surface covered thickly with dead fish. Wisps of steam rolled up from that water, and he was ready to wager that despite all of the sea to cool it the waters in that bay would remain hot for all time.

"The compound stood there," a hoarse voice said, and Sharak limped up to stand beside him. Somehow, he saw, the astrologer had kept his staff through all that had occurred. Now he leaned on it tiredly, his robes torn and his face muddy.

"I do not thing fishermen will often cast their nets in those waters," Conan replied. Sharak made a sign against evil. "Have you seen Yasbet?"

The astrologer shook his head. "I have seen many, mainly cult members leaving this place as fast as they can. I have seen Tamur and half a dozen of the Hyrkanians, wanting only to be gone from Turan, yet unsure of their welcome at home. I wager we'll find them in a tavern in Aghrapur. I saw Akman, hurrying west." His voice saddened. "Yasbet, I fear, did not survive."

"I did, too, you old fool," the girl's voice called.

A broad smile appeared on Conan's face as he watched her clamber up the hill, still leading Davinia on her leash, and Akeba following close behind. All three were streaked with mud, a condition the Cimmerian real-ized for the first time that he shared.

"I lost my sword," she announced when she reached them. A narrow length of saffron was her only garment, affording her little more covering than the tavern girls of Aghrapur, but if anything her costume seemed to add to her jauntiness. "But I'll get another one. You owe me more lessons, Conan." Her smile became mischievous. "In the sword, and other things."

Akeba coughed to hide a grin; Sharak openly leered.

"You'll get your lessons," Conan said. "But why are you still pulling Davinia about? Set her free, or kill her, if that's your wish. You have the right, for she would have killed you."

The blonde's knees buckled. She crouched weeping at Yasbet's feet, her beauty hidden by layers of filth.

"I'll do neither," Yasbet said, after studying the cringing woman. "I'll sell her to a brothel. 'Tis all she's fit for, and a fitting place for her." Davinia moaned into her gag; the horror in her eyes indicated she might rather be slain. "And thus," Yasbet added, "will I get the wherewithal for my sword."

"I am as glad as any to see the rest of you," Akeba said, "but I would as soon be gone from this place."

"Yes," Sharak said excitedly. "I must return to Aghrapur. With the powers of my staff proven, I can double, no, triple my fees. You will attest to it, will you not, Akeba?"

"Attest to what?" the soldier demanded. "Are you making claims about that stick again?"

Offering a helping hand to Yasbet, Conan started down the hill, away from the bay, toward Aghrapur. "Jhandar called you by another name than Yasbet," he said as she scrambled after him. "What was it?"

"You must have misheard," she told him blandly. "Yasbet is all the name I have." Davinia pressed forward, making urgent sounds at Conan through her gag. Yasbet glared over her shoulder. "Do you want a sound switching before you're sold?" Eyes wide with shock, the blonde fell silent, and thereafter would not even meet the Cimmerian's gaze.

Conan nodded to himself. Clearly Yasbet was lying, but some said that was a woman's right. He would not press her on it.

Snatches of conversation drifted forward from the two men behind.

"If Conan saw it, let him attest to it. I saw nothing."

"But you are a sergeant, an official as it were. Can you not see how much better your word would be? I'm certain Conan will tell you what he saw."

The smile Conan had worn since seeing Yasbet alive widened even further. For all the days before, there was much to be said for this day. He was alive, with a little gold—he checked his pouch to see if the two coins still rested there; they did—good friends, and a pretty woman. What more could any man ask for? What more?